Stellar Praise for Carl Hiaasen's

BAD MONKEY

"Hiaasen's comic thrillers come with a guarantee—broad humor that capitalizes on absurd behavior; Florida quirkiness; social commentary that rivals Jonathan Swift; and a deep concern for the environment, all wrapped in a solid plot. Hiaasen delivers all that and more in BAD MONKEY." —*Miami Herald*

"The Bard of Florida is back…Almost nobody does hot-weather reading better than Carl Hiaasen, whose novel will make you snort your seaside margarita…Read BAD MONKEY." —*New York*

"[A] rollicking misadventure in the colorful annals of greed and corruption in South Florida…Hiaasen has a peculiar genius for inventing grotesque creatures [that] spring from the darkest impulses of the id. But he also writes great heroes." —*New York Times*

"BAD MONKEY boils over with corruption and come-uppance. And yes, there's a monkey." —*O, The Oprah Magazine*

"Hiaasen is Tex Avery, fast and sinuous and able to get his grotesques down in Day-Glo colors and fastidiously minimal gestures, with a knowing voice fully earned by how much he knows." —*The New Yorker*

"A shambolic comic tale of garden-variety Florida crime…Hiaasen is laugh-out-loud funny and thoroughly entertaining." —*Booklist* (starred review)

"Carl Hiaasen's uproarious brand of Swiftian humor is on full display in BAD MONKEY." —*Seattle Times*

"Reading a Hiaasen crime novel is like returning to a favorite amusement park ride—you know what to expect, but it's always a rush." —*Pittsburgh Post-Gazette*

BAD MONKEY

CARL HIAASEN

GRAND CENTRAL
PUBLISHING

NEW YORK   BOSTON

Grand Central Publishing Edition

Copyright © 2013 by Carl Hiaasen

Grand Central Publishing
Hachette Book Group
1290 Avenue of the Americas
New York, NY 10104

www.HachetteBookGroup.com

Grand Central Publishing is a division of Hachette Book Group, Inc.
The Grand Central Publishing name and logo are trademarks of Hachette Book Group, Inc.

The Hachette Speakers Bureau provides a wide range of authors for speaking events. To find out more, go to www.hachettespeakersbureau.com or call (866) 376-6591.

The publisher is not responsible for websites (or their content) that are not owned by the publisher.

Printed in the United States of America

First international mass market edition: June 2014
First mass market edition: February 2015

11

OPM

*For all the flying fishermen of the apocalypse,
especially Jimmy*

This is a work of fiction. All the names and characters are either invented or used fictitiously.

Although most of the events depicted are imaginary, the dead-sailfish scam is based on a true-life scandal in Miami. Likewise, the odious duties of a restaurant inspector are authentically rendered.

BAD MONKEY

One

On the hottest day of July, trolling in dead-calm waters near Key West, a tourist named James Mayberry reeled up a human arm. His wife flew to the bow of the boat and tossed her breakfast burritos.

"What're you waiting for?" James Mayberry barked at the mate. "Get that thing off my line!"

The kid tugged and twisted, but the barb of the hook was imbedded in bone. Finally the captain came down from the bridge and used bent-nose pliers to free the decomposing limb, which he placed on shaved ice in a deck box.

James Mayberry said, "For Christ's sake, now where are we supposed to put our fish?"

"We'll figure that out when you actually catch one."

It had been a tense outing aboard the *Misty Momma IV*. James Mayberry had blown three good strikes because he was unable to absorb instruction. Dragging baits in the ocean was different than jigging for walleyes in the lake back home.

"Don't we need to call somebody?" he asked the captain.

"We do."

The hairy left arm was bloated and sunburned to the hue of eggplant. A cusp of yellowed humerus protruded at the point of separation, below the shoulder. The flesh surrounding the wound looked ragged and bloodless.

"Yo, check it out!" the mate said.

"What now?" James Mayberry asked.

"His freakin' finger, dude."

The victim's hand was contracted into a fist except for the middle digit, which was rigidly extended.

"How weird is *that*? He's flippin' us off," the mate said.

The captain told him to re-bait the angler's hook.

"Has this ever happened out here before?" James Mayberry said. "Tell the truth."

"You should go see about your wife."

"Jesus, I'll never hear the end of it. Louisa wanted to ride the Conch Train today. She did *not* want to come fishing."

"Well, son," the captain said, "we're in the memory-making business."

He climbed back to the bridge, radioed the Coast Guard and gave the GPS coordinates of the gruesome find. He was asked to remain in the area and look for other pieces of the body.

"But I got a charter," he said.

"You can stay at it," the Coast Guard dispatcher advised. "Just keep your eyes open."

After calming herself, Louisa Mayberry informed her husband that she wished to return to Key West right away.

"Come on, sugar. It's a beautiful morning." James Mayberry didn't want to go back to the dock with no fish to hang on the spikes—not after shelling out a grand to hire the boat.

"The first day of our honeymoon, and *this*! Aren't you sketched out?"

James Mayberry peeked under the lid of the fish box. "You watch *CSI* all the time. It's the same type of deal."

His wife grimaced but did not turn away. She remarked that the limb didn't look real.

"Oh, it's real," said James Mayberry, somewhat defensively. "Just take a whiff." Snagging a fake arm wouldn't make for as good a story. A real arm was pure gold, major high-fives from all his peeps back in Madison. *You caught a* what? *No way, bro!*

Louisa Mayberry's gaze was fixed on the limb. "What could have happened?" she asked.

"Tiger shark," her husband said matter-of-factly.

"Is that a wedding band on his hand? This is so sad."

"Fish on!" the mate called. "Who's up?"

James Mayberry steered his bride to the fighting chair and the mate fitted the rod into the gimbal. Although she was petite, Louisa Mayberry owned a strong upper body due to rigorous Bikram yoga classes that she took on Tuesday nights. Refusing assistance, she pumped in an eleven-pound blackfin tuna and whooped triumphantly as it flopped on the deck. Her husband had never seen her so excited.

"Here, take a picture!" she cried to the mate, and handed over her iPhone.

"Hold on," James Mayberry said. "Get both of us together."

Louisa watched him hustle to get ready. "Really, Jimmy? Really?"

Moments later the captain glanced down from the bridge and saw the mate snapping photographs of the newlyweds posed side by side at the transom. Their matching neon blue Oakley wraparounds were propped on their matching cap visors, and their fair Wisconsin noses practically glowed with sunblock.

Louisa Mayberry was gamely hoisting by the tail her sleek silvery tuna while James Mayberry wore the mate's crusty gloves to grip his rancid catch, its middle finger aimed upward toward the puffy white clouds.

The captain dragged on a cigarette and turned back to the wheel. "Another fucking day in paradise," he said.

The phone kept ringing but Yancy didn't answer it. He was drinking rum, sitting in a plastic lawn chair. From next door came the offensive buzz of wood saws and the metallic pops of a nail gun. The absentee owner of the property was erecting an enormous spec house that had no spiritual place on Big Pine Key, and furthermore interfered with Yancy's modest view of the sunset. It was Yancy's fantasy to burn the place down as soon as the roof framing was finished.

He heard a car stop in his driveway but he didn't rise from the chair. His visitor was a fellow detective, Rogelio Burton.

"Why don't you pick up your phone?" Burton said.

"You believe that monstrosity? It's like a goddamn mausoleum."

Burton sat down beside him. "Sonny wants you to take a road trip."

"Miami?"

"That's right."

"I'll pass." Yancy glared at the construction site across the fence. "The house is forty-four feet high—I measured it myself. The county code's only thirty-five."

"It's the Keys, man. The code is for suckers."

"Deer used to come around all the time and feed on the twigs."

Yancy offered his friend a drink. Burton declined.

He said, "Andrew, it's not like you've got a choice. Do what Sonny wants."

"But I'm suspended, remember?"

"Yeah, with pay. Is that Barbancourt?"

"My last bottle. Tell him anywhere but Miami, Rog."

"You want me to ask if you can go to Cancún instead?" Burton sighed. "Look, it's a day trip, up and back."

"They always screw me on the mileage."

Burton knew this wasn't true. Yancy had issues with the Miami Police Department, from which he'd been fired in a previous era of his life.

"Chill out. You're just going to the ME's office."

"The morgue? Nice."

"Come out to the car," said Burton.

Yancy set down his drink. "This ought to be special."

The severed arm had been bubble-wrapped and packed on dry ice in a red Igloo cooler. To make it fit, the limb had been bent at the elbow.

"That's all they found?"

"You know how it goes," Burton said.

"John Doe or Juan Doe?"

"Rawlings says white male, mid-forties, heavyset, black hair."

Dr. Lee Rawlings was the pathologist who served as the chief medical examiner for Monroe County. There were relatively few murders or accidental deaths in the Florida Keys, but Rawlings never complained. He filled his free time with golf, and was rumored to have whittled his handicap down to five strokes.

Yancy knew the sheriff was sending the arm to Miami because Miami was the floating-human-body-parts capital of America. Maybe they'd luck out and find a match, although Yancy thought it was unlikely.

"Traumatic amputation," Burton said.

"Ya think?"

"Charter boat brought it in yesterday. We checked our missing persons, all three of them. Nobody fits the description."

Yancy noticed the upraised finger on the end of the arm. "A sour farewell to the mortal realm?"

"Random rigor mortis is what Rawlings says. He took a picture anyway."

"Of course he did."

"Look, I'm late for my kid's soccer game."

"Absolutely." Yancy put the lid on the cooler and carried it up to his porch.

Burton said, "Sure you want to leave it out here all night?"

"Who's gonna jack an arm?"

"It's evidence, man. I'm just sayin'."

"Okay, fine." The island was plagued by opportunistic raccoons.

Burton drove off and Yancy moved the cooler into the house. From a kitchen cupboard he retrieved the Barbancourt bottle and ambled to the deck and poured himself one more drink. Next door, the construction crew was gone. Yancy's watch said five p.m. sharp.

For the first time all day he could hear seabirds in the sky.

The new sheriff of Monroe County was a local bubba named Sonny Summers who won office because he was the only candidate not in federal custody, the two front-runners having been locked up on unconnected rack-eteering charges eight days before the election. Sonny Summers's opponents were unable to post bond and therefore faced a strategic disadvantage during the cam-paign's final debate, which was conducted via Skype from a medium-security prison near Florida City.

During his sixteen years as a road patrol officer, Sonny Summers had received numerous commendations for not fucking up on the job. He was well-groomed, cour-teous and diligent about his paperwork. One year he led the whole force in DUI arrests, a highly competitive category in the Keys. His spelling on arrest forms was almost always legible, he never took any of his girlfriends on dates in his squad car and he smoked pot only on his days off.

Upon becoming sheriff, Sonny Summers arranged a series of get-acquainted luncheons with business leaders up and down the islands, from Key West to Key Largo. A recurring theme of these meetings was the fragility of tourism and the perils of negative publicity. The BP oil spill was often invoked, although not a drop of crude had ever reached South Florida beaches. Sonny Summers was sympathetic to the business owners, whose support he would need for future elections. Under no circumstances did he wish to be blamed for scaring customers away.

With that in mind, Sonny Summers ordered his

public-information officer not to divulge any information about the severed arm that had been brought in aboard the *Misty Momma IV*. It was the new sheriff's worry that floating body parts would be bad for tourism, particularly the waterfront trades. This was laughably untrue, as any marina owner in Miami could have assured him. Nothing short of a natural disaster discouraged people from going out on (or into) the water. One particular beach on the Rickenbacker Causeway got spunked regularly by raw sewage, yet squads of riot police couldn't keep the swimmers and kiteboarders away.

In any case, Sonny Summers was fighting a lost battle. A crime-scene van had been waiting for the *Misty Momma IV* when it docked, so news of the icky discovery spread quickly. Worse, the boneheaded angler who'd reeled in the dead arm was showing the pictures on his cell phone to everybody at the Chart Room. There was even a rumor that he'd posted a photo on Facebook.

"I'm counting on you," the sheriff said to Yancy, after Yancy finally answered the phone.

"How so?"

"I'm counting on you not to come back from Miami with that you-know-what."

Yancy said, "What if there are no matching limbs at the morgue up there?"

"I need some optimism from you, Detective. I need some can-do mojo."

"The Gulf Stream flows north."

"Duh," said Sonny Summers.

"Also, the prevailing breeze this time of year blows from the southeast."

"I was born here, Yancy. Get to the point."

"Factor in the wind and currents, the odds of that arm floating from Miami all the way down here are pretty damn slim—unless it was paddling itself."

The sheriff was aware of Yancy's employment history. "You don't want to drive up to the big coldhearted city, that's all."

"What if they won't take the case?"

"See, I'm depending on you to persuade them."

"I can't just leave a limb at the ME's office if they don't want it."

Sonny Summers said, "Tomorrow I'm announcing that the investigation has been turned over to the appropriate authorities in Miami-Dade County. That's the game plan, okay? This is officially no longer our headache."

"I would wait a day to be sure."

"Know what happened this morning? Some dickhead from Channel 7 calls up and says he heard that mangled corpses are floating up in Key West harbor!"

"Did you tell him to fuck off?"

"Call back tomorrow is what I told him. Wait for the media statement."

"Our victim's probably a rafter," Yancy said. "Drowned on the crossing from Havana and then got hit by a bull shark or a hammerhead."

"There you go!" the sheriff exclaimed brightly. "Aren't most rafters on their way to Miami to meet up with family? So that's where the goddamn arm belongs—Miami! End of discussion."

"It's not really up to me, Sonny."

"Let me put it another way: There will be no human remains on my watch. Understand? *No human remains.*"

Those close to Sonny Summers sensed that he was

sometimes overwhelmed by his elevated responsibilities. The transition from writing speeding tickets to commanding a recalcitrant law enforcement bureaucracy had been bumpy. One aspect of the new job that Sonny Summers did enjoy was putting on a blazer and schmoozing with the chamber-of-commerce types.

Yancy tried to suggest that an occasional severed limb was no cause for panic.

"Really? The two-day lobster season is next week," the sheriff said. "We're expecting, like, thirty thousand divers."

"A sea of reeking turds wouldn't keep those lunatics off the water. What are you worried about?"

"We'll speak again tomorrow," said Sonny Summers.

Yancy said, "I'll drive up there on one condition: You lift my suspension."

"Not until after the trial. How many times do I have to tell you?"

"But it's such bullshit, Sonny. I didn't even hurt the guy."

The sheriff said, "Talk to Bonnie. She's the problem."

Bonnie Witt, Yancy's future former girlfriend, was prepared to testify that he'd assaulted her husband of fourteen years with a portable vacuum cleaner, specifically a tubular attachment designed for upholstery crevices. Clifford Witt had required some specialized medical care but he was more or less ambulatory within a week.

Sonny Summers said, "Of all the women you had to get involved with. Swear to God, Andrew. All the women on these islands."

"Our love was like a streaking comet." Yancy paused. "Her words, not mine."

"Did you take a look at it? The…?"

"Arm? Yes, Burton insisted."

"Any theories?"

"No," said Yancy. "But it makes a dandy back-scratcher."

"Call me on your way back from Miami. I want some happy news."

TWO

A clawing heat settles over the Keys by mid-July. The game fish swim to deeper waters, the pelicans laze in the mangroves and only the hardiest of tourists remain out-doors past the lunch hour. Yancy's unmarked Ford was well air-conditioned but he still brought a box of Popsi-cles, which he positioned beside the disjoined limb in the cooler on the passenger side.

He was a pathologically impatient driver, and sucking on iced treats seemed to settle him. Bonnie had started Yancy on the Popsicle habit because she'd found it terrify-ing to ride with him on Highway 1. Mango was Yancy's favorite flavor beside Bonnie herself. These were the sorts of sidecar thoughts with which he tormented himself.

The drive to downtown Miami usually took ninety minutes, but Yancy had stopped along Card Sound Road to purchase blue crabs, as there was still room in the cooler.

"Is this your idea of wit?" asked the assistant medical examiner, a serious brown-eyed woman whose name tag identified her as Dr. Rosa Campesino.

"Help yourself to a Popsicle," Yancy told her. "However, the crabs are off-limits."

He summarized Rawlings's findings while Dr. Campesino removed the arm from the ice and carefully unwrapped it. She placed it on a bare autopsy table without commenting on the vertical middle digit.

"I suppose you've seen some winners," Yancy said.

"And you brought this all the way from Key West because...?"

"The sheriff thought it might belong to one of your victims."

Dr. Campesino said, "You could've e-mailed some photos and saved yourself a tank of gas."

"Want to grab lunch?"

Finally, a smile. "I'll be back in a minute," she said.

Yancy ate another Popsicle. Unless you happened to be deceased, there were worse places to hang out than a morgue in the summertime. The thermostat was turned down to about sixty-three degrees. Very pleasant.

Dr. Campesino returned with a printout of the county's current inventory of body parts, listed by race, gender and approximate age—three partial torsos, two left legs, a pelvis, three ears, seven assorted toes and one bashed skull. None of the items belonged to a chunky, hirsute white male in his forties.

"I knew it," said Yancy.

"Maybe next time."

"Are you hungry?"

"My husband's a sniper on the SWAT team."

"Say no more."

"Did you notice this?" Dr. Campesino pointed the eraser end of a pencil at a well-delineated band of pale flesh on the wrist of the darkened arm. "His watch is gone," she said.

"It probably fell off the poor fucker while the shark was mangling him."

Dr. Campesino gave a slight shake of her head. "Often in upper-arm amputations the victim's wristwatch remains attached. Not so much in homicides. The bad guys either steal it to pawn, or they remove it to make the ID more difficult."

Yancy was certain that Sheriff Sonny Summers wouldn't want to hear the word *homicide*. "Then why wouldn't they swipe the wedding ring, too?" he asked.

"You're right. It looks expensive."

"I'm betting platinum. The guy's wife would be sure to recognize it."

Dr. Campesino leaned closer to study the damaged stump of the limb.

"What now?" Yancy said.

"The end of the humerus is hacked up pretty bad."

"Maybe he fell into the boat's propeller."

"That would be a different style of wound."

Yancy said, "You're killing me."

From a tray of instruments the pathologist selected a pair of hemostats, with which she extracted a pointed tooth from one of several puncture holes in the upper biceps. She dropped the smallish gray fang into Yancy's palm.

"I'm no shark expert," said Dr. Campesino. "Some marine biologist could tell you what species this came from."

Yancy pocketed the tooth. He asked how long the arm had been in the ocean.

"Five to seven days. Maybe longer." The young pathologist took some photographs which she promised to upload in case another part of the same corpse turned up in her jurisdiction.

"Can't you keep the damn thing here?" Yancy asked. "Honestly, it would save me all kinds of grief."

"Sorry. Not our case." Dr. Campesino was mindful of the blue crabs when she returned the orphaned arm to the cooler. "I'll call you if we get something that looks like a match."

Yancy was aware that the Miami-Dade medical examiner's office sometimes assisted other jurisdictions in difficult cases. He was also aware that his boss hadn't sent him to Miami to initiate a murder investigation.

"Can we call it an accident? I mean, if you had to guess."

"Not without a more thorough exam," said Dr. Campesino, peeling off her latex gloves, "which I'd be happy to do if we had an official request from Monroe County."

"Which you won't get."

"Can I ask why?"

"I'll tell you over a strictly platonic lunch."

"Nope."

"Fine," Yancy said. "So what would you do if you were me?"

"I'd go back to Key West and advise Dr. Rawlings to pack the arm in his freezer. Then wait for someone to show up looking for a missing husband."

"And what if nobody does? It's a cold business when true love goes south. Take my word."

"Can I ask you something? Did you bend his middle finger up?"

"God, no! They found it that way!" Yancy moved the arm aside as he pawed through the cooler in search of another mango Popsicle. "Dear Rosa, what kind of sick bastard do you take me for?"

The person responsible for Yancy leaving the Miami Police Department was a sergeant named Johnny Mendez, who at the time was working with the Crime Stoppers hotline. To augment his salary Mendez would recruit friends and relatives to call in with tips on crimes that had already been solved, providing detailed information that detectives already knew. Then Mendez would backdate the tip sheet and personally sign off on the reward money, half of which he took as a commission.

Yancy had discovered the scam when he'd read a *Herald* story about a bus driver who'd received forty-five hundred dollars from Crime Stoppers for providing "crucial information" leading to the arrest of a man who stuck up a pedicure salon in Little Havana. Yancy himself had busted the robber, with no guidance whatsoever from the general public. The suspect had helpfully dropped his fishing license at the crime scene, and two days later Yancy jumped him while he was waxing the hull of his Boston Whaler.

The bus driver who'd phoned in the bogus tip turned out to be a second cousin of Sergeant Mendez's. One morning Yancy boarded the cousin's bus and sat in the first row and opened a notebook. After thirty-three blocks the driver spilled the whole story. He said Sergeant Mendez was upset to have opened the newspaper and seen the item about the reward, and had punished him by pocketing all but a grand.

That night, after too many rum and Cokes, Yancy decided it would be fabulously clever to dial the Crime Stoppers number and report Sergeant Mendez for grand theft and embezzlement. Mendez wasn't a big fan of irony, and in any case he'd been busy covering his tracks. Yancy was eventually accused by Internal Review of making up lies about a fellow officer and of trying to extort money from Crime Stoppers. Yancy's position was weakened by the transcript of his phone call to the tip line, in which he suggested that a reward of fifty thousand dollars would be appropriate for the "courageous and upright deed" of exposing a crooked cop.

Yancy had delivered that line in a snarky and facetious tone, but the review board never got to hear the original tape, which had been mysteriously damaged by magnets while in Johnny Mendez's possession. Suspended without pay, Yancy quickly ran out of money for his lawyer and had no choice but to resign from the department, in exchange for not being indicted. Sergeant Mendez denied all wrongdoing but was quietly reassigned to the K-9 division. Soon thereafter he was bitten in the groin by a Belgian shepherd trainee named Kong, and he required three operations, culminating in a scrotal graft from a Brahma steer.

Mendez retired from the police force on full disability at age forty-four. He lived on Venetia Avenue in Coral Gables. Parked in the driveway was a silver Lexus coupe undoubtedly purchased with Crime Stoppers proceeds. One solution to the severed-arm dilemma would be for Yancy to plant the limb in Mendez's car, perhaps strung to the rosary that hung from the rearview mirror. Yancy discarded the idea—if by some chance Mendez overcame his panic and called the police, the arm would end up at the county morgue, where it inevitably would be traced back to Yancy based on information provided by the exquisite Dr. Campesino.

Over the years Yancy had conjured many irrational revenge fantasies about Johnny Mendez. For a time he considered seducing Mendez's wife until he realized he'd be doing Mendez a huge favor. Mrs. Mendez was an unbearable harridan. Her features were a riot of futile surgeries, and she laughed like a mandrill on PCP. Yancy once bought her a margarita at the InterContinental, and for two solid weeks he'd slept with the lights on.

Now he was parked down the block from the Mendez marital nest. A fat Siamese was primping on the hood of the Lexus. Yancy assumed the animal belonged to Mendez, who seemed like a total cat person. The man's inability to control K-9 candidates was further evidence.

Before Yancy could make up his mind about snatching the Siamese, his cell rang. It was the sheriff, probably seeking confirmation that the severed-arm transfer was complete. Yancy let the call go to voice mail.

On the drive back to the Keys he phoned Burton and gave him the bad news.

"They didn't want the damn thing. Now what do I do?"

"Lose it somewhere," Burton said. "That's my advice."

"Listen to you."

"Seriously. Take 905 back through North Key Largo—there's a dirt road about halfway that leads to an old cock-fighting ring."

Yancy wasn't sold on the plan. "My luck, some birder will find it."

"Not before the ants and vultures do."

"What the hell's wrong with Sonny, anyway? This is no big deal."

Burton said the sheriff freaked when Channel 7 called. "Anyway, he already gave a press statement saying the case had been turned over to Miami-Dade."

"I warned him, Rog."

"Just ditch the fucking arm and come home."

"Let me think about this."

"I wish you wouldn't."

Yancy boiled the blue crabs and served them on hearts of palm, sprinkled with lemon pepper and Tabasco. Bonnie brought a bottle of Bordeaux. The fine vintage was wasted on Yancy but the gesture seemed rich with promise. Still she said: "I shouldn't have come."

They ate dinner on the back deck, where a world-class sunset was being ruined by the vulgar structure arising next door, spears of light slanting harshly through a checkerboard of window spaces and door frames.

"Where's the good doctor?" Yancy asked.

"Lauderdale. He's got a meeting tomorrow with our bankers."

"It must be nice to have bankers. As a couple, I mean. 'Here's our Christmas tree. Here's our minivan. And, oh, last but not least, here are our bankers.'"

"Shut up, Andrew," Bonnie said. Her frosted hair was in pigtails, and a touch of pink gloss had been applied to her lips.

"He's sixty, you're forty. I remain at a loss." Yancy threw up his hands.

"Don't try to flatter me. I'm forty-two and you know it."

She kicked off her flip-flops and crossed her smooth

tanned legs, which stirred in Yancy's chest a longing that almost incapacitated him. He and Bonnie hadn't slept together since the night before the vacuum-cleaner incident.

Yancy said, "The sheriff would lift my suspension if you and Cliff agreed to drop the charges."

"So that's why you invited me tonight."

"I ask you over three or four times a week, but you always say no."

"Cliff won't budge," Bonnie said. "He wants to see you punished."

Yancy pointed out that a trial would be humiliating for all parties. "Especially the alleged victim."

"Alleged? There were three hundred witnesses, including yours truly."

The assault had occurred at high noon at Mallory Square, which was packed with cruise-ship passengers. Fourteen amateur video clips of admissible clarity were in the hands of the prosecutor.

"Nobody calls you a whore and gets away with it," Yancy said.

"Well, I *was* cheating on him, as you'll recall. And I believe he used the term 'tramp,' not 'whore.'" Bonnie balanced a plate of crabs on her lap. With a silver fork she probed for morsels amid the ceramic debris. "These are pretty darn tasty," she said.

"Talk to him, darling. Please. I need my badge back."

"Why didn't you just punch him like a normal person? Why'd you have to go and sodomize him with a Hoover?"

Yancy shrugged. "You always said he had a bee up his ass. I was only trying to help."

"Are you seeing anybody?" Bonnie had no talent for

changing the subject. "I don't think you're ready yet. I think you're still recovering."

"It's true, I'm a portrait of frailty. Tell me again why Cliffy isn't divorcing you."

"He adores me, Andrew."

"Even after catching us together."

"Yes," said Bonnie impatiently.

"On his own boat."

"We've been over this a hundred times."

"In the tuna tower, for Christ's sake! His own wife and another man, lewdly entwined." Yancy inserted a crab claw in his mouth and bit down violently. "We must've looked like the fucking Wallendas up there."

The boat was a seventy-two-foot Merritt with all the bells and whistles. Dr. Clifford Witt had recently retired from the practice of medicine, having invested in a chain of lucrative storefront pain clinics that dispensed Percocets and Vicodins by the bucket to a new wave of American redneck junkies.

Bonnie said, "I wouldn't be here tonight if I didn't care."

"Yet still you intend to testify against me."

"I'll take no joy from it, Andrew." She looked down, tugging at a loose thread on her cutoffs. "Of course, you could cut a deal. Spare us all from the messiness of court."

Yancy frowned. "And lose my job? That's automatic after a felony conviction."

"Suppose I got Cliff to go along with dropping the charge to a misdemeanor? Between you and me, Dickinson's office would be thrilled."

Billy Dickinson was the local state attorney, and he had no appetite for ventilating scandals.

"Sonny could still fire me," Yancy said, "or bust me down to deputy." Still, a misdemeanor wasn't insurmountable, career-wise.

"What do you think of the wine?"

"Yeasty," said Yancy, "yet playful."

Their affair had started on a Saturday afternoon in the produce section at Fausto's, the two of them reaching simultaneously for the last ripe avocado. From there they beelined to Bonnie's car and sped up the highway all the way to Bahia Honda, where they spent the night, hiding from the park rangers and humping madly on the beach, carving their own private dunes. For breakfast they split the avocado.

Yancy had been aware of Bonnie's marital status; Cliff Witt was his dermatologist at the time, always ready with a frigid zap of liquid nitrogen whenever Yancy burst into the office to present a new, ominous-looking freckle. Yancy appreciated Cliff Witt's accessibility but knew of his reputation as a horndog perv and pill peddler.

Still, guilt fissured Yancy's conscience when he began undressing the man's wife. It was his first encounter with a Brazilian wax job, and rapture soon blinded him to the manifest hurdles in his path. Usually he avoided married women.

"I suppose I should go," Bonnie said, rising. She had pale blue eyes and reddish lashes that looked gold-tipped in the light.

Yancy suggested a detour to the bedroom, and she said no. "But I'm a little drunk. Maybe a shower would wake me up."

"There's an idea."

It was just like old times, Bonnie's bare bottom slapping against the wet tile while Yancy's heels squeaked in joyous syncopation on the rubber bath mat. Somehow they broke the soap dish off the wall and also spilled a bottle of Prell, which played havoc with Yancy's traction. Afterward they toweled each other dry and fell into bed, and there Bonnie made a peculiar revelation.

"I am wanted in Oklahoma," she said.

"You're wanted here even more."

"I'm serious. That's why I married Cliff. I was a fugitive. *Am* a fugitive."

Yancy wasn't always a good post-coital listener, but Bonnie had gotten his attention. She said, "My real name is Plover Chase."

"Ah."

"*The* Plover Chase?"

"Okay," Yancy said.

"I can't believe you don't remember the case! Stay right here."

Naked she bounded from the sheets, returning with a French handbag that Yancy judged to be worth more than his car. From a jeweled change purse she removed a newspaper clipping that had been folded to the size of a credit card. As Yancy skimmed the article, he recalled the crime and also the steamy tabloid uproar.

Plover Chase was a schoolteacher in Tulsa who'd been convicted of extorting sex from one of her students in exchange for giving him an A on his report card. The boy was fifteen at the time; she was twenty-seven. On the day of her sentencing she'd disappeared.

"The judge was a shriveled old prick. I was looking at ten years," Bonnie recapped. "So instead I hopped a plane to Lauderdale. Cliff's medical office was advertising for a receptionist, and the rest is history."

"Does he know the truth?" Yancy asked.

"Of course." Which explained why Bonnie had stayed with him.

Yancy eyed the headline on the article: WARRANT ISSUED FOR TEACHER CONVICTED IN SEX-FOR-GRADES SCHEME. He wasn't sure whether he should act shocked or jealous. Certainly he had nothing as sensational in his own past.

He said, "May I offer a couple of observations? One, you're even more beautiful today than you were then."

"That's a mug shot, Andrew. And, FYI, a dyke named Smitty had just given me a full-on cavity search, which is why my eyeballs are bulging in that photo."

Yancy plowed on. "Number two, 'Bonnie' is so much sexier than 'Plover.' I don't think I could ever be intimate with a Plover—it's just not a name that can be seriously howled in the heat of passion."

"Cody had no trouble," Bonnie said.

Yancy raised an eyebrow. "The teenage victim of your seduction?"

"Yeah, some victim. He knew more positions than I did."

"Actually, Cody's a good sturdy name. He would be, what, about thirty now?"

Bonnie said the young man had sat in the front row of her AP English class. "I have no defense for what happened. He flirted with me, fine, but so did lots of the boys. Our...whatever...only lasted a couple of weeks, and of course he blabbed to everybody. His mother was the one who went to the cops."

"Even after you gave him an A?"

"There was no trade! Cody was an outstanding student."

"I assume he took the stand."

"His parents threatened to sell his Jet Ski if he didn't testify. Apparently he'd kept a journal of everything we did and how many times we did it. His writing was quite jaunty and explicit—I should never have turned him on to Philip Roth."

"So what was the final tally? How many trysts?"

"The jury was a horrid bunch, Andrew, leering like gargoyles."

Yancy said, "I can only imagine."

"Anyway, I wanted you to know the full truth, now that we're closing the book on each other's lives."

Like a buzzard coasting through clouds, the thought crossed Yancy's mind that his lawyer might be interested to learn that the wife of the man Yancy was accused of assaulting—and a key witness against him—was herself a fugitive from a sordid felony rap. He let the notion glide away.

"Whatever happened to Cody?" he asked.

"How the hell would I know? He was a dumb mistake, that's all."

"We all make 'em."

"I'll talk to Cliff again tomorrow. Promise."

Yancy said, "Thank you, Bonnie. I like being a detective."

"In the meantime you're still getting a paycheck, right? So go fishing or something." She returned the newspaper article to her purse. Then she stood up and stepped into her denim cutoffs. "I need some ice in my wine. How about you?"

"I'm good."

Yancy lay back on a pillow and watched Bonnie button

her blouse. She always did it without looking down, her gaze clouded and faraway and dull. After she left the room, he shut his eyes and tried not to think about the supernatural frequency of erections enjoyed by fifteen-year-old schoolboys.

"Andrew!"

He lifted his head and through the doorway he saw Bonnie rigid in the glow of the open freezer. Her fists were pressed to the sides of her head.

"My God!" she said.

Yancy sat upright, thinking: *Oh fuck.*

"Andrew, what have you done?" she cried. "What on earth have you done?"

Three

After that night, Bonnie refused to come back to Yancy's house. From her line of questioning it became depressingly clear that she thought him capable of murdering somebody and hacking the corpse into pieces. Yancy took this as a sign that he'd failed, over their time as lovers, to showcase his best qualities.

He told Bonnie that the severed limb was evidence in an unsolved missing-person case and that he was storing it at home as a personal favor to Sheriff Sonny Summers, which was nearly true. Sonny didn't know Yancy still had the arm because Yancy hadn't told him, not wishing to upset the man who would soon be deciding Yancy's future in law enforcement.

Some nights, when it seemed as if Bonnie would never again be available to him, Yancy found himself wishing he'd followed Burton's advice and dumped the dead arm in the mangroves. That remained an option, of course, and perhaps one of these days he'd do it.

After a telephone plea featuring abject begging, Bonnie finally agreed to meet him for breakfast at a diner on Sugarloaf. Afterward they made love in the back of her 4Runner, sharing the cramped space with her husband's smelly golf shoes. From Yancy's vantage it was impossible not to notice that Bonnie was no longer waxing.

"We're moving to Sarasota," she explained. "Cliff's burned out on the Keys."

"But what about the trial?"

"There won't be any trial."

In jubilation Yancy rubbed his chin back and forth across her pale stubble. "You're an angel!" he chortled.

"Whoa, cowboy. It doesn't mean you're off the hook."

"No? Then what?"

"I tried my best, Andrew."

Yancy sat up quickly, bumping his head on the roof. "But they *are* offering me a deal, correct?"

"Yes, and you'll take it," Bonnie said, "because Cliff doesn't want to go to court and you don't want to go to jail. Hand me that bra, please."

"What about my suspension?"

"Look, I'm not even supposed to be talking about this. I honestly *did* try my best." She finished dressing and nimbly vaulted back to the driver's seat. "Out," she commanded Yancy. "I'm late for a facial."

He exited by the rear hatch and hurried around to her window. "I'm going to miss you," he said. When he leaned in for a kiss, she offered only a damp cheek.

"Good-bye, Andrew."

"Good-bye, Plover."

Yancy went back to his car and called Montenegro, his attorney at the public defender's office. "How soon can you be here?" Montenegro asked.

"Give me something to chew on. What the hell's going on?"

"Dude, you know how things work in this town."

Yancy sagged and said, "Damn."

"It's a good news, bad news scenario. I'm around till noon."

There was a bad wreck at Mile Marker 13, a head-on between a gravel truck and a southbound rental car that crossed the center line—somebody's Key West vacation done before it started. The fire department was still hosing the gasoline and blood off the pavement when Yancy inched past the scene in his Crown Vic. He lost a half hour in the traffic jam, but Montenegro was still waiting when he got to the office.

"What's their offer?" Yancy said.

"Just sit down and take some deep breaths."

"I need a lawyer, not a goddamn Lamaze class."

Montenegro smiled and popped a Diet Coke. He was unflappable and beyond the reach of insults, as the job of a public defender required. Although he won his share of trials, few were the days when he didn't have to deliver unwelcome, life-changing tidings to some hapless shitbird. Occasionally he had the pleasure of counseling an innocent client, although Yancy didn't quite fall into that category.

"The good news, Andrew, is that you won't have a felony on your record. Billy Dickinson's agreed to drop the assault charge to misdemeanor battery. Six months' probation, court costs and of course you'll reimburse Dr. Witt for his out-of-pocket medical." Montenegro always looked drawn and pasty. His head was as slick as an eggshell, and he peered at the world beneath veined saggy eyelids.

But the sonofabitch was sharp.

Yancy said, "Okay, get to the bad news."

"Not so fast," the lawyer said. "In addition to reducing the charges, the state agrees not to object if you continue working as a pensioned employee."

"Fan-fucking-tastic!" Yancy sat forward to give Montenegro a high-five, which was returned with a mild pat.

"However—"

"Here we go," said Yancy.

"—Dr. Witt, the victim, strongly feels that you're unfit to be a police officer." Montenegro paused for a slurp of cola. "I don't happen to agree, but I'm not the one who had a suctorial attachment inserted up his rectum."

Yancy slumped in the chair.

Montenegro went on: "Dr. Witt consented to this plea deal under two strict conditions. First, you stay away from his wife. Second, you resign from the sheriff's office. I advise you to do both."

"Let me tell you something disturbing about Mrs. Witt, something I just found out."

"Doesn't matter, Andrew. Sonny's made up his mind. He wants this mess over and done and out of the media."

Yancy said, "No, Monty. Let's go to trial."

"You'll lose," Montenegro said mildly. "You'll be mauled. Slaughtered. Eviscerated. The jury will despise you. And guess what? They won't need testimony from a naughty spouse. They've got the injured victim and, literally, a boatload of eyewitnesses. You've seen those videos taken by the cruise-ship passengers, right? Dude, you're toast."

The fact couldn't be disputed. Yancy said, "Forget what I said about Bonnie."

"Forgotten. But I'm not done with the good news."

"Your words, not mine."

"You've still got a job, Andrew, at almost the same salary." Montenegro lowered his voice. "Sonny arranged it. Be sure to thank him."

"A job doing what?"

"This is where I'm counting on you to keep an open mind."

"Oh boy," said Yancy, laughing softly in despair.

It had not been his finest moment. He'd found a shaded parking spot under a banyan tree on Front Street, where he'd spent an hour tidying up the Crown Vic. The vacuum device at issue wasn't a Hoover, as incorrectly reported by the newspapers, but rather a 14.4-volt Black & Decker cordless model with a rotating nozzle and superior suction.

Nor had the assault been premeditated. Yancy, having spotted Bonnie and her husband walking down the sidewalk, hunkered low in the front seat to avoid being seen. As they passed, he overheard arguing. In a reedy voice Dr. Clifford Witt called his wife either a tramp or a whore, at which point Yancy was certain Bonnie let out a wounded sob. She later would dispute the reason for her tears, blaming a dubiously documented allergy to night-blooming jasmine.

In any event, a misplaced sense of chivalry launched Yancy from the car and—with the vacuum in hand—he followed the quarreling couple to Mallory Square, where they began shouting at each other. Yancy later insisted that Clifford Witt had raised a fist toward his wife although Bonnie, somewhat unhelpfully, denied it.

The attack was swift and Witt was caught flat-footed. Being younger and stronger, Yancy easily pinned the doctor and yanked down his linen trousers. Tourists from the cruise liners assumed the two men were rowdy buskers, for which the city docks are famous, and whipped out cell phones to record the amusing playlet. Despite the authenticity of Witt's screams, nobody moved to disarm Yancy. The Black & Decker snorkeled mercilessly until its batteries petered out.

As officers led him away, Yancy watched Bonnie tend to her fallen husband. A local juggler offered a festive beach umbrella, which was positioned modestly over the appliance sprouting from Clifford Witt's marbled buttocks. Afterward Yancy felt truly awful.

"I admit it—I went totally batshit," he said to Sonny Summers. "It'll never happen again."

"Dr. Witt thought a trial would be embarrassing for everybody—him, his wife, you and the sheriff's department. He did us all a huge favor by going along with this plea."

"Except I lose my badge."

"But not your freedom. You should be celebrating. Monty told you to take the deal, right?"

"Please don't fire me, Sonny."

"What you did to Dr. Witt—I'm sorry, but that's totally unacceptable behavior for a detective, especially in a public venue," the sheriff said. "Did you see the editorial in the *Citizen*? They'd rip me to shreds if I cut you a break."

"But you owe me one, remember? For taking that rotting arm all the way to Miami, just 'cause you didn't want to deal with the case."

"I appreciate that, too. Which is why I made sure you have another job."

"So I lost my mind for five lousy minutes. You've seen what Bonnie Witt looks like? Now imagine her dancing around your kitchen wearing nothing but dive booties. Sonny, I was possessed!"

The sheriff shrugged one shoulder. "Her husband's connected, Andrew. He's biopsied half the county commissioners. You were lucky Dickinson didn't charge you with sodomy."

"What if I told you the On switch got stuck."

"It took us a month before YouTube agreed to pull those nasty clips."

"Fine, I get it." Yancy surrendered to the inevitable. "So, what's my new gig?"

"A good one, under the radar."

"But just until things cool off, right?"

"Sure, Andrew."

Yancy surveyed the items on the sheriff's desk: a glass leaping-dolphin paperweight from the Kiwanis Club, an oversized Rubik's Cube, a MacBook, a coffee mug from *America's Most Wanted* and a half dozen photographs featuring Mrs. Summers and their three children, the youngest of whom wore in every frame the hollow stare of a future serial killer.

"Do you enjoy a good meal?" Sonny Summers said. "The reason I ask is you're pretty thin. Unlike some of us, right?" He patted his gut and chuckled.

"I like to eat, sure."

"But you probably go out a lot, being single and all. You know where I'm headed with this?"

"No fucking clue, Sonny."

"Your new job—it's an enforcement position."

"But not *law* enforcement."

"Next best thing," the sheriff said.

Yancy said, "I'm begging you."

Sonny Summers winked. "Restaurant inspector—it's like a paid vacation, Andrew."

Yancy's jaw made a popping sound. "Roach patrol?"

"They had an opening, so I made a call. The other fella, he got sick and quit."

"He died, Sonny."

"Okay, he died. But first he got sick."

Yancy rose slowly. "I really don't know what to say."

"Thanks is enough. By the way, we'll need your Glock and the keys to the Crown Vic."

Because Sonny Summers technically was no longer his boss, Yancy thought it might be entertaining to tell him the truth about the severed arm—that the Miami medical examiner had rejected custody and now it reposed back in Sonny's jurisdiction, among the Popsicles and grouper fillets in Yancy's kitchen freezer.

Instead, all Yancy said was: "When do I start?"

He was born in South Miami and raised in Homestead. His father was a ranger at Everglades National Park and his mother worked in the dock store at Flamingo. Yancy grew up on the water and dreamed of becoming a back-country charter guide until he realized it would require almost daily contact with tourists. When Yancy was eighteen, his dad put in for a transfer to Yellowstone and Yancy chose to stay behind. The young man was anchored to Florida, for better or worse. A passion for tarpon fishing prolonged his education but eventually he earned a degree in criminal justice and wound up with the Miami Police Department. His marriage to a robbery detective named Celia expired when she accepted a job in Ann Arbor and again Yancy refused to move. They had no children, only a hyperactive border collie that had failed to bond with Yancy despite his earnest efforts. Usually dogs adored him so he was glad to see this one go, though not so much his wife.

For consolation he bought a secondhand Hell's Bay skiff with a ninety-horse outboard. He still had it, and after his dispiriting sit-down with the sheriff he spent the afternoon poling down the oceanside flats. The tide was all wrong but Yancy didn't care. A light sea breeze nudged the boat across crystal shallows, past eagle rays and lemon sharks and an ancient loggerhead turtle, half-blind and thorned with barnacles. It was a perfect afternoon, though he didn't cast at a single fish.

When Yancy returned home he saw a cream-colored Suburban parked in front of the soon-to-be mansion next door. A well-dressed man, stumpy in stature, stood in the future portico. He was slapping at bugs and speaking with agitation into a cell phone. Yancy recognized him as the owner.

The man, whose name was Evan Shook, soon came to the fence. "Excuse me," he said.

Yancy was hosing the salt rime off his boat. He nodded in a false neighborly way.

"There's a dead raccoon in my house," Evan Shook reported with gravity.

"Not good," Yancy said.

"It's huge and it's starting to rot."

Yancy winced sympathetically.

"Could you help me dump it somewhere? I've got people on their way to look at the place. They flew all the way from Dallas."

"Did you call Animal Control?" Yancy asked.

"Lazy pricks, they won't come out here till tomorrow. I could seriously use a hand."

Yancy shut off the hose. "Here's the thing. It's really bad luck to disturb a dead animal, and I can't afford any more of that."

Evan Shook frowned. "Bad luck? Come on."

"Like a Gypsy curse, which is not what I need at the moment. But you can borrow my shovel."

"The damn thing reeks to high hell!"

Yancy changed the subject. "That's quite the Taj Mahal you're building."

"Seven thousand square feet. Tallest house on the island."

"I can believe it."

"You know, anybody who might be looking to buy, now's the time to go big!" Up close, Evan Shook's cheekbones appeared to have been buffed with a shammy. When a black Town Car rolled up to the cul-de-sac, he said, "Oh shit."

The driver opened the rear door and out came an older couple, ruddy and squinting. Evan Shook hurried to intercept them.

Yancy wiped down the skiff and went inside. The Barbancourt was gone so he poured himself a Captain and Coke. He wasn't in the practice of collecting roadkill but he'd spotted the misfortunate raccoon that morning along Key Deer Boulevard. Why leave it for the birds?

From the refrigerator he took a package of hamburger

patties and two ripe tomatoes, which he placed on the counter. He turned down the AC, cranked up Little Feat on the stereo and looked out the kitchen window.

Next door, Evan Shook was attempting to herd the perplexed Texans back to their Town Car. Apparently the tallest house on Big Pine was not being shown today.

Four

Yancy received his first bribe offer at a tin-roofed seafood joint on Stock Island called Stoney's Crab Palace, where he had documented seventeen serious health violations, including mouse droppings, rat droppings, chicken droppings, a tick nursery, open vats of decomposing shrimp, lobsters dating back to the first Bush presidency and, on a tray of baked oysters, a soggy condom.

The owner's name was Brennan. He was slicing plantains when Yancy delivered the feared verdict: "I've got to shut you down."

"A hundred bucks says you won't."

"Jesus, is that blood on your knife?"

"Okay, two hundred bucks," said Brennan.

"Why aren't you wearing gloves?" Yancy asked.

Brennan continued slicing. "Nilsson never gave me no trouble. He ate here all the time."

"And died of hepatitis."

"He ate for free. That was our deal. Six years, never once did he step foot in my kitchen. Nilsson was a good man."

"Nilsson was a lazy fuckwhistle," Yancy said. "I'm writing you up."

Working for the Division of Hotels and Restaurants was the worst job he'd ever had. His appetite had disappeared the first morning, and in three weeks he'd lost eleven pounds. It was traumatizing to see how many ways food could be defiled. His first sighting of maggots put him off rice pudding forever. The opening of lobster season brought no joy because Yancy couldn't bring himself to order from a menu a crustacean of unknown provenance; all he thought about, day and night, was salmonella.

The only reason Brennan wasn't arrested for attempted bribery was that Yancy didn't want to wait around for a deputy to show up. He couldn't clear out of Stoney's fast enough. For lunch he drove home and boiled a potato.

Rogelio Burton stopped by. He looked Yancy up and down and said, "God, what do you weigh?"

"I'm down to a buck sixty."

"And you're, what, six foot two? That ain't healthy, bro."

Yancy picked up a fork and went to work on the potato. "You want half?"

Burton pulled up a stool at the kitchen counter. "The reason I came, Sonny sent me. What'd you ever do with that . . . you know . . . arm?"

"I made it into a weathervane. It's on top of my roof."

"Andrew, this is for real."

"I've still got the damn thing."

"Good. That's what I figured."

"How is that good? I'm breaking about a half dozen laws."

Burton said, "A woman came in the other day to report

her husband missing in a boating accident. He fits the general description."

"Took her long enough."

"She was in Europe for a month. Her old man was heading to the Bahamas to meet some buddies on a fishing trip. The Coast Guard found debris from his Contender a few miles off Marathon. A friend of the widow's had caught the story on Channel 7 about the *Misty* snagging a body part. Anyway, you see the problem."

Yancy did see the problem. He had a human arm in his freezer that shouldn't be there. "So, take it back to Dr. Rawlings," he said. "He can swab for DNA and close the case, or not."

"Way ahead of you. Rawlings saved a tissue sample from the day it got caught. Definitely the same dude. The wife brought in some shavings from her husband's nose-hair trimmer—Rawlings said it's a ninety-nine percent match."

"So what's the hitch?"

Burton took a beer from the refrigerator. "She wants the fucking arm, Andrew. She wants a church service and a formal burial, the whole show."

"And that she shall have." With a screwdriver Yancy began chiseling the limb from the freezer, where it was wedged among a pile of Stouffer's dinners. He placed the frosty appendage on the countertop in front of Burton and said, "All yours, amigo."

The detective used an elbow to push it away. "Rawlings won't take it back because the paperwork says it's at the coroner's in Miami. Now you get the picture? The widow went up there and, of course, they had no body pieces that belonged to her husband."

Yancy heard a door slam and looked outside. A van from Animal Control had parked in front of the half-finished house next door.

"The sheriff was highly pissed with you," Burton went on, "till I explained what happened, how the ME up there wouldn't take the case. I told him there was a chance you kept the arm."

"Lucky I did," Yancy said.

"For safekeeping."

"No, Rog, for taxidermy practice."

"Let me call him." Burton finished off his beer and went out the front door to phone Sonny Summers.

Yancy returned the severed member to its chamber among the frozen entrées. Whenever he'd thought about getting rid of it, the cop in him had said no, what if there'd been a murder, not an accident? Or what if it *was* a drowned Cuban rafter, and somebody's brother or sister in Hialeah was waiting for word? Now that the mystery was solved, Yancy was glad he hadn't followed Burton's advice and discarded it. An arm wasn't much for a wife to bury, but anything was better than an empty casket.

Through the window Yancy noticed unusual activity at the empty construction site. A uniformed officer was dragging a heavy black garbage bag across the pavers toward the Animal Control van. The officer wore a white medical mask, protective goggles and blue rubber gloves that came up to his elbows.

Burton came back inside and said everything was cool. "Sonny's telling the widow that you're the 'authorized custodian' of unclaimed remains. He said just give her the thing."

"That's it?"

"And try to behave, Andrew. She just lost her hubby."

"You ever eat at Stoney's?"

"Man, I love that place. The widow's name is Stripling—here, have her sign this."

Burton produced a Release of Property form that had been conceived with more prosaic items in mind than a severed limb—wallets, car keys, jewelry, eyeglasses, articles of clothing. Somebody had already checked the box labeled "Other."

"Does she keep a copy?" Yancy asked.

"Hell, no. In fact, once she's gone, throw away the paper. It's just for show."

"Gotcha."

Yancy said, "I get major brownie points for this, right? Sonny knows I saved his ass from a major lawsuit, not to mention some ugly press. Losing a dead man's arm!"

"You gotta stay cool."

"Tell him I want my desk back. Tell him I'm wasting away on roach patrol."

"He hasn't forgot about you," Burton said.

"Randolph Nilsson fucking died from this job!"

"Eat lots of yogurt, Andrew. Find a flavor you like."

His next stop after lunch was a Burger King. Compared to Stoney's, the place was as immaculate as a surgical suite. Yancy saw one of the cooks sneeze into a Whopper but the manager made him throw it away, so Yancy didn't write him up.

After a half-hearted inspection he sat down in a booth, where he aimed to kill the whole afternoon. With dull resolve he re-read the state's lengthy checklist of critical code violations.

Did the restaurant obtain its food from an "approved" source? Was it cooked at the proper temperature? Stored at the proper temperature? Handled with minimum contact? Did the employees wash their hands after taking a dump? Were all the restrooms equipped with self-closing doors? Was there toilet paper? Did they wash the dishes in hot water? Did they properly clean and sanitize all food contact surfaces? Were there signs of rodents or insects? Unsafe electrical wiring? Uncapped toxic substances? Did the restaurant have a current state license, and was it prominently displayed?

The manager of the Burger King hovered fretfully. He brought Yancy a cup of coffee, which Yancy insisted on paying for.

"Everything okay?" he asked.

"Relax, sport," Yancy said. "You passed with flying colors."

"Yes!" The manager, who was all of twenty-five, pumped a fist and spun a circle on one heel.

Yancy asked if he'd heard the sad news about Nilsson.

"Who?"

"The guy that had this job before me."

The manager shrugged apologetically. "We never saw him, sir."

"Of course not," Yancy said.

"What happened?"

"He passed away. Mind if I hang out for a while?"

Yancy took out a Margaret Atwood paperback Bonnie had given him. It was highly entertaining, and every now and then he would come to a dog-eared page upon which Bonnie had scribbled comments in the margins:

So funny!

So true!

Why can't I be like this?

Foolishly, Yancy dissected every marked passage in the hopes of finding clues to Bonnie's innermost feelings. On some pages he'd spy a slanted notation, always in lavender ink, that referred to their own relationship, or to him by name.

Sounds like something A.Y. would say.

Pure Andrew!

Just like a certain man I know.

No matter what the context, Yancy was warmed to be in Bonnie's thoughts, and also to know that she obviously wasn't sharing the book with her husband. On a whim he dialed her cell phone and left a lustful message that he hoped would make her blush. She hadn't spoken to him since that quickie in the 4Runner.

The manager brought a plate of fries, which Yancy accepted along with a refill on the coffee. By Keys standards it could hardly be considered a payoff. His phone thrummed and lit up, and so did his heart.

But it wasn't Bonnie calling.

"My name is Eve Stripling. Are you Detective Yancy?"

"Actually, it's Inspector Yancy." As in roach inspector.

"Sheriff Summers gave me your number."

She sounded fairly young. The accent was flat, midwestern.

Yancy said, "I'm sorry for your loss, Mrs. Stripling."

"Yes, it's awful, just awful. Where's the best place to meet up?"

Before Evan Shook's bulldozers razed the lot next door, Yancy went outside almost every evening to watch the white-tailed Key deer nibble on the hammock scrub and red mangroves. They were fantastically small and delicate-looking; even a buck was no bigger than a golden retriever. Only a few hundred of the deer remained, roaming a handful of islands. Big Pine and No Name Key had the most, but the animals were hapless when it came to avoiding cars, especially at night. Every year the *Citizen* published a gloomy scorecard of roadkills as the species teetered toward extinction. Not everyone shared Yancy's fondness for his four-legged neighbors; signs urging motorists to watch out for the critters were sometimes found spray-painted as rifle sights.

Ninety-two hundred acres had been patched together as a refuge for the remaining deer. Being unable to read, they frequently meandered beyond its boundaries. Some had become recklessly tame, mooching handouts from tourists and losing all fear of humans. Yancy never fed the small herd that appeared at dusk on the land beside his own. He didn't snap pictures, or whistle, or make up cute names for the fawns. He just sat there sipping rum and watching the deer do their thing.

Now they were gone, and Evan Shook's spec house was fucking up the sunset.

Yancy trudged inside and transferred the severed arm from his freezer to the Igloo cooler. He then toted the cooler to his personal 1993 Subaru—the roomy Crown Vic having been reassigned to a working detective—and drove to the Winn-Dixie supermarket. There he purchased two large bags of ice to make sure the limb belonging to Eve Stripling's late husband didn't thaw during her drive back home, wherever that might be.

She arrived at the store a half hour late driving a

generic Malibu. To Yancy it looked like a rental. He was leaning against the front fender of his car, sporting a red baseball cap so she could locate him in the parking lot.

"This feels like a dope deal," she said with a nervous smile. "You *are* Inspector Yancy, right?"

"And you must be Mrs. Stripling."

"Eve is fine." She was in her mid-thirties, slightly on the heavy side. The outfit was gold-strapped sandals, tight white jeans and a long-sleeved blue cotton top. Her auburn hair was tied back and her pale nose was freckled. All this Yancy could see by the light of the grocery store.

"Guess I should have a look," she said.

"You sure about that?"

"It's all I got, all that's left of my sweet Nicky."

Yancy set the cooler on the warm hood of the Malibu and removed the lid. Fortunately, the parking lot wasn't crowded. He untaped the bubble wrapping to expose the arm.

The upraised middle finger was the first thing to greet Eve Stripling.

"Who's the comedian?" She was clutching her elbows to her midsection, as if trying to stop herself from spinning into orbit.

"That's how they found it," Yancy told her. "Weird, I know."

She managed a brittle laugh. "Maybe it was Nicky flipping off the sharks."

"Is that his wedding band?"

"I'm pretty sure." She held her breath and leaned close to examine the stiffened purple hand. "You got a flashlight?"

Yancy had one in the Subaru. The batteries were weak but he shook it until the bulb lit up.

Eve Stripling gave a heavy nod. "That's his ring. It's most definitely him."

She didn't comment on the etiolated band of skin where her husband's watch had been, which surprised Yancy. Earlier he'd received a phone call from comely Dr. Campesino in Miami. Apparently the pathologist wasn't completely put off by Yancy's incompetent flirting, for in her spare time she'd digitally enlarged her photograph of the rectangular outline on the wrist of the phantom limb. In that way she was able through online resources to identify the missing watch as a limited-edition Wyler Genève Tourbillon, distinguishable by a unique clasped crown shield and also for its suggested retail price of $145,000. Yancy had assumed that the loss of such an expensive timepiece would catch the notice of a widow, even in the throes of grief. But Eve Stripling said nothing, so Yancy left the subject untouched.

A radish-eyed old geezer in hiking books walked by, pushing a grocery cart. He saw the two of them looking into the cooler and piped, "You catch some fish?"

"Lobsters," Yancy said.

"How much you want for 'em?"

"Not for sale."

"Don't be a dick."

Yancy took out the dead arm and waved it at the old man, who shuffled off quickly. Eve Stripling wore an expression of suppressed dismay. After repacking the limb, Yancy placed the cooler in the trunk of the Chevy.

He said, "What was Nick's line of work?"

Now on a first-name basis with the victim.

"Oh, he's retired."

Just like Johnny Mendez, Yancy thought, although Nick Stripling probably hadn't made his fortune looting a Crime Stoppers account.

"Did they ever find his boat?"

"Just some cushions and spare gas cans," Eve Stripling said. "Also a deflated life raft—they said it must've got popped by fish hooks."

"Was there a fuel slick?"

"Yeah, fives miles off the Sombrero Lighthouse. His body floated south, obviously."

"Anybody else on board?"

"No, just Nicky. He was on his way to Cay Sal to catch up with some friends."

A mosquito was feasting in a dimple on Eve Stripling's chin. Under more casual circumstances Yancy would have reached over and flicked it away. Instead he said, "The bugs are out of control tonight. Let's sit in the car."

"I should really be going."

"This won't take much longer."

"But the sheriff promised—"

"Just a couple more questions. All routine." That's what detectives did, they asked questions. Yancy meant to stay in practice.

He opened the door for Eve Stripling, then went around and got in the passenger side. The new smell confirmed it was a rental.

"How far's your drive?" he asked.

"Miami Beach."

A short hop not to bring your own wheels, Yancy thought, but he let it go. She'd probably rented the Chevy because she was afraid her husband's dead arm would stink up the Jaguar. "Was Nick a good swimmer?"

"So-so. He loved that damn fishing boat, though."

"How old was he?"

"Forty-six. We've got a condo on Duck Key," Eve Stripling said, "but I was in Paris when it happened."

"When did you learn he was missing?"

"The France trip was a present from Nicky. I wasn't worried when I didn't hear from him because he hardly ever calls from the islands. The cell service over there is suck-o. He was supposed to get home the Sunday after I did. When he didn't show up, I just figured the fishing must be super good and he'd decided to stay. Why aren't you writing any of this down?"

"Like I said, it's just routine."

"So, anyway, Wednesday comes and still no Nicky. That's when I started calling around and the Coast Guard told me what they found. They said it was super rough that weekend and his boat probably swamped."

"That happens."

"He called it *Summer's Eve*," she said fondly, "after me."

Also the name of a douche, thought Yancy. But, hey, it's the thought that counts.

"Are we done?" she asked.

"Almost." From a breast pocket he took the Release of Property form that Burton had given him. Eve Stripling switched on the dome light so she could read it.

"How long were you married?" Yancy asked.

"Seven years in February." She turned her head to show him the diamond studs in her ears. They were substantial. "He bought me these for our anniversary."

"Sweet. Do you have children?"

"Nicky has a grown daughter." She signed the paper and handed it back to him. "This still doesn't seem real," she said in a raw, whispery voice.

"When's the service?"

"Day after tomorrow."

"Soon, then."

"The funeral home says there's not much to do. Being it's just, you know, an arm."

"They can fix that middle finger, no problem."

Eve Stripling looked puzzled.

"Not that you'd have an open casket," Yancy added. "But just in case..."

"Oh, right. Good idea."

He got out of the car. "Again, I'm sorry for your loss."

"Thank you, Inspector."

Behind the wheel Eve Stripling appeared smaller and almost contorted. With a shudder she hunched forward, squeezing her eyes closed, and it was Yancy's impression that she was trying very hard to cry.

Five

Miguel was no beekeeper; he made that clear. He was an exterminator of bees, a highly trained assassin.

"Tell me what you've got," Yancy said.

"There's an old wood house on Ramrod, the whole east wall. I am ripping it apart tomorrow."

"I hope the hive is large."

Miguel laughed, flashing a gold-tipped incisor. "The hive is a motherfucker, Andrew. You cannot believe how big."

"But how are you going to move the damn thing?"

"Don't worry. It is what you hire me for."

"And the bees will follow? That's the part I don't understand." Yancy had a vision of Miguel's truck weaving down Highway 1 while enclouded by a seething swarm.

"They sleep at night," Miguel said. "I got a system."

"Dead bees won't do the trick. They have to be alive."

Miguel gave a sigh he reserved for thick-skulled gringos. "For sure, Andrew. Alive."

"How much do you charge?"

"For such a fucked-up job? Three hundred, plus gas."

"I can probably swing two-fifty."

"Bullshit," Miguel said. Then: "Okay, two-fifty."

Yancy handed him a piece of paper with the address. Miguel glanced at it and said, "Who lives here?"

"Nobody. It's under construction."

"Excellent, my friend. Where you want me to put the hive?"

"The master bedroom would be lovely. It's on the top floor, facing the Gulf."

"No problem." Miguel took the cash from Yancy and counted it. "Here is the thing, Andrew, because I am what you call a straight shooter. When they find that motherfucking hive, the people that own the house, I'm the one they gone to call first."

"Well, who else?" Yancy said.

"'Cause I'm the top bee guy from here to the Redlands."

"Everybody knows that, Miguel. Everybody." Yancy envied the man's pride in his work. "Shook is the owner's name. When he calls, I'm thinking maybe you could be tied up for a while—let those poor honeybees have some fun."

"I got so much fucking jobs right now, my wife she is ready to kill me."

"All right, then. Mr. Shook can wait." Yancy gave Miguel another twenty-dollar bill.

"You want, I'll e-mail to you some pictures, Andrew. For proof."

"Not necessary, amigo. I'll know when it's done."

Miguel was grinning as Yancy got in his car. "You look sharp, man, all pimped out. Must be some world-class pussy waiting up on the mainland."

"Actually," said Yancy, "I'm going to a funeral."

• • •

A short death notice had been posted on the *Herald*'s website: Nicholas Joseph Stripling, age forty-six, of Miami Beach. Survived by his loving wife, Eve, and one daughter, Caitlin Cox. Private services to be held at the Neo-Pentecostal Church of Faith, followed by interment at the St. Lazarus Gardens and Water Park in North Miami.

North Miami!

The drive took almost four hours in manic traffic, Yancy cussing humanity most of the way. He owned one dreary black suit that he'd bought years earlier for his mother's service, and he hadn't worn it since. Now the coat hung too loosely on his frame, Yancy having dropped so much weight since becoming a restaurant sleuth. The paradox wasn't lost on him—he'd worked many bloody crime scenes and never once felt queasy, yet the glimpse of a desiccated rat carcass in a vat of stale muffin mix left him poleaxed with revulsion.

So far, the only good thing about the job was that nobody complained if he didn't show up. The restaurant owners were relieved not to be inspected, and they made no inquiries to Yancy's supervisor regarding his whereabouts.

His decision to skip work and attend Nicky Stripling's burial was out of character for two reasons. First, Yancy had always been a punctual public employee and, second, he strenuously avoided graveyards. A morgue full of chilled stiffs was no problem, but for some reason a field of sunlit tombstones gave him the willies.

Ever since meeting Eve Stripling, Yancy had been sleeping poorly, nagged by the missing pieces of her story—a story of no evident interest to anyone but him. It was an easy matter to feed Nick Stripling's name through the state crime computer, revealing a single arrest and conviction at the age of twenty-seven. The colorful details were in a file at the courthouse.

Young Nicky had had a minor role in a common Florida insurance scam in which fraudsters would intentionally crash cars into innocent drivers and then submit mountains of phony medical claims, which the victims' insurance companies almost always paid off. Stripling acted as the driver and was skilled at directing each staged collision with such finesse—front bumper angled into a rear rocker panel, the impact buffered by a subtle last-second deceleration—that neither he nor any of his co-conspirators received so much as a knot on the head. Whiplash was the faked injury of choice because of its domino cascade of serial billings and easy profits. The lineup of complicit health-care providers included an alcoholic chiropractor, a senile orthopedist, an unlicensed radiologist and a battalion of nonexistent physical therapists. Nick Stripling's take for each crash was relatively paltry, so he'd turned state's witness at the first prodding from investigators. He ended up getting ninety days in the county jail and five years' probation.

From such inauspicious beginnings Stripling was somehow able to retire in his forties. Yancy was curious to know the secret of the man's prosperous turnaround.

No more than fifty hardy souls showed up for the funeral in a baking summer heat that undulated off the bright green grass. Yancy feared he might sweat through his suit. Eve Stripling wore a black dress, black heels and a veil. She sat in the shade under the canopy before a walnut coffin piled with wreaths. Yancy wondered if the mortician had prorated his embalming fee, since there was only one limb to bury.

A young blond woman, also dressed in black, sat at the opposite end of the first row. Yancy assumed she was Caitlin Cox, Nick Stripling's daughter from a prior marriage. From her body language Yancy perceived that she wasn't enamored with her father's current wife. Wearing saucer-sized sunglasses, Caitlin Cox fanned herself and every so often whispered to her buzz-cut husband, who was built like a stevedore.

Yancy kept well back from the mourners and remained standing. Shielding his eyes from the sun, he noticed he wasn't alone; two other men were maintaining a practiced distance, and their suits were charcoal gray, not black. Law enforcement of some sort, Yancy guessed. They were sweaty, too. August in the city could wilt a soul.

A generic silver-haired preacher rose and said saintly things about Nick Stripling before the coffin was lowered. Eve Stripling stood up and thanked everyone for coming. She said she'd placed in Nick's casket a childhood Bible and his favorite speargun. To Yancy it seemed a bold hobby—spearfishing—for a mediocre swimmer, as Mrs. Stripling had described her late spouse when she came to collect his left arm.

After the mourners broke into small groups and headed for their cars, Yancy approached the two cop types and said, "Friends of the deceased?"

No response except barracuda stares. Both of the men had brown hair, light eyebrows and cinder-block chins.

"You must be feds," Yancy remarked.

"Don't be an asshole," said one.

"That's bad luck, swearing in a cemetery. Like a Gypsy curse."

The men turned to leave.

"Or maybe it's blowing each other in a cemetery," Yancy said. "I forget which."

He found himself dodging Eve Stripling, although she probably wouldn't have recognized him in a suit and a tie. While waiting for her limousine to depart, Yancy drifted off among the sun-bleached headstones. Almost immediately he came across some unlucky bastard who'd been born on Yancy's very own birthday and now lay six feet under. Yancy's respiration shallowed and his palms moistened and his skin felt like it was crawling with centipedes. He stumbled a few plots farther, dropped to one knee and upchucked on the final resting site of one Marlene Suzanne Moody, who by Yancy's quick calculation had passed away at age ninety-nine and was now safe from indignity.

After wiping his cheeks and smoothing the wrinkles from his pants, Yancy made his way back to the funeral canopy. Only Caitlin Cox and her husband remained at the grave. They stood shoulder to shoulder, saying nothing.

Yancy walked up and offered his condolences.

"Were you a friend of Dad's?" she asked.

"I'm Inspector Yancy, from the Keys. I was in charge of your father's remains."

He presented one of his old detective cards. He figured what the hell—his cell number hadn't changed. Caitlin's husband asked Yancy why he'd come to the burial.

"Sometimes, in these cases, the family has questions. I just wanted to be available."

It was a smooth response, caring yet professional. Yancy had polished the wording while waiting for the funeral procession to arrive.

Caitlin put his card in her handbag. A pair of cemetery attendants hung back on the edge of the shade. They weren't allowed to start shoveling the dirt over Nick Stripling's coffin until all the mourners were gone.

His daughter said, "I do have a question, Inspector."

Yancy liked the Scotland Yard–ish ring of his new title. "I'll do my best," he said.

"We peeked at it in the funeral home—Dad's arm."

Jesus, Yancy thought. *Don't tell me they were too lazy to fix the finger.*

"It happened during rigor mortis," he said.

Caitlin Stripling Cox seemed puzzled. "What on earth are you talking about?"

Her husband spoke up. "She means the wedding ring. Tell him, sweetheart."

"Eve switched it out," she said.

"The one I saw on your father's hand looked like platinum," Yancy said.

"That's right. And the one he's wearing now is yellow gold. Fourteen karat, *maybe*." The downgrade was reported with somber disdain.

"Is it possible Eve decided to keep the original ring for sentimental reasons?"

"Lots of stuff is possible." Caitlin frowned down at the casket. Yancy hoped she wasn't expecting him to pry open the lid and appraise the substitute wedding band.

"Why don't you ask Eve about it?"

"Because she hates me and I hate her. She's a vicious cunt, by the way."

Caitlin's husband said, "Sweetheart, please." His shirt collar was soaked, and a crystal droplet of perspiration clung to one of his earlobes. Yancy didn't stare.

"A vicious greedy lying cunt," elaborated Stripling's daughter.

"It's a rough time for everyone," Yancy said.

"Is that legal—taking his ring?"

"As his wife, she's entitled."

"She probably stole his goddamn watch, too!"

Caitlin Cox was in her early twenties. Yancy figured she must have been a baby when her old man was staging auto accidents to rip off insurance companies.

He said, "The watch was already gone when they found your father's arm."

"Are you still on the case, or what?"

"I was in charge of delivering the remains. Unless some new information turns up, there's not much else to be done."

Caitlin laughed acidly. "I told you so, Simon," she muttered sideways to her husband. "Nobody wants to investigate."

"Investigate what exactly?" Yancy asked.

"Eve killed him, Inspector. She murdered my father."

Simon Cox put an arm around his wife. "Okay, that's the Xanax talking. Let's go home, baby."

Yancy offered to meet with them later in private. Caitlin said there was no point. "Don't you see? She already got away with it!"

Her husband steered her away from the grave, Yancy following.

"What makes you think she killed him, Caitlin?"

"Oh, please."

"Did your dad say something about Eve? Was he unhappy in the marriage?"

Caitlin pulled free of Simon and spun around. "How the hell would I know if he was happy or not? I haven't talked to the sonofabitch in years."

The captain of the *Misty Momma IV* was Keith Fitzpatrick, a fourth-generation Conch. His father had smuggled ganja from Jamaica, his grandfather had shipped rum from Havana and his great-grandfather had salvaged wrecked schooners that had been lured by deviously placed torches to the unforgiving reefs of Key West. Keith Fitzpatrick himself was a renowned fish hawk, booked years in advance, and therefore satisfied to abide the law. He made good money because he ran a thirty-eight-footer with only one mate.

Yancy met him for a beer at the Half Shell Raw Bar on the harbor. The motto of the place was "Eat It Raw!" Tourists went berserk for the T-shirts.

Fitzpatrick said, "Andrew, I heard Sonny canned your ass."

"Temporarily."

"That sucks." Fitzpatrick's face was boot brown except for a white goggle stripe from his sunglasses. His forearms were like glazed cudgels, his hands scarred and scaly.

"They got me doing restaurant inspections," Yancy said.

"No way. You aren't the one that shut down Stoney's?"

"Listen, man, that kitchen—it was crawling with *everything*. So gross."

"I love that place," said Fitzpatrick.

Yancy placed the small gray shark tooth on the bar.

Fitzpatrick picked it up between a thumb and forefinger and turned it in the light. "Nuthin' special," he said.

"What kind is it?"

"Looks like a bonnethead. Maybe a baby lemon."

"But not a bull shark or a tiger, right?"

Fitzpatrick shook his head and chuckled. "Not this little runt, no."

"That's what I think, too," said Yancy.

Bonnetheads, the smallest species of hammerheads, averaged only about three feet in length. It was unlikely that any shark so small would be far offshore feeding on a human body, competing with the monsters.

"Where'd the tooth come from, Andrew?"

"That arm you snagged."

"No shit?" Fitzpatrick examined it once more. "Don't make sense, unless the dead guy's boat sunk in the shallows. Which I heard he went down off Sombrero Light."

"Let's say he drowned in deep water and the body washed up on a flat."

"*What* flat?"

"Let's just say."

"Still don't explain how his whole arm got twisted off the way it did," said Fitzpatrick. "I never seen a bonnethead could do that. You?"

"Nope. I don't believe it's possible."

"So what is it you think happened? Tell me."

"I'm not sure."

"But Sonny's keepin' you on the case."

Yancy gave a misleading wink. "Let's not advertise it. Want another beer?" He ordered a couple more Budweisers.

Fitzpatrick asked if other body pieces had been found. "A leg or a head? Whatever."

"Nothing but that arm."

They were interrupted by a pushy fellow in a papaya polo shirt who recognized Fitzpatrick from a fishing website and wanted to go "load up" on mahi the next day. Fitzpatrick said he was booked until the Second Coming, but he provided the name of another charter captain.

When they were alone again, Fitzpatrick turned to Yancy and said, "How you doing on roach patrol? It's got to be different."

"Look at me." Yancy flapped his shirt collar to display his new pencil neck. "Every time I walk into a joint, all I can think about is maybe some guy in the kitchen is greasing his ass with the pizza dough. Crazy shit like that, swear to God. I can barely stand the sight of food."

"Come on, man, you gotta eat. Let's get some conch fritters."

"Go for it. I'm full."

"Promise me you won't shut this place down, too. I'm dead serious—you'd start a damn riot."

Yancy said, "You knew Randolph Nilsson, right? The last guy who had my job."

"Yeah, he was married to my second wife's third cousin. Or maybe it was my third wife's second cousin. Anyhow, I'm the one scattered his ashes out by the Mud Keys. He was only fifty-three at the end. But life ain't fair, right?"

"No, Keith, it's not."

Two more bottles of beer appeared on the bar counter, along with a platter of raw oysters. Fitzpatrick turned to scout the room, which had filled with lobster people and locals. His gaze fixed on a rangy, black-haired kid sitting beside a hard-looking blonde at a corner table. The kid wore a tight T-shirt and a scraggly pubic goatee. In his mouth bobbed an unlit cigarette, and both arms were extravagantly tattooed in a Neptunian motif. He gave Fitzpatrick a smirking salute, and the captain nodded back.

"Who's the Tommy Lee impersonator?" Yancy asked.

"He used to mate for me," Fitzpatrick said, "till a couple weeks ago."

"What boat is he on now?"

"The S.S. *Jackoff*."

"Gotcha."

"Mr. Charles Phinney, he don't need to work no more. Or so he informed me the night he quit. This was after I chewed him out for not hosin' off the tackle and wipin' down the teak. He says, 'Fuck you, old man, you can stuff this shitty job.'"

"Now he's buying you beer and oysters," Yancy said, "and dating hookers."

"Showin' off is all. He said he come into serious money, but that could mean he won eighty-five bucks on the Lotto scratch-off. Now all of a sudden he's Donald fucking Trump."

Yancy was fond of shellfish but he couldn't even look at the plate. It was tragic, what his new job was doing to him. "Was Phinney working on the *Misty* the day you caught the dead arm?"

"He was," Fitzpatrick said. "That useless sonofabitch couldn't even get it unhooked."

When Yancy looked back, the kid and the prostitute were heading for the door. Fitzpatrick slurped an oyster.

He said, "Took me a month to teach that fucking retard how to rig a bait."

"You'll hear from him again."

"Don't say that, Andrew."

"When the money runs out, he'll come begging to get back on the *Misty*."

Two gunshots rang out from the parking lot. A woman began shrieking Phinney's name.

"Or maybe not," Yancy said.

Six

The typical Key West murder is a drunken altercation over debts, dope or dance partners. Premeditated robbery-homicides are rare because they require a level of planning and sober enterprise seldom encountered among the island's indolent felons.

Charles Phinney was already dead when Yancy reached his side. He lay fish-eyed and soaked with blood, the pockets of his black jeans jerked inside out. His companion, who turned out not to be a hooker, said the killer rolled up on a blue moped, shot Phinney twice, stole his cash and took off. She said the man wore a camo sun mask and a red or orange rain poncho, which would have drawn notice anywhere except Margaret Street on a Friday night.

Because of the location of the crime, the city police—not the sheriff's office—would be handling the investigation. Uniformed officers taped off the intersection at Caroline and kept the crowd back while a paramedic pounded for show on Phinney's chest. Keith Fitzpatrick, whose leathery face had drained to gray, hung around until the kid's body was loaded into an ambulance. Then he said he was going home and drink himself to sleep.

Yancy remained at the scene with Phinney's girlfriend. Her name was Madeline and she worked at a T-shirt shop on Duval. She said the shop was owned by Russian gangsters, and that's who killed Phinney.

"They must've heard him braggin' about the money," she said.

Yancy asked how much he was carrying.

"Thousand bucks, maybe."

"Where'd he get it?"

"A job." Madeline sniffed and looked away. Tears streaked her chalky makeup.

Yancy said, "What was he dealing—coke? Meth?"

Madeline turned back with a narrow look. "You a cop or something?"

"I'm on sabbatical." Which was true enough.

She wiped her eyes. "I never seen anybody get shot before. Goddamn." She said she and Phinney had been dating only a month or so. "He was selling pot," she added.

Yancy noticed her reading his reaction, trying to figure out if he believed her.

He said, "So what happened was he made a big score and quit his job on the *Misty*."

"Yeah. Exactly."

"And you really think your bosses killed him for a grand?"

Madeline seemed to be reconsidering her theory. "Will I have to, like, go to court?"

"If there's a trial, sure."

"Thing is, Charlie was talkin' all over town. The

Russians weren't the only ones knew he had a wad." She shrugged. "Could've been anybody that shot him."

Yancy overheard one of the city detectives say that the blue moped was a rental. It had already been found, abandoned in an alley off Southard.

"I can't afford to lose my job," Madeline said. She wore her bleached hair in a spiky crop. Her hands were rough and her eyes were old-looking. Yancy figured she had fifteen years on Phinney.

"You got a smoke?" she said. "I'm comin' apart here."

"I quit a long time ago. Sorry."

"Oh. You're one of *them*."

Yancy picked a virgin Marlboro off the pavement. It was the same one Phinney was mouthing when he'd walked out of the oyster bar, the one he had paused to light when the robber on the moped shot him.

Madeline took the dead man's cigarette from Yancy's hand and said, "Why the hell not?"

That same night, 264 miles away, a man on the eastern coast of Andros Island lightly tapped on the door of a woman known as the Dragon Queen. When she let him in, the man, whose name was Neville, said, "I need some woo-doo on a white mon."

The Dragon Queen sat down in a flaking wicker chair. "What de hell's wrong wit your boy dere? He dont look right."

"Dot's not my boy," Neville said. "Dot's a monkey I look ahfta."

He'd won the animal in a game of dominoes with a sponger from Fresh Creek. The sponger told him it was the same monkey from the Johnny Depp pirate movies, which were filmed nearby in the Exumas. Neville named his new pet Driggs and he fed him too much deep-fried food. Before long the monkey got wrinkled and tufts of fur began falling out. He defiantly refused housebreaking so Neville made him wear disposable baby diapers with holes cut out for his tail. Now the nearly hairless creature was hugging Neville's left leg and chittering in dread of the voodoo woman.

She rocked forward to squint. "He sure dont favor you, suh. Bettuh talk to de missus and find out who she been messin' wit, ha!"

Neville let it go. The Dragon Queen was either far-sighted or wasted, possibly both.

"Who dis white devil you wish to be rid of?" she asked.

"He go by de name Chrissofer."

Neville presented a bottle of Bacardi 8, which he had traded for a bucket of conch meat and two hogfish with the captain of a yacht anchored in the South Bight. It was well known that the Dragon Queen was partial to good rum.

"You got any ting belongs to dis mon?"

"Piece a shoyt." Neville unfolded a teal-colored part of a sports shirt of the vented style that American sports-men wore to the bonefish lodges. Neville had recovered the fragment from Christopher's garbage can.

He said, "I want you pudda spell on 'im."

The Dragon Queen had a pink batik scarf swirled 'round her head, and a necklace strung with polished bivalves. She took the piece of the white man's shirt and sniffed it.

"I do dis ting fuh you, he might go'n die," she said.

Neville thought about it. "Whatever God's will."

"Where de white mon aht?"

"Bannister Point. Dey said yestuhdey he go eat lunch aht de conch shack in Rocky Town. 'Im and his woman."

"He like dot place, huh?" The Dragon Queen opened the rum and filled a stained coffee mug. She didn't offer any to Neville, which was fine. He was nervous being in the same house, her house, because of her reputation as a wanton man-eater. Three of her much younger boyfriends had fallen dead under murky circumstances. A fourth had fled Andros, supposedly to Cuba. Neville concentrated on avoiding the Dragon Queen's gaze, which was said to bewitch even the strongest of men.

She asked about Christopher's woman. "A white lady?"

"Yeah," Neville said. "She come 'n' go."

"Wot her name?"

"I dunno. She keep to huhself, same as 'im."

"So, tell me why you wish bod fuh dis mon." The Dragon Queen was smiling now. She had a mashed-up nose and the overbite of an ancient tortoise.

Neville said, "Juss so he get off de island, no matter how."

"All right, suh."

She traced her callused brown fingers along the strip of fabric, which was coiled like a boa in her lap. "He not a Bahamian, dis white devil. He not from Freeport or Abaco."

"No, ma'am, dot's true. He from de States."

"Den woo-doo must be extra strong. Cost more, too, you unnerstahn."

"All right."

"Bring me nodder bottle a rum."

Neville nodded. "Dot I will."

"And next time, you stay 'round to keep me comp'ny. But not tonight." The Dragon Queen pointed to the door.

Neville's heart was hammering as he got on his bike and pedaled away down the scraped coral path. The diapered monkey, riding on Neville's head, maintained his perch by clinging fiercely to Neville's ears. His tiny fingertips were moist and the nails felt sharp. Neville was grateful for the moonlight that helped him find his way.

Desperation had driven him to visit the voodoo lady. The white man named Christopher was planning to put up a resort for rich tourists on a stretch of waterfront where Neville lived, where his father and grandfather had lived before him. Recently Neville had been ordered to pack up and move. A letter was delivered saying his half-sister in Canada had sold the family property on Andros and upon closing would send Neville his share of the proceeds, which he didn't want.

What he wanted was to live and die on the beach, under the shade of casuarinas.

Nobody at the government office in Lizard Cay or even Nassau could straighten out the situation, so with trepidation Neville had turned to the Dragon Queen. He was unaware that his problem lay beyond her supernatural powers and was in fact connected to faraway criminal events in the Florida Keys, including the cold-blooded murder that very evening of a foolhardy boat mate named Charles Phinney.

Neville's bicycle jounced off a rocky divot as he coasted downhill, and a sharp pinch of pain caused him to cry out. "Bod monkey! Bod monkey!"

But the frightened animal kept his teeth buried in

Neville's scalp until they skidded to a stop in front of the house.

Yancy got home around midnight and rolled a joint. The stuff was called Trainwreck yet it failed to knock him into a proper stupor. Although he'd seen a number of dead gunshot victims, he remained disturbed by the pooled emptiness in Charlie Phinney's eyes.

A check of his cell phone revealed, to his surprise, three messages from three different women. It had been eons since such a fine thing had happened.

The first caller was Bonnie Witt, formerly known as Plover Chase, who'd called from Sarasota to leave the following voice mail: "Hey, it's me. Don't get all hot and bothered, but I've been thinking impure thoughts about you. Cliff hasn't touched me in ages because he's experimenting with autoerotic asphyxiation—you know, where guys beat off while they're faux-strangling themselves? Very classy. Anyhow, he's a total klutz, as you know, so I'm pretty sure he's going to hang himself to death one of these nights in the broom closet. Twice already I found him passed out on the floor, blue as a jellyfish. And yesterday he showed me how to use a portable defibrillator, just in case he screws up. I guess what I'm saying, Andrew— and God knows I don't expect you to wait around—I think there's a fifty-fifty chance I'll be single again soon. Anyway, give me a call."

The second voice mail was from Dr. Rosa Campesino, whom Yancy had texted during an idle period at the crime scene, while detectives were interviewing Phinney's girl-friend. The pathologist sounded very interested to hear that the shark tooth she'd tweezered from the severed arm belonged to a small specimen, possibly an inshore species:

"That definitely raises the possibility of foul play. This boat captain you spoke with, would you consider him an expert? Just to be sure, you should send the tooth to the Rosenstiel School at the University of Miami. They've got some of the top shark people in the world. Maybe you could keep me posted on how this all sorts out, okay? Also . . . well, I want to apologize for telling a small lie the day you came to the office. I'm not really married to a sniper on the SWAT team. Actually, I'm not married at all. Sorry I jerked you around—just wasn't in the mood for lunch."

The last message was from Caitlin Cox, estranged daughter of the late Nicholas Stripling, who said: "Sorry to hassle you on a weekend, *Inspector,* but remember what I told you at the funeral? About my stepmother, that greedy hose monster? Well, now I've got proof! Seriously, it's a lock. So call me right away. I mean, if you want to be a big fucking hero and solve this case."

It was an avalanche of information for a stoned person to absorb. Yancy kicked off his flip-flops and stretched out on the kitchen counter and blinked up at the curled ceiling panels. A mental picture of Dr. Clifford Witt masturbating bug-eyed with a noose around his neck caused Yancy to wonder if Bonnie's husband had actually enjoyed the vacuum-cleaner assault that had cost Yancy his detective job. The phone message gave him no reason to believe Bonnie would come rushing back to the Keys, even if freed by widowhood from Clifford's grasp. Yancy leaned toward the hard-edged view that she was regretting her tipsy confession and was angling to keep his hopes for romance alive so that he wouldn't spill the beans about her fugitive status.

The call from Rosa Campesino was more intriguing, as it opened a door to future communications and possibly a date. At least that's how Yancy chose to construe her words. He'd never wooed a coroner and wasn't sure how to read the signals. He would replay radiant Rosa's message tomorrow, when his head was clear.

Finally, there was Caitlin Cox. Yancy doubted that she had absolute proof her father had been murdered, but she might have stumbled across something worth knowing. He decided to meet with her, and not just because he was bored out of his skull on roach patrol. Yancy felt a cop-like responsibility to sort out the truth about Nick Stripling, whose severed arm had been the centerpiece of Yancy's freezer during all those days when nobody had wanted it.

Furthermore, Yancy perceived—even under the woozy sway of ganja—an opportunity for redemption in the event that Eve Stripling really had killed her husband and tried to make it look like a boat accident. If Yancy, riding solo, was able to nail the widow for homicide, what else could Sheriff Sonny Summers do but reinstate him to the force?

That was Yancy's last fanciful thought before floating to sleep on the kitchen counter, and awaking hours later to the sound of a scream.

Seven

Woodrow and Ipolene Spillwright owned three houses. The first was a spacious plantation-style spread in their hometown of Raleigh, North Carolina, where Woodrow had retired from an executive position with R. J. Reynolds. The second was a ranch-style home near Tempe, Arizona, where the arid climate was said to benefit those with pernicious lung disorders of the sort that afflicted Woodrow, a brainlessly faithful consumer of his employer's tobacco products. The third Spillwright residence was a two-bedroom lakeside cottage in Maine, where the deer flies were so bloodthirsty that Ipolene (or "Ippy" as she was known in Raleigh social circles) would spool her pudgy bare ankles with Glad wrap before scuttling to the mailbox in the morning.

In Ipolene Spillwright's opinion, three houses were two too many for a couple pushing seventy. However, her husband had recently visited Florida with his country-club buddies and managed to land a seven-pound bonefish, a seemingly prosaic event that robbed him of all common sense. He'd returned to North Carolina and proclaimed his desire to purchase a winter home in the Keys, where he could hone his skills with a saltwater fly rod. Mrs. Spillwright told Woodrow that he'd lost his marbles but he refused to give up the quest. Their arguments were brief (for he quickly ran short of breath) yet animated. Finally, after Woodrow agreed to sell the Maine cottage and place the Arizona house in a rental pool, Ipolene said she would accompany him down to "Hemingway country" to look for a place on the water.

Property in Key West was stupendously overpriced so Woodrow had Googled his way up the island chain to a place called Big Pine, where someone was advertising a multistory spec home with "breathtaking sunset views."

Ipolene Spillwright said, "It'd better have an elevator, Woody, because you don't have the strength for all those stairs. And what in heaven's name are we going to do with seven thousand square feet?"

Her husband entertained a vision of himself basking on a pearl-colored chaise, accepting a margarita from a smoky-eyed Latina housekeeper. He said, "Let's go have a look, Ippy. What's the harm?"

When they emerged from the Miami airport, the first thing Ipolene Spillwright remarked upon was the gummy, sucking heat, which she predicted would kill them both before they made it to the Avis lot. Woodrow rented a white Cadillac coupe and pointed it south. He reminded Ippy that they wouldn't be staying in Florida during the summer months and, besides, Raleigh was also a steaming armpit in August.

It was a long drive to the Lower Keys, and the Spillwrights didn't resume speaking until they crossed the Seven Mile Bridge, where Ipolene grudgingly remarked upon the view, a twinkling palette of indigo, turquoise and green stretching to all horizons. Woodrow Spillwright was practically levitating with joy.

They went directly to Key West and checked into a bed-and-breakfast a few blocks off Duval Street. Although Woody was whipped, he gassed up on bottled oxygen and took Ipolene strolling through Old Town, an excursion that nearly ended disastrously when he ambled off a curb in front of a speeding ambulance. His wife pulled him out of the road and led him back to the B-and-B as the night filled with the wailing of sirens. Another tourist couple informed the Spillwrights that a man had been robbed and shot outside a popular dockside bar, prompting Ipolene to spear her husband with a reproachful glare.

The next morning they were up at daybreak, racing up the overseas highway toward Big Pine Key. The island's many side streets confused the Cadillac's GPS unit, so Woodrow and his wife resorted to a map. At one point they passed a white-tailed deer so small that it had to be genetically defective. Ipolene decreed it was a sure sign of toxic waste spillage, and that she wouldn't be surprised if the humans living on the island were similarly stunted.

They were met at the spec house by the owner who, while short of height, was hardly circus material. He introduced himself as Evan Shook.

Mrs. Spillwright peered straight past him and said, "But the place isn't even finished yet!"

"I've brought all the plans with me. You're gonna love it."

Woodrow immediately inquired about the angling. "Bonefish is my game," he said.

Evan Shook grinned, then winked. "You, my friend, just died and went to heaven." As a precaution he'd arrived early to scout the downstairs for random carrion. He didn't want a repeat of the bloated-raccoon fiasco that had ruined his prospects with the Texans.

"The bugs are chewing me alive," Ipolene complained. "Can we please go inside? Such as it is."

The tour of the unfinished house took a while, due to Woody Spillwright's diminished lung capacity and his wife's endless questions. Sidestepping stacks of drywall and raw lumber, Evan Shook remained chipper and upbeat, at one point even volunteering that he could be flexible on the price. He was eager for the Spillwrights to experience the spectacular vista from the master bedroom suite—lush green mangroves veined with azure creeks and gin-clear tidal pools. And beyond: the Gulf of Mexico.

It was Evan Shook's belief that Mr. Spillwright would be so blown away by the exotic seascape that he would make an offer on the spot, providing he didn't collapse in a wheezing phlegm-fest before reaching the top of the steps.

Eventually they made it, Woodrow's wife shouldering him up to the final landing. After a recuperative pause, they entered the suite like wide-eyed pilgrims. Even Mrs. Spillwright seemed dazzled as she stood in the plywood frame of the unfinished bay window, a soft salty breeze on her cheeks.

"Well," she said. "This is really something."

Evan Shook wore the smile of a barracuda. "Didn't I tell you?"

"It's paradise," croaked Woodrow Spillwright. Dreamily

he took in the cries of the terns and gulls. "How soon will it be finished?"

"Depends." Evan Shook cocked a hopeful eye toward Ipolene. "Would you two be interested in a custom kitchen? I can show you some sketches."

Later, after the Spillwrights had been stabilized at the emergency room in Marathon, Evan Shook would ask himself how in the name of Jesus B. Christ he'd failed to notice the humongous beehive on the suite's interior east wall. The oozing honeycomb was immense, at least six feet high and half again as wide. Yet the bees must have been calm when Evan Shook led the Spillwrights into the bedroom—of that he was certain. Otherwise he would have heard them buzzing, there were so damn many. Thousands? Millions?

Evan Shook speculated that the swarm must have been agitated by the scent of Ipolene's perfume, which smelled like rotting orchids. Or perhaps the insects were roused by the heat of the morning sun. For whatever reason, the savage little bastards went ballistic.

With gravity now his ally, Woodrow Spillwright descended the stairway in a humping blur, his wife yowling on his heels while slapping the bees out of her hair. Evan Shook lagged behind to flail uselessly at the angry intruders. Barely a week had passed since he'd been up to the fourth floor, but evidently enough time had passed for the bees to construct a Vegas-style hive. If only his contractor worked half as fast, Evan Shook mused bitterly, the goddamn house would have been finished a year ago.

Although he got stung thirteen times, the pain was negligible compared to his distress at losing the sale.

The Carolinians hit the ground running. By the time Evan Shook caught up, they were already locked inside the Cadillac, feverishly trying to make sense of the keyless ignition. Evan Shook was tapping plaintively on the glass when the engine revved to life, and he was forced to leap clear as old Woodrow peeled out. Through the tinted windshield Ipolene could be seen shaking a bee-bitten fist.

In the driveway next door stood Andrew Yancy, a newspaper tucked under one arm. He waved amiably as the Spillwrights sped off.

"Go on. Try it," Lombardo said.

Yancy dubiously eyed the plate. Brennan was standing by their table, waiting.

"It's yellowtail," he said.

"I believe you." Yancy took a small bite. The fish had been fried whole until crispy, Cuban-style. It tasted all right.

Brennan folded his arms. "See? Ain't it the best?"

Lombardo said, "Give us a few minutes to talk."

When they were alone, Yancy said, "It's not exactly fresh, Tommy."

"Yeah, but it's not spoiled, right? It's not fucking *contaminated*."

"Last time I was here, that asshole tried to bribe me."

"For God's sake, Andrew, it's the Keys. Eat your lunch."

Yancy's official job description was "sanitation and safety specialist." Tommy Lombardo had been assigned to train him, more or less. Lombardo was FDA-certified but he was also a local. Shutting down a restaurant for code violations—not cool. In his entire career on roach patrol, Lombardo had never ordered an emergency closure. He wanted Yancy to let Stoney's Crab Palace re-open that afternoon.

"They have a thing planned for that kid who got shot. Phinney? A fund-raiser to pay for his burial. There's a country band lined up and everything," Lombardo said. "Have a fucking heart."

"The food service area is a maggot festival."

"No, they cleaned it up. Why do you think I had you drive out here on a Saturday? Brennan, he's been working like a dog."

"Which is probably what he's serving for an appetizer," Yancy said.

Lombardo was exasperated. "See, this attitude of yours? Man, just 'cause you used to be a cop.... These are hard-working people. You can't treat 'em like criminals."

"The law says no vermin in the kitchen."

"The law says? Okay, Andrew, the law also says you're supposed to be certified by the state fire marshal. Are you? Nope. The law also says you're supposed to take the food manager's exam before you can work as a state inspector. Did you do that? Nope. You got this job because the sheriff made a phone call, which is no big deal, but all I'm sayin' is let's not get carried away with what the law says and so forth. Brennan's a good guy who's just tryin' to make a fair living."

Yancy pushed the plate away. "There was a used rubber in the oysters."

"Yeah, I read your report."

"How does that even happen?"

"It's not all Brennan's fault," Lombardo said. "The

employment pool down here, it's sketchy. As a cop you should know."

Yancy stood up from the table. "Well, let's go have a peek."

The kitchen was much cleaner, he had to admit. No rancid shellfish or rodent droppings were on display. Yancy swabbed the food preparation surfaces and checked the temperature in the refrigerators and salad cooler. Brennan, who was cracking stone crabs, proudly showed off his new hairnet. Yancy dropped down and shined a flashlight under the stove, where Brennan had apparently unloaded two or three cans of Raid. Yancy scooped up a handful of dead German cockroaches and a tick, which Lombardo shrugged off.

"There's bug parts in your fucking raisin bran," he whispered. "The government says it won't hurt you."

Brennan piped up: "Nilsson was crazy about my food."

"He *died* from your food," Yancy reiterated.

Lombardo shook his head. "No, no, it was something else."

"Tommy, I read the autopsy. Hepatitis A."

Brennan said, "Then he must've caught it from that sushi pit on Cudjoe. That place is naaaasty."

Yancy nodded toward the fresh stone crabs piled on the cutting board. "Those are beauties."

"Aren't they?"

"Too bad they're out of season until October."

Brennan brought the mallet down on his thumb and yipped. "But these claws are imported from Panama. No—Mexico!"

"I think we're just about done here," Lombardo said.

"Wait a minute." Yancy walked over to the stand-up

freezer and pointed with the toe of his shoe. "Is that a tail? Tell me that's not a tail."

"Goddammit," said Brennan.

Someone had slammed the freezer door on a rat.

"Least it's not alive," Lombardo observed. He was very much a glass-half-full breed of civil servant. "Come on, Andrew, have a heart."

Yancy grunted in capitulation. Snooping for *E. coli* didn't make his adrenaline pump. He was way more interested in discovering how Nicholas Stripling got rich, and what Mrs. Stripling stood to gain from her husband's death.

Lombardo gave Yancy some forms to sign, and Stoney's was back in business. Brennan embraced Lombardo and extended an ungloved hand to Yancy, who shook it tepidly and headed straight for the restroom to scrub off the crab drippings.

When he returned to the dining area, he found Lombardo alone at a table, polishing off the remains of the yellowtail and a pitcher of sangria. Brennan stood at the bar talking to Madeline, Phinney's hard-luck girlfriend, who had come to arrange the memorial fish fry.

"Be right back," Yancy said to Lombardo.

"Hey, take your time."

As soon as Madeline spotted Yancy approaching, she bolted out the fire exit. He hurried after her but she was already on her bicycle, pedaling like a maniac down Shrimp Road.

Lombardo came out the door squinting into the sunlight. "What'd you do to scare that poor woman?"

Yancy truly had no idea. He took a ten-dollar bill from his wallet and placed it in Lombardo's hand. "Put this in the jar," he said, "for the kid's funeral fund."

"Where are you going? Brennan wants you to try the chowder."

"Not until they find a vaccine," said Yancy, and jogged for his car.

"This is exactly what I'm talking about!" Lombardo yelled after him. "You gotta work on your fucking people skills!"

Caitlin Cox stepped off the airplane in Key West without her husband. Yancy couldn't get much out of her on the drive to the Marriott—small talk about the asinine security lines at Miami International, the bumpy flight, the sweaty Canadian dude sitting next to her.

Yancy waited at the hotel bar while she checked in. Twenty minutes passed, half an hour. He felt like a cop again. Maybe she was getting a massage.

He was about to go upstairs and pound on her door when she finally made her entrance, having changed into a tank top and black capri slacks. She wore the same jumbo sunglasses that she'd had on at the funeral. She sat down on the bar stool beside Yancy and said, "You ready? Don't you have a notebook or something?"

"Just tell me what you found out."

"Dad had a two-million-dollar life insurance policy. Guess who's getting it all?"

"Doesn't mean she murdered him," Yancy said.

Caitlin looked annoyed. "That's a shitload of money, Inspector." She ordered a Grey Goose martini.

Yancy asked why she and her father hadn't spoken to each other for so long.

"What difference does that make?"

"Was it because of Eve?"

"She told him I had a drug problem, which I did. Ancient history. She also told him I was stealing from him, which I wasn't. Don't you want a drink?"

"Iced tea, thanks. How old are you, Caitlin?"

She laughed. "Almost twenty-four. I know what you're thinking."

"How long have you been straight?"

"Two years. Okay, nineteen months." She picked up a menu. "How's the swordfish?"

Yancy said, "I honestly wouldn't know." One of these days he'd be inspecting the hotel's kitchen. "Most guys like your father own big life insurance policies. That's not unusual."

"Eve told him I was snorting heroin, which was none of her business. I was a model, okay? That stuff was everywhere. But I never stole a nickel from Dad. Now, did I run up some credit card bills? Yeah, but that's not the same as embezzlement or fraud, whatever. Anyway, Dad cut me off so I told him to go fuck himself, and that was it. He never called me back, and I never called him. Do I feel shitty about that? Yeah, but I can't change what happened."

The bartender brought a tall glass of tea and some cocktail nuts. Yancy was reaching for a pecan when he thought he saw it move. He yanked away his hand and, with a straw, cautiously probed the bowl for lurking insects. None were to be found, of course. These days he was imagining crawlers everywhere, a dispiriting occupational hazard.

Caitlin said, "You some kinda germ freak?"

Yancy selected a different pecan and, in hopes of appearing normal, popped it gaily into his mouth. "Have one," he said.

"Uh, no thanks."

He chomped down forcefully with his molars to pulverize the nut, just in case. Caitlin checked her iPhone for messages. "There was this girl, back when I was modeling? She was from Austria, natural blonde, and she had a germ thing, like you. Every night she filled the bathtub with Purell and soaked for, like, an hour. Seriously."

"Did you know your dad had retired?" Yancy asked.

"Is that what my stepmother told you? That lying thundercunt. Dad wouldn't ever quit working, not ever."

"But how would you know? You hadn't spoken to him in years."

She glared. "Whose side are you on anyway?"

"Nobody's. Tell me what he did for a living."

"Eve didn't clue you in? He sold electric scooter chairs to old folks that can't walk very good. So they can motor themselves from the kitchen to the bathroom, whatever. Haven't you seen those infocommercials?"

Caitlin ordered another martini, and seemed pleased when the bartender belatedly asked to check her ID.

"They're fast little buggers, those scooters," she went on. "Dad mopped up, too. I mean—Florida? Hullo? There are *so* many geezers down here."

Yancy had seen the TV ads late at night. In addition to the chairs' compact turning radius, a main selling point was that elderly customers didn't have to pay out of their own pockets; Medicare covered the cost.

It was possible that Nick Stripling had retired honestly, Yancy thought, but more likely he'd been running a scam and shut it down before the feds nailed him. That could explain the two plainclothes Ken dolls at the graveside service.

"How do you know your father didn't just pack it in and go fishing? Sounds like a sweet retirement."

Caitlin was adamant. "Not Dad. No way."

"There were a couple guys at the funeral who looked like federal agents," Yancy said. "Was Nick having any problems with the law?"

"No! I mean, I don't think so. You should go ask Eve. Ha! Good luck with that."

"Nobody from the government ever spoke to you?"

Caitlin fidgeted. "A few years back, when Dad and I were still tight, he had some hassles with the IRS. I mean, who doesn't, right? But he got it all straightened out."

Yancy asked how she'd met her husband, and she seemed perturbed that he'd changed the subject.

"Simon worked security on some of my fashion shoots. He's the one who got me off dope. He used to be an MP in the army, did a couple tours in Iraq. But getting back to Eve, here's something else: She's already trying to get the court in Miami to declare Dad legally dead! That's how bad she wants to get her slutty paws on the insurance. But Simon says it takes five years in a missing persons case."

Yancy said, "Not if they find something."

"Even just an arm?"

"Any persuasive evidence of death. An airplane crashes, sometimes all that's left of a victim is a burned wallet or a shoe or a shred of skin. That's enough for most judges. They won't make a family wait five whole years."

Caitlin was getting more peeved. "What the fuck is your problem? Everything I say, you knock it down. How much did Eve pay you?"

"I'm holding out for new Michelins on the Subaru."

"She murdered my father for two million bucks, okay? Any jackass can figure that out."

"Dial it down," Yancy said. He nodded at the bartender, who smoothly retreated. "I'm not saying you're wrong, Caitlin. I'm saying you need more proof if you want the cops to get fired up."

She raised her hands. "I thought *you* were the cops."

Yancy made up something about following chain of command. Caitlin would be on the next flight to the mainland if she knew he was assigned to restaurant inspections.

"What about the boat sinking?" she demanded. "That story was so bogus."

A week earlier, the hull of Nick Stripling's boat had been located under seventy-five feet of water off the coast of Marathon, in the same area where the debris had been recovered. There was no money in the local Coast Guard budget to raise the *Summer's Eve,* even if investigators had wanted to. The official report said the vessel likely had capsized in rough seas.

"Somebody pulled the plug," Caitlin Cox asserted, "after Dad was already dead."

"So, hire a salvage company," Yancy said.

"How much would *that* cost?"

"A lot. It's a major job."

"Shit."

Yancy decided it was too soon to mention what he knew about the small shark tooth removed from Nick Stripling's arm. "Eve told me your father wasn't much of a swimmer."

Caitlin slammed her drink on the bar. "Are you kidding me?"

"Yet she put his favorite speargun in the casket, which seemed weird," Yancy said. "Most spear divers I know can swim like a fish."

"Dad was a damn porpoise, I'm not kidding. He could hold his breath forever. *Now* do you believe me about Eve? The reason she said he was a shitty swimmer was to make it seem like he just gave out and drowned after the boat went down. Which would never happen."

"Besides the insurance money, did she have any other reason to kill him?"

Caitlin leaned close. "Try a hot boyfriend."

"Go on," said Yancy.

"In the Bahamas!"

"You know this for a fact?"

"Let's move to a booth," she said.

Eight

The salesman at the Ford dealership informed Eve Stripling that the import duty on a new SUV in the Bahamas was 75 percent, a figure she made him repeat. After doing the math in her head, she realized that the new Explorer she'd been eyeing would cost, like, sixty-five grand.

"That's robbery," she observed.

"But I'm afraid it's the law," the salesman said sadly.

"My boyfriend'll never pay that much."

Eve walked off the lot thinking how strange it sounded when she said the word "boyfriend," strange but also sort of exciting. She took a taxi back to town, complaining to the driver about the outrageous tariffs on automobiles. The driver said he'd paid almost fifty-two thousand dollars for his cab, a used Dodge minivan he'd located on Craigslist in Hialeah. Eve was genuinely outraged on his behalf.

Stopping at an outdoor bar, she ordered a Nassau Nemesis, one of many colorful rum beverages concocted for tourists. Parked on the street was a yellow Jeep Wrangler with a hard top instead of canvas. A For Sale sign was taped to the windshield. Eve inspected the vehicle, which appeared to be in good condition except for a thumb-sized rust spot on the hood.

She drank another Nemesis and asked the bartender to play some UB40. Then she ordered fried grouper fingers and carelessly dribbled hot sauce on the crotch of her white jeans. Normally she would have been mortified, but the booze was kicking in hard. She tucked a paper napkin over her lap and asked for a basket of fried shrimp, which she was heartily demolishing when the owner of the yellow Jeep showed up carrying groceries. Eve hurried to the street, her napkin flapping.

"How much you want for it?" she called out.

The woman set her bags in the Wrangler's back seat. "Toidy towsend," she said to Eve.

"No way. Twenty-five."

"Wot!"

"Plus we need it barged down to Andros," Eve said.

"Twenty-eight if you pay'n cash. Where you ship it, dot's your prollem."

Eve went to see the Bay Street banker who was their new best friend and withdrew the money for the Jeep, which she drove sinuously to the waterfront. There she connected with a craggy white Bahamian who agreed to barge the car to Victoria Creek for a thousand dollars. Eve haggled briefly and without much starch. Her mission had been to purchase wheels and, by God, that's what she'd done.

On her way to the airport she called him in Miami. "You'll like it," she said. "It's super sporty!"

"What do you mean?"

"It's bright yellow, honey. I'm gonna call it Yellow Bird, like the song."

"And this is your idea of what a new widow should be driving? Something sporty?"

Eve sighed. "Where we're goin', who's gonna know? A whole new life is what you said. Isn't that the whole point?"

"The point is not to stand out like a couple of dumbass expats. Staying under the radar, understand? Yellow Jeep, might as well ring a fucking cowbell every time we drive to town."

He sounded on edge. Eve couldn't blame him, all the pressure he'd been under. Both of them, actually—though at the moment she was feeling exceptionally smooth and ironed out, thanks to the rum buzz.

She said, "Honey, everything's gonna be fine. Take a deep breath."

"How much did they stick you for?"

"Twenty-eight even."

"Automatic or stick?"

"You are too much."

"White would have been a smarter color. Black even."

"Boring. We're islanders now, remember? You with the orange poncho."

"When are you leaving?" he asked.

"Soon as Claspers fuels up the plane."

"Tell him to hurry."

"Does that mean you miss me?"

"I can't wait to get the fuck outta here is what it means."

Eve laughed drowsily and said, "See you soon."

A government man came all the way from Nassau to inform Neville that it was time to move. The sale of the family homestead to the white American named

Christopher was official, the closing documents filed. Neville held no voice in the matter because his half sister, Diana, was the legal trustee. She lived full-time in Toronto with her acupuncturist fiancé and rarely came back to Andros, not even for homecomings. The government man told Neville he'd soon be receiving a cashier's check for $302,000 Bahamian, which was half the property's purchase price minus the broker's commission, bank fees, lawyers and so on.

When Neville replied that he had no use for the money, the government man thought he was joking.

Neville didn't have a wife but his three girlfriends heard he was about to become rich and started making demands. To get away he took his boat down to Mars Bay and went fishing for a few days. His only companion was Driggs the almost hairless monkey, whose unnerving resemblance to a psoriatic human delinquent served to keep both friends and strangers at a distance.

The patch reefs were teeming with groupers and mutton snappers, but Neville's mood remained morose. He was deeply disappointed that the Dragon Queen's voodoo spell had failed to waylay the mysterious Christopher and his lady friend. Currently the couple was renting a private home on the water near Bannister Point. Neville had yet to lay eyes on the man, who was rumored to wear a bright poncho and carry a gun.

As for the woman, Neville saw her for the first time when she stepped off a private seaplane at Rocky Town. She was kind of chubby though pretty: dark reddish hair and fair skin, with a spray of cinnamon freckles. The doctor flies attacked her hungrily, and both legs were trickling blood by the time she made it to the car.

Neville didn't know anybody who knew her name. He didn't know it, either.

What Christopher intended to do with the beachfront property had been the topic of many rumors, but the government man confirmed to Neville that an exclusive resort was planned, a private club offering time-shares to be rented out as luxury hotel suites. The marketing would aim at wealthy Americans, Brits and Asians. There would be a geisha-style spa, two freshwater pools, a tiki bar and a four-star Caribbean restaurant. Also: cabanas, kayaks, paddleboards, snorkeling—even clay tennis courts!

The first phase of construction would be twenty-five units. Andros being the largest and most undeveloped island in the Bahamas, the prime minister himself had promised to fly in for the groundbreaking.

"Dey gon call it Curly Tail Lane," the government man told Neville.

Curly-tailed lizards were common throughout Andros. The stout little reptiles were bold and quick, and their twitchy courtship dance was always a hit with little children and tourists. Although Neville had no quarrel with the lizards, he thought Curly Tail Lane was a stupid name for Christopher's building project.

"Green Beach is wot my grandfahdda always call de place."

"Maybe once 'pon a time," the government man said.

"Dis some bullshit," Neville told him.

"Mon, you got a poymit fuh dot sick-ass monkey?"

Neville said, "Get off my land."

He spent two extra days down at Mars Bay because an east wind blew twenty knots, and Driggs was prone to seasickness. The ice in the cooler melted, so Neville ended up giving all his fish to the cook at an eco-lodge in exchange for another bottle of rum, with which he hoped to recharge the Dragon Queen.

However, upon returning to Lizard Cay, Neville saw that Christopher's crew had ripped out his wooden dock, every damn piling. He anchored his boat behind a neighbor's place, leashed Driggs's to the porch rail and hurried barefoot down the rocky cratered road. A new chain-link fence surrounded his land, complete with a padlocked gate and a No Trespassing sign. Neville scaled the fence and ran through the trees until he came to a rubble of blue cinder blocks where his family house had stood.

He fell to his knees and, because he was alone, sobbed freely. Then he pulled himself together, walked over to Christopher's backhoe and urinated copiously into the fuel tank.

Yancy's father was retired from the National Park Service though he still lived in Gardiner, Montana, at the north entrance of Yellowstone. Every summer Yancy would fly out to fish for cutthroats on Slough Creek, or do a float down to Yankee Jim Canyon. He looked forward to these visits but this year he couldn't go.

"I'm working on a big case," he told his dad on the phone. "A possible homicide."

"Well, sure. I understand."

"Sorry, Pop."

"Maybe I can come down to the Keys and throw at some tarpon. I'll stay out of your hair."

Yancy said, "It's just not a good time."

He didn't have the spine to admit that he'd lost his detective badge and gotten busted down to roach patrol. Too well he remembered his father's heartsick reaction after he was canned by the Miami Police Department, a crushing setback that had occurred shortly after Yancy's mother was lost to cancer. Yancy couldn't bear to hear such disappointment in the old man's voice again.

"Maybe we can fish together in the fall," he said.

"I'm going on a steelhead trip to BC. You'd have a ball, Andrew."

"Sign me up."

Somebody was knocking on Yancy's door. It was Miguel, the bee guy. He was wearing a full-on beekeeper suit, including a hooded veil.

He winked behind the mesh at Yancy and said, "Excuse me, sir. Tonight we will be removing a serious motherfucking honeybee hive from the structure next door. Until then perhaps you should stay inside. Unfortunately, the bees have been disturbed."

"I appreciate the warning."

Miguel winked again and cut his eyes toward the construction site. Evan Shook was watching from his Suburban, in which he had sealed himself against the ruthless swarm.

"A risky situation," Miguel said, "but we are utmostly professionals."

"That I can see."

"Your neighbor, Señor Shook, he was stung many times. Lucky for him he is not allergic."

"Nor am I," Yancy said.

"Still, I would not take chances. Do you have any pets? Smallish children? You understand I must ask these questions. Would you be owning a pacemaker?"

Yancy was happy to play along. "No, sir. And I live here all by myself."

"Excellent. We will be done by midnight." Miguel went through the motions of handing Yancy a business card. "In case you are ever likewise troubled with bees. You can phone day or night. Also I am on Skype."

"Good luck with that hive," said Yancy.

"*Vaya con Dios.*"

"Seriously?"

Miguel smiled. "Shut your fucking windows, Andrew."

Yancy buttoned up the house and headed down to Key West, where he'd set up lunch at a terrific Cuban place on Flagler with an ex–Border Patrol agent now working for Homeland Security. The man owed Yancy a favor and he stepped up big-time, bringing a printout that detailed the recent foreign travels of Mrs. Eve Stripling.

Caitlin Cox had said her stepmother was in the Bahamas, not Paris, at the time her father's boat went down off Marathon. Caitlin's proof was Eve's phone bill, which showed numerous roaming charges from a wireless company based in Nassau. To Yancy, Caitlin had admitted stealing the bill from the mailbox at her father's home in the hope of establishing the identity of Eve's secret lover. Caitlin was certain such a man existed because she'd spotted her stepmother buying a swimsuit and designer flip-flops at a Bal Harbour boutique, two days before Nick Stripling's funeral. Caitlin was there shopping for a black dress.

Mindful of her motive, which was gaining access to her late father's wealth, Yancy nonetheless found the tip intriguing. Caitlin's suspicions seemed to be partially confirmed in the records provided by his Homeland

Security connection—Eve Stripling had in fact gone to Paris, although for only a week. Then she flew back to the United States, clearing Customs at JFK before taking a nonstop to Nassau. It was nineteen days later that she returned to South Florida on a private seaplane that landed at Watson Island. There she paid duty on thirty-four hundred dollars of women's clothes and a ten-karat-gold men's wedding band, which, according to her declaration documents, had cost a whopping one hundred and ninety-nine bucks. Yancy assumed it was the same gold band Eve had switched out for Nick Stripling's expensive platinum one before burying his abbreviated remains.

Interestingly, she'd bought the replacement ring in the Bahamas before returning to Florida and reporting her husband missing at sea. The purchase made no sense unless she'd already known that Nick was dead and that his ring finger had been recovered, attached to his floating arm.

Yancy felt so energized by this disclosure that he picked up the twenty-eight-dollar meal tab, even though he'd barely touched his *picadillo* due to a suspicious-looking olive. Of late he was subsisting mostly on Popsicles and so-called energy bars, which came hygienically machine-sealed in foil although they settled in his stomach like bricks of industrial glue.

His friend from Homeland Security got up and said, "Thanks for lunch, Andrew. But anybody asks, we never talked."

Yancy grinned. "Hell, I don't even know your name."

A squall blew across the island and Yancy drove around Old Town waiting for the rain to quit. On Fleming Street he passed Fausto's grocery and thought of Bonnie, a.k.a. Plover Chase. With improbable ease he rejected the impulse to dial her number. Perhaps he was finally, at age forty-two, growing up.

He parked on Eaton Street and made his way to Duval. Even in the dead of summer it was crawling with over-fed tourists courtesy of the cruise ships, which Yancy considered a vile and ruinous presence in the harbor. After grabbing a beer at the Margaritaville café he began searching the T-shirt shops for Madeline, girlfriend of the late Charles Phinney. He found her at a place called Chest Candy, which aggressively catered to strippers, transvestites and aspiring nymphomaniacs. The display window featured a blond-wigged mannequin wearing a diaphanous tank top with sequined lettering that said: CUM TOGETHER.

Again Madeline spooked when she saw Yancy, only this time there was no place to run. She yelled for the store manager, a sallow twit named Pestov who vanished as soon as Yancy inquired about his immigration status.

After locking the front door behind himself, Yancy cornered Madeline and asked what the hell was going on.

"I got a lawyer! So watch it."

"Why do you need a lawyer?"

She said, "You told me you weren't a cop."

"I said not at the moment."

Some dork wearing Teva sandals and black socks started rattling the doorknob. Yancy shooed her away. "Tell me what's going on," he said to Madeline.

"The cops think I set Charlie up to get ripped off."

"Where'd you hear that?"

"Three times they had me in for questioning. What'd you tell them? Jesus, I need a smoke."

Yancy said, "The police never even interviewed me."

Madeline's hands were trembling as she lighted up. "I'm gonna lose my damn job."

"They'd be doing you a favor."

She said, "I wouldn't never hurt Charlie. He treated me good."

"I believe you, Madeline. But I can't help unless you tell me the truth. So let's start over, okay?"

"Not here," she whispered, glancing behind her. "The Russians, man!"

"Screw the Russians." Yancy poked his face into the back room and said, "Yo, Madeline's taking the afternoon off."

"Is fine," Pestov muttered sullenly from a closet.

"Thank you, comrade. And God bless America!"

Yancy drove Madeline out to Stoney's, which naturally had been her and Phinney's all-time favorite restaurant. They took a two-top in a corner and from the unkempt server Yancy was pleased to learn Brennan was away in Homestead, probably stocking up on frozen tilapia that would later be promoted to fresh swordfish on the menu.

Madeline asked for a vodka tonic and Yancy ordered a Coke.

She said, "I lied. I don't really have a lawyer."

"They tend to charge a fee."

"Which I have about forty bucks to my name."

"What have the cops told you?" Yancy asked.

"I got a record is the problem. Grand theft a long time ago, shoplifting, whatever. Plus they found out I'm way behind on my Visa card and also my rent, so I guess they think I lined up someone to shoot Charlie and take a cut of the cash. But I didn't!"

Yancy believed Madeline, for he knew more about the murder investigation than she did. One of his fishing pals was a city police lieutenant who'd told him that the rented moped used in the robbery had been wiped totally clean of prints, even the gas cap and side mirrors, demonstrating an attention to detail not common among the local dirtbag element. The killer's weapon hadn't been found but the .357 shell casings and bullet fragments belonged to 158-grain Winchester hollow points, a premium load for a low-rent street crime.

Yancy said, "Tell me again how much cash Phinney was carrying."

Madeline paused before answering. "Maybe twelve hundred bucks?"

"Last time you said it was a grand."

"Well, I didn't go through his fucking wallet and count it!" She took a slurp of vodka.

"You also told me he got the money from a dope deal." Yancy was watching her eyes, which flitted everywhere but in his direction. "Who was he selling to, Madeline?"

"I never met the dude. What difference does it make?"

"Maybe Charlie overcharged him. Or maybe the stuff turned out to be stinkweed and the customer got pissed off."

"No, no, that's not it," she said. "Everybody in town knew Charlie was carrying that money. He wouldn't stop talkin' about it. They probably followed us to the Half Shell that night and waited outside."

Over the years Yancy had interviewed enough witnesses to know when one was winging it. Usually they were just trying to cover their own asses, a practice also favored by law enforcement professionals although Yancy had never quite gotten the hang of it. He told Madeline she had two minutes to come clean, and right away she began to shake and cry. Yancy scooted his chair closer and put an arm around her.

"Everything I told the cops is true except about the cash," she said. "Charlie didn't get it from sellin' grass."

"Did he steal it from someone?"

"No! He would *never*." Her breath was stale and her hair smelled like an ashtray.

"Then where'd he get the money, Madeline?"

She pawed at her eyes with a cocktail napkin. "It's pretty fucked up," she said.

"I need to know before I can help."

"But you're not even a real cop."

Yancy gritted it out. "I'm on loan to another department, that's all. Temporarily assigned. Now tell me the whole story."

And Madeline was right. It was fucked up.

On the charter docks of South Florida there had evolved among a handful of unscrupulous captains a method of duping inept out-of-towners for extra money. The key prop in the scam was typically an Atlantic sailfish, caught on a previous trip and stored on ice in an aft hatch inaccessible to the paying clientele.

Once the boat was at sea, a mate first baited the outriggers and then the flat lines, which were trolled closer to the boat and often enhanced with a skirted plastic lure. Thus began a sporting day, with high hopes among the unsuspecting anglers. When the time was right, one of the mates would distract them with a clamorous false sighting of jumping porpoises or a cruising hammerhead shark, which the customers always pretended to see as they didn't wish to be regarded as clueless rubes.

Binoculars were handed out and the anglers were directed to the bow of the vessel in order to improve their view. At this juncture the mate would remove the dead sailfish from the cold hatch and covertly hook it to one of the flat lines. Once the jelly-eyed corpse was dropped in the water, the forward motion of the boat carried it back into the frothy wake.

A cry of "Fish on!" would go out, and one of the hapless sports—usually a hungover husband—would come lurching back to the cockpit, snatch the rod from the mate's grasp and begin reeling like a madman. The boat's towing of the limp billfish created enough natural drag to test the flabby muscles of most novices. Later they would brag to their pals back home that they'd whipped the sonofabitch in five minutes flat. As further testament to human vanity, no suspicions would be voiced over the odd fact that their trophy sailfish, a species renowned for its acrobatics, never once jumped out of the water.

At boatside, the mate would cap the charade by pretending to wrestle the prize into an unlocked fish box, where the entire party of numskulls could peek at it and snap pictures to their hearts' content. The coup de grâce would occur back at dockside when the captain persuaded the lucky angler to have his catch mounted, later to be displayed on the paneled wall of his real estate office or perhaps in the family den. A tidy deposit would be forthcoming, divided by the captain and mates, and a few months later the client would receive via UPS an exquisite six-foot sailfish, painted cobalt blending to indigo and airbrushed with lateral dashes of silver and gold. The replica, manufactured by the taxidermist from a standard plaster cast, would be fixed in a lifelike leaping pose, its sharp bill aimed toward the clouds and its tall dorsal fin regally flared.

Of course by then the real sailfish had been recycled profitably and eventually dumped overboard, having decomposed to chum after five or six fake captures. It was a scam to be saved exclusively for the most witless of tourists, but it worked often enough to have been passed along over decades among a certain low-pirate class of sportfishing crews.

Charles Phinney didn't learn of the trick from Captain Keith Fitzpatrick but, rather, from a stranger who'd approached him one evening at the Garrison Bight Marina while he was hosing down the *Misty Momma IV.* There was, however, a twist.

"It wasn't a dead sailfish they wanted him to hook on the line," Madeline told Yancy. "It was a dude's cut-off arm!"

"Jesus."

"I told Charlie it was the grossest thing I ever heard and he'd be crazy to do it. But he was gonna make three thousand cash."

"Three grand?"

"I'm not shitting you," said Madeline. "So he said okay."

"And got paid?"

"Same day, in hundred-dollar bills. He made me swear not to tell anyone. He said they told him it was only a practical joke, no big deal. The arm came off a dead body from some mortician school."

By now she was lapping a third vodka tonic. Yancy

felt like having a stiff one, too, but he wanted to be able to remember every word. He'd write it all down as soon as he got home.

"The night before," she said, "in Charlie's apartment? We were so fucking nervous we got stoned out of our heads. I mean *baked,* okay? He had the...you know...in this big ice cooler, I'll never forget—"

"Wait, Madeline, who gave Phinney the arm?"

"Someone brought it to the dock that same night, when he was alone on the boat. Anyway, the cooler—Charlie asks do I want to see the you-know-what and I said no freaking way, you asshole. But he takes the thing out, right? And it doesn't look real but at the same time it's too gross to be fake. And we both, I don't know why, we just start laughing. He's swingin' the thing around like a base-ball bat and I've got this half-calico kitty cat, Sheeba, all the fur on her back is stickin' up. Charlie and I both just fell out, it seemed so damn funny. Sounds pretty fucking twisted, I guess, but it's not like we put it up on YouTube or nothin'."

"So it was really good pot," Yancy said. Bonnie Witt's reaction to the severed limb had been not so jolly, though, in retrospect, they hadn't laughed very much as a couple. Again he asked: "Who brought the dead arm to Phinney?"

"Here's the worst," said Madeline. "We're so trashed, Charlie grabs the middle finger on the hand, right? The bird finger? And he bends it up like this, so it looks like the dead dude is flippin' us off! I 'bout peed my panties. But then he stuck the thing in the freezer and next morn-ing it was all iced up, and he couldn't bend the finger back 'cause he was afraid it would snap off. So that's how it stayed when he took it on the *Misty.*"

"Captain Fitzpatrick didn't know anything about this, right?"

"You kidding? He would have gaffed Charlie in the nut sack."

She wanted another cigarette so Yancy followed her outside. He stood upwind and gulped the salty fresh air. The inside of Stoney's smelled like fried sweat socks.

"Who else did Charlie tell about the arm?"

"Nobody but me," Madeline said emphatically. "Soon as he sobered up he got semi-paranoid about it. But the money, you know, that was different. The night after he got paid he took me to Louie's for dinner and bought a round for everyone at the bar, two hundred bucks." She dragged hard and then flicked the butt into a rain puddle. "Nobody said he was Alvin Einstein."

Yancy thought it was fortunate that Phinney and Madeline hadn't pooled their genes. He said: "Who got Charlie to do this thing? Didn't he mention the guy's name?"

"Wasn't a guy," Madeline said. "It was a chick that brought him the cut-off arm, Charlie said. He didn't know her name but she's the one who paid him, too. A white chick in tight white jeans. Is that wild or what? Like she was on her way to the damn mall."

Yancy patted her hand. "You need to get out of town."

Nine

They didn't call ahead, just showed up one evening at the door. Shark-gray suits, flat expressions. They told Simon Cox they needed to speak alone with Caitlin. Simon, who practically got a boner when he saw their federal shields, obediently disappeared into the small bedroom he used as a gym.

The interview only lasted twenty minutes—the agents could plainly see Caitlin wasn't living like a Kardashian, or even like the daughter of a wealthy dead medical-supply executive. She was creeped out because they knew the humiliating balance of her checking account, down to the penny. They knew Simon's car was paid off, and hers wasn't. They knew the amount on her American Express card. They even knew about one of her rehabs.

And now they knew what her house looked like, all fourteen-hundred square feet. Lebron James had closets that were bigger.

"What're you guys after?" she asked.

"Money," said one of the agents.

"Dad didn't pay his taxes again? That figures."

"It's more complicated than that. Did he ever discuss his business with you?"

"We weren't speaking for a long time. So no is the answer."

The other agent said, "Did he give you any instructions, in the event of his death?"

"What did I just say? The two of us weren't talking. He didn't even put me in his will is what I heard."

"Looks like his wife gets everything," the first agent said, "all twelve thousand dollars."

Caitlin laughed in disbelief. "Twelve grand?"

The second agent said, "Now you understand our interest."

"Dad had a shitload of money."

"That's our information, as well. However, the only American bank account with his name on it held twelve thousand and change when he passed away—basically enough for the funeral. So, we were hoping you might know what happened to the rest."

Caitlin glared at the agents. "Eve's the one you should be talking to about the money. Ask her if she killed my father, while you're at it. Because she did! Don't you guys do murders?"

"If you have hard evidence, you should call the police right away."

"Done deal," Caitlin declared. "I got a detective in the Keys working the case full-time. Yancy is his name."

The FBI men showed no reaction, no interest.

One of them said: "We tried to interview Mrs. Stripling about your father's finances, including his life insurance policy. She asked to be left alone."

"And that's what you did?" Caitlin asked incredulously.

"She's not under subpoena, Mrs. Cox."

"Good, then leave me alone, too!"

As soon as the agents were gone, Simon came out and asked Caitlin what they'd wanted. She told him it looked like Eve had ripped off her dad's estate.

"Big surprise, right?" she said. "All Dad's money is missing—who knows how much."

"They'll find it," said Simon confidently. The feds were absolutely the best.

"He was a fool to marry that greedy whore." Caitlin was still livid. "I hope they throw her ass in jail for a hundred years."

"Did they leave a card?" Simon asked, meaning the agents. He was thinking he would ask them out for a beer. Bring along his résumé.

The phone rang and Caitlin picked it up. She looked surprised by the caller. Lowering her voice, she turned her back on Simon, which he didn't appreciate.

The moment she hung up, he said, "Who was that, sweetheart?"

"You won't believe it—my former stepmother, all sweet and friendly."

"Eve?"

"Swear to God." Caitlin wore an odd smile. "She wants to get together, just her and me. A girls' day."

"That's messed up. What did you say?"

"I said, Are you paying?"

For once Yancy didn't mind driving to Miami. Dr. Rosa Campesino had agreed to meet for lunch. On the Eighteen-Mile Stretch he got stuck behind a minivan with a CHOOSE LIFE bumper sticker.

"Choose the accelerator! How's that for starters?" Yancy was shouting, pounding the horn.

He didn't mind if people advertised their religious views on their cars, but those who did invariably were the slowest, most faint-hearted drivers. It was uncanny, and all road cops knew it to be true. If God was *my* co-pilot, Yancy once groused to Burton, I'd have the fucking pedal to the metal soon as I left the garage.

Rosa arrived in her morgue scrubs at the restaurant, and she looked fabulous.

"What happened? You're so skinny," she said. "I'll order for both of us."

They were seated at a café on Miracle Mile in Coral Gables. The menu was promising, but the night before Yancy had dreamed about Stoney's Crab Palace—mouse tracks on a Key lime tart.

"I've been fighting a stomach flu," he said.

Undaunted, Rosa ordered them veal with penne pasta. She wore a fresh touch of lipstick but no other makeup, which Yancy found wildly beguiling. This he recognized as the onset of infatuation.

"Did you get fired? Tell the truth," she said.

He felt his neck get hot. "It's more like a probation."

"No, I've been checking up. You're quite the renegade, Andrew." She was smiling, thank God. "I've heard of Sergeant Johnny Mendez, by the way. Not a good guy."

"A congenital crook," Yancy said. "Disgrace to the uniform, et cetera."

"Still, you could have handled it better. Now, what happened down in the Keys?"

"That I'd rather not discuss."

"Too bad," Rosa said. "My life coach told me not to sleep with anybody who harbors a murky past."

"What about a murky present?"

"I don't really have a life coach, Andrew. However, I do believe in full disclosure."

He coughed up the whole story with a facsimile of contrition. His crude assault on Dr. Clifford Witt didn't seem to shock Rosa, but then again she was a coroner in an urban combat zone.

"Last week I did a post on a man who had a clarinet up his colon," she reported. "That's not what killed him, by the way. It was a single gunshot to the head from a jealous lover. She played the oboe."

"Shakespeare was born too soon."

"So you lost your detective job and now you're inspecting restaurants for rat poop and bacteria. Not exactly a lateral career move."

Yancy said, "I'm righting the ship, even as we speak."

The pasta and veal arrived. It was delicious, but he backed off after a couple of bites. Rosa asked for an update on the severed arm, and he told her what he'd found out. She was intrigued by the dead-sailfish scam.

"That's a classic," she said.

"I'm thinking the wife and her boyfriend killed Stripling, or had him killed."

"Before or after they sunk the boat?"

"Doesn't matter. They chop off one arm and take the expensive wristwatch, but they leave the platinum wedding band as part of the act, so that Eve can make a show of identifying it later. Then they put the arm in the shallows off some secluded beach so the bonnet sharks can gnaw on it, purely for appearance."

"How'd she pick this Phinney character to smuggle that nasty thing onto a boat?" Rosa asked.

"You hang around the docks, it's not hard to find somebody who'd sell their own mother's kidney for three thousand bucks. Once that tourist on the *Misty* reeled in Stripling's arm, Eve was golden."

"Until Phinney started blabbing about the money."

Yancy nodded. "That's why he got shot. It wasn't a robbery. Hell, he'd already blown through most of the dough."

"You said the shooter was on a moped? That's like Bogotá in the old days."

"Mopeds are all over Key West. This one was a cash rental on a stolen driver's license—somebody hired by Eve, I'm betting. Or possibly it was the boyfriend himself who pulled the trigger."

"Whose name you don't know."

"Hey, I'm just getting started."

Rosa said, "Eat your lunch, Andrew. It's sinful to waste good food. I thought you said the widow's love hunk was in the Bahamas."

"That's what I was told. It's a quick flight to Florida."

"There must be a record of that. He'd have to clear Customs."

"Only if he's an upright, law-abiding citizen," Yancy said. "A seaplane could fly in low and land anyplace. It's risky, but so is murder."

Because of the poor condition of Stripling's arm, determining the precise date and time of his death was impossible. The crime had probably occurred when Immigration records showed Eve to be in Nassau. However, with access to a floatplane and an outlaw pilot, she could have flown straight to the Keys, killed her husband, staged the boat accident and been back in the Bahamas by nightfall.

"Super bold," Rosa said.

Yancy ordered a cup of coffee that was so strong it made his eyes water. For dessert Rosa had the tiramisu.

"So, you're investigating this elaborate homicide in your leisure time? Off the reservation, as they say." She was giving him an amused, sideways appraisal.

"I want my badge back, Rosa. If I can just nail down this case—"

"Are you kidding? It doesn't work that way."

"Maybe not in Miami, but Key West is small-time. I'm tight with the sheriff."

"Oh, Andrew."

He didn't mention that he'd never before worked on an unsolved murder. During his time with the Miami police he'd been assigned to burglaries and the occasional armed robbery. In the Keys he'd been called to a total of three killings; all were domestic scenarios featuring on-scene confessions by impaired roommates.

"Now it's your turn, Doctor," Yancy said. "Tell me what led you to the cheery, life-affirming specialty of forensic pathology."

"It was either that or trauma care. I prefer patients who hold still."

"Plus you get to play cop, too."

Rosa laughed. "Some days I do."

She gave Yancy the short version of her biography: Born and raised in New Jersey; daughter of Cuban immigrants; undergrad at FSU, med school at the University of Miami; divorced, no kids, lived alone with a tank full of tropical fish. In the fall she would turn thirty-nine, and she planned to treat herself to a spa day at the Mandarin.

"Darkest secret?" Yancy asked.

Rosa thought for a moment. "Okay, this *is* dark. Once I made love on an autopsy table at the morgue."

Yancy was overjoyed to picture the scene. "How do you top that?" he said.

"Late one night, me and this guy I was dating. Those rooms are really, really cold."

"Your idea or his?"

"Mine," Rosa admitted, blushing. "Mark—my friend— he got semi-freaked. I never saw him after that. He just stopped calling."

"One of these days he'll be out of therapy."

"I love my job, but I'm pretty sure it's screwing with my head."

"Tell me about it," said Yancy. "I've dropped, like, fourteen pounds since they put me on roach patrol. I have these nauseating nightmares about filthy, putrid-smelling kitchens—bugs in the goddamn custard."

Rosa frowned and pushed away the tiramisu. Yancy paid the check and walked her to her car, some sort of sensible sedan. "I meant to thank you again," he said, "for figuring out the brand of Stripling's missing watch. That was impressive."

"Oh, I'm full of tricks." She elbowed him playfully and got in her car. "That woman whose husband you molested— are you still involved with her? This is a test, by the way."

"Bonnie has moved to Sarasota."

"Answer the question."

"No, that tawdry chapter of my life is closed. I'm in the process of rebooting." Yancy smiled hopefully.

"Maybe some night I'll come down and cook for you," Rosa said. "I bet I can make you hungry."

Then she drove off.

Midwest Mobile Medical Systems had been located in a bland office park in Doral, west of the Miami airport. The occupancy rate of the complex was only 20 percent and the few tenants no longer included Midwest Mobile, which had closed down upon the retirement of its young president, Nicholas Stripling. His daughter, Caitlin, had eagerly provided Yancy with the name and former whereabouts of the company.

The door lock was of inferior quality, surrendering to Yancy's screwdriver on the first pry. Inside the suite were eight identical cubicles, stripped bare except for the desks, IKEA knockoffs that gave the place the appearance of a telemarketing boiler room. Stripling or his staff had hauled away the files, printers and computers and, judging by a trail of white confetti, even brought in shredders.

In one desk Yancy found a color brochure advertising the "Super Rollie," a personal sit-down scooter that promised "the comfort and agility of a motorized wheelchair combined with the traction and durability of a world-class riding mower." The Super Rollie Power Chair was available in three-wheel or four-wheel models that could cruise up to nine miles per hour. Options included a headlight, a touchpad sound system and a captain's seat that swiveled 180 degrees. Prices ranged from eight hundred dollars for the basic package to four thousand for a candy-red chariot with a dashboard glucose meter. Medicare patients were assured that the vehicles could be obtained "with little or no cost to you." The main requirements were a doctor's prescription and federal form CMS-849, a Certificate of Medical Necessity for Seat Lift Mechanisms, which Midwest Mobile Medical would helpfully fill out on each customer's behalf.

"Take a ride on our Super Rollie," the brochure urged, "and recapture your independence!"

Yancy pictured himself careening down the Seven Mile Bridge aboard one of the zippy power chairs, Rosa Campesino riding on his lap.

A jowly security guard peeked in the doorway and said, "I thought you guys were done with this place."

"One more pass," said Yancy. Following his lunch with Rosa, he'd put on a necktie and a drab coat jacket to make himself appear more cop-like.

"You ever gonna arrest somebody?"

Yancy gave a thumbs-up. "Count on it, brother."

He waited until the guard was gone before he resumed searching. Probably federal agents were the ones who'd been snooping there before. Unfortunately, Nicholas Stripling had died before they could indict him.

A crumpled paper that had escaped shredding by Stripling—or confiscation by the FBI—proved to be a handwritten note: "Nicky—Dr. O'Peele says he never got paid for last month. Wants you to call him."

On his smartphone Yancy was able to access the website of the state health department, which revealed that only one medical doctor named O'Peele was licensed in Miami-Dade County. Also available online were records of the property appraiser's office, which listed a Gomez O'Peele as the owner of a three-bedroom condominium in North Miami Beach. An hour later Yancy was standing in the lobby of a high-rise, buzzing the doctor's unit number.

"Whoozair?" asked a groggy voice from the speaker box.

"Inspector Andrew Yancy."

"Oh shit. What?" Then, after a pause: "Come on up."

O'Peele was wearing a stale nappy bathrobe and one moleskin slipper when he answered the door. His eyeballs were bloodshot and his hair appeared to have been groomed with salad tongs. "Can I see some ID?" he said.

Yancy flashed his lame restaurant-inspector credentials, which drew a foggy squint from the doctor.

"Izzit morning already?" he asked.

Yancy brushed past him. "That's an unusual name, Gomez O'Peele."

"My mother's Cuban. She divorced my dad and remarried a mick. Are you FBI?"

"I'm not at liberty to say." Yancy delivered the line with a straight face. He would never have tried it on a sober person.

"How'd you find me?" O'Peele said. "Never mind. I know my rights."

The condo was piled with dirty laundry and fuzzy pizza boxes. O'Peele shambled to the disordered kitchen, which showed evidence of an active cockroach colony. Yancy found himself scanning the floorboards for signs of movement. The doctor downed a shot of bourbon and announced he had no intention of doing prison time.

"Tell me what you think you know," he said, "and I'll tell you if you're on the right track."

"Fair enough," Yancy said.

"But only if I get immunity."

"That's up to the prosecutors, not me."

"Then you'd better go. My lawyer is mean as a timber wolf."

Yancy took a safe-looking can of ginger ale from the refrigerator. He popped the tab, sat down at the kitchen table and waited patiently for Dr. O'Peele to start gabbing.

"My training is orthopedic surgery. I had a damn good practice in Atlanta—sports medicine mostly—but then there were some personal setbacks. Nothing that reflected on my work, but that medical board, what a bunch of coldhearted pricks! Finally I just said screw it and moved down here and connected with Nick."

"You never set eyes on an actual patient for Midwest Mobile Medical, did you?"

"That's true," the doctor admitted hoarsely. "All I did was sign prescriptions and fill out the 849s. A nobody is what I was. A worker drone."

Yancy said fraud was fraud. O'Peele looked wobbly. "I've got substance issues," he confided. "This is not the arc I mapped out for my life. May I sit down?"

"Of course. Let's hear more about Mr. Stripling."

O'Peele shook his head so violently that his cheeks flapped. "Request denied!"

"Then at least clue me in on how the scam worked. Where did Nick get all those Medicare numbers?"

"He bought a list of, like, ten thousand names," the doctor said. "Some clerk that worked at one of the hospitals. Mount Sinai or Baptist, I don't remember which."

As Yancy had suspected, Midwest Mobile Medical was a ghost-patient operation, billing comical sums to Medicare for electric power chairs, stair lifts, walkers and other durable home-care items that would never be delivered. The senior citizens whose IDs had been hijacked remained in the dark because the government checks were mailed directly to Midwest Mobile.

Such fraud was epidemic throughout South Florida and practically risk-free, thanks to Medicare's stupendously idiotic policy of paying out claims before asking questions. By the time the FBI zeroed in on a brazen cheat such as Nicholas Stripling, he would have already shut down his operation, banked a few million and scurried on. Had he not been killed, he by now would have resurfaced with a new storefront and a new company logo, working the same easy swindle.

"How much did he pay you?" Yancy asked O'Peele.

"Hundred bucks for every Rollie prescription."

"And you weren't the only doctor signing them."

O'Peele chuckled drily. "I was the only *live* one. The other docs, they'd been dead from old age since forever. Somehow Nicky got hold of their filing numbers. There were two girls in the office, they did all the forgeries."

Yancy had mixed feelings about what he was learning from the strung-out physician. While pleased to confirm his suspicions about Stripling, he also understood that solving the murder of a despicable felon wasn't good for as many brownie points as solving, say, the murder of a beloved Little League coach or a department-store Santa. Some people might even endorse the view that Eve Stripling had performed a service to humankind—or, at the very least, to the Medicare trust fund—by ridding the world of her larcenous spouse. A similar thought had occurred to Yancy, though he wasn't inclined to walk away from the case. Eve belonged in prison, if not on death row. She'd murdered her man for the money.

O'Peele slugged down another shot. "How much do you people pay your informants these days?"

"Not my department," Yancy said.

"A thousand dollars sounds ballpark. For all the inside stuff I just gave you? And I've got plenty more. We're talking mother lode."

When Yancy asked Gomez O'Peele how he'd heard about Stripling's death, the doctor stammered and said he couldn't recall. From a foul cranny of his robe he produced a bottle of white pills, three of which he placed under his blistered tongue.

"Sorry," he said to Yancy.

"Yes, you are."

"I used to be board-certified, Inspector. One time I got a paper published in the AMA journal."

"Wild guess: It was a woman who lured you down this squalid path."

O'Peele bared his grungy implants. "Who are you to judge?"

"A voice of experience," Yancy said. "Go back to bed."

He had one more stop before heading back to the Keys.

The phantom power-chair racket had been good to the Striplings. Their house was a Spanish-style remodel on Di Lido Island off the Venetian Causeway. It had four bedrooms, four baths, a heated lap pool, a dock on Biscayne Bay and a view of the city skyline. The landscaper was an overzealous admirer of sea grape trees and Malaysian palms.

According to the MLS website, also easily accessed by Yancy's phone, the property was listed for $2 million and had been on the market only a short time. As was sometimes the case in such upscale neighborhoods, no For Sale sign had been planted in front of the Striplings' home. This was a Realtor's ploy designed to make prospective buyers believe that they were privy to an exclusive showing, and that the owners weren't especially motivated to sell.

Yancy drove twice past the entrance and then parked in some shade down the street. While he might have been dressed like a working detective, the motley Subaru betrayed him as a civilian. He had no itch to explain his presence on Di Lido to the real police, who wouldn't be impressed by his roach-patrol ID. And although he still had good friends in Miami-Dade law enforcement, none of them were placed highly enough to spring him from a jam.

What Yancy should have done was drive home, but he loathed the evening rush hour and knew the southbound turnpike would be, in the parlance of hard-core commuters, a goat fuck. Therefore he had some time to kill. Enough time to get lucky.

It was easy to find a house that had been shuttered for the summer, and that's where Yancy left the car. He removed his coat and tie and donned a yellow hard hat that he was supposed to wear while probing the storage lofts and crawl spaces of pest-infested restaurants. Add the toolbelt and he looked somewhat like a utility-company employee.

Walking down the street, he tried to simulate the gait of an overworked stiff who'd been busting his hump all day in the blazing sun and had one last job on his ticket sheet. As he approached the Stripling residence, he spotted a cable-TV service box halfway up the property line.

Each corner of the house was equipped beneath the eaves with a security camera, so Yancy pushed the hard hat low on his head in order to obscure his face while he dismantled the cable box and pretended to repair the wires.

He was hoping to catch a glimpse of the widow's boyfriend, or at least a sign of male presence—swimming trunks tossed on a patio chair, a cigar butt in a poolside ashtray, whatever. It was possible that Eve Stripling was too careful to bring her lover to the house, but in Yancy's experience lust usually triumphed over prudence. Besides, Eve would have no reason to believe she was suspected of murder unless Nick's daughter had confronted her, which seemed unlikely.

From the back of the property wafted pleasant fragments of an old song. To Yancy it sounded like the Eagles or maybe Poco, piped through outdoor speakers. He was kneeling near the concrete pad for the air-conditioning unit and pool pump, and the motor noises made it hard to follow the melody. Unfortunately for Yancy, the motors also drowned out the low-frequency growl of the neighbor's chow-cocker-rottweiler mix, which charged from behind and clamped its jaws on his left buttock.

Later he'd recall twisting his torso while spastically attempting to whack the animal with his hard hat, at which point he must have toppled sideways and struck his head on the slab. It was dark when he awoke with a roaring skull, his pants seat shredded and sticky with blood. The Satan-hound, having lost interest, was nowhere in sight.

Yancy lay there for a while, staring up at the sky. It was a clear night, though the starlight was washed out by the vast amber glow from the city. He remembered camping many times in Everglades National Park with his father; they'd arrange their sleeping bags to face west, 180 degrees away from Miami, so they could scout for constellations on a backdrop of natural darkness. Yancy decided that, once he got back his regular job, he'd invite his dad to fly down and they could paddle kayaks along the Shark River, or maybe through the backcountry of Chokoloskee. Winter was a better season, anyway; the nights cooled off, and there was plenty of dry tinder for a fire. And no goddamn bugs! Yancy recalled his mother's aversion to insects, which made his dad's posting in the Glades somewhat of a tribulation. But she'd hung in there, even through the blast-furnace days of summer when the mosquitoes were so thick you could inhale them into your lungs.

A door slammed and Yancy blinked himself back into the present. He was surprised to feel a tear slipping down his cheek. He rolled over and crawled through a bed of manicured bushes and then along the base of a stucco wall, toward the pool patio. Peeking around a corner, he saw Eve Stripling, crammed like a pepperoni into her white skinny jeans, standing on a lighted stone path leading to the boat dock. She was speaking to a taller hatless man beside her, his features obscured by the shadows. Although Yancy couldn't hear their conversation, the elevated pitch of both voices suggested a crisis in progress.

No more than a hundred yards away, rafting like a ghost pelican in the water, was a seaplane.

Ten

Evan Shook believed that only a masochist or a moron would stay in the Keys all summer. The humidity was murderous and the insects were unshakable, yet here he was. His sons were jacking off at a soccer camp in Maryland, his wife was on an Aegean cruise with her book club and his mistress was camping at a bluegrass festival in Vermont, probably balling some goddamn banjo player.

Meanwhile the construction project on Big Pine Key loomed as one of the stickier problems in Evan Shook's untidy world. He'd purchased the lot after the real estate market tanked and two years later he broke ground, anticipating a rebound in the demand for high-end island getaways. He was mistaken. The spec house wasn't done and already he'd been forced to drop the price four times. Most buyers with real money wanted a place closer to Key West, so they could safely patronize the eateries and multitude of bars. The farther one had to drive from Duval Street late at night, the higher the risk of a costly DUI pullover. Big Pine was twenty-nine miles up the road.

Still, Evan Shook had gotten promising nibbles before

this bizarre stretch of foul luck—first the dead raccoon, then the hive of killer bees. He stormed the county offices to complain, but he couldn't find anybody in authority who would even write down his name. Eventually he was steered to some dweeb at the agricultural extension.

"They should spray the island to wipe out all the bees and wasps," Evan Shook declared. "And pay some trapper to kill those fucking raccoons. Fifty bucks a tail."

"That's not funny," the young agricultural agent said.

"Do you have any idea how much tax I pay on my property? More than you make in a year!"

"Here's some advice: Do a better job of securing the job site."

Evan Shook snapped, "Thanks for nothing, junior."

The unfinished house suffered from the absence of windows and doors, which were essential to sealing the structure from marauding wildlife. Before ordering the expensive impact-resistant glass that was required for new construction in hurricane zones, Evan Shook had been hoping to line up a buyer who'd spring for custom hardware.

As he drove back to the property, he again considered turning the whole damn thing over to a Realtor and flying home to Syracuse. However, due to a slender and ever-dwindling profit margin, Evan Shook remained opposed to paying somebody a commission to sell his spec house. Who needed a real estate agent when you had global Internet?

Two potential buyers were coming to Big Pine that very morning—a middle-aged gay couple from Oslo. One of them owned a firm that manufactured drill equipment for deep-water oil rigs, and Evan Shook smelled a cash deal. In his e-mails he'd laid it on thick about the "balmy Florida winters" and "laid-back tropical lifestyle" and "picture-postcard sunsets."

Typical Nords, the two men had arrived early for the showing. When Evan Shook pulled up, he saw them standing at the fence and conversing with his eccentric neighbor, Yancy. It was impossible not to notice that Yancy's pants were bunched around his ankles, and that the Norwegian couple was soberly contemplating his bare ass.

Evan Shook experienced a flush of dread. *What the fuck?* He remained inside the climate-controlled Suburban to mull the possibilities.

Yancy definitely liked women but perhaps he was bi-sexual. In that case, his presence next door might be a selling point for the spec house, should the Norwegians find him attractive. Evan Shook decided not to interrupt Yancy's private exhibition, just in case. He fiddled with the stereo dial and pretended to be talking on his cell. In the rearview mirror he inconspicuously checked his face for residual bee stings, and he was pleased to see that the welts were fading.

Soon Yancy pulled up his trousers and returned to his house. Evan Shook got out of the SUV and crossed the unsodded lot to greet his guests, whose first names were Ole and Peder. They were fit and fair-skinned, and they spoke better English than he did.

"I see you've met Mr. Yancy. An unusual guy."

"Yes," Ole said. "He is fortunate to be alive."

"Oh?"

The Norwegians exchanged clouded glances. Peder said, "Didn't he tell you what occurred last night?"

"No, I haven't talked with him," Evan Shook said, thinking: *This can't be good.*

"He was attacked while jogging," Ole reported.

"Yancy jogs?" Evan Shook decided it could be true. The man looked as scrawny as a scarecrow. "Did he get mugged or something?"

"Bitten," said Peder, "by wild dogs."

"A pack of them," Ole added.

Evan Shook was speechless. He'd never heard of feral hounds roaming the Keys. The Norwegians said the animals had "mauled" Yancy's rear end.

"He fought them off before they could reach his throat," Peder said.

"Where did all this happen?" Evan Shook asked.

Ole pointed. "Right there. At the corner of your street."

"That's awful," mumbled Evan Shook. *Awful in every imaginable way.*

"Mr. Yancy said it's not the first time. Usually he carries bear spray but last night he forgot."

Evan Shook bobbled helplessly. "Bear spray. Really?"

The Norwegians cast not a glance toward their future four-story island vacation house with the picture-postcard sunset view. They were grimly scanning the street for bloodthirsty canines.

"Let me assure you," Evan Shook said, "I've never seen so much as a stray Chihuahua on this island."

In the maddeningly neutral manner of Scandinavians, Peder shrugged. "Mr. Yancy showed us the bite wounds. It was a serious aggression."

"Well, I hope he's notified Animal Control. And if he hasn't, *I* damn sure will. Those mutts will be rounded up and gassed, I promise. Now, please, let me give you a tour of the palace."

Ole shook his head apologetically. "We don't wish to waste your time, Mr. Shook."

"You're not wasting my time. Are you kidding?"

Peder said, "I'm afraid we're no longer interested. This location, really, it isn't what we had in mind."

"Although your house looks quite airy and nice," Ole added. "It will make an excellent vacation home for somebody, I'm sure."

Evan Shook felt like his spine was being tapped. "Look, the price isn't locked in stone. Let's go inside and get out of the sun. The construction crew won't be back till noon."

"We have cats," Peder said. "So, you see, this neighborhood would be out of the question."

Ole elaborated politely. "They are too old to outrun a horde of dogs. Inge is eleven and Torhilda is thirteen."

"That's a pity," said Evan Shook. He sounded like a tire going flat.

The Norwegians firmly shook his hand and departed in their rental car. Evan Shook glared across the fence, where Yancy was leaning against the rail of his cedar deck. He had what appeared to be a shotgun under one arm, as if standing guard against another wolfish onslaught. Evan Shook spat on the ground and slouched off toward the chill of his Suburban.

Dr. Rosa Campesino, who insisted on examining it for herself, said: "Andrew, that's the nastiest-looking butt I've ever seen on a live person."

"The dog was a mutant brute!"

"Just hold still."

She swabbed the pulpy bite marks with Betadine while

Yancy pondered the sublime irony of being wounded in the same nether region where he'd targeted Bonnie Witt's husband.

"Looks like Fido got a mouthful," Rosa remarked, "and you didn't have much to start with."

"I have other noteworthy attributes." Yancy was flat on his belly in bed. When he reached out to squeeze Rosa's leg, she swatted his hand.

"Actually, you could use a few stitches," she said. "I brought a surgical kit, just in case."

"To cap off a truly humiliating second date."

"Hush, Andrew."

The drive back from Miami had been more nerve-grinding than usual because he'd had to tilt sideways behind the wheel, in order to keep weight off his mangled left buttock. It was worse than one of Bonnie Witt's nutty yoga positions. Contorted for nearly three hours, his brain pounding from the smack on the concrete, Yancy had emerged like an arthritic crab from the Subaru.

The next morning he'd phoned Rosa to tell her what had happened at Eve Stripling's house. She said she'd come straight down as soon as she finished the final autopsy on her schedule, a routine suicide. Yancy passed the time on his feet, because sitting was too painful. Liquor helped somewhat. He also distracted himself by initiating a useful conversation with a pair of Norwegians who were waiting to tour the monstrous spec house next door.

Rosa looked irresistible as she walked up Yancy's front steps, but he was in too much discomfort to make a move, even after she changed into a devastating sundress.

While she inspected the knot on his skull, he said, "Know what? We'd make a great crime-solving duo."

"How much have you had to drink?"

"Have mercy, woman. I ran out of Advil."

"Well, I don't sleep with drunken guys. Period."

Yancy sighed. "So many rules."

She took notice of the shotgun propped in a corner, and Yancy told her restaurant inspections could be dangerous. She informed him that for dinner she was doing blackened grouper with mashed sweet potatoes and a grilled Caesar, and that he was going to finish every bite or never see her again.

"I also stopped in Key Largo and got some homemade carrot cake," she said.

"From where?"

"What's the difference?"

"Rosa, you don't understand. I see all the health reports. I know the dirt on every kitchen."

She ordered him to be quiet while she sewed up his gnawed butt cheek. To take his mind off the intimate unpleasantries, Yancy told the story of how he was conceived during side one of *Abbey Road*.

"You mean side two," Rosa said. "The medley."

"No, side one. According to my mom, the big moment happened during 'Maxwell's Silver Hammer.'"

"It's all starting to make sense," said Rosa.

After trimming the last suture, she made Yancy stand up and drink an entire pitcher of cold water. When his head began to clear, he told her about the seaplane parked behind Eve Stripling's house.

"I ran the tail numbers on a flight-tracking website. It's a Cessna Caravan that's leased from a company in Boca Raton. Flew in from Congo Town the day before and cleared Customs at Opa-locka, all legal and proper."

"Where on earth is Congo Town?" Rosa asked.

"Bahamas." Yancy jerked a thumb toward the east. "Andros Island."

"Andrew, you'd make a darn good cop."

"That dog bite still stings like hell. You sure you know what you're doing?"

"My other patients never complain. They are, however, deceased."

That's when she kissed him. It was a good one, bordering on unforgettable.

"Only because you're injured," she said, and kissed him again.

He pulled her close. "How's this going to work with all these stitches? Do I have to keep standing?"

"Well," whispered Rosa, "I suppose you could kneel."

Yancy lifted her sundress. "You're the doctor."

The Dragon Queen asked, "How much you take fuh dot pink boy?"

Neville said he wasn't for sale.

"Too bod."

"And dot's a monkey, madam, not a boy."

"He got a name?"

"Driggs." Neville opened the brown bag. He handed her the fresh bottle of rum and a box of cheroots. "Dot woo-doo dint woyk on Chrissofer," he said. "He supposa be gone but he ain't."

"Wot!"

"Mon tore down my house!"

"Maybe den he drop dead."

"No, madam, he come in again dis morning. Got offa plane wit his woman and drove 'way." Neville had received the upsetting information from a cousin who worked at the airport.

The Dragon Queen struck a match on her bare heel and lighted one of the cigars. She assured Neville that she'd put a hideous, unshakable curse on the white devil. "Juss you wait. He be gone from Andros in due time."

"I cont wait fuh due time," said Neville. "Soon dot fella gon start puddin' up his damn hotel."

Neville had been hiding in the pines while Christopher's workers had replaced the fuel filter on the backhoe into which Neville had pissed. He asked the Dragon Queen what type of voodoo she'd used on the white American.

"Dot piece a shoyt you brought tuh me. Any minute now, his skin be fallin' off his body. Maybe his balls, too."

She twisted open the rum and took a husky slug, careful not to dribble. Then she sprang up from her wicker throne and began to dance, clapping her hands and swirling her long red-and-yellow dress. Neville glanced anxiously at the door, which he'd left ajar in anticipation of a speedy exit. Driggs bared his yellow teeth and bounded onto Neville's shoulder. It was the middle of the afternoon, broiling hot and not a murmur of breeze. The windows of the woman's shack were open and the doctor flies buzzed throughout, targeting the bald patches on the monkey's hide.

Neville was disappointed that the Dragon Queen's spell had failed, and increasingly skeptical of her claims. He'd returned to try once more only because of her considerable reputation for dark magic. He told her that stronger voodoo was needed to neutralize the man called Christopher. The Dragon Queen replied that she had needs of her own, and flapped the flowing dress up over her head. Neville was mortified to be flashed in such a crude manner. Driggs began to shriek and twitch and claw at his diaper.

"Madam, please," Neville protested.

"Wot's wrong wit dot ugly boy of yours? Am I de first grown woman he ever seen naked as God made us?"

Neville lied and said he was late to meet a boat mechanic in Rocky Town. He dug into a pocket and came up with twenty-one Bahamian dollars, which he counted out and placed on the table next to the rum. The Dragon Queen sighed, tucking the bills into her damp bony cleavage.

She said, "I will need some udder poysonal tings belonging to dis mon. Dot shoyt is all boined up."

Neville told her he'd come back with something better. That evening he would snoop in the trash cans outside the big oceanfront house that Christopher was renting. That's where he'd found the piece of shirt.

"Now, put dot sweet pink boy on my knee," she said, jabbing a dirty fingernail toward Driggs. "Lemme have a squeeze."

"No, madam, he bites."

"Wot!" She craned forward like a buzzard, studying the face of the trembling animal. "I tink someone pudda bod coyse on dis youngstah long time ago. But, see here, I kin make 'im good as new. Juss leave 'im wit me."

The monkey hissed and vaulted out of her reach. Neville followed him out the door.

Dinner was superb. Yancy cleaned his plate for the first time in weeks. Afterward he took Rosa out on his skiff. She asked why he hadn't remarried after Celia left him.

He told her he'd come close twice. Rosa's own marriage had lasted three years and fizzled with nobody to blame, or so she said.

The truth was more depressing, laid bare by Google Earth. It happened on a rare slow day at the Miami-Dade morgue, when she had only one autopsy scheduled—an elderly female tourist who had straightforwardly drowned at Key Biscayne, a tragedy witnessed by fourteen blood relatives, none of whom could swim a lick. Why a family devoid of water skills chose to vacation at a seaside resort was beyond Rosa's scope of inquiry. The postmortem was completed by lunchtime and she had the afternoon to kill.

That's when a blood tech named Gaylord showed her the Google Earth app, which he downloaded to Rosa's office desktop. Soon she was enjoying aerial views of the Hoover Dam, the Malecón in old Havana, and even—more impressively—her parents' home in Union City. From thousands of feet in the sky she could still make out the old sycamores lining each side of the driveway, the rectangular outline of her mother's flower garden and a blurred image of her backyard swing set, which her father sentimentally refused to dismantle.

Next Gaylord loaded Google Maps with a street view, which sent Rosa eagerly cruising the roadways of her youth. There was the Ferraro house—Bobby Jr. had asked her to the junior prom; the shutters were now periwinkle blue, not white like before. The two-story where Angie Fernandez and her sisters had lived looked deserted, a sign planted in the dead lawn saying the place was up for sale by some bank. Also gone were the Sotos, who'd come from Cuba with Rosa's parents; the new owners had erected a tall wooden fence and nailed up a Beware of

Dog sign embellished with the silhouette of a snarling pit bull.

It was only natural for Rosa to check out her present Miami neighborhood and the dwelling she shared with Daniel, her then spouse, who worked as a teak carpenter on yachts. The driver of the Google camera truck had chosen a sunny morning to map the streets of Morningside, and Rosa thought their small home looked tropical and welcoming—the red barrel-tile roof, the green ivy nibbling at the bright stucco walls; in the front yard, ponytail palms, crimson bougainvilleas and a birdbath carved from limestone.

The only thing out of place that day, when the Google crew with their roof-mounted cameras rolled by, was a car Rosa didn't recognize in the driveway. The car was parked next to Daniel's Ram pickup, and it appeared to be a late-model Camry or an Accord; who could tell the difference? Dark blue was the color, though, definitely. The car had a Florida license plate that was partially fuzzed in the video—Gaylord surmised that Google did that on purpose because of privacy concerns—although upon enlargement Rosa was able to identify the prefix, which was LRW.

She would never forget those three letters because, as events unfolded, they came to stand in her mind for Low Rent Whore. Having nothing better to do on that slow afternoon, Dr. Rosa Campesino fed the tag information to a cop friend, who ran a statewide computer check and found one and only one blue Honda Accord registered with a tag beginning with LRW. It came back to a Sandra Jane Finn, white female, age twenty-nine, who was known to Rosa as a freelance hotel lifeguard and stand-up paddleboard instructor. For Daniel's birthday Rosa had purchased for him a ten-foot Dragonfly and three private lessons, which had evidently evolved to include floating blow jobs on the Intracoastal Waterway.

That night Daniel broke down and admitted to the affair, lamenting his wretched luck that the Google vehicle had rolled past the marital homestead on one of the rare occasions when Sandy happened to be there. Usually they met at her place, he added ineptly. Rosa evicted him at scalpel-point, and over time she'd successfully swept him into a tiny moldy corner of her memory.

"You still talk to your ex?" Yancy asked.

"He's deceased," Rosa said, "but even if he wasn't, I wouldn't call."

A pod of dolphins rolled in the channel and Yancy patted softly on the water to draw them near. Rosa said she wasn't sure if she wanted to have children because her job presented such a depressing outlook for the human species. Yancy understood how she felt. Bonnie Witt had once tearfully begged him to impregnate her; the fact that he'd briefly considered the request was proof that he'd been crippled by romantic self-delusions. Their offspring would have been eternally fucked up, prime fodder for Dr. Phil.

The dolphins moved on, swimming leisurely with the tide. Yancy poled the skiff up on a grassy flat and staked off from the stern. He felt all right as long as he didn't sit down. A colossal thunderhead bloomed to the west, smothering the sun but spreading a lavender veil of light.

"Tell me about the other patient you saw today," he said to Rosa. "The one who didn't whine and squirm."

"You mean the suicide? It was a doctor, believe it or not."

Yancy briefly thought of Clifford, but he remembered that the Witts were in Sarasota. *Unless there was a medical convention in Miami...*

"Please tell me he didn't strangle himself with his pecker in his fist."

"No!" Rosa said. "And, by the way, that wouldn't be a suicide. That would be an autoerotic miscalculation. This fellow did the job with a handgun."

"Messy, but less embarrassing."

"He was also drunk out of his gourd, and probably loaded on oxycodone. They found prescription bottles all over his condo. We'll know for sure when the lab finishes the toxicology."

Yancy had stopped admiring the sky. "He wasn't an orthopedist, was he?"

Rosa turned in the bow and looked up at him. "How'd you know?"

"His name was Gomez O'Peele?"

"Yes, Andrew, but how on earth—"

"I went to see him yesterday, after you and I had lunch. He used to work for Nick Stripling."

"Jesus, maybe the guy freaked out after you braced him."

"That's not the reaction I got. He wanted cash money for being an informant. Did they find a note?"

Rosa shook her head.

"Then how," Yancy said, "can you be sure he killed himself?"

"Point-blank wound, right temple. His prints on the weapon. No sign of forced entry, no sign of a struggle.

His brother said he'd lost his job at a clinic and had financial problems, booze issues, drug issues." Rosa raised her hands. "It's textbook, Andrew."

"Except maybe it's not."

"Did you see a gun when you were there?"

"No. What did he use?"

"A .357 Smith."

"Let me take a guess on the ammo," Yancy said. "Hollow points, 158-grain."

"Okay, stop."

"Just like the ones that killed Charles Phinney." Yancy unstuck the pole and started pushing the skiff off the shallows. "When did this happen?" he asked.

"One of the doctor's neighbors heard a bang around seven-thirty, eight o'clock. She knocked on the door, got no answer. Didn't call the police because she had company—not her husband." Rosa was frowning. "This morning a rabbi who lives in the building found blood spots in his parking space. They'd dripped from O'Peele's balcony, where the body was found."

Yancy was disturbed to think his visit had in some way precipitated the doctor's death. Had somebody been surveilling the condo? Or maybe the shooter had followed him there. He thought of Eve and her boyfriend, their hushed and agitated conversation in the backyard on Di Lido Island. Had they been talking about O'Peele? Had they already shot him?

But why bother killing the guy, since Nick Stripling was dead and unreachable by prosecutors? A murder only made sense if Eve herself feared being indicted as a conspirator in the scooter-chair scam, and if she feared O'Peele would testify against her.

"I'll hold off signing the death certificate," Rosa said. "It should be easy to compare the bullets that killed O'Peele and Phinney. Meanwhile you should tell the homicide cops in North Miami Beach what you know. Tell them you were at the doctor's condo a few hours before the shooting and he seemed okay."

"I'm not telling anybody I was there."

"Andrew, this is serious shit."

"So is saving my career."

On the ride back to the boat ramp, Yancy mentally replayed his brief time inside O'Peele's place. He was fairly certain he hadn't left a trace of himself, besides fingerprints on a ginger ale can that the cops were not likely to dust since he'd tossed it in a Dumpster in the parking lot. Fortunately, he hadn't given the doctor one of his expired detective cards or even a phone number.

Still, there remained a slender chance that, despite the Percocets and bourbon, O'Peele had been sufficiently alert to have noted the name when Yancy flashed his restaurant-inspector ID. What if O'Peele had scrawled it down somewhere after Yancy had gone? *That* could be a problem.

Back at the house, Rosa inspected his stitches and predicted scar-free healing. Yancy attributed her unwavering Hippocratic detachment to the sorry sight of his gnawed, calorie-deprived hindquarters. When he asked her to spend the night, she declined.

"I'd never make it to the morgue on time."

"So, take the day off," Yancy said, belting his pants. "Join me on roach patrol. Tomorrow it's a gyro shop owned by Rastas who supposedly sell ganja out the back door. Lombardo thinks mice are nesting in the stash, which means they're the world's mellowest *rodentia*. Still, I could use a backup."

"Sounds like a dreamy third date," said Rosa, "but I'll take a rain check."

"When you talk to the homicide detectives in North Miami Beach, ask them if they found a cell phone on Dr. O'Peele."

"They did. In a pocket of his robe."

"I'd love to know the last number he called."

Rosa said, "Let me see what I can do." She delivered another toe-curling kiss and headed out the door.

Yancy took his time washing the dishes because standing was pain-free, making it easier to focus on the murder case. He was certain that Eve Stripling was responsible for her husband's death, yet he couldn't rule out the possibility that she'd had nothing to do with the shootings of Charles Phinney and Dr. Gomez O'Peele. Whoever said there's no such thing as coincidence never worked as a cop. The young boat mate could have been robbed and killed by some random dirtbag who'd heard him blabbing about his windfall, just as the pathetic orthopedist could have spiraled into a drug-induced abyss and ended his own life. Smith & Wesson was a popular brand of handgun in Florida, and plenty of unreliable characters favored .357s.

Like most police officers, Yancy had never in the line of duty fired his own service pistol, a lightweight Glock .40 that he'd been forced to turn in along with his resignation. At first he'd felt naked without a holster under his arm, but that had passed with time. For home protection he maintained a double-barreled 12-gauge Beretta loaded with buckshot, a habit left over from residing in greater

Miami. For life in the Keys, such a substantial weapon served mainly as a decorative fixture. Yancy would never have thought to carry it while rolling his garbage can out to the street, which is where he was ambushed by a masked bicycle rider wearing a blaze-orange poncho, no more than an hour after Rosa Campesino had kissed him good-bye.

Eleven

Yancy remembered exactly when he decided to become a police officer: It was the day of his grandmother's funeral. A gang of burglars who specialized in scouting obituaries had looted his Nanna's apartment while she was being buried. Yancy's family was sickened when they walked in on the mess, which included gratuitous defecation not uncommon in such break-ins. His mother's knees buckled and she dropped to the floor, sobbing. His father made her stay by the door while he and Yancy searched to make sure the thieves were gone. Stolen were his grandmother's television set, her wedding ring, some heirloom jewelry worth maybe two grand, and an oxygen tank that had been left by her bed.

The Homestead cops snapped some photos and told the family not to expect any miracles. Watching his mother cry while his father cleaned up the intruders' shit, Yancy experienced an overpowering anger. That such a small, shabby crime could cause so much heartache was a revelation, and he thought of how often it happened every day. The jam-packed conditions in Florida prisons seemed proof that the majority of felons eventually fucked up and got busted. Yancy imagined it would be profoundly satisfying to participate in that process, although later he'd look back on his thinking as naïve.

Still, until his third or fourth year as a detective, he continued to fantasize about capturing the assholes who'd trashed his grandmother's place on the day of her funeral. In his daydreams the burglars wildly resisted arrest and were always dealt an agonizing lesson, their window-prying fingertips crushed to pulp by a squad-car door or the butt of a pump gun.

In real life those apprehended by Yancy usually surrendered without resistance, aware that their period of confinement would be brief and only nominally tuned to their actual sentence. Savvy thieves understood that the court system went easy on the unarmed and that violence was for fools. Yancy had occasionally tackled or Tazed a fleeing suspect, but never had he been forced to fight off an attack. Although he'd punched his way out of a couple of bars, he held no special skills in self-defense or the martial arts, having quit karate classes at age twelve because they'd cut too onerously into his fishing time.

It didn't really matter, because the cyclist caught him completely by surprise.

As Yancy was placing the trash can by the road, he heard the swish of air through spokes and he turned to look. A stretch mask obscured the face of the approaching rider but the orange poncho shone even in the deepening dusk. The bike knocked Yancy to the ground, and when he looked up, the stranger was standing over him. The last image to register was a downward-swinging arm with a bulky, ornate wristwatch.

Later, as a throbbing consciousness returned, Yancy surmised that he'd been struck with an old-fashioned sap or possibly a sock filled with coins. The blow landed on the opposite side from the bruise he'd incurred at Eve Stripling's house, leaving his head with conforming knots, like raw antler nubs.

Now the man in the poncho was dragging Yancy by the collar through the lot next door, past Evan Shook's spec house. Yancy's rear end was afire with pain, the friction against the ground having shredded Rosa Campesino's delicate web of sutures. The far side of Evan Shook's property fronted a canal, and Yancy sensed what was coming next. His limbs hung uselessly, however, and failed to respond to urgent brain commands. He half-shut his eyes and pretended to be coldcocked.

The masked stranger was grunting and huffing by the time he reached the canal. Awkwardly he tried to heave Yancy headlong, but Yancy's toes snagged on a ridge of coral rock, leaving him half in and half out of the water. Swearing, the attacker kicked at the soles of Yancy's feet until Yancy slid like a comatose otter down the bank.

He knew that the man who was trying to kill him—the same man who'd murdered Charles Phinney and probably Gomez O'Peele—would be unable to see him swimming in the murky canal if he went deep enough. His arms and legs didn't awaken for several harrowing seconds, and his lungs were searing by the time he began to make progress. Fortunately the waterway was narrow and the opposite shore was fringed densely with mangrove trees. Skinny as he was, Yancy managed to slither into the embroidery of roots and poke his head up for air. He was no more conspicuous than a floating coconut or an orphaned lobster buoy.

The burly figure in the poncho stood on the other bank, staring hard in search of bubbles and scanning the length of the canal to make sure that the victim of his beating hadn't surfaced. Yancy clung to the barnacled mangroves and braced his knees, trying not to create ripples. His bruised skull clanged, and hot pulses of nausea raised the annoying prospect of a concussion. Mosquitoes swarmed his ears and eyes, but he couldn't slap them away for fear of causing a telltale splash. Eventually his attacker turned and hurried off.

Five minutes was as long as Yancy could tolerate the insects. Gingerly he extricated himself from the roots, dog-paddled across the canal and crawled out. The thick night air seemed almost as heavy as the salt water. Approaching his house, Yancy saw a light go on in the living room, revealing through a front window the masked killer in the poncho. He was handling Yancy's shotgun, checking to see if it was loaded, which of course it was.

Yancy ducked into Evan Shook's place and groped his way to what must have been a closet. The door had yet to be hung but still it was a refuge of sorts, a recessed cubby where he could hide and dry out. Maybe take a nap. The closet smelled like raw pine, and Yancy felt sawdust under his feet. His forearms and knees stung from where the barnacles had grated the skin. He touched his scalp and found a syrupy wetness. There arose an urge to strip out of his sopping clothes, and the effort exhausted him.

As he drifted away, a familiar tune entered his woozy head. It was a rocking John Hiatt number, "Master of Disaster."

• • •

Evan Shook insisted on meeting the Turbles at the Key West airport and he personally escorted them to Big Pine. The couple rode together in the second seat of the Suburban so they could snuggle. With the loss of the skittish Norwegians still fresh, Evan Shook would have donned a topcoat and chauffeur's cap if he'd thought it would help sell his godforsaken spec house.

Ken Turble, who preferred to be called Kenny, had made such a killing in the commodities markets that he remained revoltingly wealthy after losing two-thirds of his fortune in a divorce. His new wife, Tanya, was eleven years younger than the youngest Turble offspring. Kenny proudly shared this information with Evan Shook early in the car ride. As a way of backfilling, Tanya yipped, "I got a business degree from Kaplan."

By Mile Marker 7, it was clear to Evan Shook that the marriage was doomed. Behind him the Turbles were cooing and murmuring so insipidly that they couldn't possibly have anything in common. Still, Evan Shook was pleased to see the crusty old coot derailed by lust; obviously he'd buy anything for his nubile bride, including a half-finished vacation chalet in the Florida Keys. A friend in the advertising business once told Evan Shook that Viagra was the only thing keeping Tiffany's and Porsche afloat, and Evan Shook thought the same might hold true for high-end real estate. A glance in the rearview mirror confirmed that Tanya Turble was now giving her husband a peppy hand job, which could only serve to prime him for Evan Shook's sales pitch.

"Eyes on the road," Kenny Turble warbled rapturously.

"Yes, sir," said Evan Shook.

Tanya inquired if there was a Kleenex in the vehicle. Evan Shook reached back and presented his handkerchief, which happened to be monogrammed. "Keep it," he said.

She laughed. "Duh."

"I think you're gonna fall in love with this house."

"We saw a gem on Marco Island. Right, baby?"

Kenny Turble said, "Gorgeous place. Except I don't golf."

"Honestly, I can't see you two on Marco," Evan Shook commented. "The average age is, like, eighty-four. Don't get me wrong—my mother lives there and she's happy as a clam—but you don't strike me as the bridge-club-and-shuffleboard type."

"Or golf," said Kenny.

His wife rolled down the window and let fly the sticky handkerchief. "They had a cool gym in town," she said.

"Do you enjoy fishing? We've got some incredible off-shore action—tuna, mahi, even blue marlin."

"Kenny loves that stuff. Me, I just like to lay out."

"Sun we've got," Evan Shook said. "Three hundred and twenty-five days a year." It was a statistic he'd invented for the occasion; for all he knew, it might have been accurate. However, the line about his mom living on Marco Island was bullshit; she had a town house in Scottsdale.

"We almost there?" Tanya asked.

"Hey, check out the deer," Evan Shook said as they passed a doe and two fawns.

"Oh, sweet. And they're so little!"

Ken Turble grunted. "When's the season open?"

"November through January," Evan Shook replied, another lie. You could go to prison for shooting a Key deer, but he didn't want to queer the deal by telling that to Kenny, obviously an avid hunter.

Nothing seemed amiss when they got to the property; no sign of creepy Andrew Yancy in the vicinity. Tanya Turble headed for the spec house while her husband quizzed Evan Shook about windstorm insurance and flood-elevation certificates. Kenny also wanted to know if he could put in a dock, and how deep the water stood at low tide. The two men strolled to the bank of the canal, where Evan Shook was disturbed to see a discarded liquor bottle, a spinning rod and a gamey pair of flip-flops.

"What's the matter?" Ken Turble said.

"Let's go inside so I can give you and your wife the grand tour."

But the tour fizzled quickly. Upon entering the house they came upon a nude man sprawled on the floor of the future living room. He was face-up in a splayed, post-crucifixion pose. His head glistened with lumps, both knees showed fresh scabs and his outflung arms bore gashes and scrapes.

Evan Shook blurted, "Yancy, what the fuck!"

"Those dogs, man. You didn't see 'em?"

Tanya Turble stood off to the side with slender arms folded. Her husband couldn't help but observe that she was staring at the naked intruder's crotch.

"Who the hell is this character?" Ken Turble demanded. "Is he on drugs or what?"

Yancy raised his head to cough. "They went berserk again. I was lucky to get away."

Evan Shook was trembling as he hurriedly gathered Yancy's damp clothes from the bottom of the closet and threw them at his feet.

"I live next door," Yancy said, sitting up slowly.

Tanya said, "What kinda dogs?"

Kenny elbowed Evan Shook. "That's his house right there? Oh great."

"I was putting out the trash last night," Yancy continued, "and the pack was on me so damn fast, I barely made it to the canal." He rose and wriggled into his damp pants. "Soon as I got out of the water I ducked in here to hide."

In the hope of boosting Yancy's stock as a potential neighbor, Evan Shook informed Ken Turble that Yancy was a police officer. Who wouldn't feel safer with a cop living on the block? A spark came to Tanya's green eyes, which again her watchful husband detected.

"What kinda cop?" she asked.

"I'm not free to say." Yancy steadied himself against a wall. "Sorry about all the blood," he said to Evan Shook. "Your crew will be painting over it anyway, right? One of these days."

"Did you go fishing on my property last night?"

Yancy sighed. "Jesus, do I look like I went fishing?" He turned to Tanya Turble. "Wild dogs on the island. They only come out at night."

"You mean like werewolves."

"No, darling," said Kenny, stepping to his wife's side, "just a bunch of stray mutts."

Evan Shook spoke in toneless desolation. "I've never laid eyes on these animals. Not once."

Young Tanya addressed Yancy. "Would they eat a collie?"

"Are you kidding? They'd eat a fucking Clydesdale."

She pursed her lips. "Well, we could keep Barney locked up—that's our dog."

Ken Turble was wishing the cop would put on a shirt so that he might recapture his wife's attention. "No, sweetie, Barney needs open space to run. We can't leave him cooped indoors all day."

Evan Shook asked, "Don't you want to see the view upstairs?"

Kenny said no thanks. Tanya suggested they summon an ambulance for the injured police officer.

"No need," said Yancy, toddling toward the door. "My girlfriend's a doctor."

It hurt so badly that he actually screamed in the shower. Rogelio Burton arrived with nine tubes of Neosporin, the entire inventory from the local Walgreens. While Yancy gooped his multiple lacerations he told Burton everything that had happened since Eve Stripling had come to claim her husband's severed arm.

Burton said, "You need to clue the sheriff in right away."

"Not until it's a lock."

"That's insane, Andrew. You're gonna get yourself killed *and* blow the case. How did this asshole find you? The guy who tried to drown you."

"I have a guess," Yancy said.

He surmised that Gomez O'Peele had a better memory for names than most junkies. The doctor had probably phoned Eve with a shakedown in mind soon after Yancy left the apartment. Told her he'd just been questioned by a cop—how much was it worth to her for him to keep his mouth shut about the Medicare scooter scam? Eve had told him to sit tight and she'd bring some money. Instead she sent Poncho Boy with his .357. Once he pried

Yancy's name out of O'Peele, he put a bullet in the poor slob's noggin.

Tracking Yancy to his house would have been easy for Eve, who already knew he lived somewhere on Big Pine. An online check of property records would have produced the address. Google would have given her a flawless road map and, as a bonus, the news stories about Yancy's recent departure from the sheriff's office. From Eve's point of view, a disgraced ex-cop wasn't such a risky target for killing. After all, she and the boyfriend had made her husband's murder look like an accident; why not the same fate for Yancy?

"Call Sonny," Burton implored again.

"Sonny does *not* want to know about this."

"You're putting me in a helluva shitty position."

"What position? You just stopped over for a beer. Big deal." By now Yancy was shining from the ointment. He looked like an abused gummy bear.

"The widow's boyfriend jacked my shotgun last night," he informed Burton. "Oh, and here's a clever touch: He left an empty booze bottle and one of my spinning rods down by the water, so everybody would think I got drunk and fell in, whatever."

"Works for me." Burton had begun to pace. "Phinney's girlfriend is missing."

"She left town."

"Man, could you please put on some clothes?"

"I'm too sticky," Yancy said. "Hey, Rog, if I slipped you the tail numbers off a seaplane, could you find out who chartered it? I mean without sending up a goddamn flare. I'll give you the name of the leasing company."

Burton said, "I've got my job to think about, Andrew.

A wife plus two kids that might want to get off the rock and go to college someday. Why do I want to get dragged into a mess like this? Look at your victims and tell me who gives a shit. Let's see—there's a low-life Medicare scammer, a dock rat and a crooked doctor with a dope habit. Before you come close to making a case, Stripling's wife and the poncho dude will be long gone. Disappearing is no problem in the Bahamas, *mon*. You know how it goes."

"I know that anybody can be found."

"And who's gonna pay for your hotels and plane tickets, Andrew? The health department? Are they doing extraditions now, too?" Burton raised his hands. "What's the fucking point?"

"Catching a couple of murderers, that's the point," Yancy said. "Hell, it's something to do in my spare time. The tarpon run is over." He grabbed a towel from the bathroom and wrapped it around his waist. "Did I mention that Eve gave the dead husband's fancy watch to her boyfriend? He was wearing it last night when he clocked me."

Burton said, "What if Stripling was killed in Miami? You think the homicide guys up there will give you credit for solving the case? Never in a jillion years. Your name won't even be in the reports, Andrew, unless you change it to C. Informant."

"Do me a favor," Yancy said. "Next time you come over, just bring chicken soup."

"For Christ's sake, I'll check on the seaplane."

After Burton was gone, Yancy realized he should have asked to borrow a gun. Eve would be scouring the *Citizen*'s website for news of Yancy's tragic drowning. When she didn't find the story, she'd probably send the boyfriend back to Big Pine to try again. Yancy called Rosa Campesino at the morgue to tell her about his action-packed evening, but the secretary said Rosa was in the middle of an autopsy. Next Yancy tried Caitlin Cox and left a message on her voice mail.

Hearing a knock, he peeked through a window and saw a sallow, thickset fellow who was dressed like a plainclothes cop, which he was.

"John Wesley Weiderman," the man said after Yancy let him in. "Oklahoma Bureau of Investigation."

"You're shitting me."

"Can I have a glass of ice water?"

"Did you fly into Miami International?"

"Yes, sir."

"Then hard liquor is in order."

"Tap water's fine, thanks." John Wesley Weiderman opened a briefcase and took out a years-old mug shot of Plover Chase, a.k.a. Bonnie Witt. "Do you know this woman? Her husband said we might find her down here."

Yancy sat down across from the investigator. "I haven't seen her in a while. Can I assume she's in trouble?" He was wondering why Clifford had ratted out his beloved Bonnie.

"Ms. Chase is a convicted sex offender. For years she's been a fugitive."

"Well, we did have an affair, a romance, a fling, whatever you call it back home. But in no manner did she victimize me, John—may I call you John? I was a willing participant. Recklessly enthusiastic, to be truthful. But I'm sure Dr. Witt filled you in. Here in the Keys she called herself Bonnie, not Plover. I'd never sleep with a woman named Plover."

The investigator said, "What's the matter with you?"

"In general? I don't know where to start." Yancy readjusted his towel, which kept slipping off his hips due to the medicinal sheen on his skin.

"Were you in a fight?"

"There's a pack of mad dogs in the neighborhood, I'm sorry to say."

"Those don't look like dog bites."

Yancy shed the towel, spun around and bent over to display the tooth wounds inflicted by the mixed-breed fiend that lived next door to Eve Stripling. The investigator from Oklahoma took a slight step back.

"And what happened to your head?"

"I took a tumble," Yancy said, "while running for my life." He refilled John Wesley Weiderman's glass with water. "Are you folks really going to prosecute Bonnie after all this time? Hell, the bail bondsman's probably dead from old age."

"Dr. Witt said you used to be a detective."

"Tell me something—when you spoke with Clifford, did you happen to notice any rope burns on his neck? Because he likes to choke himself while he whacks off. Not that I'm passing judgment, but it's important for you to know that your complainant has oxygen-deprivation issues."

John Wesley Weiderman said, "Hey, I'm just doing my job."

Although Yancy had never been to Tulsa, he imagined any civil servant there would jump at the offer of a trip to Florida, even in the dead of summer. The investigator gave Yancy a business card, but not before asking point-blank if Plover-slash-Bonnie was the person who assaulted him.

"John, get serious."

"But it wasn't really wild dogs, was it?"

"What did she do to piss Clifford off? Or, should I say, *who* did she do?"

"Please call me if she shows up. To us, this isn't a joke."

Yancy began pawing through the open Neosporin containers on the table. "Man, the last thing I need in my life right now is a fucking staph infection." He found a tube that wasn't empty and said, "Would you excuse me for a minute?"

"Actually, I've got an appointment in Key West." John Wesley Weiderman stood up. "Can you recommend a place for lunch? The guy at Hertz said Stoney's was real good."

Yancy smiled in resignation. "So I hear."

Widowhood was a grind.

Eve Stripling thought she'd prepared herself, but there was much more paperwork than she'd expected. Also, the endless condolences—her friends, Nicky's friends, random clergy, relatives she didn't know existed. Except for Caitlin they all meant well, although Eve was ready to strangle the next person who brought her a damn casserole.

The problem was she had limited grieving experience to draw from. On numerous occasions she sensed crying was expected of her, yet the only way to make it happen was by remembering a pet turtle she'd owned when she was nine. Flash was the turtle's name; he was the size of a silver dollar. One day he trundled out of the house and her mother backed over him with the Delta 88. Eve was bereft for a week. She accused her mom of squashing Flash on purpose, the so-called accident occurring soon after a tense family conversation about bacteria on pet-store reptiles. A burial was held under a lime tree in the backyard, Eve bearing the compressed remains of her companion upon a Teflon spatula.

Years later, at Nick's funeral, all the time Eve stood sobbing by the coffin she was actually thinking of poor little Flash, whom her parents had coldly refused to replace. Every tear she shed that day was for her lost turtle, not for her husband.

Her most important task, besides mourning, was to persuade a Miami judge to declare Nicky dead. It should have been a routine order, the severed arm being more than ample evidence of his tragic demise. The hurdle was Nick's daughter, who'd been spreading a vicious whisper that Eve had murdered him and chopped off his left arm to fit a bogus story about a boating accident.

Hiring a lawyer to threaten Caitlin Cox with a slander suit might have been sound strategy for an innocent widow, a woman with nothing to hide. For Eve Stripling, the wiser course was to reach out with a peace offering— or a *piece* offering, as it happened. From past experience she knew Caitlin's hostility could be dissolved by a gush of money. At first Eve couldn't bring herself to make the phone call, but soon it became clear there was no other choice. Her nightmare scenario was Caitlin showing up at the court hearing, telling the judge that her rotten stepmother had bumped off her beloved father.

Whom she hadn't seen in years because she was a selfish, pouty, greedy—

Deep breath, Eve had said to herself before dialing Caitlin's number.

Lunch is the way to go, someplace quiet where we can talk business, neither of us having to pretend we can stand the sight of the other.

Suck it up, Eve told herself, *you're the only one who can pull this off.*

And she did.

They'd met at a small Brazilian restaurant in the Design District. Caitlin came right out and asked her if she'd killed Nick, or paid to have him killed. Eve swallowed hard, bowed her head and refocused her thoughts on Flash, her precious childhood buddy, stuck like a patty of brown chewing gum to the left rear tire of her mother's Oldsmobile. It worked like magic—Eve quickly began to cry, blubbering that she'd loved Nick Stripling more than anyone, anything in the world. He *was* her world!

Caitlin was taken aback. "Then what about that boyfriend of yours in the Bahamas?"

At which point Eve could feel the color rush from her tear-streaked cheeks. Somehow she managed to keep it together, cooking up a story about an elderly uncle that seemed to temporarily appease Caitlin. Eve then steered the conversation to the less precarious topic of money, specifically the generous benefits of Nick's life insurance policy, half of which he'd wanted his only daughter to have despite their heartbreaking estrangement.

In addition, Eve went on—Caitlin practically drooling in suspense—there was an offshore bank account that Nick Stripling had opened for the benefit of future grandchildren.

Caitlin, suddenly sentimental: "Simon and I are trying to get pregnant!"

So the deal got done. Eve ordered a bottle of white

wine, which Caitlin depleted single-handedly before the food arrived.

"I didn't kill your dad," Eve said solemnly, reaching across to touch Caitlin's hand. "He died when his boat sank, just like they said."

"I know, shit, I know." Caitlin had achieved that level of alcohol-induced volubility where no thought goes unspoken, no secret goes unshared.

And that had been when Eve Stripling learned her stepdaughter had been talking to Andrew Yancy.

Twelve

After Neville's home on Green Beach was demolished, he went to stay in Rocky Town, where he alternated sleepovers with his girlfriends. The backhoe Neville had attempted to sabotage was running fine again, joined by a bulldozer that had arrived on a barge from a bankrupt development on Chub Cay.

To watch over the Curly Tail Lane construction site, the rich American called Christopher recruited some pin-headed brute from Nassau. The fellow had a high crinkled forehead and small malformed ears that looked like fetal fruit bats. People said he used to work at Fox Hill prison but got fired for brutalizing inmates with a marlin billy. Christopher put a rusty, camper-style trailer on the property, and that's where the new man slept. Occasionally Neville spotted him in town, eating at the conch shack, but he never lingered.

On the same day Christopher's new earth-chewing machine appeared, Neville went back to see the Dragon Queen. He presented to her a man's black nylon sock that he'd snatched from the same garbage can as the shirt fragment, outside the house rented by Christopher and his woman. The Dragon Queen frowned when Neville handed her the sock, which had a hole in the heel.

"Dis all you got fuh me?"

"Please, madam. I dont have much time."

"Look how big dis mon's feet be! No wonder my udda coyse dint woyk."

Something about the Dragon Queen seemed different, and at first Neville couldn't figure it out. Then, when she reached over and deftly snatched a doctor fly from his arm, it struck him: The woman was dead sober. The hairs on Neville's neck prickled when she plucked one wing off the fly and then watched it spin helplessly across the warped plank floor.

He said, "I kin go bok and look fuh sum ting more. Wot is it you want?"

The Dragon Queen grinned. She had perhaps seven teeth in her whole mouth. "Wot do I want? I want *you,* suh."

It was a moment Neville had been fearing; the Dragon Queen's rapacious appetite for men was legendary. Not wishing to become her next doomed lover, he'd prepared a defense.

"No, madam, I got de clap."

"Lemme have a peek." She rocked in her wicker chair and lit a cigar.

Neville shook his head. "Dot's not proper."

The Dragon Queen was firm: No sex, no more voodoo curses on Christopher. Neville was angry but he held back. Instead he said, "De mon already rip down de house where my own fahdder was born. He toyn it into a heap a goddamn rocks."

She spat and said, "White devil."

"Den help me take 'im down."

"You don't got de clap. Drop off your pants, bey, so I kin see your ting."

"Wot else you take fuh pay? All I got is foity dollahs."

The Dragon Queen chuckled and shut her eyes and blew a wreath of smoke that smelled like rancid mulch. "Mistuh Neville, where's dot little pink boy a yours?"

"He's outside. Why you ask?" Neville had leashed Driggs to the handlebars of the bike.

"So, den, here's wot we do." The Dragon Queen cracked one eyelid. "You give dot boy to me, as my own, and I'll pudda coyse on dis white devil Chrissofer make 'im dread sorry he ever set foot on dis island. Maybe even kill de mon, fuh true. Dot's all I want from you. No money, no fucky, juss Driggs."

"Madam, I tole you. Dot's not a real boy."

"So you say."

"Why you want 'im fuh?"

"It's lonely here on dis dusty hill. I gotta pull de wings off flies juss so dey stay 'round to keep me comp'ny. Dot ol' Driggs, he could dance hoppy circles 'n' make me lof all night long. Nodder ting, I kin teach 'im how to pour my rum drinks and rub my feets."

"But—"

"Dot's my final offer, suh. If you want sum bigass woo-doo, either gimme de boy or every fine inch a your manhood." The Dragon Queen stubbed the cigar and dropped it inside the black sock that Neville had taken from Christopher's trash.

"Madam, he's not a very good monkey."

"Oh, I know."

Neville wasn't sure why he cared about Driggs, who had a corrupt streak and no appreciation for Neville's many acts of kindness. The animal was dexterous and conniving, but discipline was almost impossible because Driggs retaliated with filthy bites to soft-tissue targets such as calves and thighs. Even when unprovoked, the creature traveled with a septic disposition. On the streets he shrewdly singled out white tourists and approached them for handouts. Those who balked might be punished by a rabbit punch to the genitals, or the nasty twist of a nipple. On one occasion, a German teen who tried to snap a picture of the animal was flogged with her own bikini top.

Driggs's noxious attitude baffled Neville, although he suspected a dietary deficiency. He'd become worried when his little sidekick started molting, yet all efforts to wean the monkey from conch fritters and johnnycakes were vehemently rebuffed. Neville's girlfriends were scared of Driggs and demanded that the scabby demon remain tethered outdoors during Neville's nocturnal visits. The monkey's response was to dig both hands into his diaper and hurl handfuls of feces at the windows, a raucous spectacle that had pitched Neville's love life into a stall.

"He smot. Dot I kin tell," said the Dragon Queen. "I teach 'im some prime woo-doo moves."

"Butchu ain't gon hoyt de fella, right?"

"Wot!" Indignantly she flapped her hem up and down, Neville turning away.

"Hoyt dot little fella?" she cried. "Come back in a few days, see if you don't find de hoppiest pink boy in all de world. Under my roof he gern live like de Prince a Wales!"

Neville said Driggs was worth eight hundred dollars, which was what he'd been told by the sponger who'd given him the monkey years earlier at the domino game.

"Eight hundred! Dot's crazy talk," said the Dragon Queen.

"He was in de movies wit Johnny Depp. It's no lie."

"Cap'n Jack Sparrow? You fulla crap. Your boy played de bod monkey?"

"Yes, madam, in all dose pirate movies. And he *is* a monkey," Neville reiterated.

The Dragon Queen crowed uproariously. "You bring me dot boy Driggs fuh payment, I put a jumbo coyse on your white devil."

Neville was torn. "Led me tink wot to do. I come right bok."

Outside, Driggs squatted on rash-covered haunches beneath the gumbo-limbo tree where Neville had left him. It was a repugnant scene that would alter both of their lives. The Huggies diaper lay shredded on the ground, and Neville's bicycle seat was slathered with fresh shit.

Neville's outrage swelled as he appraised the stinking mess. "I fed up wit your foolishness!" he snapped. "Come den, let's go see your new momma."

The monkey stopped gnawing on his leash and looked up. His upper lip wormed into a reflex sneer, but his rosy bald brow furrowed in consternation.

"Dot's right," Neville said. "Dis is good-bye."

The owner of Big Luke's Lobsteria was Luke Motto, a former Thoroughbred jockey who stood five-two. He was called Big Luke because he was the tallest among six siblings.

The Lobsteria was Yancy's first official stop after a ten-day sick leave (ordered by Lombardo), during which Yancy went fishing alone every morning. For privacy he chose the Content Keys, and wore only his boxers while poling the skiff. The salt air hastened the healing of his gouged ass and also the mangrove scrapes on his limbs. His headaches ceased shortly after the bruises disappeared. As a treat he landed several good bonefish and an eighty-pound tarpon. Twice Rosa drove down after work and stayed the night.

"You double-clicked that fucker," Big Luke said accusingly.

"I'm afraid not."

They were arguing about German cockroaches, which Yancy was required to count during all restaurant inspections. The pest census was a challenging aspect of the job although Tommy Lombardo, Yancy's instructor, had provided little guidance. For reasons unclear to Yancy, the state of Florida required that live roaches and dead roaches be tabulated separately. Perhaps a deceased roach was deemed less repellent to diners than a crawling one, but in truth the contamination differential was negligible—insect parts versus insect droppings.

Yancy himself favored dead roaches because live ones were too quick, a coppery flash disappearing beneath a shelf or baseboard. During his first week on the job, and uncertain of protocol, Yancy included in his live-specimen tallies only those he was able to corner and kill. Many others escaped, and he was nagged by a sense of falling short in his duties.

So, to the dismay of unsanitary proprietors such as Luke Motto, Yancy developed a method of herding and capturing live roaches that allowed a more precise accounting. In his right hand he wielded a billiard cue to which he'd bolted the head of a badminton racket. In the other hand he carried a DustBuster, a lighter, updated version of the device he had ingloriously deployed against Dr. Clifford Witt in Mallory Square.

One brisk pass through the kitchen of Big Luke's Lobsteria filled the vacuum with a pulsing, melon-sized mass of roaches that Yancy neutralized by vigorously shaking the filter compartment until the captives were too addled to mount an escape. He then dumped his catch on a butcher-block cutting board, and got down to business with tweezers and a thumb-activated ticket counter he'd bought on Amazon for $2.99.

"That one right there—you did him twice!" Luke Motto insisted.

The total of live roaches was up to sixty-eight, which in Yancy's view qualified as an infestation. "And I haven't even checked the pipes under the sink," he remarked through his hospital mask.

"Don't!" Luke Motto bleated.

"I got five bucks says we break two hundred today."

"And I got a C-note and a free shrimp hoagie says you cut me some slack."

"If you had half a brain, Luke, you'd spend that money on an exterminator."

With every click of the counter, Yancy dropped another dizzy roach into a large Ziploc baggie. Lombardo hadn't instructed him to preserve the insects as evidence, so he didn't. Customarily, after presenting his inspection report to the disgruntled owner, Yancy would dispatch the roaches by placing the baggies under a tire of his car and flattening them on his way out of the parking lot. It wasn't an authorized technique for disposal, but so far none of the restaurateurs had lodged a complaint.

"You can't just barge in here and shut me down!" Luke Motto protested. "This ain't Nazi Russia!"

Yancy tuned him out while completing the order for a temporary suspension. He offered the phone number of a Marathon pest control company and told Big Luke he'd be back in three days for a re-inspection. Then he squashed the roaches with his Subaru and drove to Duck Key to view the condominium belonging to Eve and Nicholas Stripling.

The building superintendent gave up the key as soon as Yancy displayed his health department credentials. For a weekend condo it wasn't bad. The living room featured a balcony view of the Atlantic, while the bedrooms overlooked a polyp-shaped swimming pool with a slightly discolored kiddie pond. In the closets of the condo Yancy found men's and women's outdoor clothes, fishing rods, spearguns, flippers, dive masks, snorkels and a roll of clear Visqueen poly sheeting of the type used to protect carpet and furniture from splatters while a room was being painted—or a human body was being chopped to pieces.

The second scenario occurred to Yancy after he spotted a hatchet, scoured clean, inside the dishwasher. It made sense that if a woman was involved, the hatchet would have been rinsed of gore before being placed in a dishwasher rack amid wine glasses and salad bowls. Yancy reached into the opening of the garbage disposal and carefully probed the movable blades. All he recovered was the fractured chip of an olive pit.

Next he went to the double shower in the master bedroom and unscrewed the drain cover. He employed a bent coat hanger to explore the pipe, which yielded a clot of jet-black hair. Ensnared in the yucky clump were three sharp-edged, whitish fragments no larger than kitten's teeth. Yancy deposited the entire tangle in another baggie, locked up the condo, put the key under the mat and returned to his car. There he phoned Caitlin Cox and said, "I believe I know where they murdered your father."

Her reply caught him by surprise: "Actually, Inspector, we need to talk."

Yancy cranked up the Subaru's fitful AC and waited.

Caitlin said: "Look, I was wrong about Eve. There's no hot boyfriend in the Bahamas—she stopped there on the way home from Paris to visit one of her uncles. And Dad's wedding ring? The only reason she swapped it out for a cheapo? She didn't have the heart to leave it on his hand inside the coffin. She got a jeweler in Bal Harbour to hang it on a necklace and, God, I feel like such an a-hole. The more I think about it? Seriously."

Yancy was miffed at himself for not seeing it coming. "Caitlin, listen to me. Eve bought that replacement wedding band in Nassau before anyone told her your dad was missing, much less dead, which means she already knew. And, just so you're up to speed, the nonexistent boyfriend tried to kill me the other night. I'm pretty sure he was wearing your father's wristwatch."

"That's crazy."

"Okay, I made it all up. Because, truly, I've got nothing better to do."

"Look, man," she said. "I'm super sorry I got you involved, but I was so bummed about losing Dad I guess

I didn't want to believe the truth. He swamped his boat and drowned, end of story, just like the Coast Guard said. I mean, bad shit happens to fishermen all the time, right? The perfect storm, whatever."

Yancy told her about the plastic sheeting and the hatchet he'd found in the condo. "And also some white bony fragments in a shower drain."

"Oh please," said Caitlin. "Broken stone crab shells, probably."

"What about the hand axe?"

"Dad used the flat side to crack the claws. Just a couple of taps is all it took."

Yancy knew he couldn't bring Caitlin around, but he was curious to learn how the deal went down. "So you're not mad anymore about Eve getting the whole two million from his life insurance?"

"No way."

Then came the edgy pause. Yancy smiled and put the car in gear.

"Anyhow," Caitlin continued, "turns out Eve and I are what you call co-beneficiaries. We split the money fifty-fifty. So I guess Dad wasn't so pissed at me after all."

"When did you find all this out? Because last time we spoke, you expressed the view—and I'm quoting more or less faithfully—that your 'greedy slut of a stepmother' was screwing you over."

Caitlin said, "Because I was super upset, okay? I wasn't thinking straight."

"Until?"

"I saw Eve, and there was Dad's wedding ring on her neck. Then she told me about the insurance policy and other stuff."

"Other stuff?"

"You know. Inheritance stuff."

Yancy thought: *All that's missing is a winning Lotto ticket.* "And where did this healing conversation take place?" he asked Caitlin.

"She took me to lunch."

"Yes, I can picture it. Where are you now?"

"At the courthouse."

"Let me guess: Where you just finished telling the judge you totally agree with Eve—your dad should be declared legally dead."

"Yeah, so?" On the other end, Nick Stripling's daughter seemed to be clearing a chunk of cactus from her throat. After the guttural delay she said: "What the hell's wrong with you, anyway? You never heard of closure? Families are supposed to come together, no matter what."

"And nothing says closure like a million bucks."

"Dad died when his boat sunk, just like they said. Let it go, dude."

"Not possible, Caitlin. We'll chat again, you and I."

"Why? No, we won't!"

"Then tell me his name."

"Who?"

"The mystery uncle in Nassau."

Caitlin said, "You're such a dickhead."

Yancy tossed down the phone and gunned his car toward a gap in the traffic, heading up the Overseas Highway.

Thirteen

When Yancy was younger, he'd briefly considered joining the U.S. park service, like his father. "Why didn't you?" Rosa Campesino asked.

"I was too lazy. And the pay sucks."

"Andrew, you're full of shit."

"Look at it this way. If I'd become a ranger in the Everglades, we would never have met."

"Unless an alligator got you, and I was assigned to do the post."

"Assuming there was something left of me," Yancy said.

"Oh, there would be. Gators are sloppy eaters. By the way, you've healed magnificently."

"I was hoping you'd notice."

Rosa was massaging him on an autopsy table. It was half past midnight at the morgue and they were alone in the main suite, which had twelve forensic workstations. Each narrow table was made of eighteen-gauge stainless steel. Rosa had spread some towels, removed the headrest and instructed Yancy to lie still on his belly.

"What happens if somebody walks in?" he asked.

"Just play dead. I'm serious."

She was wearing a lab smock, rubber-soled white shoes, and nothing else. In theory Yancy should have been wildly aroused, but the venue creeped him out. He'd made love to women in all sorts of odd places—with Bonnie Witt, of course, high on the tuna tower of her husband's boat, but there had been other memorable trysts inside a windmill on a putt-putt golf course, the second-to-last car of a Metrorail train, an unoccupied toll booth on the Rickenbacker Causeway and a self-photo kiosk beside the manatee pool at the Miami Seaquarium. He understood the thrill of semi-public sex, but doing it among the deceased seemed more dark than daring.

The Miami-Dade morgue had been designed with a contingency for a worst-case airline crash; its five coolers were made big enough to hold all the passengers and crew from a fully loaded jumbo jet—a total of 555 bodies. Tonight there were only sixty-six in refrigeration. Yancy had declined Rosa's offer of a tour. It felt good when she pressed her knuckles into the meat of his back, but he was having trouble unwinding. The cold filtered breath of the morgue didn't smell like death, but it wasn't exactly a breeze off Monterey Bay.

"Roll over, Andrew."

"Then I can't play dead if we're caught."

"And why not?" Rosa said.

"Because dead guys don't get boners."

"Do what the doctor says."

She turned off the overhead light and climbed on top of him. The autopsy platform wasn't comfortable but it was sturdy. Soon Yancy loosened up and his thoughts began meandering, which sometimes happened when a smooth physical rhythm was established. It was no reflection on his partner; he had an incurably busy brain. Rosa herself seemed happily diverted, so Yancy kept pace while sifting through the day's events.

Except for a colorful exchange of profanity with a meth-head tanker driver on the turnpike, the ride to Miami had been uneventful. Yancy had first stopped at the Rosenstiel marine lab on Virginia Key, where an earnest young master's candidate examined the shark tooth extracted from Nick Stripling's severed arm and confirmed the species as *Sphyrna tiburo,* a common bonnethead that typically feeds inshore. The finding proved that Eve Stripling and her accomplice had placed the stump of her husband's limb in the shallows and chummed up some resident predators in the hope that their gnashing would add verisimilitude to the drowning story.

The pale shards Yancy had plucked from the shower drain at the Striplings' condo were definitely pieces of human bone, not stone crab shells as Caitlin Cox had claimed. Rosa made the determination visually over a paella at the Versailles, Yancy introducing the fragments in the same funky nest in which he'd found them. Rosa promised to order DNA tests on both hair and bones, and compare the results to the swab taken from Stripling's arm by Dr. Rawlings in Key West. Yancy had no doubt of a match. The hatchet, presumed instrument of dismemberment, he had discreetly conveyed in a Macy's shopping bag.

Later, over flan and Cuban coffee, Rosa had presented him with the only number dialed on Dr. Gomez O'Peele's cell phone the night he died. She'd obtained this key information from a North Miami Beach detective who was striving to seduce her. The call had been made minutes after Yancy had left O'Peele's apartment.

Yancy took down the number and went outside to make a call of his own, and soon he had a name: Christopher Grunion, no middle initial. The billing address on the telephone account was a post office box in South Beach. When Yancy returned to the table, he swept Rosa into his arms and kissed her exuberantly until the other diners broke into cheers. He was soaring because Christopher Grunion was the same name that Rogelio Burton had found on the charter contract for the Caravan seaplane Yancy had seen behind the Striplings' house on Biscayne Bay.

Although Grunion had no criminal record, and not even a Florida driver's license, Yancy felt certain he was Eve's secret boyfriend and co-conspirator. O'Peele had likely phoned him to demand hush money after Yancy's unexpected visit, and got shot for his greedy play. "It's Poncho Boy!" Yancy had exulted, waving a mango Popsicle while he and Rosa were driving to the morgue. "The guy who killed Phinney—the same fuckweasel who tried to drown me!"

The massage on the autopsy table had settled him a bit. Now, as he was boosting Rosa up and down with his hips, she reached up and fastened her hair into a primly perfect bun, an Elizabethan effect that revealed the flawless slope of her caramel neck and shoulders. For all her lithe athletics she stayed remarkably quiet, as if she were afraid to awake somebody in the building, which would have been quite a trick.

One advantage to fucking on immovable steel was that

it didn't squeak, unlike Yancy's sagging bed at home. The first time they'd had sex there, Rosa was so distracted by the noise that she couldn't make it happen. She said the box spring sounded like a chipmunk being skinned alive. Now, astride him on a slab where hundreds of homicide victims had been meticulously disemboweled, she shuddered suddenly, smiled and teetered forward. Pressing a moist cheek to his chest, she said, "Okay, this is pretty warped. I should probably get some counseling."

"Well, I thought it was fantastic."

"Don't lie, Andrew."

"Are you kidding? I came like Vesuvius."

Rosa sighed. "It's a freaking HBO miniseries. All I need is fangs."

Yancy kissed the top of her head. "I would've been a worthless park ranger," he said. "Disappearing for weeks at a time with just a tent and my fishing rods. The other thing? Poachers. If I caught some asshole jacklighting a fawn, I'm not sure I could restrain myself, arrest-wise. My dad, he's a very disciplined guy. I did not end up with that gene."

"I definitely don't want children," Rosa murmured. "Does that make me a selfish rotten person? Never mind. Not a fair question while you're still inside me."

"Christ, you cut up dead people for a living. Don't be so tough on yourself."

She sat up sleepily. "I should really make an effort to put on my clothes."

"Do you have video in this place?"

"Of course." Rosa pointed to a small camera mounted above the table. "Don't fret, Andrew, it has an Off switch. I'm not *that* twisted."

"Some weekend we should go camping down at Flamingo, just the two of us."

"You're very sweet," she said. "Now let's get out of here."

Yancy drove back to Big Pine the next morning and was surprised to see a car in his driveway—an old Toyota Camry with a crooked Oklahoma license tag. He took the tire iron out of his Subaru and ran through a hard rain toward the house.

Bonnie Witt stood in the kitchen, scrambling eggs. She was wearing a Sooners jersey, and her toenails had been painted gold. The fugitive life had taken a toll on her tan.

"I've still got a key," she said pertly.

"Another oversight on my part."

"I can explain everything, but first I want you to meet someone special. Honey?"

"Hey yo." A shirtless man was sprawled on the couch watching ESPN. He looked up and gave Yancy some sort of faux bro salute.

Bonnie said, "Andrew, say hello to Cody. Cody, this is my dear friend Andrew."

Yancy propped the tire iron in a corner and shook Cody's waxy hand. Whatever he might have looked like in high school, back when Bonnie was blowing his mind, the kid had grown up to be a lump—mottled skin, thinning hair and a gut that hung over unstrung board shorts. Yancy insisted on taking over breakfast duties so that the two of them could share their love story, which he anticipated to be a high point of his day.

"I just couldn't stop thinking about him," Bonnie

said, "so one day I said screw it, life's too short. Got up at four in the morning and drove nonstop from Sarasota to Tulsa, nineteen hours. This was after I'd found him on Facebook—"

"But she didn't even friend me first," Cody cut in. "One night she just shows up by the salad bar and, you know, holy shit."

"He was the number two man at the Olive Garden—"

"My boss was a major dickbrain. It was time to move on."

"When Cliff found out I was gone," Bonnie said, "he went postal. Called the OSBI and totally sold me out."

The OSBI was the Oklahoma State Bureau of Investigation, which, after Dr. Witt's tip, had dispatched Agent John Wesley Weiderman to interview Yancy about the elusive Plover Chase. Unfortunately, the lawman's investigatory mission to the Keys had been cut short when he was stricken with shellfish poisoning after eating contaminated mussels at Stoney's Crab Palace on Stock Island. Yancy felt somewhat responsible, and he looked forward to ambushing Brennan with another surprise inspection.

"So I quit my job," Cody said, "and Ms. Chase and I went seriously outlaw."

Bonnie blushed. "He still calls me that, after all these years—Ms. Chase! The police were looking for the 4Runner so we switched to Cody's car."

"Except there's no XM Radio. Bummer," he said.

"Last night we camped on the beach at Bahia Honda." Bonnie favored Yancy with a fond-memory wink. "A raccoon swiped our marshmallows."

Cody said, "I chased after him but he got away."

Yancy loaded two plates with eggs and bacon, and

he slid them across the counter. Cody inquired about the possibility of a bagel.

"Cream cheese or marmalade?" Yancy asked.

The young man beamed. "Hell, yes!"

Solemnly Bonnie said, "I never stopped loving him, Andrew. You know that."

Yancy knew no such thing, but he was savoring the plot line. "Does Clifford know Cody's back in the picture?"

"Lord, no! He thinks you and I ran off to the Seychelles. That's what I wrote in my good-bye note, just to throw him off."

"For God's sake, Bonnie."

Cody glanced up from his plate. " 'Bonnie'? So who came up with *that* one?"

Yancy was wishing that Cody would put on a shirt. His tufted breasts were droopy and mole-covered, and Yancy spied what appeared to be a fresh bite mark above his left nipple. It was increasingly difficult to keep an open mind.

"The night before I left Cliff," Bonnie was saying, "I walk into the bathroom and there he is, dangling from the shower faucet, flopping and gurgling and jerking on his little weenie. For a noose he used one of my Hermès scarves! I mean, seriously, Andrew, enough's enough."

"An intolerable situation," Yancy agreed.

Through a cheekful of mulched bacon Cody said, "Hey, Ms. Chase. If you're gonna be Bonnie then I'm changing my handle to Clyde!"

She laughed and squeezed his pudgy elbow. Yancy pried a scorched bagel from the toaster and dressed it to Cody's specifications.

"So, where are you two heading?"

Bonnie said she was hoping they could stay with him. "Until the heat's off? Please?"

Yancy told her about the visit from Agent John Wesley Weiderman. "It's not safe here," he added. "Also, my girlfriend wouldn't go for it."

"Whoa." Bonnie hitched an eyebrow and put down her fork. "Andrew has a new lady," she said to Cody, who was using a green-tinged thumbnail to remove a sesame seed from his teeth.

"She's a doctor," Yancy said.

"What kind of doctor?" asked Bonnie.

"Well, a surgeon."

"Does she have a specialty?"

"She operates on pretty much everything." It wasn't a lie; when Rosa did an autopsy, she diced up the whole works.

"Funny," Bonnie said.

"You don't believe me."

"No, I meant it's ironic: I just dumped a doctor and here you've taken up with one."

Through the window Yancy saw no sign of the construction workers next door. Wet weather was his ally.

Cody said, "Ms. Chase told me how you butt-plugged her hubby with a DustBuster. That's some awesome man-shit right there."

He reached across the counter to honor Yancy with a knuckle bump. Yancy tried to visualize the kid's photograph in the school yearbook. From Cody's present condition it seemed inconceivable that he could have made himself attractive to Bonnie at any age. Perhaps he had quieter charms, such as a nine-inch cock.

"May I ask you something?" Yancy said. "It's about Ms. Chase's trial. I read where you testified against her."

"A suck move. Mom and Dad made me do that."

Bonnie gently interrupted, suggesting a change of topic.

Cody went on: "The important thing is we're back together again. Right?"

"You kept a hot little journal of your romance is what I heard," Yancy said.

"Hey, I was fifteen. I thought I wanted to be a writer."

Proudly Bonnie chipped in: "He was wild about *Portnoy's Complaint*."

"Well, sure." Yancy smiled. "Cody, are you keeping a journal now?"

He reddened. "No! I mean, what for?"

"In case you two get caught. Bonnie goes to jail, all the tabloids would line up to pay big bucks for your story. But I'm sure you wouldn't do anything like that. Who wants coffee?"

After they were gone, Yancy walked over to the spec house and set up a Santeria shrine in the future living room. Improvising, he'd chosen a handmade doll of the warrior god Changó, and for sacrificial offerings included apples, tamales, copper pennies, a dead rooster collected on Simonton Street by Animal Control and a saucer of cat blood left over from a spaying performed by a veterinarian friend. These items were laid out upon a crude satanic pentagram that Yancy had drawn in red Krylon paint on Evan Shook's floor slab. In the center he placed a rat skull, ominously marked with the numerals 666. Students of the occult would have discounted the scene as an amateurish juxtaposition of unconnected superstitions, but Yancy believed that maintaining cultural authenticity was less important than creating a vivid first impression for potential home buyers.

At lunchtime he drove down to Stoney's and confronted Brennan, who disclaimed responsibility for Agent John Wesley Weiderman's emergency trip to the hospital. "The man's got a family history of diverticulitis!"

Yancy said, "I hope he sues your ass off."

"Sit, Andrew, sit. Try the oysters Rockefeller."

"I want to see the kitchen. You know the drill." Yancy was carrying his vacuum-equipped roach-catching device.

"I'm glad you're here." Brennan fumbled to fit on a hairnet. "Somebody came by askin' where you been. Jesus, is that a fuckin' gun on your belt?"

"Absolutely." After being nearly murdered by Eve Stripling's accomplice, Yancy had purchased a used Glock to replace his forfeited service weapon. He would have preferred another 12-gauge but that was out of his price range.

Brennan seemed agitated. "Nobody on roach patrol packs a piece! Nilsson didn't even carry a damn pocketknife."

"This can be treacherous work," Yancy said.

"The way some people do it, yeah. You got a carry permit?"

"Who was in here asking about me?"

"That girl," said Brennan. "Phinney's girl."

"Madeline? She's back?"

"For 'bout a week now. Come on, man, try the fuckin' oysters."

"Where's she staying?"

"In Old Town, with some pimple-faced Russian d-bag. Hey, are you leavin' already?"

"It's your lucky day," Yancy said, and made for the door.

Defiantly Brennan tugged off the hairnet. "I got nuthin' to hide here! Drop in anytime!"

Madeline was working at the same skanky T-shirt shop on Duval, Pestov lurking ferret-eyed among the inventory. She told Yancy she'd returned to Key West because the police no longer considered her a suspect in Phinney's murder. Yancy noticed that she'd chopped her hair even shorter and dyed it a shade of chartreuse that was popular for tarpon streamers. In addition she was sporting fresh ink—her dead boyfriend's initials, tattooed on her left wrist.

He said, "It isn't the cops I'm worried about. That's not why I wanted you to get out of town."

"Then who? Why would anyone want to hurt me?"

"Because—hold on, I'll be right back." Yancy went to the rear of the store and chased the scuttling Pestov out the door. Then he went back inside and informed Madeline that the man who'd shot Charlie had tried to kill him, too.

"Poncho Boy's feeling some heat," Yancy said.

"But he's got no cause to kill *me*. I don't know zip about zap."

"You know where Charlie got all that money."

Madeline said, "Stop tryin' to scare me. And what's with the gun?"

Yancy remembered her saying she had a sister in Crystal River. "Go stay with her until this is over. Please, Madeline."

"Millie got born-again last October."

"Oh."

"For the third fucking time. All she does when I visit is preach Jesus Christ our Lord 'n' Savior in my face, twenty-four/seven. One of her stupid cows got fried by lightning and she said it's God's will. No way can I be under the same roof with that psycho. She threw my Kools down the garbage disposer!"

Yancy said, "There must be somewhere else you can go."

"The Russians won't let anything happen to me. I already talked to Pestov."

"Pestov is a barn maggot."

"Dude, I need this job."

"Really? All the T-shirt shops in the world?"

Yancy hung back while two dancers from Teasers came in to browse for the latest in nipple clips. After they left, Madeline smiled at Yancy and said, "I'm okay here. It's kinda cool that you care, but I'll be fine."

When he returned to Big Pine, the rain had quit and the sky was clearing. Evan Shook stood on the street in front of his spec house, addressing a horseshoe-shaped gathering of the construction crew. Yancy interpreted Evan Shook's gesticulations as beseeching. Some of the workers apparently had been unnerved by the sight of the Santeria altar or the rodent skull in the pentagram, possibly both. Yancy purposely had designed the display to touch a broad socio-religious spectrum.

He was rocking to Dave Matthews an hour later when Evan Shook pounded on the door, somewhat discourteously in Yancy's view. He hid the Trainwreck he'd been smoking, unplugged his earbuds and straightened the shiny blue necktie he'd taken to wearing on restaurant inspections; the pattern on the fabric was a lateral skein of tiny silver handcuffs.

By way of a greeting, he said: "Is there news of the wild dogs? Please come in."

Evan Shook remained on the front stoop, seething in

the compressed manner of small men accustomed to bullying. Clearly he was inhibited by Yancy's height, and also the hip-mounted firearm.

"Have you been in my house again?" he asked somberly. "Somebody..."

"Yes?"

"Somebody defaced the downstairs."

"Good Lord. When did this happen?"

"Just this morning."

"That's unbelievable. In broad daylight? Kids, I'll bet." Yancy was counting on the conservative neckwear and police-model handgun to work in his favor, your average vandal being untidy and unarmed. The smell of pot, however, imperiled his credibility.

"I've been working all day," he said. "Just got home."

"So your answer is no, you haven't been over there." Evan Shook wondered if Yancy was too stoned to lie.

"Was anything stolen?" Yancy inquired. "You should hurry and hang those doors and windows, get the place buttoned up. Not just for security—it's hurricane season."

"Right." Evan Shook plainly had more to say, but his gaze kept dropping to the black butt of the Glock. The bracing accusations he'd had in mind, the harsh warning he'd composed—these would remain undelivered.

"The neighborhood's gone to hell," Yancy said supportively. "It used to be so safe and quiet."

"If you see anything unusual going on over there—"

"Of course, of course." Yancy craned his head out the doorway, as if warily scouting for a rabid dog pack or rampaging delinquents. "I'll try to keep a closer eye on things, Mr. Shook."

"Thanks."

"There used to be deer on your property, did you know that? Every evening around sundown. But now they don't come."

Evan Shook nodded witlessly. The damn mosquitoes were eating him alive.

"When I first moved here, it was mostly small houses," Yancy went on, "what you might call bungalows. Nothing as grandiose as your place. What is that, four floors?"

"I've gotta get to the hardware store," said Evan Shook, "before it closes."

Yancy stayed up listening to his iPod while the television was tuned to Animal Planet. The effect was enthralling: wildebeest migrations accompanied by Joni Mitchell and the Strokes. Yancy took no delight in Evan Shook's tribulations but wrong was wrong—the mansion was a fucking abomination. Yancy's objective was to prevent it from being sold and finished.

He ate three energy bars and weighed himself: 162 pounds, a string bean. He was surprised that Eve Stripling hadn't sent her stud muffin Christopher back to the Keys to properly finish killing him. By now she'd surely learned from Nick's daughter that Yancy wasn't drowned and that he intended to keep pursuing the case. He flipped the channel to Conan and unplugged one ear for the monologue. Afterward he turned off the TV and searched the kitchen cupboards for evidence of vermin. In some ways his roach patrol duties weren't so different from police work—the quarry was nocturnal, and unfailingly left a trail.

Marinating in a lukewarm bath, Yancy smoked the rest of the joint and dozed off. At some point he was rousted by Dr. Rosa Campesino's voice. It was rising from his cell phone, which he had apparently grabbed off the toilet seat and answered in a haze.

"Andrew, I need you here right away."

"Wadizzit? You awright?"

"Wake up!"

"Take it easy."

"That damn arm is back!" she said.

"What?"

"You heard me. *The* arm. I'm staring at it right now."

Yancy splashed out of the tub. "Stripling's arm? No way."

"Get your butt in the car," Rosa said.

Fourteen

Grave robbing was not uncommon in South Florida due to a thriving underground market for human bones, prized by Santeria priests and practitioners of extreme voodoo. The crime required muscle and nerve though no special stealth, as most cemeteries refused to spring for nighttime security guards.

Flaco Chávez and his partner, whose street name was Delta Force, were robbers by trade and had never before cracked a coffin. They'd met in prison and later shared an inattentive parole officer. Delta Force claimed to be an ex–army commando and he sometimes broke into gyms after hours to work out with the weights. Flaco Chávez specialized in mugging elderly ATM patrons, although he spoke vaingloriously of graduating to armored cars.

One night, while scouting for carjacking prospects at a BP station, the men were approached by a couple with an enticing offer: Six hundred dollars for robbing a grave—half the money up front, half when the grisly contents were delivered to a Denny's restaurant on Biscayne Boulevard. It sounded like an easy job to Flaco Chávez and his partner, who promptly stole a late-model Tahoe from a pregnant nurse and struck out for the St. Lazarus Gardens and Water Park in North Miami. Along the way they stopped to burglarize an Ace Hardware store, acquiring two shovels, a pick, canvas gloves and a flashlight.

The most challenging aspect of the heist, it turned out, was finding the correct target. Delta Force was ripped on coke and lacking in focus, so it was Flaco's chore to locate the burial plot of Nicholas Stripling, whoever the fuck *he* was. Once the site had been isolated, the excavation took barely an hour, Delta Force digging like a dervish while Flaco Chávez feigned a hamstring cramp. Heading back downtown, their stolen SUV was spotted by a county police officer, who deftly swung his squad car into a U-turn and lit them up like a disco ball. Flaco Chávez spoke out in favor of a low-key surrender but Delta Force, facing multiple parole violations and a long bus ride back to Starke, stomped on the accelerator.

Neither man could be bothered with seat belts, so their skulls spidered the windshield at exactly seventy-one miles per hour when Delta Force—showing misplaced faith in the performance-enhancing attributes of cocaine hydrochloride—attempted a cinematic off-road evasion and crashed into a banyan tree. The impact ejected from the Tahoe's rear hatch a navy-blue golf bag belonging to the husband of the pregnant carjacking victim. The golf bag spilled a full set of Callaways, three sleeves of Bridgestone balls, a speargun and an embalmed human arm, which was sent in its own ambulance to the medical examiner's office.

Ironically, the stream of emergency vehicles sped directly past the Denny's on Biscayne, where a couple armed with a stolen 12-gauge shotgun (strictly for protection) was waiting in a rented compact for the grave robbers.

After another hour passed with no contact, Eve Stripling said: "I can't believe those assholes took the three hundred bucks and bailed."

"What part can't you believe?" grumbled the man beside her, the man who was now officially a boyfriend.

"We should've offered 'em five on this end," she said.

"Or maybe we should have said you two shitheads get *nada* till we get the arm."

Eve puffed her cheeks irritably. "Okay, honey, so they ripped us off. What the hell do we do now?"

"Call the pilot is what we do. Tell him we're on the way."

Neville's friends on Andros said he was crazy not to take the money from the sale of his family's property and build a fine new beach house on another stretch of seafront. They couldn't understand his militant opposition to the future Curly Tail Lane Resort, which they gullibly believed would bring new jobs and a geyser of tourist dollars. Words didn't flow easily from Neville and he struggled without success to explain his churned feelings, the gutting sense of loss. His three girlfriends sniped relentlessly on the subject of his stubborn foolishness, to the point that he began to miss the sulfurous company of Driggs.

The monkey had been sighted around Rocky Town in the Dragon Queen's motley entourage of spurious half cousins and walleyed supplicants. Meanwhile the unwanted American, Christopher, showed no effects of major voodoo. Neville was distraught to see on his former homestead a tall pile of casuarina trees that had been felled in order to widen the beach; their scraggly dead roots looked like unclenched claws. Neville was halfway over the chain-link fence when Christopher's hired goon burst from the trailer swinging a cricket mallet and snorting like a gored hog.

Neville hopped on his bicycle and rode off shaking a fist. He hurried to confront the Dragon Queen but his angry knock on her door went unanswered. Through an open window he spied on the table an empty rum bottle and a puddle of hardened yellow wax where a candle had melted. Mingled with a smell of cigars was the familiar funk of unwashed simian.

He aimed his bike toward the wharf and wound up at the conch shack cooling his palms around a bottle of Kalik. Like many native-born Bahamians, Neville wasn't intractably aligned against progress, yet he was wary. Despite its nautical proximity to South Florida, Andros hadn't been overrun like Bimini or Freeport because its long western coast was inconveniently shallow and short of natural harbors. The island's vast middle interior was mostly boggy wilderness, a stifling outback. A slender Andros economy relied on vegetable farms, which fed most of the Bahamas, and on scattered coastal fishing settlements such as Rocky Town. One overabundant resource was fresh springwater; seven million gallons a day were shipped from Morgan's Bluff to Nassau, a place that many Androsians were content to avoid.

In Neville's view, the Curly Tail Lane extravaganza looked like another crooked Bay Street deal. That some people (his own half sister included) had been bought off was a certainty. The traditional outcome of such high-flying enterprises was, of course, bankruptcy. Christopher would be jacked up and jerked around until he ran out of patience and then money. Thereafter he would bitterly abandon the Bahamas and his half-built tourist trap, which would sit moldering in the heat until another foreign sucker came along. Green Beach was destined to be a perpetual construction site unless Neville could act swiftly to regain dominion.

A third beer was sweating on the bar before him when he spotted the Dragon Queen. Trailed by a handful of scrofulous attendants, she was motoring down the main road on a tricked-out wheelchair that gave the appearance of a mobile throne. Balanced on the steering yoke was Driggs, festively grinding his diaper against one of the rearview mirrors. He tolerated a batik head wrap that matched a flamingo-pink number worn in cool regality by the Dragon Queen. As they drew closer Neville could hear her singing low and froggishly. Her expression was governed by a style of wraparound shades once favored by the Haitian secret police.

"Madam! Stop!" Neville sprung off the bar stool and ran toward the approaching procession. "Madam, it's me!"

The monkey barked once and the Dragon Queen's ushers shifted themselves into a protective wedge around the still-rolling scooter. Neville was roughly turned away; there were filthy oaths and the threat of a stomping. Again he called out to the voodoo priestess, who dismissed his plea with a backhanded wave. The group proceeded past him along the path toward the conch hut, the Dragon Queen gliding ahead on rubber wheels.

Stunned, Neville crossed the street and sagged against a shaded coral wall. Momentarily a covered golf cart hummed into view, and out stepped the pinheaded security guard from Curly Tail Lane. He glanced at Neville long enough to scowl in recognition; then he strode directly to the palm-thatched restaurant, where the ragged assembly parted. Neville watched the goon kneel beside the electric dolly and plant a kiss on the Dragon Queen, a bobbing lip-lock that lasted long enough to draw saucy cheers. The stereo was engaged and soon the two of them were dancing to Jimmy Cliff. As the security guard pranced gaping and bear-like, the Dragon Queen used the joystick on her nimble chariot to spin fanciful circles around him. Throughout these maneuvers, Driggs—jouncing like a miniature stagecoach driver—cheeped in accompaniment.

Neville was stricken breathless from anguish. What a wretched mistake he'd made! The whore-witch Dragon Queen had taken him for both his money and his monkey.

Now she was screwing the white devil's hired man.

Sonny Summers said: "Let me tell you about my day."

"Wish I could make it better."

"Maybe you can, Andrew."

Yancy noticed some additions to the sheriff's desktop display: a photo of his wife wearing a snorkel and hoisting a distressed lobster, a brass toothpick holder from the chamber of commerce, and a small chintzy replica of the *Pilar,* Hemingway's fishing boat.

"Remember... you know... that little solid you did for me?"

"Babysitting the dead guy's left arm," Yancy said.

"Right. It was my understanding you delivered it to the widow."

"Absolutely."

"Who gave it a decent Christian burial."

"Yes, I can personally attest."

Sonny Summers slid forward. "So, this morning, I get a call from Dr. Rawlings, who says the ME's office in Miami needs the DNA swab he took off the arm."

That request would have come from Dr. Rosa Campesino, doing her job.

With false innocence Yancy said, "Maybe they found another body part from the same corpse."

"Exactly what I was thinking. Hoping for, to be honest. But then later Rawlings calls back and says guess what. You won't believe this, Andrew. They've got the actual arm in Miami. *The* freaking arm! From the *Misty*!"

Yancy of course had ID'd it himself at the Miami-Dade morgue. The distinctive watch stripe was still visible on Nick Stripling's mummifying wrist, although the embalmer had decorously retracted the middle finger. The county police were still trying to figure out how the severed limb of a drowned fisherman had ended up in the possession of two career felons, their stoved selves now occupying adjacent autopsy tables. Yancy had theorized to Rosa that Caitlin Cox had blabbed to her stepmother about the incriminating hatchet and the bone fragments he'd removed from the condo. Fearing a homicide investigation, Eve had recruited two random nitwits to dig up her husband's arm so there would be nothing for a coroner to exhume and examine.

Meanwhile, Rosa had to be careful what she told detectives. She might get fired if it became known that she was surreptitiously assisting a rookie restaurant inspector on an out-of-county murder case.

"Andrew, what the hell?" Sonny Summers threw up his hands.

"Give me back my old job and I'll get to the bottom of this."

"Christ, why would I want to get to the bottom of it? I just need it to go away."

The sheriff had come to the office in a pressed blue blazer with the requisite American flag lapel pin. He appeared to have put on a few soft pounds.

"We were dealing with a routine accident, right? Guy goes fishing, flips his boat, the sharks show up, whatever . . . and then his arm gets snagged by a tourist. See, I don't understand how we got from there to here."

"Because it wasn't an accident, Sonny."

"You're still pissed about getting canned. Is that what this is all about? Stirring the shit pot?"

Again Yancy thought of Rosa, who was definitely in the line of bureaucratic fire. Now she had real work to do, a case number and everything. Still, she hadn't urged him to retreat or even move to the shadows. A true champ, Yancy thought.

To the sheriff he said: "You're the one who wanted the guy's arm to go up the road in the first place. Now you got your wish, so what's the problem?"

"Channel 7, Andrew."

"You're killing me."

"They'll get a whiff of this. Don't think they won't."

"Who cares?" Yancy asked. "You haven't done anything wrong."

"And the fucking *Herald* will be all over it, too. My

wife, she wants me to run for state attorney general year after next. She's already looking at private schools in Tallahassee."

Yancy found himself improbably touched by the sheriff's grandiose fantasy.

"Don't you get it?" Sonny Summers said. "Everything bad's gonna come out now. Weeks ago, when that goddamn arm first showed up, I told the media that Miami had taken over the investigation. That's what Rawlings put in his report, except it wasn't true. The thing was in your—"

"Freezer."

"—personal custody. And you're not even a cop anymore."

"That you can fix," Yancy said. "Just hand over my badge."

"They're gonna say I ditched a human body part and then lied about it. That's tampering with evidence, obstruction, whatever. Now the whole damn mess looks like a cover-up."

"Naw, it's just a jurisdictional snafu. Blame it on me—no, wait, don't."

"Hang on." Sonny Summers was jotting down the phrase "jurisdictional snafu."

Yancy decided it was wiser to keep the sheriff on edge. He said, "You should be aware, however, that Stripling was murdered here in Monroe County, not in Miami."

Sonny Summers looked up, blinking like a toad in a puddle of piss.

"Chopped to pieces at his condo on Duck Key," Yancy reported heavily. "The guy was a thieving shitbird but, still, a dreadful end. I know exactly how the killing went down."

"You do?"

"The wife and boyfriend did it. Hacked up Stripling's body and sunk the boat."

Sonny Summers bit his lower lip. "Where's the rest of the corpse?"

"Who knows? Gone forever."

"But, then, the arm she had the funeral for—how'd it get back to the Miami morgue?"

"Grave robbery gone bad."

"Oh, fuckeroo." The sheriff covered his ears.

Yancy mildly raised his voice: "I'm betting they hired some mopes to dig it up."

"For God's sake, why?"

"Because," Yancy said, "yours truly was hot on their tail. The widow Stripling and her man are running scared."

Sonny Summers kicked back from the desk, the chair squealing under his fresh lard. "But you're not in homicide, Andrew. You're on roach patrol!"

"Once a cop, always a cop," Yancy said fraternally.

Given the frequency with which body parts turned up in Miami, the discovery of another hacked-off arm usually didn't draw much attention from local news outlets. However, most severed limbs were found in Dumpsters or roadside canals, not in Callaway golf bags. Such a colorful detail, if leaked to a reporter, would almost surely produce a headline. After that it would take only a bit of digging to learn that Nick Stripling had been a big-time Medicare fraudster. Next stop: *Dateline NBC*.

"I wasn't the one who said it was a boat accident," the sheriff protested. "That was the almighty U.S. Coast Guard!"

"Sonny, please let me finish this off. I'm so close."

"No way."

"Here's your story: You had me working on the case from day one, okay? On special assignment. Why? Because you're a lawman's lawman. You always had private doubts, a gut feeling there was foul play. That's what you tell the press after I bust Eve Stripling for first-degree murder—then you'll look like a star."

"Slow down, Andrew."

"I'm the only one who can put it all together!"

Sonny Summers wouldn't budge. "You can't be anywhere near this case, or any case, because you're not on the damn payroll anymore. You're an ex-detective, and you got that way by violating a prominent dermatologist with a household appliance in the middle of the business district! It made all the papers, my friend."

Yancy had one more card to play. "Remember that fishing mate who got shot? It's a city case. Charles Phinney was his name."

"Sure, I remember. The robbery near the raw bar."

"Wrong."

"Or was it the Turtle Kraals?"

"It wasn't a robbery, Sonny. The kid was killed because he knew too much about the arm."

"You're giving me a cluster migraine."

"Stripling's widow set him up. Her boyfriend was the shooter."

"Guess what? Let's stop here."

"That's three murders," Yancy said, "almost four. They tried to kill me, too."

The sheriff lowered his lamentation to a rasp. "This is *not* a productive conversation."

"Let me make it all better."

"Take a vacation, Andrew. I'll clear it with Lombardo."

"But I don't need a vacation. I need my job back."

Yancy had to cool down so he bought a ticket on the Conch Train and took a slow tour through town. A pleasant couple sat down near him, confiding a fervid interest in the polydactyl cats that roamed the Hemingway House. One of the animals was reputed to have at least twenty-six toes, and for a glimpse the Whitlocks had traveled all the way from Ashtabula, Ohio. Yancy hopped off the train near the Mallory docks and strolled to the X-rated T-shirt shop, where he emphasized to Pestov the importance of Madeline's well-being. He was able to make his point without the Glock, which he'd chosen not to wear to his meeting with Sheriff Summers, who was a chronic stickler and worrywart.

Back at Big Pine, Yancy found his home reoccupied by Cody and Bonnie Witt, who now wished to be addressed by her pre-fugitive name of Plover. The summer rains had made a swamp of the couple's camping adventure, and Cody was suffering from chiggers and an oral yeast infection. Yancy walked them next door and helped them erect their pup tent in the spacious master bedroom of Evan Shook's unfinished spec house. Although the plumbing in the structure was connected, a semi-rustic experience was guaranteed by the raw plywood flooring, unscreened windows and lack of air-conditioning.

Rosa Campesino drove down after work and met Yancy at a Thai restaurant that he extolled as sanitary. Whenever he took her out, his appetite rebounded. Afterward they went to Duck Key, where the night watchman refused to open Stripling's condo until Rosa weighed in with her Miami-Dade pathologist laminate, which was visually more impressive than Yancy's restaurant-inspector ID.

It was clear that Eve Stripling had gutted the place in anticipation of a search warrant, confirming Yancy's suspicion that Caitlin Cox had told her about his earlier visit. Rosa remained on the balcony while Yancy returned Stripling's hair and bone chips to the shower drain; the hatchet he wiped down and wedged behind the water heater, making sure its wooden handle protruded far enough to be noticed by any half-competent CSI tech.

Earlier, over noodle soup, Rosa had reported three important forensic findings, two of which Yancy had been expecting: The Duck Key bone fragments had definitely come from Nick Stripling's arm, and the odd notches on the stump of the humerus matched the blade bite of the hatchet.

"But here's the best part," Rosa said. "The hatchet isn't what severed the victim's limb."

"Then what the hell did they use?"

"A surgical saw, Andrew."

"No shit?" Instantly he thought of O'Peele, the dead orthopedist.

Rosa said, "After the amputation they whacked at the arm with the axe to obscure the saw marks."

"And make it appear that a boat propeller did it."

"The wounds really don't look much alike, but they wouldn't know that. Same with those shark nibbles—they neglected to find the right species."

"Amateur hour."

"Yeah, but they nearly pulled it off," Rosa said, "so to speak."

"The sheriff's wigging. How're things in your shop?"

"So far, so good. From now on I'll be sticking strictly to the science. Whatever else I might have heard about this case, it's only hearsay. For instance, I have no official knowledge of the hair and bones we're now illegally transporting."

"What hair?" Yancy said. "What bones?"

After reinstating the crime scene at Duck Key, he drove back to Big Pine; Rosa followed in her own car. Wheeling up to his place, Yancy looked next door and saw through the top-floor windows the yellowish glow of a kerosene lantern that he'd loaned to Cody and Bonnie-slash-Plover. He had also coached them about what to say when Evan Shook showed up, and he regretted that he wouldn't be there to observe the man's reaction.

He led Rosa into his house and put on some jazz and poured two glasses of red wine. Then he told her about his forced furlough. "Sonny strongly recommends time away. He believes my relationship with Stripling's arm is problematic, and he'd like me to be unavailable for potential interviews and depositions."

"I bet I know where you're going, Andrew."

"Can't you take some vacation days?"

"Ha, not right now. The death business is booming."

Yancy pulled his travel duffel from a closet and tossed in some swim trunks, boxers and a stack of fishing shirts. He said, "Listen, I've been having this super-kinked-out fantasy, better than the autopsy slab. Promise not to freak."

"Oh brother."

"Me. You. King-sized bed at the Biltmore."

"You are *so* warped. Cable porn?"

"And French chocolates on the pillow."

"Here, let me help you pack."

In the morning they enjoyed a room-service breakfast before Rosa left for the morgue. Yancy wrapped up a leftover slice of smoked salmon, checked out of the hotel and drove directly to the retirement residence of corrupt Miami police sergeant Johnny Mendez. Sunning on the front walk was the ex-officer's rotund Siamese. Yancy displayed the fragrant morsel of fish and the cat trailed him to the Subaru.

Next stop was the Venetian Pool, where he parked under a ficus tree and called Mendez's house. "Say, how's that bovine nut sack of yours holding up?"

"Who the fuck is this?"

"Detective Andrew Yancy from Monroe County. Good news, sir: I found Natasha." The name was embossed on the animal's collar. "She was wandering the alleys like a dazed hooker, poor thing. Lucky I came along."

"Are you nuts!"

"Don't deny that you love this critter more than your wife. What's your cell number, Johnny Boy?"

Yancy took an iPhone snapshot of the Siamese licking salmon juice off his fingertips. He texted the photo to Mendez along with a note: "She doesn't seem to miss you."

Mendez called right back and said, "You're a sick hump, Yancy."

"And you are a larcenous fuckstick. However, I need a favor—and you should view this as an opportunity to become an authentic Crime Stopper, partial atonement for all that money you embezzled."

"What kinda favor? I'm retired, you asshole."

"Yeah," Yancy said, "but I bet you can still get me a police badge."

"What happened to yours? Ha, don't tell me you got canned again."

"I guess Natasha and I will be taking a road trip."

"Jesus, you need a badge like right now? All I got is my old one."

"That'll do, Johnny Boy. Put it in your mailbox, go back inside and stay there until you hear me honk three times. That means Empress Natasha is home. Try something stupid, like calling the real cops, and you'll never lay eyes on your darling inbred feline again."

"You hurt her, you're a dead man."

Yancy, who was allergic to cat dander, sneezed volcanically. "I'd never do anything to harm Natasha, preening diva though she is. What I *would* do, Johnny, is throw away her collar and leave her with some kindly souls I know who'd find her a good home with a higher class of human companions than you and Mrs. Mendez. Now go put the fucking badge in the mailbox."

"Christ, gimme some time to look for the damn thing."

"Twenty minutes," Yancy said. "I've got a plane to catch."

Fifteen

Neville was in no condition for romance, so he tried to break up with all three of his girlfriends on the same afternoon. Each of them said he was stupid and crazy and no damn good—yet they wouldn't throw him out. Neville suspected that the women still clung to hope that he'd change his mind about the mountain of money he was refusing to accept for his family's land. They harbored dreams that he would warm to the role of rich boyfriend.

He went snapper fishing near the submarine base and caught enough for dinner, breakfast and lunch. A friend who worked at the Lizard Cay bonefish lodge, which was closed for the summer, opened the kitchen and let Neville fry up his catch. That night he slept on his boat anchored off Green Beach, where he got soaked by a squall. Shortly before dawn he guzzled two lukewarm Kaliks and a quart of water. Then he waded ashore and hid among the remaining casuarinas, where he slapped mosquitoes and waited for his bladder to fill.

Unbeknownst to Neville, the white man Christopher had responded to the first incident of diesel contamination by equipping his earthmoving machines with locking fuel caps. Therefore the tank of the Cat 450E backhoe that Neville hoped to disable with beery urine was sealed from intrusion, and the spout lid held fast under a vigorous bashing. Soon Neville's bloated gut began to ache, so he climbed to the cab, unbuttoned his fly and let loose on the gauge cluster. In his heart he understood it was an impotent gesture, the sturdy backhoe plainly engineered for all-weather operation.

In a drained state he stepped to the ground, where he was jumped by the fetus-eared security guard, who wordlessly began to pummel him. The goon's name was Egg, or so Neville had been told by a boy cleaning conchs on the waterfront. Egg outweighed Neville by fifty pounds and his sweat smelled like fermented lobster. The weapon was a short aluminum bat of the type used by offshore charter mates to subdue billfish and tuna that are dragged aboard green. Neville flopped around in the freshly turned dirt, shielding his head and moaning at every blow. The man called Egg lugged him to the beach and kicked him into the water and walked away laughing. Neville remained on all fours in the sandy shallows until he vomited. It took all his strength to swim out to the boat and pull himself over the gunwale.

The next morning, despite a fear of flying, he caught a plane to Nassau and went shopping for an attorney. None of those who met him would initiate a lawsuit without a retainer, which Neville couldn't afford. They seemed disappointed to learn he wasn't seeking any monetary compensation, only the return of family real estate that had been lawfully sold by his half-sister. The prevailing opinion was that he stood virtually no chance of winning in court.

Neville stayed overnight with a nephew who wanted to take him to the Atlantis resort for a big time, but Neville declined. He was sore and unsteady after the beating by Egg. When his nephew asked what was wrong, Neville said he'd gotten into a fight over a girl.

"Oh mon, did you hot get broke?"

"No, suh."

"Because I know plenny women kin fix dot."

"I'm okay," said Neville.

The following day he bought a pair of sunglasses at the Straw Market and rode the mail boat back to Andros.

Yancy breezed through Immigration and Customs in Nassau. All he carried through the checkpoints was his duffel and a Sage fly-rod tube that falsely announced him as a free-spending American sportsman, always a welcome breed. He took a taxi to the general aviation terminal and told a handsome woman behind the counter he was looking for a pilot friend.

"This is what he's flying," Yancy said, and showed her a picture of the white Caravan. He'd printed it out from the flight-tracker website. "I was told to meet him here."

"Are you sure, sir? That plane left a couple hours ago."

"No way. He was supposed to take me fishing!"

"They went to Lizard Cay," the woman said. "Same as usual."

"That sonofabitch. He promised to wait for me."

"There's usually a three o'clock flight on Tropical. I'll give you the phone number."

Yancy smiled. "Darling, you just saved my vacation."

It was from his father that he'd gotten not only his passion for fishing but also a love of small planes. Every year the park service would conduct aerial counts of eagle nests in the Everglades, and after turning eighteen Yancy was allowed to ride with his dad and the pilot in the government Beechcraft. He always brought his own binoculars.

While he waited for his flight Rosa called to say that she'd FedExed to Key West police the slug from the gun that killed Gomez O'Peele. Yancy was confident that ballistics tests would prove it was the same .357 used on Charles Phinney. Rosa hadn't provided the details of the doctor's death to the detectives.

"But I'll have to tell them what I know," she added, "if the bullets match."

Yancy apologized for putting her in a dicey situation. She said she was a big girl and she knew the ropes. He asked if any news reporters had called the medical examiner's office to inquire about the severed arm in the golf bag.

"Well, we might have lucked out," she said.

"I like this 'we' business."

"The man to thank would be the late, great Dawkins Brophy. The same night the grave robbers stole Stripling's arm, Mr. Brophy—"

"I thought Brophy was his *first* name."

"Whatever, Andrew. It's not even my case," Rosa said. "Anyway, the same night our severed limb reappeared, Mr. Dawkins Brophy—or Brophy Dawkins—washed down three Ecstasy tabs with a half pint of Bombay gin. Then he went racing through Government Cut on a turbocharged WaveRunner until he drove full speed into the stern of the *Duchess of the Caribbean,* killing himself and his date, a Belorussian lingerie model whose name I can't possibly pronounce."

"In other words, splat."

"Big-time splat."

"Damn," Yancy said.

Brophy Dawkins was a burly country-music star whose hit single was "Jesus Don't Speak Jihad," a defiant post-9/11 anthem. The *Duchess of the Caribbean* was one of the world's largest passenger cruise ships.

"It was a collision only in the sense that a june bug collides with a Buick," Rosa said. "Mr. Dawkins was decapitated and, consequently, his remains weren't fully recovered for a day or so due to tidal factors. Since then the media have taken an interest, Andrew. Rabid would be one way to describe it."

"Rule one: A celebrity head always trumps an anonymous arm."

"Sick but true," said Rosa. "Can I ask you something? I've been thinking about this Andros trip."

"I'll buy you a ticket. Please come."

"No, listen. Say you track down the murderous wife and her boyfriend—then what? You can't make a legal arrest over there. And the Bahamian cops won't do it without U.S. extradition papers, which you don't have in your possession because those documents don't freaking exist. The risk-reward ratio seems low, Andrew."

"Everyone needs a project."

"Soon as I hang up, know what I'm Googling? Three words: 'Nassau bail bondsmen.'"

"Come on, girl, have some faith."

In the olden days Claspers smuggled weed and later cocaine. He never got busted though he didn't stay rich for long. Now the shit was coming in on freight trucks across the Mexican border, or by air from Haiti, where Claspers refused to fly. But after four thousand hours in the cockpit, on and off the books, he could still find lawful work. The Bahama Islands he knew well, from Bimini to the Exumas. These days in small planes he delivered wealthy tourists and expats to some of the same bleached airstrips upon which he'd once landed overloaded DC-6s at night, guided only by automobile headlights.

As a legitimate aviator Claspers was doing okay—not gangbusters, but he made enough money to cover the rent on his duplex, a car payment, child support and weekly visits to a club in Lauderdale called Marbles, where a bartender one-third his age pretended to be interested in him. Claspers didn't mind being strung along. The bartender had stellar fake boobs and a quick sense of humor. He considered telling her about his years as a big-time smuggler, but he doubted it would improve his odds of getting laid. Once upon a time, sure, absolutely—but hers was a generation that grew up on homegrown or Humboldt and thought Panama Red was a merlot. Claspers suspected the young bartender would have been more impressed to meet a guy who worked for Apple, or maybe a professional skateboarder. He overtipped her anyway, because it brought back memories that made him feel good.

Lately Claspers had been piloting for a shady duck named Christopher Grunion, who disliked the formalities of the U.S. Customs service. Sometimes Grunion asked Claspers for clandestine transport between Andros Island and the lower Florida Keys. For these high-risk endeavors Claspers was decently compensated—not doper-league pay, but enough to sustain his loyalty. A secondary enticement was the opportunity to dust off his outlaw moves.

The aircraft leased by Grunion was a Cessna float-plane, a ten-seat Caravan that cruised at 160 knots. From Andros—either Congo Town or Lizard Cay—Claspers would steer a southeast course toward the Ragged Islands until reaching a singular quadrant where the seas belonged to the Bahamas while the airspace belonged to Cuba. Basically it was a neutral zone for law enforcement, and that's where Claspers would drop to four hundred feet, below radar, and swing sharply back across the Florida straits. Coming in low over the waves was the only way to cross undetected, because on Cudjoe Key the U.S. government tethered a famed surveillance blimp known as Fat Albert, which had been effectively used by the DEA to bust some of Claspers's colleagues in the aerial import trade.

Christopher Grunion seldom spoke during these flights. Often he appeared to doze with his forehead pressed against the window, causing Claspers to wonder if he was loaded, drunk or possibly ill. The girlfriend, Eve, was a nervous chatterbox who spewed questions. *Are we still in the Bahamas? What's that island down there? How fast are we going? Do we have enough fuel? What're you gonna do if the Coast Guard spots us?* Her yammering made Claspers long for the days when he flew the starry tropics in solitude, accompanied only by silent herbal tonnage and a terse Hispanic voice on the headset.

Bringing in the Caravan required a stretch of calm water, typically on the leeward side of an island. Daylight was also helpful, particularly during lobster season when the channels and bays of the Keys were clotted with small buoys that could tear up the floats and ruin a perfectly fine landing, even flip the aircraft. Once they safely touched down, Eve would call a taxi to come fetch her and Grunion. Then the two of them would inflate the rubber raft they always brought as cargo (along with a small outboard engine), and from the plane they would putt-putt to shore.

Claspers thought the well-fed couple might benefit from rowing, although Grunion would need to shed the orange weather poncho that he always wore. Surely he sweltered like a pig beneath the plastic pullover; Claspers figured he kept it on because of some weird phobia or unsightly medical disorder. A pilot friend of Claspers's had been morbidly afraid of centipedes and refused to remove his heavy woolen socks, even while bathing. Eventually the poor bastard ended up on crutches, grounded. Later a photograph of his ravaged feet was featured in an illustrated atlas of fungal infections.

Claspers enjoyed sneaking in and out of the States, but much of his flying for Grunion was routine, Andros to Nassau and back. Grunion was breaking ground on an upscale tourist resort at Lizard Cay, so Claspers would bring in architects, designers, contractors, bulldozer mechanics and even the real estate agents to whom Grunion was pitching his project. About once a week Eve would ride the seaplane to Miami but there was no cowboy stuff—it was straight into Opa-locka or Tamiami, strictly legal, her passport open and ready for stamping. Claspers looked forward to those trips because he got some time to go home and chill. Nassau wasn't hard duty, either, though he always blew too much cash at the clubs and casinos.

The toughest part of the Andros gig was cooling his heels for days at a time, waiting for Grunion or his girlfriend to call with a flight in mind. Rocky Town was the nearest settlement to the construction site, and there wasn't much to do except eat conch, drink rum and ruminate about growing old with a prostate the size of a toadstool. Marley and the Wailers were all over the radio, yet even that got stale after a while.

Grunion and the woman were renting a house on the ocean but not once had they invited Claspers for lunch or even a cocktail. He would have hired one of the local kids to take him snorkeling or grouper fishing except that Grunion insisted he hang within fifteen minutes of the plane, which stayed chocked on the tarmac at what they called Moxey's airfield.

That's where Claspers was, drinking a flat Fresca, when the late afternoon flight from Nassau landed. Three Bahamian women got off lugging shopping bags and next came a rangy guy in his late thirties, early forties. He was carrying a duffel and a fly-rod tube. Claspers knew he was American because of his tan; the Brits and Canadians were white as milk when they stepped off the planes and pink as shrimp when they left. The American paused on the apron to look at the Caravan; then he ambled up to Claspers and asked, "Do you know who owns that seaplane?"

"Private charter."

"Too bad," the American said. "I want to fly down and wade the Water Cays. I was looking for someone to take me."

Claspers told him not to get his hopes up, because there weren't many floatplanes for charter. "Wish I could help, but I'm stuck here."

"So you're the pilot."

"That's me."

The American held out his hand. "My name's Andrew."

"I'm K. J. Claspers."

"You got time for a drink?"

Claspers said thanks anyway but he had to work. "I gotta do a run for the boss."

A dented blue van pulled up and Grunion's hired man got out. He was a dome-headed hulk with shriveled-looking ears. They called him Egg but the name on his papers was Ecclestone. He wore a bleached white T-shirt that by contrast made his skin shine like onyx.

"Let's go, mon," he said to Claspers.

"In a minute." Claspers wasn't afraid of Egg and he didn't care much for him. The guy was your basic pea-brained muscle, straight from central casting. Claspers said, "I gotta take a leak. Go wait by the plane."

Egg sneered and headed across the baking tarmac toward the Caravan.

The American said, "That's some boss."

Claspers snorted. "Not him, no way—he's just the help. Poor baby's got a toothache so I've gotta take him to a dentist in Nassau. Talk about the glamour life."

The pilot went to the restroom and propped himself at the only urinal, where he spritzed and dribbled for what seemed like an eternity. A doctor back home had pre-scribed some heavy-duty pills but half the time Claspers forgot to take them. Maybe if that hot bartender at Mar-bles ever gave him a real shot, he'd get with the program and tend to his plumbing.

Claspers wanted to ask the man with the fly rod why he'd come to the island during the hottest, deadest time of summer, when the bonefish lodges were closed. It was rare to see tourist anglers so late in the season, and even more uncommon for one to arrive alone. Typically they fished in pairs to split the cost of chartering a skiff.

When Claspers emerged from the head, he tugged down the bill of his cap against the glare of the sun. He looked around and there was Egg, sitting truculently on one of the airplane's pontoons.

The American was gone.

Sixteen

Evan Shook was surprised to see a muddy Toyota parked out front. The Oklahoma tag didn't make sense; the Lipscombs had said they were from Virginia. Plus they weren't supposed to arrive for another forty-five minutes.

Inside the house Evan Shook encountered two squatters, an attractive woman with frosted blond pigtails and a flabby guy who looked younger.

"Please don't get mad," the woman began.

"Clear out right now, before I call the cops."

The man said, "Bro, we took a major hit. This is *not* where we want to be."

It was the woman doing most of the talking, some hard-luck story about her purse being stolen, all their cash and credit cards. Evan Shook wasn't even pretending to listen.

"And this was supposed to be our second honeymoon," she concluded sadly.

That part Evan Shook heard, with vexation; the woman was way too hot to be sleeping with such a zero. Evan Shook was unaware that people said the same thing about his mistress. Recently she'd been harping at him to leave his wife, demands inflicted at the cruelest bedroom moments. He couldn't afford a messy divorce, just as he couldn't afford to diddle for another six months with the Big Pine spec house. Between the construction loan and the property mortgage, the bank had him by the short and curlies.

"We tried camping," the male squatter piped up, "but, dude, the fuckin' skeeters!"

Evan Shook checked around. Except for the strange couple's tent, the place was in good shape for the Lipscombs. The menacing pentagram on the floor had been painted over by a select member of the construction crew, a Sikh carpenter who took no stock in silly Western superstitions. It was also he who'd disposed of the icky Santeria artifacts, lobbing the stiffened rooster into the canal and granulating the rodent skull with a belt sander.

The cute woman in pigtails said, "We weren't trying to make trouble. We just needed somewhere dry and safe."

"This'll be a cool-ass crib when it's done," her companion added for ingratiation.

Evan Shook nodded brusquely. "Yup. A real cool-ass crib."

Over the phone the Lipscombs had sounded like long shots. The guy claimed to be a retired hedge funder who was now raising trotters. He said he was driving all the way to Florida because the wife refused to fly ever since their Lear 45 had clipped a cow elk on the runway at Jackson Hole. He said they already owned a seaside spread at Hilton Head and a cottage up on the Boundary Waters. Evan Shook responded with cordiality but not gushing enthusiasm. It was his experience that people with serious money didn't broadcast their real estate portfolios to strangers who were angling to peddle them another property.

But maybe the Lipscombs were real. Maybe his luck would change.

The woman said, "I'm begging you, don't call the police. We have nowhere else to go."

Evan Shook opened his billfold and peeled off two, three, four hundred dollars. "Pack up your stuff and go get a room."

When the woman leaned forward to kiss his cheek, Evan Shook caught a heartbreaking glimpse down her blouse. "God bless you," she said.

What God? he thought. *In half an hour she'll be balling this slob in a hotel I'm paying for.*

Her lump-faced boyfriend solemnly took his hand. "Thanks, dude. I mean, duuuuude."

It's so tragic, thought Evan Shook. *So wrong.*

The phone number for Christopher Grunion obtained by Rosa—the last number dialed by Dr. Gomez O'Peele— was disconnected. Yancy had planned to call Grunion out of the blue, pretending to be an insurance broker or maybe a Republican pollster. He'd just wanted to hear what the prick who tried to kill him sounded like.

His room on Lizard Cay was fine; the AC was anemic but he had a striking view of the white flats, veined with tidal channels shining sapphire and indigo. Offshore Yancy could see a slow-chugging mail boat; otherwise the horizon was empty. He heard the Caravan lift off from Moxey's airstrip and pass over the motel on a slow turn toward Nassau. The pilot seemed like an okay guy although his bullet-headed passenger was bad news. Apparently the thug was connected to Grunion in a capacity of sufficient importance to warrant use of the seaplane for a dental crisis.

Yancy checked his phone and found a snide message from Caitlin Cox:

"Listen, *Inspector,* I think you oughta know what just happened. That judge in Miami declared my dad officially dead, whatever, so can you please leave us all alone and get back to your annoying life?"

The court's decision didn't surprise Yancy. Nick Stripling's mangled arm was sufficient evidence of death. That it had been unearthed later from the grave and then ejected from a stolen vehicle would have no bearing on the judge's ruling as to whether or not Stripling was in fact deceased. How he got that way—by mishap or homicide—was likewise irrelevant. Yancy wondered how long it would take Caitlin to get her slice of the insurance payoff, and whatever else Eve Stripling had promised.

He picked out a bicycle from the motel's rusty selection and rode to Rocky Town. It was critical to avoid Eve and her boyfriend, either of whom might recognize Yancy even in yuppie fishing garb. Unfortunately, he was the only white man on the streets, and the only white man at the seafood shack where he stopped to eat. A woman dicing conch behind the bar was so friendly that Yancy took a chance and said he was looking for a fellow American named Christopher. She gave a roll of the eyes and then one of those fabulous island laughs. Before long she was telling Yancy all about Grunion's ambitious project, the Curly Tail Lane Resort.

"Yeah, mon, dey gon have a spa and clay tennis and a chef dot's from some five-star hotel in Sowt Beach."

"Sounds spectacular," Yancy said.

"You friends with Mistuh Grunion back in Miami?"

"I am. Where does he usually hang out around here?"

"Ha, he dont hang no place. You see 'im drive sometime tru town but mostly he stay at Bannister Point. 'Im and his lady rent dot Gibson place. She come by every now 'n' then to pick up some chowder. Wot's your name, mon? Have another rum."

Yancy ordered one more Barbancourt with his meal. He dealt with the conch salad painstakingly; each incoming bite was picked apart by fork and then scrutinized for insect pieces. The locals who were witnessing this dour procedure snickered among themselves, but Yancy carried on. It seemed unlikely that Rocky Town was large enough to have a full-time health inspector, if such a job even existed on Andros. The conch shack was just that, an open-air bar next to a hill of gutted mollusk shells. No government health certificate was posted on the plywood menu board, only the boozy jottings of sailboaters and tourists.

Still, the food was excellent. After he finished eating, Yancy climbed on the clattering bike and set off in the starless night for the motel. At the bottom of a hill his front tire caught a pothole and he spilled sideways, landing on his back. He was sitting on the broken pavement and swearing aloud when he heard a motor.

From the crest of the roadway a single white light descended slowly. It was too small to be the headlamp of a motorcycle. Yancy leaned his bike against a utility pole. The white light weaved on its approach, the hum of the squat vehicle growing louder. Yancy still wasn't sure what he was looking at, though now he could hear a smoky voice, singing and laughing.

It was a woman piloting some sort of souped-up wheelchair, which she braked to a halt when its narrow beam fell upon Yancy. She was dressed flamboyantly and followed by heavy-lidded matrons who clapped softly and rolled their heads. On the steering bar of the motorized scooter perched a monkey wearing a doll's plastic tiara and an ill-fitted disposable diaper.

"You hoyt, suh?" the throned woman asked Yancy.

"I'm good. Took a tumble off the bike is all."

"You a white fella? Don't lie. Where you from?"

She looked bony and harmless, yet Yancy experienced a spidery chill. The woman wore a wrap of pink batik on her head and swigged from a tall glass that barely fit in the cup holder. Although it was too dark on the road for Yancy to see her features, the gleam of a gapped smile was unmistakable. Something about her pet monkey didn't seem right.

She said, "Dot's Prince Driggs. He's a movie star! You two handsome boys shake honds."

"No, that's okay."

The monkey growled and thrust out a brown paw.

"Better do it," the woman warned Yancy, "or he fuck you up bod."

Yancy shook the moist little fist and said, "Well, I'd better be going."

"Take a ride wit me, suh. I'll sit on dot strong monnish lap a yours."

"Thanks, anyway. That's a spiffy wheelchair, though."

"Ain't no fuckin' wheelchair! You tink I'm a cripple?"

To display her agility she hopped up, causing her attendants to flutter and fuss.

Indignantly the woman said to Yancy, "Wot dis ting is, boy, is lux'ry transport. Even got a iPod dock!"

"Sweet." He leaned closer to read the label on the mobile chair. It was a Super Rollie, the same brand that Nick Stripling's company had billed to Medicare in imaginary numbers.

"Can I ask where you got this?"

"From a friend. Woman like me has plenny friends." She resettled herself in the contoured seat and smoothed the folds of her colorful skirt.

Yancy said, "I'd really like to have a scooter like this."

"Maybe you lucky. Let's talk sum bidness."

The woman seized the fly of Yancy's pants and tugged him halfway on top of her. Zestfully she began to grope, her husky grunts reeking of rum and stale cigars. Yancy was shocked to feel the wiry old drunk fishing for his balls. He fought to get free but the monkey hooked three sinewy fingers through one of his belt loops. Only when Yancy pinched the hairless web of its armpit did the beast let go, screeching.

"No, no, don't hoyt my prince!" the woman cried. "Bey, I gon pudda black coyse on your soul! Black as det!"

Yancy pulled out of her grasp and jumped back from the scooter chair. The riled monkey hurled first his tiara and then the diaper, which landed in a sodden lump at Yancy's feet. As the matrons rumbled toward him, he kicked off his flip-flops and ran.

The last leg of the crossing got rough, and a few passengers began to throw up. Neville watched tall clouds building in the east as the breeze strengthened. The captain of the mail boat said a tropical storm was heading up from Hispaniola, which wasn't uncommon that time of year. He said the storm was called Françoise, which meant nobody would take it seriously. He said the hurricane forecasters in Miami should give scarier names to the storms—like Brutus or Thor—if they wanted people to pay proper attention.

Neville didn't own a television so his weather news came from the waterfront. Usually it was reliable. Some of the guides and fishermen had programmed their cellular phones to receive NOAA bulletins and radar loops; whenever they started moving their boats into the mangroves, Neville knew something big was coming. His own boat ran skinny, and he could take it up almost any creek on a low tide and tie off to the trees.

Still, he wasn't worrying about the tropical storm when the mail boat docked. Françoise could slide north or south, or fizzle to a squall line by the time it touched Andros. Neville was more concerned by what was happening at the family property on Green Beach. He needed a new strategy for halting the construction of Curly Tail Lane, his voodoo scheme having failed. By seducing Christopher's henchman the Dragon Queen had placed her own lustful urges ahead of her professional commitment to Neville. No crippling curse would be unleashed against the white devil; Christopher would have to be brought down by worldly means.

Neville's bike was at the airport so he passed on foot through Rocky Town, keeping a wary eye out for Egg. Still bruised from the beating, Neville longed to sleep on a real mattress instead of a boat deck. Among his three girlfriends the one named Joyous owned the softest bed but the hardest attitude. Neville decided he could endure another nagging if the payoff was a good night's rest. Joyous slept like a stump and seldom snored.

She lived near Victoria Creek, and the walk brought Neville close to the property on Bannister Point where Christopher and the woman were staying. On a whim he left the road and made his way to the shoreline. The wind had swung southeast, pushing white-topped surf. Neville sat down on a coral outcrop with a rear view of the Gibson place. From behind him came a soft rustle in the bushes— two plump lizards humping in the last of daylight.

Neville was thirsty and tired from the slow rolling ride on the mail boat. His chin dropped to his chest and his eyelids closed as he pondered the difficult path he'd chosen. People said he was mad not to walk away from Green Beach and take the money. They laughed about it at the conch shack and called him a simpleton, which stung. By nature Neville wasn't a troublemaker; just the opposite. Never in his life had he thrown a punch in anger or caused a scene, but here was a fight from which he couldn't turn away.

What would he ever do as a rich man that he couldn't do now? Where would he go, and for God's sake why? He already lived in the loveliest place imaginable and, besides, he didn't like to fly. That's why he took the mail boat back from Nassau, seven hours by sea being more tolerable than twenty minutes by air.

Neville couldn't think of anything to buy with all that dirty wealth. His old bicycle carried him everywhere a car could go, and it didn't cost six damn dollars a gallon. Nor did he need a new fishing boat. The one he owned ran like a champ; the motor was a Yahama 150, way past warranty, but never had it stranded him, not once. He wondered if something was mentally wrong with him for being content with what he had...

When he opened his eyes, night cloaked the shore. The lights were on inside Christopher's house. Neville got up from the rock and crept closer, approaching the landscaped edge of the lawn. Music came from speakers on the screened veranda—American rock. *Baby, we were born to run!* Neville brushed a mosquito from his nose. Through the windows he saw no movement inside the rooms. By an outside wall stood the plastic garbage can from which he'd pilfered the items he'd given to the Dragon Queen for use in her curses.

Something soft brushed against Neville's legs and he hopped backward. It was a young tabby cat, probably a stray. As he leaned down to pet it, a man spoke from the darkness behind him: "Don't move, nigger, or I'll blow your fuckin' head off."

Neville rose slowly and turned. "Don't do dot please." The gun pointed at him had a long double barrel.

"Who the hell are you? Why you sneakin' around here?" Christopher's face was difficult to see in the shadows though his orange poncho practically cast its own light. It made him appear tall and caped and spirit-like.

"I juss chasin' offer my cot," Neville said.

"That's not your fuckin' cat."

"Respeckfully, sir, it looks true like 'im."

Unfortunately, the tabby wouldn't play along. It ran off when Neville reached to pick it up. Christopher laughed.

Neville could see the whites of the man's eyeballs but not his nose or mouth. He perceived that Christopher was wearing a clinging fabric mask similar to what the local bonefish guides used to protect their faces from sunburn.

"Okay, beach nigger, what's your name?"

"Neville Stafford."

"Where you from? How old are you?"

"I'm sickty-four."

"No shit? You're in pretty good shape for an old fart."

"Dot I cont say." Neville wished he was younger and quick enough to grab for the gun. Then he would have pressed the muzzle to the man's forehead and told him to take his goddamn earthmoving machines back to Florida.

Now all Neville could do was stand still and plead for his life. In his head he said a prayer; then he asked Christopher to please kindly let him go.

"So you wanna make it to your next birthday, is that right?"

"Yah, mon," said Neville.

"My country, you get free insurance when you hit the big six-five. Government pays damn near all the bills, you get sick. They got the same deal here in the islands?"

"Dot I cont say. I ain't been sick."

Again Christopher laughed through the mask. "Good for you, nigger." He raised the barrel of the gun. "That means you can still run like a goddamn chicken."

He aimed five feet above Neville's head and a bolt of blue-gold fire punched a hole in the night. Neville ran and ran.

Seventeen

Nobody on Andros seemed especially worried about Tropical Storm Françoise. For a day the system had stalled down near Grand Turk; now it was sidling northwest again. The National Hurricane Center said atmospheric conditions were favorable for cyclonic growth. At this announcement, a TV weatherman in Miami began jabbing in febrile excitement at the floridly rendered "cone of doom"—a forecast map illustrating multiple possible pathways of the storm through the Bahamas chain and across toward Florida.

Yancy was watching on a flat-screen television in a second-story restaurant overlooking the Tongue of the Ocean. After the weather update he turned his attention to a bowl of chunky red chowder; submerged insect fragments would be hard to detect among the diced onions and celery. Yancy probed with a teaspoon. The night before he'd squashed seven adult-phase German cockroaches in his motel room; the largest was a flier that had alighted on his forehead as he slept.

The restaurant owner, an American expat with a

white-streaked ponytail, asked, "What are you doing, mister?"

"Taking my time," Yancy said.

"It's only the best soup on the island. I use fresh-growed tomatoes."

Eventually Yancy took a sip. He bowed at the man and said, "Outstanding."

"Damn right."

"How's the bonefishing?"

"Super, if you can stand the heat."

"I love the heat," Yancy said.

A plane passed overhead, the pitch of the engine dropping during descent. Yancy hurried from the restaurant and pedaled his borrowed bicycle through gusty winds to the airstrip, where he found the white seaplane parked near the small terminal building. Claspers, the pilot, was talking on a cell phone while he set the wheel chocks. Standing alone by the fence was the beefy pinhead with the crumpled ears. He wore a brown guayabera, wet moons under the armpits. One side of his mug was shiny and swollen, testifying to an eventful dental appointment.

Yancy propped the bicycle against a shaded wall of the terminal. Soon a taxi van rolled up and the pinhead squeezed himself into the front passenger side. Yancy opened the sliding door and plopped down on the bench seat behind him.

"My bike's got a flat. Can I ride back to town with you?"

"I ain't gon dot way," the big man said.

"Then we'll drop you off first. My name's Andrew. What's yours?"

It was the driver who answered. "Egg's wot dey call 'im."

The goon stared ahead, rubbing his jawbone. He told the taxi man to take him to Curly Tail Lane.

"You mean Green Beach?" the driver asked.

"Ain't wot de sign say."

"N'how 'bout you, suh?"

"Conch shack," Yancy said.

The driver chuckled. "Almost lunchtime."

Egg took a prescription bottle from a pocket and tapped out three oval pills. "Fuck lunch, mon. Juss drive."

Yancy said he was from Florida. He said he loved the Bahamas and was thinking of buying a place on Andros, maybe a time-share. Egg ignored him.

The van stopped at a construction site. Egg paid the driver, unlocked the chain-link gate and disappeared inside an Airstream trailer that looked like it had been rolled off a cliff. Yancy didn't see any signs or billboards on the property.

"Is this Curly Tail Lane?" he asked the driver.

"Yah."

"I heard it's going to be a five-star resort."

"Dot's de plon."

"They're just getting started, huh?"

The taxi driver laughed. "It's not like Miami. Tings move lil' slower here."

"You hungry?" said Yancy.

The driver's name was Philip and he was from Nicholls Town, on the north end. Yancy bought him fritters and a beer at the conch shack, where he flirted equitably with the two women behind the counter. Afterward he gave Yancy a motor tour of Lizard Cay, through the quiet old settlements of Elizabeth, Pindling's Bluff and Weech Harbor. Along the way Yancy saw a few families boarding their windows, but the prevailing mood was leisurely. When the taxi began to jerk and sputter, Philip pulled over by the ferry dock on Victoria Creek. A squall blew in while he was beating with a wrench on the carburetor, so he scrambled back into the van.

While they waited for the rain to let up, Yancy described for Philip his unsettling encounter with the old woman on the motorized wheelchair. The driver frowned and told Yancy to be careful—she was a man-eater.

"A true sex witch, mon."

"What do you mean?"

"Wonna my uncles sleep wit her and tree months later he drop dead," Philip said. "She feed 'im poison coz he won't screw her no more. Wicked bod lady—you stay 'way."

"What's the story with that monkey?" Yancy asked.

The driver said the animal starred in the Johnny Depp pirate movies until he turned rowdy and got fired—the rumor was that he had been caught masturbating on wigs in the costume trailer. Later the monkey was won in a domino game by a local man named Neville Stafford, who'd been working hard to rehabilitate his new pet. Nobody was sure why Neville had gifted him to the old voodoo hag.

"Dey call her Dragon Queen," he added.

"Where'd she get those crazy wheels?"

"From her new boyfriend, mon. He won't lost long. Nonna dem do."

Yancy suspected that her Super Rollie was a demo left over from Nicholas Stripling's Medicare-fleecing operation. Christopher Grunion could have conned the "personal mobility device" from Eve and given it to the

Dragon Queen, though it seemed far-fetched that he—or any fully sighted male—would start a romance with such a revolting loon.

"Is the lady's boyfriend a white American? About my age?"

Philip cackled. "No, bey, you already meet de fella! It's Egg."

"Oh, come on."

"Yah, dot's true. I tole you she's a witch, dot Dragon Queen. No cock is safe!"

"You know a man named Grunion?"

"Yessuh. Egg's boss."

"Show me where he lives," Yancy said.

"Why?" Philip seemed amused.

"Because...he's a friend?"

"Dot's your story, I guess. What if I say no?"

Yancy took out the Miami police badge belonging to retired sergeant Johnny Mendez and held it up briefly for Philip to see. The shield featured a lush palm tree but not the officer's name, which was convenient for Yancy.

"You cont 'rest nobody here in de Bahamas," the driver said mildly.

"I was hoping for some friendly cooperation, that's all. Wouldn't you at least like to know what crimes I'm investigating?"

"No, mon."

"Three homicides that took place in Florida. Murders."

Philip sucked in a breath and said, "God o'mighty."

Yancy gave him some cash. "I'm not here to make trouble. I didn't even bring a gun."

"Too bod. He's a mean mottafuckah."

"You're talking about Christopher."

"Egg, too. You needa be cool."

"My middle name," Yancy said.

On the return trip to Rocky Town, Philip slowed the van as they passed the oceanfront house Grunion and "his woman" were renting. Yancy saw a yellow Jeep Wrangler in the driveway but no activity. When he got to his motel room, he placed a box of bonefish flies and a water bottle in his fanny pack. Then he grabbed the tube holding his fly rod, selected another bicycle and rode back toward Bannister Point.

The tide was coming in, so the depth was fine. Under an overcast sky Yancy buttered his nose and cheeks with greasy white sunblock. Then he put on wide Polaroid sunglasses and a long-billed fishing cap with cotton neck flaps. This Unabomber style, tweaked for the tropics, ensured that neither Eve nor her boyfriend would recognize him from a distance.

He assembled the nine-foot rod, strung the peach-colored line through the guides and picked out a credible fly. Slowly he waded down the shoreline, occasionally pausing to cast at fish that weren't there. The wind was strong but he quartered slightly into it and double-hauled for more distance. It was a graceful exercise; anyone watching from a dock or a porch would have pegged him as a serious angler, not one of the usual goobers.

As he came within sight of Eve Stripling's place, Yancy spotted the widow herself. She was dragging a red kayak through the backyard toward one side of the house, where she stowed it beside a wall. Yancy continued wading, pretending to be focused on the flats. Next Eve went after a barbecue grill, which she rolled to the same sheltered location. Evidently she'd been following the TV weather reports.

Yancy put the fly rod under one arm and began the ceremony of tying on a new tippet. He took his time, hoping for a glimpse of Grunion roaming the property. The water felt warm on his bare legs, and the wind kept the ruthless doctor flies at bay. Out of nowhere a Stratocaster started twanging in his brainpan—an old Dick Dale surf riff. Offshore was a misting reef break, and Yancy could hear the waves plowing the coral ledges. Whatever he was doing on the flats of Andros Island, it sure didn't feel like work.

From land came a yell. Eve Stripling stood on a rock outcrop waving her arms. Yancy's first impulse was to flee, though the effort would be doomed to play out in slow motion. The human knee wasn't engineered to sprint hundreds of yards in three feet of water.

How the hell did she know it was me? Yancy wondered dejectedly.

Then the wind dropped, and he was able to make out Eve's words: "Help Tillie! Help her!"

He squinted at something in the water between him and the widow, something alive. To no one he grumbled, "Are you shitting me?"

A puppy no larger than a muskrat was swimming toward him like a laser-guided clump of mattress stuffing. One of those urban teacup breeds, the dog had a stunted tail that drew a pencil-thin wake in the chop. It was a brainless expedition.

"Barracudas!" Eve shrieked from the rock. "Save her! Hurry!"

"Yeah, yeah."

"Sharks!"

"I heard you," Yancy said to himself. He advanced in long splashy strides toward the weary pooch and scooped it up.

Now what? he wondered. If he carried the animal all the way to Eve, she would surely recognize him despite the sunglasses and SPF 75 war paint. And instantly she'd know why he was there—to build a murder case against her.

"Thank you, mister! Thank you!" she bleated across the shallows.

Yancy responded with a modest-seeming wave. He set Tillie back in the water and pointed her toward the spot where Eve awaited: "Now be a good little rodent and swim to Momma."

But the pup wouldn't go; it spun around and thrashed its way back to Yancy, nosing into the crotch of his shorts. He tried a second launch with the same outcome. Tired Tillie was done for the day.

Now Yancy had no choice. He couldn't abandon the dog to a certain drowning, nor could he take her ashore and risk exposing his identity. So he turned and headed up-island across the flats. In one hand was the fly rod; in the other sat Tillie.

"Hey! Hey, you! Where are you going?" Eve cried.

The wind resumed blowing and her voice faded. Yancy glanced back and saw that she'd been joined by her boyfriend, glowing like a harbor buoy in his orange poncho. Together the couple was stork-stepping along the rocky ledge, trying to keep parallel with Yancy. It wasn't difficult to do; the water was now up to his thighs. Shells and sea urchins crunched beneath his wading booties, and once the bottom skated out from under him—a half-buried stingray, streaking seaward in a gray plume of marl.

As soon as Grunion reached a sandy stretch, he broke away from Eve and began to run, his poncho flapping like an unzipped tent. Yancy knew what was coming. Fifty yards down the beach, Grunion veered ninety degrees and sloshed into the shallows on a course of certain interception. Both of Yancy's escape options were problematic—returning the opposite way, toward Eve's house, or heading out to the deep, rough water. He wasn't blind to the irony of his dilemma; he didn't even *like* runty dogs. A pertinent question was whether pet-napping would be considered a felony or a misdemeanor in the Commonwealth of the Bahamas.

Yancy elected to stand his ground, submerged though it was. He secured Tillie in his fanny pack and rapidly stripped line from the fly reel. As Grunion splashed closer, Yancy spoke up in a defective Irish accent: "Git away from me, y'arsehole!"

Then he began arcing the tapered line in fluid loops back and forth over his right shoulder, using the robust breeze to extend his distance. Visually this motion recalled the virtuoso fly-casting scenes in *A River Runs Through It,* his father's favorite movie, except that Yancy's target was a human being, not a rainbow trout.

Shining on the end of his leader was a saltwater pattern called a Gotcha, size 1/0, tied on a stainless steel hook honed to surgical efficacy. Yancy stung Poncho Boy on the bridge of his nose, drawing a dark comma of blood. Grunion swore and backed off awkwardly. The next cast pricked an unshaven cheek and the one after that whip-snapped just shy of his left eyelash. Grunion, who showed no sign of recognizing Yancy, became preoccupied with self-protection. As if buzzed by hornets, he flailed one beefy arm in front of his face.

And on that arm was the large gaudy watch Yancy had seen before, on the wrist of his assailant on Big Pine. He was sure it was the same Tourbillon missing from the severed limb of Nick Stripling.

"Call yer dog to come!" he huffed at Grunion.

"What?"

"Ye heard me, dumb shite. Gawn and call yer bloody mutt!"

Yancy deftly kept the fly whistling through the air and with his left hand reached back and lifted the clueless canine from the fanny pack. He plopped her in the water and nudged her toward Grunion. On the beach, a hundred yards away, Eve Stripling paced and whinnied.

"Tillie, come!" Grunion commanded.

The addled pup swam in circles.

"Tillie! Over here! Tillie, yo!"

Pitiful, Yancy thought. He stopped casting and tickled the dog's rump with the tip of the rod. To Eve's boyfriend he said: "Try'n whistle, ye eejit."

Grunion whistled and Tillie's cornflake ears pricked.

"Now clap yer hands," Yancy said.

The man didn't clap; he whistled again. This time the puppy turned and paddled on a zigzag course toward the sound. "Good girl! Good girl!" Grunion hollered. Minutes later he was gathering Tillie from the waves.

Yancy resumed shooting casts at an imaginary point between Grunion's eyebrows. Flinching and ducking, the killer slogged back toward the sandy mound where Eve fretted. For extra coaxing, Yancy thwacked the Gotcha against the nape of Grunion's crispy poncho, and on the subsequent cast he stuck him in the right earlobe—a keen display of aim from seventy feet in a crosswind. Yancy set the hook using a sharp strip that broke the tippet and caused Grunion to bellow vituperatively. The pink-and-white fly remained loyally embedded, sparkling in the cocksucker's punctured ear like a dainty shrimp-shaped stud.

Once safely on land, Grunion pushed the dog at Eve and, cupping his wound, stalked back toward the house. Eve followed a few paces behind, cradling Tillie and pausing intermittently to glare across the flats at the would-be abductor of her precious princess.

Yancy hurriedly waded north, reeling in his line. The homicide investigation that he'd hoped would resurrect his law enforcement career was foundering, torpedoed by bad luck and a deficit of careful planning. He expected the bright yellow Wrangler to appear any moment on the coast road, an enraged Grunion tracking him toward a fateful landfall. The man would have armed himself, probably with the 12-gauge Beretta he'd swiped from Yancy's home in the Keys. Yancy himself was a sitting duck. A graphite fishing wand, no matter how artfully deployed, was useless against a screaming load of buckshot.

However, Grunion never returned. Nor, evidently, did Eve summon the island police, for Yancy came ashore unmolested. Riding the bicycle through a fresh rain toward Rocky Town, he concluded that the widow Stripling and her consort must have dismissed him as a crank, fly anglers being notoriously irascible if their solitude is violated.

He was on his way to the motel when a thunderclap chased him off the road, into an open carport attached to a small abandoned house. The slab floor was littered with rusting Red Bull cans and green shards of Kalik bottles that threatened his bicycle's bald tires. Still, the place was dry and its roof offered material protection from the sudden electrical storm, a summertime sensation that Yancy had learned to fear and respect during his Florida childhood. One afternoon, while camping at Cape Sable, he and his father had witnessed a lightning bolt incinerate a flock of turkey buzzards roosting in the boughs of an old pine, which then flared like a sparkler and split down the midline.

The sky over Lizard Cay had closed in and the rain began to slant. Cars passed every few minutes, slowing for puddles, though none of them were yellow Jeeps. Yancy set his fly rod against a wall and stayed perched on the bicycle, pondering what to do. The sensible move would be to return to the Keys and construct his homicide case the old-fashioned way, with forensics, paper trails and dodgy self-serving witnesses.

To remain on Andros was to risk spooking Eve and Grunion, which would screw up a prosecution beyond salvation. The trip certainly hadn't been a waste—Yancy had established that the couple was hiding out together, apparently investing the late Nicholas Stripling's Medicare plunder in a resort development remote from the noses of U.S. authorities.

In the downpour Yancy no longer could see the road except during bursts of lightning. Overhead the beams of the carport began to drip so he adjusted his position, clearing away more broken glass and clutter. From somewhere inside the house came an unhappy squeak and the sounds of scuttling, which Yancy attributed to rats. His shoulders tensed when he caught a whiff of spiced tobacco smoke.

Peeking through a rotted-out doorway, he spied an unexpected shelter mate—the voodoo woman's monkey, bedraggled, sopping, undiapered. The animal squatted in a corner sucking on a meerschaum pipe that he clutched blowgun-style with four tiny fingers, the dirty kernel of a thumb clocking in an agitated motion. The whitish bowl of the pipe was carved into a miniature topless angel of the voluptuous style found on bowsprits of old sailing ships.

If the taxi driver's story was true—that the monkey was featured in the *Pirates of the Caribbean* movies— his descent from stardom had been steep indeed. Yancy hoped the little bastard had forgotten the painful pinch he'd inflicted upon him the night before during the scuffle aboard the voodoo skank's scooter chair.

The animal's expression betrayed nothing as he sucked on the pipe. Then a boom of thunder—or perhaps Yancy's stare—caused the mangy desperado to bark sharply and flash brown-stained chompers.

"Chill out, little man," Yancy said.

The monkey spat the meerschaum and flew at him, snapping and scratching at his kneecaps and bare shins. From the superior height of his bicycle Yancy kicked back in a fevered defense until the heavy toe of his wading boot caught the beast flush on his crusty chin, launching him tail over head through a charred window frame, into the squall.

With blood-streaked legs Yancy pedaled out of the carport and down the road. His visibility was so foreshortened by the deluge that there was no opportunity to dodge the endless potholes, and by the time he reached the motel he'd bitten through his bottom lip. After a hasty dismount Yancy also realized that he had left behind his fly rod, a long-ago birthday present from Celia. Disconsolately he trudged across the soggy lawn toward his room, pulling up short when he spied the door ajar.

For a time Yancy waited in the raw wet dusk, rows of fat droplets pouring off the bill of his fishing cap. *Was it Grunion himself who had come, or had he given the job to Egg?* Yancy thought. *Hell, does it really matter?*

He uprooted a cane tiki torch, unlit, and rushed through the doorway swinging like Barry Bonds. Two matching lamps and a tray of decorative sand dollars were demolished before the torch broke to pieces. Dr. Rosa Campesino stepped from the bathroom wearing lace panties and a look of consternation.

"What on earth, Andrew?"

"Oh shit. I thought you were somebody else."

"It was supposed to be a surprise. I even brought some slutty red lipstick."

"Babe, you look fantastic."

"I caught the last plane in."

"Let's light some candles."

"The last plane before the hurricane."

"What?" Yancy said.

"Take off your clothes, dummy. You're dripping all over the rug."

Eighteen

"Are you in hedge funds?" Ford Lipscomb asked without glancing up.

Evan Shook said no. He was watching with equal measures of rapture and incredulity while Lipscomb wrote out a check.

"You say fifty grand'll hold it? Call it good faith— we've still got some wrinkles to iron out."

"Fifty's just fine." More than fine. Exquisite.

"Tell me the name of your lawyer again. On the escrow account?"

Evan Shook repeated it for Lipscomb. "He's up in South Miami. Does all my real estate work."

"Stay away from hedge funds, friend. Those giddy days are over," Lipscomb went on. "I tasted the best of it, then I bailed in the nick of time. Where the heck is Jayne?"

"Upstairs enjoying the view," Evan Shook said.

"Gold is the way to go. You ever listen to Glenn Beck? Maybe he's got a few shingles loose, but that weird little crybaby is right about gold."

Evan Shook wanted to pinch himself. After only two walk-throughs, the Lipscombs were actually buying his spec house! Ford and Jayne Lipscomb from Leesburg, Virginia, on their first-ever trip to the Florida Keys, arriving in a wine-colored Bentley convertible, its rear seat backs of hand-tooled leather splattered with fresh pelican shit—a rude souvenir from their Overseas Highway crossing.

Yet these remarkable Lipscombs, these brisk and purposeful Lipscombs, acknowledged with only the mildest of frowns the pungent bird goo on their expensive import. Handsome they were as a couple, married forever, their kids surely all grown up, well-schooled, well-bred and prospering. Evan Shook suppressed a pang of envy as Ford and Jayne approached the house hand in hand, smiling the way they might have smiled on their very first date, forty-some years ago. They were eager to tour all seven thousand square feet, and they absorbed Evan Shook's sales pitch with a genial attentiveness that unnerved him at first.

Such anxiety was understandable given his run of black luck with the property—the bloating raccoon corpse, the deranged bees, the gory witchcraft altar and then that nut job Yancy, sprawled naked as a jaybird to greet the Turbles. Next came the squatters, a depressingly mismatched twosome who had cleared out only minutes before the Lipscombs' first visit.

So now, on pivotal day two, Evan Shook couldn't be faulted for anticipating another sale-killing calamity—perhaps the ghostly pack of rabid mongrels that Yancy kept nattering about. In Evan Shook's mind flashed a gothic vision of the Lipscombs being taken down by the heels—first Jayne and then Ford—while sprinting for the Bentley. He considered himself a rational person, but part of him had begun to worry that the spec house truly was jinxed, a word used by both his wife and his girlfriend in separate conversations.

Yet there was no sign of Yancy or wild dogs, and the Lipscombs' second tour was as uneventful as the first. Sweating, slapping at bugs, they remained at all times polite and uncomplaining. The few questions asked by the husband seemed deliriously naïve coming from an ex–Wall Street slick, until Evan Shook reminded himself that he was dealing with a man who'd never before witnessed a Gulf sunset, a man who'd habitually vacationed in Bridgehampton or Breckinridge before squandering the first act of his hard-earned retirement downwind from a goddamn horse barn.

Before long, Evan Shook had set aside his native wariness in order to nurture Ford Lipscomb's fantasy, which was the boilerplate back-nine fantasy of so many ultra-successful, ultra-resourceful American males: to live by the sea in perpetual sunshine, in a state with no income tax.

Jayne Lipscomb came down the stairs to report a pair of ospreys diving for fish in the tidal creeks.

"They're here every day," Evan Shook said. "Are you a birder?"

"No, but that's a thought."

"We've got a very active Audubon chapter down here."

"Did Ford tell you he's selling the trotters?"

Her husband broke in: "*We* are selling the trotters. Mutual decision."

Jayne Lipscomb sighed. "Gorgeous animals, but so much drama. My goodness."

"You'll love living in the Keys," Evan Shook said.

Ford Lipscomb handed up the check. "I'd like to buy a boat. Do a little fishing once I get the hang of it."

"First let's talk about window frames," his wife said. "Also, a skylight in the master bedroom? Is that doable, Mr. Shook?"

"Anything's doable."

A skylight inevitably would leak during the rainy season, as did all skylights in Florida, but Evan Shook felt unmoved to mention this because every whimsical add-on served to pad his wispy profit line. By the time the silicone sealant began to disintegrate, in two or three years, he'd be back in Syracuse, probably ass-deep in divorce papers.

Recently his mistress had delivered a curdling ultimatum: Dump the wife or else.

The else being a musician-slash-poet with whom she'd shared a cannabis vaporizer at the bluegrass festival—a mandolin player, she'd informed Evan Shook, knowing he would find that more threatening than a perky banjoist. The young man was *tall,* his mistress had added cruelly. Six-one in his socks.

Ford Lipscomb said, "When's the last time this island took a direct hit from a hurricane?"

Evan Shook chose to narrowly interpret the term "direct hit."

"Never," he declared. "Anyway, the building codes are much tougher now than in the old days. Heavy-duty glass, reinforced trusses—it's the law."

Jayne Lipscomb asked if he'd been keeping track of Tropical Storm Françoise on the Weather Channel. "Because this house, no offense, it's wide open. No windows, no doors, the roof could fly off to Cuba—"

"Oh, we'd board up the place," Evan Shook said with a patient-looking smile. "That storm isn't coming this way, don't you worry. It's rolling straight up through the Bahamas."

"Just what I told her," said Ford Lipscomb.

"But look at what Katrina did!" The wife, tracing an elaborate S in the air.

Evan Shook inconspicuously touched the breast pocket into which he'd tucked the couple's check, and he was comforted to feel the crisp paper rectangle beneath the fabric.

Ford Lipscomb rose. "There *is* one important detail we need to discuss."

An unpleasant contraction commenced in Evan Shook's colon.

"Fire away," he croaked, bracing for the deal breaker.

"Sewer or septic?" Ford Lipscomb said.

Evan Shook went blank, such was his apprehension. He saw the husband's lips moving but he heard not a word. Helplessly he shook his head.

"The house," Jayne Lipscomb intervened, from behind tortoiseshell frames. "Is it on a sewer main?"

Evan Shook nearly gurgled with relief. "No, no, we have state-of-the-art septic, totally aerobic," he said. "Come outside and I'll show you where the tank's buried!"

Neville took his boat up Victoria Creek ahead of the first band of heavy showers. He tied off in some mangroves, threw out an anchor, tested the bilge pump and crossed back to shore in a skiff run by some conch boys from the South Bight. The thought of being confined with Joyous for the storm's duration was withering, so he decided to walk back to Rocky Town and surprise one of his less surly girlfriends. On the way he avoided Bannister Point, feeling lucky to be alive. The white man Christopher could have shot him dead as a thief instead of firing over his head, and Neville wondered why he'd been spared. After giving it some thought, he decided there was no mercy at play; Christopher simply didn't wish to draw attention to himself.

For an American businessman needing favors from the Bahamas government, killing a local fisherman would be foolhardy and counterproductive. Neville's death would have brought the top police authorities from Nassau, generating an inquest that would have stalled the Curly Tail Lane development and poisoned public sentiment. All this Christopher must have known. Still, the ugly confrontation was a close call that had left Neville shaken and doubt-ridden. Never before had he been called a "beach nigger," and he wasn't sure what that meant beyond the obvious slur. Did Christopher know it was Neville's home that he had leveled on Green Beach? That it was Neville who'd pissed in the fuel tank of the offending backhoe, Neville who'd been stomped by Egg?

No, he cont know dot was me, thought Neville, *or he would hoff say sum ting more den juss 'hey beach nigger.' He would hoff warn me stay offa dot property, mon, or next time Egg, he gern break your goddamn arms and leg bones too!*

The rain was falling harder by the time Neville approached the settlement. He worried about the angry look of the ocean, a deep muddy purple, the furling wave tops sheared by the rising wind. Hurriedly he hiked up the hill to the shack belonging to the Dragon Queen.

The wooden shutters had been lowered and through the crooked slats came the sounds of a man and woman singing, or trying to. Neville selected the outside wall that was exposed most directly to the thumping raindrops, the noisiest wall, where his breathing wouldn't be heard by the occupants. There he positioned himself at a window and peeked through a gap between the sagging shutter and the warped pine frame.

Inside, the Dragon Queen was astride the broad lap of Egg, who had squeezed his ebony bulk into the pilot seat of her motorized scooter chair. The vehicle was rolling in tight circles around the dank little room—doing doughnuts is what the wild boys with cars called it. Neville could tell that Christopher's henchman and the hag were dizzy from their drunken orbits. Egg wore a sweat-soaked undershirt and possibly nothing else, his long yet oddly unmasculine feet protruding from beneath the Dragon Queen's rainbow skirt.

Neville muffled a gasp when his eyes fell upon Driggs, his former ward and companion. The haggard primate stood on the table amid empty rum bottles and plates of half-eaten fruit that was twitching with flies. He was holding his face over the yellow flame of a candle, lighting the bowl of a pipestem clenched in dingy teeth. Neville was appalled by this coarse new habit, and his anger swelled as the monkey studiously exhaled a train of smoke rings that dissipated in a swirl as a fresh gust rattled through the shutters. Driggs extended the pipe to arm's length and the Dragon Queen grabbed it as the scooter chair sped by, Egg cackling as he worked the joystick. The old woman got one heavy drag before losing her prize on the very next lap, Driggs reaching out to swipe it from her mottled lips.

The back of Neville's T-shirt was drenched, but the rain was warm, hurricane rain, and he didn't shrink from his spy post at the window. Inside the darkening room, Egg halted the motorized chair and snapped two fingers at the monkey, who blinked aloofly and spat into an upturned tambourine. A small commotion began, and bile rose in Neville's throat—the Dragon Queen and her new boyfriend were attempting to screw!

To and fro rocked the shiny scooter, its tires carping on the smooth-worn planks. The entanglement progressed clumsily, and soon the shack filled with adenoidal moans and raspy howls that melded into a lurid, tuneless yodel. Neville slapped his palms over both ears and turned away, the raindrops slicking his cheeks.

What is the awful nature of this woman's power? he wondered.

Thunder crashed and Neville dove to the ground as the shutter by his head banged open. Out leaped Driggs, still mouthing the pipe. Clutched in his paws were a Bic lighter and a tin of Dunhill tobacco. He never glanced Neville's way, pausing only to shed his lumpy diaper before loping down the road through the squall. Neville called the monkey's name but another thunderclap smothered his doleful cry. He sprang to his feet and gave chase, although in the downpour he soon lost sight of his fleet quarry. Spurred by guilt, Neville continued his blind pursuit, shouting miserably for the small friend he'd sold to the terrible voodoo priestess.

Sold for nothing.

His lungs were burning by the time he reached the old

Cooper place, which had been empty ever since Virgil Cooper went to Havana and fell for a tour guide named Miguelito. Neville ducked into the carport to rest and wait out the lightning. He was dripping like a horse. In a puddle at his feet floated an empty tobacco tin, which Neville picked up and examined solemnly.

Of course the brand was Dunhill.

"Driggs?" he piped excitedly. "You come out!"

But the monkey wasn't there. Neville checked every room, every closet, every cupboard of the dilapidated house. So leathered were the soles of Neville's feet—he seldom wore shoes—that he was unbothered by the rubble of broken glass and splintery planks. He found no other trace of Driggs, although upon returning to the carport he spotted something he'd previously overlooked—a fly rod propped upright in a dry corner.

It was an expensive piece of fishing equipment, too fancy and specialized for the locals. There was no rust on the metal guides of the rod, and Neville tasted wet salt when he touched his tongue to the cork. He wondered if the wealthy tourist fisherman who owned the outfit had crossed paths with the bedraggled monkey, and perhaps out of pity had adopted him.

An hour passed until the wave of thunderstorms rolled by and the rain quit. With fly rod in hand, Neville set out at full stride in the deepening night.

Rosa said, "I've always wanted to do it in a hurricane."

"Technically, this is pre-hurricane."

"Don't be a spoilsport, Andrew."

"It's six hours away, you said."

"So, consider this a warm-up."

Yancy kissed each of her nipples, then he rested a cheek on her tummy.

"If only the storm wasn't named Françoise. That is *so* weak," Rosa said. She ruffled his hair. "Hey, what was that catchy little tune you were humming earlier?"

"When?"

"While you were going down on me. You don't remember humming?"

"Oh, that was 'Yellow Submarine.' "

"So you think of me as basically your sex kazoo."

"I only hum when I'm happy," said Yancy. Sometimes he just floated off into a zone; it had happened once with Bonnie—a Paul Simon song—and she'd boxed his ears saying, "You and Julio get out of there!"

Rosa whistled. "Listen to that wind blow. Holy crap!"

"Andrew wasn't the most ferocious name for a hurricane and look what happened."

"Andrew's a fine name, Andrew. You kidding?"

"Too preppy for a killer storm. That's what they said before it hit Miami."

"Who said? Some girl you were dating?"

"Her name was Mariah."

"Oh, she was just jealous," Rosa said. " 'They call the wind Ma-rye-ah'—don't you remember that one? The poor baby wanted a storm named after herself! Tell me your age at the time of this romance."

"Twenty-two." Yancy was beginning to think in a serious way about Françoise, wondering if he and Rosa might possibly use the heavy weather to their advantage.

"When I was twenty-two I went to Paris," she said. "Graduation present from the folks. One day I went to the Rodin museum and I got totally turned on by all those sexy sculptures. You ever been there? He had a thing for nymphs and minotaurs. Incredible stuff. Anyway, I meet this semi-cute exchange student from Boston and we end up having a quickie in the bathroom."

"At the Rodin."

"There was a window. You could look out at the garden and see *The Thinker*."

"I want to believe this story," Yancy said, "with all my soul."

"Swear to God, Andrew. First and only time in a museum."

Yancy had never been to France. He imagined a misty rain falling at the time. "How was the flight today?" he asked Rosa.

"Not fun. The poor thing sitting next to me said two whole rosaries—one in English, one in Creole. Lord, what happened to your legs?"

"A monkey assaulted me."

"You mean her husband assaulted you."

"It's no joke. This was a horrible creature."

She remarked upon his recent travails with animals. "First some deranged dog in Miami practically chews your ass off, and now this. Lucky you're banging a licensed health-care practitioner."

"I did nothing to provoke the little bastard."

"Clearly it's all payback for abducting Johnny Mendez's cat. Surely you believe in karma—I never met a cop who didn't," Rosa said. "There's some goop in my kit bag. We should dress those wounds."

"The least of my problems. I capped off an otherwise productive afternoon by flogging Eve Stripling's boyfriend with a fly rod."

"And that would be your idea of stealth. Very slick."

"I'm pretty sure he didn't know who I was, but still it was a tight spot."

Rosa took a deep breath, lifting Yancy's head.

She said, "I'm afraid I've got some lousy news."

"Not right now. Please?" He blew softly into her belly button.

"I didn't mention it earlier because I didn't want to spoil the mood. Andrew, don't deny that you're susceptible to untimely distractions."

"I am," he said, "cursed with an overactive mind."

"The bullet that killed O'Peele came from the same weapon that killed Charles Phinney—the .357 they found in the doctor's condo. I saw the ballistics this morning."

"How is that bad news? It's exactly what we expected."

"The Key West police also think it's marvelous," Rosa said. "In fact, they're so overjoyed they want to close the Phinney case, ASAP. They're saying O'Peele shot the kid over drugs, then drove in a haze back to Miami. Once he sobered up and realized what he'd done, he blew his brains out. That's their story and they're sticking to it."

"Jackoffs!" Yancy sat up. "Is there any evidence that O'Peele and Phinney ever met?"

"Nope. I asked the same thing."

"Or that the doctor was down in Key West that night? Did he buy a poncho and a sun mask? Did he rent a moped on Duval Street?"

Rosa shook her head. "All they've got is the matching slug from the gun."

"And a dead boat mate that nobody cares about."

"How do you think I feel? I'm the one who sent them the bullet."

Yancy said, "They can't close the Phinney case without you ruling that O'Peele was a suicide. Otherwise their lame theory falls apart."

"It's easy to pull the plug on an investigation without officially saying so. Somehow the file just crawls into a drawer."

"Yeah, I know." Yancy put on a clean shirt and a pair of khaki shorts, Rosa cocking an eyebrow as she watched.

"Where do you think you're going, Inspector, on such a dark and stormy night?"

"I left my favorite fly rod in a vacant house up the road."

"We'll go get it tomorrow. Right now I'm craving a beer and conch salad."

"I happen to know just the place."

Rosa smiled and kicked off the sheets. "Kindly toss me my panties."

"But here's the deal—anybody asks, we're married, okay? We came to Andros to do some fishing and look around for a second home. Now we're stuck here because of the storm."

"Do we have any children? And where are we from?"

"Boca Raton, obviously. You're still a doctor—let's say a thoracic surgeon."

"Close enough."

"Our son, Kyle, just made the traveling lacrosse team at Pine Crest. We have twin daughters in the gifted program. Our dog is an incontinent pug named Cheney."

"Perfect," said Rosa, "and we all live in a yellow submarine."

She went into the bathroom and began brushing

her hair. "What's your fictitious line of work, Andrew? Should anyone ask."

"Investments, meaning I mooch off an obscene family trust fund. Shale oil—no, better, microprocessors." Yancy used the corner of a sheet to wipe the sand off his feet.

Rosa reappeared waving a crinkled white tube. "Bring me those mangled legs of yours. By the way, I demand to see your alleged assailant."

"They say he was in the Johnny Depp movies but got the axe."

"These days every movie has a monkey," she said. "Monkeys are the bomb."

"Not this mangy little psycho. Hey, Doc, take it easy."

"Hold still, please. Do you have an actual plan for trapping Eve and her murderous beau? Or are we basically flying blind?"

"Of course I've got a plan," Yancy said.

"An intelligent, fully formed plan?"

"Define fully formed."

"I knew it," said Rosa.

"Ouch, that stings! Be careful."

Yet secretly he marveled at her touch, so tender for a coroner.

Nineteen

Claspers thought it was crazy to leave the Caravan chocked on the tarmac at Moxey's in the path of a hurricane. He wanted to fly it back to Florida, but Christopher Grunion said no way, amigo, are you stranding me and my old lady on this fly-turd island. When Claspers had suggested they all leave Andros before the storm drew close, Grunion said he and Eve weren't going anywhere. He said their house was built like a goddamn fortress.

"Where I'm staying, it's a death trap," Claspers had remarked.

Either Grunion hadn't gotten the hint, or he didn't want Claspers as a guest. In any event, Claspers was stuck. Maybe the storm would miss Lizard Cay entirely, or maybe it would smash the place head-on, in which case that lovely seaplane would end up as scrap aluminum.

Claspers said, "But what do I know, sweetie? I'm only the pilot."

"Yeah, mon, dot's you. Sky King." The pretty bartender brought him his third drink of the evening.

"Is it still a Category Two?"

"Dey say trey, mebbe four."

"Lively," muttered Claspers.

The wind clawed at the palm thatching over the conch shack. No music was playing but the radio remained the center of attention because it was tuned to the Nassau weather station. The gusty conditions had disabled most of the TV dishes in Rocky Town—Claspers had seen one lying upturned in the roadway—and many residents seeking storm updates had come to the outdoor restaurant. The young Androsians, who'd never been through a hurricane, laughed and joked. The older ones positioned themselves closer to the radio and kept their voices low. Françoise was reported to be roaring along the Exuma chains; even if Andros escaped a direct hit, the island would take a battering. By daybreak it would be over.

Claspers held his glass with both hands, admiring the miniature wavelets on the coppery surface of the scotch. He was one of a half dozen white customers, including the rangy American he'd met at Moxey's airport. Andrew, the fly fisherman. Sitting next to him at the bar was a Latin woman who probably smelled as heavenly as she looked. Claspers had a serious buzz going, a down-island buzz.

The woman at the fisherman's side made Claspers think of another beauty he knew in Barranquilla, back in the old times, a woman he would have married if she hadn't already had a husband and if the husband hadn't been a macho hothead who liked to shoot people in the mouth.

Which Claspers well knew because he was working for the man at the time, running loads of grass up to South Bimini.

Donna had been the wife's name. By now she'd be in her fifties and more lovely than ever. A few years ago Claspers picked up a rumor that her husband was machine-gunned on his way to a bordello, which is what happens when you hire a half-wit cousin to armor your Escalade. On some nights Claspers fantasized about flying back to Colombia, showing up at Donna's doorstep with a grin, a hard-on and a bottle of Dom. The airstrip he remembered well, and also the Moorish-style villa at the north end; in particular, a second-floor bedroom with a balcony overlooking the valley.

To the bartender Claspers said: "Buy those two sweethearts a round on me."

Afterward the couple returned the gesture and motioned for the pilot to move down the bar and join them. Andrew introduced the Latin woman as his wife, Rosa, and said she'd arrived on a flight that afternoon.

Claspers chuckled. "Your timing sucks, no offense."

"Oh, we'll find something to do," Rosa said. "You ever flown through a hurricane?"

"Naw, but I've slept through a few. It's easier than you think." Claspers took a hearty sip, demonstrating his pre-storm preparations.

The woman said she was a surgeon. "Hopefully nobody'll get hurt, but I always travel with a kit of instruments."

"On this island," said the pilot, "that makes you the whole freaking hospital."

Somebody turned up the radio. The somber voice from Nassau reported that Hurricane Françoise was now "packing" winds of 105 miles per hour. Movement of the storm continued north-northwest.

The fisherman set a hand on Claspers's shoulder. "Can I ask you something? We heard your boss is the one who's building Curly Tail Lane. Grunion is his name?"

"That's him," said Claspers.

Leaning in close, Rosa confided that she and her husband were looking to buy in the Bahamas. "Andrew really loves this place," she added, "and I do, too."

"You should see it when the sun comes out."

"Point is," the husband went on, "do you think Mr. Grunion would mind if you introduced him to a potential customer?"

"I think Mr. Grunion would be fucking thrilled."

"We'd rather not deal with any Bay Street realtors. And we'd be paying cash, if that matters."

"Cash is never bad." Claspers liked these people, and briefly he considered telling them the truth: that Grunion's resort project wasn't exactly advancing at a breakneck pace; that Grunion was still getting hassled and tossed by the bureaucrats in Nassau; that a vandal had targeted the job site; that only two other buyers—one from Taiwan and the other from Dubai—had put down actual deposits for time-share units.

However, even in a semi-trashed condition the pilot perceived there might be something juicy in it for himself, a commission from the boss, if a sale was forthcoming. Who was Claspers to stand between this earnest young couple and their balmy vision of paradise?

Rosa said, "What about tonight? It's not raining anymore."

Claspers cast a skeptical eye skyward. There would be a few hours of lull until the next storm band, but he wasn't in the deferential mode necessary to deal with Grunion. "Now's not a real good time," he said.

The man shrugged one shoulder. "We'll be on the first plane outta here after the hurricane. I got the whole damn trust committee waiting on me back in Boca. Maybe it'll work out on another trip, if there's anything left of this place."

Claspers stood up. "Let me make a quick call. Sorry, I didn't catch your last name."

"Gates," said Yancy, "as in cousin Bill." He flinched when Rosa jabbed his ribs.

The pilot didn't notice. He took out a waterproof radio phone and stepped through the puddles toward the tall pile of conch shells by the boat ramp. Eve, the girlfriend, answered on the other end. After listening to Claspers's pitch, she accused him of being wasted.

"What are you doing? There's a hurricane coming, you idiot."

"It's just I think these folks are for real. I didn't want Mr. Grunion to miss a good opportunity is all."

"How would you know if they're real or not?"

Claspers said, "I didn't know such things, I woulda been dead a long time ago."

Thinking: *Jesus, I am drunk.*

Next Grunion got on the line and chewed him out.

"Okay. Forget I called," the pilot said.

"This guy, so where does he get his money?"

Claspers told him about the trust-committee remark. "His name is Andrew Gates, as in Bill."

"Horseshit," Grunion said.

"Fine, I'm going back to the tiki bar. See you after the apocalypse."

"Wait, tell me about the wife."

"Cuban girl, a solid nine-point-eight out of ten. Rosa's her name. Seems super smart."

"They all seem smart when you're toasted."

"Not all of 'em, trust me," Claspers said with a damp hack. "This one's a doctor."

"Whatever. You think you can find the house or should I send Egg down?"

"Christ, don't send Egg."

When the pilot returned to the bar, he informed the couple that the meeting with Grunion was on. "If we can find a damn cab," he said.

Andrew said no problem and waved to a fellow in a Rasta cap who was playing dominoes at a side table. "That's Philip, my wheelman."

Claspers recognized him from the regulars at the airport. Philip was unenthusiastic about making the run to Bannister Point, but a twenty-dollar bill from Andrew improved his outlook.

The taxi van was parked in the fluttering halo of a streetlight. Claspers sat down in the second row and Mrs. Gates got in beside him. Her husband, the fly fisherman, didn't.

"What's up?" Claspers asked.

"Rosa's taking it from here. For now I'd prefer to hang back. Don't worry—she knows what's what in the real estate game."

The pilot grunted. "Mr. Grunion will be pissed."

"Mr. Grunion will have his hands full." The fisherman winked and shut the door.

Philip stomped the accelerator and off they went. Claspers sipped from a go-cup and chatted with Mrs. Gates and thoroughly enjoyed every minute of the ride.

It had been Rosa's idea to meet the couple alone because Yancy couldn't possibly accompany her. Nick Stripling's widow would recognize him face-to-face. Yancy hadn't

argued about Rosa's decision though he should have.
Possibly his judgment had been softened by tequila;
Rosa had brought a bottle of Cuervo from Miami, and
they'd had a celebratory taste in the motel room while she
treated his monkey wounds. She'd been so jazzed about
getting a chance to play cop, selecting for the occasion a
pair of egregious Christian Louboutin sandals that were
certain to catch Eve's eye and establish Rosa as a serious
shopper for condos.

"Go big or go home," Rosa had said. "That's my motto."
For earrings she'd chosen teardrops of pure jade, a past-
life gift about which Yancy knew better than to inquire.

The plan was far from foolproof, but the start had
been promising. It didn't take an FBI profiler to predict
that Grunion's lonesome pilot would be down at the conch
shack—where else in Rocky Town would he go when
grounded by weather?

As for Grunion's receptivity to a cold call, Yancy had
counted on a condition known among developers as acute
hurricane anxiety. If Françoise flattened Lizard Cay, the
Curly Tail Lane project would be in deep trouble. Grunion would have a wretched time trying to attract new
buyers—especially those willing to overpay, a key demo-
graphic in the vacation-home market. Hurricanes being
only slightly less damaging to real estate values than volcanic eruptions and leaky nuclear plants, Grunion was
now probably glued to the Weather Channel with his gut
full of refluxed acid, wondering how in God's name to
build and promote a five-star island retreat if the island's
one-star infrastructure was destroyed.

Yancy didn't know whether Eve and Grunion had
tapped out Stripling's Medicare loot and paid cash for

the Green Beach property, or whether they'd been brazen enough to apply for a bank loan. It didn't really matter; without pre-construction sales, Curly Tail Lane would fail, which is why Grunion didn't hang up on Claspers and blow off the young American couple who were waiting out the storm in Rocky Town.

Rosa's mission was to set a trap. An acting job, as she said; no superhero shit. She'd simply let it be known that her "husband" Andrew was determined to own a piece of this gorgeous tropic isle, no matter what the hurricane did. Better still, the couple was interested in purchasing two or three condos, not just one.

Then she'd explain to Eve Stripling that, because of the family's complex asset structure, the fund transfers and contract signings must take place back in Florida. There Yancy's pal in Homeland Security would have agents waiting to detain Eve and her boyfriend, based on allegations of previous illegal border entries. The incriminating testimony would come from none other than K. J. Claspers, desperately hoping to save his pilot's certificate from revocation. It would be Yancy's task to see that Eve and Grunion remained in custody until prosecutors could assemble at least one of the murder cases.

That was the plan, anyway. By now Rosa was at the house on Bannister Point, and Yancy was worried.

Ever since the night she seduced him on the autopsy table he had wondered how to satisfy such an appetite for excitement. Sending her off to meet with a pair of murderers was one way to spice up a date weekend, but experimenting with variable-speed sex toys in a bounce house would have been safer.

Yancy knew nothing about Christopher Grunion

beyond his homicidal capacities; there wasn't a trace of the man in the public records or state crime computers. That Eve Stripling's companion might be using an alias wasn't surprising, but it heightened Yancy's anxiety about Rosa meeting with the man. If she didn't return by ten sharp, Yancy would go to Grunion's place and check on her. His watch now said eight forty-six.

The wind blew a fat palmetto bug from the thatching and it landed on the opposite bar, next to a plate of cracked conch. A tourist woman who'd been enjoying the native entrée emitted a shriek and nearly tumbled backward. Her companions, all sporting ripely sunburned cheeks, joined in the squealing and pointing. The six-legged intruder composed itself and with probing antennae began to stalk the drippings of a half-finished piña colada. Hysterically the patrons appealed to the bartender, who indicated an unwillingness to intervene.

Yancy couldn't stand the racket. He walked around to where the first woman had been sitting, and with a bare palm he flattened the insect. The crunch sounded like a boot heel on a pistachio. There was a smatter of tipsy applause and one or two supportive shouts, which Yancy didn't acknowledge. If it had happened back in Florida, he'd be writing up the place.

He used a cocktail napkin to wipe the roach bits off his hand as the aggrieved female patrons gathered up their pocketbooks and scrunchies. They departed in an ungrateful flock just as a frayed-looking older fellow walked in and propped a fully assembled fly rod against the bar rail.

"Who is that gentleman?" Yancy asked the bartender.

"Dot's Neville Stafford. Poor mon bin out all night lookin' for his monkey."

"We've all been there. Let me buy him a beer."

The American sat down beside him and Neville said thanks for the Kalik.

"Rough time?"

"Yeah, mon."

"I ran into your flea-bitten buddy," said the American.

He showed Neville the bite marks and scratches on his legs. Neville felt bad. The American said the monkey had run off in a rainstorm after a fracas at the abandoned house.

Then he said: "Mr. Stafford, I believe that's my fly rod."

Neville nodded and set it by the man's stool. He told him the errant monkey's name was Driggs and mentioned the Johnny Depp connection. The American said he'd first seen the animal riding a motorized wheelchair with the Dragon Lady.

"Queen," Neville corrected him. "Dragon Queen."

"She sort of freaked me out."

"She freak everbotty out."

"Isn't her boyfriend that huge bald dude works for Christopher Grunion?"

Neville said, "How you know Mistuh Chrissofer?"

"I heard he's building a fancy tourist resort down on the beach."

"Yeah, mon. *My* beach." Neville stopped talking and finished his beer. The American ordered him another one.

"You sell him that land?"

"He tore down my house and put up a fence with a got-tam padlock. Ain't no hoppy situation, mon. It was my hoff sister made the deal. Nobody axe me." Neville went through the story of the sale. He couldn't tell if the American, like others, thought he was crazy.

The man finished listening and said, "That's a lot of money, Mr. Stafford. You could have been rich."

"In wot way?"

The American broke into a warm smile. "Exactly. My name's Andrew."

His grip was firm when he shook Neville's hand. He said he lived on Big Pine Key, in the southernmost part of Florida. Neville said he had been twice to Miami and once to Fort Lauderdale, to have a mole on his neck removed. The American told him about his own house, about the hot-pink Gulf sunsets and the small wild deer that roamed the island. The deer were no larger than dogs, the man said, which Neville found fascinating.

"Every evening they'd come into this clearing to eat sprouts and twigs," the man named Andrew said. "I'd sit on the deck and watch them do their thing until it got dark."

"Ain't no deer on Andros dot I ever saw," Neville remarked. "Only pigs."

"But then some guy named Shook from upstate New York, he bought the lot next to mine and started putting up a huge house, a ridiculous fucking house. It's way too tall for the building codes but obviously he paid off somebody," the American went on. "Worst part? He doesn't even intend to live there, Mr. Stafford. Can't abide the heat and mosquitoes. All he wants to do is unload the monstrosity on some clueless sucker, take the money and go back north."

The American seemed deeply bothered by what his neighbor was doing to the land. Neville had never run into a tourist like Andrew, although he'd met a few like Mr. Shook.

"Wot 'bout dose lil' deer?" Neville asked.

"They don't come anymore. They can't eat plywood."

The man went still. Neville asked him what he was going to do.

"What are *you* going to do?" the American said.

Neville told him about recruiting the Dragon Queen to put a voodoo hex on Christopher Grunion. "But it dint woyk," he added. "And, at de end, she trick me outta my monkey."

"I'm not sure she got the best of that deal."

"Dot's true." Neville had to laugh.

"Movie stars, right? Nothing but trouble. Can I show you something?" The American took out a gold badge and held it close to his lap, below the bar counter, so that no one but Neville could see it.

"You police?" Neville whispered.

The man named Andrew put the badge away. He said, "Law enforcement authorities in the U.S. are very interested in Mr. Grunion—and that's not his real name. We believe the Curly Tail Lane project is being financed with moneys obtained illegally, by fraud. We also believe he's quite dangerous."

Neville nodded. "Yeah, dot asshole shodda gun at me."

"Really? When did this happen?"

"Big fucking gun, mon. Outside his house up Bannister Point."

"Shit." The man anxiously glanced at his wristwatch.

Neville drained his beer bottle thinking he and the American had something in common. Both were beset by greedy intruders destroying something rare, something that couldn't be replaced.

The light bulbs hanging from the beams of the conch

shack flickered and dimmed; soon the island would lose electricity. Neville wondered where Driggs would take shelter during the hurricane. Not with the voodoo witch, he hoped. What kind of demon skank would teach a monkey how to smoke?

"Foyst time I gon see de Dragon Queen, I bring a private ting belong to Chrissofer."

"What was that?" the American asked.

"A sleeve from a fishin' shoyt like you got on dere, 'cept it was blue. Dragon Queen supposed to pudda coyse on de mon and take care my prollem on Green Beach. But den notting hoppen—"

"It was a sleeve?" The man named Andrew planted his elbows on the bar and pressed the knuckles of his hands together. To Neville he looked a bit pale.

"Yeah, a sleeve dot been toyn off. It was in Chrissofer's garbage."

"Torn off or *cut* off?"

"I tink cut." Neville made a scissor motion with his fingers.

"Oh Jesus."

"Wot's mottah?"

"Do you have a car, Mr. Stafford?"

"No, mon. I got a boat, but—"

"Never mind." The American slapped some cash on the bar and disappeared up the road, into the swaying shadows.

Neville picked up the man's expensive fishing rod and made his way to Joyous's apartment where after a quick poke he lay awake, listening to the coconut trees shake and wondering if the American was really a policeman, and if the things he'd said were true.

Twenty

Agent John Wesley Weiderman, five pounds lighter after his bout with spoiled shellfish, had intrepidly returned to Florida on the hunt for Plover Chase. He was armed with a promising new lead supplied by the fugitive's husband, a retired dermatologist who'd contacted the Oklahoma State Bureau of Investigation.

Dr. Clifford Witt had uncovered a series of credit card charges made by the suspect under the alias of Bonnie Witt and posted on a Visa account to which Dr. Witt had access (online password: nookyluv2). The purchases, all made in Key West, included groceries, lip gloss, blond hair coloring, domestic beer, condoms, dental floss, a car rental, four jerry cans, ninety-seven dollars' worth of gasoline and a room-service charge at a Best Western on South Roosevelt.

"We run out of cash so we had to go plastic," explained the man inside the hotel room, number 217.

He gave his name as Clyde Barrow, and he seemed unflustered by having a lawman at the door. Then again, Agent John Wesley Weiderman adhered to a low-key approach.

"Do you know a woman named Plover Chase?" he asked.

"She left me, dude. Hit the bricks."

"Where'd she go?"

"Back on the run, I guess. Once an outlaw, whatever."

"Let's start with your real name."

The man said, "Okay, okay, you got me."

He was doughy and sunburned. He wore a black muscle shirt that said: OLD KEY WEST—A DRINKING VILLAGE WITH A SLIGHT FISHING PROBLEM!

"I'm Cody Parish," he said.

Agent John Wesley Weiderman didn't respond immediately. He was assessing the judicial prospects of his case, which were suddenly dimmer.

"Yo, as in Cody Parish the victim?"

"Got it," said John Wesley Weiderman.

It was the person with whom Plover Chase had notoriously swapped sex in exchange for good school grades. Now he was all grown up. He was, in fact, losing his hair.

"Ms. Chase and me, we hooked up again after all this time. Actually, she tracked me down on Facebook. Talk about a true-life fairy tale—it's all in my diary, I mean *everything*."

"May I read it?"

"First I better get with a lawyer," said Cody. "See, it's gonna be a book and then probably a movie. That's why I need to be careful nobody steals the good stuff and leaks it."

The agent asked Cody if Plover Chase had abducted him against his will. Cody said, "She's got something way more lethal than a gun. You know what they say—pussy is undefeated. That's from Merle Haggard himself."

"So she didn't threaten or physically harm you."

"Stompin' my heart to pieces, doesn't that count?"

"It was her English class where you first met, right? Back in the day."

"Not regular English but AP English," Cody said. "That means, like, super advanced."

"Got it." John Wesley Weiderman didn't have a sarcastic bone in his body.

"I love her the same now as I did back then. It's like nothing ever changed, time standing still, whatever."

"Why do you think she left you this time?"

"Dude, come on. Why do they do *anything* they do? Yesterday she shows up in a green convertible, packs her shit and off she goes up the highway. Monster hormone attack is my theory."

The agent didn't doubt that Plover Chase was gone; there were no women's clothes in the closet, no lipstick tubes or makeup items in the bathroom. On the unmade queen-sized bed lay a sad stack of men's magazines, raw jerk-off material that even a loser like Cody would have concealed had a female been in the vicinity.

"Any idea where she went?"

"Not really," said Cody. "Home maybe?"

"Was your family aware that you two re-connected?"

"Dad passed six years ago and Mom's in assisted living, thinks she's Shirley MacLaine. And guess what, bro, I'm thirty years old and I can bone whoever I want, long as she's legal age and says yes. And Ms. Chase, she said yes, yes, yes, and *more* yes, please, Cody baby! Bottom line, I didn't break any laws."

John Wesley Weiderman pointed out that it was illegal to aid and abet a wanted criminal.

"Only thing I abetted was rockin' her world. They gonna send me to the penitentiary for that?" Cody was striving to appear indignant.

"A jury might see it your way," said the OSBI agent, "but good lawyers cost money. Maybe by then you'll be rich from selling your journal, right?"

Cody Baby didn't appear to be emotionally pulverized by his lover's abandonment. He was, however, troubled by the possibility of being prosecuted.

"Listen, I just remembered," he said. "There's a guy lives on Big Pine Key, Ms. Chase had a thing with him for a while."

"I spoke with the gentleman. He used to be a police detective." John Wesley Weiderman wouldn't soon forget Andrew Yancy baring his ass to present his alleged wild-dog bites.

"Well, that's where she might be," Cody said without rancor. "With *him.*"

"He told me their affair was over."

"Maybe he's not the one calling the shots. Obviously you never met Ms. Chase."

"Someday," said the agent.

"She wasn't too jazzed about the dude gettin' another girlfriend, okay? She acted all like isn't-that-nice, but I could tell she was seriously frosted."

"So you think she went to win him back."

"You know how whacked chicks can get. The guy's new girl is a doctor, 'kay? Ms. Chase couldn't deal with that, is my theory. It's all in the diary. I do a hundred words every night, not longhand but on my iPad. That still counts, right?"

"For sure."

Agent John Wesley Weiderman fully realized that pursuing Plover Chase was an unfair burden on the taxpayers of Oklahoma. Her capture would not make the state a safer place. It would instead make a tabloid celebrity of the ex-schoolteacher, and possibly a best-selling author of her now-grown-up victim, whom John Wesley Weiderman perceived as a grubby oversexed slacker. What a circus that would be, Plover Chase returning to Tulsa in handcuffs. Plus the waste of a perfectly good jail cell.

But Agent Weiderman was a follower of orders, and there were worse places to be sent than the Florida Keys. He'd diligently scouted the health department's website and located a relatively clean seafood joint, where for lunch he had eaten grilled mahi served with Cuban plantains and black beans. It was maybe the best meal he'd ever eaten that wasn't a rib eye.

"What about those jerry cans?" he asked Cody Parish.

Parish gave a loose-jointed shrug.

"On the Visa bill were four six-gallon gasoline containers from Ace Hardware."

"Weird." Cody said Ms. Chase must have purchased the items on a day she went out alone.

"Have you ever known her to be violent?"

"No way," Cody said. "But, like I told you, we were in major love."

"Maybe she feels different about Mr. Yancy."

"There's a wild streak, for sure. It's all in my diary."

"We'll be in touch about that," the agent said. He headed toward the door.

"You catch her, don't let on it was me that told you where to look."

"Of course not. We protect our sources." Which is

what John Wesley Weiderman was trained to say, and almost always they bought it.

Flip-flops slapping on the floor, Cody Parish trailed the agent to the stairway. "Twenty gallons' worth of gas cans, what do you figure that's all about?"

"Twenty-four."

Cody's spotty lips moved as he redid the math in his head, six times four. "Maybe she's just stocking up for the drive home. Doesn't wanna waste time stopping at service stations."

John Wesley Weiderman said, "I didn't think of that."

Because only a chowderhead would think of that. People used jerry cans for fueling lawn mowers or ATVs, but there was no good reason to carry four of them unless you had a bigger job in mind.

Rosa Campesino seldom thought about Daniel, her ex-husband. What brought him to mind now, while she sipped wine with Eve Stripling on the porch of an Andros Island beach house, was a whiff of syrupy men's cologne.

Beast Down it was called, Daniel's favorite. She'd never met another man who wore the stuff. However, Rosa knew it wasn't Daniel talking on the phone in the next room because Daniel was dead, having witlessly steered his two-thousand-dollar mountain bike over a cliff. The autopsy had been performed with competence in Bozeman, Montana. As a professional courtesy the report had been faxed to Rosa, who'd made copies for the paddleboard instructor and each of the three other women Daniel had been fucking during the marrriage, the lubricious details unearthed by Rosa's divorce attorney.

"I really like those shoes," Eve Stripling said.

"Thank you. They're seriously comfy."

"What happens when all that shiny red color comes off the bottoms? Do you have to, like, get 'em spray-painted?"

Rosa said, "That's a darn good question."

This was when light chatter filled the air, before things fell apart. Eve was holding a tiny cinnamon-colored dog, probably the same runny-eyed furball that Andrew had saved from drowning.

"How much longer will Mr. Grunion be on the phone?" Rosa asked.

"He's tied up on a business call," said Eve. "How about some more wine?"

Rosa said sure. She looked at her watch—still plenty of time.

"Maybe you could tell me how the units at Curly Tail Lane are priced, pre-construction. My husband and I are interested in a couple of two-bedrooms facing the water. We'd pay cash at closing."

"No financing?" Eve looked more amused than excited.

"We'll have to do the deal back in Florida," Rosa continued, "at the office of Andrew's trust managers. They're the ones who move the money around."

"I don't think so."

"Oh, we can Skype your people in from Nassau."

"That's not what I meant," said Eve. "I don't think we're interested."

Rosa held steady. "Not interested in an all-cash deal? Seriously?"

"Honey, there's nothing serious about any of this, and we both know it."

The dog jumped down and curled up in a corner. Eve

opened another bottle of merlot. Waves rumbled out across the reef line, the wind thrashed the palms and Rosa tapped the toe of one of her French sandals.

She said, "My mistake, Eve. I thought you and your husband were in the business of selling condos."

"Thing about this place, it's easy to make friends if you treat the right people right. I'll give you a for-instance. We made a good Bahamian friend at the Immigration office, and guess what? She says nobody named Rosa Gates cleared through Nassau the last few days. Not Fresh Creek or Congo Town either. There *was* a Rosa Campesino—"

"I kept my maiden name," Rosa interjected, although she knew it was over.

"Did your 'husband' keep his maiden name, too? Because there's no Andrew Gates on the entry list, either." Eve with her stretched white jeans and tanned feet was rocking on a wooden swing, not in a lazing tempo.

She said, "Guy named Andrew Yancy came through Nassau on his way here to Lizard Cay. He used to be a cop down in the Keys. I've met the man, so just cut the bullshit."

Rosa set down her wine glass. "Tell Mr. Grunion I'm sorry to have wasted your evening. Clearly there's been a misunderstanding."

"Oh, give it up."

Calmly Rosa reached for her handbag and rose. "Too bad," she said.

Eve Stripling cocked her head. "Honey, you're not goin' anywhere."

At that moment a door to the house flung open, uncorking a fresh gust of Beast Down mixed with sweat. The smell was so strong that Rosa feared she might gag.

• • •

Against the wind he ran; uphill, downhill. Yancy was no athlete, not anymore. His lungs heaved, his legs cramped. The pocked pavement was strewn with sharp pebbles that gouged his feet.

Simple pain he could take; blood, too. It was the fucking up that was unbearable to contemplate, his own potentially disastrous failure to see the obvious.

An approaching vehicle turned out to be Philip's taxi heading back toward town, reggae thumping from the open windows. The van was dark except for the glow of a joint that Claspers the pilot was smoking in the front next to Philip. Yancy waved both arms but he was too gassed to shout. As the taxi sped past, Yancy noticed a hunched dark shape on the roof—Mr. Stafford's monkey, clinging grimly to the luggage rack.

Yancy ran on until he spotted a kid's bicycle lying beside a chicken pen in front of a cinder-block house. The windows of the place had been boarded for the storm, and through a crack Yancy saw light and heard voices. Uprighting the bike, he pedaled away on half-flat tires, his knees bumping the handlebars.

Egg loomed as a foremost concern when Yancy approached Bannister Point. Yancy reviewed his own rudimentary disabling skills, cop skills, understanding that he'd never fought a man of Egg's size whose reflexes hadn't been slowed by drugs or booze. Tonight Egg would be on full alert and sober as a hangman, not easy to surprise and bring down. In consideration of the goon's recent dental woes, Yancy planned to aim first for the jawbone.

A lead pipe or a marlin gaff would have been helpful,

but he settled for a hefty pine bough that he found where he ditched the bicycle, a quarter mile from the house. Under low purple clouds he walked the rest of the way. The property was lit up like a used-car lot; Yancy heard the rumble of a gasoline-powered generator, a luxury in the out-islands. It meant that one could spend the duration of a major hurricane in air-conditioned comfort listening to Puccini or Van Halen, as long as the walls didn't blow down.

Yancy scouted swiftly, his footfalls muted by the noise from the shuddering trees. Egg wasn't lurking out front; the backyard looked clear, too. Eve Stripling could be seen alone on the porch, untangling some wind chimes. Yancy snuck along the perimeter of the house peering in windows; no sign of Rosa, no sign of anyone. He felt a hot coal in his gut.

Then Eve's mutt started barking madly, and he thought: *Oh, what the hell.*

He opened the front door and walked inside.

Standing in the foyer clutching a broken tree branch, expecting the absurd little canine to come lunging for his ankles, a creature that would have drowned or gotten gobbled by sharks if he hadn't rescued it . . .

This is what I get for one minor act of decency.

The yapping stopped.

Yancy took a couple of steps. Paused to listen.

Peeked around a hallway corner—nothing.

A voice said, "Up here, asshole."

Yancy climbed the stairs and there the man sat on a slick burgundy Super Rollie scooter, Yancy's 12-gauge Beretta angled across his lap. Hanging from a brass hat rack in a corner, next to a full-sized print of the famous

Audubon spoonbill, was a dirty blaze-orange poncho and a couple of camo sun masks. Outside, a broken shutter banged and banged.

"Where's Rosa?" Yancy said.

"Sit down." He motioned toward a straight-backed chair.

"Where is she?"

"I've got a shotgun and you've got what—a piece of fuckin' firewood?"

"Nick, I asked you a question."

"Eve said you'd figure it out right away. I said you're not that bright."

"And I say you're bright enough not to shoot a cop." With his free hand Yancy took out the police badge on loan from Johnny Mendez. "See? I'm back on the force."

"First place," Nicholas Stripling said, "there's no law says a man can't cut off his own arm."

"Maybe not."

"I know for a goddamn fact."

"There's a law against murder," Yancy said. "You killed Charlie Phinney and Dr. O'Peele, and you tried to kill me."

"Ha, try to prove *any* of that shit."

"I will. In the meantime let's start with the Medicare rip-off," Yancy said. "Hey, guess what happens when the feds find out you're still alive."

"Who's gonna tell 'em? Not you, because you'll be disappeared."

Stripling wore a vented tan fishing shirt that was missing the left sleeve. The opening had been sewn shut to cover his empty shoulder socket. One of his ears was bandaged where it had been snagged by a bonefish fly, although Stripling obviously didn't know that the angler who'd wounded him was Yancy.

The air in the den was rank with cologne that smelled like apricots and linoleum wax.

"I remember the *Herald* didn't run a photo with your obituary," Yancy said.

"That's because we didn't give 'em one."

"Good call. They see the paper in Nassau, you're toast."

"Sit down like I told you."

"I guess I could've pulled up your mug shot," Yancy said, "but that was taken, like, twenty years ago."

"The picture on my driver's license was new. How come you didn't think of checkin' that in your God-almighty computer?"

"It didn't matter to me what you looked like because I thought you were dead. I was busy trying to catch your killer."

Stripling smiled crookedly. "That's pretty fuckin' funny, I gotta admit."

"Does your daughter know you're alive?"

"Don't worry about Caitlin. I'm gonna tell her when I'm ready."

"Make it in time for the holidays," Yancy said, "so she can order a big enough turkey."

"Is that a joke? Are you seriously standing here doing *jokes*?"

"For what it's worth, I took extremely good care of your arm. I kept it in the freezer of my refrigerator with the vodka and Popsicles. Didn't Eve tell you?"

"Thanks for nothing." Stripling's hand moved toward the trigger of the shotgun. Gleaming on his hairy wrist was a garish rose-gold Tourbillon.

"Nick, I've been very patient. Now, where's Rosa?"

Something beeped on the console of the Super Rollie. The padded footrest began to ascend, and with it rose the blue-black barrels of the Beretta, braced between Stripling's knees and pointed at Yancy's chest.

"You're right about one thing. Which, I'm not dumb enough to murder a cop." Stripling said. "But I got no problem killing a goddamn roach inspector."

Twenty-one

The decision to have his own arm amputated, a perfectly healthy arm—well, first you needed jumbo-sized *cojones*. Nobody facing a Medicare rap had ever tried it before, Nicholas Stripling was certain. Faking one's own death, sure, that happened all the time. The fuckwits usually got caught, too, whoring around Mexico or Costa Rica. Thinking they could just go missing without a trace on a whitewater raft or a solo desert hike, and the feds would say oh well and forget about them.

Which, how stupid can you be? The only way to fool-proof the scam was to disappear *with* a trace. Give the bastards something to bag up and truck to the morgue, actual human remains. So when they do the DNA, when they stare at your mauled rotting stump, there's no doubt in their minds that this poor fucker is dead as a doornail.

Because who'd be crazy enough to cut off his own arm?

Eve had begged her husband not to do it, but he had no intention of going to prison, not even a country-club joint. The feds in Miami were going hard-ass on fraud cases, and three guys Nick knew were doing heavy time, meaning double digits. One of them was an old Cuban gentleman who'd billed Uncle Sam for eighty-two hundred physical therapy sessions that he'd never performed. Stage 3 lung cancer and still they wouldn't let him out early! Nick Stripling told his wife that he couldn't do the flu in lockup, and that jail was *not* a goddamn option.

During the red-hot years of Midwest Mobile, he'd socked away eleven-plus million dollars—and don't forget this was South Florida, the Medicare-fraud capital of America, where the most experienced dirtballs came to gorge. Stripling had found himself competing against the slickest and slimiest—former mortgage brokers, identity thieves, arms dealers, insider traders and dope smugglers, all who'd switched to home-care durables because stealing directly from the government was so much easier, and the risk so small. Lots of Medicare scammers got richer than Nick Stripling, but still he'd raked in some sweet bank from all those fake orders for Super Rollies (also walkers, electric hospital beds, blood-pressure cuffs, bariatric commodes, wander alarms and sitz baths).

If he got caught the feds would demand full restitution, which wasn't going to happen in this particular universe. Stripling had made sure his ill-gotten loot was on the wing, moving it from Barbados to Luxembourg to Geneva, then finally back to a Nassau bank account belonging to one Christopher Grunion. The name had been invented by Stripling to enable an unscrutinized investment of his swindled fortune in some prime ocean-front on Lizard Cay. Eve was skeptical until he showed her an article from the *Nassau Guardian* predicting a flash turnaround of the luxury real estate market, wealthy Asians having discovered the sun-drenched charms of

Bahamian life. Which, the Chinese and so forth? Nick was still waiting for the big stampede to Andros, trying to remain patient and optimistic.

The hardest part of his plan, what scared him the most, was letting a twitchy, shot-out pillhead like O'Peele perform the operation. Again, not much choice—no legit surgeon would have agreed to the job. Man walks in says please cut off my left arm. Doctor says what's wrong with it—gangrene? Melanoma? And the guy says nothing's wrong with it, I just don't need it anymore, could you please saw it off?

O'Peele said okay because Stripling was his boss and also because he needed the money. Percocets aren't cheap when you gobble 'em like Cracker Jacks. And by then Midwest Mobile was going down. Some of the geezers whose ID numbers had been stolen got around to reading their benefit statements, and they started calling Medicare saying they'd never ordered a Rollie scooter chair but they'd sure like to try one. As soon as the FBI began sniffing around, Stripling closed the office and promised new positions in future health-care enterprises to all his loyal staff, including Gomez O'Peele.

Who was grateful for the opportunity to pocket an extra five grand, which is what Stripling offered him to cut off Stripling's left arm and then beat on the bone stump with a hatchet to make it look like a boat propeller caused the wound.

The operation was performed at the couple's vacation town house in the Keys, Eve acting as nurse, her husband blitzed on pills and hooked to a morphine drip. The surgical saw and other implements were brand-new—Stripling had made sure of that. Before they got started he had

O'Peele pee in a cup, one of those drugstore kits, to prove the doctor was clean for the day. Also: blow into a portable booze tester of the style favored by suburban parents with teenage drivers.

Admirably, the doctor had arrived totally sober, his hands steady, and he came through big-time. Afterward the town house looked like they'd been butchering hogs, but the floors had been covered with Visqueen—Nick's idea—so that all they had to do was roll up the mess and cram it in a Dumpster.

Eve sobbing behind a hospital mask flecked with her husband's blood, O'Peele chugging Gatorade pretending it was Ketel One. Stripling lying there thinking, okay, during the Civil War? Medics had to do this shit on open battlefields, hack off arms and legs. These were fucking kids, most of 'em—no anesthesia, no antibiotics. For sutures they'd rip the stitching out of boot soles, for bandages they'd tear up filthy uniforms, maggots crawling in the open wounds.

So I'll be fine is what Stripling assured himself, not that his raw shoulder socket didn't hurt like a motherfucker. Holy Christ did it hurt! But he was a new man, a free man.

This was the day after he'd sunk the *Summer's Eve,* the fuel tanks topped out, the coolers packed with ice and bait. Just like a real fishing trip. His wife had followed him offshore in a rented SeaCraft, past Sombrero Light, rough as a cob and no other vessels in sight. First he pulled the plugs and then he got her sideways in a trough and gunned her in reverse, the mighty blue Atlantic pouring over the transom and filling the cockpit. Stripling used a 5/0 hook to put a hole in the skin of the life raft (in case anyone wondered why he hadn't used it). Then Eve motored up in the SeaCraft, he jumped aboard, and together they watched the *Summer's Eve* sink: a whorl of bubbles and seat cushions and not much else, owing to the whitecaps.

The next morning Stripling went under the knife of Gomez O'Peele, and by nightfall his severed left arm was staked on a mud flat near Vaca Cut being gnawed by sharks. That's what happens when a person drowns in the Florida Keys, which is a shark's version of a Golden Corral—all you can eat, all the time.

Which, the Tourbillon? That's one reason Stripling didn't leave it on his severed left wrist after the operation. Why not, Eve had said, just drive a Rolls-Royce off a pier? Besides, you love that watch, she said, which he couldn't deny. The Tourbillon was a work of art, far as Nick was concerned. He didn't want it to end up in a hammerhead's stomach.

Some mistakes along the way, no question.

First: choosing Phinney, the pothead mate from the *Misty Momma IV*. Eve had gone to the docks and scoped out the crews and personally picked him out. Showed him the arm and said the plan was to punk her cousin, who was chartering the *Misty* the next morning. Eve said the limb came from a med-school cadaver so no worries, Charlie, everything's cool. Her cousin's crazy fraternity brothers, she said, they're the sickos who dreamed this up. And Phinney fell for the whole story, practically came in his pants when she counted out the three grand.

But then he couldn't keep his trap shut about the wad, buying rounds all over Key West, and Stripling knew it was only a matter of time before he got stoned and blabbed about the arm, too. So Nick rented a moped and ambushed the guy after he and some hooker walked out of the Half Shell. To make it look like robbery Nick even snatched Phinney's wallet—seven hundred and two bucks was all the kid had left from the biggest score of his life.

If Stripling had to do that part over again...but, see, it was the best way to make sure the fucking arm got found—arrange for some tourist to reel it in while he's trolling for tuna, whatever. At first Eve had suggested they put the limb on the shore behind somebody's house, as if it washed up with the tide. But Nick feared the coons or pouch rats might drag it off, even a stray dog. Remember, the whole plan depended on the thing being recovered and positively identified as belonging to him. Being indisputably dead would get the feds off his case, not to mention bring a sweet payoff on the life insurance.

Stripling had flapped his empty left sleeve and said to Eve: I didn't go through all this misery just for sport! Like my secret dream was to be an amputee.

So they'd recruited Phinney to do the old sailfish scam, only using Nick's arm instead of a fish. And everything would have turned out great except Phinney couldn't keep a secret. Dumbass.

Mistake number two: waiting too long to deal with the Caitlin problem.

Again, Nick's call. He and his daughter had been on the outs ever since he'd married Eve. Caitlin had a big mouth, too, and don't forget she's married to Mr. Simon Cox, ex-military. The man was so straight he'd once turned in his next-door neighbor for watering the lawn on Thursday instead of Tuesday, some lame county law, a fifty-dollar fine.

If Caitlin ever told Simon about Nick's scheme to

vanish, the buzz-cut sonofabitch would be down at the
FBI in two minutes flat. So Stripling had chosen to keep
his daughter out of the loop, planning to wait until she
got bored with Simon and divorced his hopelessly square
ass, which was inevitable. Then, when the time was right,
Nick would send the seaplane to Miami and surprise Caitlin on her birthday, some sappy move like that.

Meanwhile there had to be a funeral, and—Stripling
learns later—that's where his daughter starts talking to
Yancy, the cop who had custody of the arm. Only Caitlin
doesn't know he isn't a cop anymore, which was all over
the Keys newspapers except Caitlin doesn't read anything
besides price tags and horoscopes. Into her greedy little
skull has crept the notion that Eve murdered Nick and is
trying to screw Caitlin out of her inheritance. This she
apparently tells Yancy. Puts him on the trail of Midwest
Mobile Medical, which leads him to Gomez O'Peele,
which results in the junkie doctor calling Stripling one
night demanding more money, this time for keeping quiet.

Some detective came to see me, O'Peele said in a low
voice, asking all kindsa questions about the Medicare
stuff! I wrote down his name, you don't believe me.

The surgeon swearing on a stack of Bibles that he
didn't say boo to Yancy about the Super Rollies, or about
all those illegal prescriptions and 849s, and especially
not about surgically removing that arm to help Stripling
stage his own death. But honestly I don't know how long
I can hang tough, the doctor says, you sitting pretty and
me with the law knocking on my door. How about another
five grand, Nicky? I know you can swing it.

And Stripling tells him okay, sit tight. Then he puts
on a latex glove and drives straight to Gomez O'Peele's

condo and gives him the same surprise as Charles Phinney, only this time setting it up like a suicide.

Next move is to address the Caitlin situation as any loving parent would, by offering the scheming bitch some cash up front and half the life insurance payout. Eve isn't thrilled about sharing, but they agree it's the fastest, cheapest way out. And sure enough, Caitlin hops on board, the sorrow over losing her father dissipating like a fart at the prospect of becoming a millionaire.

Which, all her nutty talk about Eve being a murderer? Miraculously forgotten. Caitlin can't wait to call Yancy and tell him she was wrong about dear Eve, out of her head with grief and so on. My dad died when his boat sunk, end of story, says Caitlin.

Not knowing, to this day, that he's alive and well. Stripling being in no hurry to inform his one and only offspring, with her track record of indiscretion and Simple Simon on the scene.

Mistake number three—possibly the worst—was Nick trying (make that *failing*) to kill Andrew Yancy.

Eve had met the guy once, the night she went to fetch the arm. Thought he was flaky but harmless. Later they find out he got demoted from sheriff's detective to roach patrol, the Key West *Citizen* reporting it was because he'd attacked his girlfriend's husband with a vacuum cleaner in front of hundreds of tourists, which didn't strike Nick as all that harmless. But Eve said trust me, honey, the man is not a threat.

Then he showed up at Dr. O'Peele's, asking questions, after which Eve said you're right, he's gotta go. Stripling planned to thump the sonofabitch and dump him in a canal. Set it up like an accident—the man went fishing off the bank, drank too much, took a fall. Made way more sense than shooting him point-blank, because even an ex-cop? The authorities wouldn't let that slide.

But that night, when Yancy disappeared under the water, sunk like an anvil, Nick had gotten a little anxious. Like, what if I didn't hit him hard enough? What if the fucker woke up on the bottom and swam off into the mangroves?

Which, turns out, is exactly what happened. Yancy pulled himself out of the canal, now sure that Caitlin's story about Eve was true because obviously Eve had sent her new "boyfriend" after him. And what does Yancy do next? He turns up at Nick's place on Duck Key, finds the hatchet and some bone fragments in a drain—this Yancy tells Caitlin, who immediately calls Eve, who in a cold panic calls her husband.

Now they've got another problem: how to retrieve Nick's left arm from Nick's grave before Yancy obtains a court order to exhume it. Because, with all the new CSI technology, a clever coroner could aim some type of super-ionized laser-imaging ray at the putrid limb and see that the amputation wasn't accidental.

And then Eve would get arrested for murdering a spouse who wasn't even dead.

So they end up paying two random shitbirds to dig up Stripling's coffin and snatch his arm, a job Nick would have done himself except it would have taken all fucking night, a one-handed man trying to shovel packed dirt. But the grave robbers never show up at Denny's, so Nick and Eve take off.

Dawn, they're on the seaplane to Andros. That afternoon, Eve receives an urgent e-mail from the cemetery saying her husband's gravesite has been "disturbed," please call us right away. Luckily the cemetery people don't find any incriminating clues, just a hole in the ground and a pried-open casket.

Which, the arm? Who knows what those sick bastards did with the goddamn thing after they dug it up. Long as it was gone, Stripling didn't give a shit where. He had no attachment, emotional or otherwise.

Now his main concern—on top of this rotten weather—is the unexpected appearance in the Bahamas of Andrew Yancy, whom Nick is preparing to blast with the man's own shotgun.

Actually, though, the timing for a body disposal is pretty convenient. People often disappear during hurricanes, just blow the fuck away.

"... I got no problem killing a goddamn roach inspector," Nick is saying, intending for those to be the last mortal words Yancy ever hears.

Then Eve walks into the room.

"Hello there, Mrs. Stripling," pipes Yancy. "Nice to see you again."

"Don't do it here," she says sternly to her husband.

"Why not?"

"The mess is why. We'll lose our security deposit."

Stripling, barely able to contain himself. "Are you serious? So we buy 'em a new rug!"

"But meanwhile who has to clean it up? The only person in this household with two hands, that's who. Me! So, no, Nicky, you take him outside to shoot him."

Stripling is so fucking pissed off, he's having trouble steadying the shotgun. He tells Eve to go downstairs and turn up the stereo full blast.

"Wait, she's got a point," Yancy interrupts. "Bloody entrails everywhere, then you've gotta drag the body out of the house, which tends to leave a forensic trail."

"Shut the hell up."

"It's so windy outside, nobody would hear the gun go off. But you're the boss, Nick." Yancy shrugs. "Eve, where's Rosa?"

"Don't say one word," Stripling snaps at his wife.

However, he sees the benefits of doing the murder outdoors, the hurricane rains washing away the splatter. So he rises from the Super Rollie and pokes Yancy down the steps, through the foyer, out the front door. He tells Eve to switch on the floodlights—thank God for the generator—and briskly he walks Yancy to the north side of the house, Eve joining them under a pair of coconut palms.

"This'll work," Stripling says.

Yancy looking more worried now, raindrops pelting his face.

From the shadows comes a high-pitched bark, like a squirrel, then Eve is saying, "Tillie, you bad girl, come here right now."

Her spoiled runt of a dog, manically scooting between everybody's ankles.

"Get her outta here!" says Nick.

Eve pleading: "Tillie, heel! Tillie, calm down!"

Then Yancy whistles once. Real simple, like a bob-white quail.

And the retard mutt jumps into his arms.

"Nicky, wait!" Eve cries.

Yancy smiles, clutching the dog to his chest. "Shoot me, Nick, you shoot Tillie."

Eve starts to lose it. "No, Nicky, don't!"

"Unfortunately, that's how shotguns work—big noise, big crater," Yancy says in a calm expository tone.

Stripling is grinding his unshaven jaws, blinking the rain bubbles from his eyelashes. Which, the Beretta? It wasn't designed to be aimed with one arm. Beefy as Nick is, the gun's getting heavy. Slippery, too.

"Drop that goddamn dog," he says to Yancy.

Tillie's rose-petal tongue is lolling, Yancy holding her at center mass, patting her matted, spud-sized head. He matter-of-factly advises Nick to put down the gun, Nick snorting: Guy must be out of his mind.

"You really don't want to kill this scrumptious little puppy," says Yancy. "It would break your bride's heart. Clumps of bloody fuzz all over the lawn?"

"I'll buy her another one. This is not a problem."

"You bastard!" Eve shouts, and jumps between her husband and the smart-ass restaurant inspector.

Which, Nick Stripling's plan? All of a sudden it turns to shit.

Twenty-two

Tillie remembered him!

Yancy shouldn't have been so surprised. Once he'd dated a veterinary assistant who told him that dogs never forget a person's odor, even after one fleet sniff. She said the canine memory was headquartered in its nostrils, and this was as true for arctic wolves as it was for designer diva breeds. Still, with Stripling poised to blow his guts out, Yancy had been caught off guard when, in a show of improbable athleticism, Tillie bounded into his arms. He sentimentally accepted the animal's forwardness as affection, possibly even gratitude for Yancy plucking her from shark-filled waters on his faux fly-fishing visit to Bannister Point.

For him now to employ Tillie as a shield against the loaded Beretta was understandably distressing to Eve, but not for a moment did Yancy believe Stripling would vaporize the family pet in order to kill him. It wasn't a measure of compassion but rather the fear of domestic bedlam; Eve never would have forgiven Nick, and without her loyalty he couldn't sustain the complicated artifice of his new life.

Still, instead of a dog Yancy would have preferred to be holding the Glock, which he'd left at home in Florida knowing the Bahamian Customs officials took a dour view of firearms in one's luggage. Even with Tillie in his arms Yancy's kneecaps remained vulnerable to a shotgun blast. The pup would be airborne before Yancy hit the ground, giving Stripling clear aim for a kill shot.

That option seemed to dawn on Nick just as his wife stepped in front of Yancy and the dog. The span of her hips, worthy of Rubens, made it practically impossible for her husband to shoot around her.

"Tell him to drop the gun," Yancy said to Eve, "or I'll pop poor Tillie's head off."

For drama he flexed his fingers around the stem-like neck of her pooch.

"He's lying!" Stripling boomed.

"What do you care about her, anyway?" Eve cried. Then, spinning back to Yancy: "Don't hurt her, please, she has a renal condition. Let's talk this through."

"You heard what I did to Dr. Clifford Witt, the noted dermatologist. It was all over the Internet." Yancy wanted her to believe he was capable of blithe atrocities. "Eve, I'm going to ask one more time—where is Rosa?"

"Rosa's fine. Maybe we can make a trade."

"Shut your goddamn trap!" Stripling said to his wife, an unproductive approach.

She flipped him off, a robust salutation over one shoulder. Then she told Yancy that she'd lead him straight to Rosa if he freed her treasured companion.

"Only when I see Rosa alive," Yancy countered. It was difficult to preserve a threatening countenance, as Tillie was now licking his knuckles.

Craning to see past his wife, Stripling swore wildly and proclaimed that Yancy was a lying cocksucker. Stripling was hollering to be heard over the wind, which in a matter of moments had accelerated to a gale that wobbled all of them. Yancy firmed his hug on the dog to keep her from sailing away. Eve was backlit by one of the floodlights, her reddish hair dancing like an electric mop; she cupped both hands binocular-style around her eyes, for protection. The rain beat down in gusting, horizontal lashes.

"Get out of the way!" Stripling bellowed at Eve.

"No, Nicky, we're gonna do a trade!"

"The hell we are!"

Yancy wasn't surprised that Stripling refused to go along with the hostage exchange. His thoughts shifted toward escape, knowing he could outrun the lopsided mook. The shotgun had a limited range of lethality that wouldn't be improved by the fierce weather conditions.

Yet Yancy hesitated to flee, thinking: *Once I get away from here, how do I save Rosa?* Most likely she was being confined somewhere inside the Striplings' house.

If they hadn't already killed her.

The opportunity to bolt was lost when Stripling, on the edge of rage, used the twin barrels of the Beretta to somewhat firmly prod his wife. She slipped on the wet grass and fell, the sight causing Tillie to begin yipping in dismay.

Stripling shouted his intentions to shoot Yancy's legs off, at which point Yancy lowered the miniature dog from chest level to groin level. Nick's expression never changed, even as he strained with his lone arm to keep the weapon level. He seemed fully committed to pulling the trigger, Tillie or no Tillie.

Meanwhile Eve was on her knees frantically clapping

at the dog, imploring her to jump. The waterlogged lump began to wriggle and whine in Yancy's arms.

"Oh fine," he said, and he placed her on the ground.

Tillie faithfully scrambled into the emotional clinch of Eve, who shouted up at Yancy: "Thank you!"

Then, to her husband: "Okay, Nicky, now kill him!"

Among Yancy's final regrets, the most unforgivable was allowing Rosa Campesino to meet alone with a pair of known murderers. She'd been so amped about going undercover like a real cop, so calm and radiantly sure of herself—still, he should have said forget it, baby, we'll try something else. But he'd never learned to say no to the women in his life, even on those occasions when he was right—a fatal weakness, it turned out.

One lame, last stall for time: Yancy pointed at the dripping Beretta and yelled through sheets of rain: "Nick, I bet the shells got wet!"

"Let's find out, asswipe." The man looked unfazed, unworried.

Taking a breath, Yancy braced for the flash of the shotgun. He considered shutting his eyes, but that seemed like something a doomed monk would do. Yancy wasn't so spiritual or serene; nothing about death appealed to him.

So he folded his arms, directed a necrotic glare at Stripling and said: "Fuck you, Stumpy."

The response from Eve's husband was a gummy grin that showcased flawless white veneers, top and bottom, doubtlessly paid for by the Medicare trust fund. As an honest restaurant inspector Yancy could never afford a smile so luminous, and he dolefully assumed this would be the last thing he ever saw—the ill-gotten, high-end dentition of his killer.

Next came a loud crack, though it wasn't from the Beretta.

And it wasn't Yancy who went down hard in the rain.

The Lipscombs had decided on real oak floors, a thrilling development for Evan Shook. He wrung a sweet price from an outfit in Deerfield Beach, the owner himself schlepping all the way to the house to measure the interior. Evan Shook let the construction crew take an early lunch, clearing the place for the flooring dealer and his helper. Evan Shook stood in the doorway smiling to himself because he knew the square footage so precisely that he'd already calculated his inflated surcharge to the Lipscombs.

A car he didn't recognize pulled up in front. A broad-shouldered man in a dark suit got out and approached the house. Evan Shook hoped he wasn't a new building inspector. The one he'd been dealing with for months was a very reasonable guy who, in exchange for two nights at the Delano and box seats at a Marlins game, had agreed to overlook the unlawful height of Evan Shook's spec house and other flagrant code violations.

"My name is John Wesley Weiderman," the visitor said. "I'm with the Oklahoma Bureau of Investigation."

A dry handshake followed. Evan Shook couldn't imagine what a lawman from the Midwest might be doing on Big Pine Key, on the unfinished brushed-marble doorstep of the soon-to-be estate of Ford and Jayne Lipscomb.

"I'd invite you inside," Evan Shook said, "but, as you can see, it's not quite finished."

"Nice place," said Agent John Wesley Weiderman. The temperature outdoors was ninety-one degrees and he was sweating through his suit jacket. "I came here to ask if you'd seen your neighbor lately. Mr. Yancy."

"Not for a couple days." Evan Shook thinking: *Oh shit. What now?*

"Are you two friends?" the agent asked.

"Actually, I don't know him very well." Evan Shook was tempted to say Yancy was a stoned flake, but trashing one cop to another cop could be dicey. The blue brotherhood and all that.

John Wesley Weiderman said, "I have reason to believe he might be in danger."

"You're joking. Danger from who?"

"A fugitive I've been hunting."

Evan Shook felt a familiar tremor of apprehension. First wild dogs in the streets, now a murderous psychopath on the loose.

"Let's chat in the Suburban," he said to the lawman. "It's got killer AC."

The interior of the vehicle was quiet and cool. John Wesley Weiderman commented upon the ample leg room and the suppleness of the leather. He inquired about the gas mileage and seemed undaunted by the EPA estimates.

"Will you be driving north," he asked Evan Shook, "if the hurricane comes?"

"Nah. We'll have some rain and wind from it, no biggie. The Bahamas are getting clobbered, for sure."

Evan Shook had been tracking Hurricane Françoise's progress as relayed by the high-strung meteorologists on Miami TV. In the unlikely event that the storm made a hard westward turn toward South Florida, the spec house would have to be zippered up hastily. The fretful Lipscombs had been phoning Evan Shook every few hours seeking reassurance that the place wouldn't be reduced from villa to slab.

To the agent from Oklahoma he said, "Tell me about this fugitive."

Evan Shook wasn't worried about Yancy's safety but rather the tranquillity of the neighborhood and, by extension, the finalization of his real estate deal. As excited as they were about their new house, the Lipscombs would probably walk away from the closing should a gruesome homicide occur at the residence next door. Evan Shook wondered what Yancy had done to place himself in mortal jeopardy—maybe some low-life gangster he'd once busted had escaped from prison and now was vengefully pursuing him.

"Her name is Plover Chase," said John Wesley Weiderman, "most recently using the alias of Bonnie Witt. You know her?"

"I don't." Evan Shook thinking: *Yancy's desperado is a chick?*

"They were romantically involved for a while," the agent added.

"Oh no," Evan Shook said, though it was hardly shocking that his neighbor would date a nut job.

"Here's a photograph provided by her husband. Did Mr. Yancy ever introduce you to any of his girlfriends?"

"Never." Evan Shook looked at the picture and said, "She was here the other day. Some younger guy was with her, not the sharpest knife."

"They've since parted ways," reported Agent John Wesley Weiderman.

"They were squatting in my house—tent, sleeping bags, the whole deal. She said they drove all the way from somewhere and got ripped off. I gave them money for a motel." Evan Shook looked once more at the photo before handing it back; definitely the same woman. "But she never once mentioned Yancy," he said.

The lawman told him that Plover Chase had jumped bail from a sex-crimes conviction in Tulsa County.

"What kind of sex crime?" Evan Shook's imagination began to tingle.

"Sir, I'd rather not get into that."

"But she's dangerous, you say?"

"Evidently she's upset with Mr. Yancy because he's dating someone new, a doctor. It's possible she intends to harm both of them," said John Wesley Weiderman. "However, you should also know Ms. Chase doesn't have a history of violence. Her past offense was one of...I guess you'd call it exploitation."

Evan Shook clicked his tongue in fake consternation. In fact he was deeply intrigued. Never had a woman exploited him in a sexual way, but it sounded exhilarating compared to the listless bedroom comportment of his wife and even, in recent months, his mistress.

"These triangle situations can get messy," the agent from Oklahoma was saying, "and you can never predict how individuals might react. I was told Ms. Chase might be coming here to settle a score. Arson is a possibility."

"Holy Christ," Evan Shook said, although privately he felt that losing Yancy as a neighbor would be good for the subdivision; the man's dumpy-looking house definitely dragged down property values. Should the fugitive set the place ablaze, Evan Shook would manufacture a milder story for the Lipscombs—it had been a sad accident, Yancy falling asleep with a lighted cigarette or whatever.

"Please let me know if you see anything unusual going on next door," said Agent John Wesley Weiderman.

"Absolutely. Do you have a card?"

"Of course."

"And may I see her photo again? Just in case."

"Here, keep it. I've got copies."

"Thank you," said Evan Shook, trying to mask an excitement he knew was inappropriate.

Neville couldn't sleep because he couldn't stop thinking about the man named Yancy, hurrying off to the house rented by Christopher Grunion and his woman. Why had Yancy gotten so worked up when Neville told him about finding Christopher's shirt sleeve? Neville had been hoping that the American policeman—if that's what he really was—would be an ally in the fight to save Green Beach.

Yet what could Mr. Yancy accomplish tonight, all by himself, with a damn hurricane coming? Was his intention to go arrest Christopher? Egg would beat him senseless first, maybe even kill him.

So Neville put on his clothes and took Yancy's fly rod and left Joyous's place through the back door. He borrowed her daughter's bike and pumped as fast as he could toward Bannister Point. Soon headlights appeared in front of him—a car weaving recklessly, forcing Neville to veer off the road.

It was Christopher's yellow Jeep. In the driver's seat sat Egg; one massive hand was holding the steering wheel while the other gripped the hair of a frightened dark-haired woman. Neville thought she looked Cuban or maybe from Puerto Rico.

By the time he reached Christopher's place, Neville

was wind-beaten and drenched to the skin. Silvery needles of rain cut sideways through the broad wash of floodlights. The coconut palms heaved and shook like wild-maned giants. To Neville these visions appeared otherworldly though not hellish, for he'd been through hurricanes before. Drawing closer he heard back-and-forth shouts and he darted forward, careful to remain in the shadow lines.

At the north corner of the house stood three figures holding a triangular formation while the weather raged around them. One was Mr. Yancy; he was facing the others. The second person was a woman, Christopher's woman, clutching a piglet or some sort of small critter. The man with his back to Neville was large enough to be Egg but he had too much hair. It had to be Christopher, and the thing he was pointing at Yancy had to be a gun.

Unfolding in a slice of light, the scene confirmed to Neville the ruthless criminality of Christopher and also the importance of the American. Christopher wouldn't go to the trouble of shooting a man unless he posed a serious threat.

Neville had no time to search for a heavy rock or a limb. He snapped Yancy's fly rod over one knee, rushed up behind Christopher and stabbed him hard with the broken stub. The impact splintered the rod's graphite tubing down to the cork grip and unseated the reel, which fell into a puddle.

Neville wasn't a young fellow, but his arms were strong from years of conching and boat work. And while the fly rod was designed to wiggle at the tip, the butt segment was stiff and inflexible. Christopher Grunion dropped face-forward with the smallest of cries, the shotgun pinned beneath him. His woman began to caw and hop about on her knees.

Neville grabbed Yancy by the arm and said, "Come along, mon."

"I can't."

"Run!" Neville was now pushing the American ahead of him, through the hedges and trees, away from the floodlit house, down the road into the teeth of the wind.

After a hundred yards Yancy halted abruptly and bent at the waist.

"Rosa," he gasped.

"Who's dot?"

"My girlfriend. She's still back there."

"No, she ain't," Neville said.

Yancy straightened. "But she's alive?"

"Yeah, mon, I seen her."

"Okay. Okay." The cop was still panting, fists on his hips. In the sky lightning flared, giving Neville a metallic glimpse of the American's face, exactly what he was thinking.

"Tell me where she is, Mr. Stafford."

"I tink I know," said Neville, waiting for more thunder.

Twenty-three

Driggs was a white-faced capuchin born into a show-business clan. His father had worked for a few seasons on a popular television comedy called *Friends,* and an older female cousin had appeared with several look-alikes in *Ace Ventura: Pet Detective,* a high-grossing feature film starring Jim Carrey. Swinging deeper into the family tree, a great-great-grandmother of Driggs's had played the organ grinder's sidekick in an edgy Parisian musical about the Nazi occupation, the cross-dressed primate sporting hand-polished jackboots and a Hitler-style mustache clipped from Belgian broom bristles.

Born Baby Tom, Driggs was reared among other domestic capuchins on a ranch outside Santa Barbara. He showed none of his forebears' gifts for acting—his disposition was prickly, his attention span fluttering. Unlike his camp mates, he failed to outgrow an adolescent preoccupation with his own genitalia, and this too hampered his career.

A scrotum-grooming reverie, broadcast live on the stadium Jumbotron, brought an end to a short-lived stint as the official "Rally Monkey" of the Los Angeles Angels. The next morning, his team of exasperated trainers sold Driggs to a freelance animal wrangler named Martell, who hoped to cash in on the monkey boom that was sweeping through cinema and television.

Thanks to an improbable connection at Disney studios—Martell had succesfully housebroken a dwarf lemur belonging to the senior comptroller—Driggs was allowed to audition for a series of action movies based on a popular theme-park ride called Pirates of the Caribbean. The part naturally called for the garb of a pint-sized swashbuckler. Knowing Driggs was averse to costuming, Martell prepped his would-be star for the audition by spiking the animal's noontime Snapple with a shot of Wild Turkey. No more relaxed performer ever set foot on the Disney lot. Two months later, he was in the Bahamas with Johnny Depp.

Driggs had been hired as a backup to another capuchin, Dolly, who was docile, obedient and attention-loving. Martell hoped she and Driggs might become off-camera playmates, and that Driggs would begin to chill in her company. It didn't happen.

Because some of the film's stunts were staged to occur on a ship's rigging—no place for a drunken monkey—Martell had halted the palliative dispensation of bourbon. Predictably, Driggs reverted to the execrable antics that had cost him the Angels gig. From remote shooting locations on Great Exuma came reports of unprovoked biting, wanton vandalism, wardrobe destruction and of course feces throwing, the signature method of protest for unhappy simians. Depp was spared only because Driggs tolerated him, but several other actors and even one of the stuntmen refused to come on the set unless it was Dolly's turn to work.

Her demure presence, far from calming Driggs, pitched him into a state of fiendish priapism that literally came to a head when an assistant director caught him jerking off on a rack of brunette wigs. Driggs and, by association, Martell were fired within the hour. The studio agreed to pay the trainer's airfare back to Nassau though not the expensive connecting segments to Los Angeles. No return ticket was provided for Driggs, not even in cargo.

Worn out by his dissolute trainee, Martell unloaded Driggs for seventy-five Bahamian dollars to a sponge fisherman from Andros, who was bloodied and soiled by his new pet on their homeward passage. That winter, kind fate appeared as a casual game of dominoes in which the sponger happily took a flop in order to divest the horrid creature on a gullible fellow named Neville Stafford from Lizard Cay.

Neville was a gentle, patient man, and the capuchin did not despise him. The name change from Tom to Driggs was an easy adjustment, as was the dietary switch from healthy seedless fruits to batter-fried chicken, conch fritters and coconut cakes, which Driggs soon learned to crave. His skin grew scaly and then inflamed, and thereafter he began losing his fur in handfuls. The unattractive condition was worsened by the tropical heat, and by the nonstop feasting of doctor flies and mosquitoes. Wild capuchins smash millipedes and smear themselves with the guts as a natural insect repellent, but Driggs was too far removed from his Central American roots to innately know that trick. Consequently he remained wretched and welted during the summers, which possibly explained why Neville cut him so much slack.

Throughout Rocky Town the animal became notorious for his crudities and hotheadedness. The only people who thought he was cute were rum-dented tourists and of course the daffy Dragon Queen, who remained convinced he was an unusually small boy, not a monkey. No sooner had the strange old woman taken ownership of Driggs than he began to miss life with Neville. Unsentimental by nature, capuchins do possess keen memories— and Driggs was quite aware that his situation had taken a downward turn.

Never once had Neville teased or prodded Driggs the way the voodoo witch did. The animal hated human diapers but at least Neville had been diligent about changing the dirty ones; the lazy Dragon Queen would let Driggs sit for a whole day in his own shit unless he caused a scene. She also dressed him in cheap doll clothes that made him snarl at his own reflection in the coffeepot. The shack in which she lived was smelly and vile even by monkey standards, whereas Neville had always kept his house tidy and open to the sea breezes.

Driggs did enjoy riding up and down the road on the old woman's motorized scooter chair, though he disliked the capering dances that she made him perform; to defy her, however, meant there would be no fritters. And no pipe, either.

Smoking had been taught to him by the Dragon Queen as a comic stunt, diabolically reinforced with ladles of peanut M&M's. The loopy witch never told him not to inhale, so in short order Driggs became addicted to the Dunhill blend provided by the hag's companion, a hulking hairless figure whose jealousy of Driggs was as plain as the fungus beneath his toenails.

Some nights, after the Dragon Queen passed out, the man called Egg would leer at Driggs and whisper harrowing taunts. The monkey would bare his teeth and squeal until the old woman stirred; once he even hurled an empty liquor bottle that Egg deflected with a forearm. The bottle shattered on the floor and roused the Dragon Queen, who punished Driggs by lashing him with his own leash, something that had never occurred during all his time with dull, reliable Neville.

That's when Driggs began plotting an escape. An opportunity came the very next day when the old lady and her companion became tangled on the scooter chair during a braying act of human sex that the monkey mistook for a terrible fight. Swiftly Driggs made his move, snatching a pipe, lighter and tobacco stash before leaping from a window. Off he ran through a soaking rain that seemed different from other summer squalls, as did the galloping surge of the clouds.

A wild capuchin might have intuited a hurricane was coming; if not, he surely would have been alerted by senior members of his troop, who would have organized a collective refuge in heavy limbs below the forest canopy. Driggs, however, was a city monkey by birth and upbringing. He understood only that he preferred to be dry, cozy and shielded from the quaking thunder, which literally scared him shitless.

The few covered hiding places he found also attracted humans; trusting no upright species, Driggs loped on. By nightfall he was tired and famished, and he'd lost his cherished pipe during a dustup with a white man. The road was mostly empty but Driggs came upon a van that stood idling while one of the occupants urinated in the bushes. Silently the monkey climbed to the top and rode the luggage rack through buffeting gusts back to the outskirts of Rocky Town, where he hopped off and made a downcast return to the shack of the Dragon Queen.

Squeezing through a loosely hinged shutter, he entered the candle-lit hovel squinting. He was surprised to see, in addition to the witch and her boyfriend, a stranger—a younger, long-haired woman, trussed with belts to a chair. The man called Egg scowled at Driggs, but from her scooter the Dragon Queen sang out his name and joyfully welcomed him. With equine snorts she nuzzled the soggy capuchin while steering the wheelchair in gay loops until it hummed to a stop. Egg said the battery ran out and the old lady ordered him to put in another one, which he refused to do.

Driggs vaulted from the stalled scooter to the lap of the younger woman, who was unable to speak due to a gag made from one of the voodoo hag's bright scarves. The new woman's clean odor was pleasing, and Driggs pressed his face to her bosom and inhaled deep monkey breaths as a respite from the rankness in the room. Casually he foraged inside the woman's blouse for M&M's or other hidden treats. Seeing fright in her eyes, he began combing his doll-like fingers through her soft shiny hair.

An outcry rose from the Dragon Queen: "Get 'way from dot whore, my lil' prince!"

Driggs clung to the newcomer's clothing, but Egg seized his tail and yanked him away. The monkey landed on the table, where he spied another pipe and snuck a hit that made his teeth freeze. He peered into the pipe bowl and saw a foreign paste of white crystals, which confused him. The Dragon Queen rose from the scooter chair and began flapping her skirt at the tied-down woman, who looked away. Egg came around from behind and turned the woman's head with a hard slap, further upsetting Driggs.

Egg wore no clothes, the long brown thing between his legs reminding the monkey of his own. The Dragon Queen started to bob and clap while her naked boyfriend, shining with sweat, circled their prisoner. A frightened cry came from the bound woman.

Driggs heard himself chitter in agitation, meaning now he didn't want to be there, didn't want to see whatever was about to happen. The animal felt panicky and cornered. Yet outside the wind was roaring, the trees kept snapping—where could he run?

The Dragon Queen snatched him from the tabletop and buttoned him into a tiny tuxedo vest stained with coffee. She held him by the collar while shouting encouragement to Egg, who hurried to loosen the belts from the chair holding the younger woman.

"Do it! Gon now!" the hag crowed.

Once their captive was untied, Egg turned back to the Dragon Queen and struck a vulgar pose, flexing his arms. The Dragon Queen moaned theatrically and with her free hand fanned herself. When Egg took hold of the younger woman, still gagged, she began punching at his wide chest. The Dragon Queen chortled though the scene had an opposite effect upon the capuchin, who broke from the voodoo witch's grasp and launched himself in authentic jungle fury at her boyfriend.

A scream shot out from Egg—a high, full-throated

scream that overrode the low drone of the storm. The door of the shack flew open but it wasn't the wind. Standing there was a white man Driggs recognized from previous altercations.

But behind the white man, looking over his shoulder, was...Neville!

Driggs would have grinned had his incisors not been so deeply implanted in Egg's fleshy thing, to which the monkey clung as if it were the bough of a mahogany tree.

Yancy needed a moment to absorb the scene.

"Jesus," he said. "The man's got a monkey on his dick."

Neville was thunderstruck. "Dot's Driggs," was all he could muster.

Egg cast Rosa aside and feverishly commenced slapping at the capuchin, causing him to chomp down harder. Blood was dripping all over the thug's feet. He stopped flailing to appraise his tormentor, seven fuzzy pounds that might as well have been cast-iron tonnage.

The Dragon Queen railed at Driggs and hawked rheumy gobs at the intruders. Yancy shoved her backward into the seat of the Rollie scooter; then he pulled off Rosa's gag and firmly guided her toward the doorway. Neville refused to depart without his pet, who remained tenaciously attached to Egg.

From the goon came a seething croak: "Git dot fucker offa my cock or you dead mon." He was holding motionless under the most delicate of circumstances.

Once more the Dragon Queen lunged to intervene, crooning more voodoo nonsense. This time it was Neville who pushed her back onto the wheelchair.

To Driggs he gently appealed, "C'mon, boy! Poppa got fritters bok home!"

These were irresistible words to the hungry vagabond. Driggs spat out Egg and jumped to the top of Neville's head, his old riding perch. They hurried out the door behind Yancy and Rosa, chased by the fevered remonstrations of the voodoo woman.

By the time the hurricane struck, they were more or less safe—Yancy, Rosa, Neville and the monkey—inside a small house rented by another of Neville's girlfriends. Coquina was her name, and Neville fondly introduced her as half Cuban. She'd lighted two kerosene lanterns after the power went out; the windows she had boarded earlier that day with Neville's help.

The house was near the shore, the waves breaking hard enough to interrupt conversation. Coquina handed out dry clothes and a small towel for Driggs, who had torn off the tuxedo vest and was stuffing himself with johnny-cakes and orange slices.

Neville pulled Yancy to a corner and said, "You tink Mistuh Chrissofer be dead?"

"I don't know. What'd you hit him with?"

"I didn't hit 'im, mon. I stob 'im wit your fishin' pole."

Yancy said, "The fly rod?"

"Yah. In de bock." Neville demonstrated how he'd broken it and used the point of the butt section as a lance. "Wot if I hoyt 'im bod? Maybe killed 'im."

"I didn't see a damn thing," said Yancy.

"Wot 'bout his woman?"

"It was raining. It was dark. She was drunk."

"She was?"

"If anybody asks me," Yancy said. "You bet."

Outside something heavy crashed to the ground. Across the room, Rosa and Coquina were feeding Ritz crackers to Driggs. They all looked up because of the noise. Coquina said it was probably a utility pole falling in the backyard.

Yancy told Neville he had done the right thing at Bannister Point. "The man's a criminal, a murderer. All you did was save my life, Mr. Stafford."

"Dot might be so."

"His real name is Stripling. Can you remember that? It'll be important if they come to ask you questions. The woman is his wife—did she get a look at your face?"

"No," Neville said. "Who gonna come axing questions? You mean from Nassau or Miami?"

"Remember that name—Nicholas Stripling. He shot two men dead back in Florida."

"Got-tam!" said Neville.

"Before he came here, he had a surgeon take off his left arm. That's why he always wore the poncho. That's why you found the cut sleeve in his garbage—his wife stitches up his shirts to fit the nub."

Neville's voice jumped two octaves. "Why a mon get his own arm cut off? 'E muss be stone crazy!"

"No, Mr. Stafford, he did it for money. This is one cold-blooded sonofabitch."

Rosa walked over carrying a lantern. She and Yancy went into a bedroom and shut the door.

Neville sat down to think. Anyone who for pure greed would give up an arm...a true white devil, like the Dragon Queen said. Maybe her voodoo had worked, after all. What if she'd given Neville a role in the curse, and set the stabbing in motion?

He looked up at the shuddering rafters. Then he turned

back to address the monkey: "You con stay wit me like before, but tings got to change. No more smokin' and nonsense."

Coquina rolled her eyes and told Neville he was a fool.

Driggs blinked impassively and sucked an orange rind. It felt good to be out of the storm.

Yancy held Rosa close and said, "Baby, I'm so sorry."

"Totally my fault. Rule number one: Never conspire under the influence of tequila."

"Did they hurt you?"

"Not really, but it was definitely on the agenda," Rosa said. "Crazy old bat, first thing she did? Tore off my bra and poured Bacardi in the cups. The bald dude, he was just laughing and playing with himself."

"What the hell happened before that, at Stripling's house?"

"Oh, great meeting. She and the boyfriend knew we weren't for real—they've got a woman on the payroll at Immigration in Nassau. They knew 'Andrew Gates' was really you, they knew I wasn't really your wife—and they knew we were trying to set 'em up."

Yancy sat her on the bed. He kept apologizing until she told him to hush.

"Eve's boyfriend isn't a boyfriend," he said.

"I never saw him—he was in another room. The bald guy's the one who grabbed me. He's not a gentleman, either, Andrew. God bless that nasty little monkey for showing up when he did."

"What I'm trying to tell you," said Yancy, "is that the boyfriend is really the husband. Nick Stripling's alive."

Rosa flopped back on the covers. "Okay. What?"

"He had his own arm sawed off to make everybody think he was dead. It was Dr. O'Peele who did the wet work, right after Nick and Eve sank the boat."

"While Immigration has her in Nassau."

"Right. That's the beauty of the seaplane."

"They used the condo on Duck Key for the surgery, which explains the bone chips."

"Right," said Yancy. "Then, after they get some shark bites on the arm, Eve drives it down to Key West for the switcheroo on the *Misty Momma.*"

"Wow. Talk about a plan."

The wind against the ceiling beams sounded like a downhill locomotive. Yancy could feel the pressure in his eardrums.

"After the surgery," he said, "Nick came to hide out on Andros. He and Eve had already rented the house and started their big real estate project. They bought that sweet stretch of beach, probably using what Nick stole from Medicare. But he wasn't through with Florida. He snuck back to take care of Phinney and then O'Peele, and then me. Nick's the dude in the orange poncho, Rosa. He wears it to hide his stump."

Rosa ran her hands through her hair. Yancy noticed raw scrapes on both knuckles, from fighting the two freaks in the shack.

She said, "The man had his own arm amputated, Andrew. That's impressive."

"I've heard of doing a finger before."

"Oh, sure. The old Wendy's scam."

"I thought it was Burger King," Yancy said.

"Whatever. Customer starts gagging and there's a big scene. Somebody calls the local TV station. But you know it's a setup because what turns up in the cheeseburger is always a pinkie. That's the one you don't really use. An actual meat-rending accident, it's the thumb or forefinger that gets severed because those are working fingers."

"Sure, the ones nearest the blades and grinders."

"Exactly," Rosa said. "But pinkie cases are automatically suspicious. Somebody claims they found one in a bun, always check the hands of their friends and family. It's amazing how many dirtbags will chop off a pinkie just to get a piece of a lawsuit."

"You've got to admire the commitment."

"Because these fast-food companies, they'll settle almost every time. They don't want to go to a jury," she said. "Even if they know they're getting hustled, they can't take a chance."

"Not in South Florida, no way."

"Even a little finger, Andrew, that's pretty hard-core. But to give up your whole arm—that's a new one."

"We're blessed to live in such times," Yancy said.

"You think Caitlin knows?"

"Nope. Only Eve."

"And where is the fearless Mr. Stripling?"

"Not sure if he's dead or alive. He was about to shoot me when my new hero Neville stabbed him with my six-hundred-dollar bonefish rod."

"It just gets better and better," Rosa said. "And now we're in a hurricane!"

"Named Françoise, for Christ's sake."

"Don't spoil it, Andrew. Take off your pants."

The eye of the storm stayed out in the Tongue of the Ocean, feeding on the warm waters. Still there was substantial damage and disruption across Andros as it passed to the east. The winds on Lizard Cay reached seventy-one miles per hour, gusting to ninety.

Yancy found himself struggling to focus on what would have been, under calm heavens, an act of carefree and delicious reflex. The din from even a small hurricane is nerve-racking, and Yancy was additionally distracted by thoughts of the evening's frenetic events. Rosa told him to relax; Neville and his girlfriend wouldn't be able to hear them from the other side of the door, which Yancy had locked in case Neville's monkey got nosy.

It was during light-spirited foreplay when Rosa confided that she'd been reading a smutty novel in which an inexperienced woman becomes enthralled by a lover who bosses her around the bedroom with the same tone one might hear from the nail-gun operator at a slaughterhouse. The woman sportingly signs an enslavement contract, after which the fellow forces her to put on Day-Glo wetsuits and perform contortions that would daunt Olga Korbut.

Rosa said she was sort of enjoying the book. Yancy tried to act intrigued though he'd never been good at fantasy sex; it was difficult to stay in character and not make smart-ass remarks. One time Bonnie made him play the shiftless hitchhiker while she was the naïve Mary Kay associate who got lost in her imaginary pink Lexus. Yancy couldn't keep a straight face, or anything else, and Bonnie ended up steaming mad.

Adopting the role of ruthless dominator in Rosa's daydream would require some stagecraft, and in Yancy's experience there was a hazy line between daring and disgusting. Usually when making love he strived for a purely sensory, uncomplicated experience. Incorporating a game or a skit seemed too much like a class assignment.

For Rosa, however, he'd try anything—first in a morgue and now in a hurricane, the whole damn house heaving on its foundation. Fine.

"Thad always speaks to Juliette like a Russian," she was saying, referring to the characters in the novel.

"I can't do a Russian."

"Any Eastern bloc nation should work."

"Bad Irish is all I've got," said Yancy.

Rosa kissed him and said, "All right, let's hear it." In the lantern's light she looked lovely, but this wide-eyed Juliette thing she could never pull off, not with her butterscotch skin and those South Beach bikini stripes.

She said, "Ready? Now call me a mean name and order me to put my feet behind my head."

"You can actually *do* that?"

"Come on!"

"Kay, ye wortless bitch, do wutcher told or I'll spank yer arse with a boogie whip."

She broke up, giggling and kicking at the air. "It's like screwing Shrek!"

"Did I not warn you about the accent?"

"Give me some Daniel Craig."

Yancy slid over and pinned her arms. "Don't move," he rumbled.

"Oooh, baby, that's pretty good!"

It took a little time but Yancy's mind began to untorque, despite his almost having been shot point-blank and then escaping through a tropical gale to rescue his date from a voodoo den. All the heavy stuff faded as he rolled around with Rosa and finally let go. The storm made the intimacy more exotic—they were trapped but also tucked safe. When the lantern died they found their way by touch, and the knocking from a loose porch plank became their rhythm.

Later, when they had time to think about it, their recollections differed as to exactly when the top of Coquina's house blew off. Yancy thought it had happened a few moments before they finished, as Rosa's fingertips began to dig into his arms. But she said no, it was the precise instant she came that the roof had peeled away, the nails popping like firecrackers.

Yancy had known without turning what the loud noise meant. Suddenly he could see Rosa beneath him and she could see the clouds, because even at night a hurricane brings its own particular light. The wind came wailing into the open room yet the rain flew dead sideways over the gap where the boards had been, and not a drop fell upon the bed.

Rosa had laughed deeply, shaking Yancy by the shoulders and saying, "*That* is what I'm talkin' about, mister!"

Which is the part they both would remember the same way.

Twenty-four

By dawn the weather had broken and the wind dropped to nine knots. Hurricane Françoise was gone. The landing strip at Lizard Cay was littered with trees, coconuts, plywood, two-by-fours and sheets of brittle plastic roofing from a nearby chicken farm.

Along with the other debris Claspers removed two dead roosters as he walked the runway with a couple of other pilots and some neighborhood kids. Three small planes had flipped during the heavy winds, but Claspers had done a good job securing the Caravan, anchoring the tie-down stakes in a rocky patch off the edge of the tarmac. The aircraft was untouched by Françoise except for a goatee of shredded palm fronds on the propeller.

By invitation the other pilots had spent the storm inside the well-built vacation homes of their wealthy clients, while Claspers in his underwear had huddled in the shower stall of a leaky motel room expecting the entire structure to implode. Although his gutsy aviating was extremely valuable to Christopher Grunion—who these days would fly a floatplane under the radar into South Florida?—Claspers never got the call from Bannister Point inviting him to come take shelter with Grunion and his girlfriend.

Assholes.

Like they don't have a spare fucking bedroom.

Even when Claspers had delivered a potential customer for their unbuilt condos—that pretty Cuban woman, the doctor—he didn't get past the front door. Grunion's girlfriend had handed him a Heineken and said: "Here, K. J., take one for the road."

Had the motel walls crumbled during the hurricane, good luck finding another pilot who would do for Grunion what Claspers did. For the risks he'd taken he could lose his certification, or even go to prison. And where was the appreciation for all those daring moves? Where was the respect?

Claspers didn't know exactly what type of scam Grunion was running, but he knew enough to sink the man if it came to that. Like most good pilots Claspers kept a detailed log of his flights in and out, where and when—solid tracking information that could be handed over to authorities if ever he were questioned about his work for Grunion.

Because you don't earn loyalty by treating your best people like peons, not the man who flies your motherfucking airplane.

So long, K. J., have a nice hurricane!

Well, screw you, thought Claspers.

His nerves were wrung from the storm. Even half-stoned he'd been terrified to hear the windows buckle and moan. Back home he would've swallowed some pills and gone to sleep, but back home there were custom-fitted aluminum shutters and impact-resistant glass and strapped trusses. The building code on Lizard Cay was more lax, which was to say it existed only on paper. Consequently,

Claspers spent the night hugging the tiles in the shower. After Françoise passed he stumbled to his bed and found the mattress soaked, clammy rain dripping from a crooked seam in the plaster ceiling. At the first light of day Claspers was out the door.

Without electricity he was unable to recharge his cell phone, and at any minute he expected to see the yellow Jeep speeding up to the airstrip, Grunion primed to bitch him out for not taking his calls. The man would want to go to Miami until Andros Island was up and running, or maybe he'd just send Claspers back for groceries and DVDs. Grunion's girlfriend was a major fan of Matt Damon and once directed Claspers to fly low over the actor's house on Miami Beach so she might catch a glimpse. Claspers had no clue where the guy lived, so he'd randomly chosen a bayside spread with an infinity pool and buzzed the place at four hundred feet. Grunion's girlfriend had been thrilled— she couldn't wait to tell Grunion that she'd seen Matt Damon's Irish setter taking a dump on the putting green.

As Claspers removed the straps from the Caravan he thought about quitting and finding another gig. In the old days even his hard-ass cartel bosses would ask him to swing by the *finca* for drinks. Great food, late-night guitars, good times—that's how Claspers remembered it. That's how he'd first met Donna, one of the wives. The Colombians treated Claspers like an important member of the enterprise, which he was, because bales need wings. Never would they have let him hunker alone in a crackerbox motel during a hurricane.

The only bad thing about dumping Grunion—that seaplane was really fun to fly. Claspers loved it.

"You fueled up?" somebody called.

Claspers turned and saw Andrew, the American trust-fund fisherman, walking with his handsome Latina wife across the tarmac. They were carrying their bags.

"How'd the real estate meeting go?" Claspers asked.

The wife said, "Not too good. We were hoping to hitch a ride home with you."

"If I got two open seats, no problem. All depends on who else is coming. And if it's cool with the boss."

"Nobody else is coming," the fly fisherman said.

"Is that from Grunion direct?"

"We'd like to leave right now," the wife said. "Basically as soon as you can pull those chocks."

Claspers was amused by the couple's boldness. Maybe they'd been rattled by the hurricane, or maybe they'd had a brush with that caveman Egg.

He said, "It ain't my airplane, *señora*. Wish it was."

The fisherman took out a gold police badge and held it in front of Claspers's nose. "So you can appreciate the sense of urgency, Mr. Claspers. We'll pay for your gas, but the earliest possible departure is what we need. Like in five minutes."

"You're a cop?"

"The clock is ticking. Seriously," said the woman.

"You, too?"

"She's a forensic specialist," the fake fisherman explained. "We're working two homicides in which your employer is suspect *numero uno*. Also an attempted homicide, I almost forgot. Plus there's a pile of heavy federal charges that I can tell you about on the flight back. Unlike Mr. Grunion, the doctor and I don't mind the lines at Customs and Immigration, so you can take us straight to Miami International."

Claspers was feeling off balance. "I dunno what the hell you're talking about."

"It's simple. You either get this fucking plane in the air right now, or your license gets yanked back in the States and you find another profession, like driving an ice-cream truck. That's not too ambiguous, is it? Nothing fuzzy about the scenario I'm presenting. The man you call Grunion and his female companion? On several occasions you flew them nonstop from here to Monroe County, Florida—in this very same aircraft—without officially clearing at Tamiami or Key West. That's a crime, and the look in your eyeballs tells me you're aware of the possible shitstorm in your future. If you've never had the opportunity to interact with Homeland Security, you're in for a treat. I'm Inspector Yancy, by the way, and this is Dr. Campesino."

All the pilot could say was: "Grunion killed somebody?"

The pretty doctor patted his arm. "We really need to get moving."

The hurricane stayed out over the Bahamas until meandering away. It rained heavily for a day in the Lower Keys but now the sun was shining and Evan Shook's construction crew had returned to the job site. He was parked in front of the spec house talking on the phone with Mrs. Lipscomb. The topic was crown moldings.

A green Sebring convertible driven by a blonde pulled up next door at Yancy's place. Evan Shook told Jayne Lipscomb he'd call her back.

"Will you check those prices? Ford thinks we can do better."

"Sure. Right away," Evan Shook said absently.

From the glove compartment he removed a stun gun he'd purchased just in case Andrew Yancy hadn't hallucinated the wild dogs. Agent John Wesley Weiderman had said the woman didn't have a violent past, but Evan Shook pocketed his new Taser, just in case.

Before stepping from the Suburban he looked at the photo once more—there was no doubt it was the same person. She entered Yancy's house and Evan Shook moved closer to the fence separating the properties. His phone was in one hand; in the other was Agent Weiderman's card. Evan Shook knew he should make the call immediately; it would be the responsible thing to do.

Before Plover Chase burned his neighbor's house to the ground.

What a sight that would be, he thought. *A bona fide inferno.*

The fugitive came out the back door and stood on Yancy's deck. She noticed Evan Shook watching as she tied her hair in pigtails. He waved and she nodded back pleasantly. Evan Shook couldn't help wondering what sort of elaborate sex crime she'd committed—ropes? whips? manacles?—and what man in his right mind would press charges.

Back home at his club, Evan Shook was dependably conservative during law-and-order discussions: Lock up the bastards and throw away the key! Don't do the crime if you can't do the time! One quick phone call and Miss Plover Chase would be prison-bound. Possibly there was a cash reward. Agent Weiderman would know.

Then again, it was difficult for Evan Shook to imagine how such a sunny-looking soul could be a menace to society. That was his dilemma as he tapped Agent Weiderman's number into his smartphone. He was about to press Call when Plover Chase took off her cotton beach dress, under which was revealed a candy-striped two-piece swimsuit—not a bikini, yet still...

After dabbing sunblock on her nose, she stretched out on a plastic lounge chair that must've cost Yancy all of eleven dollars. To Evan Shook she seemed extremely laid-back for a would-be arsonist.

"Hi, there! I remember you!" Now she gave him a full-on wave.

Evan Shook tucked away the phone and Agent Weiderman's card as he approached the fence. Conscious of his shortness, he stood straight as an aspen. The heel lifts in his loafers helped.

"Where's your boyfriend?" he asked.

"We broke up," she said, "but thanks for the motel room."

"No problem."

"I didn't break into this place, don't worry. I've got a key." Her lips were a faint shade of pink but her toenails were the color of tangerines.

"Have you seen Andrew?" she asked.

"Not for a few days. Maybe he's out of town."

"I'm a friend of his. Really I am."

"Then he's a lucky guy. What's your name, friend of Andrew?"

"Bonnie," she said. "I tried his cell but he didn't call back. Usually he's good about returning his messages."

"My name's Evan. You want some water or a soda? It's hot as blazes out here."

"No, thanks. There's beer in the fridge."

Plover Chase had a nice figure and her legs looked naturally tanned, a feature Evan Shook appreciated. His wife got herself sprayed twice a month at a salon in downtown Syracuse, and she came out looking vinyl. Also, the stuff tasted like insecticide.

"Andrew's the one who told us it was okay to crash at your house," the fugitive confided. "Sorry about that."

"I think he likes to play practical jokes."

"Have you met his new girlfriend? The surgeon?"

Evan Shook heard himself say, "Yes, she's down here a lot."

Which was untrue.

"What's she look like?" Plover Chase asked.

"Good. She looks good." Evan Shook had never set eyes on the woman, but he said it anyway. "She's got long brown hair."

"Scale of one to ten?"

"Eleven."

"Whoa, daddy."

"They seem pretty serious," Evan Shook added.

The fugitive was looking at him over the tops of her sunglasses. "Like, how do you mean? Move-in-together serious, or get-married serious?"

"Well, you know Andrew."

"Yes, I certainly do know Andrew," she said.

Behind them, the construction site was a cacophony of hammers and table saws and sanders—even a boom box playing salsa music from Miami, heavy on the horns.

"Where you from, Emmett?"

"It's Evan." He spelled it. "I live in New York State."

"So you're down here really just to get that house built," Plover Chase said. "All by your lonesome."

"My family's up north, that's right. I fly back and forth most weekends."

Yancy's stalker crossed her killer legs, and Evan Shook found himself sidetracked by unwholesome fantasies.

"So this mansion you're putting up, Evan, it's basically a real estate investment?"

"When I'm here, I stay at the Casa Marina. That's down in Key West."

"And that's where you go at night," she said, smiling, "after a long hard day at the job site."

"They have a nice bar. Cool and private." He pointed. "Watch out, there's a horsefly on . . . well, right *there*."

"That would be my décolletage." She flicked the insect away, and with a knuckle wiped the blood dot. "How old do you think Andrew's girlfriend is?"

"I don't know. Young for a doctor," Evan Shook said. "Want to come by the Casa later for a drink? They've got a country band that's not bad."

Plover Chase sat up and swung her lovely feet to the deck. "Andrew's somewhat famous around Key West. But you probably know that already. Infamous, I should say."

"For what?"

"You don't read the papers when you're in town? Shame on you."

"There's a place on Duval where I buy the *Times*. But, really, I don't pay much attention to the local news," Evan Shook said. "So tell me what Andrew did to get his name in the headlines."

The woman laughed and said never mind, it's water under the bridge. Then she said good-bye and picked up her beach dress and disappeared into Yancy's house.

Evan Shook walked back to the Suburban thinking about the justice system. The prisons of America had become so overcrowded that hard-core cutthroats were being turned loose daily, only to strike again. Where was the logic of locking up a hot-looking babe like Plover Chase for a crime of "exploitation," whatever *that* might be?

So Evan Shook didn't dial Agent Weiderman. He still had some mulling to do.

In the meantime he called Mrs. Lipscomb back at the Pier House. He told her that the price for the carved poplar moldings was as low as he could go, regretfully, without taking a loss on the order. She put her husband on the line, and Evan Shook listened to him whine and huff about switching to fiberboard before he eventually surrendered and said okay, what the hell.

"Give her what she wants," Ford Lipscomb sighed.

"Sir, I feel your pain. But it's gonna look special when we're done."

After hanging up, Evan Shook made a U-turn in the Suburban and drove past the house next door, where the pigtailed fugitive was unloading from her car's trunk a set of red jerry cans that are normally used to transport gasoline.

Clearly she was struggling with the fact that Yancy had a brainy, beautiful new girlfriend.

Evan Shook pretended not to look at Plover Chase as he rolled by, goosing the accelerator. Sometimes it was best to let nature take its course.

Eve Stripling removed from her prone, moaning husband a broken piece of a composite-fiberglass rod blank manufactured by the Sage company. The jagged point had perforated the disc sac between the fifth lumbar vertebrae and first sacral vertebrae, at the base of Nick Stripling's spine, leaving him in bald agony, unable to stand.

Eve rushed inside to fetch the Rollie scooter chair, into which Nick one-armedly hauled himself, spitting mud and cursing his wife for not letting him shoot Andrew Yancy in the den. She guided Nick into the house and spent an hour icing his wound, which failed to restore the functionality of his legs. There followed an animated discussion that ricocheted between the subjects of urgent medical care and Eve's gross culpability for Stripling being ambushed.

Which, the guy who attacked him? Nick had no goddamn idea who it was. Never saw the man's face. Eve insisted she didn't get a good look, either.

Some black dude, is what she said—a gem of a clue, here in the Bahamas. Very fucking useful.

Eve told Nick to quit yelling and let's figure out where to find a rock-star spinal surgeon, soon as we get off this stupid island. Miami was out of the question because Yancy might beat them there and tip the feds that Stripling wasn't dead, triggering a full-on manhunt.

Yancy, who should have been safely out of the picture, a steaming pile of guts. Instead he was likely hunkered somewhere nearby on Lizard Cay, waiting for the weather to clear.

One thing Stripling had in his favor was a counterfeit U.S. passport bearing the name of Christopher Joseph Grunion. It was a superior counterfeit that had cost him nine grand—some wiseguy who ran a lunch truck in Little Haiti. The passport would remain usable for maybe three days max, depending on how long it took Homeland Security to process Yancy's information and enter Stripling's alias in the computer.

"We're going to England," Nick declared hoarsely to Eve.

"All right, honey. There's a nonstop from Nassau."

"They've got fantastic doctors. Good as New York."

Eve agreed. "I'll call British Air soon as we get cell service."

This was during the heavy part of the storm, rain hammering the roof, the electric generator grinding like a cement mixer.

To his wife Stripling said, "I better not be fuckin' paralyzed. This is all on you."

"Knock it off, Nicky."

"You know I'm right."

He couldn't stop railing about what had happened. Which, what are the odds of getting randomly stabbed in your own yard during a hurricane?

While holding a loaded shotgun.

The pain was worse than anything Stripling had ever experienced, worse even than post-amputation. Breathing hurt. Blinking hurt. Talking hurt even more.

His suspicions turned to a certain sketchy freelance employee, Mr. Carter Ecclestone, otherwise known as Egg. The meathead was supposed to return to the house after taking care of Yancy's girlfriend. However, Egg hadn't been seen since before the hurricane struck. The Jeep, however, was back in the driveway...

Maybe Egg *was* here, Nick thought, only now he was working with somebody else. Like that nutty old crone he'd been balling—what if she'd talked him into killing

Stripling and robbing the place? Maybe she put a voodoo spell on that pea-brained motherfucker.

Or maybe it was Eve who'd made Egg a better offer. Lately she'd been riding Nick's case about how boring it was on Lizard Cay, how she'd go batshit crazy living here all the time with nothing to do. She'd gotten downright surly when Nick had told her to quit bitching and get a hobby, take up snorkeling or kiteboarding. He'd said the two of them were in this thing together, up to their shiny white asses, only maybe Eve was thinking: *Not necessarily.*

Except the Egg theory didn't add up. He wouldn't have tried to murder Nick with a spindly goddamn fishing rod. He would have disemboweled him with a knife, or cracked his skull with that fish billy, or snapped his neck with those gorilla paws.

Everything about the night ambush seemed unplanned and frantic. A total amateur, but who? Stripling had made a point not to know a soul on the island.

"Oh great," he muttered. "Now I gotta take a leak."

"You can still void?" Eve said buoyantly. "That's a super healthy sign, Nicky. And I see your toes moving, too!"

"Yeah, that's right, they're dancing a tango. Now bring me something—a jar or a bowl, I don't care."

Eve went to the kitchen and came back with an empty wine bottle.

Stripling scowled. "Get serious. My dick won't fit in there."

"Sure it will."

"It's bigger than a goddamn cork!" Wretchedly he pounded on the armrests of the Rollie.

"Honey, chill. I didn't mean anything," his wife said.

"Gimme your glass before I wet my pants!"

She was holding a Waterford tumbler full of ice, peach vodka and soda. It came from a table set belonging to her maternal grandparents, now deceased. Nick could sense that Eve was reluctant to deploy the sentimental heirloom for urine collection.

Or possibly she just didn't want to pour out her cocktail.

Stripling was better at forging orders for Rollies than he was at driving one. Impatiently he toggled the joystick until the motorized chair clicked and surged forward. As it passed by Eve he made a swipe at her precious tumbler but she pulled it away. The scooter thudded hard into a wall, jarring Nick's damaged spine and also his distended bladder, which yielded a warm sour flood. With it came well-founded gloom.

Once the FBI learned he was alive, his days of freedom on Andros Island were numbered. The Curly Tail Lane project would be done, of course, as would Grunion Global Realty, Nick's mishandled stab at legitimacy. Although he still had a few million liquid, he could easily waste every penny on lawyers and bribes trying to fight extradition to the United States.

Or he could pack up and run. Purchase a new identity, find another place to hide and start over as an international fugitive. Which, talk about exhausting. He didn't want his face on the Interpol website. He wanted to stay dead.

It wasn't impossible for a clever person to get lost and stay lost in the Bahamian out-islands—if you were blessed with a spouse who was content to sit around weaving straw handbags or painting kindergarten faces on coconut husks. Keeping Eve settled would require a locale that offered shoe shopping, Pilates, sushi bars, a hair salon and a dog groomer.

A city, in other words. And living in a city would be risky.

Plus, Stripling had already ordered another Contender to replace the one he sank in the Keys. The new boat was a thirty-six-footer, sky blue, with beast triple Mercs and a sixty-gallon bait well. Delivery was due any day. He was naming it *Lefty's Revenge,* in honor of his lost arm. A goddamn fish-slaughtering machine is what it was—Nick would be able to run from the east side of Andros all the way to Cay Sal and back on a single tank.

But not if he was hiding out in Geneva or São Paulo.

He could think of just one major move that would solve everything and keep the status quo: Silence Andrew Yancy before he got to Florida and met with the feds.

It was the only way Stripling could stay officially deceased, safe on Lizard Cay. Yancy and his Cuban girl-friend, or whatever she was—they were the only ones besides Eve who knew enough to bring Nick down.

"We gotta find that cocksucker," he said to his wife.

"You can't even walk, Nicky. And, please, it's a hurricane outside!"

"In the morning I'm talkin' about. First thing."

She said, "You're hurt. We'll need to get out of here."

"Where the hell is Egg? That's who we get on Yancy's ass. Call Egg, okay?"

"He's not answering the two-way. Here, let me find you some dry pants. Not even the radio's working, honey. We should get some sleep and wait for the storm to blow through."

Stripling said, "It's all your fault, this whole cluster-fuck. Now put down your drink and roll me to the damn bathroom."

In the morning Nick felt even worse. The puncture in his lower back was oozing a fluid that didn't resemble blood. So severe was the pain that his facial muscles had seized into a grimace. But the cell phones still weren't working and there was no Internet connection, making it impossible to contact British Air. Eve proposed that Claspers should fly them to Nassau right away, so they'd be certain to get seats on the first flight to London.

But all Nick could talk about was hunting down Yancy before he escaped. Which, no way was that shit-head going to sneak out of Andros today. Bahamasair was still grounded from the storm, and none of the local boats were crossing to Florida, not with the Gulf Stream running fourteen feet.

As long as Yancy was stuck on the island, Nick said, Egg would be able to track him down and kill him. Now just find Egg!

Eve said, "First things first, honey."

She dosed her husband with Clorazepams and Tylenol 2s, left over from a knee operation, before assisting him from the Rollie to the Jeep. On the back seat sat a pair of Louis Vuitton suitcases and Tillie the dog, fussing inside her tartan travel case. During the ride to the airfield Stripling sustained a bitter monologue about people who said white-collar criminals were soft, pussies, when here he was an amputee, possibly crippled from the waist down, staring at life with no parole if he got busted.

Say the word "outlaw" and everyone thinks bank robber, but did John Dillinger cut off a limb to trick the FBI

into thinking he was dead? No, sir, he went to the movies
and got shot full of lead. Which, these days, any fuckwit
with a ballpoint pen and a Halloween mask could rob a
bank. The average take was a whopping four grand, less
than Stripling spent every year on periodontics.

Despite the hordes of health-care scammers working
in South Florida, Nick rated his felonious speciality as
elite. Defrauding the United States government of millions of dollars was no job for morons, he said. The Medicare system was chaos times ten.

Faking all those claims required cunning and precision
that was foreign to the thug world. Every patient name and
Social Security number had to belong to some real person,
which meant hacking a medical data bank or paying off
a clerk. Then the stolen names had to be transcribed cor-
rectly down to the middle initial, no typos! Same with the
Socials, otherwise a government computer in Atlanta or
Bethesda would spit the forms right back. Just the paperwork would make you nuts, sixteen fucking copies of
everything—and, Jesus, you had to be sharp with the math.

Stripling, growing fuzzy from the pills, rambled on to
Eve. Said he'd proved himself a heavy hitter. Reminded
her that he wasn't some gutless boiler-room hack who'd
copped a plea, paid back the money and ratted out his
brother scammers. No, he'd given up a healthy arm and
committed two cold-blooded murders so he could keep
his riches and stay clear of prison.

He was the real deal, an epic badass!

Yet when they pulled up to Moxey's airstrip and he saw
the white seaplane rolling toward a takeoff, Yancy blowing a kiss from behind a port window, Stripling pitched
sideways out of the Jeep and began to jabber.

Twenty-five

When the roof blew off, Neville was in the bathtub with Coquina and Driggs, covered with sofa cushions. Coquina was crying while the monkey quivered and mewled. Neville wrapped his arms around them for two hours. He knew by the ebbing pitch of the wind that the hurricane was moving away, so he wasn't afraid.

Not of the storm.

But he couldn't stop worrying about Christopher, wondering if he was dead or alive. Yancy had said Neville didn't do anything wrong, but Neville was aware that the police paid more attention when the person who got killed was rich and white. On the other hand, if Yancy was right about Christopher being a dangerous murderer, a wanted man, things might turn out all right. Maybe Nassau would reward Neville for his bravery at Bannister Point by returning the family land at Green Beach.

Then he could rebuild his house, and go back to life the way it was.

At dawn they got busy—Neville and Coquina along with Yancy and Rosa. Together they packed up Coquina's belongings and in the wilting heat carried them to her mother's place down the road. The mother wanted nothing to do with Driggs, who two Saturdays earlier had snatched a silver bracelet from her ankle outside the straw market. Neville said the monkey's manners were much improved. Coquina's mother reluctantly agreed to let the creature stay while Neville borrowed her car to drive the two Americans to the airport.

"But I hoyd ain't no Bahamasair today," she said.

The American man said, "We're flying private, ma'am."

On the ride to Moxey's, Yancy once again thanked Neville for saving his life. Neville asked what would happen next.

"Soon as I get back to Florida, I'll speak with the FBI," Yancy said. "Tell 'em where they can find Mr. Stripling— the guy you call Grunion."

"Wot if he's dead from the stobbin'?"

"Then all that's left is to arrest his wife and find the rest of the money."

Rosa spoke up: "No, Andrew, that's not all. Mr. Stafford might have to deal with the authorities here."

"Yeah, they could be a pain," said Yancy, "but I'll fly back and tell them exactly what went down. How you stopped Stripling from shooting me."

"You'd do dot?" Neville said.

"It's a promise, man."

Neville felt better. Having an American policeman on his side would be good.

"Wot about my beach?" he asked.

Yancy said he wasn't sure. "If Stripling bought it with the Medicare money, prosecutors in Miami might file a claim on it."

"But the land's mine." Neville was perplexed. "Egg stayin' dot trailer. I cont move back till he's gone."

"Egg's heading to prison, too," Rosa said. "For what he did to me."

Neville didn't know all that had occurred at the Dragon Queen's shack, but he'd never forget what he saw when he and Yancy opened the door. It would be fitting for Egg to spend time at Fox Hill as a prisoner instead of a guard. Neville pictured him being taunted in the showers by the other inmates, the ones he'd hurt with the marlin billy. Much sport would be made of his monkey wounds.

After they arrived at the airport, Yancy asked Neville to call as soon as he got information about Stripling's condition. "Dead or alive, I need to know. Meanwhile don't talk to anybody about last night at Bannister Point. You already tell Coquina?"

"No, mon."

Rosa said that was good. "For her and you."

"I dont won hafta move 'way. Home is home, you unnerstahn."

"You won't ever have to leave," Yancy said.

"I be hoppy 'f dot's true."

"It's true, Mr. Stafford."

Rosa went to the ladies' room. Neville asked Yancy about his own difficult situation back in Florida, about the large house being constructed on the land where the little deer lived—the deer that were no bigger than dogs.

"You gon stop dot fella and make 'im rip de place down?"

Yancy smiled in a tired way. "Wish I could, but it's probably too late."

"I hope not," Neville said.

Yancy said good-bye and shook his hand. Rosa did the same when she came back. She told him to take good care of Coquina, and to put Driggs on a strict fruit-and-fiber diet—no more conch fritters! Yancy said it was time to go. He and Rosa picked up their bags and went inside the terminal building.

Standing at the chain-link fence, Neville saw several overturned planes on the turnaround section of the tarmac. He also noticed, undamaged, the single-engine seaplane belonging to the man he knew as Christopher. A few white men and some local teenagers were out clearing the landing strip of hurricane litter. Soon the American policeman and his girlfriend would be able to take off, if they had a pilot who would fly them. The weather out west, toward Florida, looked all right.

The car belonging to Coquina's mother was a rust-freckled Taurus with a Salt Life decal on the back window and a fickle alternator. Neville tried the key seven times before the ignition turned over. Then, barely a mile from the airport, the engine quit. Neville got out and popped the hood hoping for something as simple as a loose wire. He fiddled with various connections but nothing worked.

Neville heard a car coming the other way and decided to flag it down. As the vehicle came into view he noticed first that it was yellow, then that it was a hardtop Jeep Wrangler, of which there was only one on the island. Neville stopped waving and backpedaled for cover behind the broken-down Taurus.

But the Jeep was moving too fast. Both occupants looked squarely at Neville as they swerved around the stalled sedan and sped on toward the airport. The bastard that Neville had stabbed in the back sat upright in the front next to his woman, who was driving. Their taut expressions displayed not a flicker of recognition, only annoyance at the roadway obstruction.

Once they were out of sight, Neville placed both hands over his heart and thanked the Lord Almighty for his good fortune. Obviously the murderous fugitive had no idea who'd speared him from behind with a fishing rod.

Minutes later Neville heard an aircraft lifting off from Moxey's. He looked up and saw the floatplane, as white and graceful as a gull. The man known to him as Christopher wouldn't have had enough time to make that flight, no matter how fast his woman was driving.

So it had to be Yancy, the American policeman, on board. Yancy and his girlfriend.

The fact was confirmed minutes later when the yellow Jeep reappeared, racing back from the direction of the airfield. This time Neville didn't wave at the Striplings as they passed, but he didn't bother to hide, either.

Rosa fell asleep on Yancy's shoulder but he kept awake, his eyes on the pilot. The flight to Miami was only forty-five minutes through a light chop. To the north, beyond Grand Bahama, towered a bank of muddy clouds, the last tailings of Hurricane Françoise.

Riding on small planes never failed to put a tune in Yancy's head, and this time it was "Mozambique." Claspers didn't ask for details of Stripling's crimes or say much of anything at the controls. Yancy figured he was preoccupied devising a story for Nick or the FAA, depending on which way he decided to play it. After the Caravan touched down at Miami International, Yancy offered him a one-hundred-dollar bill for fuel. Claspers shook his head and pointed to a gold AmEx clipped to the sun visor. The name imprinted on the card was Christopher Grunion.

When the plane taxied to a stop, Claspers tugged off his earphones.

"So, what are your plans?" Yancy asked.

"I'm not sure. Too old for prison and, man, I do like to fly."

"It won't be my call. The feds can be prickish, as you know."

Claspers said, "I had no idea he murdered anybody. Swear on the Bible, the Koran, whatever."

"Hey, I believe you."

"Then I was thinking maybe you could help. Put in a good word."

"Sure, but here's the situation," Yancy said. "Technically I'm not a cop. I'm a restaurant inspector."

"Fuck a duck!"

"It's just a temporary reassignment. The badge I borrowed from a colleague."

"Other words, you count dead flies at the Pizza Hut. This is who I got for a character witness."

"I'll be a detective again in the very near future. Meanwhile, let's not disparage the tireless civil servants who keep our public dining establishments free from vermin."

"You don't mind," said Claspers, "I got a shitload of paperwork."

Yancy woke up Rosa. They climbed out of the plane and jumped from a pontoon to the tarmac. A brief snag occurred upon re-entry when a Customs officer asked Yancy to unzip his footwear, tight nylon booties that were tailored for water wading though not ideal for travel. The fishing shoes smelled vile but the Customs man intrepidly probed their sweaty interiors in search of contraband.

Afterward Rosa called a cab to take them to the parking garages, where they kissed good-bye and set out separately to locate their cars. Twenty minutes later Yancy was in his Subaru heading up the interstate to the FBI office in North Miami Beach. He wasn't dressed for the occasion, and in fact looked like a man who'd spent the night in a hurricane. Again the booties were a liability.

Getting past the reception desk required dropping the name of a well-regarded Miami police lieutenant for whom Yancy had once worked. Eventually he ended up in an interview room with the two humorless street agents he'd encountered at Nick Stripling's funeral. They remembered Yancy with manifest unfondness, so he rather enjoyed dropping the bomb.

"Mr. Stripling isn't dead. I just left him in the Bahamas, bleeding from a fresh hole in his back."

The posture of the agents improved. They began to fashion questions. One of them asked who stabbed Stripling. Yancy said he didn't know; it was a drunken dispute.

The other agent asked if Yancy had traveled alone to the islands.

"Yep," he said, which was technically true. Rosa hadn't told him to leave her out of the recap, but that was his intention. The FBI needed to know only the basics, beginning with Stripling's whereabouts.

The taller agent was Strumberg and his partner was Liske. Their suits weren't the same shade of gray but the cut of the lapels looked identical. When Yancy told them about Stripling's self-amputation, they tried to act as if they heard such stories every day.

However, Yancy knew they were stoked because they called in an assistant to take down what he was saying. The assistant's laptop needed recharging so there was a period of lame small talk while she got on the floor to locate an electric outlet. Strumberg asked how Yancy had lost his detective job.

"Aw, come on. You guys know what happened. They let you have free Internet, right?"

"The media can exaggerate."

"Not this time," Yancy said. "In defense of a woman's honor I waylaid her husband with a portable vacuum. The gesture was unappreciated and, unfortunately, witnessed by the proverbial throngs."

The assistant's laptop beeped to life, and the important phase of the interview continued. At one point Liske asked Yancy to draw a map of Lizard Cay. Yancy politely suggested that a satellite photo would be more accurate. The assistant found one on a classified government website and zoomed in on Bannister Point.

Yancy placed a fingertip to the screen. "That's the house your subject is renting, but he won't be there much longer. You should call whoever you need to call and have him arrested. But that's probably not going to happen this afternoon, is it?"

"There's a strict diplomatic process," said Liske, "we're obliged to follow."

"Then you might lose him."

"Not for long," Strumberg asserted. "How badly was he hurt?"

"This morning I saw him in a car at the airfield. And if he's well enough to ride in a car, he can ride on a plane."

"How do you know he hasn't already left the island?"

"His pilot flew off without him," Yancy explained, "at my instruction."

"You hijacked his aircraft?"

"Not with a weapon—and I prefer the word 'commandeer.' The pilot didn't know who Stripling was until I told him. He might be in a mood to cooperate."

"We'll see." Liske looked at Strumberg. "Stripling could charter another flight to Nassau. From there it's a straight haul to London or New York."

"Or even easier to come here," Strumberg said. "Hell, we know the man's got brass balls. If he cut off his own arm, as you say."

Yancy informed the agents that the Nassau airport had gotten trashed by the storm. "But I'm guessing the runways will open by midafternoon, tomorrow morning at the latest. I were you guys, I'd be putting on my Bluetooths and workin' those phones, because that fucker's probably got a fake passport. Ask Immigration to look up a Christopher Grunion."

The quick-typing assistant piped, "Could you spell that name for me, please?"

Overall Yancy thought the debriefing went as well as he could have hoped. Although the FBI agents were riveted on the Medicare case, they showed more than polite interest in the two murders committed by Stripling in Florida. Such heavy allegations could boost him to the top of the fugitive list and, in Liske's priceless phrasing, "incentivize" the Bahamian government to apprehend him. It would help if a homicide warrant was waiting in Monroe County or Miami-Dade, the jurisdictions where the shootings took place. That would be Yancy's next project.

Back in the car he plugged in his phone and called Rosa. She was already at work, elbow-deep in an autopsy. The spare key to her house was hidden inside a fake cactus next to the back door. Yancy let himself in, fed the fish, showered and fixed a peanut-butter-and-cucumber sandwich. He left messages for Rogelio Burton and Sheriff Summers, telling them that he had big news and that he was on his way back to the Keys.

The cell rang in his hand—Tommy Lombardo at the health department.

"Hey, I know you're supposed to be on vacation and all—"

"No, I'm working," Yancy said.

"What, they got a roach emergency in the Bahamas?"

"That's hilarous, Tommy. It's a murder case."

"Sure, it is."

"I'm back in the States. What do you need?"

"You, Andrew. There's been, huh, a complaint filed on Stoney's. Worse than the usual, okay? Some widow from Ponte Vedra wound up in the ER with a three-aught hook in her watchamacallit. That pink wormy thingy hangs down in your throat?"

"The uvula," Yancy said. "She got a fish hook stuck in her uvula. I'm betting she ordered the Cuban yellowtail."

"Man, that's amazing. How'd you know?"

"Brennan doesn't check the gut for hooks when he cooks a fish whole."

"How come?"

"Because he's a bumblefuck."

"I need you pronto back in the saddle, Andrew. This one made the *Citizen*. The widow lady, she's got an in with the governor."

"Let's have lunch later in the week. Pick a place that won't poison us."

Rosa got home from the office at five-thirty. They didn't go out for dinner and they didn't make love. The autopsy she'd completed was that of a girl who had died on her birthday. Only eight years old and the parents had left her alone while they went to play the slots at the Miccosukee casino, way out on Krome Avenue. The girl was doing laps in the backyard pool when her appendix ruptured, no one there to hear the cries for help. She made it back to the shallow end but the pain doubled her up, and that's where they'd found her—the parents, so shitfaced they couldn't remember where they'd left their car keys.

Yancy spent the night holding Rosa on the bed. She cried and said not every day at her job was so awful, and all he could say was close your eyes. At dawn she was sleeping when he kissed the top of her head and slipped out the door.

First he drove to Johnny Mendez's residence and placed the crooked ex-sergeant's gold badge inside the mailbox. The Siamese was licking its paws on the hood of the Lexus, while the gargoyle visage of Mrs. Johnny Mendez watched him from the porch. She wore inappropriate heels and a sheer morning robe that revealed a gruesome topography of misspent liposuctions. Yancy felt a prick of sympathy for Mendez; embezzling from Crime Stoppers might have been the only way to pay for his wife's cosmetic overhauls. Yancy honked once and sped away.

In Homestead he steered off the turnpike at the speedway exit and drove to the apartment building where his grandmother had lived. From the road he could see the window the burglars had broken on the day of her funeral.

Whoever lived in the unit now had a small child; a tricycle stood on the walkway by the front door. Yancy called his father in Montana and left a message asking how the fishing was. He didn't mention where he was calling from.

On the drive to the Keys he kept the radio off. His thoughts tumbled in the quiet, and the miles slipped away. A fender bender on the Snake Creek drawbridge had backed up traffic, so Yancy stopped for a grouper sandwich at a café he knew to be clean. His muted phone showed two more calls from Tommy Lombardo, though nothing from Neville Stafford on Lizard Cay.

As soon as the highway cleared Yancy was back in the car, still thinking of Neville and the incident at Bannister Point. Yancy worried that Eve Stripling might have recognized the old man from Rocky Town, and that her husband would send Egg to murder him. Yancy wondered how long it would take the FBI to make a move.

His backup choice was Sonny Summers, despite the sheriff's fear of the severed-arm case. Yancy thought Sonny might be persuaded to speak with the Bahamian authorities if he saw a chance for down-range glory— assisting the capture of a runaway murderer.

Halfway across the Seven Mile Bridge Yancy heard a siren. A ladder truck loomed in the rearview, and he slowed to let it pass. Fires were so infrequent in the Keys that Yancy assumed the emergency was another head-on.

He was coming over the pass at Bahia Honda, leaving a second voice message for the sheriff, when he saw a churning spire of black smoke. It was rising on the Gulf side of Big Pine, far from the highway, which meant it wasn't a car crash. Some poor bastard's home was ablaze.

Yancy wondered if it was somebody he knew.

Twenty-six

Dear Diary,

All these years I've been wondering what ever happened to her, and tonight she walked into the Olive Garden and re-stole my heart.

She said, "Cody, you can do better than this."

I said, "You look awesome, Ms. Chase."

And she did look awesome, even hotter than I remembered from school. I'm pretty sure she got her boobs done.

"Can we go somewhere private to talk?" she asked.

I told Arnelle the hostess I was taking a ten-minute break, but there was no way. Ms. Chase grabbed my hand and led me to her car. We drove to the Bank of America near Oral Roberts, and I got the most epic BJ of all time. She parked in the tellers' drive-through so nobody could see us, and I swear I almost kicked out the windshield.

After zipping me up she told me how she'd walked out on her husband and drove all the way from Florida just to find me. She said she couldn't stay long in Tulsa because there's still a warrant left over from what happened all those years ago between me and her.

She said, "I'm a big-time fugitive, Cody."

Right away I started getting hard again, but she acted like she didn't notice.

I told her I had a girlfriend but it wasn't serious. "She's a teacher, too. AP English, same as you. Only it's a charter school."

Ms. Chase smiled and gave me a long kiss. I had a joint so we smoked it. The car smelled like McDonald's fries because that's all she ate the whole way from Sarasota. She said she didn't waste time in sit-down restaurants—she wanted to get to Oklahoma as fast as possible and track me down.

Her hair looked different because she got platinum highlights so nobody would recognize her from the Wanted poster, which I'd never seen but then I hardly ever get to the post office.

"There's a big wild world out there, Cody. Are you ready to take the ride?"

"See, they just promoted me to assistant manager."

"Congratulations."

"But the boss, he's a major dickbrain."

She said, "Life is but the blink of an eye. This is what you'll learn."

I apologized for how the trial went down, what I said about her on the witness stand. Ms. Chase said she understood and forgave me totally. I was under major pressure at the time—it was my parents who made me testify and turn over all the stuff I wrote about our love affair. My mom read every page of the diary but she didn't get most of it, thank God. She literally asked me what a "back-door job" was. I made up something about sneaking into a club.

Ms. Chase wanted to know if I'd ever got married, and my answer was almost but not quite. She told me her husband's a retired doctor with gobs of money. He knew she was running from the law but he proposed to her anyway, which I totally understand. She said he's much older than her and also he's kind of a perv. He likes to beat off while he's got a belt or electric cord around his neck, which I've heard of but sure never tried.

"Who are you reading these days?" she asked.

I told her I've sort of gotten away from books and more into Xbox.

"Oh, Cody," she said, and I took it as a cut.

She told me it was time to start thinking big, so I pointed at my all-world woody and asked, "You mean big like this?" She laughed and gave it a squeeze, which got my hopes flying, but then she started talking about inner journeys and the hand of fate.

I kept trying to pull off her skinny jeans but she wouldn't go for it. She did unbutton her top, which was pretty sweet. There were more freckles than I remembered but who cares.

"Don't you have any big dreams?" she asked, but offhand I couldn't come up with any.

"Well, you should, Cody. You're a sharp young man, an A student back in the day."

It's not easy to have a seriously deep conversation when you've got a purple hard-on that could cut a diamond. I told Ms. Chase there was a new Chipotle's opening up on North Utica and I was thinking about putting in for day manager.

"No," she said. "You're coming with me."

And that's what I did.

Yancy handed the transcript back to Montenegro, who said the sheriff's office was holding the iPad on which the diary was stored. One of the road deputies had confiscated it from the rental car.

"I knew that fuckwit was keeping a journal," Yancy said. "Should I go see Bonnie?"

The lawyer said he didn't care. "Bonnie's not her name, dude."

"Well, 'Plover' is unacceptable. I can't bring myself to say it."

"And you had no knowledge of her true identity while you were balling her?"

"The last time we were together is the first time she told me."

"And of course you felt no obligation to notify the police—or your long-suffering counsel." Montenegro rubbed both hands on his shaven orb. He was more expansive than usual but no less jaundiced. "I probably could get her six months and probation for the arson, if she wasn't already on the lam for a sex felony. Oklahoma hasn't decided whether to extradite, but I spoke to an Agent Weiderman—"

"Yes, we've met," Yancy said.

"Not a bad guy. We discussed the problems with the Tulsa case, now that Mr. Parish intends to become a published author. This new diary of escapades won't be helpful to the prosecution."

"Listen, should I go see her or not?"

"You're not as pissed as I thought you'd be."

"I am highly pissed. Supremely pissed."

"She's determined to plead insanity," Montenegro said. "Says she torched the house only because she was deranged by her passion for you. Another celestial mystery, but there you fucking have it."

"For Christ's sake, Monty, she's not insane."

"How would *you* know? I mean, of all people." The lawyer yawned. "See what you set in motion, Andrew, by sleeping with this unreliable person. The dominoes continue to fall—on my desk, unfortunately."

"Have you talked to Bonnie's husband?"

"The board-certified physician you assaulted at Mallory Square? Seems like eons ago. No, I haven't spoken to Dr. Witt because he's presently in ICU at Sarasota Memorial Hospital exhibiting the cognitive capacity of an artichoke. He was found nude from the waist down, hanging from a peewee basketball hoop at the local Kiwanis park. This was four-thirty a.m., some rookie cop called it in as a suicide attempt, which it wasn't. The bottle of virgin olive oil being a key clue. Also, the cashmere choke collar."

"Is he going to die?" Yancy asked.

"The family says the doctor's chances for recovery are about the same as the chances of him paying for his estranged wife's legal defense, which is to say remote. Go see her if you want but, here, read this first."

It was more lovesick rubbish from Cody Parish.

Dear Diary,

Ms. Chase is gone! She left the Best Western to take a walk, and came back in a rental car. I begged her to stay but I could only watch helplessly as she packed her bag.

"Don't you love me anymore?" I cried.

She touched my cheek and said, "Darling, where's my shampoo and conditioner?"

"Darling"? Seriously?

My whole world was crashing down. How could she take my heart in her hands and choke it like a baby bunny rabbit?

The last time we made love I knew something wasn't right because she didn't make a sound. Also, she didn't move her butt very much, which isn't like her. I asked what's wrong, princess, and she said nothing's wrong, everything's beautiful.

But that night in bed I had a horrible feeling she was thinking about someone else. It had to be Andrew, the man she was with before she came back to Tulsa and took me away. He's got some hot new girlfriend now and I think Ms. Chase is jealous. Supposedly the girlfriend is a doctor, like Ms. Chase's husband, and maybe that screwed with her head, too.

Or maybe it's something else. Maybe she just went batshit crazy which can happen when the monthly hormones take over. I've seen it before, and watch out!

All I know is I've lost my true soul mate. Yes, she was an outlaw and a schizo but I loved her anyway—and I would have stayed glued by her side until the law hunted us down. Every day on the road with Ms. Chase was wild lust and adventure, and I don't regret one single moment.

If she showed up on my doorstep tomorrow I'd take her back in a heartbeat, and no man alive would blame me. I'd go through the fires of Hell and follow her anywhere, except back to Tulsa because I am seriously done with the Olive Garden.

Like the book says, you can't go homeward angel. And by God I'm not.

Yancy drove out to the detention center on Stock Island, a place where as a detective he'd interviewed numerous inmates though never a former lover. He was friends with the duty officer, so he and Bonnie had a room to themselves. She was excited to see him and disappointed by his chilly reponse.

"Andrew, why are you looking at me like that? It's just a fire. Nobody died."

"You're right. It's not like you burned down an orphanage."

"Please, there's no cause for sarcasm."

Her county jumpsuit was the same blaze orange as Nick Stripling's poncho. She wore the braided pigtails but the jailers had taken away her lip gloss.

"You think they're recording us?" she said, looking around for a video camera.

Yancy said no. The phone calls usually got taped but he wasn't sure about visitations.

"Cody wants to come see me, too, but Mr. Montenegro says absolutely not."

"Why did you do this, Bonnie? So much drama."

"Oh please. It was all for you. Don't pretend like you don't get it, or I'll really be upset."

"But I truly *don't* get it."

"You were right about Cody," she said. "He was keeping a secret journal of everything we did, just like before. His notion is to do a book and get rich. He thinks he can write, which I suppose is my fault for building him up so much in class. But isn't that what teachers are supposed to do? I didn't know he would peak in eleventh grade! At first I was livid about the new diary, but then Mr. Montenegro said it's good for my case in Oklahoma because they'd have to charge him with aiding a fugitive, which would be messy for the prosecutors."

"Because he's supposed to be the victim," Yancy said.

"Exactly, Andrew. The boy I supposedly corrupted."

"Here's the thing: They don't need Cody's testimony to convict you for bail jumping. Also, Bonnie, this arson? Major felony. Nobody gets a free pass if they torch a home."

"Insane people do. Eighteen months of treatment, then we can be together again. I've done my research."

"Insanely jealous isn't the same as clinically insane." Yancy impatiently drummed two fingers on the table. "Why am I even bothering with this conversation? You *are* somewhat nuts, I'll give you that. But no judge in Florida would let you walk."

"I miss you so much, darling. Did you hear about Cliff strangling himself?"

"Yes, it was an inconsiderate choice of venue. The Kiwanians do good work."

"He probably took me out of his will when I ran off with Cody. Not that I care about the money."

"You and the doctor are still legally married. He dies tomorrow, you'll get half the estate." Yancy winked at her. "Not that you care."

"God, when did you get so mean?"

"Ever since I drove down my street and saw flames shooting into the sky."

She reached across the table and pinched him hard. "Why are you being like this? It was your idea—don't you dare say you don't remember. I did this for you!"

Yancy said, "Okay, now you are officially in lunar orbit."

"It was that night at your place when we were lying out on the deck. You put the blanket down—that wool blanket that smelled like a wet puppy—then we smoked a number and drank a bottle of cabernet." Bonnie's jaw was working and she was squeezing her hands together.

"We went out there to make love and watch the moon set over the Gulf, right? You said it was the most peaceful sight imaginable, a golden spring moon. But then it turned out that guy's new house was in the way."

Yancy lowered his forehead to the table. "You can't be serious."

"It was so tall it blocked out the whole arc of the moon," she went on. "You got real sad and then super angry, and that's when you turned to me and said—"

"I oughta burn that fucking house down."

"See, you *do* remember!"

"Word for word," Yancy muttered to the tabletop.

The worst day of Evan Shook's existence began when he sent a text message to his wife that read: "See you in Miami tonight. Don't forget to bring our little friend!"

Mrs. Evan Shook was perplexed because she had no

plans to visit him in Florida, engrossed as she was with hosting a cocktail party (including finger food) for the Republican Women's Club of Greater Syracuse. Nor did she understand her husband's reference to "our little friend," which was actually a jackrabbit vibrator belonging to his mistress, the intended recipient of the text.

Only when his wife called to accuse him of arranging illicit threesomes did Evan Shook realize his calamitous typing mistake. She said she'd been hearing lurid rumors of his cheating ways, and now she had proof! It so happened that one of the most feared divorce lawyers in the tri-state region would be attending that night's fundraiser, and Evan Shook's wife said she planned to fuck him and then hire him.

Against such a blindsiding Evan Shook rustled up what he regarded as a passable defense: The text had been meant for Ford Lipscomb, the "little friend" being a cashier's check to cover construction overruns on the Keys house. This yarn was rejected with savage derision. Evan Shook's wife advised him to hang on to his shriveled little nuts because she and her new attorney were coming with a blowtorch.

"And a Brink's truck," she added, and hung up.

So it was understandable that Evan Shook was preoccupied as he headed to Big Pine for a meeting with a landscape architect retained by Mrs. Lipscomb, also en route. On the highway his Suburban was passed by two speeding fire engines that normally would have aroused his curiosity, but he remained fogged with gloom. No internal alarms went off as he turned onto Key Deer Boulevard and saw the smoke; he thought it was just some redneck burning tires.

A green Sebring convertible went flying past in the opposite direction, and that's when Evan Shook's senses stirred: The woman at the wheel of the car was his next-door neighbor's stalker. Suddenly the billowing plume held promise, and Evan Shook drove faster. He'd never made that pledged phone call to Agent John Wesley Weiderman, never reported his encounter with the pretty fugitive on Yancy's backyard deck.

And he never would.

By the time he came around the corner of the block, Evan Shook was completely prepared to see a house on fire. He was not, however, expecting the house to be his own.

The first words from his lips were "Fuck me!" It was not an unapt metaphor for what had occurred, and he would repeat it often to no one in particular. The spec house was, in the parlance of professional firefighting, fully engulfed.

Impressive were the efforts to save it but everything except the slab was raw fuel, from the wooden baseboards to the wooden trusses. Evan Shook positioned himself upwind, leaning against one of the fire trucks and watching in a funereal stupor as the walls of his island investment buckled and turned to ash.

Mrs. Lipscomb showed up sobbing in the company of her landscaper, whose shared grief was triggered by the loss of a lucrative contract. Next to arrive on scene was Agent Weiderman, who provided the police with the name, description and automobile information of the suspected arsonist. Twenty minutes later Evan Shook was informed by a sweaty road sergeant that Plover Chase had been captured at a roadblock on Summerland Key. Four empty jerry cans smelling of gasoline were recovered from the trunk of her rental.

In the growing crowd Evan Shook recognized his insurance agent, who was scampering around snapping photographs. Although the site was covered for fire loss, Evan Shook couldn't recall the numerical terms of the policy, specifically the payoff limits. He was morbidly aware of how much of his own money he'd sunk into the property, and additionally what he owed on the mortgage and construction loan. Even with the insurance check he could lose his ass. All that remained would be a pile of charred rubble and a bare lot, which Evan Shook undoubtedly would be forced to surrender in the divorce.

The future was nauseating to contemplate. Evan Shook wished he were a clueless bystander, not the victim, so he could enjoy the blaze for the crackling spectacle it was. At some point Agent Weiderman asked if Evan Shook could think of a reason why Plover Chase would torch his house instead of Andrew Yancy's.

"No idea," said Evan Shook. "Only thing I ever did to the lady was rent a hotel room for her and her deadbeat boyfriend."

"Strange. Wonder why she picked you."

"There's the one you should ask!" Evan Shook was pointing at Yancy, who'd just stepped out of his car. He looked genuinely astounded by the sight of the fire.

Evan Shook squirted past the much taller Agent Weiderman and rushed toward Yancy yelling, "This is all your motherfucking fault! Your lunatic girlfriend burned down my house!"

Yancy surprised his neighbor by pinning him somewhat forcefully to the hood of the Subaru. "In the first place," Yancy said nose to nose, "she couldn't possibly have done this because she's in Miami. Secondly, she's not a lunatic, but on her behalf I'll accept your heartfelt apology."

"Not the doctor girlfriend," Evan Shook wheezed. "The fucked-up blonde. You know which one."

Yancy righted Evan Shook and set him on the ground like a lawn jockey. Agent Weiderman wedged the men apart and led Yancy away to brief him on the improbable particulars of the crime. Evan Shook was so upset that when the phone vibrated in his pants, he pulled out the stun gun by mistake and nearly Tazed his own ear.

After successfully extracting his cell he heard the voice of Ford Lipscomb:

"Jayne told me what happened, Evan. It's so terrible, truly awful." He was calling from the Gulf Stream aboard the *Misty Momma IV,* which he'd chartered for the day.

"It's heartbreaking for us," he continued, "but poor you! Good God, man, you must be in shock."

"Something like that," said Evan Shook.

"Jayne's completely devastated. I just spoke with her and she says the place is still burning—they couldn't save anything."

Evan Shook whimpered to himself. Three firefighters were chopping at a smoldering portico. "Is this about your deposit, Mr. Lipscomb?"

"No rush," he said. "Tomorrow's fine. Whenever the banks open."

Twenty-seven

Claspers didn't come back. The following day, the Striplings enlisted another pilot to fly them out of Andros—a
local guy with a dubiously maintained twin Beech, but
Nick said go for it. The new pilot advised them to be
ready at noon.

Cell service on the island was working again, so Eve
phoned British Air in Nassau and booked two business-
class seats to London. Her next call was to a spinal surgeon on Devonshire Street whose patients had awarded
him four and a half stars on the Internet, which was insuf-
ficiently stellar for Nick but Eve made an appointment
anyway.

While she was repacking for a longer, possibly perma-
nent stay, Egg showed up. He was haggard and limping;
Nick chewed him a new one anyway. The goon offered no
apology for disappearing the night of the storm. He said
he'd had a medical problem, so he'd brought back the Jeep
and walked to the trailer at Curly Tail Lane. He didn't
say what had been done with Yancy's girlfriend, and the
Striplings didn't ask.

Eve told Egg to look at the Super Rollie, which had been malfunctioning since Nick crashed it into the wall. Egg said the automatic steering was fucked up. Nick started hollering and cussing again because how else was he supposed to get through Heathrow if he couldn't walk. Eve said all airports offered wheelchairs.

"Not with motors!" her husband railed. "Not with a goddamn iPod dock!"

He was in ragged shape despite the painkillers. Eve told Egg to roll him outside while she finished filling the suitcases. In the hurricane's aftermath Bannister Point was an obstacle course—branches and coconuts and two-by-fours all over the place. Egg in his hobbled condition did a poor job of dodging the rubble, and even the Rollie's pneumatic suspension couldn't spare Nick from the bumps. Between groans he rehashed for Egg the saga of his ambush.

Then he asked: "It wasn't you who tried to kill me, was it?"

"No, mon. Why I do sum ting like dot?"

"You'd have to be brain-dead," Stripling agreed. "But who could it be? I don't have any enemies on this fuckin' island. I don't *know* anybody on this fuckin' island."

Egg reminded him about the vandal who'd peed on the backhoes at the construction site.

"I thought you took care of that sonofabitch," Nick snapped.

"Yah, I hoyt 'im putty bod but he ain't dead. I saw 'im utter night."

Stripling wondered aloud if the stealth urinator was the same man he'd caught snooping outside the house, the old beach nigger he'd run off with the shotgun. Which, who'd be crazy enough to come back after somebody fired a twelve-gauge over your head?

Egg made no response. It wasn't a daily occurrence that a sober white person used the n-word in his presence, but the boss man seemed clueless.

"You gotta find out who crippled me," Nick went on. "That's your number one job."

Egg said he'd ask around town.

"Yeah, right. Be careful not to work up a goddamn sweat." Nothing annoyed Stripling as much as lack of initiative. "Maybe your woman can help," he needled Egg. "Do some of her voodoo shit and pull a name out of some dead chicken's asshole."

"Dot ain't funny."

"What's with the limp?" Nick could see that the brute was hurting.

"Monkey fucked me up bod."

"No shit?" It was Stripling's first laugh in days.

Eve caught up with them on the road. When her husband saw she was out of breath, he asked what was wrong.

"You-know-who at Immigration just called," she said. "Honey, it's already in the computer—somebody in Miami flagged your passport!"

Stripling deflated in the scooter chair. "That fuckin' Yancy got to the feds."

Eve was jumpy and distraught. "So what now, Nicky? You-know-who said they won't let you out of the country, and there's nothing she can do. She said don't go near the Nassau airport."

"So screw Nassau. We'll stay right here until I line up another way out. The Bahamians can't arrest us till they get a warrant from the States, and that could take weeks.

Months even. Meantime Mr. Ecclestone'll keep an eye on Moxey's for us, right? In case a chopper full of uniforms shows up."

Egg sniffed noncommittally.

Eve said, "Arrest *us*? My passport's clean. You're the one with the fake."

Sometimes she could be so thick it drove Nick nuts. "Yes, baby, 'us' as in Mr. and Mrs. Stripling, co-conspirators. You think Yancy left you out of the story? Like maybe he didn't hear you telling me to go ahead and blow his brains out? Or maybe the Cuban babe forgot you were the one told Egg to put a gag in her mouth and get rid of her?"

"Yeah, but, Nicky—"

"Just shut up."

Worse came to worse, he and Eve could escape by water. The new Contender would be arriving soon—the boat was a damn rocketship is what it was. He could run it straight down to Grand Turk.

Nick commanded Egg to take him back to the house. Eve walked on ahead. She didn't speak again until they were alone and the new pilot had been dismissed and the bags were unpacked.

"We could fly a spine doctor over from Miami or Palm Beach," she said.

"Really. And he'll bring his own MRI and a CT scanner? Hell, all we gotta do is lease a 747 and he can haul the whole friggin' OR. That's genius, Eve." Stripling chuckled mordantly. "It's like you forget I was in the business."

"Quit being an asshole, Nicky. You weren't in the medical-care business, you were in the stealing business."

Which, he would have run over her ungrateful ass with

the Rollie except the motor didn't work because Egg had removed the battery to lighten the vehicle for pushing. After Eve stormed upstairs Stripling stewed in the scooter chair for a long time. The ice melted and turned luke-warm in the towel she'd placed upon his puncture wound. The liquid sensation caused him to squirm.

Egg had slipped away again and Eve wasn't respond-ing to Nick's yells, so he pitched forward out of the Rol-lie and worm-crawled to the nearest bathroom, where he struggled to seat himself. He noticed that his pee stream grew weaker whenever the pain got worse, which, accord-ing to MyBedsideMD.com, could be a troublesome indi-cation. Unfortunately, his wife was in possession of the codeine Tylenols, meaning Nick would have to suck it up and apologize or spend the remainder of the day in deep-ening misery.

He swung open the bathroom door and called out, "Eve, I'm sorry! Come downstairs!"

No reply.

"Eve, baby, please! I said I was sorry."

An astringent dispatch from the second floor: "Go blow yourself, Nicky."

Damn, he thought. *She's really hacked off.*

One benefit of working in a violent metropolis such as Greater Miami was superior crime-lab technology, which had advanced by leaps and bounds during decades of extreme homicidal misbehavior. The .357 Smith & Wes-son found by Gomez O'Peele's body was tested, at Dr. Rosa Campesino's request, for the presence of a corn-starch mixture commonly used on the inside of powdered latex medical gloves. Sometimes, when fitting a nervous hand into such a glove, a criminal might externally disperse microscopic particles of the cornstarch formula. That's what turned up on both the handle and the trigger of the weapon that killed Dr. O'Peele.

It was a significant finding because a person who purposely shoots himself typically doesn't worry about fingerprints, and therefore doesn't don gloves before putting the gun barrel to his temple. In any event, the hands of Gomez O'Peele were bare when his body was discovered, and the only latents on the .357 came from two of the doctor's right-hand fingers, which was instructive because his sisters reported he was left-handed.

Cumulatively the evidence was more than enough for Dr. Rosa Campesino to classify O'Peele's death as a homicide, and she signed her name on the certificate. To surprised North Miami Beach detectives she conveyed her opinion that the doctor had been shot by a person other than himself who'd staged the crime as a suicide and had worn hand protection available at any medical-supply outlet. Rosa didn't identify Nicholas Stripling as the likely killer because it would have jeopardized both her job and the case; the Bahamas excursion ranged far outside the accepted investigatory parameters of an assistant medical examiner. Yancy had to be the one to provide Stripling's name.

Rosa's ruling on O'Peele's nonsuicide was an untidy development for the Key West Police Department, which had named the dead doctor as Charles Phinney's killer since the same pistol was used in both shootings. The *Citizen* had already run a story saying the Phinney case was being closed due to the prime suspect's self-inflicted demise. Now a new story had to be written announcing that the murder of the young fishing mate remained unsolved.

Rosa e-mailed her summary of O'Peele's autopsy to numerous interested parties, including at Yancy's suggestion Agents Liske and Strumberg at the Federal Bureau of Investigation. Afterward, while Rosa was eating a tomato salad at her desk, a hearse arrived at the morgue to pick up the body of Lindy Schultz, age eight, who'd died of drowning after her appendix ruptured in the family swimming pool. Nothing complicated about the postmortem, but Rosa was having difficulty writing the report.

She got home at six p.m. and took off her lab clothes and poured a glass of white wine. When Yancy called, she told him she'd gone ahead and closed O'Peele as a homicide. He was all gung ho, saying it cleared the way for murder charges against Nick Stripling—if the police could patch together a case.

Rosa was doubtful. Yancy had been the last person to see the doctor alive, a fact any semi-competent defense attorney would exploit to cast suspicion Yancy's way. There were no known outside witnesses to O'Peele's killing and probably no physical evidence placing Stripling at the doctor's apartment. Unsurprisingly, the serial numbers had been scraped off the .357, making it impossible to trace a chain of ownership.

"And anybody can buy surgical gloves," Rosa said.

"What gave you the idea to look for that powder?" Yancy asked.

She could tell he was impressed.

"Couple years ago I had a case where a urologist down on Brickell shot her boyfriend dead. Instead of using a regular medical glove to handle the weapon, she put on those latex finger cots—five of them—because she did a lot of prostate probing and that's what she had at the office. It goes without saying she wasn't the brightest bulb in the chandelier. The techs pulled a flawless palm print off the gun but also some cornstarch from the fingerlets. She wound up pleading to murder two."

Most of the time Rosa enjoyed her work, although she was increasingly aware of the mental toll. She never watched *CSI: Miami* or any of the TV shows featuring buff forensic investigators; in fact, she didn't look at much television except *Morning Joe* and the Tennis Channel. Her now-deceased former husband had been a decent mixed-doubles partner even with a spazzy backhand.

She asked Yancy if he was glad to be back in the Keys, and he said there was never a dull moment. "The westward view out my window has been dramatically enhanced. I can't wait for you to see."

"Oh shit. What did you do, Andrew?"

"Not a thing! However, I may have unwittingly inspired a bad deed. I'll tell you all about it this weekend. You're still coming down, right? If not I might get maundering drunk and take a spill on Duval Street."

"I'll be there as promised," Rosa said. "Oh, major update on Stripling's traveling arm: It's been returned to the warm bosom of Mother Earth. The cemetery sent a man to fetch it this morning. He was dressed like a freaking Blues Brother, I swear. Said his boss sprung for a new coffin because the grave robbers 'marred' the other one. That's the word he used."

"But isn't Eve required to sign a release?"

"They got verbal consent. He said the funeral director called her this morning."

"In the Bahamas?"

"I'm not sure, Andrew."

Yancy didn't know it but Rosa was soaking in the tub. She'd been there for an hour, so the water was beginning to cool. She'd pinned up her hair and lit a candle that made the white wall tiles shine pink. It was a small candle, like the ones used for offerings in the back of the church except Rosa's was huckleberry-scented.

Yancy said, "So, how are you doing? Tell the truth."

"I'm okay, honest. But you know they're going to get away, right? Both murder cases are impossible—O'Peele and your boy Phinney. Basically zero evidence, which leaves the Medicare fraud. It'll take the feds forever to indict Stripling and get a fugitive warrant, and by then he and Eve could be in Marrakech. What the hell were we thinking, Andrew?"

Yancy said, "Look, you had a rough day."

"I suppose you've already dreamed up another plan."

"According to my new chums at the FBI, nobody calling himself Grunion has tried to leave Nassau. They believe Nick and Eve are still on Andros. And no, there isn't a new plan. It's the same ballsy, brilliant plan as before."

"For God's sake," Rosa said.

"See? I made you laugh."

"You most certainly did." She poked one big toe out of the water and found herself picturing it with a tag.

Wow, she thought, *that's pretty fucked up.* Definitely time for a career re-evaluation.

"Don't forget," Yancy was saying on the phone, "Stripling tried to kill me, too. As his only surviving victim, I intend to present myself to the county grand jury as a well-groomed, credible witness. Attempted murder is also an extraditable offense."

Rosa didn't want to derail Yancy's enthusiasm, yet she feared that his value to prosecutors would be small given the messy circumstances leading to his demotion from the detective squad to roach patrol.

"You heard from Neville?" she asked.

"Not yet," Yancy said. "I'm hoping he's just laying low."

"I feel terrible about Coquina's house. The whole roof blowing off—that was insane."

"It's what hurricanes do."

"It wasn't the hurricane, Andrew. It was us."

Rosa said good-bye and put down the phone and closed her eyes. She was smiling when the candle burned out.

Neville wasn't worried for himself. It was Driggs who was in danger.

"Some bod mon lookin' to kill you so do wot I say. Now get in!"

The monkey made a fuss but eventually he curled up inside the backpack, which Neville zipped up snug. He threaded his arms through the straps and rode his bicycle to the conch shack. Half the thatching was gone, so he sat on the shady side of the bar. A muffled chitter came from the backpack when Neville set it on the stool beside him.

Everybody in the place was talking about the storm, sharing damage reports, gossip, whose husband spent the night with who. Neville ordered fritters and out of guilt he slipped a small one to Driggs. The air was thick as glue, like always after a hurricane.

Egg came limping down the road, but Neville didn't

get up to leave. He was from Andros and Egg wasn't. The others sitting at the conch shack were locals, too. If Egg got a notion in his fat skull to start trouble, he would be heavily outnumbered.

Like a half-wit he sat down squinting in the hottest patch of sun. When he finally spotted Neville he hitched around to the shade.

"Mon, I shoulda kill you down on de beach," he said.

Neville stayed cool. He was still sore from the beating outside the trailer.

"Utter night at my old lady's place, 'member dot? She say it was your fucking monkey did a number on my cock."

"Wot! Ain't my monkey, mon. I give 'im up as pay fuh summa her big woo-doo." Neville snuck a glance at the backpack. He prayed Driggs would stay quiet.

To Egg he asserted, "Dot monkey belongs legal to her, not me."

"When I find 'im I'm gon rip 'is head off."

"No way! He wort good money. She dint tell you he was in de movies with Johnny Depp?"

Egg was conscious of his outsider status on the island. He lowered his voice. "I seen dot wicked ape run off wit you. Don't lie. Give 'im up and we be done wit dis foolishness."

"Mon, wasn't fuh me you'd still have his filty teet in you! Lucky f'you I walked in dot shack when I did!" Neville was startled by his own strong words. The plastic fork in his hand was shaking.

"Okay. I guess you wanna die," Egg said.

"Dot's *you,* mister! You beeda one must wants to die coz dot's wot hoppen to men who lay in bed wit de Dragon Queen."

"Oh bullshit."

"Axe anybotty on Lizard Cay! Go on," Neville said. "Lisbon Jones. Duncan Roxy. Lightbourne Carter, too. All strong young fellas come under her spell and now dey stone dead. Go look in de graveyard up Prince Hill, you dont believe me."

"I ain't under nobody's spell," said Egg, without much zip.

"Listen to some hard truth, mon."

Egg said Neville was a lying sonofabitch, but he didn't hit him.

"Somebody stobbed my boss in de back and put 'im in a wheelchair. Wot you know 'bout dot?"

"Mr. Chrissofer got stobbed?" Neville acted shocked.

"And why you hongin' wit dot white mon, anyhow?" Egg asked.

"Wot white mon?"

"One you was wit at de old lady's place. One who took off yest'day in boss's plane."

From the corner of his eye Neville caught movement— Driggs fidgeting inside the zippered satchel. Egg didn't notice.

"Who I choose to hong wit is my bidness," Neville said.

"Had de hawt Cuban girlfriend."

"Yah, I know who you mean. Dot white mon? He a cop from Florida."

Egg frowned. "A cop? No way." Sweat was beading on his prunish little ears.

"He gon put your boss mon in a U.S. prison," Neville said ominously. "I was you, I'd get my ahss back to Nassau look f'nudder job."

Egg gimped off at a brisk clip. Neville finished his fritters and paid the bill. On the bike ride to the dock he stopped to open the backpack. Out squirmed Driggs, funky-smelling and carping as he climbed to Neville's shoulder. He was having a bad time kicking the nicotine.

One of the conch boys in a Whaler took them up the skinny creek where Neville had left his boat during the hurricane. For bailing rainwater Neville had brought two bisected milk jugs. He handed one to Driggs, who hurled it back at him. He grabbed the monkey by the scurfy ruff and said, "Stop dis shit, or I drop you at Mr. Egg's. He boil you in a goddamn stew!"

It took more than an hour to empty the water and man-grove leaves from the boat. The engine kicked over on the first try and before long they were in open water, needle-fish scattering like shooting stars ahead of the bow. In a drooping diaper Driggs stood all the way up front, a sin-gle upraised paw shielding his wide eyes from the glare.

The tide was high, so Neville was able to run the flats all the way back to Rocky Town. He kept his face turned away, toward the ocean, as he passed by Christopher's house.

Twenty-eight

Caitlin Cox was in the shower when she heard the phone ring. She hoped it was her stepmother calling to report a bounteous transfer of funds into Caitlin's checking account. Caitlin and Simon had already listed their house and were looking for a much bigger place down in Palmetto Bay.

Two hundred grand was the amount Caitlin had been led to expect from her late father's offshore stash. A fatter chunk would be coming a bit later, when the life insurance company paid off on Nick's $2 million policy. Half of that was going to his one and only daughter, who could expedite its delivery (Eve had explained at their reconciliation lunch) if she quit making wild accusations about the manner of her father's death.

And Caitlin stopped, like, right away. The anticipated windfall had brightened her attitude toward all humanity; Simon said she was like a new person. When he got home from work every morning Caitlin would have two bagels thawing for him in the toaster oven. It was like being married to a geisha!

His job was night security on a movie shoot. *Swill* was the name of the film, about two guys and a hot vampire chick who open a juice bar on South Beach. As a surprise Simon brought Caitlin to the set, and the coolest thing happened—they asked her to play a customer who gags on a blood-and-banana smoothie. It was a short scene, no speaking lines, but still she was over the moon.

Although Simon earned a decent wage, he and Caitlin hadn't saved enough for a down payment on a fish tank, much less a house. For upward mobility they were relying on the money from Eve. But when Caitlin stepped out of the shower, she saw Simon holding her cell phone like it was a lit stick of dynamite.

"Is it her?" she asked.

"No, sweetheart, but you better take it."

Andrew Yancy was on the other end, and he got straight to the point:

"Caitlin, I've got a heart-stopping bulletin. Your dad's not dead."

"This is your idea of funny? You sick mother."

"He's hanging with Eve in the Bahamas—I tracked him down last week. He wasn't elated to see me, I won't lie. There were harsh words and gunplay."

Wrapped in a towel, Caitlin perched her bottom on the edge of a sofa. Simon was making inane hand gestures attempting to elicit information.

"I don't believe a word you're telling me," Caitlin said to Yancy. "Where in the Bahamas?"

"Andros Island. He's been using a fake name. They bought a beach, he and Eve, and they're trying to build a resort—I've given all this to the FBI, by the way. Don't waste a plane ticket, because they're going to haul your old man back here and lock his ass up. So this is sort of a good news, bad news call, but I did promise you we'd speak again."

Caitlin experienced an odd mingling of emotions, none of which was joy. "But I saw the arm in the coffin with my own two eyes. You're telling me it came from somebody else?"

"Oh no, the arm was definitely your father's. He had it removed by a surgeon. That was key to the whole scam, see? So everyone would think he's dead. The feds were getting ready to bust him, so he decided to have a quote-unquote boating accident."

"No. Way."

"Nick said he planned to let you in on the secret, when the time was right. But my feeling is that, being next of kin, you deserve to know now. I'm thinking you and Simon might want to scale down your financial plans."

Caitlin said, "Who *does* that? Cuts off their own freaking arm!"

Her husband waved at her and whispered, "I saw a really heavy flick about that! Rock climber fell down a crack—"

"Go, Simon! Get out!"

The cell phone sailed past his ear, and Simon retreated to his mini-gym. After Caitlin calmed down, she picked up the phone and spoke Yancy's name. He was still on the line.

"So, what about the money?" she asked. The deadness in her voice reminded her of how she used to sound in the heroin days. "The insurance part, I guess that's history."

"This is a lot to digest," said Yancy. "One day you're grieving for a lost parent, the next day for a lost inheritance."

Caitlin could hear the annoying clank of the weight machine in the other room. "So what happens to Eve? Sneaky lying bitch. We sat down together, just her and me, and she never told me Dad was still alive. What, like I'd rat him out or something? Know what I think? I bet it was her idea for him to give up a perfectly good arm. Sounds like her."

"Eve's in trouble, too," Yancy said.

"Good! You mean like jail?"

"Oh yes."

"Awesome!"

"We'll see."

"Then who gets all Dad's money?"

"The lawyers do," Yancy said. "Good-bye, Caitlin."

"Wait. Why are you laughing?"

Before putting his phone away he listened to a brief voice message from Neville Stafford saying Stripling was still on Lizard Cay, a big relief. Neville wanted to know when the police were coming to arrest the man. Yancy had been working to make that happen, but today he had a mundane job to do.

From the car trunk he removed his improvised roach-herding device and the portable vacuum. Alone he entered Stoney's Crab Palace. Tommy Lombardo, the coward, had texted to say he wouldn't be there; obviously he wanted Yancy to be the bad guy.

Brennan intercepted him at the door. "Not again. Are you kiddin' me?"

Shrimpy-smelling fingers twirled a hundred-dollar bill under Yancy's nose. He poked Brennan hard with the snout of the vacuum and ordered him to behave.

"But it ain't gotta be this way. Nilsson and me was like brothers!"

"Save your cash," Yancy advised. "I see oppressive legal fees in your future."

The widow who'd gulped the fish hook had tragically lost her uvula. A chopper hired by her offspring had flown her back to Jacksonville for follow-up treatment at Mayo. Brennan said that overlooking the hook had been a freak accident and he insisted that Yancy inspect his current stock of whole yellowtail snappers, seven fish. None featured honed tackle in the gullet, and Yancy made a terse notation before returning to his roach hunt.

"Aw, come on, what the fuck?" Brennan whined.

"This is coming from the top."

"Of Hotels and Restaurants? You mean like the director?"

"Higher still," Yancy said.

The downed widow was a Tea Party patroness who'd funneled ludicrous sums to the governor's election campaign. From her hospital room she had phoned the executive mansion and angrily warbled her story, and now Brennan was to be punished for serving barbed seafood.

Among many violations on the premises Yancy cataloged twelve live cockroaches, twenty-six dead flies, rodent droppings too abundant to count, a drum of rancid mayonnaise, a can of Comet stored beside the Parmesan cheese and, in a small bowl of slaw, one human toenail clipping. Over Brennan's objection Yancy wrote up another emergency closure of Stoney's.

"But we got a wedding party Saturday! Goddammit, I'm calling Lombardo."

"Take your best shot," Yancy said.

"It's that skinny chick who was dating Phinney. She's marrying that little Russian knob."

"Madeline? Oh, perfect."

Yancy drove to the T-shirt shop in town and saw an Out to Lunch sign on the door. Rogelio Burton met him at Pepe's for coffee. Yancy told his friend about the many twists in the Stripling investigation, and Burton was uncharacteristically blown away.

"Christ, I've heard of guys doing a finger before but never an arm!"

"It's trailblazing," Yancy said.

"So is you chasing this asshole through a hurricane. Best part is, you brought a date."

"That's not for general publication, Rog."

Burton advised him not to have high hopes for obtaining murder warrants on Stripling, as the evidence was less than overpowering. The detective also wasn't stunned to hear that the feds were still dicking around with the Medicare indictment, and that no decision had been made about how and when Stripling should be taken into custody.

Yancy told Burton about his latest Plan B—that he intended to give Key West prosecutors an affidavit about the night Stripling socked him and dumped him in the canal.

"That's an attempted murder, cut and dried."

"I'm not disagreeing," Burton said. "But, Andrew, you as the star witness? No offense, but the state attorney isn't what you call a risk taker. I don't see Billy Dickinson hanging a whole case on the testimony of a guy who sodomized a big-shot doctor at Mallory Square."

"It wasn't sodomy. It was a dry colonic."

"And now the doctor's wife, who you were boning behind his back, torches the house next door to yours. Please tell me you didn't put the idea in her head, 'cause I know how much you hated that place."

"No, that was all Bonnie," Yancy said. "But I've got to say, the new view from my back deck is pretty fucking fabulous. You should swing by after work on your way home."

Burton sipped his coffee. "Plus she's a fugitive on sex charges. Wait'll *that* turns up in the *Citizen*."

"Dickinson won't have to lift a finger," Yancy went on. "All he's got to do is put me in front of the grand jury. Stripling gets indicted and then there's a warrant, which is all I care about right now. The Bahamian cops snatch his ass, put him on a plane to Miami. He's a flight risk, so no bond, and there he sits in jail while the FBI puts the heat on Eve, who'll eventually cave. She, not me, becomes the star witness against Nick. What?"

"Nothing. I hope that's how it goes down."

"They nail this fucker, Rog—the guy who shot poor Charlie Phinney on the streets of Key West, horrified tourists all over the place—what else can Sonny do? He's *got* to give me back my job."

Burton said, "I like to see you radiating positivity."

"Go fuck yourself."

Yancy returned to the T-shirt shop and in the thong aisle he cornered Madeline, reeking of cigarettes as usual. She explained that Pestov had offered her thirty-two hundred dollars to marry him. He'd popped the question one afternoon shortly after an Immigration officer had stopped by the store.

"Hey, I could seriously use the money," Madeline said.

"And Pestov's an okay dude. I don't have to ball him or nuthin'." She was letting her hair grow, the roots showing brown and gray. "Charlie'd understand," she added. "He was into cash flow."

"Where's the proud groom?" Yancy asked.

"Out the back door. He saw you coming."

"Go get him, please. I need a favor."

"What kinda favor? Jesus."

"Tell him it's very important."

Madeline bit her lower lip. "Man, don't screw up this deal for me."

"Relax," Yancy said. "This one's for Charlie."

So far, the retirement years of Johnny Mendez had been uneventful, full of golf and JetBlue specials. His neighbors knew nothing of his corrupt past and treated him with the respect due a former police sergeant. That was more than Mendez could say for his wife, who had selfishly scheduled herself for yet another cosmetic procedure that his insurance plan wouldn't cover. This time it was a mentoplasty, commonly known as chin augmentation, which involved the surgical implantation of a small silicone module. In profile the face of Muriel Mendez would soon resemble a Hudson River tugboat, and her husband would once again be draining his pension account to pay for it. There was no point in arguing with her but he tried.

He was on the losing end of another shouting match when Andrew Yancy rapped on the door. It was a tailor-made opportunity to exercise the state's Stand Your Ground law and shoot Yancy dead as an intruder, and Johnny Mendez might have done it if Muriel could have been counted on to support an embroidered account of the incident.

"Hide the fucking cat," he said to his wife, who shooed the obese Siamese to another room.

"But Natasha loves me," said Yancy. "Come outside, Johnny, let's chat."

Mendez went to the bedroom and from the nightstand got his .38 Special, which he stuck in the waist of his golf shorts. Yancy was waiting on the porch. He said he was sorry for abducting the cat and thanked Mendez for the use of his sergeant's badge.

"I want to make it up to you," he said.

"No, you don't. You hate my fucking guts."

"Well, yes, that's impossible to deny. The truth is, I'm here because I need you to do something."

"What now? The answer's no effin' way. Are you serious?" Mendez couldn't believe this jerk showing up at his door.

"One phone call, Johnny. Five grand in your pocket." Yancy grinned and held up five fingers.

Mendez was suspicious, but there seemed no harm in listening. His wife came out complaining that the garbage disposal was jammed again. She was heading straight to Home Depot to purchase a new one, and for the errand she'd dressed in a short canary-yellow tennis ensemble.

Yancy said, "You are lookin' good, Muriel."

"Thank you. This is Stella McCartney—Johnny says it cost too much but I say he's a lucky duck." She laughed, a jungle hooting that spooked a pair of mockingbirds from the cherry hedge.

Yancy said, "He is the luckiest of lucky ducks. Don't let him give you any shit."

Mendez felt like shooting both of them. After his wife drove off he showed Yancy the pistol and told him to start talking fast, or else. Yancy punched him in the gut, shoved him inside the door and whisked the .38 from his pants.

"What kind of drooling moron threatens a man who's just offered him an easy five grand? Don't answer, Johnny Boy, that's rhetorical."

Mendez was bent double, huffing to catch his breath. Yancy helped him into a BarcaLounger and laid out the arrangement.

"Tomorrow there's going to be an item in the Key West newspaper—you should look it up online. It'll say Crime Stoppers is offering five thousand dollars for information leading to the arrest of the person or persons who murdered a man named Charles Phinney in Key West. I'd appreciate it if you call that hotline number, Johnny, and tell them who did it. Strictly as a concerned citizen, you understand."

Mendez, still clutching his midsection, was wary. "You know the killer, how come *you* don't call up for the reward?"

"Because I might end up as a witness in the case. It wouldn't go over so good with the jury if they knew I benefited financially from the defendant's capture. His lawyers would cut me to ribbons, am I right?"

"Only if you're dumb enough to tell 'em the truth."

Yancy emptied the bullets from the gun and tossed it back to Mendez, just like in the movies.

"Johnny, I picked you for three reasons: experience, experience, experience. Nobody can work Crime Stoppers like you," Yancy said. "The killer's name is Nicholas Stripling. He's hiding out in the Bahamas. It's all right here."

Yancy handed Mendez a paper that listed every important detail, from the suspect's DOB to his alias to the color Jeep he was driving. It was more like a dossier than a tip. Mendez knew that the cops in the Keys couldn't brush it off as a crackpot lead. There would have to be a follow-up.

He said, "They don't catch him, I don't get any money. You're aware how that works."

"Then what—you wasted a phone call? Big deal."

"I'm just saying."

"Stripling is the right man, Johnny. Everything I'm giving you is gold. Plus he's only got one arm, which is what the Wanted posters would call a noticeable feature."

"Okay, yeah. But I still don't believe you won't be takin' a cut."

"All I want," Yancy said, "is to see this shithead in handcuffs. That's it. That's all."

"Guy who died—he was a friend of yours or something?"

"Never met him. Just some kid worked on a fishing boat."

Mendez thought about it from all angles, and he really couldn't see a downside to making the call. He'd get a code number, like all the tipsters; nobody would ask his name.

And the five grand would cover most of Muriel's chin work.

"One thing you didn't tell me," he said. "Who put up the reward?"

Yancy looked amused. "You never cared before."

"Don't be a douche. Is it the dead kid's family came up with the money?"

"You'll love this," said Yancy. "It's the Russian mob."

Twenty-nine

The airstrip outside Barranquilla was stubbled with weeds from years of disuse, although the pale Moorish villa looked the same as Claspers remembered it. He circled back toward the coast and set the Caravan down on a flat sapphire bay. After mooring to a crab pot he dove from the starboard pontoon and swam to shore, where he flagged down a taxi, which took him first to a liquor store and then to the countryside.

His clothes were still damp when he knocked on the tall carved door. Donna was more breathtaking than ever, as he'd known she would be. He said he'd been shocked to hear of her husband's death, such a terrible crime, and then he asked if she'd remarried. She said no and invited him to come inside. Her English was still very good. He was careful not to throw his arms around her until he was sure she was alone. He iced the bottle of Dom and then she led him up the stairs.

Later, sitting in the twilight on the bedroom balcony, they drank the champagne and watched a pair of emerald-colored parrots courting in the treetops. When Donna asked if he was still in the business, Claspers laughed and said no, not for a long, long time.

"Then what are you doing here?"

"Dropping off an airplane."

"When are you going back?"

"I don't know," he said. "You need a pilot?"

The next morning he phoned Palm Aviation Options in Boca Raton and told the leasing agent where the Caravan could be found. The man was displeased to learn that the aircraft was way down in Colombia. Sending a person to retrieve it would be inconvenient and expensive.

"Your client's glad to pay," Claspers said, and read off the numbers on his former employer's gold AmEx.

"Thank you, but I should speak directly with Mr Grunion."

"He's a busy guy," Claspers said.

"And who are you? I didn't get your name."

"Nobody special. I'm fond of that seaplane is all."

The leasing agent put down the phone and turned to the men sitting in his office.

"Speak of the devil," he said. "The aircraft you were asking about is in South America when it's supposed to be in the Bahamas. Can somebody please tell me what the hell's going on?"

"Sorry," said Special Agent Liske.

"We appreciate your cooperation," added Special Agent Strumberg.

There was a fundamental disagreement about the future of Driggs. Egg wanted to twist the little monster's head off. The Dragon Queen wanted him found and brought back alive.

"Dot's my sweet pink boy," she said warmly.

"Ain't no boy. Dot's a goddamn wild-ass monkey."

The Dragon Queen told Egg to quit talking that way or she would unleash a black curse on his soul. She ordered him to search the island and made him take one of the meerschaum pipes, packed with Dunhill, which she said Driggs would be unable to resist.

Now Egg sat by himself at the conch hut wondering what to do. He didn't strictly believe in Caribbean magic, but the woman possessed some kind of mystic power. What else would account for him being seduced by such a moldy-smelling crone?

Since the night of the storm Egg had been avoiding sex due to the tender state of his cock, which the monkey had mauled like an ear of corn. Tumescence was a hydraulic impossibility, yet the Dragon Queen gave Egg no sympathy, pestering him crudely whenever he stopped by. At first he'd been merely annoyed but now he was worried. The girl behind the bar had confirmed the eerie story told to Egg by Driggs's owner—three young men on the island had died shortly after breaking off a romance with the ill-tempered old witch. Poison was the rumor.

Egg decided the monkey man was right—it was time to move on. Soon he'd be out of a job, anyway. Grunion was in deep shit with the American authorities, his days as a Bahamas real estate tycoon running out. Even before the stabbing the man had been obnoxious, a loud racist bastard. Egg didn't care what happened to him.

Nassau beckoned—not only the girls but the air-conditioning. There was always a bar or a tourist hotel where you could cool off. Here on Lizard Cay the grip of deep summer was unbreakable; the conch shack's ceiling

fan had only one blade. In the absence of casino income
the puny island's infrastructure doddered; two-thirds of
the power poles knocked down by the hurricane still lay
where they'd fallen. Even when the electricity worked,
the trailer on the construction site was a toaster oven,
the prehistoric wall unit blowing warm, dog-fart air. Egg
couldn't get any sleep there, and now he was too creeped
out to crash at the Dragon Queen's.

So, after three beers and a shrimp hoagie, he made
up his mind to fly home and valet cars at Atlantis, until
something easier came along.

"Mr. Ecclestone."

Egg spun himself on the stool. "Wot hey, mon."

It was a fellow named Weech, who'd been a rookie
guard at Fox Hill prison when Egg worked there. Now
Weech was with the Royal Bahamas Defence Force,
which Egg knew was more than a navy. The RBDF did
big cases with the American DEA and FBI.

"You here chasin' druggers?" Egg asked lightly.

Weech wore full camos, boots, wraparound shades
and a black beret. He was carrying an assault rifle with
a jumbo clip. Egg noticed that he'd bulked up and lost his
sense of humor. Weech said he'd received information
that a suspected murderer from Florida was living with
his wife near Rocky Town. The American was using the
name Grunion and, although he was missing an arm, he
was described as extremely dangerous.

"No shit?" Egg said.

"Dey say you woik fuh 'im."

"I juss quit."

"You smot fella," said Weech.

Three other RBDF officers appeared, every one as

muscled and heavily armed as Weech. Egg looked toward the harbor but he didn't see the government patrol boat. They must have used a different dock.

Weech was studying a printout. "De house is on Bannister Point," he said. "He's up dere now? Don't lie."

"You gon grob 'im?"

"Yah, mon. Soon as my orders from Nassau come tru." Weech skimmed the paperwork again. "Where's his floatplane? It's not at Moxey's."

Egg said, "Plane's gone. He pissed off 'bout dot, too."

Weech and the other officers stepped away, into the sunlight, to converse out of earshot. Egg thought their balls must be roasting in those combat uniforms.

On the other side of the bar stood Philip, the taxi man. Egg waved him over and arranged a ride later to the airport. First he had to pick up a gold necklace he'd left at the Dragon Queen's place last night. Hanging on the chain was a miniature gold anchor inlaid with real diamonds. The piece was quite expensive, and Egg couldn't believe he'd forgotten it. The Dragon Queen had told him to remove it so she could lather him head to toe with some smelly green cream she'd said would stop the pain in his privates.

"Mr. Ecclestone, one more ting." It was Weech again, standing beside him. "Be wise you don't tell your boss we're here."

Egg said, "Mon find out soon enough. Dot's his old lady."

He jerked his chin toward the water. Eve was at the wheel of a gleaming new fishing boat idling toward the ramp at the conch hut. Egg recalled she was crazy about the chowder, seasoned with sherry. She'd piled her hair under a blue ball cap, and she was wearing the flowered top of a two-piece swimsuit and white jeans. Her husband wasn't aboard.

The RBDF officers were hard to miss, and Eve spotted them right away. Instantly the three loud outboards began rumbling in reverse. As she spun the boat's bow toward the bight, the name painted on the stern came into view: *Lefty's Revenge.*

Eve gunned the throttles.

Weech said, "No prollem. She ain't goin' no place we cont find her."

Egg believed that to be true. He set the wicked monkey's pipe on the bar top and walked off.

Plover Chase already had received the Miranda spiel, but Agent John Wesley Weiderman recited it again.

"My lawyer advised me not to talk with you," she said.

"I'll leave the minute you ask me to."

"Cody said you seem like a decent sort. Open-minded. Straight shooter."

"I was sorry to hear about your husband," John Wesley Weiderman said.

"Oh, let's not go there."

"I spoke with the hospital. The nurses said he moved his right hand yesterday."

"I don't doubt it. That's how he got where he is," said Plover Chase.

The agent told her the prosecutors in Key West would agree to probation on the arson, but only with a guarantee that she'd go back to Oklahoma and do at least two years for the old charges.

"Two years for what?" she said. "This time around, Cody won't be testifying. He's saving it all for his book."

"We don't need Cody. You jumped bond, Ms. Chase. That's a separate crime."

"But I'm not going back to Tulsa. I plan to stay right here and be near Andrew." She pulled an orange thread from the sleeve of her jumpsuit. "I'm not scared of a trial. It isn't like I tried to kill somebody. Nobody was in the house when I lit the match."

She was something of a surprise to John Wesley Weiderman, the level way she looked at him, her poise and confidence seemingly unshaken by the grubby experience of jail. For some reason he'd been expecting despondency or a teary plea for lenience.

Instead Plover Chase came across as a strong, composed woman who'd just happened in a heartsick lapse of judgment to torch an unoccupied structure. Clearly she was rehearsing for court.

"I'm in it for the long haul," she added.

"Your lawyer will advise you that's a foolish choice. The judge in your old Tulsa case is deceased. The lead prosecutor is now farming soybeans. There's no longer much interest back home in making an example of you. The state just wants to close the file. Two years is a real fair deal."

"And lose Andrew forever? No, sir, I won't be going anywhere."

It was warm in the interview room. John Wesley Weiderman felt like loosening his necktie, but he didn't. After twelve years on the job he was still puzzled by people who were determined to live in turmoil. Plover Chase wasn't a career criminal, yet she was making it impossible for her to be treated as anything less. Oklahoma wanted her sent back as soon as possible, the arson having upended the assumption that she was harmless.

The agent explained to Plover Chase that she was fortunate to be offered basically a free pass out of Florida. It happened that the Monroe County state attorney was unenthusiastic about expending his limited resources on a flaky love-triangle case while a cold-blooded murder remained unsolved.

"I read about that," she interjected. "They're good about letting us see the newspapers."

"The young man—Phinney was his name—he was shot down in cold blood. There's heavy pressure to find the killer and put him away."

"God, I hope so."

"Point is," the agent said, "they're happy to ship you home and save the taxpayers here some money. However, if you insist on fighting extradition, forcing a trial, talking to reporters—"

"Hey, she called *me*—"

"—then you're going to aggravate these Key West prosecutors, and they'll come down hard on you. You could get five years for burning that house and, when your hitch is done, *then* they'll send you back to Tulsa to face the music."

Plover Chase was undaunted. "I plan on being acquitted of the arson," she said.

John Wesley Weiderman put forward his opinion that she wasn't insane.

"I was at the time of the crime!" She was a plucky one.

"That's a long shot with juries."

"Now you sound like Andrew."

It was time to go. The lawman stood up and buttoned his suit jacket.

"Well, good luck," he said.

She gave a little smile that wrinkled her nose. "How long have you been chasing me, Agent Weiderman?"

He was halfway to his car when a cab pulled into the parking lot of the stockade. The driver chose a spot in the shade of a tree, and a rear door was flung open. Cody Parish got out holding a brown grocery bag. He clutched the bag with both hands as he headed toward the front doors of the building.

John Wesley Weiderman thought it odd that the cab stayed to wait. Running the meter was expensive, and Cody Parish didn't give the impression of a young man with a bankroll. He braked like the cartoon coyote when the lawman called out his name.

"Oh. Yo!" Cody lifted one hand off the brown bag to wave, sort of.

John Wesley Weiderman crossed the parking lot unknotting his tie. The heat shimmered off the pavement like a vapor.

"I just had a visit with Ms. Chase," he said.

Cody was antsy, shuffling in his flip-flops. "Yeah? That's where I'm goin' now."

"Bet you're wondering how all this will turn out."

"Sure, dude. Absolutely." His cheeks were flushed and his chubby neck was moist.

"Okay, here it is," said John Wesley Weiderman. "Ms. Chase is going back to Tulsa, no matter what she thinks. The prosecutors here will drag out the arson case for months and she'll wake up one day understanding that she's basically rotting in that cell, that Mr. Yancy is no longer infatuated with her, and that she might as well be in Oklahoma working off her sentence. Her lawyer here will be relieved that she came to her senses, and the very next day we'll be on a plane home, she and I."

Cody looked as if his face had locked in the middle of a sneeze. "Huh," was all he said.

"You all right?"

"Yeah, I'm...I'm good. Holy shit, it's like two hundred friggin' degrees out here."

"What's in the bag?"

"Books and stuff. She's a major reader."

"Me, too. May I have a look?" John Wesley Weiderman took the bag from Cody and opened it. He said, "See, this is what I was afraid of."

"Dude, come on. Don't, please..."

"Oh, I'm not about to touch anything," the agent said. "Neither are you."

There was a rubber Liberace mask and a chrome cap pistol. Cody had intended to bust his true love out of jail.

"I thought it'd be a super-cool thing for my diary, for when they make the book and movie. Her breaking out with some mystery man," he whispered. "See, all I got so far is fifty-three pages and this agent I called in New York? She said that's not enough. She said I need more material."

The lawman closed the paper bag and handed it back.

"And that taxi would be your getaway car?"

"I know, right?" Cody was about to break down. "Sometimes I can be, like, a total fucking idiot."

"That doesn't begin to cover it," said John Wesley Weiderman. "Get back in the cab and go straight to the bus station."

"Yes, sir."

"Buy yourself a ticket to anywhere."

"Okay, dude. Thanks, like, so much. I totally mean it."
As Cody was stepping backward, he dropped the brown
bag and kicked it away from his feet. "Yo, would you tell
Ms. Chase I still love her like crazy?"

"If it ever comes up," said John Wesley Weiderman.

Yancy lay out watching a thunderhead bloom in the Gulf.
Every afternoon it was a new show, now that the house
next door was gone. Earlier a convoy of dump trucks had
hauled away the rubble and ashes, Evan Shook watching blankly from his Suburban. He'd told Yancy that the
insurance payoff was tied up in his divorce, as was the
property. He and his future ex-wife couldn't even agree on
a real estate broker. Meanwhile his mistress had dumped
him for a bluegrass player who had his own fucking website. Yancy couldn't make himself feel sorry for Evan
Shook. Bonnie shouldn't have burned down the man's
house, but the house shouldn't have been built to start
with.

Not nine feet over code.

Not big enough to block out a setting moon.

Rosa was caught in Miami traffic, so Yancy put in his
earbuds and smoked half a joint and opened a new bottle
of Barbancourt. His name was in the papers again, thanks
to Bonnie's birdbrain interview with the *Citizen*. The
headline: FIERY CLIMAX TO SEX FUGITIVE'S ROMANCE. To
the reporter Bonnie had decoded the arson as a misguided
act of love for Yancy. Then she'd rehashed their whole
affair, a lowlight being the foolishness at Mallory Square.

The article made a racy splash, and Yancy could hardly
blame Sheriff Sonny Summers for not taking his calls.
He would be more approachable after Nick Stripling was

arrested and returned to Florida, and there was credit to be claimed.

Meanwhile, the toxic new publicity had demolished Yancy's chances of testifying at the grand jury; his role in the capture and prosecution of Stripling would have to be strictly invisible. Under no other circumstances would Yancy have enlisted the thieving though adroit Johnny Mendez. It was a backdoor move, using Crime Stoppers, but Yancy had grown impatient with the deliberate, over-cautious duo at the FBI.

He downloaded the new Steve Earle and watched the high-stacked clouds turn purple. By the time Rosa arrived the bugs were insane, but she wanted to stay outside and see the crime scene next door. It had been a regular day at work, all grown-ups on the table, and Rosa was in a fair mood. The squall stalled offshore, so Yancy fired up the grill. Burton had dropped off some lobsters, most of them legal.

"Some men would be flattered," Rosa said playfully, "if a sexy woman did something that dramatic to win back their love."

"Oh yes, torching a stranger's house. Hallmark should do a valentine."

"Obviously she still cares for you, Andrew."

"All I want out of a relationship is neutral buoyancy. Is that asking too much?" He was lightly buzzed.

"Maybe she just missed being the center of atten-tion during those boring years as the doctor's wife. Once you're in the headlines it's like a drug. That's what they say."

"Oh, is that what they say?" Yancy was grinning.

"Hey, I'm serious," Rosa said.

"You're adorable is what you are."

"Wow, how much did you smoke?"

The lobsters were excellent. After dinner they tossed the shells into the canal and watched a swarm of mangrove snappers go berserk. Then Yancy walked Rosa back to the house and in the dark they took a long bath, the faraway weather strobing through the windowpanes. While she was moving on top of him, her hair flying, Yancy spied a palmetto bug on the shower curtain. For once he kept quiet and stayed in the moment. Deep space was what it seemed like, weightless and slow motion.

At midnight he and Rosa were dancing in their towels when his cell phone rang. He didn't recognize the number, so he didn't answer it. Early the next morning it began ringing again; this time he picked up. It was Neville Stafford calling from Lizard Cay.

"Are you okay?" Yancy asked thickly.

"Yah, mon. How soon you come?"

"Why? What happened?"

Neville said, "Wot hoppen is Chrissofer gone."

"What do you mean 'gone'? Define 'gone.'"

"I try'n call loss night."

Yancy said, "This is un-fucking-believable." Except it wasn't.

"Tink you should come, mon."

"Right away." He put down the phone and looked hopefully at Rosa.

"Andrew, I love you," she said, "but not enough to go back."

Thirty

Key West homicide detectives reacted to the anonymous Crime Stoppers tip the way Yancy had expected they would. They didn't go through diplomatic channels in Nassau, as was required of the FBI, but chose the more direct and efficient approach. They picked up the phone and called Lizard Cay.

There the Bahamian police contingent consisted of a single easygoing officer named Darrick. He was rattled to learn that the reclusive American developer of the Curly Tail Lane Resort was a fugitive murderer. As soon as Darrick got off the line with Key West, he made an agitated call to his superior at Andros Town, who made a more agitated call to a nephew of high rank on the Royal Bahamas Defence Force. A patrol boat refueling at Fresh Creek was dispatched to Rocky Town, triggering events that neither Yancy nor Neville Stafford could have foreseen.

The authority to detain foreign nationals rested at higher levels of the Bahamian government and required a tedious exchange of paperwork. In the meantime, Nicholas Joseph Stripling was put under a military surveillance that was highly visible, the purpose being to discourage thoughts of flight. The presence of the Defence Force commandos produced in Stripling round-the-clock anxiety and improvident behavior, including the constant berating of his wife, Eve. In actuality she'd had little to do with the hell-bound spiraling of his fortunes.

On the deciding night, Neville went snapper fishing at the mouth of the bight. The sea was velvet, the stars tucked behind thick clouds. He carried a large flashlight that connected with rusty alligator clips to the boat's battery. Driggs was a reluctant crew; huddled in the bow, he crossly labored to peel off a nicotine patch Neville had affixed to a bald spot on his chest.

Near one of the navigational markers the channel bottom dropped off into a deep gouge. There were giant cuberas, too powerful for Neville's tackle, and also hogfish, excellent to eat but difficult to fool with a baited hook. Neville missed several strikes because he was too distracted, replaying in his mind a frightful finishing skirmish with the Dragon Queen.

It had happened on the road to the docks. The voodoo woman was drunk, slumped in her electric scooter chair and attended as usual by her murmuring matrons. At the sight of the monkey she began to keen, reaching for him with stained crooked fingers. Driggs yeeped and ducked behind Neville.

This rejection brought from the Dragon Queen a mortifying wail. Neville tried to dart past but she nimbly manipulated the joystick to keep the wheelchair in his path. She said Egg had gotten sick and she needed a new boyfriend, and she commanded Neville to come see her later for sex.

"You owe me, bey," she said.

"Fuh wot I owe you?"

The Dragon Queen huffed. "Fuh dot woo-doo. Ha! You'll see."

She held up a gold chain strung through a small, diamond-studded anchor. "Dis here fuh my lil' pink boy."

"No need, madam."

"Take it, mon, 'less you hungry fuh pain."

Neville was ashamed that he still feared her dark magic. He accepted the chain and handed it to Driggs, who began scratching at a scab with the prongs of the anchor charm. The Dragon Queen frowned and levered herself from the scooter. From the depths of her dress she produced a small meerschaum, which she waggled like a lollipop at Driggs.

"Don't!" Neville warned, but the monkey wore a rictus leer as it flew toward the old woman's ankles swinging the anchor necklace like a mace. She commenced a queer jig, kicking left and right at the frenetic creature while chanting in a voice as deep as pure evil.

Neville was not too preoccupied to notice Philip's taxi van jouncing at a loose clip down the hill. He tackled Driggs and in a tangle they rolled clear. The Dragon Queen's supplicants had also seen the speeding van and—rotund as they were—parted as fleetly as sparrows. Their excited shouts, loud enough for a tent revival, failed to pierce the voodoo woman's boozy trance.

The taxi slammed hard into her bony frame as Philip stomped uselessly on the brake pedal. In a sinusoidal path the van petered on down the road. Through its punctured windshield jutted the Dragon Queen's legs, her vivid raiments flapping like a broken beach umbrella. Terrified,

Neville lowered a shoulder and barreled through her cow-like retinue, Driggs galloping after him.

Now they sat in the boat solemnly waiting for a fish to bite. On shore Rocky Town looked smaller than usual because half the lights were still out from the hurricane. As the tide rose, the current grew stronger and the ripples ticked against the bow. Neville's rod bent, and he reeled in a good five-pound hogfish. He placed it inside a Styrofoam cooler, where it flapped loudly, startling Driggs. With a sigh the monkey pantomimed a pipe-smoking motion, which Neville ignored.

An hour passed without another nibble. Neville was preparing to move to a different spot when he heard high-powered engines. Initially he believed it was the Royal Defence Force patrol boat he'd seen earlier near the public wharf. Then he saw a bright light moving rapidly up the shoreline from Bannister Point—a foolhardy route in darkness across tricky water. The danger was grounding on the flats or smashing into a coral head. Nobody in the government fleet would make such a run, even with a spotlight.

Neville figured it must be drug smugglers, so he lay down flat on his seat. He groped for Driggs's silhouette and pulled the monkey to his chest. The sound of the fast boat got louder and louder. Driggs smelled awful but Neville didn't let go. He knew that his own small boat, with its low profile and dark hull, would be difficult to see on a starless night.

Abruptly the oncoming engines shut down. Neville waited a few minutes before peeking over the gunwale. Anchored on the edge of the shallows, perhaps two hundred yards away, was a sleek light-colored boat. Neville guessed the length at thirty-five, maybe thirty-six feet. It had a V-hull, three big outboards, and a pair of tall outriggers for trolling. The finish on the sides of the craft looked bright and new.

A faint light glowed in the cockpit, and Neville discerned movement—a hunched figure emptying a bucket over the transom again and again. There was no conversation rising from the deck and no two-way radio crackle, which seemed odd. Voices carried a long way across open water and, in Neville's experience, dopers were always yakking to each other.

At Neville's feet, Driggs issued a sequence of warning chirps. Neville hastily snatched up the monkey and held him over the side for a pee. It was a small milestone in Neville's dogged campaign to housebreak his unruly pet, and his hushed praise for Driggs was heartfelt. He set the animal in the bottom of his skiff and returned his attention to the gleaming boat across the channel, where there was finally noise.

The person on the aft deck was grunting as if moving bales. Something heavy made a splash near the stern. Neville figured the smugglers were dumping their load, yet he counted no other splashes. Soon the triple outboards thundered and the boat sped away, cutting a long, foamy stitch in the sea.

Neville struggled to pull up his anchor, which had snagged on the ledge of the hogfish hole. He started the motor and backed upcurrent with the rope in one fist. When the anchor came free, Neville hauled it aboard.

Then he aimed his flashlight and chugged toward where the other vessel had been. It wasn't clear why the smugglers had spooked, but they were a jumpy breed.

Neville expected to see a fifty-pound bale of grass or a bundle of cocaine floating in the tide. What he found instead was something else, and a dread turbulence of sharks drawn to the surface by buckets of rotting fish heads.

The following afternoon, when Yancy stepped off the plane, the first thing he saw on the tarmac at Moxey's was a pickup truck with a wood coffin in the flatbed. The driver said the dead man was called Egg though his real name was Ecclestone. He'd been found sprawled on Prince Hill, near the graveyard. Heart attack most likely, the driver said. The corpse was being flown back to Nassau, where Mr. Ecclestone was from. None of the freezers on Lizard Cay were large enough to hold a person that size.

Yancy said he was a friend of the deceased, and he asked the driver if he could say good-bye. The driver lifted the lid of the coffin. It was Egg inside.

He was stark naked, the monkey bites still visible on his sad-looking cock. Both his eyes were wide open and so was his mouth. Yancy could see that a chunk of tongue had been bitten off. From each of the goon's nostrils trailed a crust of dried blood. Whatever killed him wasn't a heart attack. Dr. Rosa Campesino could have solved the mystery if Egg had been lucky enough to die in Miami. For show, Yancy flicked one of the thug's crimped ears and said, "Adios, wild man." The pickup driver offered a respectful nod.

Down at the waterfront a crowd was collecting. Yancy didn't see Neville though it looked like most of the island's population had turned out to watch a Bahamian patrol boat escort a barge to the government docks. Upon the barge sat a light-blue Contender, outriggers drooping, the hull showing a stoved hole with the diameter of a garbage-can lid. The bridge of the damaged fishing boat had been covered with a yellow tarp, meaning the accident victim, or victims, were deceased and still aboard.

Yancy was working his way through the onlookers when he felt a sharp tap on one shoulder—it was Neville. He wore amber sunglasses and a faded Peter Tosh T-shirt.

"Come along," he said to Yancy.

"I'm right behind you, brother."

The ride in his skiff was choppy but the breeze felt good. Andros was so vast that it made its own weather, and a squall line thickened over the center of the island. Yancy was eager to hear Neville's story even though he knew the ending. He'd known it the moment he laid eyes on the monkey.

To manage the bumpy waves Driggs balanced up front in the hinged pose of a surfer, his ropey arms extended. Yancy smiled though he remained wary, for his shins still bore the beast's claw marks from the attack at the vacant house. Yet today Driggs wore a different look, and it wasn't just the new bling.

Near the channel marker Neville cut the engine and dropped the anchor and let the wind push the bow toward the cut of the bank. The tide was dead low. Yancy stood to snap a picture with his phone for Rosa.

The Super Rollie had uncannily come to rest upright on the flats, its spoked wheels glinting. As they looked out across the ocean, the empty scooter chair was the only object above the waterline all the way to the horizon.

Yancy could envision his photo as an artsy advertisement in some medical-supply catalog.

Neville told him everything he'd seen the night before, everything he'd heard later in Rocky Town.

"It's big woo-doo, mon."

"Sounds more like Stripling seriously pissed off his wife."

"Was me who paid fuh dot coyse on 'im! Finally it hoppen!"

"What about Egg?"

"Dot I dint do," Neville stated somberly. "Dragon Queen got mod and spike 'is rum. I told 'im stay 'way."

"Well, she's done her last voodoo dance."

"Yah, mon," said Neville. "But Philip need a new toxie."

Yancy had a few questions but there was no one left alive to answer them. He asked Neville if they could take a ride down the coast before returning to the dock. He wanted to see the place where Eve Stripling, surely believing she was free, had at a fatal velocity steered the *Lefty's Revenge* into a coral outcrop known to islanders as Satan's Fist.

It had happened only a few minutes after she rolled her husband off the stern into night waters churned by sharks, the fatal splash witnessed by a local fisherman and his pet monkey. The makeshift ramp used to launch the scooter chair was discarded by puzzled authorities, who had no inkling of its purpose. It had been found on board the impaled Contender along with Eve, whose brains were splashed all over the interior windshield.

Neville couldn't picture the man he knew as Christopher going overboard without a fight, even having only one arm and a severely injured spine. Yancy surmised that Eve had incapacitated her husband with painkillers before wheeling him onto the boat. The sharks she'd chummed had finished the job, interrupted momentarily when Neville motored up on the scene and made his daring grab.

As they prepared to set out for Satan's Fist, Yancy remarked that Driggs looked like an honest-to-God movie star.

Neville craned forward. "Same ting as if I found it at de bottom of de sea."

"Absolutely. The maritime law of salvage."

Stripling's wrist was fatter than the monkey's neck, so with a jeweler's screwdriver Neville had removed several links from the watchband. Now the Genève Tourbillon fit Driggs splendidly as a collar.

Yancy said, "Nobody'll try to steal it, that's for sure."

"No, he fuck 'im up bod."

"It's a gorgeous watch, Mr. Stafford. This will do wonders for his self-esteem."

"Yah, mon. He hoppy fella."

The monkey did seem uncharacteristically mellow, as if his demons were lulled by the inner ticking of the rose-gold timepiece. He plucked leisurely at his nicotine patch as he eyed the marooned Rollie, its tires licked by the tide.

Neville said, "I dint tell a soul wot hoppen out here loss night."

"And why should you?" Yancy shrugged. "It's over. Everyone's dead."

"Yah, dot's right."

"I assume there was nothing left of the bastard."

Neville scratched the silvery stubble on his jaw. He looked uneasy.

"Don't tell me," Yancy said.

The fisherman flipped open the Styrofoam cooler. "Here's wot de shocks dint eat."

"Oh Christmas! Of course!"

It was Nick Stripling's other arm.

Thirty-one

The sheriff, not wishing to be seen with Andrew Yancy, insisted on an off-site meeting. They agreed that Yancy's house was the safest place.

"Is this any way to treat an international crime buster?" Yancy said.

Sonny Summers squeezed out a chuckle. "Walk me through this mess, okay?"

They sat in the cheap lounge chairs on the backyard deck. The sheriff was known to sweat like a warthog so Yancy had preemptively chosen a shady spot.

"The man who murdered Charles Phinney is dead. Would you like the official version first?"

Sonny Summers said, "Oh, why not."

"Nicholas Stripling and his wife perished two nights ago in a boating accident off the coast of Andros Island. Foolish Americans, sporting around in unfamiliar shallows."

"Okay. What really happened?"

Yancy popped a beer and delivered a nearly complete account.

"Oh, fuckeroo," the sheriff said, and grabbed a bottle for himself.

"There's a karmic symmetry you've got to appreciate. Not quite Shakespearean, but close."

"Were you on Andros when this happened? Did you—what's the word—contribute to these events in some way?"

"No, Sonny. I was here on Big Pine."

"Well, thank God for that."

Yancy set up his pitch. "If Stripling hadn't drowned he'd be going to prison. Nobody in the States knew where he was until I told them. Nobody had a clue he was alive."

The sheriff rolled the chilled beer bottle between his palms and stared at the scorched patch of land where Yancy's sex criminal ex-lover had torched his neighbor's extravagant spec house.

"Sonny, are you even listening? I flew to the islands on my own dime and found this shitweasel. He almost blew my head off point-blank, you understand? I risked my freaking life to solve this case."

"You want your badge back. I get it."

The muddy response reminded Yancy that he was talking to a politician. "But there's a big 'however,' right? I can smell it."

"However," said Sonny Summers, "the situation isn't that simple. Yes, you did some first-rate police work. Ballsy, man. *Scary* ballsy. But what you just told me, man, I can't put that in a press release."

"No kidding. Who said anything about a damn press release?"

"Oh, I'll need a good one," said the sheriff, "the day I rehire you. See, you're what the media calls a controversial figure. And now Bonnie Witt's plastered all over the *Citizen* again, just when I thought this shit was fading away."

"Meaning Mallory Square."

"Everything, all of it," the sheriff said in a beleaguered tone. "Consorting with a fugitive, whatever."

"Like I knew? Come on, Sonny."

"Some people are saying this arson was all your fault. Just bar talk, but still. They say you put Bonnie up to it because that house"—Sonny Summers nodded grimly toward the burned lot—"was screwing up your precious sunsets."

"Absurd."

"Look, we're shipping her crazy ass back to Oklahoma. Maybe in a year or two, if you can stay out of the damn headlines, I'll bring you back on the force."

"But I thought you were going to quit and run for attorney general."

Sonny Summers shifted his bulk. "Then I'll be sure and tell the new sheriff to put you on the short list for detective. Same rank as before. Meanwhile, I hear you're tearing it up on roach patrol. Gangbusters is what Tommy Lombardo said."

"Did he now."

"He tells me you bring a firearm on these restaurant inspections. Is that true?"

"It sets a certain tone."

"But you haven't actually shot anything, right? Rats and so forth."

"Not yet, Sonny."

"Try not to. That's my advice."

"Thanks. You've always been like a father to me." Yancy was barely holding it together.

The sheriff said, "I've got to ask—where'd they find Stripling's other arm? I mean, after all the screwed-up shit that happened with the first one."

"I was there, remember? Chauffeuring it up the highway on your secret orders. That was the start of it all."

Sonny Summers wanly acknowledged the fact.

"Stripling's right arm," said Yancy, "was recovered in the water near the spot where the boat wrecked."

Where Yancy had dumped it from Neville Stafford's fish cooler, a detail with which he chose not to burden the sheriff.

"And the sharks ate the rest? They're sure about that?"

"Sonny, they were big fuckers. Bulls and lemons. Whatever was left of Stripling, you could probably scoop it with a guppy net."

"I'll call Key West homicide—they'll be jazzed about closing the Phinney case. We can set up a joint press conference tomorrow. Our prime suspect is dead, et cetera."

All of a sudden it was *our* suspect. Miraculously Yancy held his tongue.

He said, "The right arm is being sent back to Miami to be buried with the left one. There's plenty of room in the coffin." Caitlin Cox was handling the arrangements. Yancy had hung up on her when she'd asked whom she should call about her father's life insurance.

Sonny Summers put down his beer bottle. "Okay, then. Anything else?"

"Just my police career is all. My self-worth and future sanity."

"Be patient, like I said."

"You ever spent a day on your knees counting mouse turds?"

The sheriff winced. "Enough already. Good Lord."

Later Yancy trailered his skiff down to Sugar Loaf and poled the Gulfside flats. He'd forgotten to bring a fishing rod, but that was all right. The sun on the back of his neck felt good enough. A salty clean breeze on his cheeks. For a while he staked up to spy on a great blue heron wading along the mangroves spearing minnows and shrimp.

When he got back to Big Pine, the FBI men were waiting in front of the house. They'd made the trip in a new black Tahoe, pretty sweet for a government ride. Yancy remembered his dad always drove a puke-green utility vehicle, standard issue for the park service.

"Howdy, gentlemen," he said to the partners.

While he rinsed his boat they inquired about his latest trip to Andros Island. Agent Strumberg divulged that they'd spotted his name on a list of travelers provided by Homeland Security. Yancy explained that in the absence of prompt federal action he'd returned to Lizard Cay to check on Nicholas Joseph Stripling.

Agent Liske warned him that he was acting recklessly. "You could jeopardize our whole case. We're getting very, very close to making a move."

In a bombshell whisper Strumberg divulged that the seaplane Stripling was leasing had turned up in Colombia.

Yancy started laughing. The agents stiffened.

"What's so damn funny?" asked Strumberg.

"It's too late to catch that asshole!"

"Just watch us," Liske said.

"Guys, you're killing me." Yancy turned off the hose and dried his hands on his pants. "Your suspect, Mr. Stripling, is deceased."

"Shit," said the FBI men, one after the other.

Yancy brought them into the house and fixed a couple of iced teas. For himself he unwrapped a grape Popsicle. The agents found the circumstances of Stripling's demise somewhat mind-bending. Strumberg walked out to the Tahoe and started making calls. Yancy put on some music, a Springsteen concert.

Liske surprised him by saying he'd seen Bruce twice at the Meadowlands. "The band can't be the same without Clarence."

"I hear it's still a great show."

"The gun—is that loaded?" He pointed at Yancy's Glock on the kitchen counter.

"I'm fully permitted," Yancy said. "The Russian mob is very active in Key West."

"Is that cannabis?"

Near the sink lay a half-smoked doobie.

"Medicinal," said Yancy. "Self-prescribed."

Strumberg returned, having confirmed the details of the fatal boat accident in the Bahamas. Eve Stripling's corpse had been identified at the scene. Fingerprints taken from the hand of the recovered arm matched those from Nick's long-ago arrest as a car-crash scammer.

"Incredible," said Liske. "Just when we're about to nail the sonofabitch, he really dies—and the exact same way he wanted us to think he died before."

Once more from Strumberg: "Shit."

The agents were bummed because there was nobody to arrest. Yancy felt their pain. After all, it was his case, too.

"You boys had him by the balls," he said, to boost morale. "It was a done deal."

Peevishly Strumberg reported that someone other than an authorized FBI official had tipped the Royal Bahamas Defence Force that Stripling was living on the island.

"Wasn't me," said Yancy. "You might check with the Key West police. They've been working the murder of that fishing mate pretty hard."

"Whatever. Our boy got sketched out by all the pressure. Word was that he and the wife were plotting to escape in their new boat. The RBDF thinks they were on a practice run the night they crashed."

Yancy saw no reason to enlighten the agents about what really happened. "What's your next move?" he asked. "Or do you have a next move?"

"Chasing the assets, of course," said Liske, "starting with his bank accounts in Nassau."

"Plus all that prime beachfront he was developing on Andros," Strumberg added.

"Don't get your hopes up," Yancy said. "Stripling had a silent partner in that resort deal. I don't know the guy's name but I heard he's got a Bay Street lawyer, the brother of an MP. Try to execute a property forfeiture over there, they'll tie you up in the courts forever."

The FBI men bore this setback stoically. In the absence of prolonged legwork they would never discover there was no silent partner in Curly Tail Lane, no high-powered Bay Street barrister.

Yancy said, "Stripling hadn't put up any buildings, anyway. Just chopped down some trees."

"It's way easier to go after the money," Liske muttered to Strumberg, who agreed with leaden resignation.

As soon as the agents drove away, Yancy phoned the conch shack in Rocky Town and left a message. He looked forward to telling Neville Stafford that it was safe to move back to Green Beach.

Rosa got in around seven. "Your tongue's purple," she said.

"But my heart is true blue."

"Take your hand out of there. I'm hungry."

They cruised down to Stoney's, which Yancy had cleared for reopening in time for Madeline's pre-wedding party. Madeline was glad to see him and Pestov was less furtive than usual, buoyed no doubt by the future upgrade of his citizenship status. Rosa and Yancy gave the happy couple a three-speed juicer, though a better gift was the news that Charles Phinney's killer had drowned in the Bahamas.

Madeline sniffled in relief, while Pestov emitted a chuff of glee that had nothing to do with seeing justice for the murdered charter-boat mate. Because Nick Stripling had died before he could be arrested, Pestov wasn't obligated to cough up the five thousand dollars he'd grudgingly committed to the Crime Stoppers reward.

And retired sergeant Johnny Mendez would have to find some other means to pay for his wife's new chin.

Brennan acted insulted when Yancy and Rosa departed before even the apps were served. They went to a pizza joint that always passed inspection, then back to Yancy's house, where they made love on Rosa's pink yoga mat, which stuck to Yancy's butt like an oversized Post-it note.

"What did the sheriff say about your job?" she asked later, after they showered.

"Be patient, he told me. Maybe a year or two."

"That sucks, Andrew. I'm sorry."

"Monday I'm doing an Italian joint down on Ramrod,"

he said. "Some customer, retired navy, you don't even want to know what he found in his calzone."

Rosa dried off. "I'm applying for a pediatric residency at Jackson. It's time."

"Uh-oh. What happened?"

She said, "I'm burning out is all. It'll be nice to have patients who can talk back."

"Did another kid come in today?"

"A child, Andrew. He stepped in front of the school bus. Eleven years old."

"Aw Jesus."

"You know what? Let's go look at the moon."

Outside they held on to each other. Rosa's hair was still wet, and the drops felt cool on Yancy's arms. The sky was clear and the air was still, though in the far Caribbean a new tropical cyclone had begun to churn.

Gerardo, for God's sake. Already the TV weathermen in Miami were fibrillating.

Rosa said she wanted to come stay with Yancy if the storm veered toward Florida. "Hurricane sex is the best," she whispered. "You'd better agree, by the way."

"Off the chart."

"Hey, I brought the movie."

"Finally," Yancy said.

His career troubles were placed in cosmic perspective by the sight of a barefoot woman in a Foo Fighters T-shirt popping popcorn in his kitchen. Beyond the window hung a crescent moon, lighting the Gulf of Mexico. Life was fine. All that stood between him and his detective badge was a few thousand cockroaches.

"The DVD's in my purse," Rosa said.

She'd rented the first of the Johnny Depp pirate films,

which they'd both seen before. Yancy paused the action on a close-up of the scraggly buccaneer monkey, costumed in a velvet waistcoat and a bell-sleeved shirt.

He and Rosa edged forward for a close look.

"I don't think that's Driggs," Yancy said.

"But he was younger then. Before his fur fell out."

"Check out those chompers. What a psycho."

"Don't you dare," said Rosa, "talk that way about my little hero."

The next day Captain Keith Fitzpatrick took them fishing offshore on the *Misty Momma IV*. It was a free trip, Keith said, in honor of Yancy finding Phinney's killer. Rosa reeled in mahi until her arms got sore. Yancy caught a tuna on a gorgeous new fly rod that he couldn't afford but had bought for himself anyway.

That evening he fixed a plate of sashimi while Rosa grilled the fillets. They drank a manageable amount of tequila and made plans for Gerardo, just in case. As the sun slipped below the mangroves a Key deer—a grown buck, antlers in velvet—appeared in the yard. Not even three feet tall at the shoulder, the deer nosed silently along Evan Shook's fence line looking for shoots. Rosa was taken by its grace.

Yancy pulled out his cell phone and snapped a picture for Neville.

A NOTE ABOUT THE AUTHOR

Carl Hiaasen was born and raised in Florida. He is the author of twelve previous novels, including the best-sellers *Star Island, Nature Girl, Skinny Dip, Sick Puppy,* and *Lucky You,* and four best-selling children's books, *Chomp, Hoot, Flush,* and *Scat.* His most recent work of nonfiction is *The Downhill Lie: A Hacker's Return to a Ruinous Sport.* He also writes a weekly column for the *Miami Herald.*

VISIT US ONLINE AT

WWW.HACHETTEBOOKGROUP.COM

FEATURES:

**OPENBOOK BROWSE AND
SEARCH EXCERPTS**

•

AUDIOBOOK EXCERPTS AND PODCASTS

•

AUTHOR ARTICLES AND INTERVIEWS

•

**BESTSELLER AND PUBLISHING
GROUP NEWS**

•

SIGN UP FOR E-NEWSLETTERS

•

**AUTHOR APPEARANCES AND TOUR
INFORMATION**

•

SOCIAL MEDIA FEEDS AND WIDGETS

•

DOWNLOAD FREE APPS

BOOKMARK HACHETTE BOOK GROUP
@ WWW.HACHETTEBOOKGROUP.COM

Devastated by the news that her beloved grandmother has died after hip surgery in New Delhi, UCLA medical student Jennifer Hernandez flies to India, desperate for answers. Jennifer's grandmother appears to be another victim of medical tourism—uninsured first-world citizens traveling to third-world countries for more affordable surgery. With revelations of other unexplained deaths and pressure from Indian hospital officials for a hasty cremation, Jennifer reaches out to her mentor, New York City medical examiner Dr. Laurie Montgomery.

Laurie, along with her husband, Dr. Jack Stapleton, rush to the younger woman's side, only to discover a sophisticated medical facility with little margin for error. But as the death count grows, so do the questions, leading Laurie and Jennifer to unveil a multilayered conspiracy of global proportions.

FOREIGN BODY

"Does for hypochondriacs what Ludlum does for paranoiacs . . . Cook is a master of pacing."
—*The Raleigh News & Observer*

"Interesting characters, plenty of medical background, a fast pace, and increasingly unbelievable events."
—*Library Journal*

"Cook well knows that a spoonful of sugar helps the medicine go down. After all, he's been coating very serious medical ethics debates in fast, fun, escapist thrillers for more than three decades."
—*The News-Press*

continued . . .

Praise for
CRITICAL

"A top-notch thriller . . . vivid and memorable."

—The Associated Press

"*Critical* might scare you to death . . . his prescient plotting is far from far-fetched." —*The Tampa Tribune*

"[A] lively new thriller . . . An entertaining mix of suspense, action, and education about medical issues."

—*Publishers Weekly*

CRISIS

"Mixes relevant social issues with murder and mayhem . . . A completely unexpected ending."

—*USA Today*

"Shocking." —*Booklist*

"A timely topic." —*Publishers Weekly*

MARKER

"A highly entertaining read." —*USA Today*

"A master of medical mystery . . . a fun page-turner . . . a perfect, explosive ending." —*The Boston Globe*

"[A] gripping medical chiller . . . the denouement crackles to an electric edge-of-the-seat finale."

—*Publishers Weekly* (starred review)

Praise for
ROBIN COOK
and his bestselling novels

"Gripping."   —*The New York Times Book Review*

"Holds you page after page."   —Larry King, *USA Today*

"Shocking and thought provoking."
—The Associated Press

"Dr. Robin Cook certainly knows how to tell a story."
—*The Detroit News*

"Fast . . . exciting . . . spine tingling."   —*The Denver Post*

"Stern and bracing . . . [a] suspenseful thriller."
—*San Francisco Chronicle*

"A real grabber."   —*Los Angeles Times*

"A riveting plot, filled with action."
—*The San Diego Union-Tribune*

"Straight out of today's headlines."   —UPI

"A spellbinder . . . unbearable tension."
—*Houston Chronicle*

FOREIGN BODY

Robin Cook

BERKLEY BOOKS
NEW YORK

THE BERKLEY PUBLISHING GROUP
Published by the Penguin Group
Penguin Group (USA) Inc.
375 Hudson Street, New York, New York 10014, USA
Penguin Group (Canada), 90 Eglinton Avenue East, Suite 700, Toronto, Ontario M4P 2Y3, Canada
(a division of Pearson Penguin Canada Inc.)
Penguin Books Ltd., 80 Strand, London WC2R 0RL, England
Penguin Group Ireland, 25 St. Stephen's Green, Dublin 2, Ireland (a division of Penguin Books Ltd.)
Penguin Group (Australia), 250 Camberwell Road, Camberwell, Victoria 3124, Australia
(a division of Pearson Australia Group Pty. Ltd.)
Penguin Books India Pvt. Ltd., 11 Community Centre, Panchsheel Park, New Delhi—110 017, India
Penguin Group (NZ), 67 Apollo Drive, Rosedale, North Shore 0632, New Zealand
(a division of Pearson New Zealand Ltd.)
Penguin Books (South Africa) (Pty.) Ltd., 24 Sturdee Avenue, Rosebank, Johannesburg 2196,
South Africa

Penguin Books Ltd., Registered Offices: 80 Strand, London WC2R 0RL, England

This is a work of fiction. Names, characters, places, and incidents either are the product of the author's imagination or are used fictitiously, and any resemblance to actual persons, living or dead, business establishments, events, or locales is entirely coincidental. The publisher does not have any control over and does not assume any responsibility for author or third-party websites or their content.

FOREIGN BODY

A Berkley Book / published by arrangement with the author

PRINTING HISTORY
G. P. Putnam's Sons hardcover edition / August 2008
Berkley premium edition / August 2009

ISBN: 978-0-425-22895-1

BERKLEY®
Berkley Books are published by The Berkley Publishing Group,
a division of Penguin Group (USA) Inc.,
375 Hudson Street, New York, New York 10014.
BERKLEY® is a registered trademark of Penguin Group (USA) Inc.
The "B" design is a trademark of Penguin Group (USA) Inc.

PRINTED IN THE UNITED STATES OF AMERICA

10 9 8 7 6 5 4 3 2 1

Acknowledgments

I would like to acknowledge several Indian doctors who were exceptionally hospitable to me on my visit to India, particularly Dr. Gagan Gautam, who took an entire day out of his busy schedule to show me both private and public Indian hospitals. There was also Dr. Ajit Saxena, who not only showed me his private hospital but also invited me into his home to meet his family and enjoy a wonderful, home-cooked Indian dinner. And finally there was Dr. Sudhaku Krishnamurth, who introduced me to the two previously named individuals.

At the same time as acknowledging these physicians I would like to absolve them of any responsibility for the story line, descriptions, or slight exaggerations in *Foreign Body,* for which I take full responsibility. For example, upon reading the manuscript, Dr. Gautam commented, "I haven't seen people riding on the roof of a bus in Delhi. Hanging from them, yes . . . but not on the roof." After some thought I realized he was correct. When I saw the phenomenon, it was indeed outside the city limits.

Finally, I would like to acknowledge the country of India itself. During my visit I found it to be an overwhelmingly fascinating mixture of contrasts: rich yet poor, serenely beautiful but insidious, modern yet medieval. It is a country living in three centuries all at once, with a fascinating history I knew little about, and populated by creative, intelligent, beautiful, and hospitable people. In short, it is a country I can't wait to revisit.

This book is dedicated to Daksh Gautam,
in hopes that his generation
and the previous will live in respectful harmony.
Have a great life, little guy!

If one thinks of oneself as free, one is free,
and if one thinks of oneself as bound, one is bound.
Here this saying is true, "Thinking makes it so."

—*Ashtavakra Gita,* 1:11,
translated by John Richards

Prologue

OCTOBER 15, 2007
MONDAY, 7:00 P.M.
DELHI, INDIA

Only those long-term residents of Delhi who were extraordinarily sensitive to the vicissitudes of the city's traffic patterns could tell that rush hour had peaked and was now on the downward slope. The cacophony of horns, sirens, and screeches seemed undiminished to the tortured, untrained ear. The crush appeared unabated. There were gaudily painted trucks; buses with as many riders clinging precariously to the outside and on the roof as were inside; autos, ranging from hulking Mercedes to diminutive Marutis; throngs of black-and-yellow taxis; auto rickshaws; various motorcycles and scooters, many carrying entire families; and swarms of black, aged bicycles. Thousands of pedestrians wove in and out of the stop-and-go traffic, while hordes of dirty children dressed in rags thrust soiled hands into open windows in search of a few coins. Cows, dogs, and packs of wild monkeys wandered through the streets. Over all hung a smothering blanket of dust, smog, and general haze.

For Basant Chandra, it was a typically frustrating evening commute in the city that he had lived in for his entire forty-seven years. With a population of more than fourteen million, traffic had to be tolerated, and Basant, like everyone else, had learned to cope. On this particular night he was even more tolerant than usual since he was relaxed and content from having stopped for a visit with his favorite call girl, Kaumudi.

In general, Basant was a lazy, angry, and violent man who felt cheated in this life. Growing up in an upper-caste Kshatriya family, he felt his parents had married him down with a Vaishya woman, despite his father's obtaining a management position at the in-laws' pharmaceutical firm as part of the union, while he was afforded a particularly well-paying sales manager position in place of his previous job selling Tata-brand trucks. The final blow to Basant's self-esteem came with his children, five girls, aged twenty-two, sixteen, twelve, nine, and six. There had been one boy, but his wife had miscarried at five months, for which Basant openly blamed her. In his mind, she'd done it on purpose by overworking as a harried medical doctor, practicing internal medicine at a public hospital. He could remember the day as if it were yesterday. He could have killed her.

With such thoughts in mind, Basant pounded his steering wheel in frustration as he glided into the reserved parking slot in front of his parents' house, where he and his family lived. It was a soiled three-story concrete structure that had been painted white at some indeterminate time in the past. The roof was flat and the window frames metal. On the first floor was a small office where his wife, Meeta, occasionally saw her few private patients. The rest of the first floor housed his aging parents. Basant and his family occupied the second floor, and his younger brother, Tapasbrati, and his family were on the third.

As Basant was critically eyeing his house, which was hardly the style that he expected to be living in at this stage of his life, he became aware of a car pulling up behind him, blocking him in. Gazing in the rearview mirror, he had to squint against the car's headlights. All he could make out through the hazy glare was a Mercedes emblem.

"What the hell?" Basant spat. No one was supposed to park behind him.

He opened his door and climbed from the car with full intention of walking back and giving the Mercedes's driver a piece of his mind. But he didn't have to. The driver and his two passengers had already alighted and were approaching ominously.

"Basant Chandra?" the passenger in the lead questioned. He wasn't a big man, but he conveyed an indisputable aura of malevolent authority with his dark complexion, spiked hair, a bad-boy black leather motorcycle jacket over a tight white T-shirt, exposing a powerful, athletic body. Almost as intimidating was the driver. He was huge.

Basant took a reflexive step back as alarm bells began to sound inside his head. This was no chance meeting. "This is private property," Basant said, trying to sound confident, which he clearly wasn't.

"That's not the question," the man in the motorcycle jacket said. "The question is: Are you the piece of donkey crap called Basant Chandra?"

Basant swallowed with some difficulty. His internal alarms were now clanging with the utmost urgency. Maybe he shouldn't have hit the hooker quite so hard. He looked from the Sikh driver to the second passenger, who'd proceeded to pull a gun from his jacket pocket. "I'm Basant Chandra," Basant managed. His voice squeaked, almost unrecognizable to himself. "What's the problem?"

"You're the problem," the man in the motorcycle jacket said. He pointed over his shoulder. "Get in the car. We've been hired to talk some sense into you. We're going for a little ride."

"I . . . I . . . I can't go anyplace. My family is waiting for me."

"Oh, sure!" the apparent leader of the group said with a short, cynical laugh. "That's exactly what we have to talk about. Get in the car before Subrata here loses control and shoots you, which I know he'd prefer to do."

Basant was now visibly trembling. He desperately looked from one threatening face to the other, then down to the gun in Subrata's hand.

"Should I shoot him, Sachin?" Subrata asked, raising his silenced automatic pistol.

"See what I mean?" Sachin questioned, spreading his hands palms up. "Are you going to get into the car or what?"

Wanting to flee off into the darkness but terrified to

do so lest he be shot in the back, Basant forced himself forward, wondering if he should run out into the middle of the congested street. Unable to make up his near-paralyzed mind, he found himself at the black Mercedes, where Subrata opened the passenger-side rear door with his free hand. Subrata forced Basant's head down and his torso into the car before walking around and climbing in on the other side. He was still holding on to his gun and made certain Basant saw that he was.

Without another word, Sachin and the driver climbed into the front seat. The car pulled out into the street as fast as the congested traffic would allow.

"To the dump?" the driver asked.

"To the dump, Suresh," Sachin agreed.

Acutely aware of the firearm, Basant at first was too terrified to say anything at all, but after ten minutes he was more afraid of not saying anything. His voice wavered at first but then gained some semblance of strength. "What is this all about?" he questioned. "Where are you taking me and why?"

"We're taking you to the dump," Sachin said, turning around. "It's where we all agreed you belonged."

"I don't understand," Basant blurted. "I don't know you people."

"That's going to change, starting tonight."

Basant felt a modicum of hope. Not that he was happy about the prospect, but Sachin was suggesting a long-term relationship, meaning they weren't going to shoot him. As a drug-sales manager, it crossed his mind that these people might be interested in some kind of drugs. The problem was that Basant had access only to drugs his in-laws' firm made, which were mostly antibiotics, and this kind of shakedown for antibiotics seemed extreme.

"Is there some way I can help you people?" Basant asked hopefully.

"Oh, yeah! For sure!" Sachin responded without elaborating.

They drove in silence for a while. Finally, Basant spoke up. "If you would just tell me, I'll be happy to help in any way I can."

Sachin swung around and glared at Basant for a beat but didn't speak. Any slight diminution of Basant's encompassing panic evaporated. His trembling returned with a vengeance. His intuition assured him this was not going to end well. When the driver braked to a crawl behind one bullock cart passing another, Basant considered opening the car door, leaping out, and sprinting off into the dark, dusty haze. A glance into Subrata's lap at the nestled gun resulted in a quick response.

"Don't even think about it," Subrata said, as if reading Basant's mind.

They turned off the main road after another fifteen minutes and headed into the enormous landfill. Through the windows they could see small fires with flames licking up through the mounds of trash, sending spirals of smoke up into the sky. Children could be seen scampering over the debris, looking for food or anything of even questionable value. Rats the size of large rabbits were caught in the headlights as they scurried across the roadway.

Pulling up between several story-high piles of garbage, the driver made a three-point turn to direct the car back toward the way they'd come. He left the motor running. All three of the toughs climbed out. The driver opened the door for Basant. When Basant didn't respond, the driver reached in and, grabbing a handful of his kurta, dragged him stumbling from the car. Basant couldn't help choking from the smoke and stench. Without letting him go, the driver continued to drag him into the illumination provided by the headlights, where he released him roughly. Basant did all he could do to stay on his feet.

Sachin, who was pulling a heavy glove on his right hand, walked up to Basant and, before Basant could react, punched him viciously in the face, sending him stumbling backward, losing his balance, and falling into the fetid garbage. With his ears ringing and blood dripping from his nose, he rolled over onto his stomach and tried to get up, but his hands sank into the loose trash. At the same time he felt broken glass cut into the flesh of his left arm. He was yanked by the ankle from the soft garbage out onto the firmly packed truck track. He was then forcibly kicked in the stomach, causing him to lose his wind in the process.

It took Basant several minutes to catch his breath. When he had, Sachin reached down and grabbed the front of his kurta and yanked him to a sitting position. Basant raised his arms in an attempt to try to shield his face from another blow, but the blow didn't materialize. Hesitantly, he opened his eyes, looking up into the cruel face of his attacker.

"Now that I have your attention," Sachin snarled, "I

want to tell you a few things. We know about you and what kind of piece of shit you are. We know what you've been doing to your oldest daughter, Veena, since she was six. We know you've been keeping her in line by threatening to do the same to her four younger sisters. And we know what you've been doing to her mother."

"I've never—" Basant began but was interrupted by a vicious slap to the face.

"Don't even try to deny it, you bastard, or I'll beat you to a pulp and leave you here for the rats and the wild dogs to eat."

Sachin glared down at the cowering Basant before continuing. "This isn't some kind of trial. We know what I'm saying is the truth, you slimy bastard. And I'm going to tell you something. This is a warning! If you ever touch one of your daughters inappropriately or your wife in anger, we will kill you. It's that simple. We've been hired to do it, and knowing what I do about you, I'd just as soon do it and get it over with. So I actually hope you give me the excuse. But that's the message. Any questions? I want to be certain you understand."

Basant nodded. A glimmer of hope appeared in his terrified mind. This current nightmare was only a warning.

Sachin unexpectedly slapped Basant once more, sending the man onto his back, his ears ringing and his nose rebleeding.

Without another word, Sachin took off his leather glove, glared down at Basant for a beat, waved for his companions to follow, and returned to the black Mercedes.

Sitting up with a sense of utter relief when he realized he was being left, Basant proceeded to get to his feet. A moment later he had to leap back into the loose trash and out of the way as the large sedan surged toward him, missing him by inches. Basant stared after the goons' car while the red taillights receded into the smoke and haze. Only then did he become truly aware of the darkness and stench surrounding him, and the facts that his nose and arm were bleeding, that he'd gathered a small audience of silent, staring landfill urchins, and that the rats were inching closer. With sudden new fear and revulsion, Basant struggled back onto his feet, extricated himself from the soft trash, and regained the firmness of the track, all the while grimacing from the pain in his side from the kick he'd suffered. Although it was very difficult to see, because of the moonless night, he hurried forward, hands outstretched like a blind man. He had a long way to walk before reaching a road that would have transportation. It wasn't pleasant and was definitely scary, but at least he was alive.

SAME TIME IN A SECTION OF NEW DELHI

On a busy business street, wedged between typical, three-storied, reinforced-concrete commercial buildings whose façades were almost completely covered by signs in both Hindi and English, stood the starkly modern five-story Queen Victoria Hospital. In sharp contrast to its neighbors, it was constructed of amber-mirrored glass and green marble. Named after the beloved nineteenth-century British monarch to appeal to the modern medical tourist as well as the rapidly expanding Indian upper middle class, the hospital was a beacon of modernity thrust into the center of India's timelessness. Also in contrast to its neighboring plethora of small businesses, which were, for the most part, still open, busy, and casting harsh blue-white fluorescent light into the street, the hospital looked bedded down for the night, with little of its soft, interior illumination penetrating the tinted glass.

Except for two tall, traditionally costumed Sikh doormen standing at either side of the entrance, the hospital could have been closed. Inside the day was clearly winding down. As a tertiary hospital with no real emergency department, the Queen Victoria handled only scheduled elective surgery, not emergencies. The soiled dinner dishes had long since been picked up, washed, and hidden away in their cupboards, and most of the visitors were gone. Nurses were handing out evening medications, dealing with drains and dressings from the day's surgeries, or sitting within bright cones of light at nurses' stations to finish up their computerized charting duties.

After a hectic day involving thirty-seven major surgeries, it was a relaxed and quiet time for everyone, including the one hundred and seventeen patients: everyone, that is, except Veena Chandra. While her father was trudging out of the rank, loathsome landfill, Veena was struggling in the half-light of an anesthesia room in the empty operating-room suite, where the only light was filtering in from the dimmed central corridor. Veena was attempting with trembling fingers to stick the needle of a 10cc syringe into the rubber top of a vial of succinylcholine, a rapidly paralyzing drug related to the curare of Amazonian poison dart fame. Normally, she could fill such a syringe with ease. Veena was a nurse, having graduated from the famous public hospital the All India Institute of Health Sciences almost three months ago. Following graduation she'd been hired by an American firm called Nurses International, which had, in turn, hired her out to the Queen Victoria Hospital after providing her with some specialized training.

Not wishing to stick herself with the needle, which could prove deadly, Veena lowered her arms for a moment and tried to relax. She was a ball of nerves. She truly didn't know if she was going to be able to do what she'd been tasked with and had agreed to do. It seemed incredible that she'd been talked into it. She was supposed to fill the syringe, take it down to Maria Hernandez's room, where the woman was hoped to be sleeping off the anesthesia from the hip-replacement surgery she'd had that morning, inject it into her IV, and then beat a rapid retreat, all without being seen by anyone. Veena knew that not being seen by anyone on a nearly full hospital floor was highly unlikely, which was why she was still dressed in her traditional white nursing uniform she'd had on all day. The hope was that if someone did see her, they wouldn't think it odd she was in the hospital even though she worked days, not evenings.

To help her calm down, Veena closed her eyes, and the moment she did so she was instantly transported back four months to the last time her father threatened her.

They were at home, his parents in the living room, her mom at the hospital, and her sisters out indulging in Saturday-afternoon activities with friends. Totally unexpectedly, he had cornered her in the bathroom. While the television blared in the next room, he began shouting, then cursing at her. He was very clever in how he hit her, never leaving a mark on her face. His rage was unexpectedly volcanic, and it was all Veena could do not to cry out. Since it hadn't happened for more than a year, Veena had assumed that the problem was over. But now she knew for sure it would never be over. The only way to escape her father's clutches was for her to leave India. Yet she feared for her sisters. She knew he was unable to control his urges. If she left, he would undoubtedly single out one of her sisters and start anew, and that she could not abide.

The sudden crash of metal against the composite floor brought Veena back to the present, her heart skipping a beat. Feverishly, she stashed the vial and syringe in a drawer packed with IV needles. Suddenly, the bright lights came on in the main corridor of the OR. With her pulse pounding, Veena went to the small wired-glass window and glanced out. Within the darkened anesthesia room, she was confident she would not be visible. To the right she saw that the main doors to the outer hall were momentarily propped open. A second later two members of the janitorial crew appeared, wearing hospital scrubs. Both men carried mops. They picked up the empty buckets they'd dropped moments before and started down the corridor, passing within feet of Veena.

Relieved to a degree that it was only a cleaning crew, Veena turned back into the room and retrieved the vial and syringe. She was now more nervous than she'd been just moments earlier. The unexpected arrival of the janitors reminded her how easy it would be for her to be caught in the OR, and if she was caught, how hard it would be to come up with an explanation of what she was doing there. With her trembling even worse, she persisted and managed to guide the needle into the vial. Exerting negative pressure, she filled the syringe to the level she'd predetermined. She wanted a good dose, but not too big.

Veena's short, unpleasant reverie had reminded her with painful clarity why she had to do what she'd been tasked with. She'd agreed to put to sleep an aged American woman with a history of heart problems in return for a guarantee from her employer that her mother and her sisters would be protected into the foreseeable future from her abusing father. It had been a difficult choice for Veena, made impulsively with the idea that it would be the only opportunity she would have to obtain any kind of freedom, not only for herself but also for eleven of her friends, who had all joined Nurses International at the same time.

Putting away the vial and throwing away the packaging from the syringe, Veena walked toward the door. If she was going to go through with the plan, she had to concentrate and be careful. Above all, she had to try to avoid being seen, especially near her victim's room. If she happened to be confronted in any other part of the hospital, she would explain that she'd returned that evening to use the library facility to study Maria Hernandez's condition.

Veena cracked the door and slowly eased it open to get her head out to see up and down the corridor. Presently, several of the cleaning people could be seen chatting and mopping. As they had started at the very end and were working toward the doors, their backs were conveniently turned in Veena's direction. Stepping into the corridor, Veena let the door close gently before silently heading out of the OR area. Just before she let the main entrance doors swing shut, she glanced back at the cleaning crew. She felt palpable relief. They were oblivious to her presence.

Forgoing the elevator lest she not only run into someone but be forced to converse, Veena used the stairwell to descend to the fourth floor. There she again cracked the door before gazing the length of the dimmed corridor in both directions. No one was in view, even at the nurses' station, which was by contrast an oasis of bright light in the center of the floor. Apparently, the nurses were out in the rooms attending to their charges. Veena hoped no one would be in Maria Hernandez's room, which was in the opposite direction. From where she was in the stairwell, it was on the right, three doors down. All she could hear were muted sounds from multiple TVs and distant beeping from the nearby monitors.

To gather her resolve, Veena let the door slip shut while she closed her eyes and leaned her head back against the concrete block of the stairwell. Step by step, she went over what she was about to do to avoid any possible errors, thinking back to how she had reached this unimaginable point in her life. Everything had fallen into place this afternoon, as she returned to the bungalow after work. She and the other eleven nurses hired by Nurses International were required to live at what sounded like a small cabin in American English but was in reality an enormous British Raj–era mansion. They lived there in luxury along with the Nurses International four-person administration. Yet coming through the front door she had felt her pulse quicken and her muscles tense just like she always did. Veena had to be constantly on guard.

As an acculturated Hindu woman, Veena recognized she had a powerful inclination to bow to male authority. When she joined Nurses International, mainly for their promised help in her goal of emigrating to America, she naturally treated Cal Morgan, the head of the organization, as she was expected to treat her own father. Unfortunately, this natural response was not without problems. As a typical thirty-two-year-old American male, Cal interpreted Veena's culturally motivated attention and respect as a come-on, which created numerous episodes of misunderstanding. The situation was difficult for both of them and persisted because of a continued lack of communication. Veena feared compromising her chances of Nurses International giving her her freedom by helping her emigrate, and Cal feared losing her because she was their best employee and the leader among the others.

That afternoon, like all workday afternoons, once inside the mansion and despite the tension between them,

Veena sought out Cal in the paneled library, which he
had commandeered as his office. At the end of each shift
the nurses were required to report to one of the four
principals of the firm, President Cal Morgan, Vice President Petra Danderoff, Computer Head Durell Williams,
or Psychologist Santana Ramos, whichever individual
had hired the nurse in question. Veena had to report to
Cal because she had been his hireling some two months
earlier, when the company was being formed. Each day
Veena and the others were tasked, in addition to their
normal nursing duties, to surreptitiously download
reams of patient data from the central computers of the
six private hospitals where they'd been hired out and
bring it back and report it to their assigned administrator. During their month of U.S. training, they had been
specifically instructed in this activity. As an explanation,
they had been told that one of the primary functions of
Nurses International was to obtain surgical outcome
data. Why the company was interested in such data had
not been explained, and no one particularly cared. The
complicated, clandestine effort seemed a small price to
pay to be already compensated with American nurse
salaries, which were ten times what their Indian cowork-
ers were being paid, and, more important, to be given
the promise of being relocated to America after six
months.

Already tense as usual, when Veena had walked into
Cal's office that afternoon, he had magnified her anxiety
by ordering her to close the door behind her and sit
down on the couch. Fearful of another seduction scene,
she'd done as she was asked, but he shocked her with

something else entirely. He had told her that he'd learned that day the whole story about her father and how he was extorting her. Stunned and humiliated, Veena was also furious at her best friend, Samira Patel, because she knew instantly it had to have been she who'd revealed Veena's darkest secret. Samira was a nurse who'd trained with Veena and who'd joined Nurses International along with her. She too wanted to emigrate to the United States, but for a more generic reason. Familiar with the freedoms of the West from images on the Internet, she despised what she considered the restrictions life in India placed on her. She was what she liked to describe as a free spirit.

After Cal had revealed what he knew, Veena had stood up with the idea of fleeing without even thinking of where she would go, but Cal had grabbed her arm and urged her to sit back down. To her surprise, in lieu of blaming her and condemning her as she had always feared, he'd convincingly sympathized with her, and had been angry that she thought she was somehow responsible for her father's behavior. He'd then gone on to persuade her that he could help her if she'd help him. He'd guaranteed that her father would never again lay a hand on her, her sisters, or her mother. And if he did, he would disappear.

Convinced Cal was being deadly serious, Veena had asked what she was to do for him. Cal had then gone on to explain that the surgical-outcome data they were amassing was proving to be disappointing. The data was too good, and they had come to realize they needed to create some of their own bad data, and he'd told her how they envisioned doing it using succinylcholine. At first Veena had been shocked by the plan, especially since she had no idea why they needed this "bad data," but the more Cal talked, saying that she would have to do it only once, and that she would be free from her father and able to emigrate without the guilt of putting her sisters and mother at risk, and the more she recognized she would never get such an offer again, she had impulsively decided to cooperate. And not only did she agree to cooperate, she wanted to do it immediately, that very night, lest she think too much about what she was actually doing.

With a renewed sense of determination to get the business over with and a clear idea of the sequence of events she needed to follow, Veena took a deep breath. She then straightened up from where she was leaning against the stairwell wall, opened her eyes, and checked again to be sure the corridor beyond was empty. With tension quickening the pulses in her temples, she started toward the Hernandez room at a brisk walk. No sooner had she taken several steps when one of the evening nurses emerged from the room directly opposite Hernandez's, bringing Veena to a sudden halt. Luckily for Veena, the nurse was unaware of her presence. Concentrating on the medication tray in her hands, she headed farther down the corridor, away from the nurses' station. As suddenly as she had appeared, she disappeared into another patient room.

Breathing a silent sigh of relief, Veena checked in the direction of the nurses' station. All was quiet. She hurried on, reaching Hernandez's door in seconds. Pushing it open, she stepped in and returned the door to its near-shut position. Although the TV was on, the volume was low. The overhead lights were dimmed, causing the corners of the room to be lost in shadow. Veena had no trouble seeing Mrs. Hernandez. The woman was fast asleep, with the head of her bed elevated about forty-five degrees. The fluorescent-like light emanating from the TV dimly illuminated her facial features while leaving her orbits in deep shadow, giving her a ghastly appearance, as if she were already dead.

Thankful the woman was asleep, and wanting the anxiety-producing affair over with as soon as possible, Veena rushed to the bedside, pulling the syringe from her pocket. She was careful not to nudge the noisy, metal bed rails as she reached for the IV line. She was also careful not to pull on it for fear of attracting the patient's attention and waking her. Holding the IV port in one hand, she used her teeth to remove the needle cover. Then, holding her breath, she inserted the needle. When she could see the needle tip within the lumen of the IV line, she prepared to slowly depress the plunger. Instead, she almost leaped out of her shoes. For no discernible reason, Mrs. Hernandez rolled her head in Veena's direction and looked up into Veena's face. A slight smile played across her lips.

"Thank you, dearie," she said.

Veena felt her blood run cold. Knowing she had to act that instant or she'd never be able to do it, she forcibly depressed the plunger of the syringe, shooting the bolus of succinylcholine into the patient's bloodstream. What had pushed her over the edge was sudden, inappropriate defensive anger that the woman had the insensitivity not only to wake up but to thank her, apparently thinking Veena was giving her medication to help her.

Although Veena hadn't seriously thought about what she'd be forced to witness after injecting the paralyzing drug, she was horrified by what she did see. Contrary to a peaceful, cinema-like passing, which had been her general assumption and what Cal had intimated, it was anything but. Within seconds Mrs. Hernandez's body reacted to the large dose of succinylcholine with rapid fasciculation of her musculature. It started with her facial muscles giving her waves of grotesque facial contortions. Adding to the unexpected horror was the intense fear that clouded her eyes. As her hand lifted in a vain attempt to reach out to Veena for help, it too started to jerk about uncontrollably. And then came a sudden ominous, purple darkness that spread over her face like the shadow that seeps across the face of the moon during a lunar eclipse. Unable to breathe yet fully conscious, Mrs. Hernandez was being rapidly suffocated and turning deeply cyanotic.

Horrified at what she had wrought and wanting nothing more than to flee, Veena was forced by her guilt to remain rooted to her spot and watch her patient's death throes. Luckily for both it was soon over, and Mrs. Hernandez's eyes gazed blankly out at eternity.

"What have I done?" Veena whispered. "Why did she . have to wake up?"

At last breaking free from her psychologically induced

paralysis, Veena turned and raced from the room. Without even thinking of the consequences, she ran headlong down the hall, only vaguely aware that the nurses' station was still empty. During the day there was always at least a ward clerk, but not in the evening and not at night.

In the elevator Veena was only dimly aware that she was alone. She kept seeing Mrs. Hernandez's face in all its twitching horror. There were people in the hospital lobby, even a few ambulating patients and their family members, but no one gave Veena a second look. She knew what she had to do, and that was to get away from the hospital as soon as she possibly could.

Outside, the doormen opened the glass doors for her when they saw her coming. They said good evening as she rushed out, but she didn't respond. Originally, she had planned on leaving through the staff-and-delivery entrance, but now, in her mind, it didn't matter. As far as she was concerned, whether people saw her or not did not make any difference.

Out in the street Veena hailed one of the yellow-and-green auto rickshaws, which were nothing more than three-wheeled covered scooters with bench backseats and open sides. Veena gave the bungalow's address in the swank Chanakyapuri section of the city and climbed in. With a sudden jerk the driver took off as if he were joining a race, sounding his horn intermittently, despite the lack of need. Since the traffic had now lessened considerably, they made good time, especially when they reached the residential area of Chanakyapuri. Staring straight ahead during the journey, Veena tried not to think, yet she couldn't get the violent contortions of Mrs. Hernandez's face out of her mind's eye.

At the mansion, Veena was unable to convince the driver to enter the driveway to take her to the porte cochere. He argued that he didn't believe she lived there and didn't want to get in trouble with the police. Since a similar episode with an auto rickshaw driver had happened twice before in the little less than a month she'd lived there, Veena didn't try to argue. She paid the man and hustled through the gate into the walled and fenced property. Reaching the front door, she didn't go immediately to the room she shared with Samira, but rather went directly to the library in the hope of finding Cal still there. When she didn't find him there, she looked for him in the formal living room, where Nurses International had added a large flat-screen TV. She found Cal and Durell absorbed in a rebroadcast of one of the previous day's American football games. Both were draped across respective formal sofas with bottles of Kingfisher beer in their hands.

"Ah!" Cal exclaimed, catching sight of Veena. He let his legs fall from the sofa's arms. "That was fast! Is it done?"

Veena didn't talk. With a somber expression, she merely waved for Cal to follow her and started back toward his library office.

When Cal walked into the library, Veena was standing just inside the door. She closed it behind him, which he found curious. "What's going on?" he asked. For the first time he sensed something was decidedly wrong. He looked at her more closely. From his perspective and most everyone else's, Veena was an extraordinarily beautiful combination of both angular Aryan and rounded Hindu features, with exotically shaped, strikingly blue-green eyes, blacker-than-night hair, and golden bronze skin. Normally, she appeared quite peaceful. But not now. Her usually full, dark lips were pressed together and pale. Cal couldn't tell if it reflected anger, determination, or some combination. "Is it done?" he questioned again.

"It's done," Veena said handing him a keychain with a USB storage device containing Maria Hernandez's medical record. "But there was a problem."

"Oh?" Cal questioned, eyeing the storage device, wondering if it was the problem. "Was there trouble getting the data?"

"No! Getting the woman's medical record was easy."

"Okay," Cal said, extending the word. "So, what's the problem?"

"Hernandez woke up and spoke to me."

"So?" Cal questioned. He could tell Veena was highly upset but didn't think the fact that the woman spoke with her was so unusual. "What did she say?"

"She thanked me," Veena said, as tears welled up in her eyes. She took a deep breath and looked off, trying to keep her emotions in check.

"Well, that was nice," Cal said in an attempt to lighten the conversation.

"She thanked me just before I injected her," Veena added angrily. Her eyes blazed as she turned back to Cal.

"Calm down!" he half urged and half ordered.

"It's easy for you to say. You didn't have to look into

her eyes or watch her face contort. You didn't tell me she was going to twitch grotesquely and turn purple as she suffocated in front of my eyes."

"I didn't know."

Veena glared at Cal and shook her head in apparent disgust.

"The people who told me how to do it implied the patient would just die peacefully because they would be completely paralyzed."

"Well, they lied."

"I'm sorry," Cal said with a shrug. "I'm proud of you anyway. And like I promised, I heard just a few minutes ago that the conversation my colleagues had with your father went very well. They are very, very confident he will follow their advice to the letter. So from now on, you don't have to worry about him misbehaving with you, your sisters, or your mom. The men I sent are utterly convinced, but they're still going to check in every month or so to remind him he'd best behave. You're free."

For several beats Cal returned Veena's glare. He had expected some positive reaction from her, but it wasn't forthcoming. Just when he was about to question why she wasn't more pleased to be free, she shocked him by hurling herself at him. Before he knew what was happening, she grabbed his shirt at the collar with both hands and proceeded to tear it open. Buttons popped off with explosive force.

Reflexively, Cal grasped her forearms but not before she'd peeled his shirt back from his shoulders and yanked it down. At that point, in utter confusion, Cal let her pull his shirt completely off, ball it up in a tight bundle, and toss it to the side. He tried to catch her eyes in hope of some explanation, but she was too preoccupied. Without a second's hesitation, she put both her palms on his bare chest and pushed him stumbling backward until his heels slammed up against the foot of the couch. At that point his knees buckled, and he ended up in a sitting position. Still without hesitation or any explanation, she grabbed one foot, lifted it, and pulled off his shoe, tossing it in the direction of the abandoned shirt. Next came the second shoe. Once the shoes were history, she attacked his belt and zipper, and after grabbing both cuffs, the pants went in the direction of the shoes and shirt.

"What the hell?" Cal questioned as she unabashedly slipped her thumbs inside the waistband of his briefs. Cal's athletic body in all its glory was in full view. This was beyond even his most lascivious fantasy. It was true that Cal Morgan had been attracted to Veena Chandra from the moment he'd interviewed her nine weeks earlier and had pursued her sexually but with no luck. Cal had been perplexed. Having been voted sexiest man in his Beverly Hills high school graduating class as well as valedictorian, and with similar accolades at UCLA, Cal had never lacked for female companionship and sex, which he thought of as a sport. But he'd never made any headway with Veena, which was confusing, since she always acted as if she truly cared for him, with small favors and special consideration.

"Why are you doing this?" Cal questioned with un-camouflaged bewilderment, although he wasn't about to tell her to stop. At the moment, Veena was rapidly unbuttoning her nurse's uniform. She had now locked eyes with Cal, and her expression was one of angry determination. For the first time since he'd met her, the thought went through Cal's mind that she might be truly emotionally unbalanced. The fact that he'd learned just that day that she'd been victimized by her father for sixteen years was not lost on him.

Veena did not speak as she stepped out of her uniform. Nor did she take her eyes from Cal's as she undid her bra and set her shapely breasts free. In contrast, Cal let his eyes drop to take in the full glory of Veena's nakedness. Cal had known she had a knockout body from seeing her in a modest bikini when they'd brought the nurses to California for their month of computer and cultural training, but this was infinitely more captivating.

Still, Veena did not speak, nor did she slow down. The second she was out of her clothes, she advanced on Cal, straddled him, and directed him inside. She then proceeded to put her hands on his shoulders and to rock rhythmically.

Cal raised his eyes to hers. She was still glaring at him with the same determined expression. If it hadn't been so pleasurable, he would have thought she was punishing him for her experience that night at the hospital. Without any letup on Veena's part, Cal lost voluntary control and climaxed. When Veena still didn't stop, Cal had to urge her to do so. "You have to give me a rest," he managed.

Veena responded immediately by climbing off, and

without even a moment's hesitation began dressing. Her facial expression still had not changed.

In a postcoital fog of physical pleasure, Cal watched her and progressively became even more confused. He sat up straight. "What are you doing?"

"I'm getting dressed, obviously," she said, speaking for the first time since she'd launched her aggressive lovemaking. Her tone was challenging, as if she thought Cal's question idiotic.

"Are you leaving?"

"I am," Veena said, while hooking her bra.

Cal watched her pick up her dress. "Did you enjoy this experience?" he questioned. It was obvious she'd not had an orgasm. It had been so mechanical on her part that Cal likened her behavior to that of a motorized mannequin.

"Why, am I supposed to?"

"Well, yes, of course," Cal said, a little hurt but also perplexed. "Why don't you stay. I need to file the story about Mrs. Hernandez, but then we can talk about your experience tonight at the hospital. I sense you need to talk about it."

"How would we talk about it?"

"Well, discuss the details."

"The details were that she woke up, thanked me, and she didn't go quietly."

"I'm sure there's more than that."

"I've got to go," Veena said with emphasis. She glanced around to make sure she had everything and started for the door.

"Wait! Why did you make love to me tonight, and why did you do it the way you did?"

"How did I do it?"

"Well, aggressively. That's the best way to describe it."

"I wanted once in my life to prove my father wrong."

"What can you possibly mean?" Cal questioned, with a short, cynical laugh. He was beginning to feel totally used, not that it had been unpleasant physically.

"My father always told me that no man would want me if he knew my secret. You knew my secret, and you still were willing to make love. My father was wrong."

Oh, for crissake, Cal thought irritably but didn't utter. He said with a fake smile, "Wonderful, now you know. See you around the mansion." He got up and began dressing. He was aware Veena was watching him, but he avoided her eyes. A moment later she was gone.

Cal let out a slew of expletives under his breath as he pulled on the rest of his clothes. At age thirty-two, he had no intention of getting serious romantically, and experiences like he'd just had made him wonder if he'd ever feel like getting serious. Women truly were mysterious and even crazy as far as he was concerned.

With the USB device in hand he left the library and sought out Santana Ramos, who was their psychologist-in-residence and also their media guru. Although Cal had had significant media experience running Superior-Care Hospital Corporation's PR department, where he worked prior to Nurses International, along with Petra Danderoff, he didn't have inside network connections, but Santana did. She'd worked at CNN for almost five years. He found Santana in her room reading one of her beloved psychology journals, and without the gory details Veena had related, he told her that the first patient had been taken care of. He handed over the USB device for the patient's history. He didn't mention a word about the aggressive lovemaking.

"Call your friends at CNN," Cal said. "It's about ten a.m. there. Get the story to them, puff it up as a big inside scoop, saying the Indian government is trying to keep such stories under wraps. Tell them there will be more because there are now moles in place, and encourage them to get it on the air ASAP."

"Perfect," Santana said, hefting the USB device. "I think this is going to really work," she added, as she stood.

"I do too," Cal said. "Get right on it."

"Consider it done."

Confident she would be true to her word, Cal gave Santana an encouraging couple of taps on the shoulder. Leaving her room, he headed in the direction of the formal living room with full intention of getting back to the NFL game he'd been watching with Durell. But while he walked, his mind went back to his disturbing episode with Veena. Despite her being their best employee, he wondered if he should bring up with the others her obvious emotional instability. What gave him pause was that he knew Petra, who was against any dalliance between Cal or Durell and any of the nurses, would end up gloating and torture him with her invariable "I told you so" routine. On top of that, it was also downright embarrassing to have been used so flagrantly. Suddenly, Cal stopped. His mind had replayed Veena's last comment that she "wanted once in her life to prove her father wrong."

Why once? Cal questioned. He raised a knuckle to his mouth and absently chewed on it. "Oh my God!" he voiced suddenly. Turning from the direction of the formal living room, he raced toward the guest wing, where the nurses were housed. Arriving at Veena and Samira's room, he pounded on the door as he yelled Veena's name. When she didn't answer immediately, he tried the door, all the while hoping that his fears would prove groundless. Unfortunately, they didn't. He found Veena peacefully sprawled on her bed, her eyes closed. In her hand she clutched an empty plastic container of Ambien.

Grabbing Veena's shoulders, Cal rudely sat her up. Her head lolled, but her eyes opened with heavy lids.

"God, Veena!" Cal shouted. "Why? Why did you do this?" He knew that if she died, the whole enterprise he had so carefully set up would be over.

"It's appropriate," Veena murmured. "A life for a life."

Veena tried to lean back, and Cal let her flop back onto the bed. He pulled out his cell phone and speed-dialed Durell. When Durell answered, complaining about being interrupted while watching the game, Cal blurted out for him to get an ambulance ASAP as Veena had just ODed and would need to be pumped out.

Tossing the phone aside on the bed, Cal dragged Veena's limp body to the edge, allowing her head to hang down, he used his index finger to get her to vomit. It wasn't pretty. The good part was that more than a dozen intact Ambien tablets as well as a few broken ones appeared on the doomed carpet. The bad part was that he ended up puking himself.

Chapter 1

It was a glorious day in Los Angeles. The heat, smog, and smoke from the inevitable wildfires of late summer and early fall had finally been blown inland to be replaced by the first clear air in months. Not only had Jennifer Hernandez been able to see the nearby Santa Monica Mountains on her way to the UCLA Medical Center, but she'd even caught a glimpse of the more distant San Gabriel range, beautifully backlit by the rising sun.

Jennifer was excited on this crisp morning, and not just because of the weather. It was the first day of a new rotation in general surgery. Jennifer was a fourth-year medical student at UCLA who'd enjoyed the third-year program in surgery enough to consider it as a specialty, but she felt she'd not been exposed to enough surgery to make the decision. Although more women were studying surgery than did in the past, they were still a minority. It was not an easy decision. General surgery was particularly demanding time-wise, particularly for a woman with goals of having both a career and a family, and Jennifer thought she wanted a family. Needing more experience so she could make an intelligent decision, she'd selected general surgery as one of her fourth-and-final-year electives. On the plus side, she was confident she was decisive of mind and good with her hands, both qualities needed for surgery, and from her experience during her third-year course, she knew that surgery was both challenging and exciting.

The plan for the first day was for the assigned medical students to change into scrubs and meet their respective preceptors in the surgical lounge at eight in the morning. Jennifer was early, as was her habit. Consequently, although it was only seven-thirty-five, she'd already changed and was sitting in the surgical lounge, mindlessly flipping through an outdated *Time* magazine. At the same time she was keeping an ear to CNN on the TV while watching the comings and goings of the doctors, nurses, and other staff. The surgical day was definitely already in full swing. She'd been told Mondays were always busy, and she could tell from the whiteboard that every one of the twenty-three operating rooms was currently occupied.

Jennifer sipped her coffee. The anxiety about being late was now comfortably fading, and she began to wonder if she'd be accepted in the excellent UCLA surgery program if she decided on it as her specialty of choice. The exciting thing was that in the upcoming year, the whole hospital was moving into the new Ronald Reagan facility across the street, where the ORs were to be the

latest and the best. As one of the hardest-working students, Jennifer was one of the top students in her class,
and as such, she was confident she had a good chance to
be asked to stay on if she applied. But in actuality, staying in L.A. wouldn't be her first choice. Jennifer wasn't
from Los Angeles; she wasn't even from the West Coast
like the vast majority of her fellow students. Jennifer was
from New York and had come west to take advantage of
a four-year scholarship that had been established by a
grateful and wealthy Mexican whose cancer had been
cured at the UCLA Medical Center. The scholarship
was for a needy Hispanic woman. Being all three, Jennifer had applied and won, and so began her unexpected
foray to California. But now that her medical schooling
was winding down, she wanted to go back east. She
loved the Big Apple and considered herself a New Yorker.
That's where she'd been born, and as hard as it had
been, that's where she'd grown up.

Jennifer took another sip of her coffee, and switched
her full attention to the TV. The two CNN talking
heads had said something that caught her interest.
They had said that medical tourism seemed to be
threatening to become a growth industry in the developing world, particularly in South Asian countries like
India and Thailand, and it wasn't just for cosmetic or
quack procedures, such as untested cancer cures, as it
had been in days of yore. It was for full-blown twenty-
first-century procedures, such as open-heart surgery and
bone-marrow transplants.

Leaning forward, Jennifer listened with growing interest. She'd never even heard the term *medical tourism*.

In her mind it seemed like an oxymoron of sorts. Jennifer had certainly never been to India, and with scant knowledge she envisioned it to be an appallingly poor country whose majority population was skinny and malnourished, dressed in rags, and lived in a hot, humid monsoon for half the year, and a hot, dry, dusty desert for the other half. Although she was smart enough to know such a stereotype was not necessarily true, she thought it most likely had an element of truth, or it wouldn't be the stereotype. What she was certain of was that such a stereotype hardly suggested the appropriate destination for someone to go to for the latest surgical skills, modern and expensive technology, and twenty-first-century techniques.

To Jennifer it was apparent the newscasters shared her disbelief. "It's shocking," the man said. "In 2005, more than seventy-five thousand Americans traveled to India for major surgery, and since then, according to the Indian government, it's been growing more than twenty percent per year. They expect by the end of the decade, it will be a two-point-two-billion-dollar source of foreign exchange."

"I'm amazed, totally amazed!" the woman newscaster said. "Why are people going there? Does anyone have an idea?"

"Lack of insurance here in the States is the main reason, and cost is the second," the man said. "An operation that would cost eighty thousand here in Atlanta might cost twenty thousand there; plus, they get a vacation at a five-star Indian resort to boot."

"Wow!" the woman commented. "But is it safe?"

"That would be my concern as well," the man agreed, "which is why this story that's just come in is so interesting. The Indian government, which has been supportive of this medical tourism with economic incentives, has claimed over the last number of years that the results are as good as or better than anywhere in the West. They say the reason is that the surgeons are all board-certified, and the equipment and hospitals, some of which are accredited by the International Joint Commission, are state-of-the-art and brand-new. However, there've never really been much data and statistics in any of the medical journals to back up such claims. Just a few moments ago CNN learned from a known, reliable source that a generally healthy sixty-four-year-old American woman from Queens, New York, named Maria Hernandez, who'd had an uncomplicated hip replacement some twelve hours earlier, suddenly died at seven-fifty-four Monday night, India time, at the Queen Victoria Hospital in New Delhi, India. Of particular interest, the source said she was certain that this tragic passing of a healthy sixty-four-year-old was merely the tip of the iceberg."

"Very interesting," the woman said. "I trust we'll be hearing more."

"That's my understanding," the man agreed.

"Now, let's move on to the interminable '08 presidential campaign."

Jennifer sat back, dazed. In her mind she repeated the name: Maria Hernandez from Queens, New York. Jennifer's paternal grandmother, the most important person in her life, was named Maria Hernandez, and more worrisome, she lived in Queens. Even more worrisome, she had a bad hip that had been progressively worsening. Just a month ago, she'd asked Jennifer's opinion if she should get it repaired. Jennifer's advice had been that only Maria could answer such a question, since it depended, at this stage, on how much disability and discomfort it caused.

"But India?" Jennifer shook her head. The fact that it seemed so totally unlikely that her grandmother would go to India without discussing the idea with her was Jennifer's main source of hope that the story was just a coincidence and didn't involve her Maria Hernandez but some other Maria Hernandez who also lived in Queens. Jennifer and her grandmother were extremely close, since Maria was Jennifer's ersatz mother. Jennifer's real mother had been killed when Jennifer was only three, as the tragic victim of a hit-and-run driver on the Upper East Side of Manhattan. Jennifer, her two older brothers, Ramón and Diego, as well as her good-for-nothing father, Juan, had lived in Maria's tiny one-bedroom rowhouse apartment in Woodside, Queens, almost from the day of the accident.

Jennifer had been the last child to move out, and that hadn't happened until she'd left for medical school. In Jennifer's mind, Maria was a saint whose own husband had abandoned her. Maria had not only allowed them all to live with her, she'd supported and nurtured them all while working as a nanny and housekeeper. Jennifer and her brothers helped with after-school jobs as they got older, but the main breadwinner had been Maria.

As for Juan, he had done nothing for as long as Jennifer could remember. Supposedly having suffered an old incapacitating back injury before Jennifer was born, he'd been unable to work. Before her death, Jennifer's mother, Mariana, had been the only wage earner, a buyer for Bloomingdale's. Now that Jennifer was nearing the end of medical school and knew something about psychosomatic illness and malingering, she had even more reason to question her father's supposed disability and despise him even more.

As the lounge chair she was sitting in was low with high arms, Jennifer had to struggle to get to her feet. She couldn't just sit there with the disturbing worry about her grandmother. She also knew that even the slight possibility that the news release involved her grandmother was going to make it near impossible to concentrate when she met her new preceptor. She had to find out for certain, which meant she was going to have to do something she was loath to do—call her hated, lazy-ass father.

Jennifer had barely spoken to her father since she was nine, preferring to pretend he didn't exist, which was somewhat difficult, as they were all living together in such tight quarters. In that regard, it had been a relief since she'd come to L.A., as she hadn't spoken to him at all. During her first year, if he ever happened to answer the phone when she'd called Maria, she just hung up and would try later when she was certain her grandmother would be home. But mostly she let her grandmother call her, which her grandmother did on a regular basis. Even the phone was no longer a problem when her grandmother, at Jennifer's insistence, got a mobile phone and allocated the land line to Jennifer's father.

As far as Jennifer visiting New York was concerned, she hadn't done it for four years. It was partly because of her father and partly because of the expense. Instead, she'd had her grandmother come out to the West Coast every six months or so. Maria had loved it. She'd told Jennifer that for her, coming to California to see Jennifer was the most exciting thing she'd done in her whole life.

Inside the women's locker room, Jennifer undid the safety pin that held her locker key, opened her locker, and got out her cell phone. After walking around the room and searching, she was happy to find a hot spot with an adequate signal. She dialed, and as she waited for the call to go through, she gritted her teeth in anticipation of hearing her father's voice. As it was seven-forty-five in L.A., she knew it would be ten-forty-five in New York, just the time Juan usually raised himself from the dead.

"Well, well, my uppity daughter," Juan scoffed after the initial hellos. "What's the occasion I get a call from the snooty doctor-to-be?"

Jennifer ignored the provocation. "It's about Granny," she said simply. She was insistent that she wasn't going to be baited into expanding the conversation beyond the issue at hand.

"What about Granny?"

"Where is she?"

"Why do you ask?"

"Just tell me where she is."

"She's in India. She finally had her hip repaired. You know how hardheaded she is. I've been asking her to do it for a couple of years since it was really getting in the way of her work."

Jennifer bit her tongue about the comment concerning work, knowing her father's history. "Have you heard from the doctor or the hospital or anything?"

"No. Why should I?"

"They have your telephone number, I assume."

"Certainly."

"How come you didn't go with her?" It pained Jennifer to think of her grandmother going all the way to India by herself and facing major surgery when the most distant travel she'd ever done was come to California to visit Jennifer.

"I couldn't go with my back the way it is and everything."

"How was this surgery set up?" Jennifer questioned. She wanted to get off the phone. The fact that no one had called Juan was definitely encouraging.

"By a company in Chicago called Foreign Medical Solutions."

"Do you have the number handy?"

"Yeah, just a sec." Jennifer could hear the receiver drop onto the tiny side table. She could picture it by the entrance door in the part of the apartment that was supposed to be used for a dining table but which contained Juan's bed. A minute later Juan came back and rattled off the Chicago number. As soon as Jennifer had it, she hung up. She didn't feel like hypocritical small talk or even saying good-bye. With the number in hand she dialed Foreign Medical Solutions, and after telling an operator who she was and what she was calling for, she was switched to an individual named Michelle, whose title was case manager. The woman had an impressively deep, resonant voice with a slight southern accent. After Jennifer repeated her story, Michelle asked her to hold the line. For a few moments Jennifer could hear the unmistakable sound of a computer keyboard in use as Michelle pulled up Maria Hernandez's file.

"What is it you were hoping to learn?" Michelle asked, coming back on the line. "As a medical student, you're probably aware that HIPAA rules limit what we can give out, even if you are who you say you are."

"First I wanted to make sure she's okay."

"She's doing very well. She had her surgery, which went smoothly. She spent less than an hour in the PACU, and then was moved to her room. It's indicated she's already started fluids by mouth. That's the latest entry."

"Was that recently?"

"It was, indeed. Just a little more than an hour ago."

"That's good news," Jennifer said. She was even more relieved than when Juan said he'd heard nothing. "Do most of your patients from the Queen Victoria Hospital do well?"

"They do. It is a popular hospital. We've even had one patient insist on going back to the Queen Victoria for his second knee."

"A testimonial is always good," Jennifer said. "Can I call the hospital and try to talk with my grandmother?"

"Certainly," Michelle said, and rattled off the number.

"What time is it now in New Delhi?" Jennifer asked.

"Let's see." There was a pause. "I often get this mixed up. It's nine-fifty-five a.m. here so I believe it is nine-twenty-five p.m. in New Delhi. They are ten and a half hours ahead of us here in Chicago."

"Would it be an okay time to call?"

"I really couldn't say," Michelle responded.

Jennifer thanked the woman. For a moment she thought about trying her grandmother's cell phone but then nixed the idea. In contrast to Jennifer's AT&T phone, she didn't think her grandmother's Verizon would work in India. She called the Queen Victoria Hospital. As the call went through in literally seconds, Jennifer couldn't help being impressed, especially since she had no idea how cell phones, or any phone for that matter, worked. A moment later she found herself conversing in English halfway around the world with a woman with a pleasantly melodic and distinctive Indian accent. It was somewhat similar in Jennifer's ear to an English accent but more musical.

"I can't believe I'm talking to someone in India," Jennifer effused.

"You are welcome," the hospital operator said somewhat inappropriately. "But you probably talk to India more than you realize, with our many call centers."

Jennifer gave her grandmother's name and asked if she could be connected to her room.

"I'm very sorry," the operator answered, "but we are not able to forward calls after eight in the evening. If you had the extension, you could call direct."

"Can you give me the extension?"

"I'm sorry, but I'm not allowed, for obvious reasons. Otherwise, I would connect you."

"I understand," Jennifer said, but she still felt there hadn't been any harm in asking. "Can you tell me how she is doing?"

"Oh, yes, of course. We have a list right here. What is the surname again?"

Jennifer repeated "Hernandez."

"Here she is," the operator said. "She's doing very well and already taking nourishment and has been mobilized. The doctors say they are very pleased."

"That's terrific," Jennifer responded. "Tell me, does she have someone there at the hospital who is in charge of her case?"

"Oh, yes, indeed! All our foreign visitors have a host-country case manager. Your grandmother's is Kashmira Varini."

"Can I leave a message for her?"

"Yes. Would you prefer I take it or would you like to leave it on her voicemail? I can connect you."

"Voicemail would be fine," Jennifer said. She was impressed. Her brief exposure to an Indian hospital suggested it was quite civilized and certainly equipped with contemporary communications.

Following Kashmira Varini's pleasant outgoing message, Jennifer left her name, her relationship to Maria Hernandez, and a request to be kept informed of her granny's progress or, at the very least, to be informed if there happened to be any problems or complications. Before disconnecting, Jennifer slowly and distinctly gave her cell phone number. She wanted to be certain there would be no mistakes because of accent. Jennifer knew she had a strong New York accent.

Flipping her phone closed, Jennifer started to put it back into the locker but then paused. She thought the likelihood of another Maria Hernandez from Queens having surgery at nearly the same time as her grandmother in the same hospital in India was quite small. Actually, it seemed completely far-fetched, and the idea of calling CNN and telling them as much crossed her mind. Jennifer was an activist, not a ponderer, and didn't hesitate to speak her mind, which she felt CNN deserved for not adequately vetting their story before putting it on the air. But then a more intelligent, less emotional frame of mind prevailed. Who could she call at CNN, and what were her chances of getting any kind of satisfaction? Besides, she suddenly looked at her watch. Seeing that it was now after eight, a shiver of anxiety descended her spine like a surge of electricity. She was late for her first day of her surgery elective, despite her efforts to the contrary.

Jennifer slammed the locker closed, and as she ran for the door, she put her phone on vibrate and slipped it into her scrub pants pocket along with the safety pin and the key. She was truly worried. Being late was not the way to begin a new rotation, especially with a compulsive surgeon, and from her experience in third-year surgery, they were all compulsive.

Chapter 2

an you see them?" Dr. Shirley Schoener asked. Dr. Schoener was a gynecologist who had specialized in infertility. Although she'd never admitted it, she'd gone into medicine as a way of superstitiously dealing with her fear of disease, and she went into infertility for fear of suffering it herself. And it had worked on both fronts. She was currently healthy and had two great kids. She also had a thriving practice, as her statistics for successful pregnancies were superb.

"I suppose," Dr. Laurie Montgomery said. Laurie was a medical examiner who worked at the Office of the Chief Medical Examiner for the city of New York. At forty-three, she was a contemporary of Dr. Schoener's. They'd gone to medical school together and had even been friends and classmates. The difference between them, other than their professional specialties, was that Shirley had married relatively early—at age thirty, just after completing her residency—and kids had come in due course, with Shirley popping out one after the other. Laurie had waited until age forty-one, two years ago, before marrying a fellow medical examiner, Jack Stapleton, and stopping what she'd come to call the "goalie," which was a euphemism for various methods of contraception she'd employed over the years. Without contraception, Laurie had assumed that she would promptly become pregnant with the child she always knew she would have. After all, she had mistakenly become pregnant while relying on the rhythm method by merely cutting things a bit too close. Unfortunately, the pregnancy turned out to be ectopic and had to be terminated. But now that conception was supposed to happen, it hadn't, and after the requisite year of unprotected "goalie"-free sex, she'd come to the unpleasant conclusion that she had to face reality and be proactive. At that point she'd contacted her old friend Shirley and started treatments.

The first stage had involved finding out if there was something wrong anatomically or physiologically with either Jack or herself. The answer had turned out to be no. It had been the only time in her life that she'd hoped medical tests would find something wrong so it could be fixed. They did find, as was expected, that one of her fallopian tubes was nonfunctional from her ectopic pregnancy, but the remaining fallopian tube and its apparent function were entirely normal. Everyone felt one tube shouldn't have been a problem.

At that point Laurie had tried the drug Clomid along with intrauterine insemination, whose old name, artificial insemination, had been changed to make it sound less unnatural. After the requisite Clomid cycle attempts, all of which were unsuccessful, they'd gone on to the follicular-stimulating hormone injections. Laurie had now begun her third cycle of injections, and if this was unsuccessful, as the two earlier ones had been, Laurie was scheduled for in vitro fertilization as the last hope. Consequently, she was understandably on edge and even a touch clinically depressed. She had never guessed how stressful infertility treatments were going to be or the emotional burden they were going to entail. She was frustrated, let down, angry, and exhausted. It was as if her body was toying with her after she had made so much effort over so many years not to get pregnant.

"I don't know why you can't see them," Dr. Schoener said. "The follicles are very apparent, at least four of them, and they look terrific. They are a good size: not too big, not too small." Grabbing the ultrasound screen with her free hand, she turned it forcibly to make it more perpendicular to Laurie's line of sight. She then pointed to each follicle in turn. With her right hand under a modesty sheet, she was directing the ultrasound wand into the left vertex of Laurie's vagina.

"Okay, I see them," Laurie said. She was propped up on the examining table with her feet in stirrups and her legs apart. The first time she'd experienced a fertility-style ultrasound she'd been mildly taken aback, since she'd expected the sensor to be placed externally on her abdomen. But now, having had the procedure every couple of days through the first half of five cycles, she took it in stride. It was mildly uncomfortable but certainly not painful. The biggest problem was that she found it humiliating, but then again, she found the whole infertility rigmarole humiliating.

"Do they look any better than they have in earlier cycles?" Laurie asked. She needed encouragement.

"Not remarkably," Dr. Schoener admitted. "But what I particularly like is that the majority in this cycle are in the left ovary rather than in the right. Remember, it's your left oviduct that is patent."

"Do you think that's going to make a difference?"

"Am I detecting some negativity here?" Dr. Schoener said, as she removed the wand and pushed the ultrasound screen out of Laurie's way.

Laurie let out a short mocking laugh while she removed her feet from the stirrups, swung her legs over the side of the exam table, and sat up. She was clutching the sheet around her midsection.

"You have to stay positive," Dr. Schoener went on. "Are you having some hormonal symptoms?"

Laurie repeated her sham laugh with a touch more forcefulness. She also rolled her eyes. "When I started all this, I promised myself I wouldn't let it get to me. Was I wrong! You should have heard me yesterday bawl out an octogenarian who tried to cut in front of me at the checkout line at Whole Foods. As the saying goes, it would have made a sailor blush."

"How about headaches?"

"Those, too."

"Hot flashes?"

"The whole shebang. And what bothers me the most is Jack. He acts like he's not even part of this. Every time

I get my period and feel crushed that I'm not pregnant, he just blithely says, 'Well, maybe next month,' and goes about his business. I feel like hitting him over the head with a frying pan."

"He does want children, doesn't he?" Dr. Schoener asked.

"Well, to be truthful, he's probably going through this mostly on my behalf, although once we have them, if we have them, he'll be the world's greatest dad. I'm convinced. Jack's problem in this regard is that he had two lovely daughters with his late wife, but the wife and the kids were all tragically killed in a commuter plane crash. He suffered so he's afraid of making himself vulnerable again. It was even hard to get him to commit to marriage."

"I didn't know," Dr. Schoener said, with true sympathy.

"Very few people know. Jack's not forthcoming with his personal emotional issues."

"There's nothing strange about that," Dr. Schoener said, as she snatched up the paper debris from the ultrasound test and stuffed it into the wastebasket. "Unless the male is demonstrably the source of the infertility, which he then takes very seriously, he deals with infertility and its treatment very differently than a woman."

"I know, I know," Laurie said insistently. She stood up, still keeping the sheet wrapped around her. "I know it, but it still bugs me that he doesn't act more committed and understanding of what I'm going through. All this ain't easy by any stretch of the imagination, especially with the threat of hyperstimulation hanging over my head. The trouble is as a doctor I know what to be afraid of."

"Luckily, there doesn't seem to be any threat of hyperstimulation in this cycle or those in the past, so I want you to continue with the same dosage with your injections. If your hormone level is too high in the blood sample we drew today, I'll call and make the necessary adjustments. Otherwise, stay the course. You're doing terrific. I feel good about this cycle."

"That's what you said last month."

"I did say that because I did feel good last month, but I feel better this month with that left ovary of yours getting more into the act."

"What is your guesstimate in terms of my taking the trigger injection and having the intrauterine insemination? Jack likes a little warning about when he's going to be required to step up to the plate."

"Considering the current size of the follicles, I'd say maybe five or six days. Have the front desk schedule another ultrasound and estradiol for two or three days from now, whatever's most convenient. I'll be able to give you an even better estimate."

"And one other thing," Laurie said, as Dr. Schoener was about to leave. "Last night I was lying in bed unable to go back to sleep when the question dawned on me about my job. Do you think that there could be any environmental issues at the morgue that could be contributing to this infertility problem, like fixatives for tissue samples or something like that?"

"I doubt it," Dr. Schoener said without hesitation. "If pathologists had more infertility than other docs,

I think I would have heard of it. Remember, I see a lot of docs around the med center, including a few pathologists."

Laurie thanked her friend, gave her a quick hug, and then ducked into the changing room where she'd left her clothes. The first thing she did was get out her watch. It was not quite eleven-thirty, which was perfect. It meant she'd be getting back to the medical examiner's office just about noon, the time she gave herself her daily hormone shot.

Chapter 3

The cell phone's vibration caught Jennifer completely off guard because she'd totally forgotten she'd slipped it into the pocket of her scrub pants instead of leaving it in her locker. As a consequence she jumped, and it was enough to catch her new preceptor's attention. His name was Dr. Robert Peyton. Since he'd made her adequately aware that she'd started on the wrong foot in his estimation when she'd been almost four minutes late on the first day, the vibrating phone, which could be heard faintly, was a potential disaster. She shoved her hand into her pocket to try to calm the insistent device, but she couldn't. Unable to determine quickly enough the phone's orientation, she couldn't connect with the appropriate button.

Jennifer, along with Dr. Peyton, who was an elegant man with marquee good looks, and seven of Jennifer's classmates who'd signed up for the same elective, was standing in the mausoleum stillness of the anesthesia supply room situated between operating rooms number eight and ten, discussing the coming month's schedule. The eight-person group was to be divided into four pairs and assigned weeklong rotations in various surgical specialties, including anesthesia. To Jennifer's chagrin, she and another student had been assigned to anesthesia. She felt that if she'd wanted anesthesia, she would have chosen it for the whole rotation. But because of the bumpy start she'd had from being late, she'd not complained.

"Is there something the young lady would like to share with the group in reference to her very apparent startle and her apparent need to bring her cell phone into the OR?" Dr. Peyton questioned, with a taunting tone and with what seemed to Jennifer an uncalled-for hint of sexism. She was tempted to give the man an appropriate response but thought better of it. Besides, the continuing vibration of the phone dominated her thoughts. She could not imagine who could be calling her unless it had something to do with her grandmother. Impulsively and despite everyone's attention directed at her, she pulled the phone from her pocket, mainly to quiet it, but in the process glanced at the LCD screen. Instantly, she could see it was an international call, and having called the number so recently, she knew it was the Queen Victoria Hospital.

"I beg everyone's pardon," Jennifer said. "I have to take this call. It's about my grandmother." Without waiting for a response from Dr. Peyton, she rushed out through the door into the OR's central corridor. Sensing that even having a phone in the OR might have been considered a major no-no as she flipped it open and put it to her ear, she said, "Hold the line for a moment!" Then she ran toward the double bidirectional entrance doors. It wasn't until she got to her earlier location in the locker room that she tried to have a conversation. She started by apologizing.

"It is no bother," a rather high-pitched Indian voice said. "My name is Kashmira Varini, and you left a message on my voicemail. I am Maria Hernandez's case manager."

"I did leave a message," Jennifer admitted. She could feel her abdominal muscles tense as to why the woman was calling. Jennifer knew it wasn't a social call, since it must have been close to midnight in New Delhi.

"I'm calling you as you instructed. I have also just finished speaking to your father, and he advised me to call as well. He said you should be in charge."

"In charge of what?" Jennifer asked. She knew she was playing dumb to an extent and postponing the unthinkable. The call had to be about Maria's condition, and there was little chance of it being good news.

"In charge of arrangements. I'm afraid Maria Hernandez has passed away."

For a moment Jennifer couldn't speak. It seemed impossible that her grandmother could be dead.

"Are we still connected?" Kashmira questioned.

"I'm still here," Jennifer answered. She was thunderstruck. She could not believe a day that had started out so promising was turning out so disastrous. "How can this be?" she complained irritably. "I just called your hospital maybe an hour and a half ago and was assured by the operator that my grandmother was doing just fine. I was told she was even eating and had been mobilized."

"I'm afraid the operator did not know. All of us here at the Queen Victoria Hospital are terribly sorry about this most unfortunate state of affairs. Your grandmother was doing splendidly, and the operation to replace her hip was a complete, unqualified success. No one expected this outcome. I hope you will accept our most sincere sympathies."

Jennifer's mind was in a near paralysis. It was almost as if she'd been hit on the head.

"I know this is a shock," Kashmira continued, "but I want to assure you that everything was done for Maria Hernandez that could have been done. Now, of course—"

"What did she die of?" Jennifer suddenly demanded, interrupting the case manager.

"I'm told by the doctors it was a heart attack. With no warning whatsoever of any problems, she was found in her room unconscious. Of course a full resuscitation attempt was made, but unfortunately with no response."

"A heart attack doesn't seem to me to be particularly likely," Jennifer said, as her raw emotions spilled over into anger. "I happen to know she had low cholesterol, low blood pressure, normal blood sugar, and a perfectly normal cardiogram. I'm a medical student. I made sure she'd had an A-plus physical here at the UCLA Medical Center only months ago when she visited me."

"One of the doctors mentioned she'd had a history of a heart arrhythmia."

"Arrhythmia my ass," Jennifer snapped. "Oh, she had a few PVCs way back when, but it was found to be due to ephedrine in an over-the-counter cold remedy she was taking. The important thing is that the PVCs disappeared as soon as she stopped the med, and never came back."

It was now Kashmira's turn to be silent, necessitating for Jennifer, after a pause, to question if the call had been dropped.

"No, I'm still here," Kashmira intoned. "I'm not quite sure I know what to say. I'm not a doctor; I only know what the doctors tell me."

A touch of guilt softened Jennifer's response to the horrid news. Instantly, she felt a slight embarrassment about blaming the messenger. "I'm sorry. I'm just so upset. My grandmother was very special to me. She was like a mother."

"We are all truly sorry for your loss, but there are decisions to be made."

"What kind of decisions?"

"Mainly concerning disposition of the body. With a signed death certificate, which we already have, we need to know if you plan to have the body cremated or embalmed and whether you plan to ship it back to the States or have it remain here in India."

"Oh! Good God," Jennifer murmured under her breath.

"We know it's hard to make decisions under the circumstances, but these decisions must be made. We asked your father, since he is listed in the contract as next of kin, but he said you, as a near doctor, should handle it, and he's faxing us a statement to that effect."

Jennifer rolled her eyes. Such a trick to avoid responsibility was so typical of Juan. He was shameless.

"Considering this awful circumstance, we had expected Mr. Hernandez to come here to India forthwith at our expense, but he said he was unable to travel because of a back injury."

Yeah, sure, Jennifer silently mocked. She was well aware that every November he could drive all the hell up to the Adirondacks to hunt and climb over mountains with his other worthless buddies with no trouble at all.

"We will surely extend the same invitation to you as the new next of kin. The contract your grandmother signed included airfare and lodging for a relative to accompany her, but she had said it was not needed. Anyway, funds are still available."

Jennifer felt herself getting choked up, imaging her grandmother dying in far-off India, and her body alone on some cold slab in a mortuary cooler. With travel, room, and board available, she knew instinctively she could not let her granny down, never mind the inconvenience of her personal responsibilities—namely, medical school and her new surgical rotation. She'd never forgive herself, despite the fact that her grandmother had not conveyed to Jennifer that she was going in the first place.

"Arrangements could be made through the American

embassy and documents signed from afar, but your presence is definitely preferable. It is safer under such circumstances when a family member is present to avoid any mistakes or misunderstanding."

"Alright, I'll come," Jennifer said abruptly, "but I want to come immediately. That means today if possible."

"That should not be a problem if there are seats on the late-afternoon Singapore flight through Tokyo. We've had American patients from the L.A. area before, so I'm familiar with the schedule. The bigger problem will be the visa, but I should be able to arrange that through the Indian health ministry for a special emergency M visa. We can let the airline know from this end. I will need your passport number just as soon as possible."

"I'll head to my apartment and call you with it," Jennifer promised. She was glad she had one, and the only reason she did was because of her grandmother. Maria had taken her and her two brothers to Colombia to meet relatives when she was nine. She was also glad she'd made the effort to renew it.

"Perhaps I'll have most of the arrangements done by the time you call back. Despite the hour here in India, I will do it right now. But before I let you go, I want to ask again whether you want your grandmother's body cremated, which we recommend, or embalmed."

"Don't do either until I get there," Jennifer said. "Meanwhile, I'll ask my two brothers what they think." Jennifer knew that was a lie. She and her brothers had gone in opposite directions in life, and they rarely talked.

She didn't even know how to get a hold of them, and for all she knew they were still in prison for dealing drugs.

"But we need an answer. The death certificate is already signed. You must decide."

Jennifer hesitated answering. As a matter of habit whenever someone pushed her, she pushed back. "I assume the body is in a cooler."

"It is, but our policy is to take care of it immediately. We don't have the proper facilities, as Indian families claim their deceased kin immediately to cremate or bury, but mostly cremate."

"A good part of the reason I'm coming is to see the body."

"Then we can have it embalmed for you. It will be far more presentable."

"Look, Ms. Varini," Jennifer said. "I'm coming halfway around the world to see my grandmother. I don't want her disturbed until I arrive. I certainly don't want her sliced and diced by an embalmer. I'll probably have her cremated, but I don't want to decide until I see her one last time, okay?"

"As you wish," Kashmira said, but with a tone that suggested she strenuously disagreed with the decision. She then gave Jennifer her direct-dial number with the insistence that Jennifer get her passport details back to her just as soon as possible.

Jennifer flipped her phone closed. Her perplexity and annoyance at the case manager's inappropriate and continued insistence that she make a decision about what to do with her grandmother's body, when she clearly indicated she didn't yet know, at least had the effect of taking the edge off her grief. But then Jennifer shrugged her shoulders. The situation was probably just another example of how some people lacked common sense in regard to social skills. Kashmira Varini was probably one of those midlevel administrators who had a box next to "dispose of body" that needed to be checked off.

Leaving the locker room at a fast walk, she planned her next few hours, which she sensed would also help take her mind off her grandmother's passing. First she would need to go back into the OR suite to seek out Dr. Peyton and explain the situation. She would then rush to her apartment, get her passport, and call in the number. Then she would head over to the medical school and explain everything to the dean of students.

After passing through the main OR doors, Jennifer stopped at the main desk. While she waited to ask one of the busy head nurses if Dr. Peyton and his students were still in the anesthesia room where she'd left them, she found herself pondering a perplexing issue: How was it that she learned of her grandmother's death from CNN, of all places, some hour and a half before she heard it from the hospital? Since she couldn't think of a single possible explanation, she decided that once she got to India, she was going to try to ask the hospital authorities. It was her general understanding that next of kin were supposed to be notified before names were given out to the media, although it occurred to her that this might be the case only in the United States and not in India. But that thought led to another: Why was CNN even interested in putting her grandmother's name on the air? It wasn't as if she were a celebrity. Was it just as a lead into the issue of medical tourism? And who was this known, reliable source who claimed that her grandmother's death was merely the tip of the iceberg?

Chapter 4

OCTOBER 15, 2007
MONDAY, 11:40 P.M.
DELHI, INDIA
(SIMULTANEOUS WITH JENNIFER'S QUESTIONING HER GRANDMOTHER'S
DEATH BEING ANNOUNCED ON CNN)

Kashmira Varini was a slim, sallow, no-nonsense woman who rarely smiled and whose skin tone was always in sharp contrast to the saris that she inevitably wore. Even late in the evening, having been called back to the hospital on an emergency basis to deal with the death of Mrs. Hernandez, she'd made the effort to dress in a freshly pressed, richly colored red-and-gold outfit. Although almost lifeless in appearance and not particularly sympathetic, she was good at what she did by conveying to patients a strong, reassuring proficiency, efficiency, and commitment, especially with the help of her superb command of English English. Although patients coming from afar for surgery were invariably scared and therefore nervous, she put them at ease the moment they got to the hospital.

"Could you hear enough from my side of the conversation to guess what Ms. Hernandez said?" Kashmira questioned. She was sitting in the hospital CEO's office at a library table. He was seated across from her. In contrast to her elegant ethnic costume, Rajish Bhurgava, the rounded, mildly overweight CEO, was attired cowboy-style with ill-fitting jeans and a plaid flannel shirt that snapped rather than buttoned. He had his legs crossed and his cowboy boots precariously balanced on the corner of the table.

"I could tell you were not able to get permission to embalm or cremate, which was the major goal of the call. That's unfortunate."

"I tried my best," Kashmira said, in her defense. "But the granddaughter is distinctively pertinacious in comparison with the son. Maybe we should have just gone ahead and cremated without asking her."

"I don't think we could have taken that risk. Ramesh Srivastava was very clear when he called me that he wanted this case to disappear. He specifically said he did not want any possible continued cause for media attention, and if the granddaughter is bullheaded, as you suspect, cremating the body without permission could have caused a blowup."

"You mentioned Ramesh Srivastava earlier when you called me about Hernandez's death and told me we had to deal with it tonight. Who is he? I've never heard the name."

"I'm sorry. I thought you knew. He's a top-level administrator who's been placed in charge of the department of medical tourism in the health ministry."

"Is he the one who called you about the death?"

"He is, which was shocking. I've never met the man,

but he's an important individual. His appointment shows how vital the government thinks medical tourism is becoming."

"How did he hear about the death before we did?"

"That is a good question. One of his subordinates saw it on CNN International and felt it serious enough, considering its possible effect on the PR campaign the Ministry of Tourism and the Indian Healthcare Federation have been co-sponsoring, to inform Srivastava immediately despite the hour. What impressed me was that Srivastava then called me directly instead of delegating it to one of his underlings. It shows how serious he thinks it is, which is why he wants the case to disappear, which, of course, is why he wants rapid disposition of the body. To help, he said he'd call to have the death certificate signed without delay, which he did. He also ordered that no one from the hospital staff on any pretext should talk to the media. He said that on the air there was a hint of some kind of investigation. He does not want an investigation of any sort."

"I got that message loud and clear, as did everyone else."

"So," Rajish said, letting his legs fall to the floor and slapping the table for emphasis, "let's get the body cleared for cremation or embalming and out of here."

Kashmira pushed back her chair, the legs of which screeched against the floor in protest. "I will get the process started immediately by making the travel arrangements for Ms. Hernandez. Are you planning on talking to Mr. Srivastava again tonight?"

"He asked me to call his home with an update. So, yes, I will be calling."

"Mention to him we might need his support to get an emergency M visa for Ms. Hernandez."

"Will do," Rajish said, jotting down a quick note to himself. He watched Kashmira walk out the door. Returning his attention to the phone Kashmira had used to call Jennifer and taking out Joint Secretary Srivastava's phone number, which Rajish had written on a piece of scratch paper, he made the call. It made him feel proud to be calling someone so high in the health bureaucracy, especially at such an unorthodox hour.

After answering on the first ring, suggesting he was waiting by the phone, Ramesh Srivastava wasted no time with small talk. He asked if the body had been taken care of as he'd requested. "Not quite," Rajish had to admit. He went on to describe how they'd asked the son but that the son had designated the granddaughter but the granddaughter had demurred. "The good part," Rajish explained, "is that the granddaughter will be on her way to Delhi within a few hours and that as soon as she arrives they will press her for a decision."

"What about the media?" Ramesh questioned. "Has there been any media patrolling around the hospital?"

"None whatsoever."

"I'm surprised and encouraged. It also brings me to the issue of how the media got news of the death in the first place. In the context the piece was presented on the air, it seems to us that it had to have been a left-wing student who is against the rapid increase in private hospitals in India. Are you aware of any such person or persons at Queen Victoria Hospital?"

"Absolutely not. I'm certain we in the administration would be aware of such a person."

"Keep it in mind. With public hospital budgets stagnant, particularly for infectious disease control, there are people who feel quite emotional about the issue."

"I will certainly keep it in mind," Rajish said. The idea that one of their medical staff could be a traitor was troubling, and the first thing he was going to do in the morning was raise the issue with the chief of the medical staff.

Chapter 5

Jennifer was in the process of making her way from the medical school back to the main building of the UCLA Medical Center and felt amazed at what she'd been able to accomplish despite her emotional fog. From the moment she terminated the conversation with the Queen Victoria Hospital case manager a little over an hour ago, she'd dealt with her new preceptor, dashed home, called back to India to give her passport number, made her way to the med school, got the blessing of the dean for a week off, arranged a replacement for her gainful-employment blood-bank job, and was now hoping to solve her emotional fears, economic concerns, and the problem of malaria prophylaxis. Although she'd taken out the almost four hundred dollars she had in savings, she was worried it might not be enough even with her credit card and Foreign Medical Solutions of Chicago paying her major expenses. Jennifer had certainly never been to India, much less on a mission dealing with a dead body. The possibility she would need a significant amount of cash was hardly far-fetched, especially if cremation or embalming was not something that could be charged.

Being as busy as she'd been over the hour-plus had had the secondary benefit of keeping her from obsessing about the reality of her grandmother's passing. Even the weather helped, since it was as glorious as the dawn had predicted. She could still see the mountains in the distance, although not with quite the same startling clarity. But now that she was almost finished with her errands, reality began to reassert itself.

Jennifer was going to miss Maria terribly. She was the person with whom Jennifer was the closest, and had been since Jennifer was three years old. Besides her two brothers, neither of whom she spoke with for months on end, her only relatives that she knew were in Colombia, and she'd met them only once back when her grandmother had taken her there for that expressed purpose. Relatives on her mother's side were a complete mystery. As far as Jennifer was concerned, her father, Juan, didn't count.

Just as Jennifer had passed through the revolving entrance of the main redbrick hospital building, her cell phone sounded. Checking the screen, she could see it was India calling back. She answered the phone and in the process stepped back outside into the sunlight.

"I have good news," Kashmira said. "I've been able to make all the arrangements. Do you have a pencil and paper?"

"I do," Jennifer responded. Getting a small, stiff-backed notebook from her shoulder bag and tucking her phone into the crook of her neck, she was able to write down the flight information. When she learned she'd be leaving that afternoon but not arriving until almost the wee hours of Wednesday, she was appalled. "I had no idea it would take so long."

"It is a long flight," Kashmira admitted. "But we are halfway around the world. Now, when you land here in New Delhi and reach passport control, go to the diplomatic corps line. Your visa will be waiting there. Then once you have your baggage and come out of customs, there will be a representative from the Amal Palace Hotel holding a sign. He will handle your luggage and get you to your driver."

"Sounds simple enough," Jennifer said, while she was trying to figure out from the departure times and the arrival times just how many hours she would be in the air. She quickly realized she couldn't do it without knowing all the time zones. In addition, she found herself confused by having to cross the international date line.

"Wednesday morning we will arrange a car to pick you up from the hotel at eight. Will that be alright with you?"

"I guess," Jennifer said, wondering how human she would be feeling after being on a plane for nine years and having no idea how much sleep she would be able to get.

"We look forward to meeting you."

"Thank you."

"Now I'd like to ask you once again if you have made up your mind between cremation and embalming?"

A wave of irritation washed over Jennifer just when she was beginning to like the case manager. Didn't she have any intuition? Jenifer wondered with amazement. "Now why would I change the way I thought just a couple of hours ago," she questioned irritably.

"The administration made it clear to me they believe it would be best for everyone, even best for your grandmother's body, if we got on with it."

"Well, I'm sorry. My feelings have not changed, especially since I have been so busy that I haven't had time to think about anything. Furthermore, I don't want to feel like you are pushing me. I'm coming just as soon as I can."

"We certainly are not pushing you. We are just recommending what is best for everyone."

"I don't consider it the best for me. I hope you people understand, because if I get there and my grandmother's body has been violated without my consent, I'm going to make a big stink. I'm serious about this, because I can't believe your laws are that much different than ours in this kind of situation. The body belongs to me as the responsible next of kin."

"We certainly would not do anything without your expressed approval."

"Good," Jennifer said, recovering to a degree yet surprised about the vehemence of her response. It wasn't lost on her that she was probably experiencing a significant amount of transference with her emotions, blaming the hospital and even Maria. Not only was she sad about her grandmother, she was also mad. It hardly seemed fair that Maria had not confided in her about running off to India, having major surgery, and then getting herself killed.

After terminating the call, Jennifer stood where she was, recognizing it was probably going to take her some time and effort to sort through her psychological issues. But then she realized what time it was and that she had to catch a flight whose departure was not that many hours away. With that in mind, she hustled back through the revolving door and headed for the emergency department.

As per usual, the emergency room was bedlam. Jennifer was looking for Dr. Neil McCulgan, who had risen in rapid fashion from chief emergency-medicine resident to his current position as an assistant emergency-room director in charge of scheduling. Jennifer had met him during her first year, when he was still a resident. As a character unknown on the East Coast, he was entirely unique to her, and she found him intriguing. Neil was a stereotypical Southern California "surfer dude" sans blond hair, which, in his case, was nondescript brown. What Jennifer found so distinctive was his openly friendly laid-back attitude that was in total contrast to his being a closet intellectual and a compulsive studier with a near photographic memory. When she'd first met him she truly couldn't believe he'd been attracted to a tense, highly demanding medical specialty like emergency medicine.

Although Jennifer was well aware she didn't share his social graces, she did share his general interest in knowledge for knowledge's sake and his study habits, and found him a fertile source of all sorts of information. Over a period of a year Neil became the first man with whom she felt she could truly converse, and not only about medicine. As a consequence, they became best friends. Actually, Neil had become her first real boyfriend. She thought she'd had boyfriends before, but after meeting Neil she realized that was not exactly true. Neil had been the first person to whom Jennifer had been willing to confide her most private secrets.

"Excuse me!" Jennifer called out to one of the harried nurses at the chaotic central station. The nurse had just shouted something to a colleague who was leaning out a doorway several rooms down the main corridor. "Can you tell me where Dr. McCulgan is?"

"I haven't the faintest," the man said. For some reason he had two, not one, stethoscopes draped around his neck. "Did you try his office?"

Taking that suggestion, Jennifer hurried over to the triage area, where the office was located. Glancing in, she felt lucky. He was sitting at his desk with his back to her, dressed in a starched white coat over green scrubs. Jennifer plopped herself down in the chair squeezed between the desk and the wall. Startled, he looked up momentarily.

"Busy?" Jennifer managed, with a catch in her voice. Her question only elicited a scoffing chuckle from the man, whose attention had returned to the massive ER schedule for the month of November that he was poring over.

Neil had pleasant features, intelligent eyes, and a slight

dusting of premature gray along his temples. He also had the broad shoulders and exceptionally narrow waist of a surfer. On his feet he wore white-leather wood-soled clogs. "Can I talk to you for a moment?" she questioned. As she spoke she had to choke back tears.

"If you can make it quick," he said, but with a smile. "I have to have this schedule ready for the printer in one hour." He looked up again and only then became aware that she was struggling with her emotions. "What's wrong?" he said with sudden concern. He put down his pen and leaned toward her.

"I had awful news this morning."

"I'm so sorry," he said, reaching out and gripping her arm. He didn't ask what the news was about. He knew her well enough to know that she would tell him if she was inclined but wouldn't tell him if she wasn't, despite any amount of cajoling on his part.

"Thank you. It was about my grandmother." Jennifer pulled her arm free and reached across Neil's desk to grab a tissue.

"I remember. Maria, right?"

"Yes. She died just a few hours ago. It was even announced, believe it or not, on CNN."

"Oh, no! Gosh, I'm truly sorry. I know what she meant to you. What happened?"

"I'm told a heart attack, which definitely surprises me."

"I can understand why. Didn't the medical department here recently give her a remarkably clean bill of health?"

"They absolutely did. They even gave her a stress test."

"Are you going to head home, or is that a problem? I mean, didn't you start your new surgery rotation today?"

"No and yes," Jennifer said cryptically. "The situation is a bit more complicated." She then went on to tell Neil the whole story about India, about being needled concerning cremation or embalming, about getting the dean to grant a week's leave, about a medical-service company paying her expenses, and about leaving in just a few hours.

"Wow," Neil said. "You've had quite a morning. I'm sorry you are going to India for such a sad reason. As I told you last May when I came back, it's a fascinating country, full of unbelievable contrasts. But I guess this won't be a pleasure trip." Neil had been to India five months before to speak at a medical conference in New Delhi.

"I can't imagine anything about this trip being pleasurable, which brings me to the issue of malaria. What do you think I should do?"

"Ouch," Neil said, wincing. "I'm sorry to say you should have started something a week ago."

"Well, there's no way I could have anticipated this. I'm okay on everything else, even typhoid, from the scare last year with my patient in internal medicine."

Neil grabbed a prescription pad from his drawer and rapidly wrote one out. He handed it to Jennifer, who looked it over.

"Doxycycline?" Jennifer read out loud.

"It's not the number-one choice, but the coverage starts immediately. The best part is you probably don't need it. It's the south of India where malaria is a true problem."

Jennifer nodded and put the scrip into her shoulder bag.

"Why did your grandmother go to India for her surgery?"

"Purely cost, I assume. She didn't have health insurance. And I'm sure my bastard of a father encouraged it big-time."

"I've read about medical tourism to India, but I've never known someone who actually did it."

"I wasn't even aware of it."

"Where are they putting you up?"

"A hotel called the Amal Palace."

"Wow!" Neil said. "That's supposed to be five-star." He chuckled, then added, "You'd better be careful; they must be trying to buy you off. Of course I'm kidding. They don't need to buy you off. One of the negatives about medical tourism is you have no recourse. There's no such thing as malpractice. Even if they screw up big-time, like taking out the wrong eye or killing someone by mistake or incompetence, there's not a thing you can do."

"It's my guess they've negotiated some kind of deal with the Amal Palace. It's just where they put people up. I mean, it's not like I'm getting a special deal. Apparently, they pay airfare and hotel for one relative. That's why I'm getting the trip. My lazy father claimed he couldn't go."

"Well, I hope something positive comes out of this journey," Neil said. He gave Jennifer's wrist one last squeeze. "And keep me informed. Call me anytime: morning, noon, or night. I'm so sorry about your grandmother." He picked up the pen as a signal he had to get back to work.

"I have a couple of requests," Jennifer said, maintaining her seat.

"Sure. What's on your mind?"

"Would you consider coming with me? I think I need you. I mean, I'm going to be completely out of my element. Except for a trip to Colombia when I was nine, I've never been out of the country, much less to some exotic place like India. Since you were just there, you already have a visa. I can't tell you how much more comfortable I'd feel. I know it is asking a lot, but I feel so provincial; even going to New Jersey used to make me anxious. I'm kidding, but I'm not a traveler by any stretch of the imagination. And I know that one of the benefits of emergency-room medicine is that you can take time off, especially since you covered for Clarence a couple of weeks ago, and he owes you."

With a sigh, Neil shook his head. The last thing he wanted to do was wing off to India, even if he could get time off. In truth, it had been part of his initial motivation for the specialty, and he'd specifically set up a twenty-four-hours on, twenty-four-hours off schedule for himself so that when his workweek started seven a.m. Monday it was essentially over seven a.m. Thursday, unless he wanted overtime. The four remaining days of the week were available for his true love, surfing. At that very moment he was looking forward to a surfing meet over the weekend in San Diego. It was also true that his friend, colleague, and fellow surfer Clarence Hodges did owe him for a Hawaiian trip he'd made. But all that didn't matter. Neil did not want to go to India because of a dead grandmother. If it had been Jennifer's mother who had passed away, maybe, but not her grandmother.

"I can't," Neil said, after a pause, as if he'd given the idea true consideration. "I'm sorry, but I can't go. Not now, anyway. If you can wait a week, maybe, but it's not a good time." He spread his hands awkwardly in the air over the schedule he was working on as if it was the problem.

Jennifer was taken aback and disappointed. She'd given a lot of thought about whether to ask him or not and if she truly needed him. What had tipped the balance was the realistic question in her mind whether she could actually handle the situation once she got to India. What was clear to her was that after the initial shock of learning about Maria's death, she'd marshaled significant defenses, including all the rushing around, making the plans to take the trip, and what psychiatrists called "blocking." So far things had worked reasonably well and she was functioning. But as close as her grandmother had been to her, she feared there would be problems when the reality of the loss set in. She truly feared she could get to India and be an emotional train wreck.

Jennifer stared daggers at Neil. Surprise and disappointment had instantly metamorphosed into anger. Jennifer had been so confident that if she asked him directly and admitted she needed him, which she felt she had done, he would surely acquiesce as a direct spin-off of the confidences they shared. The fact that he was turning her down so promptly and with a flimsy, ridiculous explanation, something she never would have done had the situation been reversed, could mean only that their relationship was not what she thought it was. In short, like men in general, in her mind he was demonstrating he couldn't be counted on.

Jennifer stood abruptly and without saying anything walked out of the tiny office and back into the crowded emergency room. She could hear Neil call her name, but she didn't stop or respond. It tormented her that she knew now that it had been a mistake to confide in him. As for asking to borrow some cash, at this point she wouldn't even consider it.

Chapter 6

Cal Morgan was a deep sleeper and needed a powerful alarm to wake up. What he employed was a clock radio with a CD player, and the CD he used was martial music. At three-quarter volume the player was capable of vibrating the night table enough to move itself and other objects on its crowded surface. Even Petra in the neighboring master suite could hear it as if it were in her room. So when it sounded, Cal made an effort to turn it off the moment he became adequately conscious. Even so, he occasionally fell back into deep sleep.

But that was not going to happen this morning. He was much too keyed up about the previous night's activities for more sleep. He stared up at the high ceiling and thought about what had transpired the evening before.

What bothered him was how close Veena's suicide attempt had come to bringing his whole project down. If he hadn't gone in to check on her when he did, she would have died, and there was little doubt that her death would have resulted in an inquest, and an inquest would have been a disaster. It would certainly have closed Nurses International, and in the process, at the very least, slowed his progress toward his ultimate goal of becoming truly wealthy as the CEO of SuperiorCare Hospital Corporation.

Cal hadn't been interested in healthcare initially, and he still wasn't interested in taking care of patients or nurses, for that matter. He just liked the money involved, two trillion per year in the United States alone, and the field's record of sustained growth. Back when he was in high school, advertising had been his first career choice, and he had gone through UCLA and the Rhode Island School of Design in preparation. But briefly working in the field caused him to recognize its limitations, especially financially. Giving up on advertising, but not its principles of deception, he sailed through Harvard Business School, where he was introduced to the mind-boggling money involved in healthcare. When he finished business school he sought and got an entry-level job at the SuperiorCare Hospital Corporation, which was one of the biggest players in the field. The company owned hospitals, feeder clinics, and healthcare plans in almost every state and major city in the United States.

To best utilize his creative bent, Cal entered the company via the public relations department, where he saw the best opportunity to make a name for himself and thereby attract the attention of the company's officers. On his first day he boasted he would lead the company in ten years, and after two it appeared as if his prophecy might have merit. Along with a striking woman five years his senior and an inch taller than his six feet named Petra Danderoff, who'd been part of PR when he joined, he found himself co-running the entire department thanks to a series of extremely successful ad campaigns the two had contrived that had nearly doubled the enrollment in several of the company's healthcare plans.

Some people had been surprised at his meteoric rise, but not Cal. He was accustomed to success from an early age, partly as a self-fulfilling prophecy of the confidence and competitiveness that was part of his genetic makeup, and which had been honed to an obsession by his equally competitive father. From early childhood he'd wanted to win at everything, especially in competition with his two older brothers. From board games like Monopoly to school grades, from athletics to the presents he gave his parents at Christmas, Cal insisted on being number one with a kind of single-mindedness few could match. And success only reinforced his appetite for more success, to the extent that over the years he lost all vestiges of the need for moral principles. In his mind cheating, which he didn't refer to as such, and ignoring ethics, which he considered mere limitations for the faint of heart, were simply tools to advance one's agenda.

SuperiorCare Hospital Corporation officers were not aware of these details of Cal's background and personality. But they were very aware of his contributions to the company and were eager to reward him, particularly the CEO, Raymond Housman. By coincidence this recognition had materialized more or less at the same time a mounting financial problem had been brought to the CEO's attention by his CFO, Clyde English. To their collective horror, accounting had determined that the company had lost, in 2006, about twenty-seven million dollars from its bottom line because India's growing medical tourism industry had caused a disturbing number of American patients to shun SuperiorCare hospitals and wing off to the Asian subcontinent for their surgeries.

Linking the two issues, Raymond Housman had invited Cal to a secret meeting in his office. He'd explained the medical tourism issue and the need to somehow turn it around. He'd then offered Cal an unparalleled opportunity. He said SuperiorCare was looking to lavishly fund through a secretive bank in Lugano, Switzerland, a company with the express purpose of seriously diminishing demand for patients to go to India for surgery, if he would agree to form it. Raymond was very clear that SuperiorCare Hospital Corporation wanted no ostensible connection with such a company and would strenuously deny there was a connection if asked, nor did they want to know how the company accomplished its goal. What Raymond didn't say but what Cal definitely heard was that his termination at Superior-Care Hospital Corporation was temporary and that his success in the current venture would be a cause for him to be welcomed back into the corporate fold with open arms at an extremely high level, essentially leapfrogging the corporate ladder.

Despite having no idea how he was going to engineer the new company's objective, Cal had accepted immediately with the proviso that Petra Danderoff, then his

co-director of the public relations department, would be
included in the deal. At first Housman had balked with
no one to run SuperiorCare's PR, but after being reminded of the seriousness of the medical tourism problem, he relented.

Two weeks later, Cal and Petra were back in Cal's
hometown of Los Angeles, brainstorming their company-
to-be's modus operandi. To help, each had hired a gifted
friend: Cal had chosen Durell Williams, an African-
American whom he had befriended at UCLA and who
had gone on to specialize in computer security; and Petra had asked Santana Ramos, a Ph.D. in psychology
who had joined CNN after she'd worked in private practice for a half dozen years.

Most important, all four people were equally competitive, equally dismissive of ethics as a limiting weakness, and equally convinced that their current challenge
of curtailing medical tourism for a Fortune 500 company was an opportunity of a lifetime, and each vowed
that they would do whatever it took to denigrate medical tourism. Quite expeditiously, the group had settled
on a company plan of promoting patients' fears as the
best way to lower demand. Until patients were subjected
to propaganda to the contrary, everyone facing surgery
had strong reflex reservations about going to India or
another developing country for an easily understandable
complex of reasons. First was the concern of the country's general lack of cleanliness, raising the specter of
wound infection and catching any one of a number of
dreaded infectious diseases. Next there was an obvious
question of the skill of the surgeons and the other per-

sonnel, including nurses. In addition, there was the question of the quality of the hospitals and whether the necessary high-tech equipment was available. And finally there was the question of whether the operations that were performed were generally successful.

When the group looked into the propaganda the India Tourist Office was actively putting out, they discovered the office was clearly addressing these specific issues. Consequently, it was decided that Cal's new company would create ad campaigns to do the opposite and take advantage of people's fears. Everyone was certain this plan would be successful, since ad campaigns are always easier when the goal is the support of people's existing beliefs and prejudices.

Unfortunately, no sooner had they settled on a strategy and begun trading ideas when they ran into a serious problem. They had realized that with India spending serious money and effort promoting their medical tourism, the Indian government would surely investigate if someone started doing the opposite, and an investigation of any sort would invariably cause significant problems if ad campaign claims could not be substantiated.

What had been quickly recognized was that real data were needed involving private Indian hospitals, particularly in relation to outcomes, mortality, and complications, which included such statistics as infection rates. Yet the data were not available. The group had checked the Internet, medical journals, and even the Indian health ministry, which they soon discovered was dead set against releasing any such information, even refusing to admit if it existed. In their own ads they used no data whatsoever, merely claiming their outcomes were as good as or better than outcomes in the West.

Stymied for a time, the group had suddenly realized they needed a fifth column inside the private Indian hospitals participating in the highly profitable and growing medical tourism industry. What would have been best were accountants, but the efficacy of that idea seemed questionable at best. Instead, they had hit on the idea of using nurses, mainly because Santana knew something the others didn't—namely, that there existed a worldwide business in nurses. In the West there was a shortage. In the East, particularly in the Philippines and India, there was a surplus, with many young nurses desperately wanting to emigrate to the United States for economic and cultural reasons but facing significant, almost insurmountable, hurdles.

After extensive research and much discussion, Cal et al. had decided to go into the nurse business by founding a company called Nurses International. Their plan, as was accomplished, was to hire a dozen young and vulnerable, attractive, impressionable, newly graduated Indian nurses, pay them U.S. nurses' wages, and bring them to the States on tourist visas, specifically to California, for a monthlong training session with the idea of turning them into a team of beholden and therefore easily manipulated spies. In California they had been purposefully spoiled to maximize their manipulability and to take advantage of their wish to emigrate. At the same time, they had been trained in computers during the morning hours, particularly in regard to computer-hacking techniques. In the afternoons they had worked for a few hours as nurses in a SuperiorCare hospital to improve their American English as well as acquaint them with American patient expectations, both of which, it had been assumed, would make it easier to hire them out to private Indian hospitals.

Everything had gone miraculously according to plan, with teams of two nurses currently in six private Indian medical tourism hospitals. For housing, all had been required to live together in a mansion rented by Nurses International in the diplomatic area of New Delhi, to the initial chagrin of the nurses' families. Since the money the nurses were providing continued, however, family complaints vanished.

After they had been working for a week, with all of them complaining they wanted to go back to California sooner than the six months they were required to remain in India, they had been instructed to begin extracting patient-outcome data from the computers in their respective hospitals. The goal was to be able to begin to calculate infection rates, adverse outcome rates, and death rates for their future ad campaigns. To Cal and the others' surprise, none of the nurses questioned this activity, and they were wonderfully successful. But then disaster had struck. Something had happened that no one had anticipated. The stats had turned out to be quite good, even strikingly excellent in several of the institutions.

For a few days Cal and Petra had been depressed and unsure of what to do. After all the money they'd gone through to set up the elaborate spy system, they had begun to feel pressure for results. Raymond Housman had even sent a secret representative a week earlier for an update on when they could expect something to happen. It seemed that the bottom-line losses from medical tourism were continuing, and ticking upward at an alarming rate. Cal had promised results would soon be forthcoming, since at the time of the envoy's visit, the outcome data were just beginning to flow in.

But then, by tapping into his creativity and urge to win, Cal had come up with a second idea. If there were no bad statistics to be found for the basis of a negative ad campaign, why not create their own bad-outcome, hard-luck stories with the help of their installed fifth column and feed the stories to the media in real time. With the unsuspecting help of an anesthesiologist and pathologist whom he'd gotten to know in Charlotte, North Carolina, while he'd worked at SuperiorCare's corporate office, Cal had settled on succinylcholine as his drug of choice to cause sudden death. The idea was to find patients who'd had a history of some sort of heart disease and who'd had succinylcholine as part of their anesthesia, and inject them with an additional bolus of the muscle-paralyzing drug the evening following their operations. Cal had been assured the drug would be undetectable, and if it was detected, it would be assumed to be from the patient's anesthesia. Best of all, there'd be an immediate diagnosis of a fatal heart attack because of the cardiac history.

As soon as Cal and Petra had polished the scheme, they presented it to Durell and Santana. Although Durell had taken the plan in stride, Santana had initially been hesitant. For her, stealing privileged data was one thing, but killing people was something else entirely. Still, she had eventually given in, partly as a function of the others' enthusiasm; partly because of everyone's commitment to success, including her own; partly because she'd become convinced the scheme could not be discovered; and partly because there was going to be a limited number of victims; but mostly because she and the others believed it to be the only way to salvage Nurses International, which, as it turned out, they were all counting on to be a key step in their careers and in obtaining the wealth they thought they deserved. A lesser reason for her change of heart was the intense study of Hinduism she'd undertaken since she'd arrived in the country. She'd found herself attracted intellectually to the concept of punarjamma, or the Hindu belief in rebirth, meaning death was not the end but merely the door to a new life, and a better one if the individual had adhered to his dharmic responsibilities. And finally was the fact that she, along with the others, had vowed to do whatever it took to denigrate medical tourism.

Once the new strategy had been accepted, the problem had then switched to the nurses' reactions and the question of their cooperation. Although the group had become so acculturated to American culture from their month in Los Angeles, so addicted to the money they were being paid for the benefit of their families, and were so looking forward to emigrating that they would most likely do whatever was asked of them, Cal, Petra, and Durell were unsure. Santana, on the other hand, thought the nurses would have no problem, as they would be aided by their belief in samsara and particularly their belief in the importance of the organization and the group over the individual. Santana had then said the key was Veena and getting her to accept that it was her dharma to "put to sleep" an American patient. The idea was that if she was willing to do it, as the de facto leader, the rest would unquestioningly follow suit.

But Veena's cooperation was not a given. While everyone agreed she was the most committed to the team and the most desirous of emigrating, everyone had sensed a disconnect of her obvious keen intelligence, her inborn leadership ability, and her exceptional beauty, with her equally apparent poor self-image and lack of self-esteem. With such a thought in mind, Santana had gone on to explain it was her professional opinion that Veena was burdened with serious psychological baggage of some sort on top of a strongly ingrained attachment to traditional Indian culture and religiosity. She also had suggested that learning the issue and offering to help her with it, whatever it was, might be key in obtaining Veena's cooperation.

At that point all had looked to Durell. It was common knowledge he was intimate with one of the nurses, Samira Patel. Although this affair had been looked upon with disapproval by Petra and Santana, suddenly it became useful. Since Samira had been Veena's roommate as well as her best friend, they believed that if Veena had confided in anyone, it would have been Samira. Consequently Durell had been tasked to find out, which he did by convincing Samira that Nurses International needed to help Veena, and if they weren't able to do so out of ignorance of what was troubling her, the whole program, including helping the nurses to emigrate to the United States, would be in peril.

Samira clearly believed every word and, despite having been sworn to secrecy, related Veena's painful family history. Armed with this information, Cal had approached Veena the previous afternoon with his offer to stop the abuse once and for all in return for her cooperation and leadership in regard to the new strategy. Veena had initially demurred but then had changed her mind, because of the promise of eliminating the threats to her sisters and mother. That had always been the biggest concern standing in the way of her being able to emigrate.

Cal Morgan sighed. Having rehashed this history, he realized the whole program of discouraging Americans to come to India for surgery had hardly been the walk in the park that he'd initially assumed it would be. He shook his head and wondered what else was going to happen. Recognizing there was no way to anticipate the unexpected, he decided he needed an exit strategy. If worse came to worst, he needed to have a plan and resources to get out of India, at least for himself and the other three principals. He promised himself he'd bring it up that morning at the eight-o'clock meeting he'd scheduled.

Rolling over, Cal looked at the face of his alarm clock. At six-forty-five it was time to get up if he wanted to get in a run before breakfast, and he could check on Veena to make sure she was up and planning to go to work. Although the doctors had cleaned her out the night before in the emergency department and thought she'd absorbed a minimum of the Ambien because of Cal's rapid efforts, he had to be certain. Her not showing up for work the very next day after Mrs. Hernandez's passing might attract some attention if there was any reason for someone to doubt the patient's death was natural. There was also the concern that Veena had been noticed at the hospital well after her shift had been over.

With his jogging gear on, Cal headed in the direction of the guest wing. Rounding the last turn, he saw Veena's door was ajar, which he thought encouraging. Once at the entrance he knocked on the jamb, said hello, and leaned into the room all at the same time. Veena was sitting on her bed in a robe. Except for the slight reddish color of the whites of her eyes, she appeared normal and as gorgeous as ever. She wasn't alone. Santana was sitting on Samira's bed opposite Veena.

"I'm glad to say the patient feels fine," Santana said. Santana was five years Cal's senior. Like Cal, she was dressed in a jogging outfit, but unlike Cal's, the outfit was stylish, with black, shiny, skintight pants and an equally tight, black short-sleeved shirt made of synthetic fabric. Her dark, thick hair was in a ponytail pinned up against the back of her head.

"Terrific!" Cal said, and meant it. "You are going to work, I presume?" he asked Veena.

"Of course," Veena said. The voice reflected the mildly drugged feeling she was experiencing.

"We've been talking about what happened last night," Santana said forthrightly.

"Terrific," Cal repeated, but without the same enthusiasm. He couldn't help but feel reluctant discussing an issue he'd be uncomfortable talking about if he'd been the one involved.

"She has assured me that she will not try it again."

"That's nice," Cal responded, while thinking *She'd damn well better not.*

"She said she did it because she felt the gods would look kindly on her: sorta a life for a life. But now, because the gods saved her, she feels they want her to stay alive. In actuality, she believes the whole episode is her karma."

Like hell they saved her, Cal thought but didn't vocalize. In its place, he said, "I couldn't be happier, because we certainly need her." Cal studied Veena's face and wondered if she'd told Santana about the aggressive lovemaking episode or about the patient's disturbing agonal death throes, but her face appeared as inscrutably serene as usual. When Cal had spoken with the other principals the night before after returning from the ER, he hadn't mentioned it either—exactly why, he didn't know. His best guess was that he was embarrassed at having been so clearly taken advantage of by Veena's sexual aggression. Cal was accustomed to manipulating women, not vice versa. In regard to the kind of death the succinylcholine had apparently caused, which was far different from the peaceful paralysis that had been described to him and he'd relayed to the others, he was afraid any discussion might dampen general enthusiasm for the scheme.

Cal had then excused himself and left, despite being mildly concerned the women might take the opportunity to discuss him. But he didn't worry about it for long.

Exiting the bungalow and running out through the front gate, he began his jog. Chanakyapuri was one of the few areas of the city other than the coastal ridge reserved forest where running was enjoyable. Unfortunately, he was later than usual, and the traffic was already heavy and increasing with every passing minute. The dust and pollution were already almost to midday levels. In response, he exited the main road in favor of backstreets. There the air was better, but not far from the clogged main road he ran into a large group of monkeys, which always scared him. Delhi monkeys were remarkably bold, at least from Cal's experience. It wasn't that he thought they would attack him en masse, but more because he worried they carried some exotic diseases that he might catch, especially if one bit him. That morning, as if sensing this unease, the animals chased after him, baring their yellow teeth, chattering, and screeching as if they were crazed.

Deciding that monkeys and pollution were more than enough reason to consider the jog that morning a bust, Cal abruptly switched directions, causing the monkeys to flee in panic. Like a horse intent on returning to the barn, Cal rapidly retraced his route back to the mansion. After being outside for less than a half-hour, he was happy to be inside and particularly happy to step into his shower. While he lathered and shaved, and despite the disappointing jogging experience, he thought of the morning in a positive light. The short conversation with Santana had significantly relieved a concern about Veena. The suicide gesture had scared him, and until Santana's reassurance to the contrary, he'd been worried she might try it again. Now he was confident that wouldn't happen, and by involving the concept of karma, Veena apparently now thought of what she'd done to Mrs. Hernandez as part of her fate, which boded well for the cooperation of the other nurses.

After enjoying a breakfast of ham and eggs prepared by the bungalow's chef, Cal headed toward the glass-enclosed conservatory at the back of the house. When they had moved into the house, the room had only chairs, but they had added a round table and used the space as their morning conference room.

When Cal walked in, the other three were already seated and their lively conversation trailed off. Cal took his usual chair, facing directly out into the garden with his back to the mansion's interior. The others had taken their usual chairs as well, suggesting all four to be creatures of habit. Santana was to Cal's right, Petra to his left, and Durell directly across. Each of their postures reflected to a degree their personality. With quiet confidence, Durell was slouching, cradling his chin in his hand with his elbow on the arm of the chair. He was a powerful-appearing, heavily muscled man with mahogany-colored skin and a dark pencil-line goatee and mustache. Petra was sitting bolt upright on the edge of her chair as if in grammar school with the need to impress the teacher with the degree of her attention. She was a remarkably tall, handsome woman, high-colored and high-spirited. Santana was sitting back comfortably in her chair with her hands folded in her lap like the professional psychologist she was, waiting for the patient to begin speaking. She always appeared calm, with her emotions under strict control.

Cal opened the meeting with Veena's suicide attempt to be certain everyone was well informed. He had Santana relate what she had learned that morning when talking with Veena, particularly about Veena insisting she would not try it again and why. Cal admitted the episode had frightened him to the point he believed they needed a rapid exit strategy in place in case it was needed. "If she had succeeded in killing herself," Cal continued, "there would have been an investigation and an inquest, and any sort of investigation would have spelled big trouble for Nurses International."

"What exactly do you mean by exit strategy?" Petra questioned.

"Exactly what the phrase implies," Cal said. "I'm not talking about something philosophical here. I'm talking literally. In a worst-case scenario, such that if we have to get out of India at a moment's notice, all the details should be prearranged. There shouldn't be any need for improvisation, for there might not be time."

Petra and Santana nodded in agreement. Durell merely raised his eyebrows questioningly. "By land, sea, or air?" he asked.

"I'm open to suggestions," Cal responded. He looked at each in turn, settling on Petra, who was a stickler for this kind of detail.

"By air would be too difficult," she said. "Passport control at Gandhi International is too experienced. We'd have to pay off too many people, since we wouldn't know what time of day it might end up being. If we were trying to secretly escape, it would have to be by land."

"I agree," Durell said. He leaned forward, elbows on

the table, hands working at each other. "I think we should plan to go northeast with a car or SUV that we buy expressly for this purpose and keep it gassed, packed with necessities, and ready to go. We could plan to cross the border into Nepal at a place we decide beforehand that is the best, although there really isn't a lot of choice. And finally, we should also put in the car an appropriate amount of cash for bribes. That's key."

"You mean buy a vehicle, prepare it, and then keep it out of sight?" Cal asked.

"Exactly," Durell responded. "Start it up once in a while but put it into that big garage on the grounds and leave it there."

Cal shrugged. He looked at each woman in turn to sense their reactions. No one spoke. Cal turned back to Durell. "Can I put you in charge of arranging what you are suggesting?"

"No problem," Durell said.

"Now let's turn to our new strategy. Have we gotten any feedback at all?"

"We most certainly have," Santana said. "I heard back from my contact at CNN in only a couple of hours. They had gone ahead and put the story on the air right after they got it just as I'd hoped. The response was terrific and apparently much more than they had expected, with a flood of e-mail from the word go. It was more than they've had on any story other than presidential primary politics for a week. They are dying for more."

Sitting back, Cal let a slight smile spread across his face. What he was hearing was the first good news their collective efforts had generated for the whole project.

"When I woke up this morning, there was another message from Rosalyn Beekman, my CNN contact. She said that all three networks' news shows expropriated the story to put together pieces on medical tourism in general. At the end of all three segments, the anchors left the question of the safety of surgery in India very much in question."

"Terrific," Cal exclaimed, lightly punching the surface of the table with his fist several times for emphasis. "It's music to my ears. It also brings up the question of when we should do it again. If CNN is, as Santana says, dying for more material, it seems to me we shouldn't deny them."

"I agree," Durell said. "No question. If the fish are biting, it's time to fish. And I have to tell you guys, Samira is ready. It hurt her feelings that Veena had been selected to be the first over her. She says she has a patient with some kind of heart history having surgery this morning who would be perfect."

Cal gave a quick chuckle. "And I was worried we'd have trouble getting the nurses to cooperate, and here they are spontaneously volunteering."

Turning from Durell, Cal glanced at Petra and Santana in turn. "What about you women? What are your thoughts about doing another? Last night when I found Veena had ODed, I never guessed I'd be asking whether we should do another tonight, but here I am."

"Rosalyn was emphatic about wanting more material," Santana said, looking across at Petra. "Since we know the news will be guaranteed to go right on the air, I'd have to vote yes."

"What's the chance Samira will have an overreaction like Veena?" Petra asked, staring back at Santana. "We don't want another suicide attempt."

"Certainly not Samira," Durell said. He was emphatic. "She might be Veena's age, her roommate, and her best friend, but personality-wise, they are two completely different people, which in some respects might be why they are tight, or at least used to be tight. Yesterday afternoon before Veena left to do her thing, she reamed Samira out for sharing her family secrets."

"Do you agree, Santana?" Petra asked.

"I do," Santana said. "Samira is very competitive, but she's not a leader. More important, she's more self-centered, and not so bottled up."

"Then I'll agree to it," Petra said.

"What about the event being in the same hospital two days in a row?" Durell asked. "Does anybody see that as a problem?"

"That's a good question," Petra said.

All eyes switched to Cal. He shrugged. "I don't think it matters. I was assured it would not be discoverable for a bunch of reasons. Second of all, the hospital authorities and their business backers are going to want to bury these deaths ASAP, excuse the pun, to avoid negative publicity as much as possible. India doesn't have a medical examiner system, but even if by some astronomically thin chance someone suspected foul play, and for another astronomically thin chance even thought of succinylcholine, the drug would be long gone and any residuals, or whatever they call it, would be explained away as coming from the anesthesia they'd had from surgery."

"Actually," Santana said, "two deaths in two days is an even bigger story. I think it helps our cause."

Nodding his head in agreement, Cal looked at both Petra and Durell. Both nodded. "Wonderful," Cal said with a smile, placing both hands on the table. "It's wonderful to have unanimity. Let's make it happen." Then, looking at Durell, he added, "Then you'll give Samira the good news when she returns from work."

"It will be my pleasure," Durell responded.

Chapter 7

Neil McCulgan put down his pen to rub his eyes. The schedule he'd been working on was still unfinished. The software company whose program was supposed to do the schedule had recently changed hands, and without the original CEO's keeping everything under control, the software was getting things mixed up, ergo the need for Neil to painstakingly redo it by hand. He looked at his watch. It was already close to eight and he was supposed to have been off at seven, and he was exhausted.

The fact that he'd not managed to get the schedule completed was based on two things. The first was a major pileup on the 405 freeway causing several deaths and a number of very serious injuries, all of whom had begun to arrive in their respective ambulances less than a half-hour after Jennifer Hernandez had childishly stalked out of his office. All that took a number of hours to handle, meaning separating the dead from the living, stabilizing the most seriously injured and sending them up to the OR, and finally dealing appropriately with the less severely hurt by setting and casting broken bones and suturing lacerations.

The second reason the reworked schedule wasn't done was because he wasn't concentrating well. "Damn!" he shouted at the wall, then felt guilty and foolish. Spinning around in his chair, he looked out into the triage area. Two patients were looking in his direction with raised eyebrows. Embarrassed at his outburst, Neil got up from his chair, and after giving the two startled patients a reassuring wave, he closed the door and sat back down.

Neil couldn't concentrate because of Jennifer. Although he'd inevitably used what he called her puerile behavior as further justification for his decision not to go to India, he slowly began to admit that he'd handled the situation miserably. First off, the real reasons were simply more selfishly motivated. He eventually admitted that the excuse he'd given her—namely, the reworking of the ER schedule—had been a transparent lie. He should have been more up-front so that there could have been, at a minimum, an honest discussion. And finally, the part that made him feel most guilty was that the excuse he gave himself—that he would have been more receptive if the death involved her mother, not her grandmother—was also a lie. He was well aware that Jennifer's grandmother, for all intents and purposes, had been her mother.

At one point Neil called Jennifer's cell phone, but she

didn't answer. He had no idea if it was because she noticed it was he who was calling or if she'd already departed, and there was no way to find out. He even thought, in a moment of irrationality, about running out to LAX to catch her before she did leave, but he dismissed the idea because he had no idea which airline she was taking. From having made travel arrangements to India five months ago, he knew there were multiple carriers flying from L.A. to New Delhi.

All afternoon Neil progressively chastised himself for having handled Jennifer so badly, to the point that he began to accuse himself of exhibiting the immature, selfish behavior he'd blamed on her. He had even gotten to the point of believing she'd acted entirely appropriately by walking out and not looking back. By then he had good reason to suspect that had she done otherwise, he probably would have dug in his heels and made an even bigger fool of himself.

Impulsively, Neil stood up, sending his desk chair rolling backward on its casters to collide with the door. Taking a fresh white coat from the hook behind the door, he pulled it on and went out to the central desk. He asked the first nurse he could corner if she knew whether Clarence Hodges had left. He was officially off duty the same time as Neil, but like Neil, he rarely left on time. Happily, Neil was told he was in one of the bays, sewing up a laceration. For Neil's benefit, the nurse pointed to the appropriate curtained area.

"Wow!" Neil exclaimed when he looked over Clarence's shoulder. Clarence was in the process of sewing a right ear back onto the side of a patient's head. He was doing a meticulous plastic repair with what looked like hundreds of tiny sutures of gossamer-like black silk thread. Neil had recruited Clarence. He had been a classmate of Neil's in high school. For college they had chosen rival schools, with Neil going to UCLA and Clarence to USC, but for medical school both had chosen UCLA. What made them special friends was their shared love of surfing. "That's quite a laceration!"

Clarence leaned back and stretched. "Bobby here and his skateboard had a little argument with a tree, and I think the tree won." Clarence picked up the edge of the drape and looked in at his patient. He was surprised to find him asleep. "My goodness, I guess I have been at this for a while."

"Why didn't you have one of the plastic-surgery boys come down and handle it?" Neil asked.

"Because of Bobby," Clarence said, as he got another stitch in the claws of his needle holder. "When I suggested that, he said he was going to leave, despite his ear hanging off by a few threads of tissue. He said he'd been here so long he wasn't going to wait. He wanted me to do it even though I told him I wasn't a plastic surgeon. He was persistent and even stood up from the table as if he was heading for the door. So to make a long story short, that's why I'm doing it."

"Do you mind if I ask your opinion about something while you work?"

"Not at all. With Bobby sleeping, I could use the company. Of course, two seconds ago, I didn't know he was sleeping."

Neil rapidly told Jennifer's story, which Clarence lis-

tened to without comment while he continued to reat-
tach Bobby's ear. "So that's it in a nutshell," Neil said
when he'd finished.

"What do you want my opinion about? Whether I'd
go to India to have a hip replacement: The answer is
no."

"That's not the issue. The issue is how I handled Jennifer's request. I think I did a lousy job. What's your
take?"

Clarence looked up into his friend's eyes. "Are you
serious? How else should you have handled it?"

"I could have been more honest."

"In what regard? I mean, I can't imagine you want to
go all the hell way over to India for someone's grandmother, do you? I mean, it's not like you could bring her
back to life or anything."

"It's true I'm not wild about going all the way to
India at the moment," Neil admitted.

"Well, there you go. You handled it just fine. It's her
problem the way she responded. She shouldn't have
walked away."

"You think so?" Neil asked. He was unconvinced.
After explaining the episode to Clarence, he actually felt
guiltier about his behavior, not less guilty.

"Wait a minute," Clarence said, holding up the suturing and staring back up at Neil. "I'm beginning to think
there's something you're not telling me here. What's
your relationship with this woman? Are you sweet on
her or what? Are you guys dating?"

"Sort of," Neil admitted. "Actually, I'm not sure. It's
like she's been holding me at arm's length. We have been

getting together a lot, and it's wonderful. We never run out of things to talk about, and she's been really open with me, telling me things she's never told anyone else. I know that for a fact."

"Have you guys ever hooked up?"

"No, but it's not for not trying. I mean, we tried once, but it was awkward. It's kind of strange. We can be talking about the most intimate things, and as soon as I try to move in on her, wham! This wall comes up."

"That doesn't sound good."

"I know, but on the other hand she's really smart, and she works and studies her butt off, and she's terrific to be with. I've never been with a girl quite like her."

"If she's who I think she is, she's also a piece of ass."

"I can't deny that. She caught my eye the first time I saw her as a first-year med student."

"Okay," Clarence said. "This all changes everything. What I'm hearing is you love this woman."

"Let's just say I'm interested, but since she's got some baggage, there's more that I've got to learn."

"Are you thinking about chasing after her to India? Is that what I'm hearing you want my opinion on?"

"It is. The one thing I do know about her with absolute certainty is, she's headstrong. She makes up her mind about things instantaneously and then holds on to her decision like a dog with a bone. At the moment she's royally pissed at me, and I can understand why. She took me into her confidence, and now that she's asked me to support her, I, in a sense, confirmed her worst fear by not doing so. If I don't go over there, I have to kiss good-bye any chance of learning anything more about her."

"Then do it! That's my advice. Handling the arrangements for the grandmother's body will probably take all of a half-hour, and it's over. Then you guys can make up. That way you won't be burning bridges over this affair."

"So you think I should go?"

"Absolutely. And you told me you found India fun, so you can kill two birds with one stone."

"I told you it was interesting."

"Interesting or fun, what's the difference? As far as your responsibilities here are concerned, don't worry about it."

"I do have the next four days off."

"See what I mean. It was meant to happen. Go! As far as your obligations here are concerned, after your four days, don't worry about it. I owe you. I'll cover for you, and when I can't, I'll see that someone else does."

"I'll certainly need more than four days. The travel alone takes four days."

"Don't worry about it. Okay? I said I'd cover. Do you know where she's staying?"

"I do."

"That's all you need. When will you leave?"

"Tomorrow, I guess," Neil said, wondering if he'd allowed his friend to talk him into something that might end up being more complicated and more stressful than he'd anticipated.

If he only knew . . .

Chapter 8

By reflex Samira Patel smiled coyly at the two tall Sikh doormen at the Queen Victoria Hospital's front entrance. She was dressed in her nurse's uniform, just as Veena had been the night before. They did not return her flirtatiousness. But there was no doubt they recognized her. Each silently reached out and pulled open his respective door and, with a bow, allowed her to enter.

Durell had coached her for several hours that afternoon before Samira had set out on her mission, which had included what to do once she was inside the hospital. Despite her excitement, she followed the suggestions to the letter. She marched across the lobby, avoiding eye contact with anyone. Instead of the elevator, she took the stairs up to the second floor, where the library was located. After turning on the lights, she got down from the shelves several orthopedic books and spread them out on one of the tables, even opening one to the section on knee replacement, which was the procedure her patient, Herbert Benfatti, had had that morning. All this was Durell's idea. He wanted her to have a clear, confirmable explanation for being at the hospital after hours if one of the more senior nurses questioned it.

Once the library was prepared to her liking and she'd downloaded Benfatti's chart from the library's workstation onto a USB storage device, she returned to the stairwell and climbed up to the fifth floor, where the OR suite was located. By now her excitement had built to the point of true anxiety, even more than she had expected, and it caused her to question why she'd been so eager to volunteer. At the same time, she knew exactly why she'd volunteered. Although Veena Chandra had been her best friend since they'd met each other in the third grade, Samira had always felt inferior. The problem was that Samira envied Veena's beauty, which Samira knew she could not compete against, ergo her wish to compete in every other way. Samira was convinced Veena's hair was darker and shinier than hers, and Veena's skin more golden, her nose smaller and shapelier.

Yet despite this competitiveness, about which Veena was totally unaware, the girls had developed a keen friendship based on the shared dream of someday emigrating to America. Like their other friends at school, both had had early access to the Internet, which Samira had availed herself of much more than Veena but which had provided both girls an oculus to the West and an introduction to the idea of personal freedom. By the time they'd reached their teenage years, they'd become inseparable and shared their secrets, which for Veena included abuse by her father, something she'd never shared with anyone else for fear of bringing shame to her family. Samira's secret, sharply contrasting with Veena's, was that she was fascinated by pornographic websites, and consequently sex, finding it hard to think of anything else by its denial. She was dying to experience sex herself and felt like a caged animal, especially because of her strict Muslim upbringing. Ultimately, what cemented the relationship between the two young women was their willingness to cover for each other. Each would tell her parents she was sleeping at the other's home, enabling them to go to Western-style clubs and stay out all night. Instead of embracing the traditional Indian karmic values of passivity, obedience, and acceptance of life's difficulties based on expectations of reward in the next life, both Samira and Veena progressively wanted the rewards in this life, not the next.

Yesterday, when Samira heard that Veena had been selected as the first of the nurses to carry out the new strategy, she'd been immediately jealous. That was why she'd acted as she had, volunteering for the next task with the claim she'd do it better and without hesitation. The reason she felt so confident was that there was one arena in which she had made more progress than her friend, and that was in the degree to which she'd abandoned the old culture of India and embraced the new culture of the West. Her affair with Durell was clear evidence.

With a trembling hand, Samira pushed open the stairwell door on the fifth floor. It was relatively dark.

For a few seconds, Samira merely listened. She heard no sounds except the constant omnipresent low hum of the HVAC machinery. She stepped out into the hallway and allowed the door to close behind her.

Confident she was alone, Samira walked in the direction of the operating suite while trying to keep the sound of her heels striking the composite floor to a minimum. The lighting was dim but adequate. Passing through the outer double doors, she made certain the surgical lounge was empty. She knew that it was occasionally used during the evening, and that the night-shift staff used it to take breaks and catch some TV, even though officially it was off-limits. She moved on to the double doors to the OR suite itself and cracked them. Unfortunately, the hinges complained with a screeching noise, making Samira cringe. She could feel her heart throbbing in her chest and could hear it in her ears. After pausing for a few seconds to check for any kind of response to the sound of the doors, Samira stepped into the operating suite itself. When the same screech occurred as the door closed, she cringed again. But the earlier tomblike silence immediately descended like a heavy blanket.

Samira was eager to get this portion of the task over with. She could now feel perspiration on her face despite the OR's being over-air-conditioned. She was not fond of feeling anxious, and because of the long-term duplicitous life she'd led as a teenager with her parents, she'd felt it all too often.

Once in the OR and confident she was alone, Samira made quick work of getting the syringe full of succinylcholine. The only potential problem was that in her haste she nearly dropped the glass bottle containing the paralyzing drug. If it had broken, hitting against the hard floor, it would have been a calamity, since she would have hesitated cleaning it up. Each sliver of glass would have been the equivalent of a curare poison dart in the jungles of Peru. It wasn't lost on her how ironic it would be if she'd end up being found dead in the OR in the morning.

It was with great relief that Samira retraced her steps back to the stairwell. With this portion of the assignment out of the way, she thought she was home free, but little did she know.

Descending two floors, she checked the time. It was a tad past eight. Her only concern at that point was Mrs. Benfatti, whom she had met that afternoon. Would she still be visiting? On the positive side, it was the night of Herbert Benfatti's surgery, and the chances were he was still feeling the results of the anesthesia, meaning he'd probably be seriously sleepy or sleeping. The only way to find out was to check.

Opening the third-floor stairway door, Samira glanced up and down the corridor. Two nurses could be seen in the brightly lit nurses' station, which meant the other two were either off in patient rooms or taking a break. There was no way Samira could know.

With her anxieties again mounting, she told herself it was now or never. Taking a deep breath, she stepped out into the hall and headed toward Mr. Benfatti's room. All went well until she arrived at the man's door, which was open about six inches. Eager at that point to get the whole thing over with, Samira raised her hand to knock when she found her hand poised in midair. To her utter shock, the door had been pulled away the instant Samira had expected to make contact with its surface. Reflexively, Samira let out a yelp of surprise as she was unexpectedly confronted by one of the evening nurses, whom Samira knew only by her first name. It was the remarkably obese and brusque Charu, and she completely filled the doorway.

In contrast to Samira's reaction of surprise, Charu acted irritated that someone was in her way. She looked Samira up and down as if evaluating her and said, in not too friendly a manner, "What are you doing here? You work days."

Charu and Samira knew each other only from nurses' report during the shift change when the day nurses communicated to the evening nurses each patient's status and specific needs.

"I just wanted to check on my patient," Samira said, her voice more hesitant than she would have preferred. "I've been in the library studying up on knee-replacement surgery."

"Really?" Charu questioned, with a tone that suggested doubt.

"Really," Samira echoed, trying to sound forceful.

Charu eyed Samira with a look of disbelief but didn't voice it. Instead, she added, "Mrs. Benfatti is visiting."

"Will she be leaving soon? I wanted to ask Mr. Benfatti a few questions about symptoms."

Charu merely shrugged before pushing past Samira.

Samira watched her as she headed in the direction of the desk. Samira was in a quandary about what to do.

She couldn't hang around the floor waiting for Mrs. Benfatti to leave, yet if she returned to the library, she wouldn't know when the wife departed. On top of that, she wondered if running into Charu meant she should abort the effort altogether. Of course, the trouble with doing that was that it might be a week before she had another American patient with some kind of history of heart trouble who would make an appropriate target. By then the benefits of competing with Veena probably wouldn't accrue.

Samira was still debating the issue when she was surprised yet again. This time it was Mrs. Lucinda Benfatti, who was a moderately tall, heavyset woman in her mid-fifties with tightly permed hair. Having met Samira that day, she recognized her immediately. "My word, you do put in a long day."

"Sometimes," Samira stammered. Her mission during which she was to avoid being seen was devolving into a bad joke.

"What time do you work until?"

"It varies," Samira lied. "But I'll be heading home shortly. How is the patient doing? I wanted to stop by and check."

"Well, aren't you a dear! He's doing reasonably well, but he's not good with pain, and he's having a lot of pain. The nurse who was just in here gave him an additional pain shot. I hope it works. Why don't you go in and say hello. I'm sure he'd be glad to see you."

"I'm not sure that's appropriate, since he just had a pain shot. I don't want to bother him."

"It'll be no bother. Come on!" Mrs. Benfatti took

Samira by the elbow and walked her into her husband's room. The lights had been dimmed, but the overall level of illumination was reasonably bright, since the large, flat-screen TV was on and tuned to the BBC. Mr. Benfatti was propped up in a semi-recumbent position. His left leg was encased in a device that was slowly but constantly flexing the knee joint thirty degrees several times a minute.

"Herbert, dear," Mrs. Benfatti called out over the sound of the TV. "Look who's here."

Mr. Benfatti lowered the TV's volume with the remote and looked over at Samira. He recognized her and, like his wife, commented on the impressive length of Samira's workday.

Before Samira could comment, Mrs. Benfatti intervened. "I don't know about the rest of you people, but I'm exhausted. I'm going back to the hotel and collapse. Good night again, dear," she said, kissing Herbert's broad forehead. "Hope you sleep well."

Mr. Benfatti's right hand waved weakly. His left hand, with the IV going into his arm remained perfectly still. Mrs. Benfatti said good-bye to Samira and departed.

Samira found herself in an awkward predicament. She wasn't interested in getting into a conversation with the man if she was going to go through with her plan, yet she couldn't just stand there. Plus, having run into Mrs. Benfatti, was there more reason to cancel? The only thing that was for certain was what she'd thought was going to be so simple was turning out to be anything but. Unable to make up her mind, Samira just dumbly remained rooted to her spot.

Mr. Benfatti waited for a moment before inquiring: "Is there something I can do for you, like run down to the kitchen and rustle you up a snack?" He chuckled briefly at his own attempt at humor.

"How is your knee feeling?" Samira questioned, while she tried to organize her thoughts.

"Oh, great," Mr. Benfatti scoffed. "I'm ready to go for a jog."

Unconsciously, Samira's hand slipped into her pocket, and her fingers encountered the full syringe. With a start, she was reminded why she was there.

While Mr. Benfatti carried on about the details of the pain he'd been suffering, Samira struggled with what to do. Recognizing there was no rational way to make a decision short of the crystal ball she didn't have, she opted for the more simple choice of acknowledging her impetuosity and just proceeding as planned. The deciding factor was the realization that Mr. Benfatti would not be discovered for hours maybe, since his wife had just left and the nurse had just given him a shot. What that meant was that Samira would have lots of time to be far from the scene when he was discovered. She pulled the syringe from its hiding place. Using her teeth to remove the needle cap, she reached for the IV port below the millepore filter.

Mr. Benfatti had seen Samira suddenly approach the bed, had caught sight of the syringe, and had stopped his diatribe about pain. "What's this?" he questioned. When Samira ignored him and raised the needle up to the IV port to inject, he reached out with his right hand and grasped Samira's right wrist. In the next instant, their eyes locked. "What am I getting?"

"It's something for your pain," Samira nervously improvised. The fact that Mr. Benfatti was holding her terrorized her. For a second, she irrationally worried that what she was about to give Mr. Benfatti would pass into her from the contact.

"I just got a pain shot two seconds ago. Isn't this overdoing it?"

"The doctor ordered another. This is more, to get you to sleep longer."

"Really?"

"Really," Samira repeated, reminding her of the unpleasant conversation she'd just had with Charu. She looked down at Mr. Benfatti tightly gripping her wrist. The man was strong, and although she wasn't yet experiencing pain, it was close. He was restricting her blood flow.

"Is the doctor here?"

"No, he's gone for the day. He called this in."

Mr. Benfatti maintained his grip for several more seconds and then suddenly released it.

Samira let out a silent sigh of relief. The very tips of her fingers had begun to tingle. Without wasting another moment, she struggled to get the needle inside the port, being especially careful in her haste not to prick herself. With succinylcholine, even a small amount could create problems. Without delay, Samira emptied the syringe. A second later a cry began to issue from Mr. Benfatti's lips, causing Samira to clamp a free hand over the man's mouth.

Mr. Benfatti responded by reaching for the nurses' call button clasped to the edge of his pillow, but Samira was able to yank it out of reach with the hand holding the syringe. Almost immediately, she felt the resistance she'd had against her hand cupped over the man's mouth melt away. Taking her hand away, Samira noticed a kind of wriggling under the man's skin, as if suddenly his face had been infiltrated by worms. At the same time, his arms and even his free leg began to briefly and uncontrollably jerk. The next second, the twitching stopped. In its place was a darkening of his skin that was particularly apparent due to the white light from the TV. It had started slowly, then picked up speed until all of Mr. Benfatti's exposed skin was an ominous dark purple.

Although Samira had purposely avoided looking into the man's eyes while he'd gone through his rapid death throes, she did now. The lids were only half open and the pupils blank. Backing up toward the door, Samira collided with a chair and grabbed it to keep it from falling over. The last thing she wanted was for someone to appear, questioning a crashing noise. Taking one last look at Benfatti from the doorway, Samira was momentarily hypnotized by the fact that the man's leg was still rhythmically being mechanically flexed and extended as if he were still alive.

Turning around, Samira fled from the room but then forced herself to slow to a walk by sheer will to keep from attracting attention. Maintaining her eye on the nurses' station, where she could see all four nurses, Samira made her way to the stairwell. Only when she was inside did she allow herself to breathe, surprised that she'd been holding her breath. She'd been totally unaware.

After picking up the books and turning out the light in the library, Samira descended to the lobby floor. She appreciated that the lobby was empty and appreciated even more that the doormen had gone off duty. Out on the street Samira caught an auto rickshaw, and as they pulled away, she glanced back at the Queen Victoria Hospital. It looked dark, shadowy, and, most important, quiet.

During the ride home, Samira felt progressively better at what she had accomplished, and the fear, anxiety, and indecision she had experienced rapidly faded into the background. As the auto rickshaw reached the bungalow's driveway, it seemed to her that such problems were mere blips on the radar screen.

"I have to leave you here," the driver said in Hindi, as he pulled to a halt.

"I don't want to get out here. Take me up to the door!"

The driver's eyes nervously flashed in the darkness as he looked back at Samira. He was clearly afraid. "But the owner of such a house will be angry, and he might call the police and the police will demand money."

"I live here," Samira snapped, followed by choice Internet-learned expletives. "If you don't take me, you won't be paid."

"I choose not to be paid. The police will demand ten times as much."

With a few more appropriate words, Samira climbed from the three-wheeled scooter, and without looking back started hiking down the drive. In the background she heard a burst of equivalent profanity before the auto rickshaw noisily powered off into the night. As she walked, Samira mulled over how she was going to describe her experience taking care of the American. It didn't take her but a moment to decide to leave out the minor concerns and concentrate on the success: Mr. Benfatti had been taken care of. That was the important thing. She surely wasn't going to complain like Veena had.

Entering the house, she found everyone, all four officers and all eleven other nurses, in the formal living room watching an old DVD called *Animal House*. The moment she walked into the room, Cal paused the movie. Everyone looked at her expectantly.

"Well?" Cal questioned. Samira was enjoying teasing the group. She'd taken an apple and sat down as if to watch the movie without providing a report.

"Well what?" Samira questioned, extending the ploy.

"Don't make us beg!" Durell threatened.

"Oh, you must mean what happened to Mr. Benfatti."

"Samira," Durell playfully warned.

"Everything went fine, exactly as you all suggested it would, but then again, I didn't expect anything different."

"You weren't scared?" Raj asked. "Veena said she was scared." Raj was the only male nurse. Despite his bodybuilder appearance, his voice was soft, almost feminine.

"Not in the slightest," Samira said, although while she spoke she remembered how she'd felt when Benfatti was gripping her arm hard enough to hinder the blood flow.

"Raj has volunteered for tomorrow night," Cal explained. "He's got a perfect patient scheduled for surgery in the morning."

Samira turned to him. He was a handsome man. In the evenings he wore his T-shirts a size too small to emphasize his impressive physique. "Don't worry. You'll do fine," Samira assured him. "The succinylcholine works literally in seconds."

"Veena said her patient's face twitched all over the place," Raj commented with a concerned expression. "She said it was horrid."

"There were some fasciculations, but they were over practically before they began."

"Veena said her patient turned purple."

"That did happen, but you shouldn't be standing around admiring your handiwork."

Some of the nurses laughed. Cal, Petra, and Santana stayed serious.

"What about Benfatti's computerized medical record?" Santana asked. Since Samira hadn't yet mentioned it, Santana was afraid she'd forgotten. She needed the history to make the story more personal for TV.

By leaning back against the couch and straightening her body out, Samira was able to reach into her pocket and pull out the USB storage device, similar to the one Veena had provided Cal with the evening before. She then flipped it in Santana's direction.

Santana snatched the storage device out of the air like a hockey goalie, hefted it as if she could tell whether or not it contained the data, then stood up. "I want to get this story filed with CNN. I've already given them a teaser about it, and they are waiting anxiously. My contact assures me it's going right out on the air." While the people who had been sitting next to her on the couch raised their legs, Santana worked her way from behind the coffee table and started for her office.

"I do have one suggestion," Samira offered after Santana had departed. "I think we should get our own succinylcholine. Sneaking into the OR is the weakest link in the plan. It's the only place in the hospital where we don't belong, and if any of us were to be discovered, there would be no way for us to explain."

"How easy would it be for us to get the drug?" Durell asked.

"With money, it's easy to get any drug in India," Samira said.

"It sounds like a no-brainer to me," Petra said to Cal.

Cal nodded in agreement and looked over at Durell. "See what you can do!"

"No problem," Durell said.

Cal couldn't have been more pleased. The new strategy was working, and everyone was on board, even offering suggestions. He couldn't help thinking that starting the scheme with Veena had been brilliant, despite the suicide scare. Just a few days before, he'd been afraid to talk with Raymond Housman, but now Cal couldn't wait. Nurses International was beginning to pay off, which he couldn't have been more pleased about, even if it wasn't in the way he'd expected. But who cared, Cal thought. It was the results that counted, not the method.

"Hey, who wants to see more of the movie?" Cal called out, waving the remote above his head.

Chapter 9

The wheels of the wide-body jet hit hard as they touched down on the tarmac of the Indira Gandhi International Airport and jolted Jennifer awake. She'd been awakened twenty minutes earlier by one of the cabin attendants to raise the back of her seat as the plane had started its initial descent, but she'd fallen back asleep. The cruel irony was that during most of the final leg, she'd not been able to sleep until the last hour.

Pressing her nose against the window, Jennifer tried to appreciate her first images of India. She could see little more than the runway lights streaking by as the powerful engines reversed. What surprised her was what looked like fog obscuring the view toward the terminal. All she could see were hazy, individually illuminated airplane tails rising up out of a general gloom. The terminal itself was a mere smudge of light. Raising her eyes, she saw a nearly full moon in the apex of a dark gray sky with no stars.

Jennifer started arranging her things. Lucky for her, the neighboring seat had been vacant, and she'd taken full advantage with the surgery book, the India guidebook, and the novel she'd brought for the flight—or, more accurately, the three flights. Her itinerary required two stops, which she'd actually appreciated as an opportunity to stretch her legs and walk, but only one change of aircraft.

By the time the big plane had nosed into the gate, and the seat-belt sign had gone off, Jennifer had her carry-on items packed away in her roll-on but then had to wait while others closer to the exit slowly filed out. Everyone looked as she felt: exhausted, yet having landed in a strange and exotic country, she could feel herself enjoying a second, or maybe a third or fourth, wind. Despite the fact that she was coming to deal with her beloved grandmother's death, she couldn't help but feel a certain excitement as well as nervousness.

The flights themselves, although remarkably long, had been endurable. And contrary to her initial worry that their duration might give her too much free time to obsess about the loss of her closest friend, it seemed to have been the opposite. To some degree, the forced solitary time had allowed her to come to terms with the loss by tapping into one of the lessons she'd learned from studying medicine: that death was very much a part of life, and its existence was one of the things that makes life so special. Jennifer wasn't going to miss her grandmother any less, but her loss wasn't going to paralyze her.

Once off the plane, Jennifer walked through the mildly dilapidated and dingy terminal building, finally appreciating that she was truly in India. On the plane everyone had been in Western clothes. Now she started to see bright-colored saris and equally bright-colored outfits on women she would later learn were called salwar-kameezes. On men she saw long tunics called dhotis over either voluminous lungis or pajamas, which were loose pants snugged at the ankles.

With some concern that she might face a problem, Jennifer approached her first potential hurdle: passport control. She couldn't help but notice that the lines were long and moving slowly for the few booths occupied by border agents both for citizens and for tourists. On the other hand, the line in front of the diplomatic booth was completely free. Its occupants were either chatting or reading newspapers. With little confidence in bureaucracy in general, and India's in particular, thanks to what she'd recently read in the guidebook, Jennifer fully expected to have a problem because she was not carrying a visa, even though the airline had been so apprised. It all depended on Mrs. Kashmira Varini and whether she'd made the call she promised and whether she had spoken to the right people.

"Excuse me," Jennifer had to call out at the booth's window to get attention. Conversations stopped and newspapers were lowered. The rather large group manning the diplomatic line, in sharp contrast to the other booths, which were occupied by single agents, all stared blankly at Jennifer as if shocked that they had business. All the agents were wearing saggy brown uniforms, and although the clothes were not obviously soiled, everybody appeared mildly disheveled.

As directed, Jennifer handed over her passport and began to explain the situation, when the border agent slid back the passport, and without speaking motioned for Jennifer to use one of the other lines.

"I was specifically told to come to the diplomatic window," Jennifer explained. Her heart sank as she began to worry about possibly not getting into the country after such a long trip. Hurriedly, she related that she'd been instructed that a visa would be waiting for her specifically at the diplomatic window.

Still without speaking a word to Jennifer, the border agent picked up his phone. Even from where she was standing outside the booth, she could hear some shouting on the other end of the phone line. A minute later, she watched as the agent opened a drawer beneath the countertop he was sitting at and extracted some papers. He then motioned for Jennifer to hand back her passport, which Jennifer was happy to do. The agent then glued into it what she assumed was a visa, initialed it, and then stamped it. Only then did he slide it back out to Jennifer while motioning for her to pass. With relief at being allowed to enter the country after fearing for the worst and surprised at not having to pay for the visa, Jennifer grabbed her roll-on and quickly moved on in case they changed their minds. It was curious the episode had happened without the agent's speaking one word to her, which reminded her why she disliked bureaucracy.

Next was baggage, which surprisingly turned out to be more efficient than it was at JFK. By the time Jennifer had located the correct carousel, her wheeled bag was there, having already made several circuits.

The customs agents appeared even more rumpled than the passport people, and even less engaged. They all were sitting on the edges of the long countertops that had been built to facilitate opening and examining luggage, but no one was doing either. Dutifully, Jennifer slowed, but they merely waved her on.

Jennifer then pushed through the customs security doors and entered the terminal's main arrival area. Immediately, she had a presage of one of India's main characteristics: an impressive population. The place was mobbed. Although the arrivals part of the terminal had been crowded thanks to multiple international flights landing almost simultaneously, it was nothing like the rest of the terminal. Just beyond the doors was a thirty-foot-wide upward-sloping ramp more than eighty feet in length and lined with a metal handrail. Pressed against the handrails and pancaked against one another like sardines were hordes of expectant people, most holding up crude signs. About half the crowd was in Western dress, including a large number outfitted in fancy uniforms with visored hats sporting hotel insignias.

Jennifer stopped in her tracks, taken aback by this new quandary. Having been told she would be met by an Amal Palace Hotel employee holding up her name, she'd not concerned herself with this aspect of the journey. Clearly, that had not been a wise move. From her vantage point there could have been thousands of signs and even more people.

Never happy to be the center of attention, Jennifer nonetheless tried to make herself apparent as she gradually made her way up the incline. As she vainly looked for her name, she invariably briefly locked eyes with strangers, each of whom appeared to be more foreign and exotic than the next. As a young single woman with essentially no travel experience, it was intimidating, even a little scary, especially with no police or other authorities in sight.

Just stay cool, Jennifer silently advised herself, hoping at any second to hear her name being called out over the din. Unfortunately or fortunately, Jennifer was not sure whether anyone had accosted her by the time she reached the top of the ramp. Unwilling to press into the mob, she turned around and as slowly as she'd risen up the incline, she now descended. No one had called out to her by the time she reached the exit doors, or if they had, she hadn't heard it.

With the idea of returning inside to see if there was any kind of information available for hotels, the doors burst open and out came a youthful man in a porter's uniform that was a step down in appearance from those worn by the custom men. He looked more like a student than a professional porter, and the uniform was not only tattered but also much too big. He was pushing a four-wheeled cart loaded with luggage. As he came through the doors, he had built up speed to get up the incline. As a consequence, he almost ran into Jennifer.

"I beg your pardon," the porter exclaimed, catching sight of Jennifer and with some difficulty pulling his cart to a stop.

Jennifer stepped aside. "It's my fault. I shouldn't be trying to enter an exit. Can you tell me if there's an information booth around? Someone from my hotel was supposed to be meeting me, but I don't know where."

"What hotel?"

"The Amal Palace."

The porter whistled. "If someone was supposed to pick you up from the Amal, they will be here no doubt whatsoever."

"But where?"

"Go up to the top of the ramp and turn right. There'll be a number of them for sure in that general area. They'll all be in dark blue uniforms."

Jennifer thanked the man and headed back up the ramp. Although she still felt mildly reluctant to push into the crowd, she did so, and as the porter promised, she immediately found the Amal greeters in their highly pressed sartorial splendor. Although Jennifer thought it odd they didn't make themselves more apparent, she now confronted the man with her name on his chalk board. He introduced himself as Nitin and took her two pieces of luggage. He also called Rajiv, who was to be her driver, on his cell phone before ushering Jennifer out of the terminal. As they walked, he kept up a friendly banter.

When Jennifer and Nitin got outside and were standing on the curb waiting for Rajiv to bring the car around, Jennifer again noted the heavy foglike haze that blanketed the area and hung heavy halos around the airport's streetlamps and the headlights of cars. It was exactly as she'd seen from the plane, but now with the addition of an acrid smell.

"Is this haze typical?" she asked Nitin, while she wrinkled her nose.

"Oh, yes," Nitin said. "At least at this time of year."

"What time of year is it not around?"

"During monsoon."

"Is that it?"

"That's it."

"What causes it?"

"Dust and pollution, I'm afraid. We have eleven and a half million people in Delhi now, more or less officially, with more people moving into Delhi every day than are born here. Unofficially, I think it's more like fourteen million. It's a mass migration from the countryside, which is straining everything, and causing increased traffic. The smog is from exhaust and dust from the streets mostly, but the factories here in the outskirts add to it, too."

Jennifer was horrified but didn't comment. She thought L.A. was bad in September, but Delhi made L.A. seem like springtime in an Alpine pasture.

"Here comes Rajiv," Nitin said as an ultra-shiny black Ford Explorer with darkly tinted windows pulled up to the curb. Rajiv leaped from the driver's seat, came around the vehicle, and greeted Jennifer in the typical Hindu fashion of pressing his palms together, bowing over them, and saying "namasté." He was attired in a splendid, spotlessly clean, freshly pressed white uniform complete with white gloves and a white visored cap. While he opened the rear door for Jennifer, Nitin loaded her two bags in the back. A moment later, she and Rajiv were on their way into New Delhi.

Passing the first car heading in the opposite direction took Jennifer by complete surprise. Although the Explorer's steering wheel was on the right, the implication hadn't dawned on her. When the headlights of the approaching car appeared out of the gloom and headed for them, she assumed they would pass on the right, but as the vehicles sped closer together, the oncoming car did not move to Jennifer's right. On the contrary, it appeared to be drifting to the left. The moment the two cars passed, Jennifer had to suppress a scream, expecting they were about to collide head-on. It was only then that she figured it out. In India, like in Great Britain, autos kept to the left and passed on the right.

With her heart thumping in her chest, Jennifer sat back. She was ashamed of her travel naïveté. To calm down, she used the cold towel Rajiv had given her to mop her brow and took a sip from the iced bottle of water he had provided. Meanwhile, she stared out the window in amazement about what she was seeing.

Once they had reached the main highway from the airport access road, their progress slowed to a crawl. Despite being after midnight, the road was choked in both directions with all manner of vehicles, but mostly trucks, every one of them overloaded in the extreme. Over all hung a choking layer of both exhaust fumes and dust plus the din of unmuffled engines and each vehicle's horn sounding every few seconds for no reason other than the mere whim of the driver.

As Jennifer looked out on the scene, she found herself shaking her head in disbelief. It was like a wild dream, and if this was the way traffic was at midnight, she couldn't even conceive of what it was going to be like during the day.

The driver spoke reasonable English and was more than willing to play tour guide as they worked their way into the city. Jennifer peppered him with questions, particularly when he turned off the main road and entered the residential section of Chanakyapuri. Here at least there were no trucks or buses and the traffic moved more freely. Jennifer noted block after block of relatively similar huge white mansions, which appeared to be mildly dilapidated but still impressive. She asked about them.

"They are British Raj–era bungalows," the driver said. "They were for the British diplomats and are still used by some diplomats." Soon the driver was pointing out the various foreign embassies, for which he seemed proud. He pointed out the American embassy, which looked rather ugly to Jennifer when compared with those of many of the other countries. Its main characteristic was that it was large. Jennifer turned as it passed by on her left to get a better view. She imagined she'd probably have to make a visit for help dealing with her grandmother's remains.

Next the driver pointed out the Indian government buildings, which were stunningly impressive. He said they had been designed by a famous English architect, whom Jennifer had never heard of. A few minutes later they reached the hotel and pulled up its ramp to the front entrance. At first she was disappointed. The structure was merely a modern high-rise that could have been anywhere in the world. She'd expected something more typically Indian.

But inside it was another story. To her surprise, the hotel's public spaces were buzzing with activity despite the hour, and Jennifer had to wait in line to check in. Actually, it wasn't a line per se but a comfortable chair where she was offered refreshments and given a chance to gaze around the lobby area. Instantly, Jennifer could see why the porter at the airport had responded as he had when she'd named where she was to stay. Jennifer had not stayed in many hotels in her life and certainly never in one like the Amal Palace. It was, in her own words, sumptuous, even decadent.

Twenty minutes later the formally dressed guest manager who'd shown her to her room on the ninth floor backed out and closed the door behind him. En route to the room he had described the hotel's facilities and services, which included a fully staffed twenty-four-hour spa/exercise facility with an outdoor Olympic-size pool. Jennifer decided that she was going to make an effort to enjoy her stay at least a little, as Neil had suggested. Briefly thinking about Neil raised her hackles, so she put him out of her mind.

After fastening the safety lock on the door, Jennifer opened her bags, unpacked, and took a long, hot shower. Once out of the shower, she puzzled over what to do.

Although she knew she must be exhausted, the excitement of the arrival and the knowledge it was midday in L.A. had given her yet another wind. She knew that if she tried to sleep she'd toss and turn and become frustrated. Instead, she donned one of the luxurious Turkish robes hanging from behind the bathroom door, turned down the comforter in the expansive king-size bed, propped herself up with a clutch of down pillows, and turned on the impressive flat-screen TV with its remote. She had no idea what she would find on the TV, but she didn't care. The idea was to relax and fool her body into thinking it was time to sleep.

What she did find was a lot more English-speaking channels than she expected, so channel surfing was quite entertaining. When she stumbled on the BBC she almost stopped to actually watch the news. But finding it difficult to concentrate, she moved on and soon found CNN. Surprised to find an American cable network, she watched it for a while, since she didn't recognize the news anchors. After fifteen minutes had gone by and she was about to move on, the female anchor caught her attention by beginning a piece on medical tourism similar to the one that Jennifer had heard while waiting in the UCLA Medical Center's surgical lounge. Wondering if her grandmother's name would again be mentioned, she listened carefully. But her grandmother was not part of the segment. It was another patient's name, but it was the same hospital, the Queen Victoria.

Mesmerized, Jennifer sat up straighter as the news anchor continued. "The Indian government's claims that their surgical results are as good or better than those anywhere in the West received another blow last night when a Mr. Herbert Benfatti of Baltimore, Maryland, as we mentioned, passed away with a heart attack slightly after nine p.m. New Delhi time. This tragic result happened after the gentleman had had an uncomplicated knee replacement some twelve hours earlier. Although Mr. Benfatti had had a history of an arrhythmia, he'd been in good health and had even had a normal angiogram in the past month in preparation for his surgery. Our sources tell us that such a death is not an infrequent phenomenon in private Indian hospitals. It's just that the Indian authorities have managed to keep a lid on such information leaking out. Our sources tell us further that they plan on continuing to report future as well as past deaths so prospective patients can have the information they need to make informed choices of whether or not they want to take such risk merely to save a few dollars. CNN, of course, will bring such information forward the moment it is available. Now let's turn to . . ."

Jennifer's first reaction was sympathy for the Benfatti family and the hope they hadn't had to hear the tragic news from the TV as she did. It also made her wonder about the hospital. Two unexpected deaths from elective surgery two nights in a row was definitely excessive and, as such, most likely preventable, and thereby more poignant. She also found herself wondering if Mr. Benfatti was married; and if he was, whether Mrs. Benfatti was in India, and if so, whether she was staying there at the same hotel. It was Jennifer's thought that if there was a Mrs. Benfatti it might be nice for Jennifer to convey her sympathies in person if she could marshal the nerve. The last thing Jennifer wanted to do was bother whoever was the next of kin, yet because of her ongoing experience with her grandmother's death, she thought she could commiserate better than anyone.

Chapter 10

Jennifer climbed from the black Mercedes sedan that the Queen Victoria Hospital had sent to fetch her from the Amal Palace Hotel. The outdoor temperature was warm but not hot. The anemic morning sun was working hard to penetrate the haze, and it reflected only weakly off the hospital's mirror-like façade. Jennifer didn't even need to shelter her eyes as she examined the building. It was five stories tall, and although it was cold and ultramodern, its pleasing combination of copper-colored glass and complementary-colored marble made her admire it to an extent. What made it stand out so sharply was the neighborhood. The ostensibly expensive structure was wedged cheek-to-jowl against the most run-down, white but heavily stained, nondescript concrete commercial block, housing an assortment of small stores selling everything from Pepsi to crude washtubs.

The street itself was a mess, potholed and filled with trash of all sorts, along with several cows that were oblivious to the crush of traffic and beeping horns. As Jennifer had expected, the traffic was even worse than it had been the night before. Although there seemed to be fewer of the gaudily painted, beat-up trucks, there were significantly more packed-to-overflowing buses, cycle rickshaws, regular cyclists, pedestrians, and what Jennifer found particularly disturbing, packs of young shoeless children dressed in soiled rags, some deformed, others sick and malnourished, all of whom were dangerously darting between the slow-moving vehicles while begging for coins. As if that wasn't enough, a few doors down from the hospital on the other side of the street was an empty lot filled with broken pieces of concrete, dirt, rocks, all kinds of rubbish, and even true garbage. Even so, the space was the home of multiple families, their hovels formed by pieces of corrugated metal, cardboard boxes, and scraps of cloth. Adding to the ambience were a number of stray dogs and even a rat.

"I will wait for you here," said the driver, who'd come around to open the car door for Jennifer. "Do you know how long you will be?"

"I haven't a clue," Jennifer responded.

"If I'm not sitting here, please call me on my mobile when you are ready to leave."

Jennifer agreed to do so, although her attention was focused on the hospital. She didn't know what to expect and realized her emotions were raw. In place of feeling merely sad about her grandmother's passing, she was progressively irritated now that she was finally here. Having heard of a second similar death occurring in so many days, she couldn't help but think the death could have been prevented or at least avoided. She knew it wasn't a completely rational thought and maybe was more because of her general state of mind, but she felt it anyway. The main problem was that Jennifer was exhausted and more jet-lagged than she had expected she would be. She'd slept poorly if at all.

Then, to make matters worse, her driver had been late, something she was going to learn was an Indian tradition, forcing her to cool her heels in the hotel's lobby. Fearful that sitting down would cause her to fall asleep, she used the time to inquire about Mrs. Benfatti and whether the woman was staying at the same hotel, which it turned out she was. Jennifer hadn't necessarily decided to call the woman but wanted to know just the same in case she decided to do so.

Jennifer found the two towering, traditionally costumed, turbaned doormen as imperturbable as the hospital building itself. Each offered a traditional palms-pressed Indian-style greeting before pulling open his respective door, neither spoke nor changed his neutral expression.

The interior of the hospital was markedly over-air-conditioned, as if trying to proclaim the hospital's luxuriousness by itself, and as modern and rich-looking as the outside. The floors were marble, the walls a highly finished light-colored hardwood, and the furniture a combination of sleek stainless steel and velvet. To the left was a smart coffee shop that could have been in a five-star Western-style hotel.

Unsure of what exactly to do, Jennifer approached the information counter, which looked more like the front desk of a Ritz-Carlton or a Four Seasons than a hospital, especially with the attractive young women dressed in impressive saris, not pink volunteer smocks. One of them had noticed Jennifer's entrance and, as Jennifer approached, graciously asked if she could be of assistance. Knowing how the harried employees and volunteers of American hospitals acted, Jennifer was already impressed with the institution's consumer orientation.

The second Jennifer said her name, the receptionist told her that Mrs. Kashmira Varini was expecting her, and that she would let the case manager know that Jennifer had arrived. While the receptionist made the call, Jennifer took in more of the lobby. There was even a cute bookstore and gift shop.

Within moments, Mrs. Varini appeared at the door leading into one of several offices located behind the information counter. She was dressed in a particularly eye-catching sari of exceptional fabric. Jennifer sized her up as she approached. She was slim and somewhat shorter than Jennifer's five-six-and-a-half, although not markedly so. Her hair and eyes were all significantly darker than Jennifer's, and she wore her hair up and clasped tightly at the back of her head with a piece of silver jewelry. Although her facial features were generally pleasant, her lips were narrow and would have appeared hard had she not been sporting a beatific smile that Jennifer would later discover to be false. Reaching Jennifer, Kashmira used the typical Indian greeting. "Namasté," she said.

Although Jennifer felt self-conscious, she returned the greeting.

Kashmira then embarked on the usual socially acceptable questions concerning the trip and how Jennifer liked her room and the hotel, and whether the transportation had been acceptable. Even after such a quick exchange, the smile had essentially disappeared except for a few short, subsequent de rigueur bursts at appropriate junctures.

At that point Kashmira became extremely serious as she conveyed the sympathies of herself, the doctors, and, indeed, the whole hospital staff for Jennifer's grandmother's passing. "It was a totally unexpected tragic event," she added.

"That it was," Jennifer said, eyeing the woman and experiencing a reburst of the anger she'd felt that morning about the whole affair, not only losing the person closest to her in all the world but also having been dragged away from possibly one of the most important rotations in her entire medical-school career. She knew her pain-in-the-ass father was probably as guilty as anyone for the current situation, but at the moment she leveled it all at Queen Victoria Hospital in general and Kashmira Varini in particular, especially since Jennifer's immediate impression was that she was conveying less-than-sincere sympathy to boot.

"Tell me," Kashmira said, totally unaware of Jennifer's sleep-deprived state of mind, "where should we go to get the unpleasant arrangements business out of the way? We can either go into the coffee shop or into my private office. It's totally your decision."

Taking her time, Jennifer looked beyond the information counter at the open door where Kashmira had emerged and then, turning in the opposite direction, glanced into the glass-fronted coffee shop. What made the choice was concern that if she didn't have another cup of coffee, she might fall asleep. When Jennifer communicated her verdict to Kashmira, the case manager acted quite pleased, which was the cause of one of her brief smiles, since it suggested Jennifer would prove easy to manipulate.

Jennifer did get coffee, though it failed to have much of an impact, and she soon decided it was imperative she get back to the hotel for a nap. As a further explanation of how bad she was feeling, a quick computation told her that had she still been in L.A., she would be soon settling in for the night.

"Mrs. Varini," Jennifer said, interrupting her host, who was describing the hospital's lack of mortuary facilities. "I'm very sorry, but I'm finding it hard to concentrate due to lack of sleep, and I'm certainly less capable than normal to make any significant decisions. I'm afraid I'm going to have to return to my room for a few hours of rest."

"If it's anyone's fault, it is mine," Kashmira said, not particularly convincingly. "I shouldn't have scheduled things so tightly. But we can make this short. We really only need a simple decision from you, and we can do the rest. We just need to know if you intend to embalm or cremate. Just tell us! We'll make it happen."

Jennifer rubbed her eyes and audibly sighed. "I could have done that from L.A."

"Yes, you could have," Kashmira agreed.

Jennifer opened her eyes, blinking enough to get the foreign body sensation to disappear, then regarded the expectant Mrs. Varini. "Okay, I need to see my grandmother. That's why I came."

"Are you certain?"

"Of course I'm certain!" Jennifer snapped before she could control herself. She hadn't meant to be quite so demonstrable. "She's here, isn't she?"

"She is here for sure. I just wasn't certain you'd want to see her. It's been since Monday evening."

"She's been in a cooler, hasn't she?"

"Yes, certainly. I just thought maybe a young girl like yourself would not want—"

"I'm twenty-six and a fourth-year medical student," Jennifer interjected irritably. "I don't think you have to worry about my sensibilities."

"Very well," Kashmira said. "As soon as you finish your coffee, we'll have you see your grandmother."

"I've had enough coffee. I'm starting to get jittery." Jennifer pushed her half-filled cup and saucer back from the edge of the table and stood up. While Kashmira did the same, Jennifer paused for a moment to let a touch of dizziness pass.

Using one of the silent, ultramodern elevators, they descended a floor to the basement level, where there were mechanical rooms, a modern staff cafeteria, a staff locker room, and various and sundry storerooms. Down the central corridor and past the cafeteria was a freight dock. A single elderly guard in an oversized uniform sat in a straight-backed chair tipped against the wall.

There were two coolers, both sited on the elevator side from the cafeteria. Without comment, Kashmira led Jennifer to the nearer one and struggled to open it. Jennifer lent a hand. It certainly wasn't a mortuary cooler, as Kashmira had admitted. The interior was filled with shelving that ran from the floor to the ceiling along the cooler's forty-foot length. A quick glance from Jennifer told her that it contained mostly sealed foodstuff but also some sealed medical supplies that needed refrigeration. In the center was a hospital gurney whose occupant was completely covered with a clean hospital sheet. The cooler's smell was mildly cloying.

"There's not a lot of space," Kashmira said. "Perhaps you'd like to go in yourself."

Without a word, Jennifer stepped inside. The temperature felt adequate at somewhere near freezing. Now that Jennifer was actually in her grandmother's presence, she wasn't so confident she actually wanted to look at her. Despite the suggestion to the contrary, Jennifer, the medical student, had never gotten accustomed to looking at dead bodies, even after she had the chance to spend a week observing in a morgue in middle school. She glanced back at the case manager, who caught Jennifer's eyes and wrinkled her brow as if to say, *Well? Are you going to look or what?*

Realizing she could not delay any longer, Jennifer grabbed the edge of the sheet and, fighting back tears, pulled the cloth up to expose her grandmother's face. At first the shock was that she looked so normal. She appeared to be the warm, generous, white-haired grandmother and the always-sympathetic and in-your-corner-no-matter-what stalwart that Jennifer had known. But then when Jennifer looked more closely, it wasn't fluorescent light that made her skin and lips the color of alabaster except along the side of her neck where there was dark purple lividity. Her color was truly a lifeless, translucent, blotchy, peachlike tan, and she was without a doubt dead.

In keeping with her fragile emotions, Jennifer's sadness switched back to anger. She let the sheet drop and looked back at Kashmira Varini, and the woman's false sympathy irritated her further. Jennifer walked out of the cooler and watched Kashmira struggle to close the heavy door. Jennifer didn't offer to help.

"There!" Kashmira said, standing up straight and wiping her hands after the door had clicked shut. "You can see why you need to come to a decision for your loved one. She can't stay here any longer."

"Is there a death certificate?" Jennifer asked, seemingly out of the blue but more because Mr. Benfatti's fate suddenly reoccurred to her.

"Most definitely. There would have to be a death certificate if either cremation or embalming were being considered. The death certificate was signed by Mrs. Maria Hernandez's primary surgeon."

"And the cause of death was definitely a heart attack?"

"It was!"

"What caused the heart attack?"

For several seconds, Kashmira stared back at Jennifer. Jennifer couldn't tell if the woman was shocked, irritated, or simply frustrated by Jennifer's question or by what might appear to her as Jennifer's foot-dragging regarding the body deposition.

"I don't know what caused your grandmother's heart attack. I'm not a doctor."

"I'm about to become a doctor, and I can't imagine either what could have caused her to have a heart attack. Her heart was literally and figuratively one of her best features in lots of ways. What about an autopsy? Did anyone think of that? I mean, if the doctors don't know what happened to their patient, they usually want to know, and that's a good indication for an autopsy."

Kashmira was surprised at such a suggestion, but so was Jennifer. Up until the moment Jennifer had said it, she'd not considered an autopsy, nor did she even know she wanted one. She'd said it more for Kashmira's sake, and probably because Kashmira and maybe even the hospital were trying to bully her into making a decision. Autopsy, cremation, and even embalming were violent events, and Jennifer hated to think she was somehow responsible, no matter how irrational such a feeling was. But there was also a new thought as well: How similar was Herbert Benfatti's death to Maria's, and could both have been prevented?

"The police or a magistrate are the only people in India that can ask for an autopsy, not the doctor."

"You're joking."

"I'm certainly not joking."

"That's like asking for collusion between the police and the magistrates, if you ask me. What about learning something from my grandmother's passing, something that could keep another, future patient alive? I mean, after all, you had a pretty similar death again last night. If they knew what had caused my grandmother's heart attack, could Mr. Benfatti's heart attack possibly have been prevented and the man saved?"

"I don't know anything about a Mr. Benfatti," Kashmira responded, almost too quickly. "What I know is that we have a body in this cooler, which has been in there too long and has to be removed. Our experience is that families claim bodies immediately, so we have to reach a resolution now. As you can plainly see, the body cannot stay in here. It's simply not meant for bodies, and the body has been in here since Monday night."

"That is your problem," Jennifer said. "I'm shocked your hospital doesn't have better mortuary facilities. I just got here to India after flying for almost twenty-four hours, and I'm just learning the details. My difficulty is that I'm mentally and physically exhausted. I'm going to go back to my hotel and sleep for a few hours before I make my decision. I'm also going to visit my embassy and talk to them about logistics. I know you feel confident what they are going to say, but I don't, and I like to hear such things from the horse's mouth."

"The horse's mouth?" Kashmira questioned.

"It's an expression. It means directly from the person or persons involved. I'm going to take a nap, visit the American embassy if I can, and then I'll come back."

"That's too late. A decision has to be made now."

"Listen, Ms. Varini, to be honest, I'm getting a bad feeling here like I'm being pushed too hard. And now with this second death last night, which seems a wee bit too similar to my granny's, I'm even less likely to make a hasty decision. I mean, you say you don't know anything about it, which is probably true, but I want to know something about it. It's too close to my grandmother's death and sounds too similar."

"I'm sorry, but other people's records are confidential. And in regard to yourself, I was specifically told that I had to obtain your decision this morning. We simply cannot have your grandmother's body in this cooler another hour." For emphasis, Kashmira reached out a hand and made renewed contact with the cooler's door. "If you are not willing to cooperate, I'm afraid you will have to speak with our president directly, because he has the authority to speak to a magistrate and petition the court to make the decision for you."

"I'm not speaking with anyone for a few hours," Jennifer snapped back. Now she was truly angry. Earlier, she had the opinion Queen Victoria Hospital was trying to push her, and now she was sure of it. Although on the one hand such an action was understandable because of their lack of proper storage, on the other hand it seemed provocative, especially their unwillingness to even consider an autopsy if she expressly indicated she wanted one. "I'll give you a call when I'm able to think a little better, and I'll come back. Meanwhile, let me warn you people: Don't defile my grandmother's body without my permission unless you are willing to deal with one very unhappy camper."

"An unhappy camper?" Kashmira questioned, totally confused.

Jennifer rolled her eyes. "It means someone who's really pissed."

Chapter 11

Jennifer stared out the Mercedes's window. She was so embroiled in her own thoughts she didn't even notice the traffic. The reality was that she had been what she called "pissed" far sooner than she'd admitted. There was no doubt Queen Victoria Hospital was jerking her around, and having been a victim long enough in her relatively short life, she didn't relish the role. Breaking out of the role had been her major challenge. The seminal event had occurred in middle school, where truancy and fighting had become the rule for her. At loose ends, her grandmother, who had been a particularly proud woman, did something she normally would not have done: She begged for someone's help. The person she turned to was Dr. Laurie Montgomery, a New York medical examiner whom the grandmother had practically raised from age one to age thirteen as her nanny.

At the time Jennifer had found it big-time weird to meet a stranger who called her own grandmother "Granny." But Granny had been Laurie Montgomery's nanny for twelve years. Not surprisingly, Dr. Montgomery had fallen in love with Granny and considered her family. So when Jennifer's demons drove her over the cliff, Granny pleaded with Laurie Montgomery to try to stop Jennifer's downward spiral.

With as much love and respect as Laurie held for Maria, she was happy to help. What she did was invite the wayward Jennifer to the Office of the Chief Medical Examiner after school for one week to follow her around and see what her job was all about. The other medical examiners had been skeptical of a twelve-year-old girl having a career week at the morgue, but Laurie had prevailed, and the result beat expectations. The situation had been sufficiently "weird" and "yucky," in Jennifer's own terms, to capture her adolescent imagination, especially since it was the first academic career to which she'd been even slightly exposed. Jennifer took it all in stride—until the third day. That day, a girl just her age was brought in with a perfectly clean, round red dot in her forehead. She'd been shot by a rival gang.

Fortunately, Jennifer's story went on to have a happy ending. Jennifer and Laurie had clicked more than either would have imagined, prompting Laurie to check with both her philanthropic mother and her own private school as to the possibility of Jennifer's getting a scholarship. A month later, Jennifer found herself in a demanding academic environment with no gang affiliations, and the rest was history.

"Of course!" Jennifer said loud enough to startle the driver.

"Is there a problem, madam?" the driver asked, while looking at Jennifer through the rearview mirror.

"No, no problem," Jennifer said, as she reached for her shoulder bag and began rummaging for her phone. She had no idea what it would cost to call New York, but she wasn't going to worry about it. She was going to call Laurie Montgomery. Laurie didn't even know Granny had died, and that was reason enough to call. On top of that was the decision issue, and even the autopsy idea. Now that she had thought of calling Laurie, Jennifer had trouble explaining to herself why she hadn't thought of it earlier.

While trying to figure out how to dial the United States, Jennifer had another question: What time was it on the East Coast? She knew it was nine and a half hours' difference, but in which direction? Despite her exhaustion, Jennifer forced herself to concentrate. She reasoned that since New York was ahead, then time should go back, and as crazy as that sounded to her at the moment, the more confident she was, but not over-confident. She went through the reasoning again, and then decided to accept on faith it was close to midnight the evening before in the Big Apple.

Knowing from the distant past that Laurie was an inveterate night owl, Jennifer was willing to make the call. Despite the subject of the call, she found herself getting excited as she heard it go through. It was astounding to think she was about to talk to Laurie halfway around the world, and she hadn't spoken with her for more than a year. The phone was picked up on the first ring.

"I hope I'm not calling too late," Jennifer said without preamble.

"Heavens no," Laurie responded. "Is this Jennifer?"

"It is."

Laurie was demonstrably pleased to hear Jennifer's voice and assumed she was in California. For a few minutes, the women made small talk. Jennifer asked about Jack. Laurie, for her part, apologized for not calling Jennifer since the wedding and used the infertility turmoil as her prime excuse. Jennifer wished her luck.

"So," Laurie said when there was a pause, "is this a mere social call or what? Not that it isn't great to hear from you, but is there something I can help with, like a letter of recommendation for a residency?"

"Unfortunately, there is a specific reason for my call, but it doesn't have anything to do with my medical training," Jennifer said. She went on to explain that she was in India and why. At several places she had to stop and pull herself together.

"Oh, no!" Laurie said when Jennifer finished. "I hadn't heard a word. Oh, I'm so sorry!"

Jennifer could hear a catch in Laurie's voice as she waxed nostalgic about how much Maria had added to her childhood. She closed her spontaneous eulogy with a question: "Did you go to India to bring back her body or her ashes to the States, or are you planning on leaving her there? After all, India might be the world's most spiritual country. If I died in India, I think I'd like my ashes placed in the Ganges with the billions of other souls."

"Now that's one thing I didn't think of," Jennifer admitted, explaining that she was having trouble deciding between cremation or embalming, much less what she was going to do with the remains afterward. "Sometime today I'm going to try to get over to the American embassy. I imagine they'll have the scoop on comparative costs and all the diplomatic details."

"I imagine that will be the case. Gosh, I'm sorry you have to do this yourself. I wish I were there to help. She truly was like a mother to me, so much so, I think there were times my real mother was jealous, but it was my mother's own fault. She was the one who handed me over to begin with."

"I can assure you the feelings were mutual," Jennifer said.

"I'm pleased to hear it, but I'm not surprised. Children can sense it, like I did."

"There's something else I want to run by you. Do you have a few more minutes?"

"By all means. I'm all ears."

"The hospital authorities have really been pushing me hard, which I freely admit I don't respond well to, and they do have reason. I mean, the private hospital involved is spectacular and very high-tech. Yet when they built it, they passed on building any mortuary facilities. Because in India bodies are claimed very rapidly by both Hindus and Muslims, for religious reasons."

"And maybe the hospital's owners thought that in spiritual India with all the gods on their side, they wouldn't have any deaths."

Jennifer managed a chuckle then went on. "Granny's

body is in a walk-in cooler, but the cooler is down near the cafeteria and contains mostly sealed food containers. Apparently that's the only place to leave a body."

"Yuck," Laurie voiced.

"Why I'm telling you this is because from their vantage point they have a real reason to want to dispose of Granny, especially since they already have the death certificate in hand."

"I should say."

"But they tried to force me to decide even before I got here, and once I did get here, and I've only been here for hours, it's been push, push, push, cremate or embalm. I mean, they literally wanted to do it yesterday for fear the sky would fall. Initially, maybe I was just being obstructive from being angry because they killed my granny. Now it's something else."

"Like what? What are you implying?"

"I asked them what killed Maria, and they said heart attack. Then I asked them what caused the heart attack, given that she came out to visit me in L.A. not too long ago, and while she was there, she got a very thorough physical at UCLA Med Center. I was told her cardiovascular system got an A-plus report. Now, how can someone with an A-plus get an F a few months later, twelve hours post–elective surgery. I mean, during the procedure it might be understandable for idiosyncratic drug toxicity but not twelve hours later. At least I don't think so."

"I agree," Laurie said. "With no apparent risk factors, you have to ask the question why."

"And that's why I did ask the question, but I certainly

did not get a satisfactory answer, at least from the case manager. She just told me she wasn't a doctor and apparently considered that adequate. It was then that I suggested the autopsy."

"Good for you," Laurie commented. "That is exactly what is needed if you have questions."

"Fat chance," Jennifer scoffed. "The case manager, Kashmira Varini, said whether or not there is going to be an autopsy is not up to the doctors or next of kin but the police or the magistrates. She went on to say that since Granny had been issued a death certificate, then there was not going to be an autopsy, case closed!"

"I've heard that the Indian forensic pathology system is behind the times. It's too bad. It creates a circumstance where miscarriages of justice are waiting to happen. In many developing countries, the police and the judiciary are almost invariably corrupt and often in cahoots."

"There's more," Jennifer said. "For the second night in a row, there's been a death at the same hospital that sounds strangely similar. First it was my granny, then last night it was a man named Herbert Benfatti. Both were apparent heart attacks the night of their surgery, and like Granny, Mr. Benfatti had been recently cleared by an essentially normal pre-op angiogram."

"Did they do an autopsy on the second patient?"

"I have no idea. When I asked the case manager handling Granny's case, she told me she didn't know about any death last night, but I didn't believe her."

"How come?"

"Mostly intuition, I guess, which is hardly scientific.

She just does not strike me as a truthful person. She wanted me to decide on the disposition of my grandmother's body and didn't want the issue to be diluted. I don't know."

"Do you think you are going to be able to keep stalling them?"

"I truly don't know. As irritated as I am, I know they're irritated, too; at least the case manager is. Why do you ask?"

"Because I'm going to come over there as soon as I possibly can and give you a hand. I don't think I'd forgive myself if I didn't come. Remember, she was as much a mother to me as she was to you and your brothers. Listen, I'll come unless you think you won't be able to deal with a hormone-addled crazy woman."

Jennifer was stunned. Laurie being willing to come all the way to India had never even occurred to her. "Hormones or no hormones, it wouldn't make a particle of difference, but it's one hell of a long flight," she warned. "I mean, I'd love to have your help and support. Don't get me wrong!"

"I don't doubt that it is one of the longest," Laurie said, "but how bad can it be? I just read that Air India has New York–Delhi nonstops."

"I suppose that would have been better than the two stops I was relegated to."

"Where are you staying?"

"It's called the Amal Palace, and it's the best hotel I ever stayed in. Of course, I've stayed in very few hotels."

"Wait a second!" Laurie suddenly said, sounding disgusted with herself. "What am I thinking? I can't wing off to India. I'm in the middle of an infertility cycle."

"Right! You told me, and I forgot, too," Jennifer said. Selfishly, she felt a big letdown. Having Laurie there with her would have been terrific.

"Actually," Laurie said, "I believe I can do it after all, providing I can bring my sperm factory. That's what Jack has been calling himself the last few months. That means it will be up to Dr. Calvin Washington, the deputy chief. I know he'd let me go, but whether he'd let both of us go without more warning, I have no idea. But it's worth a try. Here's the plan: We'll both be coming or neither will come. I'm sorry about that. Can you live with the uncertainty?"

"Of course," Jennifer said. "Tell Dr. Washington I'm asking him pretty please to let you guys come."

"That's a good ruse. He's never gotten over your week stay fourteen years ago."

"Neither have I, and I'm finally getting a payoff this June with my M.D. diploma."

"And I'll be there to see you get it," Laurie said. "Now, what about timing? How soon can we get there, presuming we're coming? Do you have any idea?"

"I do," Jennifer said. "Correct me if I'm wrong: It's still Tuesday there."

"It is. It's a little before midnight."

"If you leave tomorrow night, which is Wednesday, you will get here Thursday night late."

"Do you think you can hold them off until we get there? We don't want Granny cremated or embalmed if we are considering an autopsy."

"I'll certainly do my best. Hey, I'll even come to the airport to pick you up."

"We can discuss that when we know for certain we'll be coming."

"Laurie," Jennifer said, just moments before the call was to be terminated, "can I ask you a personal question?"

"Of course."

"Do you think any less of me that I've let all this undoubtedly superfluous stuff overwhelm the grief I feel for Maria? What I mean is that most people would be so overwhelmed by their emotions that they would be incapable of worrying about whether their loved one should be subject to an autopsy or not. Am I weird?"

"Absolutely, totally, one hundred percent no! It's exactly the way I would have responded. Normal people love the person, not the body. The body is a mere receptacle guaranteed to wither and die. The fact that you loved your grandmother to the extent that you are sensitive to issues way beyond the details of dealing with funeral concerns, I believe, is a tribute."

"I hope so."

"I know so," Laurie said. "As a medical examiner, I've seen a lot of bodies and the reactions of a lot of family members."

A few minutes later, after an appropriate good-bye, Jennifer disconnected. Despite not being superstitious, she quietly thanked her lucky star that she'd even thought of calling Laurie Montgomery. She was thrilled Laurie might come, and the fact that Laurie was as willing as she was emphasized to Jennifer what a piece of dog crap her fair-weather friend Neil McCulgan had turned out to be. Jennifer literally crossed her fingers for a few moments and gestured with them in the air that Laurie and Jack would be given the time off.

"We are nearing your hotel," the driver announced. "Am I to wait?"

The thought of asking him to wait hadn't occurred to her, but since the health management company that killed her grandmother was paying, why not? After all, she had to go back to the hospital. "You can wait or you can come back to the hotel in a few hours. One way or the other, I'll give you a call when I have to go back to the Queen Victoria Hospital."

"Very well, madam," the driver responded.

Chapter 12

"Jack!" Laurie called. "Wake up!"

Laurie had turned the bedroom lights on but for Jack's benefit had kept them at their dimmest. Since she'd been on the computer in the fully illuminated study, it seemed exceptionally dark.

"Come on, dear," she continued. "Wake up! We have to talk."

Jack was on his side, facing Laurie. She had no idea how long he'd been asleep, maybe almost two hours. Their usual evening routine was a light dinner after Jack's run on the basketball court. While they ate, they watched half a DVD for an hour or so, the rest the next night, before tidying up. At about nine they generally moved into their double study that looked out over 106th Street and the neighborhood basketball court and the rest of the small park that Jack had paid to have renovated and lighted. At about ten Jack would invariably begin yawning, give Laurie a peck on the top of her head, and supposedly retire to bed to read. But in reality, not much reading ever got done. No matter what time Laurie might poke her head in, he'd invariably be asleep, sometimes with a book or a medical journal precariously propped on his chest and his bedside light ablaze.

"Jack!" Laurie called again. She knew it was going to be hard to wake him, but she was determined. She began to nudge his upper shoulder until she was shaking it. Still, he stayed asleep. Laurie had to smile. His sleeping ability was of Olympic caliber. Although in some situations she could find it frustrating, generally she found it a trait to envy. Laurie was a light sleeper until the morning hours, when she had to get up. Then she slept soundly.

Laurie gave a final good shake to Jack's stocky shoulder and called out his name sharply. One eye, then the other, popped open. "What time is it?" he asked in a gravelly voice.

"It's around one-fifteen, I think. We need to talk. Something has come up." Initially, after Laurie had gotten off the phone with Jennifer, she wasn't going to bother Jack. She assumed he was asleep, as he proved to be. What she'd done was go on the Internet to learn what she could about traveling to India, and she'd learned a lot.

"Is the house on fire?" he asked, with his usual sarcasm.

"No! Be serious. We have to talk."

"It can't wait until morning?"

"I suppose it could," Laurie admitted. "But I wanted to give you a heads-up. You've warned me you don't like surprises. Especially big surprises."

"Are you pregnant?"

"I wish! But good guess. No, I'm not pregnant. Just a few moments ago I got a call from that young woman who's graduating from UCLA Medical School this coming June, Jennifer Hernandez. Do you remember her? She came to our wedding. She wore a luscious red dress. Can you picture it? She has one of the world's best figures."

"Jesus H. Christ," Jack mumbled. "It's almost midnight, and you woke me up so you can quiz me about what someone wore to our wedding? Give me a break!"

"The dress doesn't matter. I'm just trying to get you to remember this medical student. She's the one who spent the week at OCME when she was twelve, and also the one my mother and I got a scholarship for the same year."

"Okay, I remember her," Jack said, making it apparent he was lying. He was clearly much more interested in going back to sleep.

"She called me an hour or so ago from India. She's there because her grandmother died after having surgery in New Delhi. The hospital is pressing her to decide how she wants to deal with the body."

Jack lifted up his head, and his eyes opened wider. "India?"

"India," Laurie repeated. She then told the whole story to Jack as Jennifer had related it to her. When she got to the end she added, "I don't know if you'll remember, but Maria Hernandez was my nanny until I was thirteen, and the only reason she stopped was because my own mother became too jealous. I was crushed at the time. I preferred Maria's opinion to my mother's, like with clothes and things. I loved that woman. She was a mother to me for a lot of crucial years. I used to sneak over to Woodside, Queens, to visit her."

"Why did she go to India for her surgery?"

"I don't know for sure. Probably mostly financial."

"Do you really think there is some conspiracy here?" Jack asked in a skeptical tone.

"Of course not. I was supporting Jennifer because she seems to think so. If there's a problem at this hospital, it's undoubtedly some systems error. As far as the hospital putting pressure on Jennifer, I'm certain they are. The body has been in the cooler since Monday night, but it's not even a mortuary cooler. It sounds like mostly an overflow storage cooler for the cafeteria."

"You mean there's food in with the corpse?"

"That's the story. And it is the other way around. It's more accurate to say the corpse is in with the food and some medical supplies. But it's sealed food, which sounds worse than it is. Anyway, Jennifer is thinking there might be some sort of conspiracy involved."

"That's crazy! I think Ms. Jennifer Hernandez might be in a tiny bit over her head and a touch paranoid because of it."

"I couldn't agree more, which is one of the reasons you and I hopefully will be heading over there tonight."

"Come again?" Jack asked. He thought he'd heard but wasn't sure.

"First thing tomorrow morning I'm going to head into Calvin's office. What I'm hoping is that this emergency will justify him giving us a week or so off together. If he gives the green light, I'll go directly over to the organization that handles Indian visas, then I'll pay for our tickets, which I have already reserved online. Then I'll—"

"Wait a sec!" Jack said. He sat up and drew the blankets around his waist. The eyes were wide open now. "Hold your horses. Have you already committed us to this journey halfway around the world?"

"If you mean have I told Jennifer we're going to make every effort to come, then the answer is yes. I told her we had to get clearance from Calvin."

"Because a grieving young girl has become paranoid under stress is hardly justification to fly umpteen thousand miles to hold her hand."

"Giving Jennifer our support is not the only reason we are going," Laurie responded, her ire rising.

"Run by me another reason!"

"I told you!" Laurie spat. "Maria Hernandez was like a mother to me for twelve years. Her passing is a true loss."

"If it's that much of a loss, how come you haven't seen her since God knows when?"

Laurie saw red and for a second didn't say anything. Jack's comment made the growing confrontation much worse, as it effectively fanned Laurie's guilt. It was true she hadn't visited or even talked with Maria for a very long time. She'd thought about it and meant to do it but hadn't.

"I'm on a deadline about my research paper," Jack said. "And we have a neighborhood b-ball game on Saturday that I've been anticipating for weeks. Hell, I helped arrange it."

"Shut up about the stupid basketball," Laurie roared. She gritted her teeth and snarled at Jack. Like a volcano, all the resentment bubbling below the surface about the stress of infertility treatment emerged like a pyroclastic explosion. She also hated the fact that he continued to play basketball, which she thought was a dangerous game.

Jack was the first to remember that Laurie was currently undergoing daily injections of hormones, and although he actually had no inkling Laurie had been harboring resentment about his attitude, which he had had the delusion was fine, he had already experienced a number of surprising hormone-induced outbursts from Laurie, which she was plainly having at the moment. Recognizing this reality, he raised his hands in surrender. "I'm sorry," he said, trying to sound sincere. "I forgot about the hormones."

For a brief moment Jack's comment made things worse. Irrationally, Laurie thought Jack was merely trying to blame the current disagreement on her. But as she thought more about it, she could see the similarities between her current state of mind and when she'd torn into the eightysomething grandmother at the checkout counter at Whole Foods. A second later, the insight caused her to burst into tears.

Jack moved over to the side of the bed and put his arm around her. For a moment he didn't say anything.

From past trial-and-error experience, he knew it was the best thing to do. He had to wait for her to calm herself.

After a minute or so Laurie reined in her tears. Her eyes were bright red and watery when she looked at Jack. "You really haven't been supporting me with this infertility stuff!"

Jack had to fight to resist rolling his eyes. From his perspective, he'd tried to do everything, and there wasn't anything else for him to do except provide the sperm when required.

"When I get my period each cycle, you are so damn blasé," Laurie said, choking back tears. "You just say, 'Oh, well, maybe next time,' and that's it. You make no effort to mourn with me. For you it's just another cycle."

"I thought I was helping by making an effort to be nonchalant. Frankly, it would be easier to express despondency. But I never imagined that could be a help. I distinctly remember Dr. Schoener saying so herself. Hell, it's the indifference I have to manufacture."

"Really?" Laurie questioned.

"Really," Jack said, as he brushed some strands of damp auburn hair away from her forehead. "And about India. I have nothing against you going, I don't know Maria Hernandez or her granddaughter, Jennifer. For me, flying halfway around the world just doesn't make sense for the time or the money, but mostly the money. Of course, I'll miss you, and I would go if you needed me."

"Are you just saying that?" Laurie questioned.

"No. If you needed me, I'd go. That's for certain but—"

"I do need you," Laurie said, with sudden enthusiasm. "You are indispensable."

"Really?" Jack said. His bushy eyebrows knitted together questioningly. "I can't imagine how."

"The cycle, silly," Laurie said excitedly. "Yesterday Dr. Schoener thought it would only be four or five days before I give myself the stimulating shot and follicular release will occur. At that point it will be your turn at bat."

Jack exhaled fully. In his mind the infertility issue had not meshed with the proposed trip to India.

"Don't look so glum. Maybe we should count on dispensing with the turkey-baster part and do it the real way. But I'll tell you something, with the effort and stress involved, I'm not going to have you sitting here and me in India when this current crop of follicles bursts. Dr. Schoener is particularly optimistic because the left ovary fronting my good fallopian tube is the one that's going great guns this time around."

Lifting his arm from Laurie's shoulder and sitting back against the headboard, Jack said, "Looks like we're in for a quick trip to India, provided our fearless second-in-command lets us go. Maybe I can bribe him to say no!"

Laurie playfully swatted Jack's thigh through the covers as she got up. "I just had a good idea. Since I'm going to need an ob-gyn consult to follow my follicles and do my blood work, maybe I can find one in the same hospital, the Queen Victoria. It might be helpful with Jennifer's problem if we had a friend on the hospital staff."

"Could be," Jack said, as he shimmied down under the covers and then pulled them up around his neck. "A question about logistics: If we need visas, we'll be needing passport photos."

"In the morning we can use that all-night shop with the photo section up on Columbus Avenue."

"That's exactly what I was thinking," Jack said, after taking a deep breath and letting it out noisily.

"Are you going back to sleep?"

"Of course I'm going back to sleep. What else am I going to do after midnight?"

"I wish I could sleep like you can. The problem is, now I've gotten myself all worked up."

Chapter **13**

Jennifer felt totally frustrated. Despite how ex-hausted she was, even to the point of being slightly nauseated, she could not fall asleep. She'd drawn the heavy lined draperies, so the room was dark enough. The problem was that she was overtired and excited at the same time. The idea that Laurie might come was almost too good to be true and had her mind buzzing. Finally she thought, *Screw it,* and climbed from beneath the covers.

Dressed in only her panties, which was the way she'd gotten into bed, she went to the window and reopened the draperies, flooding the room with urban India's hazy sunshine. Absently, she wondered how much hotter it would have been outside had all the pollution not blocked out a significant portion of the sun's rays.

Looking down, Jennifer checked out the swimming pool. There were quite a few people enjoying it, although it was far from being crowded. It was a large pool. All at once Jennifer regretted not having brought a suit. It had never even crossed her mind when she'd packed for the trip, although now, looking down at the impressive expanse of blue water, it should have. After all, she knew she was going to a fancy hotel in a hot country. Jennifer shrugged. The idea they might have simple suits for sale occurred to her, but then she shook her head. As fancy as the hotel was, if they were to have suits for sale, they'd undoubtedly be designer and very expensive. It was unfortunate, because Jennifer thought some exercise might be just what the doctor ordered as far as helping her jet lag.

Thinking of exercise reminded Jennifer of the hotel's gym. It occurred to her to put on jogging clothes, which she did bring, and ride a stationary bike and lift some weights. She was about to follow her own advice when she glanced at the time. It was closing in on noon, which gave her another idea: lunch. Despite the lingering mild jet-lag-induced nausea, she thought it best to try to normalize her diurnal eating pattern as a way of helping to deal with the completely topsy-turvy sleep situation.

Having no interest in impressing anyone that morning, least of all the Queen Victoria people, Jennifer had worn a simple polo shirt over fitted jeans to the hospital, and after her nap attempt, she pulled on the same clothes. As she did so, she had an idea to see if Mrs. Benfatti might be willing to have lunch with her. Of course there was always the chance the woman might be in deep mourning and very depressed and not wish to be seen in public. At the same time, such a possibility was an indication of the appropriateness of asking her. As a medical student, Jennifer had witnessed all too often how death and sickness could actually isolate people in our society just when they most needed support.

Jennifer picked up the phone before she lost her nerve. She had the operator connect her to Mrs. Benfatti's room, wherever it was in the hotel. Jennifer briefly held the receiver away from her ear for a moment while it was ringing to see if Mrs. Benfatti's room was close by. She heard nothing.

Just when Jennifer was about to hang up, the connection went through. A woman whose voice was rough and slow answered. Jennifer guessed she had been crying.

"Mrs. Benfatti?" Jennifer questioned.

"Yes," Mrs. Benfatti answered warily.

Jennifer launched into a rapid description of who she was and why she was in India. She thought she heard Mrs. Benfatti draw in a breath when Jennifer explained that her grandmother had died in similar circumstances as her husband only the night before.

"I am so sorry about your husband," Jennifer continued. "Given my grandmother's death only the night before, I can truly sympathize with you."

"I'm equally sorry for your loss. It is such a tragedy, especially being so far from home."

"Why I was calling in particular," Jennifer said, "is the hope that you might feel like having lunch with me."

Mrs. Benfatti didn't respond immediately. Jennifer waited patiently, fully understanding that the woman was probably engaged in an internal argument with herself. Jennifer imagined that she probably looked a wreck from crying and being depressed, which was a big argument for her to stay in her room. At the same time, she'd be intrigued by the coincidence and would jump at the chance to talk with someone who was in the same awful situation.

"I need to get dressed," Mrs. Benfatti said finally, "and to do something with my face. I checked myself out a little while ago, and as the expression goes, I look like death warmed over."

"Take your time," Jennifer said. She liked this woman already, especially if she was strong enough to mock herself at a very difficult time. "There's no rush. I can wait for you here or in one of the restaurants, say the main one just off the lobby, or would you prefer Chinese?"

"The generic restaurant is fine. I'm not very hungry. I'll be there in half an hour, and I'll be wearing a violet blouse."

"I have on a white polo and jeans."

"I'll see you there, and by the way, my name is Lucinda."

"Sounds good. I'll see you there, Lucinda."

Jennifer slowly hung up the phone. She didn't know why, but she had a good feeling about Lucinda and was suddenly looking forward to lunch. Somehow, the nausea had mysteriously disappeared.

Having taken a seat in the multileveled restaurant that had a clear view of the hostess table, Jennifer saw Mrs. Benfatti the moment she entered from the lobby—at least, she was quite confident it was Mrs. Benfatti. The woman was wearing a carefully pressed violet top over a darker purple skirt. She was a large woman with an ample frame. Her mousy-colored hair was medium-length and tightly permed. If pressed, Jennifer would have guessed mid-fifties or thereabouts.

Jennifer watched as she stopped to speak with the maître d'. When the maître d' motioned for Mrs. Benfatti to follow and turned to head in Jennifer's direction, Jennifer waved and Mrs. Benfatti waved back. As they approached, Jennifer continued to watch the woman. She was impressed by the way Mrs. Benfatti was walking with her head held high. It wasn't until the woman got close and Jennifer could see her bloodshot eyes that it was at all apparent she'd just lost her life partner.

Jennifer rose and stuck out her hand. "Mrs. Benfatti," she said. "So nice to meet you, though I'm sorry about the circumstances. Thank you for being willing to join me for lunch."

Mrs. Benfatti didn't speak right away. She let the maître d' pull out her chair and then push it in once she was seated.

"Sorry," she said when the maître d' had left the table. "I'm afraid I have to struggle to keep myself under control. It's all been so sudden. Yesterday when he came out of the anesthesia so easily and then had such a good day, I thought for sure we were out of the woods, and then this had to happen."

"I understand, Mrs. Benfatti," Jennifer started to say.

"Please. It's Lucinda." The woman dabbed at the corner of her eyes before sitting up straighter, visibly trying to regain and maintain control.

"Yes, of course. Thank you, Lucinda!" Jennifer said. Taking relative command of the lunch, Jennifer suggested they order their food to get it out of the way. Once they had that accomplished, Jennifer began talking about herself, how she was about to graduate from medical school, about losing her mother, and having been raised by her grandmother. When Jennifer paused as the food came, she was pleased that Lucinda asked a question. She asked about what had happened to Jennifer's father, since Jennifer had not mentioned him.

"I didn't?" Jennifer said with a humorously exaggerated questioning expression. "I'm shocked. Well, maybe I'm not shocked. That's too strong. Probably the reason I didn't mention him is because we never do, neither my two older brothers nor I. He doesn't deserve it."

In spite of herself, Lucinda chuckled, gently covering the lower part of her face with her hand. "I know the type. We have one of those in our family, too."

To Jennifer's delight, Lucinda picked up from there, and as they ate their respective lunches, Lucinda talked first about the disowned uncle who'd been sent to prison for a time. Next she talked about her two sons. One was an oceanographer at Woods Hole, Massachusetts, with one child, and the other a herpetologist at the Museum of Natural History in New York City, with three children.

"And your late husband?" Jennifer questioned with some hesitancy. She didn't know what Lucinda's reaction would be, but Jennifer was interested in eventually talking about the deaths of their relatives. She wanted to find out how far the similarities went.

"He had a pet store for many years."

"Then I can see where the biologists came from."

"It's true. The boys loved the store and loved working with the animals, fish and all."

"Why did you come to India for his surgery?" Jennifer asked, holding her breath. If Lucinda was capable of fielding such a question about a decision that had it been different, her husband might still be alive, Jennifer was confident there would be no holds barred as far as other questions were concerned.

"It's simple: We didn't think we could afford a knee transplant Stateside."

"I think it was the same with my grandmother," Jennifer said. She was pleased. Although there was a slight catch in Lucinda's voice, there were no tears. "Tell me," Jennifer continued, "how have you found the Queen Victoria Hospital? Have they been easy to deal with? Are they professional? I mean, the hospital itself looks fantastic, which you can't say about the neighborhood."

Lucinda offered another one of her soft chuckles, which Jennifer was beginning to think was one of her idiosyncrasies, particularly the way she tried to hide the smile with her hand. "Isn't all that trash just terrible? The hospital staff, including the doctors, act as if they just don't see it, especially the child beggars. Some of them are demonstrably ill."

"I'm equally mystified. But how have you been treated by the staff?"

"Excellent, at least at first."

"How do you mean?"

"When we first got here, we were treated extremely well. Just look at this hotel." Lucinda gestured around the restaurant. "I've never stayed in a hotel this nice. It was the same at the hospital. In fact, the service at the hospital reminded us of a hotel. Herbert specifically said so."

Mentioning her husband so casually made Lucinda pause for a moment. She cleared her throat. Jennifer let her take a moment. "But it was a bit different this morning."

"Oh?" Jennifer questioned. "How was it different?"

"They are frustrated with me," Lucinda said. "Everything was fine until they insisted I make a decision whether to cremate or embalm. They said I had to do it right away. When I said I couldn't since my husband refused to discuss it out of superstition, they tried to force me. When I told them my two boys were coming and that they would decide, the hospital representative said they could not wait for someone to come all the way from America. They needed to know today. I could tell they were truly upset."

Now it was Jennifer's turn to chuckle. "I'm in the same circumstance," she said, "and they are irritated at me for the same reason."

"That's a coincidence."

"I'm beginning to wonder about that," Jennifer said. "Where is your husband's body?"

"It's in a cooler someplace. I'm not really certain."

"It's probably in one of two walk-in refrigerators in the basement near the staff cafeteria. That's where my granny is while we wait."

"Why are you waiting?"

"A very good friend of mind is coming. At least, I

hope she's coming. She's a forensic pathologist who works as a medical examiner. She's going to help me and look at my granny. I'm thinking that my grandmother might need an autopsy, and the more they push me, the more I think she does. You see, my granny was not at risk for a heart attack. I'm quite confident in that."

"We didn't think Herbert was, either. His cardiologist examined him a little over a month before we came. He said he was fine and had a terrific heart and low cholesterol."

"Why did your husband have a cardiologist?"

"Three years ago he and I took a trip to Africa to see the animals. Both of us had to take a bunch of shots and also an antimalaria medication called mefloquine. Unfortunately, he experienced a side effect where his heart beat irregularly, but it went away by itself."

"So your husband had a normal heart for all intents and purposes," Jennifer said. "Well, it was the same with my granny. She had remembered being told that she had had a heart murmur when she was a child, and had always thought there was something wrong with her. I had her seen at the UCLA Med Center by a top cardiologist, and he figured out that she'd apparently had what they call a patent ductus, which embryos need but are supposed to close. Granny's stayed open but then mostly closed later. She also had some irregularity like your husband, but that was determined to have been caused by a cold remedy and went away. Her heart was perfectly normal, and for her age quite remarkable. With your husband and my granny having cardiac histories like that, it's enough to make you paranoid."

"Do you think your friend may be willing to take a look at my Herbert?"

While the waiter took their coffee order and cleared the dishes, the women leaned back and didn't speak, both rehashing the conversation. When the waiter left, both leaned forward again. Jennifer spoke. "I can certainly ask her if she'd take a look at your husband. She's a terrific person, and I think a famous medical examiner, both she and her husband. They work together in New York." She paused. "When did you find out about your husband?"

"That was the most bizarre thing," Lucinda said. "I had gotten a call, which had awakened me, from a family friend in New York, who'd wanted to convey his condolences about Herbert. The trouble was, at that point I'd not heard anything. I thought Herbert was just fine, like I'd left him some three hours earlier." Lucinda stopped talking, and her lips quivered as she fought back tears. Finally, she sighed audibly and dried the corners of her eyes. She looked at Jennifer, tried to smile, and apologized.

"There's no need to apologize," Jennifer assured her. In truth, Jennifer was feeling a tad guilty, pushing Lucinda as much as she was. Yet the similarities between the two cases seemed to grow. "Are you alright?" Jennifer asked. Without really thinking about what she was doing, Jennifer reached out and gripped Lucinda's wrist as a spontaneous gesture of support. The move surprised even Jennifer; she hardly knew the woman, and here she was touching her. "Maybe we should talk about something else," Jennifer suggested, withdrawing her contact.

"No, it's okay. Actually, I want to talk about it. Up in the room I was just brooding, which wasn't helping anything. It's good for me to talk."

"So what did you do after you talked with your friend from New York?"

"Of course, I was taken aback. I asked him where on earth he'd heard such a thing. Well, he'd heard it on CNN as part of a piece on medical tourism. Can you imagine?"

Jennifer's lower jaw slowly dropped open; she had seen the same segment as Lucinda's friend, although possibly not at the same time.

"Anyway," Lucinda continued with progressive control over her fragile emotions, "while I was still talking to my friend, insisting that Herbert was just fine, the second phone line began to ring. I asked the friend to hold for a moment while I pressed the other button. It turned out that it was the hospital—specifically, our case manager—informing me that Herbert had indeed died."

Lucinda paused again. There were no more tears, just some deep breathing.

"Take your time," Jennifer urged.

Lucinda nodded as the waiter came over to inquire if they wanted more coffee. Both women shook their heads, totally preoccupied with their private conversation.

"I thought it was horrid that CNN knew about my husband before I did. But I didn't say anything at the time. I was too overwhelmed by the news. All I did was tell Kashmira Varini I'd come right to the hospital."

"Hold up!" Jennifer said, raising her hands for emphasis. "Your case manager's name is Kashmira Varini?"

"Yes, it is. Do you know her?"

"I can't say I know her, but I've met her. She was Granny's case manager, too. This is getting stranger still. This morning I asked her about your husband's death, and she told me she wasn't aware of it."

"She certainly was aware of it. It was she whom I met last night."

"Good grief," Jennifer voiced. "I had a feeling the woman wasn't trustworthy, but why would she lie about something I could easily find out about?"

"It doesn't make sense."

"I can tell you one thing. When I see her this afternoon, I'm going to ask her directly. This is ridiculous. What does she think we are, children, that she can just out-and-out lie to our faces?"

"Perhaps it has something to do with their need for confidentiality."

"Bullshit!" Jennifer said, and then caught herself. "Pardon the language. I'm just getting progressively ticked off."

"You don't have to apologize. I raised two boys."

"Maybe so, but most people don't give women the same latitude. But getting back to CNN. Something very similar happened to me." Jennifer went on to explain how she, too, had heard about her grandmother's passing on CNN and had actually called both the healthcare company that had arranged everything and the hospital itself only to be reassured that her grandmother was doing fine. It was only later when she got a call back from the hospital by Mrs. Varini that she learned the truth and that her granny had indeed passed away.

"How bizarre! It sounds as if the right hand doesn't talk to the left hand at the Queen Victoria."

"I'm wondering if it might be worse than that," Jennifer replied.

"Like what?"

Jennifer smiled, shook her head, and shrugged her shoulders all at the same time. "I haven't the foggiest idea. Of course, we could just be suffering from grief-driven paranoia. I'm the first one to admit I'm far from my right mind with the shock of losing my best friend, mother, and grandmother—all at once. On top of that, I'm learning that jet lag is not for kids. I'm exhausted, but I can't sleep. Maybe I'm not thinking so well, either. I mean, it could be that elective surgical deaths are so uncommon for the Queen Victoria that they don't quite know how to handle it. After all, they didn't even build mortuary facilities."

"What are you going to do?"

"Pray that my friend Laurie Montgomery comes. If she doesn't come, I truly don't know what I'll do. Meanwhile, this afternoon I'm going back to the hospital. I'm going to ask Mrs. Varini why she lied to me, and I'm going to make it absolutely clear, if I haven't already, they are not to touch Granny. What about you? Would you like to have dinner tonight?"

"What a thoughtful invitation. Can I let you know later? I just don't know where my emotions are going to be."

"You can let me know whenever you like. It probably

will have to be early. I think what's going to happen is that I'll just run out of gas and then sleep for twelve hours. But what are you going to do about the hospital? Are you just going to wait until your sons get here and let them make the decisions?"

"That is exactly what I am going to do."

"Maybe you should give our friend Mrs. Varini a call and make sure she can't claim a misunderstanding and do something without your expressed approval. When the next of kin are grieving, it's easy to bully them. Ironically, it's usually about doing an autopsy, not about not doing one."

"I think I'll take your advice. Last night I wasn't myself."

"Are you done with lunch?" Jennifer asked. "I'm going to head back to the hospital. I was going to go to the embassy, but I think I'll put that off. I want to pose a few questions to the case manager, like why she lied to me. I'll let you know if I learn anything startling."

Having already signed their respective checks, the women stood, and several busboys ran over and pulled out their chairs. The restaurant was now full, forcing them to weave among a crowd of people waiting for tables. Out in the lobby, they said their good-byes with a promise to talk later. Just as they were about to separate, Jennifer thought of something else. "I think I'm going to look into the CNN connection if possible. Would you mind terribly finding out from your New York friend exactly when he saw the segment about your husband, New York time?"

"I'd be happy to. I'd planned to call him back. I know he felt terrible about having broken the news."

They were about to separate again when Lucinda said, "Thank you for encouraging me to come out of my room. I think this was a lot healthier, and I'm afraid I wouldn't have if left to my own devices."

"It was my pleasure," Jennifer responded. She was holding her phone in preparation for calling her car and driver.

Chapter 14

How long will you be, madam?" the driver asked. He was holding the car door as Jennifer climbed out. During the ride from the hotel to the hospital she had managed to fall asleep for some twenty minutes or so, and now felt distinctly worse than she had when she'd started. Still, she wanted to talk with Kashmira Varini.

"I'm not sure," Jennifer said, looking up at the hospital. She'd just gotten the idea to go up to the fourth floor where she'd been told her grandmother's room had been and see if she could find the day nurse who'd been assigned to her case. "But it won't be long, not the way I feel."

"I'll try to stay here," the driver said, pointing down at the ground, "but if the doormen chase me, you'll have to call my mobile."

"No problem," Jennifer said.

As had been the case on the earlier visit, the two colorful doormen opened the double doors without Jennifer having to say a word. Because it was hotter outside than it had been that morning, it felt colder inside. As far as she was concerned, it was definitely over-air-conditioned.

At that time there were forty to fifty people in the lobby, all either upper-middle-class Indians or well-to-do foreigners. Near the admitting desk were a handful of prospective patients, some sitting in wheelchairs. A number of hospital staff were in evidence with their charges in varying stages of the admitting process. Glancing into the coffee shop, Jennifer could see it was full, with some people standing and waiting for tables.

With the aplomb garnered from all the hours she'd spent in a hospital, Jennifer didn't hesitate in the slightest from making her way over to the elevators. When she boarded, she made certain the button for the fourth floor had been pressed, and then melted into the background.

For Jennifer, the patient floor was one of the most pleasant she'd seen, and she'd seen her share. The floor itself was covered with attractively colored high-quality sound-absorbing industrial carpet, and combining it with a high-tech acoustic ceiling and walls constructed of sound-dampening material, the ambient noise was muffled down to almost nothing. Even the sound of a large, fully loaded food tray cart was minimal as it passed behind Jennifer while she walked over to the nursing station.

Several patients had just returned from surgery, so

most everyone was busy, including the floor clerk. Jennifer just watched. She was impressed how similar the protocols for running the floor seemed to be to what she'd experienced at UCLA Med Center, despite her being halfway around the world in a developing country.

In a relatively short time the immediately postoperative patients had been settled in their rooms, stabilized, and returned to the company of their next of kin. As abruptly as it had started, the flurry of activity dissipated. It was then that the floor clerk, whose nametag said merely "Kamna," happened to notice Jennifer. "Can I help you?" she asked.

"I believe you can," Jennifer responded. She wondered if Kamna was a proper name or meant something like clerk. "My name is Jennifer Hernandez, and I am Maria Hernandez's granddaughter. I believe she was a patient on this floor."

"You are correct," Kamna said. "She was in room four-oh-eight. I'm very sorry."

"I am, too. Is this a common problem here?"

"I'm not sure what you mean."

"Are deaths relatively frequent?"

Kamna jerked almost as if Jennifer had hit her. Even the head of one of the nurses using a computer terminal bobbed up with a shocked expression on her face.

"No, it is very rare," Kamna said.

"But there was another one just last night around the same time. That's two in a row."

"That's true," Kamna agreed nervously. She looked down at the nurse for support.

"I'm Nurse Kumar," the woman said. "I'm the head nurse on this floor. Can I be of assistance?"

"I wanted to speak to whoever was taking care of my grandmother."

"There were actually two. First there was Ms. Veena Chandra, who is new to our staff, and since she is new, a senior nurse by the name of Shruti Aggrawal was assigned to supervise."

"I suppose it would be safe to say that Ms. Chandra would have been the person actually interacting with my grandmother."

"That's correct. Everything had gone entirely normally. There had been no problems whatsoever. Mrs. Hernandez had been doing excellently."

"Is Ms. Chandra available?"

Nurse Kumar paused while giving Jennifer a moment of scrutiny, perhaps worried that Jennifer could possibly have been a deranged woman in the hospital to exact revenge. Everyone was acutely aware of the Hernandez demise. But apparently, Jennifer had passed muster. "I don't see why not. I'll see if she can speak with you now."

"Perfect," Jennifer said.

Nurse Kumar got up, walked down the corridor a way, and after a quick glance back at Jennifer, disappeared into a patient's room.

Jennifer glanced back at Kamna, who'd not moved a muscle. She was clearly still unsure of Jennifer's mindset and intentions. Jennifer flashed a smile, intending to calm the woman, who appeared like a rabbit ready to flee. The woman flashed a smile back, one even more fake and fleeting than Jennifer's. Before Jennifer could try to put the woman at ease, she saw Nurse Kumar emerge from the patient room with a young nurse in tow. Jennifer blinked. Even in a nursing uniform, the newly hired nurse looked like a beauty queen or a movie star, or even more irritating, as far as Jennifer was concerned, a lingerie model. She was the kind of female who never failed to make Jennifer feel fat. She had a perfect body and a photographer's dream face.

"This is Nurse Veena Chandra," the head nurse said when the women had reached the station. At the same moment, the elevator arrived and out stepped one of the uniformed guards Jennifer had seen downstairs. Since he just seemed to be lingering in the background, Jennifer sensed that the head nurse had called down when she'd been out of sight.

Veena greeted Jennifer, palms together. Jennifer tried to imitate the gesture. Veena was even more beautiful up close, with flawless bronze skin and stunning green eyes, which Jennifer found mesmerizing. The problem was the eyes didn't engage hers except for fleeting moments before looking away, as if Veena was bashful or somehow self-conscious being in Jennifer's presence.

"I'm Jennifer. Mrs. Hernandez's granddaughter."

"Yes, Nurse Kumar has told me."

"Do you mind if I ask you a few questions?"

Veena exchanged a quick uncertain glance with her head nurse, who nodded that it was okay.

"I don't mind."

"Maybe we could step over to those chairs by the window," Jennifer said, pointing to a small sitting area with a modern couch and two chairs. Jennifer felt crowded by the head nurse and the clerk, who were standing like statues, hanging on every word.

Veena again looked to Nurse Kumar, which began to confuse Jennifer. The woman was acting as if she were twelve, whereas Jennifer guessed she was in her twenties, even if just barely. She was acting as if she would have preferred being anywhere but where she was, facing a conversation with Jennifer.

Nurse Kumar shrugged and gestured toward the sitting area.

"I hope I'm not making you uncomfortable," Jennifer said to Veena as they walked over and sat down. "I didn't even know my grandmother was in India when I learned she had died. So I'm not very happy about her death, to put it mildly, and I'm looking into it to a degree."

"No, you're not making me uncomfortable," Veena replied tensely. "I'm fine." For a brief moment the image of Maria Hernandez's contorting face flashed in her mind's eye.

"You are acting very nervous," Jennifer commented, trying vainly to make sustained eye contact.

"Maybe I'm afraid you are angry with me."

Jennifer reflexively laughed, not loud but more in surprise. "Why would I be angry with you? You helped my grandmother. My goodness. No, I'm not angry. I'm thankful."

Veena nodded but seemed unconvinced, although she did allow herself more eye contact.

"I just wanted to ask you how she was? Did she seem happy? Did she suffer at all?"

"She was fine. She wasn't suffering. She even talked about you. She told me you were becoming a doctor."

"That's true," Jennifer said. She wasn't surprised. Her grandmother was extremely proud of what Jennifer had done, and to Jennifer's chagrin bragged about it to anyone who would listen. Jennifer tried to think of what else to ask. She actually hadn't given it a lot of prior thought. "Was it you who found Maria after her apparent heart attack?"

"No!" Veena said comparatively explosively. "No, no," she repeated. "Mrs. Hernandez died on the evening shift. I work days. I'm off at three-thirty. I was home. This is my first month working here. I work days with supervision."

Jennifer regarded the young nurse, who was, in actuality, a contemporary. Jennifer couldn't help but feel there was something amiss, as if they weren't quite on the same wavelength. "Can I ask you a couple of personal questions?"

Veena nodded hesitantly.

"Have you recently graduated from nursing school?"

"About three months ago," Veena said, nodding.

"Is my grandmother the first patient you've lost?"

"Yes, she was," Veena said with another nod. "The first private patient."

"I'm sorry. It's never easy, whether you're the doctor, the nurse, or even the medical student, and I'm certainly not angry with you. The fates, maybe, but not you. I don't know if you are religious, but if you are, doesn't your religion provide a source of comfort? I mean, apparently, it was my grandmother's karma to leave this life, and maybe in her next life she won't have to work quite so hard. She really worked hard all her life, and not for herself. She was truly a generous person. The best."

When Jennifer saw Veena's eyes glaze over with tears, she felt she had figured out the source of the nurse's distress. Granny had been her first death as a real nurse, a difficult milestone, which Jennifer could certainly relate to. "You are a dear for caring so much," Jennifer added. "I don't mean to make you feel uncomfortable. But I do have a few more questions. Do you know much about my grandmother's actual death? I mean, like, who found her and what were the circumstances? Even what time it was?"

"It was Theru Wadhwa who found her when he went in to see if she wanted sleep medication," Veena said, wiping the corners of her eyes with a knuckle. "He thought she was asleep until he noticed her eyes were open. I asked him about it last night when he came to work, since she was my patient and all."

"What time was it, do you know?" Jennifer asked. Having uncovered the young woman's secret and broached the issue, Jennifer expected she'd relax. But such was not the case. If anything, she seemed even more anxious. Her hands were working at each other in her lap as if in a wrestling match.

"Around ten-thirty."

"Since you talked directly with the nurse, did he describe her in any particular way? I mean, did she look calm, like it was an easy death? Did he say anything like that?"

"He said she looked blue when he turned the lights on and called a code."

"So they tried to revive her?"

"Only briefly. He said it was apparent she was dead. There was no cardiac activity at all, and she was cool and already a little stiff."

"That's dead, alright. What about the blueness? Do you know if he meant more gray or really blue?"

Veena looked off as if thinking. Her hands detached from each other and gripped the arms of the chair. "I think he meant blue."

"Cyanosis-like blue?"

"I think so. That's what I assumed."

"That's curious for a heart attack."

"It is?" Veena asked, somewhat surprised.

"Did he say allover blue or just, like, blue lips and blue fingertips."

"I don't know. I think allover blue."

"What about Mr. Benfatti?" Jennifer asked, rapidly switching the subject. She'd suddenly remembered stories of so-called angels of death, healthcare serial killers, who also were the ones who "found" their victims after the fact, sometimes to try to save them.

"What about Mr. Benfatti?" Veena questioned, startled.

"Did Nurse Wad-something happen to find him as well last night?" Jennifer asked. She knew the answer would be no, but she had to ask it anyway.

"No," Veena blurted. "Mr. Benfatti wasn't on this floor. He was on three. I don't know who found Mr. Benfatti."

"Ms. Hernandez!" a voice called from behind Jennifer. Startled, Jennifer turned and looked up. It was Head Nurse Kumar, who'd walked over from the central desk.

"I'm afraid Ms. Chandra has to get back to her patient. Also, I called down to Mrs. Kashmira Varini to let her know that you were here. She asked me to ask you to come by her office. She said you knew where it was. I'm sure she can handle any more questions you might have." Nurse Kumar motioned for Veena to return to her charge.

Both Jennifer and Veena stood.

"Thank you very much," Jennifer said. She reached out and shook hands with the woman and was surprised that her hand was like ice.

"You are welcome," Veena said hesitantly, reverting back to acting like a shy girl. Her eyes darted self-consciously between the two women. "I'll get back to work."

Jennifer watched her walk away, lamenting just how little she'd be able to eat and how much she'd have to exercise to have an equivalent body. She then turned her attention and acknowledged as much to Nurse Kumar: "A beautiful woman."

"You think so?" Nurse Kumar questioned stiffly. "You do know where Mrs. Varini's office is, I trust."

"I do," Jennifer agreed. "Thank you for your help in allowing me to speak with her."

"You are entirely welcome," Nurse Kumar said, but she then abruptly spun on her heel and headed back toward the nurses' station.

Sensing a snub of sorts, Jennifer walked over to the

elevators. She thought briefly of asking to see her granny's room but changed her mind. She knew it would
look like any hospital room, just upscale. When the elevator came and she boarded, she noticed the guard
who'd come to the floor earlier did, too. She was clearly
being treated with great suspicion.

As the elevator descended, Jennifer thought over the
conversation she'd had with the newly hired nurse. She
was touched the woman was still so emotional about
Granny's passing, since she probably had spent only
hours over the course of several days in Granny's presence. Of course, the most interesting part of the conversation was about Granny's reputed cyanosis. Closing
her eyes for a second, Jennifer transported herself back
to physiology class and tried to scientifically think
what kind of heart attack might cause generalized cyanosis. Unfortunately, she couldn't think of any. The
only thing that came to mind was possible aspiration
and choking on food. To get generalized cyanosis,
Granny's heart would have had to have been pumping
fine; it would have had to be her lungs that weren't doing their part.

Jennifer opened her eyes. Such thinking raised the
issue of smothering. Someone could have smothered her
grandmother and produced generalized cyanosis, but as
soon as the idea occurred to her, Jennifer actively swept
it from her mind. She couldn't believe how paranoid she
was becoming. She felt embarrassed. She knew, just as
she knew where her next breath was coming from, that
no one had smothered Granny.

The elevator landed at the lobby and most everyone got out, including Jennifer, who made it a point to lock eyes for a moment with the guard, who was holding the doors ajar. "Why, thank you," Jennifer said brightly. The guard acted surprised to be addressed but didn't return the nicety.

Wasting no time, Jennifer headed to the marble front desk, rounded it, and walked to Kashmira Varini's open door. Jennifer rapped on the jamb. Kashmira was at her desk, filling in a form. "Come in, please," she said when she looked up in response to Jennifer's knock. She stood and went through her usual greeting, which Jennifer merely acknowledged with a slight bowing of her head. Kashmira then motioned to a seat and Jennifer dutifully sat. Jennifer looked at Kashmira.

"Thank you for coming back," Kashmira said. "I hope you had a refreshing nap."

"I didn't sleep a wink."

"Oh!" Kashmira voiced, apparently expecting a more positive reaction to what she meant more as a rhetorical question. She was definitely hoping to begin the discussion on a more favorable note than it had ended that morning in the basement. "Did you get something to eat? I could order you a small sandwich or a salad."

"I had my lunch, thank you."

"Did you see your consular officer at your embassy?"

"Nope," Jennifer said and then added, "Mrs. Varini—"

"Please call me Kashmira."

"Okay, Kashmira. I think we should clear the air.

This morning I specifically asked you about Mr. Benfatti. You lied to me. You said you didn't know anything about a Mr. Benfatti, and then I learn you are his case manager. What gives?"

For a moment, Kashmira pondered her words. She cleared her throat before speaking. "I apologize for that. It came out of a sense of frustration. I was trying to convince you to stay on the subject of your grandmother and the dire need to make a decision, which should not be so difficult. I'm sure you know we do not talk about other patients. That's what I should have said. I must confess I was exasperated with you, and still am to a degree. I just got a call from Lucinda Benfatti, and she has informed me that you specifically advised her to wait with her decision as well. Now, I know she'd thought about waiting until her sons got here, but I was hoping that after the shock wore off, I could ask her to ask them their preference before they started their trip so the body could be dealt with appropriately. That's how it has always worked in the past. This kind of problem has never come up before."

"Are you saying that dealing with patient death is a common problem here?"

"Quite the contrary," Kashmira said forcefully. "Don't read something into my words which is not there."

"Okay, okay," Jennifer said, afraid she might have pushed the woman a little too far. "Thank you for your apology, and I accept. Actually, I'm impressed how you explained it. I was very curious how you were going to, because I didn't think you could."

"This issue about your grandmother has me entirely flummoxed."

"It's nice to know we at least see eye-to-eye about something," Jennifer mumbled.

"Excuse me?"

"Forget it," Jennifer added. "I was making a bad joke. But there is something I would like to see. I'd like to see my grandmother's death certificate."

"What on earth for?"

"I just want to see what it has on it as the cause of death."

"It has heart attack, just like I said."

"I'd still like to see it. Do you have it, or at least a copy?"

"I do. It's in the master folder."

"May I see? I assume I'll be getting a copy at some point anyway. It's not a state secret."

Kashmira thought for a moment, shrugged, and pushed herself in her chair over to a bank of file cabinets. Pulling out one of the drawers, she scanned the tabs and eventually pulled out an individual file. Opening it, she found a very Indian-looking government document. She returned to the desk, handing the document across to Jennifer.

Jennifer took it, and seeing her grandmother's name gave her a stab of emotion. The languages were Hindi and English, so she had no trouble going over it. She scanned the hand-lettered entries to alight on the cause of death, heart attack, and the time of death, ten-thirty-five p.m., October 15, 2007. Jennifer committed it to memory and handed the paper back to Kashmira.

Kashmira returned it to the file and the file to its rightful place in the cabinet.

Scooting her chair once again back to the desk, Kashmira glanced over at Jennifer. "Now! After all is said and done, are you ready to tell me what we are to do, cremate or embalm?"

Jennifer shook her head. "I'm at my wit's end as well. But there's hope on the horizon. My grandmother was nanny to a woman who has conveniently become a forensic pathologist. I spoke with her, and she's on her way here, which will, I believe, have her arriving tomorrow night. I'm going to defer to her and her husband, who is a medical examiner as well."

"I remind you, forensic pathologists or not, it will make no difference. There's to be no autopsy, period. It has not and will not be authorized."

"Maybe, maybe not. At least I'll feel like I've got someone on my side. I know I'm not thinking too well. I'm utterly exhausted, but I can't sleep."

"Perhaps I could get you some sleeping medication."

"No, thanks," Jennifer said. "What I would like is a copy of my grandmother's hospital records."

"That can be arranged, but it might take twenty-four hours."

"Whatever! And I'd like to talk to the chief surgeon."

"He's very busy. If you have some specific questions, write them down, and I'll try to get some answers."

"What if there was malpractice involved?"

"There is no such thing as malpractice in an international setting. Sorry."

"I have to say you're not being very helpful."

"Listen, Miss Hernandez. You would undoubtedly find us more helpful if you would be cooperative with us."

Jennifer stood up.

"Really," Kashmira said. "I could get you something for sleep. Perhaps after a good night's rest you'd come to your senses and realize you must make a decision. Your grandmother cannot stay in our cooler."

"I already realize that," Jennifer said. "Why not transfer the body to a regular city mortuary?"

"That would be impossible. Public mortuaries in our country are in frightful condition thanks to our byzantine bureaucracy. Mortuaries are administered by the home ministry, not the ministry of health, as they should be, and the home ministry cares little about them and grossly underfunds them. Some have no refrigeration, others only intermittently, and bodies routinely rot. To be brutally honest, we cannot allow that to happen even to your grandmother because of the potential negative media consequences. We're trying to help you. Please help us!"

All at once, Jennifer felt off-balance. She got to her feet. Although still being less than tactful, Queen Victoria Hospital seemed to be going from trying to bully her to pleading with her. "I'm going back to the hotel," Jennifer managed. "I need to rest."

"Yes, you go have a long sleep," Kashmira said. She stood as well and bowed over her pressed-together hands.

Jennifer stumbled out into the confusion of the lobby, where a dozen more admissions were waiting to be processed. She went to the front glass wall and looked for her car and driver in the hospital's small turnout. Not seeing him, she pulled out her cell phone and punched in the numbers.

Chapter 15

Kashmira had watched as Jennifer navigated her way through the people in the lobby. Never had Kashmira been more aggravated by a next of kin. When she'd been able to talk the woman into coming to India, she'd thought the problem of Maria Hernandez's body was essentially over; now it was ascending to another level of urgency, with not one but two forensic investigators on their way to lend their thoughts. Kashmira knew that CEO Rajish Bhurgava was not going to be happy.

The second Jennifer exited from the lobby Kashmira walked out of her office and down the hall to where Rajish's corner office was located.

"Is he available?" Kashmira questioned Rajish's private secretary.

"I believe so," the secretary said. "But he's not in a good mood." She checked, using the intercom, and then waved Kashmira by as another call came in on an outside line.

Between calls, Rajish was reading over a stack of letters and then signing them with his rapid scrawl. In contrast to his casual cowboy outfits he wore when called in at night, he was wearing a Western designer suit, white shirt, and Gucci tie.

"Did she come back this afternoon?" Rajish demanded when Kashmira shut his office door and approached his desk. Over the lunch hour she had briefed him about Jennifer's intransigence that morning and how self-willed she was, but had ended by saying she was optimistic Jennifer would be more reasonable after some sleep. She'd also conveyed to Rajish Jennifer's brief talk of an autopsy. This new information had provoked Rajish to comment irritably that there would be no autopsy under any circumstances. He added that the last thing he wanted to do was take the risk of some true pathology's being found that should have been known before the surgery. Kashmira also had told him that Jennifer had brought up the name of Benfatti, and Rajish had questioned how Jennifer had learned about the death. Kashmira had confessed she had no idea. All in all, Rajish was no fan of Jennifer Hernandez.

"She just left," Kashmira said with a nod in answer to Rajish's question.

"And?" Rajish snapped. With a second death in so many nights, he was in a foul mood. Once again the night before he'd been called by the powerful Ramesh Srivastava and informed that CNN International had reported another death at Rajish's hospital before the hospital had called him. Although the highly placed public servant hadn't actually threatened Rajish directly, the implication of blame had been uncomfortably clear.

"It's getting worse, I'm afraid. She now says that she wants to wait until Friday before making a decision. Apparently, the dead woman worked for someone who has subsequently become a forensic pathologist. This forensic pathologist is apparently arriving tomorrow night."

Rajish slapped a hand to his forehead and forcibly rubbed his temples with his thumb and forefinger. "This can't be happening," he moaned.

"It gets worse. The woman is bringing her husband, and he is also a forensic pathologist."

In a minor panic, Rajish lowered his hand and stared at Kashmira. "We'll be dealing with two American forensic specialists?"

"It appears that way."

"Did you make it absolutely clear to Ms. Hernandez that there will be no autopsy?"

"I did, both this morning and this afternoon. It's my understanding that the fact that this woman who is on her way is a forensic pathologist is incidental to why she is coming. So we shouldn't jump to conclusions."

Rajish tipped back in his chair until he was looking directly up at the ceiling. "What did I do to deserve these problems? All I'm trying to do is keep it all out of the media beyond the initial CNN segments."

"In that regard, things are still quiet. There's been no media people here yesterday or today."

"Thank the gods for small favors, but that might change at any moment, especially now with two deaths."

"Ms. Hernandez is potentially interfering in that situation also."

There was a loud squeak as Rajish suddenly tipped forward and gaped at Kashmira. "How is she managing that?"

"Somehow the widow and she got together. Lucinda Benfatti called back a little while ago to reemphasize that she, too, doesn't want her husband's body touched until her sons get here Friday. As you know from last night she'd already said that, but both of us thought the chances were good that she'd change her mind today when I spoke with her. No deal. In fact, she mentioned Jennifer's forensic pathologist friends coming, and that she'd asked Jennifer if her friends could look at her husband's case as well. If the media get wind of this, they might jump on it."

Rajish slammed his palm down on his desk. Several of the letters waiting to be read swooped off into the air. "This woman is a scourge spreading her stubbornness to others. I worry this situation is rapidly growing beyond our capability to keep it under wraps. Most people who are grieving are too emotionally paralyzed to cause trouble. What is wrong with this Hernandez girl?"

"She's self-willed, as I mentioned," Kashmira agreed.

"Is she spiritual?"

"I haven't any idea. She's not said anything to make me think one way or the other. Why do you ask?"

"I was just thinking that if she were spiritual, we could tempt her with her grandmother's body."

"How so?"

"Offer to have it cremated at the world-famous burning ghats of Varanasi and the ashes placed in the Ganges."

"But that is a privilege reserved for Hindus."

Rajish made a gesture as if swatting a fly. "Some extra consideration for the Brahmin of the Ghats of Jalore would solve that issue. Perhaps Ms. Hernandez could be tempted. It could be touted as an extra favor to the departed. We could offer it to Mrs. Benfatti as well."

"I'm not optimistic," Kashmira said. "Neither strikes me as particularly religious, and being cremated in Varanasi only has true meaning for Hindus. Yet I'll give it a try. The Hernandez girl herself admitted she might think differently after she'd gotten some sleep. She is exhausted and suffering jet lag. Maybe such a bribe would push her over the edge."

"We must get these bodies out of that cafeteria cooler," Rajish emphasized. "Especially with the hospital currently under observation by the International Joint Commission. We can't afford to fail for such an incidental violation. Meanwhile, I will give Ramesh Srivastava a call back and report we are having a particularly difficult time with the Hernandez woman."

"I have tried my best with her, I assure you. I've been very direct. More so than with any other next of kin."

"I know you have. The problem is we have limited resources. That's not the situation with someone like Ramesh Srivastava. He has the weight of the entire Indian bureaucracy behind him. If he so desired, he could even keep the two forensic friends of Ms. Hernandez out of the country."

"I'll keep you informed of any changes," Kashmira said as she turned to go.

"Please do," Rajish said, with a brief wave. He used his intercom to ask his secretary to get Mr. Ramesh Srivastava on the line. He wasn't looking forward to it. He knew how powerful Srivastava was and how he could get Rajish fired with a snap of his fingers.

Chapter 16

It had not been a good day for Ramesh Srivastava. Starting the moment he got into his office in the morning, the deputy secretary of state for health had called to tell him that the secretary of state for health was furious about the second CNN International segment being aired concerning India's nascent medical tourism industry. Then the calls had never stopped. They came from half a dozen joint secretaries of the Ministry of Health and Family Welfare, the president of the Indian Healthcare Federation, and even the secretary of state for tourism, all reminding him that he happened to be presiding over the department of medical tourism when it was experiencing the most negative international PR that it had ever experienced. All the callers also reminded him that they had the power to end his career if he didn't do something and do it fast. The problem was, he didn't know what to do. He'd tried to figure out how CNN International was getting the tips, but without success.

"A Mr. Rajish Bhurgava is online at this moment," Ramesh's secretary said as Ramesh came through his office door, returning from his three-hour lunch. Ramesh dashed into his inner office and snatched the receiver off the hook. "Have you found the leak?" he demanded straight off.

"Just a moment," Rajish's secretary said. "I'll put Mr. Bhurgava on."

Ramesh silently cursed as he flopped down in his desk chair. He was a large balding man with watery eyes and deep scars on his cheekbones from adolescent acne. He tapped his fat, impatient fingers on his desk. As soon as Rajish Bhurgava came on the line, Ramesh blurted out the question again and with equal emotion.

"We haven't," Rajish admitted. "I've spoken yet again at length with the chief of the medical staff. We still believe the most likely culprit is one of the academic doctors who also have admitting privileges here for their relatively few private patients. We know some of them are rabidly against the government's granting us the incentives and tax breaks it has at the expense of adequately funding the control of communicable diseases in rural areas. What he's doing now is trying to see if any of the most outspoken ones were here in the hospital both Monday night and last night."

"What does he say about the deaths themselves?" Ramesh grumbled. "Two in two nights is intolerable. What are you people doing wrong? With CNN beaconing these fatalities around the world seven or eight times a day, you have essentially negated six months of our ad campaign, especially in America, our biggest target."

"I asked him the same question. He's entirely baffled. Neither patient had warning symptoms or signs, either from their home doctors or during our admitting tests."

"Did they have cardiograms here preoperatively?"

"Yes, of course they had cardiograms, and both arrived with clean reports from American cardiologists. Our chief of the medical staff said that even in retrospect there would have been no way to predict what happened. Both surgeries and postoperative courses were without incident."

"What about the problem with the Hernandez girl? Has that at least been taken care of?"

"I'm afraid not," Rajish admitted. "She's not decided on the disposition of the body, and she now has begun talking about possibly wanting an autopsy done."

"Why?"

"We're not entirely certain other than her belief that her grandmother's heart was in fine shape."

"I don't want an autopsy," Ramesh stated categorically. "There's no way it could help us. If the autopsy were to be clean, they wouldn't use it to exonerate us because there's no story, and if the autopsy shows pathology we should have known about, they would crucify us. No, there is to be no autopsy."

"To complicate things, Ms. Hernandez has apparently contacted a former client of the deceased, and she and her husband, both of whom are forensic pathologists, are on their way and will be in Delhi on Friday."

"Good grief," Ramesh said. "Well, if they make formal

application for an autopsy, make sure it is taken by one of the magistrates we are accustomed to dealing with."

"I'll do my best," Rajish said. "But perhaps with your connections you might question whether we want them here at all."

"I would need more warning. Otherwise, they get stopped only at the airport, and that, in and of itself, could cause a media problem if it gets associated with the already notorious private hospital deaths reported by CNN. A free media is such a bore, and they love these gossipy-type stories."

"There's one other way that the Hernandez girl is causing mischief. She had seemingly sought out the Benfatti woman this morning and convinced her to delay giving us permission to dispose properly of her husband's body in the same way she is denying us access to her grandmother's."

"No!" Ramesh exclaimed with disbelief.

"I'm afraid so. I'm beginning to think as I hear from my case manager that she is deliberately trying to cause trouble. I'm even beginning to believe she's starting to become paranoid and hold us accountable, as if we have caused this tragedy deliberately."

"That's it, then," Ramesh said. "We cannot let this go on."

"Is there something you can do, sir?" Rajish asked hopefully.

"Perhaps," Ramesh said. "We cannot sit passively and let this woman have free rein until her paranoia is somehow satisfied."

"I couldn't agree more."

"Keep me informed of any and all developments," Ramesh said.

"Absolutely," Rajish answered.

Ramesh hung up the receiver and turned to the keyboard at his workstation. Going into his address book, he found the mobile number of Inspector Naresh Prasad of the New Delhi police, who headed up the small, clandestine Industrial Security Unit. Picking the phone receiver back up, he placed the call. Since the men hadn't spoken in almost six months, they traded some personal information before Ramesh got around to the reason for the call. "We here at the department of medical tourism have a problem that needs your expertise."

"I'm listening," Naresh said.

"Is this a good time to talk?"

"It doesn't get much better."

"There is a young woman named Jennifer Hernandez, whose grandmother passed away Monday night at the Queen Victoria Hospital of an unfortunate heart attack. Somehow CNN got ahold of the story and put it on the air as a way of questioning our record of safety."

"That's not good."

"That is an understatement," Ramesh said. He then went on to tell Naresh the entire problem, including the details of the second death. He then enumerated all the things that Jennifer had done and was doing to make herself persona non grata. "This affair is beginning to have a serious deleterious effect on our medical tourism ad campaign, which could then impact our ability to meet our goals. I don't know if you have been kept completely up to date, but we have upped our estimates such that Indian medical tourism is to be a two-point-two-billion-dollar-a-year industry by 2010."

Naresh whistled into his phone. He was duly impressed. "I hadn't heard those figures. Are you people aiming to catch IT? The information technology people are going to be envious, as they believe they have become the hereditary kings of foreign exchange."

"Unfortunately, this current problem could seriously impact our goal," Ramesh said, ignoring Naresh's question. "We need help."

"That's what we're here for. What can we do?"

"There's two parts. One part for your unit in general and one part for you in particular. Concerning your unit, we need an investigation to uncover who is supplying CNN International with confidential information. The CEO of Queen Victoria and his chief of the medical staff believe it to be a radical academic M.D. who also has admitting privileges. How many there are at the Victoria I don't know, but I want them investigated now. I want to know who this person is."

"That can easily be arranged. I will put my best men on it. What is my part?"

"The girl, Jennifer Hernandez. I want her taken care of. It shouldn't be difficult. She's staying at the Amal."

"Why not call up one of your equals in immigration. Have her picked up and deported. Problem over!"

"My sense is that she is feisty, stubborn, and resourceful. If immigration picks her up, I'd worry that she'd make a fuss, and if the media associates her case with the death reported by CNN, there could be an even bigger story about a governmental cover-up. That could make everything decidedly worse."

"Good point. What exactly do you mean 'taken care of'? Let's be specific."

"I leave that to your well-earned reputation for creativity. I want her to stop being a potential thorn in our side. However you can accomplish that, I'm content. Actually, it's better if I don't know. Then if I'm asked at a later date, as one who was interested in her behavior, I don't have to lie."

"What if I can assure you she means no harm and her current apparent threat is bogus?"

"That would be satisfactory, of course. Particularly if your team can provide us with the physician mole. I need to attack this problem from both ends."

"Can I assume my compensation will be the usual?"

"Let's say comparable. Check things out. Follow her. Remember, we don't want her to become the news, and we surely don't want her to be any kind of martyr. As for the compensation, it should depend on degree of difficulty. You and I go back a ways. We can trust each other."

"You'll hear from me."

"Good."

Ramesh disconnected the call. Toward the end of the conversation with the industrial policeman, he'd had another idea about the Hernandez problem, a possible solution that would be easier, cheaper, and probably better, as it wouldn't involve the government. All he had to do was get someone he knew angry enough, and it so happened that the individual Ramesh had in mind was easy to get angry when the issue involved money. Ramesh was surprised he'd not thought of Shashank Malhotra earlier. After all, the man regularly paid him off and had even taken him on a memorable trip to Dubai.

"Hello, my good friend," Shashank enthused several octaves louder than necessary. "Wonderful to hear from you. How is the family?"

Ramesh could visually imagine Shashank in his palatial office overlooking the fashionable Connaught Place. Shashank was one of India's new-style businessmen who were into a wide variety of pursuits, some legal, some less so. Of late he'd become particularly enamored of healthcare and saw medical tourism as the path to an easy second fortune. Over the last three years he'd invested a substantial sum and was the principal stockholder in a company that, appropriately enough in relation to the current problem, owned the Queen Victoria Hospitals in Delhi, Bangalore, and Chennai, and the Aesculapian Medical Centers in Delhi, Mumbai, and Hyderabad. It was also he who had recently contributed the lion's share of the cost of the recent ad campaign in Europe and North America touting India as a twenty-first-century healthcare destination. Shashank Malhotra was a major player.

After an appropriate amount of niceties had been exchanged, Ramesh got down to business. "The reason for my call is a problem at Queen Victoria Hospital here in Delhi. Have you been briefed?"

"I heard there was some sort of minor problem," Shashank said warily. He had heard the change in Ramesh's voice and was famously sensitive to the word *problem*, as it usually meant the necessity of spending money. And he was particularly touchy about problems associated with both the Queen Victoria Hospital group and the Aesculapian Medical Centers, as they were the newest members of his financial empire and had yet to reach profitability.

"It's more than minor," Ramesh said. "And I think you should know about it. Do you have a minute?"

"Are you kidding? Certainly I want to hear it."

Ramesh told Shashank the story pretty much the same way he'd told it to Inspector Naresh Prasad but minus the optimistic government economic predictions for medical tourism, as Shashank was already well aware of those. As Ramesh progressed, he knew Shashank was appreciating both the importance and the urgency of the situation because of the pointed questions he posed as Ramesh continued.

When Ramesh finished and fell silent, Shashank remained silent as well. Ramesh let him stew, particularly about the part of erasing most of the gain from the ad campaign.

"I think you should have told me all this a little sooner," Shashank growled. He sounded like a completely different person. His voice was low and menacing.

"I think that everything should be fine if this young woman will make up her mind about her grandmother's body, and then she heads home. I'm sure you know someone qualified to make those suggestions, someone whom she might listen to."

"Where is she staying?"

"At the Amal Palace."

Ramesh found himself holding a dead line.

Chapter 17

Veena glanced at her watch. Report had never seemed to take so long. She was supposed to have been off at three-thirty, and it was already a quarter to four.

"That's it, then," Nurse Kumar said to the evening head nurse. "Any questions?"

"I don't believe so," the evening head nurse said. "Thank you."

Everyone stood. Veena made a beeline to the elevator while the others erupted in casual conversation. Samira saw her and had to hurry to catch up.

"Where are you going?" Samira questioned.

Veena didn't answer. Her eyes darted from elevator to elevator to see which one would be arriving first.

"Veena!" Samira voiced with emotion. "Are you still not going to talk with me? I think you are carrying this too far."

Veena ignored Samira and stepped over to the door of the arriving elevator. Samira followed.

"I know it is reasonable for you to be angry with me initially," Samira whispered after moving behind her friend. Several of the other nurses joined them, chattering about the day's events. "But after you'd had time to think about it, I thought you'd understand I did it for you as much as for myself and the others."

The elevator arrived. Everyone boarded. Veena moved to the back of the car, turned, and faced forward. Samira joined her. "This silence is not fair," Samira continued in a whisper. "Don't you even want to know the details about last night?"

"No," Veena replied, also in a whisper. They were the first words she'd spoken directly to Samira since Monday, when Cal had revealed to Veena that he knew about her family's problems. The only other person in the world who knew about it was Samira, so the source was obvious.

"Thank you for talking to me," Samira said, keeping her voice low over the babble of the others. "I know I wasn't supposed to tell about your father, but this seemed different. Durell told me our emigrating depended on it. I was also promised your problem would be taken care of and you'd be free, and so would your family."

"My family has been shamed," Veena said. "Irreversibly shamed."

Samira didn't say anything. She knew that Veena initially would be absorbed in thinking about her extended family and its reputation instead of rejoicing in her newly gained freedom and that of her sisters from a horrid father. But she expected her to promptly see the light. More than ever, Samira wanted to escape what she thought were the cultural shackles of current-day India. She couldn't wait for Nurses International to help her emigrate.

With the shift changing, the elevator stopped on every floor.

"I'm not going directly back to the bungalow," Veena said, keeping her eyes glued to the floor indicator. "I'm going to stop in and see Shrimati Kashmira Varini."

"What on earth for?" Samira questioned in a whisper.

"The granddaughter of my victim came to see me this afternoon, and I found it very uncomfortable having to speak with her. Cal never suggested I'd have to do anything like that. She scares me. She told me she's not happy about her grandmother's death and she's looking into it. I don't like it."

The elevator came to a bumpy stop at the lobby level and disgorged its full load of passengers. After only a few steps, Veena came to a halt. Samira did the same.

"Maybe it would be best if you didn't do anything until we talk with Cal and Durell," Samira said after making certain no one was listening.

"I want to find out where she is staying in case Cal wants to know. I'm sure the case manager knows."

"I imagine she does."

"The granddaughter mentioned your victim as well."

"In what regard?" Samira asked with increasing alarm.

"She wondered if the same person who'd found Mrs. Hernandez also found Mr. Benfatti."

"Why would she care?"

"I don't know."

"Now you have me concerned," Samira said.

"I'll wait for you here," Samira said, as Veena turned and headed toward the information desk. She merely waved acknowledgment over her shoulder. Rounding the desk, Veena peered beyond Kashmira Varini's open door. She was hoping the case manager would be alone, and she was.

"Excuse me," Veena called out, and bowed as Kashmira looked up. "May I ask you a question?"

"Of course," Kashmira replied, returning the greeting.

Veena advanced to the desk. "I spoke with Mrs. Hernandez's granddaughter, Jennifer, this afternoon."

"Yes, so Nurse Kumar informed me when she called to let me know she was here. Sit down!" Kashmira pointed with her chin toward one of the free chairs in her office.

Although Veena was planning on staying only for a few moments, she sat down.

"I'm interested in your reaction to her. We are finding her difficult to deal with."

"In what regard?" Veena asked, feeling progressively more unsettled toward the American.

"In most every regard. We need her simply to stipulate what she wants us to do with her grandmother's body and be done with it so we can dispose of the body. But she refuses. I'm afraid she has some paranoid notion this tragedy was either a medical error or intentional. She'd even arranged that several American forensic pa-

thologists are coming for heaven knows what. I've re-
peatedly made it clear there is to be no autopsy."

Veena had reflexively sucked in a bit of air when she'd
heard Kashmira say "intentional" and hoped it hadn't
been apparent. Her sense that Jennifer Hernandez was
potential trouble had ratcheted up several notches.

"Are you alright?" Kashmira asked, leaning toward
Veena.

"Yes, I'm fine. It's been a long day is all."

"Do you need a drink of water or anything?"

"I'm fine. Why I stopped in was to find out where
Jennifer Hernandez is staying, because I was thinking of
calling her. I want to be certain I've answered all her
questions. When she was here I was very busy, and Nurse
Kumar had to interrupt to get me back to my patient."

"She's at the Amal," Kashmira said. "During the
time you were talking with her, how did she seem? Was
she hostile at all? With me she goes back and forth. I
don't know if it is because she is exhausted or angry."

"No, not hostile. In fact, the opposite. She acted
sympathetic that her grandmother had been my first
patient death since my graduation."

"That seems out of character."

"But she did specifically say she was unhappy about
her grandmother's death, whatever that meant, and that
she was looking into it to a degree. She used those words
but quite matter-of-factly."

"If you end up talking with her, please encourage her
to decide about her grandmother's body. It would be an
enormous help."

After promising to put in a good word if the opportunity presented itself about the cremation/embalming issue, Veena bid Shrimati Varini good night and hustled out into the lobby. She found Samira and guided her outside.

"What did you learn?" Samira asked, as they walked down the driveway.

"We have to talk with Cal about this Hernandez woman. She worries me. Even Kashmira Varini is having trouble with her. She said that she believes Jennifer Hernandez suspects the death of her grandmother was either medical error or somehow purposeful. In other words, not natural."

Samira stopped, suddenly grabbing Veena by the elbow and pulling her up short. "You mean she thinks her grandmother might have been murdered."

"In so many words," Veena said.

"I think we better get back to the bungalow."

"I couldn't agree more."

Despite the pre–rush hour traffic clogging the street, the women were lucky to find a free auto rickshaw. They climbed into the bench backseat, gave the driver the bungalow address, and then held on for dear life.

Chapter 18

"You got a sec?" Durell asked from the library door. Cal looked up from the spreadsheets of Nurses International expenses. The burn rate was impressive, but with things going so well at the moment, he was not as concerned as he'd been just two to three days before.

"Of course," Cal said. He leaned back and stretched his arms over his head. He watched Durell saunter in and spread several maps on the library table that Cal used as a desk. There were also photos of a number of vehicles, which he carefully positioned with his large, powerful hands. Durell was dressed in one of his signature stretch black T-shirts, which molded over his muscles as if it had been sprayed on.

"Okay," Durell said, standing straight and rubbing his hands together with relish. "Here's what I've found."

Before he could continue, the front door slammed

shut in the distance hard enough not only to be heard but also to rattle Cal's espresso cup in its saucer on his desk. The two men shared a look. "What the hell?" Cal questioned.

"Somebody wants us to know they are home," Durell said. He looked at his watch. It was almost four-thirty. "Must be one of the nurses who have had a bad day."

No sooner had the words escaped Durell's lips than Veena and Samira came through the library door. Both started talking at once.

"Hey!" Cal called out, motioning with both hands for them to calm down. "One at a time, and this better be important. You've just interrupted Durell."

Veena and Samira exchanged glances. Veena spoke. "There's a possible problem at the Queen Victoria—"

"A *possible* problem?" Cal questioned, interrupting her.

Veena nodded excitedly.

"Then I think you should show some consideration. Durell was speaking."

"We can go over this later," Durell said, gathering up the car photos.

Cal grabbed his wrist to restrain him and made eye contact. "No, continue! They can wait."

"Are you sure?" Durell said, leaning over to speak directly in Cal's ear. "I thought this escape stuff was privileged information."

"It's okay. If Armageddon arrives, I want them with us anyway. Let them hear. They could help."

Durell flashed a thumbs-up sign and stood back up.

"Listen up," Cal said. "Durell has been working on

what is called a contingency plan for a worst-case scenario. But it's privileged information. No telling the others."

Their curiosity piqued, the women crowded in against the table, looking at the maps.

"I hope you realize that including them will add a new level of complexity to get us all hooked up if and when the plan is activated," Durell told Cal.

"You can work that out at a later date," Cal said. "Let's hear the pitch!"

Durell went back to setting out the photos of the vehicles. While he did so, he explained to the women that he'd come up with an idea of how to get out of the country if the need arose.

Veena and Samira exchanged a nervous stare. This was a subject related to what they had come to talk about.

"First, these are a few potential vehicles to buy and store in that fortress garage we have on the property. The idea would be to have it fueled, packed, and ready to go. I believe it should be four-wheel drive because the roads on my proposed route are not in the best of shape."

"What's the route you are recommending?" Cal asked.

"We'd head southeast out of Delhi and use the main highway to Varanasi. From there we'd head northeast to cross the border into Nepal at the Raxaul-Birgunj border crossing." Durell traced the route on the maps.

"Is that a good place to cross?"

"I think the best. Raxaul's in India, and Birgunj is in

Nepal. They apparently are both sprawling shithole cities only a few hundred meters apart, whose major industry, as far as I can tell, is the commercial sex trade for the
two-thousand-plus truckers who use the crossing each
day."

"Sounds delightful."

"For what we're looking for, I think it sounds perfect. It's such a backwater crossing, they don't even require visas. It's really just a customs stop."

"Is this in the mountains?" Cal asked.

"No, it's tropical and flat."

"It does sound perfect. Then what, once we cross?"

"It's a pretty straight drive up the Prethir Highway
on the Nepalese side to Kathmandu and an international
airport. At that point, we'd be home free."

"There'll be mountains in Nepal, I suppose?"

"Oh, yeah!"

"Then I recommend the Toyota Land Cruiser," Cal
said, picking up the photo and brandishing it. "We got
our six seats plus four-wheel drive."

"You got it," Durell said, picking up the other photos. "It was my first choice, too."

"Buy it, get it ready, and put it out in that garage.
Have the groundspeople start it once a week. Also, let's
all pack an overnight bag."

"If the car keys are going to be left out there, I'm not
sure I recommend leaving our bags out there. The fence
at the far rear of the property has fallen down in one section."

"Let's use that dungeon-like room below. The door
that goes down to it locks, doesn't it?"

"It's got a big old key that looks like it belongs to a medieval castle."

"That's what we'll do. We'll each prepare a small suitcase and lock them in the dungeon."

"What will we do with the key?" Durell asked. "We all should know where the key is. If a major problem happens like this plan is supposed to cope with, we all should know where the key is located. One hang-up could be a problem."

Cal glanced around the library. Besides the sizable collection of antique books, there were many knick-knacks on tables and shelves. Cal's eyes soon came to rest on an antique Indian papier-mâché box sitting on the marble mantel. He got up and went over to it. It was intricately painted and glazed and certainly large enough. After a bit of a struggle, he got it open. It was conveniently empty. "The key will go in here. What do you say?" He held the box up so everyone could see.

Everyone nodded as Cal put the Indian craft box back in its original position. As he came back to his chair, he regarded the women. "Are you okay with all this? You can get a small bag together and get it to Durell? And I mean small, just for a couple of days."

The women nodded again.

"It all sounds terrific, Durell," Cal said, "especially since the chances of needing it are about zero, but it's best to be prepared." Cal thought but didn't say that the stimulus had been Veena's suicide gesture, which certainly had not been anticipated. He glanced at her, amazed at her apparent turnaround. Yet now knowing the story of abuse that she'd had to quietly suffer, he couldn't help but wonder if she was as stable as he needed her to be.

"I'll let Petra and Santana know the details," Durell said to Cal, as he gathered up the maps. Then, to the women, he said he'd get back to them later about how they would all hook up in the unlikely case the emergency plan had to be activated.

Cal nodded to Durell, but his attention was now directed at Veena and Samira. "Okay," he said. "It's your turn. What's this possible problem?"

Veena and Samira erupted together, stopped, and started again before Samira gestured that she'd give the floor to Veena. Veena described her meetings with Jennifer Hernandez and the Hernandez case manager.

Cal raised a hand to stop her and then called out, "Durell, maybe you should listen to this!" Durell was on his way out the door, wrestling to get his maps folded. He turned around and came back. Cal summarized what the girls had already said, then motioned for Veena to continue.

Veena went on to tell how Jennifer was thwarting the hospital's ability to deal with the Hernandez body and, more important, that she was actually investigating her grandmother's death. Veena said that the case manager even used the words *error* and *intentional* to describe how Jennifer thought the death had been caused. "I'm afraid she doesn't believe it was natural," Veena summarized. "And you told me that that could not happen, that it was impossible for someone to even imagine such a thing. But this Jennifer Hernandez is doing just that, and it gives me a bad feeling about all this—"

"Okay, okay," Cal said, raising his hand and gesturing for Veena to calm down. "You are getting yourself too worked up here." Cal looked at Durell. "How the hell could this Hernandez girl be thinking the way she is?"

Durell shook his head. "Beats me, but I think we'd better find out. Could there be some aspect of this succinylcholine strategy we're not taking into consideration?"

"I can't imagine," Cal said. "The anesthesiologist was very specific in our hypothetical case. He said the victim should have a history of some kind of a heart problem; exactly what it was didn't matter. The person should have had general surgery within twelve hours, and the drug be given in an existing intravenous line. That was it, wasn't it?"

"That's what I remember," Durell said.

"She's a medical student," Veena added. "She knows about this stuff."

"That shouldn't matter," Cal said. "We got the plan from an anesthesiologist, and he said it was foolproof."

"She has arranged for two medical examiners to come to India," Samira said.

"That's right," Veena agreed. "It's not just she we have to think about."

"And she mentioned my patient, Benfatti, to Veena, meaning she already knew about him," Samira added.

"Once the information has been on CNN, anyone can know about it," Cal said. "That's not an issue."

"But aren't you worried about the medical examiners coming?" Veena asked. "They are forensic pathologists. It certainly worries me."

"The medical examiners don't worry me for two reasons: one, it sounds like from what you've said the Queen Victoria has no intention of allowing an autopsy to take place, and two, even if one was done and they found some evidence of succinylcholine, it would be attributed to the succinylcholine the patients are known to have been given as part of their anesthesia. The only thing that worries me to an extent is this Hernandez having a suspicion in the first place. What could have caused her to suspect anything?"

"Maybe it's just paranoia on her part," Durell suggested. "And the fact that there were two deaths back-to-back."

"That's an interesting idea," Cal said. "You know, that could be it. Think about it. Out of the blue she finds out her grandmother is dead after surgery in India, of all places. She has to fly all the way here. Then the hospital pressures her to make a decision about what to do with the body before she's ready. On top of that, there's another, similar death. It's enough to make anyone paranoid. Maybe the only lesson we should be learning here is not to do two in a row at the same hospital."

"But Samira had a perfect patient," Durell said, defending his girlfriend. "And she was eager. We have to reward that kind of initiative."

"No doubt, and we did. You did a terrific job, Samira. It's just from now on let's not do the same hospital two nights in a row. We have to spread them out. After all, we have nurses in six hospitals. It doesn't make sense to take any risks whatsoever."

"Well, we're not taking that kind of risk tonight," Durell said.

"Is there another one tonight?" Veena asked apprehensively. "Don't you think we should let things slide for a few days or a week, or at least until Jennifer Hernandez leaves?"

"It's hard to stop with the success we're seeing," Cal said. "Last night in the States, all three networks picked up on CNN's lead and ran segments about Asian medical tourism with the theme it might not be as safe as assumed. It was powerful."

"It's true," Durell said. "The message is hitting home in a big way. Santana has heard from her CNN contact that they are already getting reports of medical tourism cancellations. You can't argue with success, as my daddy always used to say."

"What hospital is going to be involved tonight?" Veena asked, in the same serious tone. She was not trying to hide her opposition to another case so soon after the first two, especially since it had been she who had started the program.

"The Aesculapian Medical Center," Cal said. "Raj called today to say that his patient David Lucas, who's in his forties, was a terrific candidate. He'd had abdominal surgery to control obesity this morning. Cardiac-wise, he couldn't be better. He had a stent inserted three years ago, so he's known to have obstructive disease."

"We've also made it easier," Durell said. "We took Samira's excellent suggestion about the succinylcholine. We now have our very own supply, so there will not be any dangerous sneaking around the ORs."

"That's right," Cal said. "We got it today. Those are the kinds of suggestions we need to make this plan better and safer. I think we should pay bonuses for them to encourage such constructive thinking."

"Then I think Samira should get a bonus," Durell said, giving Samira a congratulatory squeeze.

"And Veena a bonus for breaking the ice," Cal said. He gave Veena an equivalent hug, and the shapeliness and firmness of her body beneath her nurse's uniform instantly turned him on.

"Does this mean you don't plan on doing anything about Jennifer Hernandez?" Veena asked. She immediately pulled away from Cal. She was surprised Cal and Durell weren't as concerned as she was about Jennifer's interest in looking into her grandmother's death. "I made the effort to find out where she was staying, thinking you'd want to know."

"Where is she staying?"

"At the Amal Palace."

"Is she now! What a coincidence, since that's where we all stayed when we interviewed you women for Nurses International."

"Cal, I'm being serious."

"So am I. But I'm not going to have anything to do with that woman, not as one of the principals of Nurses International. Whereas you could without arousing any suspicion. If you are so concerned, why don't you come up with a reason to meet her again and find out the source of her suspicions. I'm sure you'd find Durell is right, that it's her own paranoia, and it will be a relief for you and for us to know there isn't some clue we're missing."

"I couldn't," Veena said, with a shake of her head as if shivering off a touch of nausea.

"Why not?"

"Even just thinking of her gives me flashes of her grandmother's face, contorting as she was dying, and even worse, I hear the grandmother thanking me all over again."

"Then by all means don't meet with her," Cal said, with an edge to his voice. "I'm just trying to suggest how you can deal with your anxieties."

"Maybe I shouldn't be doing this at all," Veena said suddenly.

"Now, let's not go off the deep end. Remember, you don't have to 'do' any more patients. You're done. You were to start the ball rolling, that's all. You're in a supporting role now."

"I mean, maybe none of us should be doing this."

"It's not your role to decide," Cal stated. "Just consider it your dharmic duty to support the others. And remember, this activity has freed you from your father, and it is going to bring you and your colleagues, including Samira here, to a completely new freedom in America."

Veena stood for a moment, nodding as if agreeing, then turned and left the room without saying anything additional.

"Is she going to be alright?" Durell asked, looking back at the others after watching Veena silently exit.

"She's going to be fine," Samira said. "It's just going

to take a while. She suffers more than the rest of us. Her problem is that she hasn't had nearly the Westernizing Internet experience we've had, and as such she's still way more an acculturated Indian than we are. As an example, when she finally started talking to me today after being mad at me for revealing her deep, dark secret to you guys, one of the first comments she made was not to rejoice at finally being free at last of her father and able to follow her dreams but that her family had been shamed."

"I think I'm beginning to understand," Cal said. "What worries me, though, is the suicide thing. Is there any chance she'll try that again?"

"No! Definitely not! She did it because she felt she was expected to do it in the context of her religion and her family, but you saved her. So that's that. It wasn't to be her karma to die, even if she had thought it was. No, she won't try it again."

"Let me ask you something else," Cal said. "Since you're her best friend, does she ever talk about sex?"

Samira laughed hollowly. "Sex? Are you joking? No, she never talks about sex. She hates sex. Well, let me amend that. I know she wants to have kids one day. But sex for sex's sake, no deal. Not like other people I know." Samira winked at Durell, who snickered behind a closed fist.

"Thanks," Cal said. "I should have asked you these questions weeks ago."

Chapter 19

OCTOBER 17, 2007
WEDNESDAY, 6:15 A.M.
NEW YORK, USA

Before ever opening his eyes, Dr. Jack Stapleton heard a sound that was foreign to his ears. It was a distant hushed roar, the likes of which he found hard to describe. For a moment he tried to think what could be making it. Since their 106th Street Manhattan brownstone, which was actually brick, had been renovated only two years ago, he thought it could have been a sound that was normal to the newly configured house but that he'd just never appreciated. Yet on further thought it was too loud for that. Trying harder to characterize it, he suddenly thought of a waterfall.

Jack's eyes blinked open. Sweeping his hand under the covers on his wife's side of the bed and not encountering her sleeping form, he knew what the sound was: It was the shower. Laurie was already up, an unheard-of phenomenon. Laurie was a dyed-in-the-wool night owl and often had to be dragged kicking and screaming from her bed in order for her to get to the OCME, also known as the Office of the Chief Medical Examiner, at some reasonable time. As for himself, Jack liked to arrive early, before everyone else, to give him the opportunity to cherry-pick the good cases.

Mystified, Jack tossed back the covers, and completely naked, which was the way he liked to sleep, he padded into the steamy bathroom. Laurie was practically invisible within the shower stall. Jack cracked the door.

"Hey in there," Jack called out over the sound of the water.

With suds in her hair, Laurie leaned out of the spray. "Good morning, sleepyhead," she said. "It's about time you woke up. It's going to be a busy day."

"What are you talking about?"

"The India trip!" Laurie said. She leaned her head back into the torrent and vigorously rinsed her hair.

Jack leaped back to avoid being splashed and let the shower door close. It all came back to him in a rush. He'd vaguely remembered snatches of the conversation in the middle of the night when he'd first awakened, but he'd thought it all had been a nightmare.

Jack had not seen Laurie so motivated since she and her mom had teamed up for planning their wedding. A little later Jack learned that Laurie had stayed up and essentially made all the travel and lodging arrangements, pending Calvin's permission for the two of them to take a week off. They were to leave that evening, change planes in Paris, and arrive in New Delhi late the following night. As far as the hotel was concerned, they were booked in the same place Jennifer Hernandez was staying.

By seven a.m. Jack found himself staring into the lens of a digital camera in a shop on Columbus Avenue. When the flash went off, he jumped. A few minutes later he and Laurie were back on the street.

"Let me see your photo!" Laurie said, and giggled when she looked at it. Jack grabbed it back, miffed that she was making fun of it. "Want to see mine?" Laurie asked, but she extended it to Jack before he had a chance to respond. As he'd expected, hers looked better than his, with the flash catching the auburn highlights in her brunette hair as if the clerk was a professional photographer. The biggest difference was the eyes. Whereas Jack's light brown, deeply set eyes looked like he was hung-over, Laurie's blue-green eyes were bright and sparkly.

When they got to the OCME at seven-thirty, Laurie thought things looked auspicious. She imagined that if it had been a particularly busy day, Calvin would be less inclined psychologically to let them both take a week. But it was not busy, at least not yet. When she and Jack walked into the ID office, where the day began for all the medical examiners, the medical examiner in charge of reviewing the cases that had come in during the night, Dr. Paul Plodget, was sitting at the ID desk reading *The New York Times*. In front of him was an unusually small stack of folders that had already been reviewed. Next to him in one of the brown vinyl club chairs sat Vinnie Amendola, one of the mortuary techs whose job it was to come in early to help with the transition from the night techs. He also made the communal coffee. At the moment he was reading the *New York Post*.

"A light day today?" Laurie questioned to be certain.

"One of the lightest," Paul said, without appearing from behind his newspaper.

"Any interesting cases?" Jack asked as he started rummaging through the short stack.

"Depends on who's asking," Paul said. "There's one suicide that's going to be a problem. Maybe you saw the parents. They were parked out in the ID room earlier. They are part of a prominent, well-connected Jewish family. To put it bluntly, they don't want an autopsy, and they are pretty adamant." Paul glanced around the edge of his paper at Jack to make sure he'd heard.

"Does the case really need an autopsy?" Jack asked. By law, suicides demanded autopsies, but the OCME tried to be sensitive to families, especially when religion was involved.

Paul shrugged. "I'd say yes, so there needs to be some finesse involved."

"That leaves out Dr. Stapleton," Vinnie commented.

Jack roughly flicked the back of Vinnie's paper with his fingernails, causing the man to jump. "With that kind of recommendation, mind if I take the case?" Jack asked Paul.

"Be my guest," Paul said.

"Has Calvin arrived yet?" Laurie asked.

Paul lowered his paper so he could look at Laurie with an exaggerated questioning expression that said, *Are you crazy?*

"Jack and I are possibly having to take some emergency leave starting later today," Laurie said to Paul. "If it's not a problem, which it doesn't look like it will be,

I'd like to take a paper day to sign out any and all cases I can."

"Shouldn't be a problem," Paul agreed.

"I'm heading out to talk with these parents," Jack said to anybody and everybody while holding the case file aloft.

Laurie grabbed his arm. "I'm going to wait for Calvin. I want a yes or a no as early as possible. If it's yes, I'll pop down to the pit before heading out to get our visas."

"Okay," Jack said, but it was apparent he was already preoccupied by the purported case.

After a quick detour out to Marlene at reception to ask to be informed the minute Calvin arrived, Laurie took the elevator up to her fifth-floor office. Sitting down, she dove into the stack of cases she had pending. But she didn't get far. It was only twenty-two minutes later that Marlene informed her that Calvin had just come in through the front door, much earlier than usual.

The deputy chief medical examiner's office was sited next to the chief's much larger one near the building's front entrance. At that time, prior to eight, the secretaries had yet to arrive, and Laurie had to announce herself.

"Come on in!" Calvin said when he saw Laurie at his door. "Whatever is on your mind, make it fast. I'm due down at City Hall." Calvin was an enormous African-American who could have played in the NFL had he not been quite so interested in studying medicine when he graduated from college. With his ability to intimidate combined with a stormy temperament and streak of perfectionism, he was a very effective administrator. Despite the OCME being a city agency, things got done and got done efficiently under Calvin Washington, M.D.

"Sorry to bother you so early in the day," Laurie began, "but I'm afraid Jack and I have a kind of emergency."

"Uh-oh," Calvin intoned, as he gathered the material he needed to take to the mayor's office. "Why do I get the feeling I might have to do without my two most productive pathologists. Okay, give me the short version of the problem!"

Laurie cleared her throat. "Do you remember that young girl, Jennifer Hernandez, whom I invited here fourteen years ago?"

"How can I forget. I was totally against it, and somehow I let you talk me into it. Then it turned out to be one of the best things this office has ever done. Has it been fourteen years? Good lord!"

"It has been that long. In fact, Jennifer is graduating this coming spring from UCLA Medical School."

"That's terrific. I loved that kid."

"She sends her regards."

"Likewise," Calvin said. "Laurie, you have to pick up the pace. I've got to be out that door five minutes ago."

Laurie told the story of Maria Hernandez's death and Jennifer's difficulty trying to deal with the body. She also told Calvin how Maria had been like a mother, not only to Jennifer but to herself as well from infancy to early teens, and concluded by saying that she and Jack wanted to go to India and needed a week to do so.

"My condolences," Calvin said. "I certainly can understand your wish to show your respects, but I'm not sure I understand why Jack has to go. To lose both of you at the same time puts us under a degree of strain unless we have significant warning."

"The reason Jack has to go is actually unrelated to the Hernandez death," Laurie explained. "Jack and I have been undergoing infertility treatment for about eight months. Currently, I'm in a cycle where I have been injecting myself with high levels of hormones, and within days I'll be giving myself the follicle-releasing shot. At that point—"

"Okay, okay!" Calvin exclaimed, stopping Laurie in midsentence. "I get it. Fine! You guys take your week. We'll manage." Calvin picked up his briefcase.

"Thank you, Dr. Washington," Laurie said. She felt a shiver of excitement. The trip was really going to happen. She followed the deputy chief out of his office.

"Give me a call when you'll be returning to work," Calvin called over his shoulder on his way to the front door.

"Will do," Laurie called back, as she headed for the elevators.

"One more thing," Calvin called, halfway out the door, keeping it open with his butt. "Give me a souvenir; get pregnant." With that he left, and the door swung shut.

Like the arrival of a sudden summer storm, a cloud swept over Laurie's nascent excitement. Calvin's last comment infuriated her. Turning back to the elevator, she let loose a barrage of expletives. With all the pressure she'd been putting on herself to get pregnant and the despondency it engendered, she didn't need more. For her, Calvin's weighing in on the issue was akin to sexual discrimination. After all, he wasn't about to put equivalent pressures on Jack.

Inside the elevator, she slammed the fifth-floor button with the heel of her fist. She could not believe how insensitive men could be. It was inexcusable.

Then, almost as soon as the fury had arrived, it dissipated. Sudden clairvoyance made Laurie know it was the hormones at work again, similar to her response last night with Jack and in the grocery store with the elderly woman. What surprised and embarrassed her was the speed with which such episodes took place. There wasn't time to be rational.

Once back in her office and feeling more in control of her emotions, Laurie put in a call to her friend Shirley Schoener. She knew it was a good time, because Shirley set aside eight to nine as the time to be available for phone and e-mail communication with her infertility patients. She answered immediately.

Knowing other patients would be calling, Laurie got right down to business, telling Shirley that she and Jack were leaving for India that evening and why.

"I'm jealous," Shirley responded. "You are going to find it so . . . interesting."

"That's how someone would describe something he or she didn't like but felt the need to be diplomatic about," Laurie responded.

"It's just that it is difficult to characterize your response to India," Shirley explained. "The country evokes such a wide range of emotions; it makes simple, generic descriptions useless. But I loved it!"

"We're not going to have time to really see India," Laurie said. "It's going to be in and out, I'm afraid."

"It doesn't matter. India is so full of contradictions all over that you'll sense what I'm talking about irrespective of how long you are there and no matter whether you go to Delhi, Mumbai, or Kolkata. It's so complex. I was there a year ago for a medical conference, and I just haven't been the same since. There's sublime beauty and urban ugliness all mixed together. There's extreme wealth and the most wrenching poverty you can imagine. I tell you, it takes your breath away. It's impossible not to be affected by it."

"Well, we'll certainly keep our eyes open, but we're going to be there to deal with Maria Hernandez's death. But we have to deal with my cycle as well."

"My goodness," Shirley exclaimed. "In my enthusiasm about India, I momentarily forgot about that. I feel so positive about this cycle; I don't want you to go away. I won't be able to take any credit for when you get pregnant, which I think you are going to do."

"Now, don't you put any extra pressure on me," Laurie said with a chuckle. She related her recent reaction to Calvin's innocent comment.

"And you were the woman who doubted you'd have a problem with hormones!" Shirley laughed.

"Don't remind me. But I really didn't think I would. PMS was never the bother that it is with some of the people I know."

"So we are going to need you to be seen by someone

in New Delhi the first full day after you arrive. We don't want to take any risk of hyperstimulation."

"That's the reason I'm calling. Do you know anyone in New Delhi you could recommend?"

"Lots," Shirley responded. "Thanks to my having been there for that meeting, I'm in contact with a number. Indian medicine is quite advanced, more than most people realize. I know at least a half dozen docs I'd feel comfortable recommending for you to see. Any specific requirements, like male or female, or any particular location in the city?"

"What might be handy is if any of those you recommend are associated with the Queen Victoria Hospital," Laurie said. "It might be helpful to know someone on the staff when we're dealing with the administration."

"I couldn't agree more. I tell you what. I'll make some calls right now. It's around quarter-to-six in the evening in Delhi, which is a perfect time. I could e-mail, too, but I think telephoning and talking directly will be better, and I don't seem to have any incoming calls."

"Thanks, Shirley," Laurie said. "I'm certainly going to owe you for all this, but I don't know how I'm going to repay. I seriously doubt you want any in-kind professional services."

"Don't even joke like that," Shirley said. "I'm too superstitious."

Disconnecting, Laurie reflexively checked her watch. The Indian visa place didn't open until nine, so she had some time. The first thing she did was call up the airlines and use her credit card to pay for the tickets she had reserved. Next she called Jennifer. The phone rang four or five times, and when it was finally answered, Laurie expected voicemail. It was Jennifer, who sounded out of breath.

Laurie identified herself and then asked if she were calling at a bad time, because she could easily call back.

"No, this is fine," Jennifer said, breathing deeply. "I'm having dinner in a fancy Chinese restaurant here in the hotel, and when the phone rang, I ran out here to the lobby to answer it. Guess who I'm having dinner with?"

"I couldn't begin to guess."

"A Mrs. Benfatti. She's the wife of the man who died at the Queen Victoria last night."

"That's a coincidence."

"Not really. I looked her up and we had lunch. I have to say his death has some strange parallels with Granny's."

"Really?" Laurie questioned. She wondered if they were real parallels or imagined.

"Gosh, here I am blabbing away, and you called me. Please tell me you are coming to India."

"We are indeed coming to India," Laurie said, the excitement showing in her voice.

"Terrific!" Jennifer cheered. "I'm so pleased, you have no idea. Tell Dr. Washington thank you, thank you, thank you."

"He did send you his regards," Laurie said. "Have there been any big changes in the situation there?"

"Not really. They are still trying to push me to give them the green light. I did tell them that you guys were coming and will be there Friday morning sometime."

"Did you mention that we happen to be forensic pathologists?"

"Oh, yeah, most definitely."

"And their response?"

"Another lecture that there will be no autopsy. They are very adamant."

"We'll see," Laurie said.

"I made it a point to talk with the nurse who took care of Granny. She's this beauty queen you won't believe with a figure to die for."

"Coming from you, that's quite a compliment."

"I'm not in her league. She's the kind of woman who probably can eat anything, and she just looks better and better. She's also really nice. At first when I met her she acted weird."

"How so?"

"Shy or embarrassed, I couldn't tell which. It turns out she was afraid I would be angry at her."

"Why would you be angry?"

"That's what I asked her. You know what it turned out to be? Granny was the first patient she has lost since she'd graduated from nursing school. Isn't that touching?"

"Did you learn anything about your grandmother from her?" Laurie asked. She didn't comment on Jennifer's rhetorical question. At first blush, Laurie didn't understand how Maria being the nurse's first nursing death meshed with the nurse's being worried Jennifer might be mad at her. Laurie assumed it had to be a cultural thing.

"Not really," Jennifer said, but then corrected herself.

"Except she said Granny was cyanotic when she was found."

"True cyanosis?" Laurie questioned.

"That's what she said, and I asked her specifically. But she was relating this secondhand. Granny didn't die on her shift but on the evening shift. She had learned it from the nurse who had come upon Granny after Granny had already died."

"Maybe you'd better not play medical investigation," Laurie suggested. "You might ruffle too many feathers."

"You're probably right," Jennifer agreed, "and especially not with you guys coming. What are your flight details?"

Laurie gave the flight numbers and the expected arrival time. "Now, you don't have to come to the airport like you suggested," Laurie said. "We can just jump in a taxi."

"I want to come. I'll take a hotel car. I mean, my expenses are being covered."

Under those circumstances, Laurie agreed for Jennifer to come out to fetch them when they arrived. "Now I better let you get back to your dinner and your dinner companion."

"Speaking of Mrs. Benfatti, I offered that you would look into the situation with her husband. I hope you don't mind. There are parallels, as I've said."

"We'll look first at the parallels and then decide," Laurie said.

"One more thing," Jennifer said. "I went to the U.S. embassy this afternoon and spoke to a very nice consular officer who was very helpful."

"Did you learn anything?"

"It turns out that the case manager at the Queen Victoria was giving me the true story about bringing bodies back to the States. You have to jump through a lot of bureaucratic hoops, and it is expensive. So I'm leaning in the direction of cremation."

"We'll discuss it more when I get there," Laurie said. "Now get back to your dinner."

"Aye-aye, sir. See you tomorrow night," Jennifer said gaily.

Laurie replaced the receiver. For a moment she kept her hand on it, thinking about a heart attack and general cyanosis. When the heart fails, the pumping action stops, and you don't get general cyanosis. Cyanosis generally comes from the lungs failing and the pumping continuing.

The phone under Laurie's hand rang harshly, causing her to start. With her pulse racing, she snapped the receiver back up and blurted a hurried hello.

"I am looking for Dr. Laurie Montgomery," a pleasant voice said.

"This is she," Laurie answered with curiosity.

"My name is Dr. Arun Ram. I just spoke with Dr. Shirley Schoener. She said you were imminently coming to New Delhi and are in the middle of an infertility cycle using hormones. She said you will need to have the size of your follicles followed and your estradiol blood levels checked."

"That's true. Thank you for calling. I expected to hear back from Dr. Schoener with some numbers so I would have to make the calls."

"It is no bother. It was my suggestion, since Dr. Schoener said she had been just speaking with you. I wanted to let you know I would be honored to be of assistance. Dr. Schoener told me a little about you, and I am very impressed. There was a time in my early training when I aspired to become a forensic pathologist from watching American TV shows. Unfortunately, I became disenchanted. The facilities in this country are very bad because of our infamous bureaucracy."

"That's too bad. We need good people in the specialty, and India would be well served if the facilities and the field were improved."

"Dr. Schoener had first called a colleague of mine, Dr. Daya Mishra, who is obviously a woman, if you would prefer. But Dr. Schoener said you were interested in someone with admitting privileges at the Queen Victoria Hospital, so Dr. Mishra recommended me."

"I would be very grateful if you would see me. My husband and I have other business at the Queen Victoria Hospital, so it will be convenient."

"When are you coming exactly?"

"We are leaving this evening from New York and scheduled to arrive in Delhi late Thursday night, October nineteenth, at twenty-two-fifty."

"Where are you in this current infertility cycle?"

"Day seven, but more important, on Monday, Dr. Schoener estimated five days before the trigger shot should be given."

"So the last time you were seen was Monday, and everything was fine."

"Everything was fine."

"Then I believe I need to see you Friday morning. What time would you prefer? Anytime is good since Friday is a research day and my calendar is clear."

"I don't know," Laurie said. "How about eight a.m."

"Eight a.m. it is," Dr. Arun Ram said.

After terminating the call with Dr. Ram, Laurie called Shirley back and thanked her for the referral.

"You'll like him," Shirley said. "He's very smart, has a great sense of humor and good stats."

"One can't ask for much more than that," Laurie said before ringing off.

With all the calls out of the way, Laurie glanced briefly at her watch. It was time to head over to the company to which India had outsourced its visa service. She got out her and Jack's passports from her briefcase and wedded them with the photos they'd had taken that morning.

With the passports and photos tucked into her shoulder bag along with her mobile phone, Laurie stepped back out of her office and headed for the elevators. When she heard the elevator door open ahead, she quickened her step to catch it and bumped head-on into her office-mate, Dr. Riva Mehta, exiting. Each apologized. Laurie actually laughed.

"My, you are in a good mood," Riva commented.

"I guess I am," Laurie responded cheerily.

"Don't tell me you are pregnant," Riva said. Not only were Riva and Laurie officemates, they were also confidantes. Riva was the only person other than Shirley with whom she had shared all the stresses of the infertility treatment.

"I wish," Laurie said. "No, Jack and I are making an emergency trip to India." Laurie struggled with the elevator door that desperately wanted to close.

"That's terrific," Riva said. "Where in India?" Riva and her parents had emigrated to the United States when she was eleven.

"New Delhi," Laurie said. "Actually, I'm on my way over to get our Indian visas. I'll be back in a half-hour or so. I'd love to talk to you about it and maybe get some tips."

"By all means," Riva said with a wave.

Laurie ducked into the elevator car and let the insistent door close. As she descended, she thought about Riva's comment regarding her mood and realized that she was truly on a high, magnified by the low she'd been on over the last two to three months. Vaguely, she hoped that the strain of infertility wasn't making her bipolar.

Getting off at the basement level, Laurie hurried down to the autopsy room. Knowing she was going to be in there for only a few moments, she grabbed just a gown and a hat, and pushed in through the main double doors. Although it was almost eight-forty-five, Jack and Vinnie were the sole team working. Several other mortuary techs were preparing cases and putting out bodies, but the associated docs had yet to appear. Jack and Vinnie were well along. The body they were working on already had the large Y incision over the chest and abdomen sutured. At the moment, the individual's skull cap was off and they were working on the brain.

"How's it going?" Laurie asked, coming up alongside Jack.

"We're having a ball as usual," Jack responded, straightening up and stretching.

"A typical gunshot suicide?" Laurie asked.

Jack let out a short laugh. "Hardly. At this point, it's pretty clear it was homicide."

"Really?" Laurie questioned. "How so?"

Jack reached over to the corpse and grabbed the reflected and inverted scalp and pulled it from covering the face back into its original position. High on the side of the head and in the center of a shaved area was a sharply defined circular deep-red entrance wound surrounded by a number of two-to-three-inch black speckles.

"My word," Laurie exclaimed. "You are right. This is not suicide."

"And that is not all," Jack said. "The path of the bullet is steeply downward such that it ended up in the subcutaneous tissues of the neck."

"How can you guys read so much into this?" Vinnie asked.

"It's easy," Laurie said. "When someone shoots themselves, they almost always place the barrel against the skin. What happens then is the explosive gases go into the wound along with the bullet. The resultant entrance wound becomes raggedly stellate as the skin blows away from the skull and tears."

"And you see this stippling?" Jack said, pointing with the handle of a scalpel to the ring of black spots around the wound. "That's all gunpowder residue. In a suicide, all that goes into the wound." Then, turning back to Laurie, he asked, "How far away do you think the barrel was when the gun was fired?"

Laurie shrugged. "Maybe fifteen to twenty inches."

"That's exactly my thought," Jack agreed. "And I think our victim was lying down when it happened."

"You'd better let the boss know as soon as possible," Laurie advised. "This is the kind of case that invariably has political fallout."

"That's my plan," Jack said. "It's amazing, isn't it, how many cases we see where the manner of death is different after the autopsy than what it was thought to be before."

"It's what makes our job so important," Laurie said.

"Hey!" Jack voiced. "Did you get to see Calvin yet?"

"Oh, yeah!" Laurie said remembering her mission. "That's why I popped down here. I'm on my way to Travisa to get our Indian visas. Calvin has given us the green light for a week."

"Damn," Jack said, but then he laughed before Laurie could get miffed.

Chapter 20

OCTOBER 17, 2007
WEDNESDAY, 7:40 P.M.
NEW DELHI, INDIA

Raj Khatwani cracked the door from the stairwell and peered out into the wedge of the third-floor corridor of the Aesculapian Medical Center hospital that was visible. There was no one in his line of sight, but he could hear a medication cart approaching with its characteristic rattling of glass against glass. He let the door close. Through its fire-resistant thickness, he heard the cart roll past.

Leaning back against the concrete-block wall, he tried to control his breathing. With the tension he was experiencing, it was difficult. Sweat dotted the upper part of his forehead. All he could think of was his new respect for Veena and Samira. Now that he was in the middle of putting his first patient to sleep, he realized it was a lot more stressful than he had anticipated, especially after Samira had told him it was a breeze. *Some breeze,* he thought grudgingly.

When an adequate amount of time had passed, he cracked the door again. Not seeing anyone or hearing anything, he opened the door farther and slowly stuck his head out, looking up and down the hallway. The only people he saw were two nurses a distance down the main corridor at the central desk, talking to an ambulatory patient. They were far enough away so that Raj could just barely hear them. In the opposite direction, there were only three more patient rooms on either side of the corridor before a terminal conservatory. There were conservatories at both ends of the long corridor, each filled with plants and chairs for those patients able to use them.

In his mind, Raj could hear Samira's advice: Don't be seen, but if you are, act normally. Let your nurse's uniform do the talking. *Don't be seen!* Raj scoffed silently. Since he was a big man, slightly more than two hundred pounds, not being seen was particularly difficult, especially on a full hospital floor with nurses and aides scurrying about on any one of myriad possible errands.

Raj had gone to Samira and Veena's room to seek advice that evening before he'd left for the Aesculapian Medical Center. He didn't think he'd really need help and did it more out of respect for his female colleagues, but now that he was there, he was glad he did. Samira had finally admitted she had been nervous, which was good to know, since he, too, was definitely nervous. Veena, however, had said nothing.

Of the twelve nursing employees of Nurses International, as the only male, Raj provided a stark foil for the other eleven attractive and quite feminine females. He had medium-dark flawless skin, very dark closely cropped hair, darkly penetrating eyes, and a pencil-line mustache beneath a slightly hooked nose. But his most characteristic physical feature was his physique. He had broad shoulders, a narrow waist, and bulging muscles. He looked every inch the enthusiastic weight lifter and black-belt martial arts expert he was. But despite his appearance, Raj was not a masculine-acting individual, but nor was he feminine, at least in his mind. Nor was he gay. He thought of himself as just Raj. The seemingly out-of-character weight lifting and martial arts had originally been his father's idea. Recognizing early his son's social proclivities, his father had wanted him to have some protection in a socially cruel world. As he got older, Raj liked the weight lifting, as looking buff had become enjoyable because of the attention it engendered from his mostly female friends, and he liked the martial arts because, in his mind, it was more like dance than an aggressive sport.

Suddenly Raj heard loud footsteps against bare concrete. To his horror, he realized that someone was behind him in the stairwell, descending from above. From the proximity of the noise he could tell the person was imminently going to reach and round the landing between the third and fourth floors, at which point Raj and his loitering would be in full view! Raj knew he had two choices if he didn't want to be seen: either he could run back down the stairs, maybe as far as the basement, or he could exit onto the third floor and take the risk of being seen there.

The footsteps were rapidly descending; Raj had to

decide! He was in a panic. He heard the more hollow sound as the approaching individual reached the landing. In an even greater panic, Raj opened the door to the third floor only enough to step through and then used his hip to push it closed. Not realizing he'd been holding his breath, Raj allowed himself to breathe as he glanced up and down the corridor. Behind him, in the stairwell, he could hear the now muffled steps descending toward the third-floor landing. For fear whoever it was might try to exit on the third floor, Raj pushed off the stairwell door and headed for his patient's room. He'd been forced into action. It had been like standing at the edge of a pool afraid of the water and then being pushed in. Raj did not look back until he'd reached David Lucas's door. Just ahead, two nurses emerged from the next patient room, in deep conversation about the individual's care. Luckily, they immediately turned toward the central desk. Had they looked in the opposite direction, they would have locked eyes with Raj a mere ten feet away, and he would have had some serious explaining to do.

Luckily, he was able to slip unseen into the room, but then he stopped just inside the door. He heard hushed conversation. Mr. David Lucas was not alone!

Confused about whether to stay or flee, Raj froze. A second later a wave of relief spread over him. It wasn't a visitor; it was the TV. With a surge of confidence, Raj walked farther into the room, rounding the outer wall of the bathroom, affording him a view of the strikingly obese patient propped up in the hospital bed. The patient was asleep. A nasogastric tube issued forth from one nostril and was connected to suction. About a half-cup of yellowish, blood-tinged fluid could be seen in the collecting bottle. A cardiac monitor on the wall behind Mr. Lucas played out a regular rhythm. All in all, the entire scene looked identical to how it had looked when Raj had left for the day a little after three that afternoon.

Raj reached into the pocket of his white nurse's trousers and pulled out the syringe he'd prepared back at the bungalow. In contrast to Veena and Samira, he'd not had to go to the empty operating room to get the succinylcholine, and for that he was pleased. He knew he had Samira to thank, and had already done so.

After checking the syringe to be certain none of the fluid had leaked out, a distinct possibility, since he had actually overfilled the 10 cc syringe, Raj was ready to go. He'd overfilled the syringe on purpose, thinking that the last thing he wanted to do was not give enough.

Returning to the door, Raj gave one last look up and down the corridor. There was one nurse walking toward him, but she turned into a room and disappeared. Sensing the time was never going to be better, he returned to the bedside. Carefully picking up the IV line without pulling on it, he took the cap off the needle with his teeth, and then gently poked the needle through the IV port. There was no need to worry about sterile technique.

Thus prepared, Raj paused for another moment, listening if there were any telltale sounds from the hall that he could hear over that of the lowered TV. There weren't, so he used both hands to discharge the entire contents of the syringe into the IV line in a large bolus. Having not stoppered the upper part of the IV line beforehand, the first thing he noticed was a rapid rise in the level of fluid in the millepore chamber. But that effect was overshadowed by the patient's response. As Samira had warned, there were almost instantaneous fasciculations of the facial muscles combined with David Lucas's eyes shooting open. He also started to cry out as his extremities began a series of myotonic jerks.

Raj took a step back, shocked by what he was observing. Although he'd been cautioned, the reaction had been more rapid and more disconcerting than he'd expected. He watched for another beat as the patient tried to sit up but immediately collapsed back like a freezer bag full of fluid. With a sense of revulsion, Raj turned and fled. The problem was, he didn't get far. As he yanked open the door to the corridor, he literally ran into a white-coated figure who'd just raised his hand to push open the door that because of Raj was no longer there.

Raj grabbed the man in a bear hug to keep from knocking him over as his inertia carried them out into the corridor. "I'm so sorry," the befuddled nurse blurted. The collision had been so unexpected, and making it even worse, he recognized the man. It was Dr. Nirav Krishna, David Lucas's surgeon, on late rounds before heading home.

"My God, man," Dr. Krishna snapped. "What the bloody devil is the rush?"

For a brief moment of utter panic, Raj tried to think of something to say. Realizing there was no way out, he told the truth. "It's an emergency. Mr. Lucas is having an emergency."

Without saying anything, Dr. Krishna pushed by Raj and dashed into the room. Coming to the bedside, he saw David Lucas's beginning cyanosis. Out of the corner of his eye he saw from the monitor the heart was beating relatively normally. It was then that he realized the patient was not breathing. He did not see any fasciculation, because they had already stopped.

"Get the emergency cart!" Dr. Krishna yelled. He yanked out the nasogastric tube and threw it to the side. Grabbing the bed control, he began to lower the head. Seeing Raj glued to his spot, he again yelled for him to get the crash cart. They were going to have to resuscitate.

Raj recovered from his paralysis but not his terror. He raced from the room and ran headlong down the corridor toward the nurses' station, where the emergency cart was stored. As he ran he tried to think of what he should do. He couldn't think of anything other than to help. The surgeon had gotten a good look at him, and if he just disappeared, he'd surely be implicated.

Reaching the central station, Raj blurted out to the two nurses sitting at the desk that there was a code in room 304. Without stopping, Raj threw open the door to the storeroom where the crash cart was kept, grabbed it, backed out with it in tow, and then raced back down to David Lucas's room, making an enormous racket in the process. When he got there, the lights had been turned up. Dr. Krishna was doing mouth-to-mouth, and to

Raj's added horror, Mr. Lucas didn't look so bad; his cyanosis had faded to a large extent.

"Ambu bag!" Dr. Krishna shouted. One of the floor nurses who'd raced after Raj grabbed it from the cart and tossed it to the doctor. Dr. Krishna repositioned the patient's head, applied the bag, and began respiring the victim. Now the chest was moving even better than it was with the mouth-to-mouth. "Oxygen!" Dr. Krishna barked. The other floor nurse got the cylinder over to the head of the bed, and between Dr. Krishna's compressions, she connected it to the breathing bag. Within seconds Mr. Lucas's color improved dramatically; it was now actually pink.

As these activities progressed, Raj had an opportunity to appreciate just what kind of disaster he was in. He didn't even know for certain whether it would be better if the patient died or was saved. Nor did he know if it would be better for him to slink away or stay, and the uncertainty kept him riveted in place.

At that point the evening house doctor, Dr. Sarla Dayal, arrived at a run. She crowded in at the head of the bed, and Dr. Krishna gave her a rapid summary of what had happened.

"When I got here he was definitely cyanotic," Dr. Krishna said, "and the cardiac monitor looked reasonable, but it's only one lead. The problem was, he'd stopped breathing."

"You think it was a stroke?" Dr. Dayal questioned. "Maybe a heart attack precipitated a stroke of some sort. The patient has a history of occlusive cardiovascular disease."

"Could be," Dr. Krishna agreed. "It does look now like the cardiac monitor is telling us something. The rhythm is certainly slowing."

Dr. Dayal placed a hand on the patient's chest. "The heart rate is slowing and feels rather faint."

"It's probably the patient's obesity."

"The patient also feels really hot. Take a feel. I'll breathe for a while."

Dr. Krishna turned the ambu bag over to the house doctor and felt David Lucas's chest. "I agree with you." He looked over to one of the floor nurses. "Let's get a temperature!" The nurse nodded and got the patient's thermometer.

"Do we have a cardiologist on call?" Dr. Krishna asked.

"We certainly do," Dr. Dayal said. She called over to the other floor nurse to give Dr. Ashok Mishra a call and ask him to come in immediately. "Tell him it's an emergency," she added.

"I don't like that the heart rate keeps slowing," Dr. Krishna said, watching the monitor. "Let's get a stat potassium level."

The floor nurse who was not on the phone drew some blood and rushed it off to the lab herself.

To stay out of the way, Raj had slowly backed away until he'd hit up against the wall. He was thankful that people were so involved in the resuscitation activity that he was being virtually ignored. He again began to think about slipping out, although the specter of drawing attention to himself made him stay put.

"Dr. Mishra will be in as soon as he can," the nurse

yelled out while hanging up the phone. "He's finishing up with another emergency."

"That's not good," Dr. Krishna said. "I have a bad feeling. With this progressive bradycardia, it might be over by then. This heart is definitely having trouble. It looks to my untrained eye as if the QRS interval is widening."

"The patient definitely has a fever," the nurse blurted, staring at the thermometer in disbelief.

"What is it?" Dr. Krishna demanded.

"It's over one hundred and nine."

"Shit!" Dr. Krishna shouted. "That's hyperpyrexia. Get ice!"

The floor nurse ran out of the room.

"You must be right, Dr. Dayal," Dr. Krishna moaned. "We must be dealing with a heart attack and a stroke."

The nurse who'd dashed up to the lab returned on the run. She was out of breath but managed to say, "The emergency potassium level is nine-point-one milliequivalents per liter. The tech says he's never seen it that high, so he's going to repeat it."

"Yikes!" Dr. Krishna exclaimed. "I've never seen a potassium level like that. Let's give some calcium gluconate: ten milliliters of a ten percent solution. Draw it up. We'll give it over a couple of minutes. Plus, I want twenty units of regular insulin. And do we have cation-exchange resin available? If so, get it."

The floor nurse came back with ice. Dr. Krishna dumped it over the patient, and a lot clattered to the floor. The nurse then ran back out to try to get the resin while the other began to draw up the medication.

"Damn!" Dr. Krishna shouted as the blip on the monitor flatlined. "We lost the heartbeat." He climbed up on the bed and began closed-chest massage.

The CPR attempt went on for another twenty minutes, but despite the medication, the ice, the cation-exchange resin, and a lot of effort, a heartbeat was not regained. "I think we are going to have to give up," Dr. Krishna said finally. "It's intuitive what we are doing is not working. And I'm afraid rigor mortis is setting in already, probably from the patient's hyperthermia. It's time to stop." He let up from compressing the chest. Although Dr. Dayal had offered to relieve him ten minutes earlier, he'd refused. "It's my patient," he'd explained.

After thanking the two floor nurses for their help and Dr. Dayal for hers, Dr. Krishna pulled down the sleeves of his white coat from where he'd pushed them up at the outset of the resuscitation attempt, and started for the door. "I'll do the paperwork," he called over his shoulder as the others began to pick up the debris, put the room in order, and prepare the body. "As per that e-mail directive that came out just today from admin about reporting deaths immediately, I'll also call CEO Khajan Chawdhry to give him the bad news."

"Thank you, Dr. Krishna," the two nurses echoed.

"I'll do the phoning to Khajan, if you'd like," Dr. Dayal offered.

"I think I should do it," Dr. Krishna rejoined. "He was my patient, and I should take whatever heat this is going to create. With those deaths over at the Queen Victoria garnering international media attention, this episode is going to be looked upon as very inconvenient, to say the least. I'm sure there'll be great pressure to keep it under wraps and dispose of it promptly. It's too bad, because under more normal circumstances, I'd actually like to learn the physiological sequence of events, starting with the patient's history of obstructive heart disease, right up to the hyperpyrexia and the massively elevated potassium level."

"I doubt we'll ever know," Dr. Dayal said. "I agree with you about the admin wanting to keep this quiet. But if Khajan wants to talk to me, tell him I'm here at the hospital and can be paged."

Dr. Krishna waved over his shoulder to indicate he'd heard. He was about to turn down the short corridor to the room's door to the hall when his eyes passed over Raj. Reflexively they snapped back to the statue-like nurse. "My gosh, son, I forgot all about you. Come with me!" Dr. Krishna waved for Raj to follow, then preceded him out the door.

Vainly hoping he would have continued to be ignored as if he were invisible, Raj reluctantly followed the surgeon. Once again, his heart was racing. He had no idea of what to expect, but it was going to be bad.

Out in the hall, Dr. Krishna had waited for him. "Sorry to have ignored you, young man," the surgeon said. "I've been seriously preoccupied, but now I recognize you. I saw you this morning when I stopped down here to check on Lucas. You're the day nurse, if I'm not mistaken. What was your name again?"

"Raj Khatwani," Raj hesitantly said.

"Oh, yes, Raj! My, you have long hours."

"I'm not working. I get off after three."

"You're still here at the hospital and you certainly look like you are working, uniform and all."

"I came back to the hospital to use the library. I wanted to learn about the surgery you did on Mr. Lucas. Obesity surgery was not included in our nursing-school curricula."

"That's very impressive! You remind me of myself when I was a student your age! Self-motivation is key to success in medicine. Come, walk with me down to the central desk."

The two men began walking, with Raj having trouble resisting the temptation to flee. He knew that the longer he stayed and the more he said, the more apt he was to incriminate himself. He could even feel the succinylcholine syringe in his pants pocket, pressing against his thigh.

"Did your research result in any questions I might answer for you?"

Desperately, Raj tried to think up a question he could ask to make it seem believable that he'd truly been studying. "Umm . . ." he voiced. "How do you know how small to make the stomach?"

"Good question," Dr. Krishna said, switching to a professional mien as he answered it with the help of elaborate hand gestures. He caught Raj's eyes longingly taking in the stairwell door, which they were passing. The surgeon stopped, interrupting himself. "I'm sorry," he said. "Do you have to be someplace?"

"I do have to get home," Raj said.

"Don't let me hold you up," Dr. Krishna said. "But I

do have a question. How was it you were in Mr. Lucas's room just when he suffered his terminal event?"

Raj's mind desperately raced for an explanation. Making the tension even worse, he knew that every moment he hesitated, the less convincing he would be. "After the reading I'd done, I had some questions for the patient. But the second I got into his room, I knew there was something seriously wrong."

"Was he conscious?"

"I don't know. He was writhing around as if in pain."

"That was probably the heart attack. It's what usually kills these overweight patients. Well, you almost saved the day. Thank you."

"You're welcome," Raj said with a gulp, almost giving himself away. He couldn't believe he was being thanked.

"I have some good journal articles on obesity surgery I can loan you if you'd like."

"That would be terrific," Raj managed.

After a quick shake of hands, the two men parted, Raj disappearing into the stairwell and Dr. Krishna heading for the central desk to fill out the death certificate and call the care manager and Khajan Chawdhry.

Once inside the stairwell, Raj had to pause. His heart was beating at such a rate that he felt mildly dizzy. Squatting down on his haunches for twenty or so seconds relieved the dizziness, and after wiping the cold sweat from his forehead he stood back up, holding on to the handrail. Relieved, he took a few steps down, and when he sensed he was back to normal, he let himself run down the rest of the stairs to the lobby floor.

Pleased that the lobby was as deserted as it was, Raj

half ran across the room to the main exit door and left the building. Outside, he forced himself to slow to a rapid walk, finding it difficult not to give in to his panic and bolt. He felt like a bank robber exiting a bank with all the cash and every eye on him. At any moment he half expected to hear a shrill whistle and a shouted command to stop.

Reaching the still-crowded street, Raj hailed an auto rickshaw, and it wasn't until the Aesculapian Medical Center faded from view out the small rear window that he could begin to relax. Facing forward in a near trance, Raj terrorized himself by rehashing the whole unfortunate episode. He was afraid to tell the others, but he was more afraid not to tell them, unsure of what the ultimate fallout was going to be.

After passing through the front door of the bungalow, Raj stopped to listen. He could feel the vibration of the large subwoofer of the video system pumping out the bass in the formal living room, so he headed in that direction. He found Cal, Durell, Petra, and Santana, along with Veena, Samira, and two other nurses, watching a taut action DVD. Durell was enthusiastically into it and cheering on the protagonists, who were facing insurmountable odds.

Raj went up behind Cal, and after a moment's hesitation gently shook his shoulder.

Tense from the movie, Cal jumped when he felt the nudge, took one look at who'd caught his attention, and then paused the movie. "Raj! We're glad to see you back. How did it go?"

"I'm afraid it did not go well at all," Raj admitted, and dropped his eyes from Cal's to the floor. "It was a disaster."

There was a moment of silence as all eyes regarded Raj.

"I thought we shouldn't have gone ahead with another so soon," Veena blurted out. "You should have listened to me!"

Cal raised his hand to quiet her. "I think we should hear from Raj before we jump to any conclusions. Tell us what happened, Raj. Don't spare the details."

Without much embellishment, Raj told the whole story, from colliding with the doctor to being thanked by the doctor in the hospital corridor after the failed resuscitation attempt. When he was finished he fell silent, still looking down at the floor and avoiding eye contact with anyone.

"That was it?" Cal asked, after a brief silence. Cal was relieved. He and everyone else had expected something a lot worse, like Raj being accused of doing what he in reality did do. "And let me review. The working diagnosis was heart attack and stroke of some sort. That's what will be on the death certificate?"

Raj nodded. "That's my understanding."

"And you heard nothing about an inquest, an autopsy, or any investigation?"

"No. Nothing like that. What I did overhear from the surgeon was that an e-mail had come out that obligated him to call the hospital CEO and report the death immediately. Apparently there's concern because of the two deaths at the Queen Victoria Hospital causing international attention. They are going to want to suppress any attention toward tonight's death."

"That sounds almost too good to me," Cal said. "Under the circumstances I can't imagine that this kind of potential disaster could have any better outcome. Raj, it seems as if you did a terrific job."

Raj began to perk up. He even made eye contact with several people. Led by Cal, there was even spontaneous applause. "Let's get a bunch of Kingfisher from the fridge and make a toast to Raj," Cal said.

"What about stopping any more episodes?" Veena questioned. "I think we should decide now to stop them, at least for a few days. Let's not push our luck."

"That seems reasonable," Cal said, "but let's get full advantage of this one. Did you get the patient's hospital record?" Cal asked Raj. Raj went into one of his pockets and pulled out his USB storage device and the succinylcholine syringe. Cal took the storage device and handed it to Santana. "Let's get this death episode right to CNN. With the failed resuscitation attempt, it should make good copy and have even more impact. Encourage them to get it on the air ASAP."

Santana took the storage device. "It will only take me a few minutes, then I'll be back for that beer. How about waiting."

Chapter **21**

Jennifer's sleep pattern had never been so out of whack. When she'd returned to her room from having dinner with Lucinda Benfatti, she was so tired she'd almost fallen asleep brushing her teeth. But once she'd gotten into bed and turned out the lights, her mind started waking up. Before she knew it, she was anticipating Laurie and Jack's arrival with great excitement and wondering whether she should have already reserved one of the hotel cars to pick them up. It seemed that ten p.m. to two a.m. was when most of the international flights arrived, so the demand for the hotel's vehicles was the highest then.

· Worried that she might already be out of luck, Jennifer sat up, turned on the light, and called down to the concierge's desk. Talking with the concierge, she learned something she didn't know. An airport pickup for Amal

Palace guests was complimentary, and a vehicle was already scheduled to pick up Laurie and Jack. Asking if she could join the pickup, the concierge assured her she could, told her when it would be leaving, and promised to let transportation know that she would be going along.

With that job out of the way, Jennifer turned the light off again and wriggled down under the covers. At first she started out on her back with her hands comfortably folded on her chest. But with her mind activated from making the car reservation, she found herself puzzling over whether Laurie and Jack would have more luck dealing with the case manager than she did, and what that would mean in regard to a possible autopsy.

A few minutes later, Jennifer turned on her side while she thought about cyanosis and wondered if Herbert Benfatti had been cyanotic, and how she might find out.

Five minutes later, she was on her stomach thinking about what she should do the following day. She certainly had no intention of hanging around the Queen Victoria Hospital and being badgered all day. She thought she might try to do a bit of sightseeing, even though, as preoccupied as she was, she thought she might find it tedious. She knew herself well enough to know that even in the best of circumstances, she wasn't much of the sightseeing type as far as old buildings and tombs were concerned. What she did find interesting was people.

At that point she started thinking about how little she knew about India, Indians, and Indian culture.

"Damn!" Jennifer suddenly said to the darkness. Despite her body's insistence that it was exhausted, her mind was buzzing like a beehive. With frustration Jennifer sat up, turned the bedside lamp on, and got out of bed. In the walk-in closet she located the several Indian guidebooks she'd gotten at LAX, brought them back into the room, and tossed them onto the bed. She then went over to the TV and angled it from pointing at the couch to point at the bed. Leaping back into the bed, she used the remote to tune in CNN International. She then cursed again, realizing she'd forgotten water. Climbing back out of bed and going to the minibar refrigerator, she got herself a bottle of cold mineral water and popped the top. Back in the bed, she puffed the pillows and eased herself against the headboard. Finally comfortable, she cracked one of the guidebooks and turned to the section on Old Delhi.

As the CNN anchors droned on about clever French entrepreneurs dreaming up Disney-themed hotels for Dubai, Jennifer read about the Red Fort built by Mughal emperors. There were lots of facts and figures and names and dates. On the next page there was the description of the largest mosque in India, with equally boring statistics, such as how many people it could hold for Friday services. But then she came upon something that did really interest her: a lengthy description of the renowned bazaar of Old Delhi.

Jennifer was trying to locate the world-famous spice bazaar on the guidebook's cutaway map when the TV caught her attention. The woman anchor announced, "Following up on the news of two deaths in the heretofore vaunted Indian medical tourism hospitals, there has now been a third only an hour or so ago. Although the first two deaths occurred at the Queen Victoria Hospital in New Delhi, tonight's tragic death occurred at the Aesculapian Medical Center, also in New Delhi, and involved a healthy, although obese, forty-eight-year-old from Jacksonville, Florida, named David Lucas. He'd undergone stomach-stapling surgery this morning. He is survived by a wife and two children, aged ten and twelve."

Mesmerized, Jennifer sat up straight.

"Such a tragedy," the male anchor agreed, "especially with the children involved. Did they say what the cause of death was?"

"They did. It seems that it was some sort of heart attack/stroke combination."

"It's awful. People going to India to save a few bucks, and wham, they come home in a box. If I were facing surgery and had to choose between it costing a little less and dying versus spending a bit more and living, there's no doubt what I'd chose."

"No question. And apparently a number of other clients are reacting the same way. CNN has been getting a rising blizzard of reports and e-mails of people canceling surgery scheduled to be done in India."

"I'm not at all surprised," the male anchor said. "As I said, if it were me, I certainly would."

When the anchors switched to another subject dealing with Halloween coming up in a mere two weeks, Jennifer lowered the TV's volume. She was again stumped. Another cardiac death in a private Indian hospital involving a healthy American occurring about the same time postsurgery.

Jennifer looked at the clock and tried to figure out

what time it was in Atlanta. She came up with about eleven-thirty in the morning. Impulsively, she grabbed her phone, and by using AT&T directory assistance got herself connected to CNN. After explaining what she was interested in and being switched around from several different departments, she finally got a woman on the line who seemed to know what she was talking about. The woman introduced herself as Jamielynn.

"I just saw a segment on CNN International about a medical tourism death," Jennifer said. "What I'd like to know is, who—"

"I'm sorry, we don't divulge anything about our sources," Jamielynn said, interrupting Jennifer.

"I was afraid of that," Jennifer said. "But what about the time the story came in. That wouldn't compromise your source in any way."

"I suppose not," Jamielynn agreed. "Let me ask! Hold the line!" Jamielynn was gone for a few minutes before coming back. "I can tell you when it came in but that's all. It came in at ten-forty-one a.m. EST and was broadcast the first time at eleven-oh-two."

"Thank you," Jennifer said. She wrote it down on the pad by the phone. She then called down to the concierge and asked for the phone number of the Aesculapian Medical Center. Once she had it, she dialed it. She had to wait for a number of rings. When it was answered, she asked to be connected to David Lucas's room.

"I'm sorry, we are not allowed to ring patient rooms after eight."

"How do family members call after eight?" Jennifer thought she knew but wanted to ask anyway.

"They have the direct-dial number."

Jennifer hung up without saying good-bye. She felt she was on a roll, and called down to the front desk. She asked if there was a guest in the hotel by the name of Mrs. David Lucas. As she waited, she wondered if she'd be able to muster the courage to call the woman so soon after the event.

"I'm sorry, but we have no Mrs. Lucas registered at the hotel," the front desk clerk said.

"Are you certain?" Jennifer questioned. She felt an immediate letdown.

The clerk spelled the name and asked if Jennifer had an alternate spelling. Jennifer said no and discouragingly was about to hang up when she thought of something. "I'm here at the Amal Palace Hotel because of the Queen Victoria Hospital. Do other private hospitals put their international patients' next of kin at other hotels?"

"Yes, they do," the clerk said. "Even the Queen Victoria does as well if we are fully booked."

"Can you tell me what hotels I might try?"

"Yes, of course. Any of the other five-star hotels. The Taj Mahal, the Oberoi, the Imperial, the Ashok, and the Grand are the most popular, but the Park and the Hyatt Regency are used as well. It depends on availability. If you'd like to be connected to any of these hotels, the operator will be happy to do it."

Taking the clerk's advice, Jennifer called the other hotels in the order in which they had been given. It didn't take long. Jennifer scored on the third hotel, the Imperial.

"Can I connect you?" the Imperial operator asked.

Jennifer hesitated. She would be seriously disturbing and upsetting the woman, no matter whether the woman was aware of her husband's status or not. Yet with the similarities between her grandmother's case, Mr. Benfatti's, and this current one, she felt she had little choice. "Yes," Jennifer said finally.

Jennifer grimaced as she heard it ring. When it was answered she rapidly jumped and initially stumbled over her words as she explained who she was and apologized effusively for being a disturbance.

"You are not disturbing me," Mrs. Lucas said. "And please call me Rita."

You won't be asking me to call you Rita as soon as I tell you why I'm calling, Jennifer thought to herself as she struggled to find the courage to begin. It was already clear to her that like herself and Mrs. Benfatti, Rita had not yet been informed of her husband's fate, even though CNN already had it on the air. To soften the blow, Jennifer went ahead and explained to the woman what had happened to her and Lucinda vis-à-vis CNN.

"That's awful learning like that," Rita said sympathetically, but her voice trailed off as if she reluctantly sensed why Jennifer was calling her after nine at night.

"Yes," Jennifer agreed, "especially since in the U.S. the media go to great lengths to avoid it because they want the family informed first. But Mrs. Lucas, just a few moments ago I had CNN International on, and the anchors discussed the tragedy of your husband's passing."

After finally getting herself to say it, Jennifer fell silent. As the seconds ticked by, Jennifer didn't know if she should express sympathy or wait for Mrs. Lucas to respond. As the time passed, Jennifer could no longer stay silent. "I am so sorry to have had to be the one to tell you this awful news, but there is a reason."

"Is this some cruel prank?" Rita demanded angrily.

"I assure you it is not," Jennifer said, feeling the woman's anger and pain.

"But I just left David only a little more than an hour ago, and he was perfectly fine," she yelled.

"I understand how you feel, Mrs. Lucas, with a stranger calling you up out of the blue. But I assure you it was broadcast around the world that a David Lucas of Jacksonville, Florida, passed away at the Aesculapian Medical Center an hour or so ago, and he is survived by a wife and two children."

"My God!" Rita voiced in desperation.

"Mrs. Lucas, please call the hospital and make sure of this. If it is true, which I hope it isn't, please call me back. I'm only trying to help. And if it is true, and they try to pressure you into agreeing to cremation or embalming immediately, please do not do it. Because of my experience with the hospital where my granny and Mr. Benfatti had had their surgery, I'm thinking there is something wrong, something very wrong, with Indian medical tourism."

"I don't know what to say!" snapped Rita, angry but confused that Jennifer sounded so sincere.

"Don't say anything. Just call the hospital, and then call me right back. I actually already called the hospital, but they wouldn't give me any information, which is silly, since it has already been on international television. I'm staying at the Amal Palace Hotel and will stay here by the phone. Once again, I'm sorry to be the one to have had to call you when it was the hospital's responsibility."

The next thing Jennifer knew, she was listening to a dial tone. Rita had hung up on her. Thinking she might have done the same had the situation been reversed, Jennifer slowly hung up the receiver. It gave her a terrible feeling to have been the messenger with such bad news, and she found she hated the role. At the same time, as a physician in training she knew that she might have to do it a number of times over the course of her career.

Knowing that sleep was now completely out of the question, Jennifer wondered what she should do. She thought about reading more in the guidebook but then gave up. She couldn't concentrate. She began to worry that even if the CNN report had been correct, Rita might leave her in the dark and not call her back in a kind of passive-aggressive reaction, blaming the messenger.

Without coming up with a better idea, Jennifer turned up the volume on the TV and blankly began watching a CNN segment on Darfur. But no sooner had she gotten herself comfortable when her phone rang. She snatched it up practically before the first ring terminated. As she hoped, it was Rita, but Rita's voice had changed. She was now choked up to the point that it was difficult for her to speak.

"I don't know who you are or what kind of human being you are, but my husband is dead."

"I'm terribly sorry, and I certainly didn't get any pleasure from having had to be the one to tell you. The only reason I was willing to do so is to warn you about the hospital possibly trying to bully you into giving them permission to cremate or embalm."

"What difference does that make?" Rita snapped.

"Only that if either is done, an autopsy can't be done. It seems already that there are similarities between your husband's unexpected passing and my grandmother's and Mr. Benfatti's. I would assume your husband's death was unexpected?"

"Absolutely! We had him cleared by his cardiologist only a month before."

"It was the same with my grandmother and Mr. Benfatti. To be honest, I'm concerned these deaths are not natural. That's what I meant when I said something was wrong."

"What do you mean exactly?"

"I'm concerned these deaths might be intentional."

"You mean someone killed my husband."

"Somehow, yes," Jennifer said, realizing just how paranoid such a statement sounded.

"Why? No one knows us here. There's no way for someone to benefit."

"I've no clue, I'm afraid. But tomorrow night two forensic pathologists who are friends of mine are arriving. They are going to help me with my grandmother. I could ask them to check your husband's case, too." Jennifer knew she was going out on a limb offering Laurie and Jack's services without consulting them, but she thought they'd be willing to help. Jennifer also knew that in trying to solve a conspiracy, the more cases there were, the more chances of success.

Jennifer could hear Rita blow her nose before coming

back on the line. There were catches in her breathing as she tried to control her grief.

"Please, Mrs. Lucas. Don't let them destroy any potential evidence. We owe it to our loved ones. Also, you could ask whoever found your husband if he was blue. Both my granny and Mr. Benfatti were blue."

"How would that help?" she demanded, fighting tears.

"I don't know. In this kind of situation, if what I fear is true, there's no predicting what facts might solve the mystery. I've learned that studying medicine and trying to make a diagnosis. You just don't know what's going to be important."

"Are you a doctor?"

"Not yet. I'm in my last year of medical school. I'll graduate in June of '08."

"Why didn't you tell me?" she demanded, although with considerably less acrimony.

"I didn't think it mattered," Jennifer said, although when she thought about it, she had experienced episodes where people seemed inappropriately to give her opinion more credence, even about issues unrelated to medicine, when they found out she was a medical student.

"I'm not going to promise anything," Rita said. "But I'm on my way to the hospital now, and I'll think about what you said. I will call you in the morning."

"Fair enough," Jennifer said.

The fact that Rita went on to say good-bye gave Jennifer reason to be optimistic. The woman would not only get back in touch with her but would also cooperate. But as Jennifer thought about this third death in so many nights and its implications, it reminded her of a famous Shakespearean quote: "Something is rotten in the State of Denmark." At the same time, it did cross her mind that she could be using this conspiracy idea as another way of blocking the real impact of her grandmother's passing.

Chapter 22

Ramesh Srivastava did all he could to keep his composure. Here it was after ten at night and he was getting yet another call. To him it has seemed like he'd been on the phone all evening. First it had been his deputy of the department of medical tourism calling to say that his immediate subordinate deputy had called him only minutes earlier with the disappointing news that there'd been a report on CNN of yet another American patient death in a private Indian hospital. It was the third in three days, this time at the Aesculapian Medical Center. What made it particularly newsworthy was that the patient, David Lucas, was only in his forties. No sooner had Ramesh finished that unsettling call than he got a call from Khajan Chawdhry, the CEO of the involved hospital, with all the details as he knew them. Now here was the phone ringing yet again.

"What is it?" Ramesh demanded, with no attempt at

sociability. As a high-ranking Indian civil servant, he didn't expect to be working this hard.

"It is Khajan Chawdhry again, sir," the CEO said. "I'm sorry to bother you, but a slight problem has developed in relation to one of your specific orders—namely, your insistence there should be no autopsy."

"How can there be a problem?" Ramesh demanded. "It's a very simple order."

Earlier, Khajan had explained the bizarre sequence of events involving David Lucas's demise, starting with the incipient cyanosis with no airway obstruction, followed by the changes in the heart's conduction system and a sudden rise in the patient's temperature and potassium level. As a nonphysician, Ramesh had asked for a translation of the irritating doctor gobbledygook and had been told the man had died of some sort of heart attack/ stroke combination as a best-guess hypothesis. Ramesh's response had been for the attending surgeon to sign the death certificate as exactly that, and under no circumstances ask for an autopsy to be authorized.

"The problem is the wife," Khajan said sheepishly. "She said she may want an autopsy."

"People generally do not want autopsies," Ramesh said irritably. "Did the surgeon talk her into requesting one after I specifically ordered him not to do so?"

"No, the surgeon is well aware of the general negative feeling about autopsies in the private sector, and specifically aware of your feelings in this case. It wasn't he who has spoken to the wife about an autopsy, but rather another American, by the name of Jennifer Hernandez, who had called her prior to the wife's even hearing about her husband's death. It was this Hernandez woman who raised the issue of a possible autopsy by saying several American forensic pathologists were on their way to look at her grandmother, and could look at her husband as well, provided the husband's body was not cremated or embalmed."

"Not her again!" Ramesh groaned out loud. "This Hernandez woman is becoming intolerable."

"What should I do if Mrs. Lucas insists on the autopsy?"

"Like I told Rajish Bhurgava over at the Queen Victoria, make sure the autopsy request gets picked up by one of the magistrates we're accustomed to working with, and inform him there's to be no autopsy. Meanwhile, try your best to get Mrs. Lucas to agree to cremate or embalm. Lean on her! Is she still at the hospital?"

"She is, sir."

"Do your best."

"Yes, sir."

Ramesh disconnected and immediately called Inspector Naresh Prasad.

"Good evening, sir," Naresh said. "I don't hear from you for months, then twice in one day. What can I do for you?"

"What have you learned?"

"What have I learned about what?"

"About the mole in the Queen Victoria Hospital and the thorn in my side, Jennifer Hernandez."

"You're joking. We just spoke today. I haven't started looking into either issue yet. I'm just putting a team together for tomorrow."

"Well, both problems are getting worse, and I want some action."

"How are they getting worse?"

"There was another death, and again CNN had it on the air almost immediately. I heard about it from a deputy whose assistant happened to catch it on TV not much later than the CEO of the hospital heard it directly from his staff doctor who'd tried to resuscitate the patient."

"Am I to assume it was the same hospital, the Queen Victoria?"

"No, this time it was the Aesculapian Med Center."

"Interesting! Changing hospitals might help if the culprit is a staff physician. He or she would have to have privileges at both hospitals. That could narrow the list down quite nicely."

"Good thought. That hadn't occurred to me."

"Maybe that's why you're a bureaucrat and I'm a police investigator. What about the woman? What's she done to irritate you further?"

Ramesh told Naresh what Khajan had told him about Jennifer talking the wife into requesting an autopsy even before the hospital had informed the woman her husband had died.

"How did the Hernandez woman know the man had died?"

"I don't know for certain, but I'd have to guess she saw it on CNN International."

"Maybe she knows someone at CNN who is informing her. What do you think of that idea?"

For a moment Ramesh did not respond. He found

himself getting vexed at wasting his time with such mental gymnastics. That was Naresh's job, not his. What he wanted was results. He wanted to be rid of the whole mess so that the public-relations damage could be fully assessed and then, he hoped, repaired.

"Listen!" Ramesh said suddenly, ignoring Naresh's question. "What it all comes down to is this. Jennifer Hernandez is making a supreme nuisance of herself, and in the process putting the future of Indian medical tourism in jeopardy, particularly from the perspective of the United States, which promises to be our biggest potential market because of its idiotic healthcare system and the out-of-control medical inflation it fosters. I want you to take care of this woman, either yourself or some agent you trust. Tail her for a couple of days and keep me informed in real time who she sees, who she talks with, and where she goes. I want a full report, and most of all I want a reason to deport her without causing a scene or publicity of any sort. If she's not doing anything wrong, conjure it up. But for heaven's sake don't make a martyr of her, meaning no strong-arm tactics. Understood?"

"Quite so," Naresh said. "I will start in the morning with the Hernandez woman, and I will see to it myself. I will also put a trusted agent on the issue of who is tipping off CNN."

"Perfect," Ramesh said. "And as I said, keep me informed."

As he hung up the phone, Ramesh noisily exhaled in exasperation. Although he felt good about having built a little fire under Naresh and took the man at his word, meaning he expected him to follow Jennifer Hernandez around starting in the morning, the question of whether it would be enough and soon enough dogged him. In his mind he considered Naresh dependable and reasonably competent but certainly not the sharpest knife in the cutlery drawer. At the same time, Ramesh worried what the effect of yet another death reported by CNN was going to have on the higher-ups who'd called him that very afternoon to complain about the other two. It was clear it wasn't going to be positive, and it cast more doubt on the efficacy of Naresh's methodical but slow style. Such thinking reminded Ramesh of his call that afternoon to Shashank Malhotra, who was anything but slow and methodical. Believing it couldn't hurt to rile the rash businessman a little more, Ramesh picked the phone back up and made what he hoped would be the last call of the day.

"Are you calling me with some good news this time?" Shashank demanded as soon as he knew who was calling.

"I wish that were the case," Ramesh responded. "Unfortunately, there was another medical tourist death tonight that has already been reported on CNN International."

"Was it again at Queen Victoria?" Shashank demanded. It was clear he was in no mood for small talk.

"That's the single aspect of the event on the positive side," Ramesh said. "It was at the Aesculapian Med Center on this occasion." In a way, Ramesh was provoking Shashank with this comment, knowing the Aesculapian Med Centers were just as much a part of Shashank's holdings as the Queen Victoria Hospital. "The bad aspect is that the patient was young and leaves behind a wife and two children. Such a story frequently garners more media attention because of the sympathy angle."

"You don't have to tell me what I already know."

"The other problem is this Jennifer Hernandez. Somehow she's got herself involved in this case as well as the last one, even though it was at a different hospital."

"What has she done?"

"You understand that on sensitive cases like this we want to avoid autopsies, because autopsies are like feeding wood to a fire. The less attention the better, so we avoid the media and specifically avoid giving them anything newsworthy, which frequently autopsies are."

"I understand. It makes sense. Don't make me ask again!" Shashank growled. "What has she done?"

"She's somehow convinced both widows to demand autopsies."

"Shit!" Shashank snapped.

"I'm curious," Ramesh said, trying to sound nonchalant. "I asked you this afternoon if you could find someone who could talk with her and convince her that what she is doing is not in her best interests and that maybe, just maybe, it would be far better for her to take her grandmother's remains back to America before she severely impacts Indian medical tourism. Later this afternoon, I was informed of quite a number of patients making last-minute cancellations of their scheduled surgeries, not only from America but also Europe."

"Cancellations, you say."

"Yes, cancellations," Ramesh repeated, knowing that

Shashank's business mind closely associated cancellations with lost revenue.

"I must confess that this afternoon I put off taking your suggestion," Shashank growled, "but I'll look into it right now."

"I think you'd be doing Indian medical tourism a big favor. And in case you've forgotten, she's staying at the Amal Palace Hotel."

Chapter 23

Excuse me, sir," the cabin attendant said as she gently shook Neil McCulgan's shoulder. "Could you raise the back of your seat? We're in the final approach, and we'll be landing at the Indira Gandhi International Airport in just a few minutes."

"Thank you," Neil said, and did as he was told. He yawned, then pushed back in his seat and wiggled around to get comfortable. Despite having left Singapore almost an hour and a half late, they were arriving only an hour late. Somehow they'd managed to pick up a half-hour, even though they'd been flying into the jet stream.

"I'm impressed with how well you sleep on a plane," Neil's immediate seat neighbor said.

"I'm lucky, I guess," Neil responded. He had spoken with the gentleman for the first hour, learning that the man sold Viking kitchen appliances in northwestern India. Neil had found the man interesting, since their conversation made him realize, as an emergency-room doctor, how little he knew about the world in general.

"Where are you staying in Delhi?" the stranger asked.

"Amal Palace Hotel," Neil said.

"Would you like to share a cab? I live in the neighborhood."

"I have a hotel car picking me up. You're welcome to join, provided you don't have to wait for luggage. I just have carry-on."

"Same with me." He stuck out his hand. "The name's Stuart. I should have introduced myself earlier."

"Neil. Nice to meet you," Neil said, giving the man's hand a quick shake.

Neil leaned forward and tried to look out the window.

"Nothing yet to see," said Stuart, who was sitting at the window.

"No lights or anything?"

"Not this time of year, not with the haze. You'll see what I mean on our drive into town. It's like a dense fog but is mostly pollution."

"That sounds nice," Neil said sarcastically.

Neil leaned back against the headrest and closed his eyes. Now that he was nearing his journey's destination, he started to think about how he should meet up with Jennifer. During the two stops he'd had to make en route, he'd debated calling her. What he couldn't decide was whether it was best to surprise her in person or by phone. The benefit of the phone call would be to give her some time to adapt to the idea. The problem with it was that there was a good chance that she might simply tell him to turn around and go home. Ultimately, it was such a fear that made him opt not to call.

The huge plane's wheels touched down with a thump that caused Neil's eyes to pop open in surprise. He gripped the armrests to keep himself back in the seat as the plane braked.

"How long are you staying in Delhi?" Stuart questioned.

"Not long," Neil said evasively. He wondered briefly if he should disinvite the gentleman from sharing his ride. He was in no mood to get into any kind of personal conversation.

Apparently taking the hint, Stuart didn't ask any more questions until they'd passed through both passport control and customs. "Are you here on business?" Stuart asked, as they waited for the hotel car to be brought around.

"A little bit of both," Neil lied while being less than receptive. "And yourself?"

"The same," the man said. "I'm here often and keep an apartment. It's quite a city, but for my purposes, I prefer Bangkok."

"Really," Neil said with little interest, although he vaguely wondered what the man's "purposes" were.

"If you have any questions about Delhi, give me a call," the man said, handing Neil a Viking kitchen appliance card.

"I'll do that," Neil said insincerely, pocketing the card after a quick glance.

Both weary travelers settled into the hotel SUV's backseat. Neil closed his eyes and returned to musing about how he was going to hook up with Jennifer. Now that he was in the same city as she, he found himself even more excited than he'd expected. He was truly looking forward to seeing her and to apologizing for not coming the moment she'd asked him.

Neil opened his eyes long enough to check the time. It was five after midnight, and he realized that as excited as he was to see Jennifer, it would have to wait until morning. But then he began to wonder how he would surprise her then, an issue complicated by his acknowledging he had no idea of her schedule. He suddenly had an uncomfortable fear. Although it seemed unlikely enough for him not to have thought of it before, she might have concluded the business about her grandmother during the course of Wednesday, her first full day in Delhi, and could be flying out at that very moment: maybe even on the same plane he'd just flown in on.

Opening his eyes, Neil shook the thought from his mind. He laughed at himself and looked out the window at the haze his fellow traveler had described earlier. It was enough to make health-conscious Neil feel congested.

Shortly thereafter, the hotel car pulled up the ramp to the hotel's main entrance. Several porters and doormen surrounded the vehicle, opening the doors.

"Give me a call if I can help in any way," Stuart said, shaking hands with Neil. "And thanks for the ride."

"Will do," Neil responded. He got his carry-on bag from a porter with some effort, insisting he'd prefer to bring it into the hotel himself—not only was it not heavy, it had wheels.

Check-in was accomplished sitting down at a desk, and as Neil handed over his passport, he asked the formally dressed clerk who'd introduced himself as Arvind Sinha if they had a Jennifer Hernandez registered. Unseen by the clerk, he actually crossed his fingers.

"I can check for you, sahib," Arvind said. He used a keyboard that he pulled out from beneath the desk's surface. "Yes, we do, indeed."

Yes! Neil said to himself. Ever since he thought about the possibility of Jennifer's having already left, he'd been torturing himself. "Can you tell me her room number?"

"I'm sorry, I cannot," Arvind apologized. "For security purposes, we cannot give out guest room numbers. However, the operator can connect you, provided Ms. Hernandez hasn't a block on her phone and provided you think it is appropriate to call. It is past midnight."

"I understand," Neil said. As excited as he was now that he knew she was there, he couldn't help but be mildly disappointed. At the very least, he'd planned on going to her door and putting his ear against it. He'd decided that if he heard the TV, he was going to knock. "Can you tell me if she's scheduled to check out in the next day or so?" Neil asked.

Arvind went back to the keyboard, then checked the monitor. "There's no scheduled departure date."

"Good," Neil said.

After a few more minutes of formalities, Arvind stood up and his chair rolled back. "May I show you to your room?"

Neil stood up as well.

"Do you have a luggage tag?"

"Nope, this is it," Neil said, hoisting his carry-on. "I travel light." As he followed the clerk past the main entry doors toward the elevators, he wondered how he was going to surprise Jennifer in the morning. Since he didn't know her plans, it was hard to decide, and ultimately he thought he'd just play it by ear.

"Excuse me, Mr. Sinha," Neil said as they rose up in the elevator. "Could you see to it that I get a wake-up call at eight-fifteen?"

"Absolutely, sir!"

Chapter 24

Jennifer was embroiled in a recurrent nightmare involving her father that she often got when she was stressed. She'd never told anyone about the dream for fear of what people might think of her. She wasn't quite sure what she thought of it herself. In the dream her father was stalking her with a cruel expression on his face while she yelled to him to stop. Ending up in the kitchen, she grabbed a butcher knife and brandished it. But still he came at her, taunting her that she would never use it. But she did. She stabbed him over and over, but all he did was laugh.

Normally she woke at this point, finding herself drenched in sweat, and so it was on this day, too. Disoriented, it took her a few moments to realize she was in India and that the phone was ringing. Jennifer snatched up the receiver in a minor panic while irrationally thinking that whoever was calling had been a witness to her murderous activities.

The called turned out to be Rita Lucas, and she sensed the anxiety in Jennifer's voice. "I hope I'm not calling at a bad time."

"No, it's okay," Jennifer said, becoming more oriented to reality. "I was just dreaming."

"I'm so sorry to be calling so early, but I wanted to be certain not to miss you. I've actually waited. I never went to sleep. I was at the hospital for most of the night."

Jennifer checked the analog clock radio. It took her a moment to figure out the time, as the little hand and the big hand were not too different in size.

"I was hoping we could have breakfast together."

"That would be fine."

"Could it be soon? I am exhausted. And can I impose on you to come here to the Imperial? I'm afraid I look the wreck that I feel."

"I'd be happy to come. I can be ready in less than a half-hour. How far is the Imperial hotel from the Amal Palace? Do you know?"

"It's very close. It's just up the Janpath."

"I'm afraid I don't know the Janpath."

"It's very close. Maybe five minutes in a taxi."

"Then I should be able to be there close to eight," Jennifer said, throwing back the covers and swinging her legs off the bed.

"I'll meet you in the breakfast room. When you come through the front door, continue straight across the lobby. The breakfast room is to the right."

"I'll see you in a half-hour," Jennifer said.

After hanging up, Jennifer put herself in high gear. As a medical student, she'd perfected the process of getting ready. Early on she decided that the aggravation of hurrying was worth enduring for fifteen minutes more sleep.

She was pleased that Rita Lucas was willing to see her. Jennifer was eager to learn about this third American medical tourist death and exactly how much it resembled the first two.

During the process of showering and throwing on her clothes, she thought about the rest of the day. She wanted to steer clear of the Queen Victoria Hospital so as not to be further aggravated by the pesky case manager. That meant she had to think of something to do for the better part of the morning, lunch, the afternoon, and dinner to avoid obsessing about the frustration of not being able to move forward on her grandmother's situation until Laurie arrived. As for the late evening, she knew exactly what she was doing and looked forward with great zeal to heading out to the airport.

As she stepped out of her room carrying one of her guidebooks, she felt proud of herself. It was only seven-fifty-three, possibly a new record for her. On the way down in the elevator she went back to thinking about the day's plans. She had decided to contact Lucinda Benfatti for lunch or dinner or both. In the morning, provided breakfast didn't drag on, she thought she'd sightsee, even though she wasn't much of a sightseer. She thought it would be a shame to have traveled as far as she had without seeing something of the city. In the afternoon she thought she'd work out and then just lounge around the pool, a rare treat.

One of the Amal Palace doormen, when she told him she was going only to the Imperial hotel, advised her to walk down the hotel driveway and hail a yellow-and-green auto rickshaw if she was adventuresome. Taking the advice as a challenge of sorts, Jennifer did just that, especially when he told her that it would be significantly quicker than a regular cab during the morning rush hour.

At first Jennifer thought the vehicle quaint, with its three-wheel, open-sided design. But when she settled herself on the slippery vinyl bench seat and the conveyance took off as if it was joining a race, she had second thoughts. Being thrown forward and backward as the driver rapidly shifted, Jennifer scrambled for appropriate handholds. Once reaching speed, she was then thrown side to side as the driver began to weave among the exhaust-belching buses. The final indignity occurred from a large pothole that threw Jennifer skyward with enough velocity that her head made contact with the molded fiberglass top.

But the worst episode occurred when the driver accelerated between two buses that were converging. Seemingly oblivious to the possibility of being squished by vehicles fifty times the rickshaw's size, the driver did not slow in the slightest despite the rapid disappearance of space, such that people clinging to the sides of the buses could have shaken Jennifer's hand.

Convinced that the auto rickshaw and the buses were going to touch, Jennifer let go of the hand railing, pulled in her arms, and switched her grip to the edge of the seat itself. She closed her eyes and gritted her teeth, certain she was about to hear the grinding noise of actual contact. But it didn't happen. Instead, she heard the deafening screech of the buses' brakes as they rapidly slowed for an upcoming red traffic light. Jennifer reopened her eyes. The auto rickshaw driver, able to stop in a much shorter distance, rocketed forward, shooting out from between the braking buses before applying his own brakes.

The moment the auto rickshaw came to a lurching halt, it was surrounded by a small horde of shoeless, dirty children dressed in rags, ages three to twelve, thrusting their left hands in at Jennifer while making an eating gesture with their right. Some of the older girls were carrying swaddled infants on their hips.

Jennifer shrank back, looking into the children's sad, dark eyes, some of which were crusted with pus from obvious infection. Afraid to give them any money lest she cause a riot of sorts, Jennifer looked to the driver for help. But the driver did not move or even turn around. Absentmindedly, he raced the vehicle's tiny engine while keeping the clutch disengaged.

Feeling almost sick facing such in-your-face wrenching poverty, Jennifer was alternately repulsed and awed that Hinduism, with its creeds of punarjanma and karma, could inure its adherents to such contrasts and injustices.

To Jennifer's relief, the traffic light changed to green and the swarm of auto rickshaws, scooters, motorcycles, buses, trucks, and cars surged ahead, mindless of the children, who had to dodge the vehicles to save themselves.

As promised, the ride from the Amal Palace to the Imperial was short, but after Jennifer paid her fare and started to walk up the Imperial hotel's drive, since she'd been informed by the auto-rickshaw driver that he was not allowed on the Imperial's property, she felt as though she'd been through a marathon both physically and mentally. On top of everything else, she had a slight headache from all the diesel fumes she'd been forced to breathe.

As she approached the hotel, she found herself appreciating the building's appearance, which had a colonial aura, but not the site. In that sense it reminded her of the Queen Victoria Hospital, as it, too, was wedged in among rather unattractive commercial establishments.

Dhaval Narang felt he had the best job in the world because most of the time he just sat around and played cards with several other people who worked for Shashank Malhotra. And when he was called on to do something, it was always interesting and often a challenge, and the current assignment was no different. He was supposed to get rid of a young American woman by the name of Jennifer Hernandez. The challenging part was that he had no idea what she looked like. All he knew was that she was staying at the Amal Palace Hotel. How long she would be staying was also unknown, so he did not have the luxury of spending a lot of time looking for the woman, observing her, and learning her habits. Shashank's orders had been to get it done and get it done fast.

With the radio playing contemporary Bollywood-inspired music, Dhaval, dressed in a black open-necked shirt with a number of gold chains, steered his beloved black Mercedes E-Class sedan into the Amal Palace's driveway and drove up under the porte cochere. In the locked glove compartment was a Beretta automatic fitted with a three-inch suppressor. It was one of his many disposable guns. It was Dhaval's rule that when he made a hit, the gun disappeared or was left at the scene. Back when he'd just been hired, Shashank had complained that such a habit was too expensive, but Dhaval had insisted, and even threatened to quit if he was not allowed to follow it. Shashank had eventually relented. In India it was a lot easier to buy guns than to find people with Dhaval's résumé.

Dhaval was from a small rural town in Rajasthan and had joined the army to escape the inexorable grip of provincial life. In so many ways the decision was life-altering. He came to love the army life and the thrill of potential sanctioned killing. He applied for and was accepted into the newly formed Indian Special Forces, ultimately ending up as a Black Cat in the elite National Security Guards. His career progressed stupendously, at least until he saw real action in the 1999 Kashmerian ops. During a night raid on a suspected Pakistani-supported group of insurgents, he demonstrated such unbridled ruthlessness by killing seventeen suspects who were trying to surrender that the command considered him an embarrassing liability and removed him from the operation. A month later he was discharged from the service.

Luckily for Dhaval, his story, which the National Security Guards tried to keep quiet, appeared on the radar screen of Shashank Malhotra, who was rapidly diversifying his business interests and making enemies in the process. Needing someone with Dhaval's training and attitude, Shashank actively pursued the ex–special forces agent, and the rest was history.

Dhaval lowered his window as the Amal Palace's head doorman approached, holding his book of parking stickers in one hand and a pencil in the other. "How long will you be?" the doorman demanded. He was busy, as businessmen were arriving in ever-increasing numbers for breakfast meetings.

Palming a roll of rupees, Dhaval handed them over. They rapidly disappeared into the doorman's scarlet tunic. "I'd like to park up here near the entrance. I'll probably be an hour or so, certainly less than two."

Without saying anything to Dhaval, the doorman pointed at the last parking spot just across from the hotel's entrance, then waved for the next car to pull forward. Dhaval rounded the outer columns that supported the porte cochere and took the designated spot. It was perfect. He had an unobstructed view of the hotel entrance and his vehicle was pointing down toward the driveway's exit to the street.

After climbing from the car, Dhaval went into the lobby and, using the house phones, placed a call to Jennifer Hernandez. He let it ring a half dozen times, got voicemail, and hung up. Walking over to the main restaurant used for breakfast, he asked the maître d' if Ms. Jennifer Hernandez had been seen yet that morning.

"No, sir," the gentleman said.

"I'm supposed to meet her, and I have no idea what she looks like. Could you possibly give me an idea?"

"A very pretty young woman, medium-height; dark, thick, shoulder-length hair; and nice figure. She tends to wear tight jeans and cotton shirts."

"I'm impressed," Dhaval said. "That is a much more complete description than I expected. Thank you."

"I must admit I remember the attractive women the best," the maître d' said with a smile and a wink, "and she is indeed an attractive woman."

Dhaval wandered out of the restaurant, mildly confused. It was only a little after eight, and Jennifer was not in her room and not in the breakfast area. Dhaval stopped near the center of the lobby and glanced around to see if anyone might fit the description given by the maître d', but no one did. Then his eyes wandered out the large windows and he saw a half dozen or so people swimming laps in the pool.

Exiting the hotel, Dhaval checked the swimmers. There were two youngish women. One had medium-brown hair but would not qualify as having a nice figure. The second swimmer was blond, so she was out as well. Returning to the hotel, Dhaval used the lower entrance to check out the spa and workout room. There were two people using the weight machines and exercise bikes, but they were both men.

Mildly discouraged, Dhaval returned upstairs to the lobby and went over to the transportation desk. The hotel employee who ran it was called Samarjit Rao. Sam, as he was known, was on Shashank Malhotra's under-the-counter payroll. When Shashank brought business-men to Delhi, he always put them up at the Amal, and often he found it important to know where these people went.

"Mr. Narang," Sam said respectfully. "Namasté." Sam knew who Dhaval was and was appropriately scared of him.

"There is a young woman, supposedly attractive, at least according to the maître d', who is registered here at the hotel. Her name is Jennifer Hernandez. Do you know this person?"

"I do," Sam said, nervously glancing about. There were several other hotel employees who knew who Dhaval was.

"I need someone to point her out for me. Think you could do that?"

"Of course, sir. When she comes back."

"She is out of the hotel?"

"Yes, I saw her leave a little before eight."

Dhaval sighed. He'd hoped to meet up with her early enough so that when she went out he could follow her.

"Well, I'll wait around for a few hours," Dhaval said. "I'll get a paper and sit over against the wall." He pointed to several free club chairs. "If and when she comes in, let me know."

The wake-up call at 8:15 a.m. woke Neil from a deep sleep, and he answered in a panic, not quite knowing where he was. But his mind cleared rapidly, and he thanked the operator before bounding out of bed. The first thing he did was open the draperies and look out at the hazy sunshine. Directly below was the pool, with a handful of people swimming laps. Neil looked forward to doing the same sometime during the day. It would be good treatment for his anxiousness and jet lag.

With his anticipation building, he rushed into the bathroom and jumped into the shower. He brushed his teeth, combed his hair into some semblance of order, and pulled on a fresh shirt and clean jeans. Thus prepared, he sat on the edge of the bed and pressed the operator button with a trembling finger. His idea was to pretend he was calling from L.A., and during the course of the conversation, try to find out her day's plans. From that information, he'd figure out how to surprise her.

It seemed like it was taking forever for the operator to answer. "Come on!" he urged impatiently. When the operator finally answered, he gave Jennifer's name. The next thing he heard was the phone ringing in her room, and expecting to hear her voice at any second, his excitement grew.

After almost a dozen rings, Neil was convinced she wasn't going to pick up, so he replaced his receiver. Next he tried her cell, but got her voicemail after only one ring, suggesting she'd not turned it on. He hung up. With some disappointment, he contemplated his next step. He did think that there was a chance she was in the shower and he should call her room again in five to ten minutes, but as agitated as he'd become, he wasn't about to just sit there. Neil got his key card, left his room, and descended down to the lobby level. His next thought was that she could be having breakfast.

The restaurant was nearly full, and as he waited in line to talk to the maître d', his eyes scanned the entire multilevel room. To the left on the highest level against the back wall was a substantial buffet.

To the right, down several levels, were the picture windows facing the gardens and the pool. Again, Neil had to suffer disappointment. He didn't see her.

"How many persons?" the maître d' asked when it was Neil's turn.

"Just one," Neil said.

As the maître d' got out a menu to give to one of the seating hosts, Neil asked, "Would you by any chance be familiar with a hotel guest by the name of Jennifer Hernandez? She is—"

"I am," the maître d' said. "And you are the second gentleman looking for her this morning. She has yet to come in for breakfast."

"Thanks," Neil said, encouraged. She must have been in the shower when he called earlier. Neil allowed the host to lead him to a table for two near the windows but didn't sit down. "Where is the nearest house phone?"

"There are several in the hallway leading to the restrooms," the young woman said. She pointed.

Neil thanked her and hurried over. His heart was again pounding in his chest, which surprised him. He hadn't anticipated getting as excited as he was, and it made him wonder if he was more attached to Jennifer than he was willing to admit. When the operator came on the line, Neil again asked for Jennifer's room. Feeling confident he was going to get her this time, he even began to ponder an opening line. But he didn't need one. The same as earlier, the phone just rang and rang.

Finally, Neil disconnected. As sure as he'd been that she'd answer, he was even more disappointed than he'd been earlier. He even experienced a touch of paranoia by irrationally wondering if she'd been warned he was coming and was deliberately avoiding him. "That's utterly ridiculous," Neil murmured when his more sane self intervened.

Deciding that a good breakfast was in order, Neil headed back to his table. As he walked, he wondered if her absence had anything to do with the other gentleman who had been looking for her, and as he pondered the question, he realized something else. He felt jealous.

Positioning himself at his table so he could see the hostess stand, he picked up the menu and motioned for the waiter.

Inspector Naresh Prasad directed his government-issue vintage white Ambassador automobile into the Amal Palace Hotel driveway and accelerated up the ramp to the hotel's entrance. As it was nearing nine a.m., there was a profusion of other cars arriving and discharging their businessmen occupants.

When it was Naresh's turn, one of the resplendently attired and turbaned doormen waved him forward, then put up a hand for him to stop. He opened the Ambassador's door, straightened up, and saluted as Naresh alighted from the car.

Having gone through this ritual before, Naresh had his billfold open, displaying his police identification. He held it up almost at arm's length so the impressively tall doorman could read it and check the photo if he so chose. Naresh recognized there was an element of humor in the scene as he was on the short side. At five-foot-three, he made the nearly seven-foot Sikh look like an absolute giant.

"I want the car parked up here by the door and ready for a quick departure if it is needed," Naresh said.

"Yes, Inspector Prasad," the doorman said, indicating he had carefully checked Naresh's ID. He snapped his fingers and directed one of the uniformed parking valets on where to put the car.

Naresh self-consciously tried to make himself as tall as possible as he walked up the few steps toward the hotel's double doors and past a group of hotel guests waiting for transportation. Once inside, Naresh glanced around the expansive lobby, trying to settle on how to proceed. After a moment of deliberation, he decided enlisting the help of the concierge made the most sense. Wanting to avoid making any scene, he waited his turn as several guests kept the two concierges busy making dinner reservations.

"What can I do for you, sir?" one of the formally dressed concierges asked with a charming smile. Naresh was impressed. The man and his partner conveyed an alacrity that suggested they truly enjoyed their work, something Naresh rarely saw in the vast Indian civil service that he had to deal with on a daily basis.

Continuing to be careful not to make a scene, Naresh

subtly flashed his identification. "I am interested in one of your hotel guests. There is nothing serious. It's just a formality. We are only interested in her safety."

"What can we do to help, Inspector?" the concierge asked, lowering his voice. His name was Sumit.

The second concierge, finishing with a guest, leaned forward to be included in the conversation after having seen Naresh's police identification. His name was Lakshay.

"Are either of you acquainted with a young American woman who is a guest of the hotel named Jennifer Hernandez?"

"Oh, yes!" Lakshay said. "One of our more pleasant, attractive guests, I might add. But she has only come to the desk to request a city map so far: no other services. It was I who assisted her."

"Seemingly very friendly woman," Sumit added. "She always has a smile when she passes and makes an effort to make eye contact."

"Have you seen her today?"

"Yes, I have," Sumit said. "She left the hotel about forty minutes ago. You had left the desk momentarily," he said to Lakshay, in response to his partner's questioning expression.

Naresh sighed. "That's unfortunate. Was she accompanied or alone?"

"She was alone, although I do not know if she met anyone outside."

"How was she dressed?"

"Very casual: a brightly colored polo shirt and blue jeans."

Naresh nodded as he weighed his possibilities.

"Let me run out and ask our doormen. They might remember her." Sumit came out from behind the concierge's desk and briskly walked outside.

"He acts like he's enjoying himself," Naresh commented, watching the concierge through the glass, noticing the man's tails flapping in the breeze.

"Always," Lakshay said. "Has the young lady done something wrong?"

"I'm really not at liberty to say."

Lakshay nodded, mildly self-conscious about his obvious curiosity.

They watched Sumit and one of the Sikhs have a short, animated conversation. Sumit then returned inside.

"It seems that she only went as far as the Imperial hotel, provided we're talking about the same woman, which I'm pretty sure we are."

A middle-aged English couple approached the concierge's desk. Naresh stepped aside. While the English couple asked for a lunch recommendation in the old section of Delhi, Naresh mulled over what he thought he should do. At first he thought about rushing over to the Imperial, but then he changed his mind, realizing it had been close to an hour that Jennifer had been away, and that he might miss her, especially with no one there who could make a positive identification. He decided to stay at the Amal in hopes she was not out for the day and would soon return. At least at the Amal he had the concierges available for identification purposes.

"Thank you for your help," the English woman said after Sumit handed her a lunch reservation. The moment the English couple turned to leave, Naresh moved in to regain his spot.

"Here's what I've decided to do," he said. "I'm going to sit here in the center of the lobby. If Miss Jennifer comes in, I want you to signal me."

"We will be happy to do that, Inspector," Sumit said. Lakshay nodded as well.

Jennifer looked across the breakfast table at Rita Lucas and was impressed with how well the woman was holding up. When Jennifer had first arrived at the Imperial hotel, the woman had apologized for her appearance, explaining that she'd been unwilling to look at herself after being up all night, first at the hospital for a number of hours, then on the phone with family and friends.

She was a slim, pale woman, the opposite of her late husband. She reflected a kind of shy, desperate defiance in the face of the tragedy in which she'd found herself.

"He was a good man," she was saying. "Although he could not control his eating. He tried, I have to give him credit, but he couldn't do it, even though he was embarrassed at how he looked and embarrassed at his limitations."

Jennifer nodded, sensing that the woman needed to talk. Jennifer got the impression that it was she more than her husband who was embarrassed and who had urged him to undergo the obesity surgery, which had now resulted in his death.

Earlier Rita had admitted that the hospital had tried to push her into making a decision about disposition of the body. She said they presented it as a suggestion at first but then became progressively more insistent. Rita admitted that had she not spoken with Jennifer first, she surely would have given in and had the body cremated.

"It was their inability to explain how he died that really influenced me," Rita had explained. "First it was a simple heart attack, then a stroke with a heart attack, then a heart attack causing a stroke. They couldn't seem to make up their minds. When I suggested an autopsy, that's when they got almost belligerent; well, at least the case manager got angry. The surgeon seemed unconcerned."

"Did they mention whether he had turned blue when he had his heart attack?" Jennifer had asked.

"He did mention that," Rita had responded. "He said that the fact it cleared so dramatically with artificial respiration had made him optimistic he was going to pull through."

Rita paused for a moment before asking, "What about your forensic pathology friends who are on their way here to help with your grandmother? You mentioned they could check my husband's case as well. Is that still a possibility?"

"They're en route, so I haven't had a chance to ask them. But I'm sure it will be fine."

"I would really appreciate it. The more I thought about your comment about us owing it to our loved ones, the more I agree. From everything you've told me, I've become suspicious, too."

"I will ask them tonight when they arrive and get back to you tomorrow," Jennifer said.

Rita sighed, and as a few new tears welled up, she carefully pressed a tissue against each eye in turn. "I think I'm talked out, and I know I'm exhausted. Maybe I'd better head upstairs. Luckily, I have a couple of old Xanax tablets. If I ever needed one, this is the time."

Both women stood and spontaneously hugged. Jennifer was surprised at how frail Rita felt. It was as though if she squeezed too hard, some bones might crack.

They said good-bye in the lobby. Jennifer promised to call in the morning, and Rita thanked her for listening. Then they parted.

As Jennifer exited the hotel, she promised herself a real taxi, not an auto rickshaw, on her ride back to the Amal.

Chapter 25

On the relatively short run from the Imperial hotel back to the Amal Palace Hotel, Jennifer decided the regular taxi wasn't that much more relaxing than the auto rickshaw except for having sides, providing at least the impression of being safer. The taxi driver was as aggressive as the auto rickshaw driver had been, but his vehicle was slightly less maneuverable.

En route and after checking the time, Jennifer reconfirmed her plans of doing some sightseeing during the morning and exercising and lying around the pool in the afternoon. After her breakfast with Rita, she was even more convinced something weird was afoot, and she didn't want to obsess. As she looked out the cab's window, she was becoming familiar enough with Delhi traffic to recognize that the morning rush hour was beginning to abate. In place of stop-and-go it was crawl-

and-go, so it was as good a time as any for her to drive around the city.

Back at the hotel, she didn't bother going up to her room. Using the house phone, she called Lucinda Benfatti.

"Hope I'm not calling too early," Jennifer said apologetically.

"Heavens, no," Lucinda said.

"I just had breakfast with a woman whose husband died last night, not at the Queen Victoria but at another similar hospital."

"We can certainly sympathize with her."

"In more ways than one. The whole situation resembles our experience. Once again, CNN was aware before she was."

"That makes three deaths," Lucinda stated. She was shocked. "Two can be a coincidence; three in three days cannot."

"That's my thought exactly."

"I'm certainly glad your medical examiner friends are coming."

"I feel exactly the same, but I feel like I'm treading water until they get here. Today I'm going to try not to think about it. I might even try to act like a tourist. Would you like to accompany me? I really don't care what I see. I just want to take my mind off everything."

"That's probably a good idea, but not for me. I just couldn't do it."

"Are you sure?" Jennifer asked, unsure if she should try to insist for Lucinda's sake.

"I'm sure."

"Here I am saying I want to take my mind off everything, and I have a couple of questions for you. First, did you find out from your friend in New York what time he learned about Herbert's passing on CNN?"

"Yes, I did," Lucinda said. "I wrote it down somewhere. Hold on!"

Jennifer could hear Lucinda moving things around on the desk and mumbling to herself. It took about a minute for her to come back on the line. "Here it is. I wrote it on the back of an envelope. It was just before eleven a.m. He remembered because he'd turned the TV on to watch something scheduled at eleven."

"Okay," Jennifer said as she wrote down the time. "Now I have another request. Do you mind?"

"Not at all."

"Call up our friend Varini and ask her what time is on the death certificate, or if you are going out there, ask to look at the death certificate yourself, which you are entitled to do. I'd like to know the time, and I'll tell you why. With my granny, I heard about her passing around seven-forty-five a.m. Los Angeles time, which is around eight-fifteen New Delhi time. Here in New Delhi, when I asked to see her death certificate, the time was ten-thirty-five p.m., which is curious, to say the least. Her time of death was later than it was announced on television."

"That is curious! It suggests someone knew she was going to die before she did."

"Exactly," Jennifer said. "Now there could have been some screw-up here in India that could explain the discrepancy, like someone writing ten-thirty-five p.m. when they were supposed to write nine-thirty-five, but even that is too short an interval for CNN to get the tip, verify it in some way, write the piece about medical tourism, and get it on the air."

"I agree; I'll be happy to find out."

"Now, the last thing," Jennifer said. "When my granny was discovered having passed away, she was blue. It's called cyanosis. I'm having trouble explaining that physiologically. After a heart attack sometimes the patient can be a little blue, maybe the extremities, like the tips of the fingers, but not the whole body. With all the other similarities between Granny and Herbert, I'd like to know if he was also blue."

"Who would I ask?"

"The nurses. It's the nurses who know what goes on in a hospital. Or medical students, if the hospital has them."

"I'll give it a try."

"I'm sorry to be giving you all these tasks."

"It's quite alright. I actually like having things to do. It keeps me from obsessing over my emotions."

"Since you're not up for sightseeing, how about dinner? Are you going out to the airport to meet your sons, or are you going to wait for them here?"

"I'm going to the airport. I really am anxious to see them. As for dinner, could I let you know later?"

"Absolutely," Jennifer said. "I'll call you in the afternoon."

After appropriate good-byes, Jennifer hung up the house phone and hastened over to the concierge desk. Now that she had decided to sightsee, she wanted to get on her way. Unfortunately, there was a line at the desk, and she had to wait. When it was her turn and she had stepped up to the desk, she couldn't help but notice the reaction of the concierge. It was like he'd just recognized an old friend. What made it particularly surprising was that he wasn't even the concierge who'd given her the city map the day before.

"I'd like some advice," Jennifer said, while watching the man's dark eyes. Rather than make proper eye contact, he seemed to be intermittently looking over Jennifer's shoulder out into the lobby, so that even Jennifer herself turned to see if there was something going on, but she saw nothing unusual.

"What kind of advice?" the man asked, finally engaging Jennifer with normal eye contact.

"I want to do a little sightseeing this morning," she said. She noticed the man's name was Sumit. "What would you recommend for two to three hours?"

"Have you seen Old Delhi?" Sumit inquired.

"I haven't seen anything."

"Then I suggest Old Delhi for certain," Sumit said, while reaching for a city map. He opened the map with a practiced shake and smoothed it out on the desktop. Jennifer looked down at it. It was identical to the one she'd gotten the day before.

"Now, this is the area of Old Delhi," Sumit said, pointing with his left index finger. Jennifer followed his pointing finger but out of the corner of her eye she saw Sumit wave with his right hand over his head as if trying to get someone's attention. Jennifer turned to look into the lobby area to see who Sumit was waving at, but no one seemed to be returning the gesture. She looked back at the concierge, who seemed mildly embarrassed and lowered his hand like a child being caught reaching for the cookie jar.

"Sorry," Sumit said. "I was just trying to wave at an old friend."

"It's quite alright," Jennifer said. "What should I see in Old Delhi?"

"For sure, the Red Fort," he said, poking a finger at it on the map. He took her guidebook and flipped it open to the proper page. "Perhaps second only to the Taj Mahal in Agra, it might be India's most interesting landmark. I particularly like the Diwan-i-Aam."

"It sounds promising," Jennifer said, noticing that the man no longer seemed to be distracted in the slightest.

"Good morning, Ms. Hernandez," the second concierge said when he'd finished with his last client and was waiting for the next to step up. It had been he who had given her the city map the day before.

"Good morning to you," Jennifer responded.

"Ms. Hernandez is going to visit Old Delhi," Sumit said to Lakshay.

"You'll enjoy it," Lakshay said, while waving for the next hotel guest to approach.

"What about after the Red Fort?" Jennifer asked.

"Then I recommend you visit the Jama Masjid mosque, built by the same Mughal emperor. It is the largest mosque in India."

"Is this area near these two monuments a bazaar?" Jennifer asked.

"Not only a bazaar but *the* bazaar. It is the most wonderful labyrinth of narrow galis and even more narrow katras where you can buy most anything and everything. The shops are tiny and owned by the merchants, so you must bargain. It is marvelous. I suggest you walk around the bazaar, shop if you are so inclined, and then walk here to a restaurant called Karim's for lunch," Sumit said, pointing at the map. "It's the most authentic Mughlai restaurant in New Delhi."

"Is it safe?" Jennifer asked. "I'd prefer not to get Delhi belly."

"Very safe. I know the maître d'. I'll call him and tell him you might be stopping in. If you do, ask for Amit Singh. He will take good care of you."

"Thank you," Jennifer said. "It sounds like a good plan." She tried to fold the map into its original form.

Sumit took the map and expertly collapsed it. "May I ask how you plan to travel to Old Delhi?"

"I hadn't gotten to that yet."

"May I recommend using one of the hotel cars. We can arrange for an English-speaking driver, and the car will be air-conditioned. It is somewhat more expensive than a taxi, but the driver will stay with you, although not while you visit the monuments or the bazaar. Many of our female guests find it very convenient."

Jennifer liked the idea immediately. Since the sight-seeing outing might be her one and only, she thought she should do it properly, and for a babe-in-the-woods tourist, it might make the difference between enjoying herself or not. "You say it's not much more than a taxi?" Jennifer asked, to be reassured.

"That's correct if you are hiring the taxi by the hour. It's a service for our hotel guests."

"How do I make the arrangements? It's not going to work for me unless there's a car available now."

Sumit pointed across the hotel's main entrance to a desk similar to his. "That's the transportation desk just opposite, and my colleague, attired similar to myself, is the transportation manager. I assure you he will be most helpful."

Jennifer wove through the people coming in and going out of the hotel and approached the transportation desk. She was unaware of a balding, round-faced man behind her, more than three inches shorter than her, who stood up from a club chair in the center of the lobby and approached the concierges. But a few moments later she did happen to see him while the transportation manager finished up a phone conversation. She noticed him only because he was talking with one of the turbaned, towering doormen, and by comparison appeared considerably shorter than he actually was.

"May I help you?" the transportation manager said as he hung up his phone.

As she started to speak, she noticed the man had a similar reaction on confronting her as the concierge: a kind of distracted recognition. Jennifer felt instantly self-conscious, worrying something must be amiss with her appearance, like something was stuck between her teeth. As a reflex, she ran her tongue across them.

"Can I help you?" the man repeated. Jennifer noticed his name was Samarjit Rao. She certainly didn't remember meeting him.

"Have we met?" Jennifer asked.

"Unfortunately, we have not—not in person, anyway. But I did arrange for your airport transportation Tuesday evening, and I know you are to accompany an airport pickup this evening. And we are encouraged by management to learn our guests' names and faces."

"I'd say that is impressive," Jennifer said. She then went on to ask how much a car and driver would be for three hours or so, and if one was currently available with a driver who spoke English.

Samarjit quoted Jennifer a price, which was less than Jennifer expected. As soon as he was able to ascertain a car with an English-speaking driver was available, Jennifer said she'd take it. Five minutes later she was sent out to the porte cochere and told a Mercedes would soon be up from the garage for her. She was also told the driver's name would be Ranjeet Basoka and that the Sikh doormen had been informed and would direct her to the right vehicle.

As she stood waiting for the hired car to appear, she amused herself by observing the mix of nationalities, but in so doing she didn't make particular note of a man dressed in black with several gold chain necklaces exit the hotel, weave his way through the crowd, and climb into a black Mercedes. Nor did she notice that the man did not start the car but merely sat in the driver's seat, drumming his fingers on the steering wheel.

"Would you care for more coffee?" the waiter asked.

"No, thank you," Neil said. He folded the newspaper he'd been given, stood up, and stretched. The breakfast had been terrific. The buffet had been one of the most extensive he'd ever seen, and he'd tried just about everything. Having already signed the check, he walked out into the busy lobby, wondering what his plan should be. Catching sight of the concierge desk, he thought he'd start there.

It took a while before it was his turn. "I'm a guest in the hotel . . ." he began.

"Of course," Lakshay said. "You are Sahib Neil McCulgan, I presume."

"How did you know my name?"

"When I arrive in the morning, if there's time, I try to acquaint myself with the new guests. Sometimes I'm wrong, but usually I'm right."

"Then you must be aware of Miss Jennifer Hernandez."

"Absolutely. Are you an acquaintance?"

"I am. She doesn't know I'm here. It's sort of a surprise."

"Just a moment," Lakshay said as he rushed out from behind the desk. "Wait here," he added, as he ran out the door.

Bewildered, Neil watched him though the glass as he made a beeline to one of the colorfully dressed doormen. They had a quick conversation, and then Lakshay ran back inside. He was slightly out of breath. "Sorry," he said to Neil. "Miss Hernandez was just here two minutes ago. I thought maybe I could catch her, but she just got into her car."

Neil's face brightened. "She was just here at the concierge desk a few minutes ago?"

"Yes. She asked for some recommendations for sightseeing. We sent her to Old Delhi's Red Fort, the Jama Masjid mosque, and the Delhi bazaar, with lunch possibly at a restaurant called Karim's."

"In that order."

"Yes, so I believe you could catch her at the Red Fort if you hurry."

Neil started for the hotel exit when the second concierge called out, "She's using a hotel car. A black Mercedes. Ask the transportation manager its tag number. It might be useful."

Neil nodded and waved that he'd heard, then headed to the transportation desk, got the vehicle tag number and the mobile number of the driver, and then rushed out to snare a taxi.

Jennifer was instantly grateful she'd allowed the concierge to talk her into hiring a hotel car for her outing. Once she was nestled within the muffled air-conditioned comfort of the Mercedes, it was like being on a different planet, compared with either the auto rickshaw or the regular taxi. For the first fifteen minutes she enjoyed gazing out at the spectacle of the Indian streets with their fantastic collection of conveyances, crush of people, and admixture of animals, from restive monkeys to bored cows. She even saw her first Indian elephant.

The driver, Ranjeet, was dressed in a fitted, carefully pressed dark blue uniform. Although he spoke English, his accent was so strong Jennifer found it hard to understand him. She tried to make an effort as he pointed out various landmarks, but she eventually gave up and re-sorted to merely nodding her head and saying things like "Very interesting" or "That's wonderful." Eventually, she opened her guidebook and turned to the section dealing with the Red Fort. After a few minutes the driver noticed her concentration on the book and fell silent.

For almost a half-hour she read about the architecture and some of the fort's history to the point of being unaware of the traffic or their route. Nor was she aware of two cars that were following hers: one a white Ambassador, and the other a black Mercedes. At times these trailing cars were very close, especially when they all stopped for a red light or backed-up traffic. At other times they were quite far away but never out of sight.

"We'll soon be seeing the Red Fort on the right," Ranjeet said, "just beyond this traffic light."

Jennifer looked up from her reading, which had switched from the Red Fort to the Jama Masjid. What she immediately noticed was that Old Delhi was significantly more crowded than New Delhi, with both people and conveyances, especially more cycle rickshaws and animal-drawn carts. There was also more trash and debris of all sorts. Plus, there was also more activity, such as people getting shaves or haircuts, medical treatment, fast food, massages, their ears cleaned, clothes cleaned, shoes repaired, and teeth filled—all in the open, with very little equipment. All the barber had was a chair, a tiny cracked mirror, a few implements, a bucket of water, and a large rag.

Jennifer was mesmerized. Everything about living life

that was secreted away behind closed doors in the West was being done out in the open. For Jennifer, it was visual overload. Every time she glimpsed an activity and wanted to question her driver what people were doing or why they were doing it in the open, she saw something else more surprising.

"There's the Red Fort," Ranjeet said proudly.

Jennifer looked out the windshield at a monstrous crenellated structure of red sandstone, far larger than she'd imagined. "It's huge," she managed. Her mouth was agape. As they drove along the western wall, it seemed to go on forever.

"The entrance is up here on the right," Ranjeet said, pointing ahead. "It's called the Lahore Gate. It's where the prime minister addresses the Independence Day rally."

Jennifer wasn't listening. The Red Fort was overwhelming. When she'd read about it, she'd envisioned something about the size of the New York Public Library, but it was vastly larger and constructed with marvelously exotic architecture. To explore it adequately would take a day, not the hour or so she'd intended.

Ranjeet turned into the parking area in front of the Lahore Gate. A number of huge tour buses were parked along one side. Ranjeet motored by them and stopped near a group of souvenir shops.

"I will wait just over there," he said, pointing to a few highly stressed trees providing a bit of shade. "If you don't see me the moment you come out, call me and I will come directly back here."

Jennifer took the business card the driver extended

toward her, but didn't answer. She was gazing at the immensity of the fort and recognizing the futility of trying to see a famous edifice the size of the Red Fort in an hour. It certainly would not do it justice. Adding to that negative feeling was the general exhaustion she felt with her jet lag, the lulling sensation the car had provided, and her admission she was not much of a sightseer of old buildings. Jennifer was a people person. If she was to make an effort, she'd prefer to see people than crumbling architecture any day of the week. She was far more interested in the spectacle of Indian street life, a portion of which she'd just witnessed from the car.

"Is there something wrong, Miss Hernandez?" Ranjeet asked. After handing her his card he'd continued looking at Jennifer. She'd made no effort to move.

"No," Jennifer said. "I've just changed my mind. I assume we're close to the bazaar area?"

"Oh, yes," Ranjeet said. He pointed across the road running the length of the Red Fort. "The whole area south of Chandni Chowk, that main street leading away from the Red Fort, is the bazaar area."

"Is there somewhere convenient for you to park so I can wander in the bazaar?"

"There is. There is parking at the Jama Masjid mosque, which is at the southern end of the bazaar."

"Let's go there," Jennifer said.

Ranjeet made a rapid three-point turn and accelerated back the way they'd come, raising a cloud of yellowish dust. He also hit his horn as they bore down on a man dressed in black and carrying a jacket over his arm. What Ranjeet didn't see was a short man standing at a refreshment stand toss away a canned soda and sprint for his car.

"Is Chandni Chowk both a street and a district?" Jennifer asked. She had gone back to reading her guidebook. "It's a little confusing."

"It is both," Ranjeet said. Although stopped at the traffic light, he hit his horn again as a taxi turned into the parking area for the Lahore Gate more rapidly than appropriate, came within inches, and sped past. Ranjeet shook his fist and shouted some words in Hindi that Jennifer assumed were not used at "high tea."

"Sorry," Ranjeet said.

"That's quite alright," Jennifer said. The taxi had alarmed her as well.

The light changed and Ranjeet accelerated out into the broad multilaned Netaji Subhash Marg that fronted the Red Fort, turning south. "Have you been on a cycle rickshaw, Miss Hernandez?"

"No, I haven't," Jennifer admitted. "I've been on an auto rickshaw, though."

"I recommend you try a cycle rickshaw, and specially one here at the Chandni Chowk. I can arrange for one at the Jama Masjid, and he can take you around the bazaar. The lanes are called galis and are crowded and narrow and the katras are even more narrow. You need a cycle rickshaw; otherwise, you'll get lost. He will be able to bring you back when you wish."

"I suppose I should try one," Jennifer said, without a lot of enthusiasm. She told herself she should be more adventuresome.

Ranjeet turned right off the wide boulevard and was promptly engulfed in the stop-and-go traffic on a narrow street. This was not the bazaar per se, but it was lined by modest-sized shops selling a wide variety of merchandise, from stainless-steel kitchen utensils to bus tours in Rajasthan. As the car slowly moved along, Jennifer was able to gaze at the myriad faces of the local population reflecting the dizzying variety of ethnic groups and cultures that have miraculously become glued together over the millennia to form current-day India.

The narrow street butted into the exotic-appearing Jama Masjid mosque, where Ranjeet turned left into a crowded parking lot. He jumped out and told Jennifer to wait for a moment.

While Jennifer waited, she took note of something about the Indian temperament. Although Ranjeet had left the car in the middle of the busy parking area, none of the parking attendants seemed to care. It was like she and the car were invisible despite blocking the way. She couldn't imagine what a firestorm it would have caused to do something similar in New York.

Ranjeet returned with a cycle rickshaw in tow. Jennifer was horrified. The cyclist was pencil-thin with protein-starved, sunken cheeks. He didn't appear capable of walking very far, much less pumping hard enough to move a three-wheeled bicycle supporting Jennifer's hundred and fourteen pounds.

"This is Ajay," Ranjeet said. "He'll take you around the bazaar, wherever you might like to go. I suggested the Dariba Kalan with its gold and silver ornaments. There's also some temples you might like to see. When you want to come back to the car, just tell him."

Jennifer climbed out of the car and then with some reluctance up into the hard seat of the cycle rickshaw. She noticed there was little to hold on to, making her feel vulnerable. Ajay bowed and then started pedaling without saying a word. To her surprise, he was able to propel the cycle with apparent ease by standing up and pedaling. They rode along the front side of the Jama Masjid until they were soon engulfed by the extensive bazaar.

By the time Dhaval Narang got back to his car at the Lahore Gate at the Red Fort, Ranjeet had already gotten a green light and had accelerated southward to join the traffic coming from Chandni Chowk Boulevard. Hurrying, Dhaval was able to get to the light before it turned red. Accelerating as well, he rushed after the hotel's car, trying desperately to keep it in sight. Since the traffic was heavy, it was not easy, even though he was driving very aggressively in an attempt to catch up. He was doing well until a bus pulled away from the curb in front of him and blocked even his view.

Forcing himself to take even more of a chance, Dhaval pressed down on the gas pedal, cut in front of a truck, and managed to get around the overly crowded bus. Unfortunately, by the time he could again see ahead Ranjeet had disappeared. Slowing to a degree, Dhaval began looking down the side streets that headed west as he passed them. A moment later he had to stop at a traffic light, allowing crowds of people to surge forth to cross Netaji Subhash Marg.

Dhaval was disgruntled, impatiently tapping the steering wheel while waiting for the light to change. Originally, he'd been happy about the Red Fort, as it was big and packed with tourists, making it easy to do a hit and melt into the crowd without fear of being caught. But then Ranjeet had suddenly driven away, giving Dhaval no idea where he was going or why.

When the traffic light turned to green, Dhaval had to wait impatiently while the vehicles in front of him slowly accelerated forward. At the corner, he glanced down toward the Jama Masjid mosque and made a rapid decision. Halfway down toward the mosque and mired in traffic was what looked like the Amal Palace's Mercedes.

Suddenly throwing the steering wheel to the right, Dhaval recklessly turned into the oncoming traffic, forcing several vehicles to jam on their brakes. Gritting his teeth, Dhaval half expected to hear the crunch of a collision, but luckily it was only screeching tires, horns, and angry shouts. Whether the car ahead was the hotel's or not, he'd decided to check the mosque. If Jennifer Hernandez wasn't there, then he'd head back to the hotel.

Moving slowly in the stop-and-go side-street traffic, it took some time to get to the front of the mosque, where Dhaval turned left into a parking area. As soon as he did so he recognized the hotel car as it was being parked. Quickly glancing over his shoulder in the opposite direction, he was rewarded with catching sight of

Jennifer on a cycle rickshaw just before she disappeared into one of the crowded galis.

Having been told the order in which Jennifer was planning on touring Old Delhi, Inspector Naresh Prasad merely assumed she'd changed her mind about the Red Fort and was moving on to the Jama Masjid. Although still hurrying to a degree, he felt there wasn't the need to put himself in jeopardy. At the same time, he didn't want to lose her, even though he was progressively questioning the need to follow her while she was acting like a tourist. He would have much preferred to see whom she'd had breakfast with that morning than follow her on a sightseeing junket.

As he pulled into the parking lot and parked, he noticed a man in black climbing from his Mercedes. He was the same man Naresh had seen only a few minutes earlier rushing for his car as Jennifer Hernandez was driving out from the Red Fort's parking area. Curious, Naresh rapidly got out himself.

Neil had to smile at himself as he ran along the face of the Jama Masjid mosque. He was certainly having a devil of a time surprising Jennifer, and wondered what had happened at the Red Fort. When he had visited India five months ago, the Red Fort had been one of his favorite tourist sites, but apparently Jennifer had felt otherwise.

A minute earlier, by sheer luck, Neil had just caught sight of Jennifer, poised on a cycle rickshaw and about to be swallowed up by the labyrinthine Delhi. Yelling to the driver to stop, Neil had tossed the fare into the taxi's front seat, and had leaped from the vehicle, only to be bogged down by the milling crowds massed at the mosque's entrance. When he'd finally broken free, Jennifer had disappeared.

When Neil entered the bazaar, he had to slow to a jog. At first he wasn't sure which way she'd gone, but a minute or so of further jogging brought her back into sight. At that moment she was about fifty feet ahead of him.

Jennifer was not enjoying herself. The cycle rickshaw seat was hard and the alleyway bumpy. Several times she was concerned she might fall as the cycle's tires fell into potholes. The alleyways, narrow lanes, and even narrower katras were horribly crowded, noisy, frenetic, vibrant, and chaotic all at the same time. Myriad electrical wires, like spider webs, hung above, as did water pipes. There was a symphony of smells both delightful and sickening, involving, among other things, spices and urine, animal feces and jasmine.

As she held on for dear life she thought she probably would have found the experience more engaging if it hadn't been for her grandmother's death, which she couldn't quite displace from the forefront of her consciousness, despite the bombardment on her senses. Although she was dealing with the tragedy far better than she had imagined before arriving in India, it was still affecting her negatively on many levels. As such, it seemed to her that the part of the bazaar she was seeing was dirty—filled with too much trash and sewage, and teeming with far too many people. The shops themselves for the most part were mere holes in the walls, their junk tumbling out into the lane. Although she recognized she'd yet to see the section selling the gold and silver or the spice area, she'd had enough. She just wasn't in the right mind-set.

Jennifer was about to try to tell the cyclist she wanted to go back—in fact, she'd leaned forward, holding on with her left hand and keeping her shoulder bag in her lap, to attempt to get the man's attention—when she noticed a kind of commotion out of the corner of her eye. As she turned to her left and looked down, she found herself staring down the barrel of a gun. Over the top of the barrel was a man's hard, thin, expressionless face.

The next thing everyone in the crowded galis heard was the startling noise of the gun being fired twice. Those close to the victim, who happened to be looking in his direction, also had to witness the awful destructive power at close range, of a nine-millimeter bullet traversing the skull and exiting the left side of the man's face. In this instance, most of the victim's left cheek was blown away, laying bare the upper and lower dentition.

Chapter 26

For a moment, time stood still. All was silent. Everyone in the immediate area was dumbstruck for almost a full beat. With the gun going off in the narrow, close-quartered alleyway, their ears were ringing. The next instant it was like being next to a tornado, with everyone screaming and running headlong away in a complete panic.

The protein-starved cyclist ferrying Jennifer was one of the very first to flee, literally leaping from his tricycle and dashing off, heading down the galis, not even holding on to his dhoti. He might have appeared malnourished, but he had a strong sense of self-preservation.

The instant the driver left the cycle rickshaw and forcefully pushed off with his feet, the front wheel turned sharply and the tricycle's momentum heaved it forward. As it crashed it hurled Jennifer straight ahead onto the filthy pavement. With her shoulder bag looped over her shoulder, it stayed with her as she sprawled spread-eagle on the ground, scraping the side of her nose and her right elbow in the process. At the time she didn't care what she'd fallen into. Almost the second she'd touched down, she was up and running with everyone else.

Within seconds the bazaar became a building tide of people rushing forward like a wave, engulfing the shops, which acted like clams. As soon as the disturbance touched them, their doors instantly slammed shut from within; locks were secured, leaving merchandise to be stumbled over and trampled in the street.

Jennifer had no idea where she was going but was content to let her shocked feet take her anyplace quickly, as long as it was away from where the gun had gone off. All she could think about was the fleeting image of the man in black aiming a gun at her face. At the last nanosecond she saw the man's left cheek literally disappear; one second it was there, the next it was gone. At that instant the man appeared to be the embodiment of the Grim Reaper.

Jennifer became aware of other people running, everybody in a slightly different direction, although most down the street and bearing to the right at the first corner. Rapidly tiring from running full-tilt, she noticed a number of people disappearing into the doorway of one of the larger shops beyond the corner. The owner was complaining and trying to get his door shut, but the half dozen or so people were ignoring him. Jennifer pushed into the store behind the others, as ahead she saw two policemen, scruffily dressed in khaki, trying to stop the panic by beating people with their long bamboo staffs as they ran headlong into them.

As she dashed into the shop and stared around at the merchandise, she realized it was a butcher shop. Toward the front were stacks and stacks of tiny crates stuffed with live, cackling chickens and a couple of ducks. A little farther inside were some pigs and a lamb. The place stank and was horribly dirty. The floor was covered with dried crusted blood. Flies were all over everything. Jennifer found it hard to keep them out of her face.

While the proprietor was arguing with the other strangers who had run in, Jennifer looked for a hiding place of sorts, where she could get her breath and reprogram her mind. She was still overwhelmed by fright. Knowing she could not be choosy, she encountered a soiled curtain. With no hesitation, she pulled it aside and stepped beyond.

As her foot came down, Jennifer realized belatedly she had to direct it onto one of two bricks. The same with the other foot. She had inadvertently stepped into a makeshift toilet. Balancing herself, she pulled the curtain back into place. Next she managed to turn herself around without stepping off the bricks. The facility was just a hole, two bricks, and a faucet.

The argument between the owner and the interlopers was still going on out in the narrow store. Jennifer assumed the language was Hindi. She tried not to breathe through her nose. The smell was repulsive.

Now that she was stationary, Jennifer shivered. She looked at her hands and then tentatively smelled. It didn't smell good, whatever it was that she'd landed in when she'd pitched out of the tricycle. At least it wasn't feces. She looked down at the faucet, shrugged, and bent down to rinse off her hands. At that point it sounded as if a new person had gotten into the shop and was arguing with the owner. This time it was in English. But the individual said little. It was mostly the owner carrying on very angrily. Then there was a crash, and the pigs began squealing and the lamb bleating.

Worrying about what was happening, Jennifer stood up, turned, and listened. It sounded like the owner was trying to get up. Just when Jennifer had generated the courage to peek around the curtain, it was rudely whipped to the side, causing her to cry out, as did the person doing the whipping.

It was Neil McCulgan.

"God, you scared me half to death," Neil complained with a hand pressed to his chest.

"You?" Jennifer complained with equal vehemence. "What about me? And what in God's name are you doing here?"

"There'll be time to explain," Neil said. He extended a hand for Jennifer to step off the bricks. Behind him, the owner was busy trying to extricate himself from a stack of the tiny chicken cages where he'd presumably been pushed. Several of the cages had broken, and the released chickens were nervously pacing around the immediate area.

She shook her head and raised her hands as a warning. "You don't want to touch me. I was tossed out of a tricycle into some—"

"I know. I saw."

"You did?" Jennifer stepped off the bricks. She briefly glanced at the half dozen Indians she'd followed into the shop.

"I most certainly did."

"I want you Americans out of here," yelled the owner, after catching the chickens and cramming the poor birds into occupied cages. "I want everyone out of here!"

"Let's go!" Neil said, keeping himself between the owner and Jennifer. "There's nothing to be running from."

Outside, things had pretty much returned to normal. People were no longer in a panic and were beginning to drift back into the street. Shops were reopening, and the two policemen were no longer beating anyone. Best of all, it seemed no one had gotten hurt other than the person who was shot.

"Alright, this is far enough!" Jennifer said, halting in the middle of the alley. She was trembling now that she'd had a moment to think about what she had experienced. It had all transpired so fast. "Do you know what happened?"

"Sort of," Neil said. "I was behind you trying to catch up when the shooting occurred. I've been trying to catch you from the moment you left the hotel. I missed you at the Red Fort."

"I couldn't handle visiting it," Jennifer confessed. "And it turned out that I couldn't handle the bazaar, either. I was trying to get the cyclist to turn around and take me back to my car when the shots rang out."

"Anyway, I got to the mosque and I just caught a glimpse of you disappearing on the cycle rickshaw. I had to run through all those people in front of the mosque to try not to lose you in this labyrinth." Neil made a sweeping gesture with his hand. "I wasn't even sure which direction you'd gone. But I hurried best I could despite the crowd. Then the moment I did see you, I noticed someone go right up behind you and take out a gun. I yelled bloody murder and started running faster, but a short guy behind the first was faster. He was like a gunslinger. He whipped out his own gun and blam, blam, then yelled 'Police!' and held up a badge. That was it. I saw you pitch from the cycle and dash off. It was all I could do to keep you in sight. You really can sprint."

"You think the guy with the gun was going to shoot me?" Jennifer asked anxiously. She started to raise her hand to her face in consternation but thought better of it.

Neil pressed his lips together and shrugged. "It sure looked like it. I mean, he could have been planning on robbing you, I suppose, but I kinda doubt it. He acted too motivated. Is there anyone that might actually want to kill you?" Neil let the question trail off, suggesting that he couldn't believe what he was actually asking.

"I've kinda frustrated a couple of people, but not enough to want to kill me. At least I don't think so."

"Maybe it was a case of mistaken identity?"

Jennifer looked away, shook her head, and laughed humorlessly. "God, what I've been doing is certainly not worth getting killed for. No way. If it's not a mistake, then I'm outta here, Granny and all."

"Are you certain there's no one really, really angry at you?"

"My granny's case manager, but it's her freaking job. It's not the kind of thing you kill someone over."

"One way or the other, you are mighty lucky that plainclothes policeman was where he was."

"You are so right," Jennifer said. "Come on! Let's go meet this guy. Maybe he'll know something. Maybe he was even following the other guy. Now that they have the body, maybe they might know if he was following me or not. It's worth a try to get some answers."

Neil reached out and restrained Jennifer. "I don't advise it."

"Why not?" Jennifer said, pulling her arm free from Neil's grasp.

"When I was here last for my medical meeting, I learned a lot about the Indian government and the Indian police from my hosts. It's best, unless absolutely necessary, to stay clear of both. Corruption is a way of life here. It's not viewed from the same moral perspective as it is in the West. Whenever you get involved, it costs you money. The CBI, which is the equivalent to our FBI, is supposed to be very different. But in this situation you'll get yourself caught up with the regular local police. I'm not even certain they wouldn't put you in jail for inciting someone to pull a gun."

"Don't be silly," Jennifer said, thinking Neil was joking. She started walking back to where the episode occurred. "You're exaggerating."

"I'm exaggerating a little," Neil admitted, catching up to Jennifer. "But the fact that the local police are corrupt to some degree is apparent to everyone in the know, trust me. Also, so are many of the civil servants for the most part. It's best not to get involved. If you make any specific request about a crime, they have to fill out an FIR, or First Information Report, and, of course, it has to have five million copies. It makes work for them, and they hate it and hate you, too."

"A man was killed. There needs to be an FIR."

"Yeah, but that's his FIR."

"The more I think about it, he must have been after me in some form or fashion."

"Maybe, maybe not," Neil said. "I'm telling you, you're taking a risk. I was told under no uncertain terms not to get involved with the local police."

It was hard to walk side by side in the crowd, especially as the crowd got more and more dense the closer they came to the scene. Neil let Jennifer go ahead. Suddenly, she stopped and turned around. "Wait a sec!" she said. "Although I've been blown over and distracted by this episode, let me ask you again: What in God's name are you doing here in India? I mean, the question has popped into my mind several times, but this attempt on my life has tended to dominate my attention."

"No doubt," Neil said, trying to think what exactly to say at this point. If it hadn't been for the excitement, he was going to come right out and apologize first thing. He shrugged, thinking, *What's the difference.* "I'm here because you asked me to come and because you suggested you needed me. I didn't really take that seriously back in L.A. I was more concerned, I'm afraid, about a surfing meet that's taking place today in La Jolla. Unfortunately, when you walked out prior to any discussion, I got mad, and it took me a while to get unmad, and by the time I did, you were gone."

"When did you get here?" Jennifer asked.

"Last night. I wasn't going to disturb you if you were asleep. The problem is they wouldn't even tell me your room number, so I couldn't put my ear against your door."

"Why didn't you call me to let me know you were coming?"

"Easy," Neil said with a short laugh of self-mockery. "I was afraid you'd tell me to turn around and go home. I mean, I wasn't even confident you'd take my call, or if you did take it, knowing you as I do, I wasn't sure you wouldn't just tell me to drop dead and that would be that."

"I might have," Jennifer acknowledged. "I was more than disappointed at your response. I can tell you that."

"I'm sorry I didn't give the situation the significance it deserved at the time," Neil said.

Jennifer was thoughtful for a moment, chewing on the inside of her cheek. Then she turned around again and pushed through the crowd. The cycle rickshaw was still lying on its side. The body was still there as well, uncovered. With the left side of the face gone and the teeth visible, it looked like it was grimacing.

"That's the driver," Jennifer whispered, motioning with her chin toward the emaciated cycle rickshaw driver squatting on the ground. There were several policemen in khaki uniforms standing on either side of him.

"See what I mean!" Neil whispered back. "The poor guy's probably under arrest."

"You really think so?"

"I wouldn't be surprised."

"It looks to me as if that short guy is in charge. What do you think?"

Naresh Prasad was talking to several other uniformed police officers standing near the body.

"He must be some kind of plainclothes detective or something."

"You really think I shouldn't talk to them?" Jennifer asked.

"Put it this way: What do you know? Nothing. You don't even know if this guy followed you from the Amal Palace, or just saw you here and said there's a millionaire Westerner."

"Get out of here!" Jennifer said.

"There's no way for you to know. That's the point. They don't know, either. If you insist on getting involved, you're not going to learn anything and you're not going to add anything, and it will possibly cost you some money. Besides, if you change your mind, you can tell them tomorrow, or this afternoon for that matter. No one is going to fault you for getting the hell out of here under the circumstances."

"Alright," Jennifer snapped. "You've talked me out of it, at least for now. Let's get back to the hotel. I think I need a drink or something. I'm still shaking."

"Good choice!" Neil commented. "What we can do is head over to the American embassy at some point either today or tomorrow and get their take. If they think you should file an FIR, we'll do it, because then they will be involved and there won't be any screwing around."

"Fair enough," Jennifer said.

The crowd near the killing blocked most of the galis. On one side, several policemen were keeping a narrow right-of-way open against the far wall. To create it, the police had required the local merchants to clear the street of merchandise. Jennifer and Neil again had to walk in single file.

As Jennifer passed, she looked back at the cycle rickshaw still lying on its side. She could see where in the street she'd fallen. She glanced briefly again at the driver. He'd not been allowed to move, which tended to give further credence to Neil's point about not getting involved unless there was some compelling reason. Her eyes also briefly passed over the short plainclothes policeman as they came abreast of where he was standing, causing her to do a double take. The officer was looking at her.

For several beats Jennifer and Inspector Naresh Prasad's eyes locked together before Jennifer self-consciously looked away.

"Don't look now," Jennifer said in a low voice over her shoulder at Neil, "but that short policeman was staring at me."

"Let's not get paranoid."

"Really, he was. Do you think he recognizes me from being in the cycle rickshaw?"

"I haven't the slightest idea. Stop and turn around. Let's see what he does. I mean, if he recognizes you from being involved, we don't have a lot of choice. We have to talk to him."

Jennifer stopped but didn't immediately turn around. "I feel nervous," she said.

"Turn around!" Neil said under his hand to keep from being overheard. They were only about twenty feet from the policemen. If the bazaar hadn't been quite so noisy, they might have been able to hear parts of the man's conversation.

Taking a breath, Jennifer slowly turned. At that point it was not a clear line of sight between herself and Inspector Prasad. When she and Neil had abruptly stopped, they had blocked the right-of-way, and people trying to pass were backing up. Still, Jennifer could see the side of the policeman's face, and if he turned his head only ninety degrees, he would be looking directly at her. But he didn't turn his head, nor did he interrupt his conversation with the uniformed officers.

"He's not looking at you," Neil said.

"He doesn't appear to be," Jennifer agreed.

"Let's get out of here before he does," Neil said, grabbing Jennifer's arm and giving it a tug.

As the crowd thinned, they were able to pick up the pace and soon emerged from the shadows and tunnel-like atmosphere of the bazaar. The enormous Jama Masjid was now in front and to the right. Jennifer slowed and glanced back over her shoulder into the depths of the bazaar, although she couldn't see far.

"I feel more exposed out of the bazaar than in it," she said. "Let's get out of here."

"I'm with you," Neil agreed.

They both started to run, but as they did so, Jennifer kept glancing back over her shoulder.

"You're really becoming progressivly paranoid, I'm afraid," Neil commented between breaths.

"You'd be paranoid, too, if someone pointed a gun at you and got killed in the process."

"I can't argue with you there."

Around the front entrance of the mosque they had to slow with the crowds of tourists and those who preyed on them. Jennifer continued checking over her shoulder, and as they neared the parking area, it paid off.

"Don't look!" Jennifer said, continuing forward. "But that short plainclothes policeman is actually following us."

Neil stopped, but didn't turn around. "Where is he?"

"Behind us. Come on! Let's get out of here."

"No. Let's see if he approaches us," Neil said. "Hey, I'm responsible for you leaving the scene of a crime. I don't want you getting into trouble for it."

"Now you're saying conflicting things."

"I'm not. Really. As I said, if he recognizes you as having been in that cycle rickshaw, we need to talk to him. Can you still see him?"

Jennifer turned around and scanned the crowd. "No, I don't."

Neil turned around and looked. "There he is, moving away from the mosque. Another false alarm."

"Where?"

Neil pointed.

"You're right."

They watched as Inspector Prasad disappeared up the street that butted into the Jama Masjid.

Jennifer glanced at Neil and shrugged. "Sorry!"

"Don't be silly. Until he turned up that street I would have thought he was following us as well."

Jennifer and Neil continued on, entering the parking lot. Neil, as the taller one, was able to rise up on his toes and see over the sea of cars. The first black Mercedes they saw was not the Amal Palace car, but the second one was. Then it took the parking attendants almost twenty minutes to move all the cars boxing it in. Five minutes after that Jennifer and Neil were back on the main road heading south toward the Amal Palace.

"I thought you were going to go to Karim's," the driver said to Jennifer, while glancing at her in the rearview mirror.

"I lost my appetite," Jennifer called from the backseat. "I just want to go back to the hotel."

"Have you seen any sights here in Delhi?" Neil asked Jennifer.

"None," Jennifer said. "This was to be my big attempt. Unfortunately it was a bust." She held out her hand. It was trembling, not as much as it had been right after the shooting event but grossly shaking nonetheless.

"Despite this disaster, I gather you are doing much better dealing with your grandmother's issues than you thought you would be able to do."

Jennifer took in a deep breath and let it out through partially pursed lips. "I guess I am. I didn't realize how much of a separation I would be making between my grandmother's body and her soul or spirit. I don't know if it is a side benefit of going to medical school and having worked with cadavers or what. Of course, when I looked at Granny's body the first time, it got to me. But since then, I've been thinking of it as just a used body, and what it can tell us about how she died. At this point I really want there to be an autopsy."

"Are they going to do an autopsy for you?"

"I wish. No, no autopsy. They have a signed death certificate, and once that's signed, they want the body embalmed or cremated. My grandmother's case manager is dead set, so to speak, on getting the body disposed of and has been ragging on me from day one, which for me was Monday morning."

"Where is the body, in a morgue?"

"Yeah, sure," Jennifer voiced with a mocking laugh. "Granny's body and that of a man named Benfatti are in a cafeteria cooler. Yesterday morning, I actually saw my granny's body in there. It's not a perfect location for lots of reasons, but it's okay. It's cold enough."

"What's this other body you mentioned?"

"There have been two other similar deaths. One was so similar to my grandmother's it seems eerie. The other is sorta similar, but my guess would be that he was discovered immediately after he suffered whatever the other two suffered, because on the third one they actually went through a real resuscitation attempt."

"How do you know all this?"

"I've met the wives. I also talked both of them into not allowing their husbands to be embalmed or cremated. I think we have three bodies of people who have suffered some kind of a fatal medical crisis. The hospitals want to call it a heart attack, whether it's warranted or not, because all three have each had some kind of cardiac history. To tell you the truth, it has been my sense that the hospitals just want to get rid of these cases as soon as possible, and frankly, that has made me suspicious from day one."

"Could any of this be a kind of defense on your part as a way of helping you deal with the emotional aspect of losing your grandmother?"

For a moment Jennifer turned and stared out the car window. It was a good question, even though her first response was irritation that Neil would be capable of thinking she was making all this up. She turned back to Neil. "I think that there is something wrong with these three deaths. I think they were not natural. I do."

It was now Neil's turn to stare. He chose to stare out the front window. When he looked back at Jennifer, she was still looking at him. "It would be something hard to prove without autopsies. I assume you've been trying to get one."

"To some degree," Jennifer admitted. "As I said, once the death certificate is signed, they don't think about autopsies. They just want to get the body out of the cafeteria cooler. But the reason I'm treading water today is because something is happening tonight that could turn this all around."

"What do I have to do, guess?" Neil complained when Jennifer paused.

"I just want to make sure you are listening." Jennifer said. "Did I ever mention to you that Granny was a nanny to a woman who's become quite well known as a medical examiner?"

"I believe so, but remind me again."

"Her name is Laurie Montgomery. She works as a

medical examiner in New York City along with her husband, Jack Stapleton."

"I can recall your mentioning Laurie Montgomery
but not Jack."

"Well, they just got married a couple of years ago. I
called her Tuesday, right after I'd seen Granny. I just
wanted to run some things by her, and she shocked me by
offering to come immediately. I guess I didn't know that
Granny meant so much to her. I should have. Maria had
that kind of effect on people. But then a problem arose:
Laurie and Jack are in the middle of an assisted reproduc-
tion cycle, meaning Jack's got to be around to perform."

Neil rolled his eyes.

"Anyway, to solve the problem they both are coming
and are scheduled to land tonight."

"The fact that they are coming won't hurt," Neil
said. "But I'm not so sure you should put such hope on
it. If you've been unable to move the authorities here, I
wouldn't count on a couple of medical examiners doing
much better. I happen to know that forensic pathology
is not a really popular field here in India, and whether or
not an autopsy is done is not up to the doctors."

"I've heard the same. And to add to the trouble,
there is some controversy over which ministry oversees
what. The morgues are under the ministry of home,
while medical examiners who use them are under the
ministry of health. Also, the decision of whether an autopsy is indicated in a specific case is up to the police and
the magistrates, not the doctors."

"That's my point. So I wouldn't get your hopes up

too high just because a couple of sharp medical examiners are coming to town. I get the feeling that you have done just about as much as anyone could do."

"Maybe so, but I'm not going to give up, although I'm tempted after this episode today. I tell you, if Laurie and Jack weren't coming tonight, I'd be out of here."

"I'd be the one trying to get you to go, and I'm not sure it wouldn't be the most sensible idea."

They rode in silence, each lost in thought and each looking out their own window at the kaleidoscopic view of the Delhi street scene. After a while Jennifer hazarded a glance in Neil's direction. She was still shocked by his presence. He was perhaps the last person on earth she'd expected to see when the curtain was whipped back while she was cowering in the toilet in the filthy butcher shop. She studied his profile. There was very little indentation where his nose abutted his forehead, like a head on a Greek coin. His lips were full, his Adam's apple large. She thought he was a handsome man, and she was flattered that he came. But what did it mean? She had essentially given up on him because of the way he had brushed her off. Although Jennifer was unaccustomed to vacillating once she'd made up her mind, Neil's effort in coming nine thousand miles suggested this might be the time to start.

"Are you planning on going out to the airport to welcome your friends?" Neil asked suddenly.

"I am. Would you like to come along?"

"Don't you think you'd be safer staying in the hotel?"

"Maybe so, but security is high at the airport and at the hotel. I think I'll be alright."

"I'll go with you, if I'm invited."

"Absolutely," Jennifer said.

Jennifer held her hand up. It was still shaking like she'd had eleven cups of coffee.

Every so often, Jennifer glanced out the back window. She was concerned about being followed, as she apparently had been when she left the hotel. Unfortunately, with the dense traffic and general chaos of the street, it was difficult to tell. But when they reached the Amal Palace Hotel and turned up the lengthy ramp, something mildly out of the ordinary happened.

Once again, she had glanced out the back as they rose up the driveway, and she was about to face around when a small white car pulled into the driveway behind them. But then it stopped, blocking the drive. Jennifer tried to see how many people were in the car, but she couldn't, as the hazy sun was reflecting off the windshield.

Looking forward, she could see they were about to reach the porte cochere. Glancing back, she saw the small white car back out of the drive and drive away after causing a lot of honking, beeping, and angry shouts. Someone must have made a wrong turn, was all Jennifer could think, yet in her sensitized state it seemed out of the ordinary.

"Are you finished with the car?" the driver asked Jennifer, pulling her attention away from the curious antics of the white car.

"Absolutely," Jennifer said, eager to get into the hotel. "Thank you."

"I'm impressed you took a car," Neil said as they walked toward the entrance doors.

"I don't know if I'll get away with it," Jennifer admitted. "The company, Foreign Medical Solutions, out of Chicago, is paying my hotel bill, but I don't know whether it's for extras or not. If not, it will have to go on my credit card."

Inside the lobby they hesitated. "Are you hungry?" Neil asked.

"Not at all," Jennifer admitted. "I feel like I ODed on caffeine."

"What would you like to do? Or would you like me to make a suggestion, since you're so wired?"

"The latter," Jennifer responded without hesitation. She didn't feel capable of thinking about practical issues.

"When I checked in last night, I was told they have a full spa with weights, stationary bikes, the works. Do you have some gym clothes?"

"I do."

"Perfect. Maybe a little workout is what you need. After we do that, maybe you'll be hungry for something, and if so, we can have it out by the pool. Then, later this afternoon, if you are up to it, we could go over and meet with someone in the consular section at the American embassy. They can give you their take on the episode in the bazaar and what you should do."

"I don't know if I want to go to the embassy, but the idea of a workout and going out to the pool was my original plan. I'm definitely up for it."

"Miss Hernandez!" a voice called out. Jennifer turned in its direction. She could see one of the concierges waving a slip of paper. She excused herself from Neil and stepped over to his desk.

"You are back early," Sumit said. "I hope you enjoyed your sightseeing."

"It wasn't quite what I had in mind," Jennifer said, reluctant to tell him exactly what had happened.

"I'm very sorry," Sumit said. "Is there something we could have done differently?"

"I think it was my problem," Jennifer admitted, and then changed the subject. "Do you have something for me?"

"Yes, we do. We got this urgent message for you. You are to call Kashmira Varini, and here is the message and the number." Jennifer took the number. She was vexed to be bothered. On her way back to Neil, she opened the message. It said, "We have arranged to do something very special for your grandmother. Please call Kashmira Varini." Jennifer stopped and reread the message. She was mystified. The first thing that went through her mind was that perhaps they had seen the light and were planning on doing an autopsy. Continuing on, she showed the message to Neil.

"This is the lady who's been my bête noire," Jennifer said.

"Give her a call!" Neil responded, handing the paper back.

"You think so? I just cannot believe that she might be doing something appropriate."

"There's only one way to find out."

The two of them walked back to the concierge desk. Jennifer asked if there was a phone in the lobby that she could use to make a local call. Without a second's hesitation, Sumit grabbed one of the several phones he had, lifted it up on top of the counter, and gave it a push to-ward Jennifer. As if that wasn't enough, he lifted the re-ceiver, handed it to her, and then punched an outside line with his index finger. All this was done with a gra-cious smile.

Jennifer tapped in the number and stared up at Neil while the call went through. She truly did not know what to expect.

"Ah, yes," Kashmira said when Jennifer identified herself. "Thank you for getting back to me. I have excel-lent news. Our CEO, Rajish Bhurgava, has arranged something extraordinary for your grandmother. Have you ever heard of the burning ghats of Varanasi?"

"I can't say that I have," Jennifer responded.

"The city of Varanasi, or Banaras, as the English called it, or Kashi, as the ancients did, is by far India's holiest Hindu city, with a religious legacy that goes back more than three thousand years."

Jennifer shrugged at Neil, indicating she still had no idea what the hospital had in mind.

"The city is sanctified by Shiva and the Ganges and is by far the most sacred place for rites of passage."

"Perhaps you could tell me how this all relates to my grandmother," Jennifer said impatiently, recognizing it had nothing to do with an autopsy.

"Of course," Kashmira said enthusiastically. "Mr. Bhurgava has arranged something unheard of for your grandmother. Although the burning ghats of Varanasi are reserved for Hindus, he has obtained permission for your grandmother to experience her rite of passage in

Varanasi. All I need is for you to come to the hospital and sign a release."

"I don't mean to offend anyone," Jennifer said, "but whether Granny is cremated in Varanasi or New Delhi doesn't make a lot of difference to me."

"Then you don't understand. Those people cremated in Varanasi gain particularly good karma and a markedly good rebirth in the next life. We just need your permssion to proceed."

"Mrs. Varini," Jennifer said slowly, "tomorrow morning we will be coming to the hospital. I will be with my medical examiner friends, and we will come to some kind of agreement."

"I believe you are ill-advised not to take this special opportunity. There will be no cost. We are doing this as a favor to you and your grandmother."

"As I said, I don't want to hurt anyone's feelings. I appreciate efforts on my behalf, but I would have preferred an autopsy. The answer is no."

"Then I must inform you that the Queen Victoria Hospital has gone to the courts, and we imminently expect, around noon tomorrow, a writ of authority from a magistrate to remove, send to Varanasi, and cremate your grandmother, Mr. Benfatti, and Mr. Lucas. I am sorry that you have pushed us to this extent, but your grandmother's body, as well as those of the others, is a threat to the institutions' well-being."

Jennifer's head rebounded slightly with the force of the disconnect. She handed the phone back to Sumit and thanked him. To Neil she said, "She hung up on me. They are going to get legal permission to remove Granny tomorrow and have her cremated."

"Then it's a good thing your friends are coming in tonight."

"You can say that again. If I were here on my own, I have no clue what I'd do."

"Then it's a good thing. . . ." Neil said, teasing Jennifer by actually repeating his comment the second time as she'd rhetorically asked him to do.

"That's quite enough!" she said with a suppressed laugh, giving his arm a shake with both hands.

"Why don't we head up to our rooms and change into some exercise clothes."

"That's your best suggestion so far," Jennifer said, and they both headed for the elevators.

Chapter 27

Inspector Naresh Prasad entered the health ministry building and noted the difference between it and the one that housed the New Delhi police department. Whereas peeling paint and a certain amount of trash were the norm in his building, the health ministry was comparatively clean. Even the security equipment was new, and the people manning it seemed somewhat motivated. As usual, he had to leave his service revolver at the entrance.

Exiting on the second floor, Naresh walked down the long, echoing hall to where he knew the relatively new medical tourism office was. He entered without knocking. The contrast between his office and Ramesh Srivastava's was even greater than that between their respective buildings. Ramesh's offices were freshly painted and had new furniture. The fact that Ramesh

was part of a significantly higher level of civil bureaucracy was apparent in most everything, including the
equipment on the secretaries' desks.

As he fully expected, Naresh had to wait for a certain
amount of time. It was part of the mechanism bureaucrats used to exert their superiority over colleagues, even
if they were available. But Naresh didn't mind. He expected it. Besides, there was a waiting area with a new
couch, a rug, and magazines, even if the reading material was outdated.

"Mr. Srivastava can see you now," one of the secretaries said fifteen minutes later, pointing the way toward
her boss's door.

Naresh heaved himself to his feet. A few seconds later,
he was standing in front of Ramesh's desk. Ramesh
didn't invite him to sit down. The man had his fingers
intertwined, elbows on his desk. His watery eyes regarded Naresh irritably. It was obvious there was to be
no small talk on this occasion.

"You said on the phone you wanted to see me because there was a problem," Ramesh said sulkily. "What's
the problem?"

"I got on Miss Hernandez first thing this morning. I
didn't get there early enough to tail her to breakfast at
the Imperial, so I don't know whom she met there. But
right after that, not too much after nine, she came back
to the Amal and then took a hotel car, apparently to go
sightseeing."

"Do I have to hear all this?" Ramesh complained.

"If you want to know how the problem happened,"
Naresh said.

Ramesh made a rotating motion with his index finger for Naresh to continue.

"She stopped briefly at the Red Fort, but it didn't appeal to her. Next she went to the bazaar, parked at the Jama Masjid, and hired a cycle rickshaw."

"Can't you just tell me the problem?" Ramesh complained again.

"It was at that moment that I came into the parking area just after someone in a new E-Class Mercedes. I vaguely noticed him because he'd been tailing her as well from the Red Fort."

Ramesh rolled his eyes at Naresh's lengthy rendition.

"He took off after Miss Hernandez, which I thought curious, so I redoubled my efforts and ran after both. From then on everything happened in the blink of an eye. He didn't hesitate. He ran up behind Miss Hernandez and pulled a gun. It was right in the middle of the crowded bazaar, with people all around. He was going to shoot, no questions asked. I had two seconds to decide whether to intervene. All I could hear was your telling me not to let her become a martyr. Well, that's what she was about to become, so I shot and killed the would-be killer."

Ramesh's mouth slowly dropped open. Then he slapped a hand across his forehead and leaned on his elbow while he shook his head in short arcs. "No!" he cried.

Naresh shrugged. "It all happened so fast." Naresh reached into his pocket and took out a piece of paper. On it was written *Dhaval Narang*. He placed it on the desk in front of Ramesh.

Without removing his head from his hand, Ramesh reached out and picked up the paper. He read the name. "Do you know who this guy is?" Ramesh blurted. He raised his eyes and looked irritably at Naresh.

"I do now. It is Dhaval Narang."

"That's right. It is Dhaval Narang, and do you know whom he works for?"

Naresh shook his head.

"He works for Shashank Malhotra, you bungling idiot. Malhotra was getting rid of the girl. It would have been ascribed to thieves. The martyr issue is only if we, the Indian civil services, killed her, not Malhotra."

"What should I have done? I was trying to follow your orders. Why didn't you tell me Malhotra was going to take care of her?"

"Because I didn't know. At least I didn't know for sure." Ramesh rubbed his face vigorously. "Clearly, now everything's worse. Now she's warned she's been targeted. Where is she?"

"She went back to her hotel."

"What happened at the site?"

"The shot caused a general panic. She fled with everyone else. I stayed at the site to help the local constables restore order and get the victim's ID."

"Did she come back and talk to the police and to you?"

"She came back and was accompanied by an American man. I don't know where or how they teamed up. But she didn't talk to the police, which is somewhat strange. I thought about pulling her in, but I wanted to talk to you first."

"That just shows how suspicious she is."

"Maybe she will just leave after such an experience?"

"Wouldn't that be nice, but not according to her grandmother's case manager or the CEO of the hospital. For whatever reason, this young woman is motivated no matter what happens."

"Well, what do you want me to do?"

"Have you had any luck in regard to finding out who is the source providing the material to CNN?"

"I put two people on it this morning. I haven't spoken with them since."

"Give them a call while I call Shashank Malhotra. Also, there was another death but at the Aesculapian Medical Center. Once again, CNN got it extremely early."

Ramesh picked up his phone. He was not looking forward to talking with Shashank Malhotra. Despite what he said to Naresh, Ramesh knew that he was ultimately responsible for Dhaval Narang's demise. As Naresh said, he should have been informed.

"I hope you are calling me up to thank me for solving your problem," Shashank said when he came on the line. His tone was neutral. It wasn't as cheerful as it had been the day before, nor as menacing.

"I'm afraid not. I'm afraid there's an additional problem and an extension of the old one."

"What?" Shashank demanded.

"First, Miss Hernandez has talked the spouse of the third patient into wanting an autopsy. And second, Dhaval Narang was shot and killed this morning in the Old Delhi bazaar."

"You're not serious?"

"Did you send him to talk to the Hernandez woman, to get her to leave India?" Naresh asked.

"He's truly dead?" Shashank questioned, with anger and disbelief.

"I have it from a good source."

"How could this have happened? He was a professional. He was no amateur."

"People make mistakes."

"Not Dhaval," Shashank growled. "He was the best. Listen, I want this woman taken care of."

"We feel similarly, but she's now been alerted that someone wants her dead. I think we better handle this problem from this end."

"You'd better!" Shashank groused. "I don't want you to have to start looking over your shoulder to and from work." With that said, he hung up.

Ramesh dropped the phone back into its cradle. He looked up at Naresh, who'd finished his call as well.

"Nothing yet," Naresh said. "But they've barely begun the investigation. It's not going to be easy. There are lots of private academic doctors who have admitting privileges at other nonacademic private hospitals, and most have admitting privileges at more than one. It's more for convenience's sake for the patients in terms of location, and they apparently don't admit that many, as they are not supposed to have private patients."

"Your people are going to continue to work on it, I presume?"

"Very much so. What do you want me to do?"

"Keep tabs on the Hernandez woman. Supposedly, a friend is coming tonight who is a forensic pathologist. Remember, there are to be no autopsies. Luckily, in this situation, we have the law on our side."

Chapter 28

Cal had his legs crossed and his feet on the corner of the library table. Santana had gotten him a bunch of articles about medical tourism that had been springing up in the U.S. newspapers. They had all picked up on the three CNN segments about the New Delhi deaths, and on the three networks' evening news broadcasts. People were eating it up. Cal's favorites were those laced with personal stories of people canceling scheduled trips, mostly to India but also to Thailand.

With everything suddenly going so well, Cal should have been ecstatic, but he wasn't. Like a toothache, the issue involving the Hernandez woman had been bothering him all day. Early that morning, he'd called back the anesthesiologist and the pathologist, and again had gone over the hypothetical scenario involving succinylcholine. If the two doctors had been at all suspicious, they didn't show it in the slightest, and in certain respects competed with each other in making certain the diabolical scheme was foolproof.

When he had hung up from the conference call, he'd felt reassured. Unfortunately, it hadn't lasted, and the issue had slowly wormed its way back into his consciousness. What could it have been that the pesky medical student had come across that had initiated her suspicions? Even after the Hernandez woman's departure, there were bound to be others who'd be just as curious and stumble on the same mysterious and potentially fatal flaw.

"Hey, man!" Durell called out from the library doorway.

Cal waved. "What's up?"

"You want to come out and take a look at the organization's new ride?"

"Why not," he said. He let his feet fall to the floor with a plop and stood up.

The front door to the mansion then slammed shut.

"Can we hold off just for a few minutes?" Cal asked. "If that's Veena and Samira, I'd like to get a debriefing. I've been worrying over that Hernandez chick all day, ever since you rightly said we should find out what made her suspicious. I imagine it has something to do with her being a medical student, but I cannot for the life of me figure out what it could be. I even called the two doctors we originally consulted in Charlotte, North Carolina. As far as I can figure out, we've thought of everything."

"I'm for finding out," Durell admitted. "Otherwise, it's going to be a constant worry, you know what I'm saying?"

"I know what you're saying," Cal agreed, as Veena, Samira, and Raj came into the library. They were in a good mood, singing a song they all knew from childhood. Samira broke off and went up to Durell for a hug and a real kiss. Veena went to Cal but availed herself of only a French-style peck on each cheek.

Raj literally threw himself laughing onto the couch as he finished the last refrain of the childhood ditty.

"You guys are happy," Cal commented, with the suggestion he wasn't.

"It was an easy day for all of us," Veena said. "Raj was the only one assigned a patient, and he was just a hernia repair. Samira and I had to look for things to do."

"How come?"

Veena and Samira looked at each other. "We're not sure. Maybe a few cancellations. Maybe Nurses International is doing too good a job." They laughed.

"Wouldn't that be ironic," Cal said. "Anyway, what's the status with the Hernandez woman? Any feedback today?"

"I was free around two-thirty," Veena said, "so I went down to talk to the case manager. I asked her about Maria Hernandez's body and whether it had been taken care of. She cackled mockingly and said, 'Of course not.' Apparently, they had gone to the extent of offering to have the body taken to Varanasi to have it cremated on the banks of the Ganges, but the granddaughter turned it down, so they are completely frustrated. Tomorrow the medical examiner friend is coming to the hospital, which shouldn't make the slightest difference because they absolutely refuse to do an autopsy.

But there's clear sailing in sight. The case manager told me they are getting a writ tomorrow from a magistrate to remove and cremate the body. So it should be over tomorrow sometime."

"Same for Benfatti," Samira said.

"Same for David Lucas," Raj said. "The magistrate writ is to cover all three bodies."

"You all haven't been inquiring about your bodies, have you?" Cal asked, with mild alarm.

"Yes, we have," Samira said. "Is that a problem? We will all feel better when the bodies are gone."

"Please, no more! Don't call any attention to yourselves by asking specifically about the bodies."

All three shrugged. "We didn't think we were causing undue attention," Samira said. "The situation is general hospital gossip. It's not as if we are the only ones talking about it."

"Do me a favor and don't participate," Cal said.

"My patient's death certificate was signed today," Raj said. "But still the wife wants an autopsy on the advice of Jennifer Hernandez."

"What was the official cause of death?" Cal asked.

"Heart attack," Raj said. "Heart attack with emboli and stroke."

"With all three bodies still around," Cal said, "maybe we should put off doing any more patients for a few days."

Veena sat up straight from where she'd collapsed into a leather club chair. "I agree wholeheartedly. No more deaths until all this chaos caused by Jennifer Hernandez is cleared up."

"Someone should let Petra know," Cal said. "One of her nurses called in today to say she had a good candidate."

Veena bounded out of the chair. "I'll do it. I didn't even think we should have done one last night." Without waiting for a response, she left the room.

Raj got up from the couch. "I think I'll take a shower," he said.

"Likewise," Samira said. She gave Durell a final hug and followed Raj out of the room.

Cal glanced at Durell. "Let's see those wheels," he said.

"You got it," Durell responded.

"I'm thinking we should do something proactive about this Jennifer Hernandez," Cal said as they passed out of the library and headed toward the front door.

"I told you, if we don't find out what has made her suspicious, we're always going to feel like we have our dicks hanging out. Someone else is going to see it and call us on it."

"That's exactly what has me worried. It's a bummer it has to be now, just when everything else is going so smoothly."

"What do you have in mind?" Durell asked. He opened the mansion's front door and held it for Cal.

"I thought I'd call Sachin, Mr. Motorcycle Jacket. He handled Veena's father perfectly. I thought of him because he called me yesterday to say he checked on Basant Chandra Wednesday and the guy panicked. He doesn't think he has to see him again for a couple of weeks. I think he could handle Jennifer Hernandez with ease. It's a much more simple job."

"What would you have him do?"

"Snatch her and bring her here. We can lock her in that room under the garage until she talks."

"Then what?" Durell asked. He was standing next to a burgundy Toyota Land Cruiser. It had seen some miles and had its share of dents, but the wear and tear only seemed to give it character.

Cal put his right hand lightly on the vehicle's metallic surface and walked a complete circuit around it, letting his fingers trail along. He then opened the driver's-side door and glanced inside. The interior was equally worn.

"I like it," Cal said. "How does it run?"

"Just fine. It's been a workhorse for an architectural firm."

"Perfect," Cal said. He shut the door firmly, and there was a reassuring click.

"So what will you do with Hernandez after you learn what you want her to tell us?"

"Nothing. I'd just pay Sachin to have her disappear. I don't really want to know where, but my guess is that she'd end up somewhere at the bottom of the landfill."

Durell nodded. He wondered how many people had already disappeared there. It was so convenient.

"Hey, man! I love the car," Cal said, his spirits rising. He gave one of the front tires a kick. "If we need it, it will be perfect. Good job."

"Thanks."

Chapter 29

Juggling all her injection paraphernalia, Laurie made her way to one of the plane's lavatories. After locking the door, she spread out her gonadotropin pharmacopeia on the tiny shelf. She deftly filled the syringe with the prescribed amount of follicular-stimulating hormone and then equally deftly gave herself the subcutaneous injection on the anterior aspect of her thigh. Ten-thirty p.m. Indian time was only an hour later than noon in New York City, which was when she gave herself her shot each and every day. At that moment they were flying over northwestern India, soon to begin their approach into New Delhi.

Finishing with the injection, Laurie regarded herself in the mirror. She looked terrible. Her hair was an absolute mess, and the dark circles beneath her eyes were drooping down in the direction of the corners of her mouth. Worst of all, she felt just generally dirty. But no wonder. First there'd been the overnight flight to Paris, during which she'd managed to sleep only a couple of hours. Then there'd been the three-hour layover, which was mostly needed to get to the next departure gate. And then there had been this current eight-hour marathon. What had her irritated was Jack, who had no trouble sleeping. It just didn't seem fair.

Laurie picked up the debris from her shot and poked it into the trash. The used needle went back into her purse, where she carried the medications and the fresh syringes. She didn't want to be irresponsible. She washed her hands and again looked at herself in the mirror. It was hard not to, since most of the wall behind the sink in the Lilliputian bathroom was a mirror. She couldn't help but wonder what effect this sudden trip was going to have on her infertility saga. She had absolutely no idea why she'd not gotten pregnant so far, and hoped the travel wouldn't add to whatever her problem was.

She opened the door and stepped out. Sensing that between her reaction to Jack's sleeping and her pondering her inability to get pregnant, she was getting herself worked up, she made a conscious effort to calm down. She hoped that over the course of the visit she would be capable of keeping her fragile emotions in check so she'd be able to provide the support Jennifer needed, which was the major stimulus for making the trip. At the same time, Laurie admitted to herself that she was also there to appease her own conscience. Maria's passing had definitely provoked a certain amount of guilt.

Back in her seat, Laurie looked at Jack. He was still sound asleep and in the exact same position as he was when she left him five minutes earlier. He was the picture of relaxation, with a slight insouciant smile on his handsome face. His hair was certainly messed up, but since he wore it short in a kind of Julius Caesar style, it didn't look nearly as bad as her tangled mop.

As swiftly as the irritation about Jack's sleeping ability had come over her a few minutes earlier, now the opposite feeling surged through, bringing a smile of appreciation to her own face. Laurie loved Jack more than she had thought she was capable, and felt blessed.

At that moment the plane's intercom crackled to life. The captain welcomed everyone to India and announced that they had begun their descent into the Indira Gandhi International Airport and would be arriving in twenty minutes.

With a surge of love, Laurie reached down and cradled Jack's head in both hands and gave him a sustained kiss on the lips. His eyes popped open and blinked, then he returned the gesture. Laurie gave him a broad smile. "We're here," she said.

Jack sat up, stretched, and tried to look out the window. "I don't see a damn thing."

"You won't. Remember, it's ten-forty at night. We're landing around eleven."

The landing was unremarkable. Both Laurie and Jack felt a definite excitement as they exited the plane and walked through the terminal. There was no problem at passport control, nor did they have to wait for luggage since they hadn't checked any. They were waved through customs without hesitation.

As Laurie and Jack came up the ramp outside the

customs area, Jennifer began waving wildly and shouting their names. Her impatience was such that she ran down a few steps to meet them, enveloping Laurie in a hug. "Welcome to India," Jennifer said gleefully. "Thank you, thank you for coming. You have no idea how much it means to me."

"You're welcome," Laurie said, laughing, somewhat taken aback by Jennifer's exuberance. Until Jennifer let go, she was unable to walk.

Jennifer then hugged Jack with equal enthusiasm. "You, too," she said.

"Thank you," Jack managed, trying to keep the Boston Red Sox baseball hat his sister had given him from falling off his head.

Jennifer transferred one arm back to Laurie's shoulder so that she had one on Jack and one on Laurie. In that awkward configuration, they walked the rest of the way up the ramp to where Neil was standing. He had not run down when Jennifer had. Jennifer introduced them, and they all shook hands.

Laurie was instantly confused as to who Neil was, and said as much. She thought Jennifer was in India alone.

"Neil is a friend from L.A.," Jennifer explained, still overexcited with Laurie and Jack's arrival. "I met him my first year. He was the chief resident in the ER. Now he's already one of the head guys. Kind of a meteoric rise, if I say so myself."

Neil blushed.

Laurie smiled and nodded but was still in the dark.

"Listen, guys," Jennifer said with great animation.

"I've got to run and use the facilities. It takes maybe an hour to get to the hotel. Anybody else need to use the bathroom?"

"We used them on the plane," Laurie said.

"Terrific. I'll be right back," Jennifer said. "Don't go away! Stay right here! Otherwise, we might lose each other."

Jennifer dashed off. The other three watched her go. "She's really wound up," Laurie said.

"You have no idea," Neil said. "She's been so excited you were coming. I've never seen her like that. Well, that's not true. The last time her grandmother came to L.A. she was like that. I was with her at the airport then, too."

"The people-watching is fantastic," Jack said. "I'm just going to walk around this general area. Okay?"

"Okay, but don't get yourself lost. We'll stand here. But I don't think Jennifer will be long."

"Neither will I. Can I leave my carry-on with you?"

"Sure," Laurie said. She took the bag from Jack and stood it next to hers. Both she and Neil watched Jack wander into the crowd.

"It's a pleasure to meet you," Neil said. "Other than her late grandmother, you are the only one she talks about from her childhood. You must know her really well."

"I suppose."

"As I said," Neil added, "I'm glad to meet you."

"Jennifer didn't tell me you were here," Laurie said. She wasn't sure how she felt about Jennifer having company.

"I know she didn't," Neil said, "because she didn't know I was coming. I got here last night and didn't meet up with her until today."

"I also didn't know she was seeing anyone seriously."

"Well, don't jump to any conclusions. I don't even know how serious it is. I guess it's one reason why I'm here, so as not to burn any bridges. I really do care for her. I mean, I came all this way for a grandmother. But I'm sure you know Jennifer and how difficult she can be, given her relationship with her father."

"I'm not sure I follow."

"You know: self-esteem issues."

"I've never thought of Jennifer as having self-esteem issues. She's bright, attractive—just a great girl."

"Oh, yeah. She's got them, and it can make relationships kind of bumpy. And she definitely doesn't think of herself as beautiful as other people think she is, no way. I mean, she's textbook with the entire recognized complex, but not without hope."

"What exactly are you talking about?" Laurie demanded, squaring off in front of this stranger who was openly criticizing someone she cared deeply about.

"She's confided in me, so you don't have to pretend. I'm talking about the abuse she suffered at the hands of her delinquent father after her mother died. I mean, she's done amazingly well, thanks to her intelligence and general strength of character. She's very tough, and her father is lucky she didn't kill him, as headstrong as she is."

Laurie was stunned. She'd had no inkling that Jennifer had been abused. For a second she wondered if she should be honest with this man or play along. She decided to be honest. "I was not aware of any of this," Laurie said.

"Oh my gosh!" Neil blanched. "Obviously I shouldn't have said anything. But the way Jennifer has always spoken of you as her only and closest mentor, I assumed you would have been the only one to know besides myself."

"Jennifer never told me. Never even hinted at it."

"Gosh, I shouldn't have assumed. I'm sorry."

"Don't apologize to me. You'll have to apologize to Jennifer."

"Not unless you mention it. Can I ask you not to?"

Laurie thought about the request, trying to decide what was best for Jennifer. "At some point I reserve the right to tell her, if I thought it were in her best interest."

"Fair enough," Neil said. "But I'm here because she came to me and asked me to come with her. My first response was to say no. I had too much on my plate to drop everything and go to India. Then she walked out on me. I thought we were done. I mulled over it for a few hours, couldn't get in touch with her, then decided to come after all."

"Was she pleased?"

Neil shrugged. "Well, she didn't tell me to leave."

"That's all you got for coming halfway around the world?"

"She's prickly. But it's a good thing that I did come. Today, in the Old Delhi bazaar, trying to catch up to her to let her know I was here, I came upon a man trying to accost her in the worst possible manner. He seemed too well dressed to be your stereotypical thief."

"What do you mean he tried to accost her in the worst possible manner?"

"I mean with a silenced handgun, like he was an assassin."

Laurie's jaw dropped open. "What happened?" she demanded.

"We have no idea what this guy's intentions were, because out of the blue, almost right in front of me, another guy who we later realized was some kind of plainclothes policeman blew the first guy away at point-blank range."

"What happened next?" Laurie asked. She was horrified. She'd warned Jennifer about too much amateur sleuthing, and it seemed that she'd been right.

Neil told her, how Jennifer had been thrown from the cycle rickshaw, how she'd bolted with the masses, and how he'd managed to find her hiding in a butcher shop.

"Good Lord," Laurie murmured. She brought a hand up to her face to cover her mouth.

"It was quite a day," Neil said. "The rest of the day we hid in the hotel. I didn't even want her coming out here tonight, but she was adamant."

"Jack!" Laurie called out suddenly, shocking Neil. She'd seen him emerge from the crowd and look in their direction. Laurie waved. "Come back, Jack."

"This changes everything," Laurie said to Neil, as Jack made his way over.

"The concern is," Neil added, "that this possible attempt on her life is because of her activities in relation to her grandmother's death."

"Exactly," Laurie said, waving for Jack to hurry.

"Neil has just told me a very scary episode that happened today," Laurie said to Jack as he joined them. "Something that I believe is going to change our visit."

"What?" Jack asked.

Before Laurie could begin, Jennifer appeared out of the crowd and hurried over. "So sorry, everyone. The first ladies' room was just too crowded, so I had to find another. Anyway, I'm back." She paused, looking from Laurie to Jack to Neil. "What's going on? Why the long faces?"

"Neil just told me about your experience today in the Old Delhi bazaar."

"Oh, that," Jennifer said with a wave. "I've got a lot to tell you. That's just the most dramatic."

"I think it's very serious and has serious implications," Laurie said soberly.

"Wonderful," Jennifer said, waving over her head. "I was hoping you'd feel that way. Sorry, but here come the Benfattis, who I told you about."

"Good evening, folks," Jennifer said as Lucinda directed her two sons over to Jennifer and her group.

All of them introduced themselves, and hands were shaken all around.

Jennifer eyed the two boys. Louis was the older and the oceanographer. Tony was the herpetologist and the younger, and he looked more like his mother.

"Jennifer told me about you," Lucinda said to Laurie and Jack. "She suggested that you might be willing to have a look at my husband, Herbert, before we tell them to go ahead and cremate him."

"My understanding, at this point, is that your husband's and Jennifer's grandmother's cases are strikingly similar," Laurie said. "If that's the case, we would like very much to check it out. Whether an autopsy might be in the offing, I cannot say. Hold off on giving them the green light with the cremation until you hear from us. We'll be at the hospital tomorrow morning."

"We'll be happy to do that," Lucinda said. "Thank you very much."

"There's not going to be an autopsy," Jennifer said. "Mrs. Varini reminded me of that again today under no uncertain terms. Not unless something very unusual happens. Here in India the doctors cannot make that decision. It's up to either the police or the magistrates. Did you hear from her today, Lucinda?"

"I did. She made the offer to take Herbert to Varanasi if I'd give the green light. Between you and me, I don't give a hoot about Varanasi. Anyway, I reminded her my boys were coming tonight, and I told her she would hear from them tomorrow."

"Did she threaten you at all about tomorrow?" Jennifer asked.

"Yes, something about getting a court order but not until the afternoon. I merely repeated about my boys calling her before noon and hung up. She's very tiresome."

Jennifer laughed. "That's an understatement."

After agreeing to chat in the morning, the two groups walked over to the Amal Palace Hotel area and found their respective greeters. The greeters in turn called the respective drivers, and the group went outside to wait for their respective rides.

Inside their SUV, Jennifer had taken the front seat, Laurie and Jack the middle, and Neil had climbed into the back row. Although she responsibly had her seat belt on, Jennifer had twisted herself around, facing the rear, essentially sitting on her right leg.

"Okay, you guys," Jack said, once they got under way. "You've kept me in suspense long enough about whatever happened today that was scary and is going to change our visit."

Jennifer rolled her eyes in the direction of the driver, suggesting it might be best if they held off on discussing sensitive issues until they were back at the hotel. Laurie caught on immediately and whispered as much to Jack. Instead, what they ended up carrying on was an animated discussion about India, and New Delhi in particular. They also talked about Jennifer's imminent graduation from medical school and how she'd been considering surgery, possibly eyeing New York–Presbyterian for a residency. Jack found the view of the traffic outside the window fascinating for the entire fifty minutes.

When they pulled up to the front of the hotel, Neil called out, "Let's all group around Jennifer as a safety precaution."

"What for?" Jack questioned.

"It's part of what we have to tell you," Laurie said. "It's not a bad idea. One can never be too careful."

Laurie, Jack, and Neil got out of the car before Jennifer, who was cooperating under protest. When she self-consciously followed, the others were grouped around her door as she emerged. In a tight group, they made their way inside.

"Why don't you guys check in, and then we'll all have a cold beer?" Jennifer said, recovering her dignity. "Neil and I will wait for you."

As it was well past midnight, the bar crowd had thinned. There was some kind of live music, but the group was on a break. Jennifer and Neil found a table as far from the music as possible, around a bend and away from the main seating area. A waitress appeared as soon as they sat down. They ordered a round of Kingfishers for everyone and settled back into overstuffed chairs.

"This is the first time I've felt relaxed all day," Jennifer said. "I even may be a little hungry."

"I like your friends," Neil said. He thought briefly about confessing how he had mistakenly shared Jennifer's secret with Laurie, but then chickened out. After the stress of the day, he was afraid of what it might do to her mental state. The problem was, he didn't want it coming from anyone other than him if she were to be told, but he felt he could trust Laurie. Neil was confident he'd never do anything to make Laurie feel she had to tell.

"I don't know Jack very well, but since Laurie thinks he's terrific, he must be."

The waitress brought the beers.

"Do you have any prepared finger food?" Jennifer asked.

"We do, and I can bring you a nice selection."

Fifteen minutes later, Jennifer had a large platter of exotic appetizers, and a few minutes after that Laurie and Jack joined them. Jack took a few sips and sat back. "Okay," he said. "You've all teased me enough about the scary episode. Let's hear it."

"Let me tell it," Laurie said. "Then, if I have something wrong or a misconception, you can correct me. I want to be sure I understand exactly what happened."

Jennifer and Neil both motioned for her to go ahead.

Laurie then told the Old Delhi bazaar episode, requiring only a few explanations and corrections from Jennifer and Neil. When Laurie finished, she looked at the young couple for any final additions.

"That's it," Jennifer said, nodding. "Well done."

"And you didn't go to the police?" Jack asked.

Jennifer nodded. "Neil, who's been here before, to a medical meeting, pretty much talked me out of it."

"The local police are often corrupt," Neil explained. "And besides, something I did not mention to you today, Jennifer, and another reason I didn't want you going back to talk to the police, is that I think they are somehow actively involved."

"How so?" Jennifer asked. She was taken aback by the idea.

"I can't imagine it was by chance the plainclothes policeman was behind you. It's too much of a coincidence. My sense is that he was either following you or following the victim. If I had to guess, I'd put my money on you."

"Really?" Jennifer intoned. "If that were the case, then I'd be willing to bet the policeman was following us when we were leaving."

"Who knows. The point is that the police might not be innocent bystanders in all this, which isn't reassuring, since, as I said, corruption is not unknown."

"Well," Jack said. "A threat to Jennifer's life certainly

does change the complexion of her granny's case and what we are going to have to do."

"You think the threat is related?" Laurie asked.

"You have to assume so," Jack said, "and, as Neil says, a threat that involves possibly corrupt police is very disturbing."

"Let me tell you the main thing that has made me suspicious about this whole situation," Jennifer said. "This threat, or whatever it was today, is just the icing on the cake. What really caught my attention, not only with Granny but with the other two deaths as well, is the disconnect between the time of the victims' deaths as reported on their death certificates and the time that the death was a centerpiece of a CNN segment about medical tourism. Take Granny! I saw the piece on television at approximately seven-forty-five in the morning in L.A., which is about eight-fifteen the same night here in India. When I got to see the death certificate, I found out it said she died at ten-thirty-five, two hours and twenty minutes later."

"The death certificate is just the time a doctor declares the person dead," Laurie said. "It doesn't aspire to be the actual time the person died."

"I understand that," Jennifer said. "But think about it. It's a two-hour, twenty-minute separation, but you have to add to that the time for someone to put the story together, call CNN, and report it. Also, you have to add the time it takes CNN to do whatever authentication they are going to do, write the story, and then schedule it. We're talking about a lot of time. In fact, I'd probably guess more like two hours."

"I see her point," Jack said. "Did this happen with the other two deaths as well?"

"Exactly the same with the second one, Benfatti. The earliest I had it being on TV in New York was eleven a.m., which is eight-thirty p.m. in India. The time on the death certificate is ten-thirty-one p.m. Again, that's two hours' difference. It almost seems like someone is reporting these deaths to CNN before they even happened. On top of that, consider the similar time frames. Could that be a coincidence, or something else?"

"What about the third death?" Laurie asked.

"The third death was somewhat different than the other two, and the reason why was, the victim wasn't discovered essentially cold and blue like the first two. But in other ways the same, including the time frame. The third patient was discovered still alive by his surgeon, and a full resuscitation was attempted that unfortunately was not successful. I happened to catch the CNN segment a little after nine p.m., and the anchors reported that the death had been sometime earlier. This afternoon I talked to the wife. The death certificate has nine-thirty-one p.m."

"It does seem as if someone has been tipping off CNN way before anyone else seems to even know about the deaths, especially on the first two cases," Jack said. "Now, that's odd."

"All three of us—myself, Lucinda Benfatti, and Rita Lucas—learned of our loved ones' death from CNN after the network had known about it long enough to make it into a story and schedule it to be on the air and seemingly before the hospital knew about it. If it hadn't been for this very strange timeline situation, I might have already had my granny's body treated. But as it is, I cannot help but think these deaths are not natural. They're purposeful. Someone is doing this and then is very eager to proclaim it around the world."

When Jennifer stopped speaking, no one spoke for several minutes.

"I'm afraid I have to agree with Jennifer," Laurie said, breaking the silence. "It's starting to sound to me like an Indian version of an angel of death. We've had a few of those in the U.S.: healthcare workers who go on a murdering spree. This has to be an inside job. But usually the victims have some consistent association with one another. From what you've said, that doesn't appear to be the case here."

"That's right," Jennifer said. "They range in age from Granny at sixty-four down to David Lucas, who was in his forties. Although two were at the same hospital, the third was at another institution. Two were orthopedic procedures, the third was obesity surgery. The only constant is that they are all Americans."

"It does seem that the time of death is approximately the same," Laurie added. "And presumably the mechanism, with slight individual variations."

"Is there any relationship between the two hospitals?" Jack asked.

"They are both the same kind of hospital," Jennifer said. "There are essentially two types of hospitals in India: the run-down public hospitals and these new, impressively equipped private hospitals that are being built for the medical tourism industry and secondarily for the newly emergent Indian middle class."

"How big is the Indian medical tourism movement?" Jack asked.

"It's going to be very big," Jennifer said. "The little I've been able to look into it has suggested some people think it might eventually challenge information technology for foreign exchange. By 2010 it's supposed to produce two-point-two billion. It was growing somewhere around thirty percent per year last time accurate figures had been obtained. It's interesting to speculate if these recent deaths will impact such an impressive growth. There have been a number of cancellations reported."

"Maybe that's why there's such eagerness on the part of the powers that be to sweep these cases under the proverbial rug," Jack suggested.

"Jack asked if there was any relationship between the two hospitals," Laurie said. "You didn't quite answer the question."

"Sorry," Jennifer said. "I got sidetracked. Yes. I found out on the Internet that they both belong to the same sizable holding company. There are big profits to be made in Indian healthcare, especially with the government providing strong incentives, like various kinds of tax breaks. Big business is becoming more and more involved as a consequence of the high profits yet high start-up costs."

"Jennifer," Jack said, "when you started to tell us about the timeline discrepancy, you said that it was the main source of your suspicion the deaths weren't natural. That suggests there were other sources. What were they?"

"Well, first it was that they were pushing me too hard

to make a decision about cremation or embalming right from the word go. Since I'm aware that autopsies either can't be done or are significantly less useful after either procedure, their dogged persistence eventually raised a red flag. Next was the pat and all-too-convenient diagnosis of heart attack after I'd just had Granny evaluated by the UCLA Medical Center, and she'd been given a blue-ribbon report, especially in relation to her heart."

"They didn't do any angiography or anything like that, did they?" Jack asked.

"No angiography, but they gave her a stress test."

"Anything else that has made you suspicious?" Jack asked.

"The cyanosis that was reported on both Granny and Benfatti when they were found."

"This is interesting," Laurie said, nodding her head.

"Not the third patient?" Jack asked.

"Him, too," Jennifer said. "I asked Rita Lucas, the wife, to ask. There was cyanosis, but it was only when they first found him, and he was still alive but in extremis. When they started resuscitation, the cyanosis cleared rapidly, giving them a false impression that the resuscitation was going to be more effective than it was."

"How long did the resuscitation go on?"

"I don't know exactly, but my impression was not that long. The patient started getting rigor mortis while they were still trying to revive him."

"Rigor mortis?" Laurie questioned. She looked at Jack. Both were surprised. Normally rigor mortis didn't set in for hours.

"The wife said that the surgeon told her that so she

wouldn't think they'd stopped too soon. She said he attributed it to the hyperthermia."

"What hyperthermia?" Jack asked.

"It was a very difficult resuscitation attempt. The patient's temperature shot up sky-high, and so did his potassium. They tried to treat both without much result."

"Good grief," Jack said. "What a nightmare."

"So it turns out that all three had generalized cyanosis, which didn't make a lot of sense to me with the diagnosis of a generic heart attack."

"That doesn't make any sense to me, either," Neil said, speaking up for the first time. "That's got to be a respiratory problem more than a cardiac problem."

"Or a right-to-left shunt," Laurie said.

"Or a poisoning," Jack said. "It's not going to be a right-to-left shunt: not with three patients. One, maybe. But not three. I think we're looking at a toxicology problem here."

"I agree," Laurie said. "And I thought I was coming merely to be supportive."

"You are being supportive," Jennifer added.

Jack looked at Laurie. "You know what this means, don't you?"

"Of course," Laurie responded. "It means there definitely needs to be an autopsy."

"They are not going to do one," Jennifer interjected. "I'm telling you. And let me tell you something else, which is what I was talking to Mrs. Benfatti about. This afternoon I got a call from my favorite case manager, Kashmira Varini, and she had a new offer that she and the hospital administration thought would entice me to give cremation a green light. She said that the hospital CEO pulled some strings and had gotten permission for Granny, along with Benfatti and Lucas, to be taken to Varanasi to be cremated and her ashes placed in the Ganges."

"Why Varanasi?" Jack asked.

"I looked it up in my guidebook," Jennifer said. "It is interesting. It's the holiest Hindu city; it's also the oldest. It's been occupied for over three thousand years. If you are cremated there, you get extra karma for your next life. When I didn't jump up and down and agree instantly to the Varanasi offer, she then threatened me just like she threatened Mrs. Benfatti. She said the hospital intends to seek a magistrate's writ to deal with Granny's body as they see fit and have the writ in hand by noon tomorrow."

"That means somehow we have to manage to do an autopsy in the morning," Laurie said. She looked at Jack.

"I agree," Jack said. "Looks as if tomorrow might be a full day."

"I'm telling you they won't authorize one," Jennifer insisted. "I told this to Laurie on the phone. The Indian autopsy situation is horrid. It's a kind of bad legacy system with no independence for the forensic pathologists. The police and the magistrates are in control of deciding if and when an autopsy is to be done, not the doctors."

"It's an extension of the British inquest system," Laurie said. "It's very much behind the times. It's hard for medical examiners to provide the necessary oversight they are supposed to provide without freedom from law enforcement and the judiciary, especially if the police and the magistrates are in cahoots."

"We'll have to do the best we can," Jack said. "You mentioned a death certificate. Is there a signed death certificate for your grandmother?"

"Yes, there is," Jennifer said. "The surgeon was apparently only too happy to sign it out as a heart attack."

"It probably was, ultimately," Jack said. "What about the other two cases?"

"As I said, there are death certificates on all three," Jennifer added. "It's part of the reason I feel the ministry of health just wants these cases to disappear."

"That's confusing if it is true," Laurie said to Jack. "What we are thinking about here is an Indian healthcare angel of death. Why would the hospitals, and even the ministry of health, want to help cover it up, which it is doing by avoiding an autopsy. It doesn't make much sense."

"I don't think we're going to be able to answer too many questions until we are reasonably sure our hypothesis about these deaths being murders is confirmed," Jack said. "So let's talk about tomorrow."

They all glanced at their watches.

"Oh my goodness," Jennifer said. "It's already tomorrow. It's after one. You guys better get some sleep."

"I have an infertility appointment at eight a.m.," Laurie said, agreeing.

"That's at the Queen Victoria Hospital," Jack said. "That's going to get us there early."

"I made it there so we'd have an in of sorts."

"That was a great idea," Jennifer said.

"I understand your grandmother's body is in a basement cooler," Jack said to Jennifer.

"That's correct. Very close to the staff cafeteria."

Jack nodded, deep in thought.

"What time should we meet up in the morning before heading out?" Jennifer asked. "And where? Should we breakfast together?"

"You, young lady," Jack said with authority, "are going to stay here at the hotel. After what you experienced today, it is too dangerous for you to be running around outside. You really shouldn't have come to meet us at the airport."

"What!" Jennifer demanded. She leaped to her feet, arms akimbo, challenging Jack.

"I have to give you credit," Jack said calmly. "It seems that your suspicions and persistence have opened a can of worms here in New Delhi, but in so doing you have put yourself in jeopardy. I think Laurie will agree with me."

"I do, Jennifer."

"You have to let us try to prove what you've managed to uncover," Jack continued. "I can't participate unless you are willing to step back. I refuse to have your life on my conscience for this possible conspiracy."

"But I've put—" Jennifer tried to complain, but she knew Jack was right.

"No buts!" Jack said. "We can't even be sure we'll be able to do much. Is that worth risking your life?"

Jennifer shook her head, then slowly sat back down. She glanced at Neil, but Neil nodded that he agreed with Jack.

"Okay," Jennifer said with resignation.

"That's it, then," Jack said while slapping his thighs.

"We'll keep you guys informed. I'd prefer you stay in your room, but I know that's asking a bit much, and it's probably not necessary. Just stay within the hotel."

"Can I help?" Neil asked.

"We'll let you know," Jack said. "Let me have your mobile number! Meanwhile, you can keep Jennifer entertained so she won't be tempted to leave the premises."

"Don't be patronizing," Jennifer complained.

"You're right. I'm sorry," Jack said. "That did sound condescending. I truly didn't mean it that way. Sarcasm is my reflex style of humor. As I already said, I do give you a lot of credit for getting this investigation to this point, in spite of your grief. I doubt I could have done it."

After saying good night to one another, Jack and Laurie got up and left the other two to finish their beers. As they walked out into the lobby, Jack said he wanted to stop at the concierge desk to reserve a van for the morning if it was possible.

"What do you want with a van?" Laurie asked.

"If we want to take a body from point A to point B, I want us to be prepared."

"Good thinking," Laurie said with a smile, guessing what Jack had in mind.

A few minutes later, as they were rising up to the seventh floor in the elevator, Laurie said, "I learned something tonight I didn't know before. Jennifer's father apparently abused her as a child."

"That's a tragedy," Jack said, "but she's certainly high-functioning."

"At least ostensibly."

"Did she tell you?"

"No, he did. It was by accident. At least I think it was by accident. He had convinced himself that from my mentoring position, I would have known, but I didn't. So don't say anything to anyone."

Jack made an exaggerated questioning expression. "Who would I tell?"

"Are you done?" Neil asked, after Jennifer had taken the last pull on her beer. She nodded as she placed the empty bottle back on the table. She stood up and offered him a hand. They started for the elevators.

"I don't like the idea of being confined to the hotel."

"But it is the smartest thing to do. Why take a chance at this point. I thought about it but hesitated to suggest it."

Jennifer gave Neil a quick testy glance.

They boarded the elevator. "Floor, please," the operator intoned.

Jennifer and Neil exchanged a glance, unsure who was going to speak.

"Nine," Jennifer said, when Neil failed to respond.

They didn't talk as they rode up, nor when they walked down to Jennifer's room. At her door, they stopped.

"I hope you are not expecting to come in," Jennifer said. "Not at one-thirty in the morning."

"When it comes to you, Jen, I don't allow myself to expect anything. There are always surprises."

"Good. I got pretty angry at you back in L.A. I had expected a different response."

"I realized that after the fact. At the same time, there could have been a bit more discussion."

"To what end? I could tell you weren't going to come, even after I expressed how much I thought I needed you."

"But you did fine without me. Doesn't that change to some degree how you feel about the original event?"

"No," Jennifer said, without hesitation.

"How do you feel that I came to India even though I said I wasn't? You haven't told me."

"I appreciate it, but I'm also confused. I guess the jury is still out whether I can really trust you, Neil. I have to be able to trust you. For me, that's a big, big requirement."

Neil inwardly cringed when he thought about how he revealed her secret to Laurie just that evening. He was absolutely certain had he confessed it to Jennifer she'd decide he couldn't be trusted. With the thought came a certain exhaustion. Was it all worth it? At the moment he didn't even know, as there was no guarantee she would ever be capable of a normal give-and-take relationship. He worried that in her mind he was always going to be either totally good or totally bad, whereas in reality he was somewhere in between, like everyone else.

"Who should call whom in the morning?" Neil asked, trying to lighten the atmosphere. Any vague thoughts of possible intimacy had vaporized the moment she said she hoped he was not expecting to come into her room.

"Why don't we set a time?" Jennifer said. "How about we meet down in the breakfast room at nine?"

"Sounds good," Neil said. He was about to leave when Jennifer launched herself at him, enveloping him in a sustained hug.

"Actually," Jennifer said, with her head buried against his chest, "I really do appreciate that you're here. I'm just afraid to show it for fear of being disappointed. I'm sorry I'm so skeptical." With that she pulled away, gave him a quick kiss on the lips, and then disappeared into her room.

For a second Neil stood there, caught off guard by her actions. As he had said, there were always surprises.

Chapter 30

Inspector Naresh Prasad drove up the Amal Palace Hotel ramp. While he did so he checked his watch. It was earlier than his arrival was yesterday, although not as early as he had been shooting for. He'd conveniently forgotten that the rush-hour traffic Friday morning was always a little worse than it was on other days, and it had taken him longer to get to his office and from his office to the hotel than he'd planned.

The head Sikh doorman recognized him, and he pointed with his stack of parking tags to the same spot Naresh had used the day before. Naresh drove through the porte cochere, angled around it, and parked. He waved to the doorman as he walked into the hotel. The doorman saluted in return.

"Back again, Inspector!" Sumit said cheerfully as Naresh approached the concierge desk.

"I'm afraid so," Naresh admitted irritably. In truth,

Naresh was not happy with his assignment. Just like yesterday, which led to a disaster, his instructions were hopelessly vague. What did it really mean to keep tabs on Jennifer Hernandez? It was kind of like babysitting. And the more Naresh thought about yesterday's calamity, the more convinced he was that the fault lay squarely on Ramesh's shoulders.

"You're in luck today," Sumit said. "I have yet to see Miss Hernandez, although I did see her companion."

"Is he staying here as well?"

"Absolutely."

"What is his name?"

"Neil McCulgan."

"Are they staying in the same room?"

"No, separate rooms."

"Did he go out already?"

"No. He was in exercise clothes. He's down in the spa."

"I believe Miss Hernandez spotted me yesterday, so I think I'll have to wait in the car."

"Very good," Sumit said. "We will try our best to keep you informed."

"Thank you," Naresh said. "Meanwhile, I'd appreciate if you brought me some tea."

"Of course. Coming right up."

"It's a travesty that the Indian civil service can sleep in their beds at night and allow those children to beg in the streets," Laurie said indignantly, as she and Jack entered the Queen Victoria Hospital. She had been incensed by the plight of the children on the ride over to the hospital. Remembering her hormonal sensitivity, Jack had been careful to agree wholeheartedly with her response.

"What do you think of this hospital?" Jack asked, trying to get her to change the subject.

Laurie looked around the large sumptuous lobby with its modern furniture and marble floor. "It's very attractive." She looked into the coffee shop. "Very attractive indeed."

"Here's the deal," Jack said. "While you head up to your appointment with Dr. Ram, I'm going to check out Maria Hernandez's body."

"You're not coming up to see the ultrasound?" Laurie asked plaintively. "You've never seen it."

"I'll be there," Jack assured her. "I just want to check out the body so we'll know what we're dealing with. Then I'll be up to see the ultrasound. I promise."

Reluctantly, Laurie let Jack go to the elevators while she approached the busy hospital front desk.

Jack was very impressed with the hospital. From his perspective it was not only modern but constructed with great care and with superior materials. It was obvious no money had been spared when the hospital had been designed. As he waited for the elevator, he noticed that the nurses were dressed in old-fashioned white uniforms, complete with hats. There was something nostalgic about it. Since most people were going up in the elevators, Jack had a car to himself going down.

Emerging onto the basement level, Jack walked down the hall and peered into the modern cafeteria. There was a handful of doctors and nurses having coffee. No one paid him any heed. Backtracking toward the elevators, Jack opened the first of two walk-in coolers. There were no bodies. Closing the heavy door, he stepped on to the next. The fairly ripe aroma told him he was in the right place.

There were two gurneys and two bodies, both covered with sheets. Luckily, the temperature was fairly cold—Jack guessed just about freezing. Grasping the edge of the sheet on the first gurney, he flipped it back. The patient was an obese man who appeared to be in his mid-fifties. Jack assumed it was Herbert Benfatti.

After re-covering Benfatti, Jack moved to the second gurney. He pulled back the sheet and found himself staring at Maria Hernandez. Her broad, full face had collapsed somewhat, pulling her mouth down in a grimace. Her color was a mottled greenish-bluish gray. Pulling the sheet down more, Jack could see that she was still wearing her patient's johnny. Even her IV was still in place. Jack returned the sheet back over her. For a minute he pondered how to handle the situation. As far as he was concerned, he didn't feel he had a lot of choice.

Returning to the door, Jack stepped back outside. He looked down the long corridor and saw a guard in an oversized baggy uniform sitting in a chair next to a pair of double doors he was ostensibly guarding. Without hurrying, Jack walked down to the elderly man, who'd watched him approach but otherwise didn't move.

"Hello," Jack said with an insouciant smile. "I'm Dr. Stapleton."

"Yes, Doctor," the aged guard said. Except for his

eyes, he was motionless. He was like a statue until Jack caught a partially suppressed pill-rolling tremor. Jack surmised the man had Parkinson's disease.

Jack pushed through the doors and stepped out onto the loading dock. There was one van in the small parking area. On its side in careful lettering it said *Queen Victoria Hospital Food Service*. Satisfied, Jack turned back inside. He smiled again at the guard, who smiled back. Jack was confident they were now old friends.

Back on the elevator, Jack pressed the button for floor four. He wasn't particularly choosy; he just wanted a patient floor, and when the door opened, he knew he'd chosen wisely. He walked over to the busy central desk. The first wave of patients had been sent up to surgery a little more than an hour earlier, and the second wave was being readied. It was mild pandemonium.

"Excuse me," Jack said to the harried ward clerk. "I need a wheelchair for my mother."

"The closet next to the elevators," the clerk said, pointing with the pen in his hand.

Without hurrying, Jack went to the designated closet and wheeled out one of the chairs. It had a waffle-weave blanket folded on its seat, which he left in place. He took the chair to the elevators and brought it down to the basement. Once there, he wheeled it into the cooler with the two bodies and left it.

Returning to the front door of the hospital on the lobby level, Jack walked out into the parking area, climbed into the van that the Amal Palace Hotel concierge had arranged, and drove it around the back of the hospital and down the ramp. He parked it next to the hospital's food-service vehicle with its rear butting up against the freight dock.

When he entered the hospital from the loading dock, he again smiled and said hello to the elderly guard. Jack was confident they were even better friends now. The guard's toothless smile was even broader.

As he walked down the hall to the elevator, which was going to take him to the lobby so that he could get directions to Dr. Ram's office, he took out his mobile phone and the piece of paper with Neil McCulgan's number and dialed it.

"I hope I'm not waking you guys," Jack said once Neil had answered.

"Not at all," Neil said. "I'm in the gym riding the stationary bike. I'm supposed to meet up with Jennifer at nine."

"You asked if you could help last night."

"Absolutely," Neil said. "What do you need?"

"I imagine they've already given Jennifer her grandmother's belongings. What I need is a set of her clothes. Could you ask Jennifer for them and then run them over here to the Queen Victoria Hospital? Laurie and I will be in seeing Dr. Arun Ram. I don't know where his office is, or I would tell you."

"Clothes? What do you want clothes for?"

"She needs them, not me. She's being discharged in an hour or so."

When Veena had left the bungalow for work that day, Cal had given her specific instructions to artfully find out at some point what had transpired with Maria Hernandez's body. He'd asked her to do this even though last evening he'd specifically told her, Samira, and Raj not to call attention to themselves in regard to their victims' remains. But with the American forensic pathologists coming, he knew that it was going to be the critical day.

As he laced up his jogging shoes in preparation for a run, his mind was busy mulling over what Veena might tell him that evening. He hoped and was reasonably confident that the day's events would be the end of the problem. He wanted to hear that the body was cremated or at the very least embalmed.

While he was thinking about Maria Hernandez, he couldn't stop obsessing about Jennifer Hernandez, either, and what it was that had aroused her suspicion. During the morning meeting in the conservatory he almost brought up the subject of what he was planning, but at the last minute changed his mind. He was afraid of Petra's and Santana's responses, particularly Santana's, in relation to the necessity of having the Hernandez woman disappear after he had learned from her what he needed to learn.

Cal ran in place for a couple of seconds. His shoes were new, and he wanted to make sure they were comfortable. Everything seemed fine. He grabbed his water bottle and headed for the door. He didn't quite make it. His phone's insistent jangle brought him to a halt and initiated a rapid debate: Do I get it or do I let voicemail get it?

With so much happening all at the same time, he thought he'd better answer it, but it irritated him. "Yeah!" he said gruffly.

"It's Sachin," an equally gruff voice responded.

"Ah, yes, Mr. Gupta," Cal said with a more business-like tone.

"You called last night."

"I did. We have another job. Are you available?"

"It depends on the job and on the compensation."

"The compensation will be more than the last time."

"Give me an idea of the scope of the job."

"It's an American. A young woman. We'd like to entertain her here for perhaps twenty-four hours, and then we would like her to leave."

"For good?"

"Yes, for good."

"Do you know where she is, or is that part of the job?"

"We know where she is."

"It will be double last time's charge."

"How about one and a half times?" Cal suggested. Even though he didn't care about the cost, he had an irrepressible urge to bargain.

"Double," Sachin said.

"Alright, double," Cal responded. He wanted to get out for his run. "But I want it to happen today, if possible."

"I'll be by for half the compensation now and for the rest tonight."

"I'm going out for a run. Give me a half-hour."

"What is the name, and where do I find her?"

"Her name is Jennifer Hernandez, and she's staying at the Amal Palace Hotel. Is that a problem?"

"No. It shouldn't be. We have friends who work in maintenance. We'll let you know. I'll give you a call before we bring your guest over for her visit."

"It's nice doing business with you."

"Likewise," Sachin said before disconnecting.

"That was easy," Cal said to himself, hanging up the receiver.

"Of course I can see them," Jack said. He was bending over Laurie, who was semi-recumbent on the examination table. Dr. Arun Ram was standing between her legs, which were draped with an examination sheet, directing the ultrasound probe with one hand and pointing at the screen with the other. He was a short man with honey-colored skin and remarkably dark, thick, medium-length, carefully groomed hair. He was also young: Jack guessed early thirties. What Jack noticed most was the singular gentleness and serenity he projected.

"I'm amazed I can see them so well," Jack added with excitement. "Laurie, can you see them?"

"If you stop hogging the screen I can."

"Oh, sorry," Jack said. He backed up a foot or so. Using his index finger, he counted four in the left ovary alone.

"It's a wonderful crop," Arun agreed. His voice matched his composure.

"How much longer with the injections?" Jack asked.

"Let's measure," Arun said. Then, to Jack, he added, "Could you hold the probe while I get a ruler?"

"I guess," Jack said, not sure he wanted to play doctor with his own wife. But he took the handoff of the probe from Arun, and he took it blindly. The image rapidly distorted.

"Careful!" Laurie complained.

"Sorry," Jack said contritely. Watching the screen, he managed to reposition the probe where it had been. He felt nervous.

Arun opened the exam-table drawer and pulled out a ruler. Placing it directly on the screen, he read out the diameters of the follicles: "Seventeen millimeters, eighteen millimeters, sixteen millimeters, and seventeen millimeters. That's terrific!" He put the ruler away. "I think we can substitute the gonadotropin trigger injection for your injection shot today." He took the probe from Jack and removed it. He gave Laurie a reassuring pat on the top of her knee. "We're done. You can get up, and we'll meet in my office." He waved for Jack to follow.

"The trigger will be today?" Laurie asked. "I'm thrilled."

"We don't need for them to be much bigger than they are," Arun said from the doorway, gesturing for Jack to precede him. Inside his office, he moved a couple of chairs over to his desk. Jack took one. Arun sat down and recorded his finds in the chart he'd started for Laurie. "This looks like a very auspicious cycle, with four such healthy-looking follicles poised over the functioning oviduct. Dr. Schoener will be pleased. If the trigger shot is done today, which I'm going to recommend, then the fertilization should be tomorrow. Are we going to utilize intrauterine insemination, or what is your preference?"

"I think we should wait for Laurie," Jack said.

"Fine," Arun commented, finishing up and tossing the chart aside. "Did your wife happen to mention that there was a time I aspired to be a forensic pathologist here in India?"

"I don't believe she did."

"It's not important. The reason I didn't is because the facilities for forensic pathology have been traditionally very bad, for bureaucratic reasons."

"I notice even a hospital like this one lacks any mortuary facility."

"That's true," Arun said. "There's little need. Hindu and Muslim families claim their departed immediately for religious reasons."

"Here I am," Laurie said brightly, coming into the room. "I'm so excited about reaching the trigger injection. I can't tell you how much I hate taking hormones."

"I asked your husband about IUI," Arun said to Laurie. "He wanted to wait for you."

Laurie glanced at Jack. "Why did you want to wait for me?"

Jack shrugged. "He asked what our preference was."

"Well, natural is much nicer. There's no doubt. But intrauterine gets all those little guys where they need to be. With this much effort, we cannot take any chances. I'm afraid we have to do IUI."

"Fine," Jack said, waving his hands in the air.

"Then let's make an appointment for tomorrow. How about around noon?"

Laurie and Jack looked at each other and nodded. "That's fine," Laurie said.

"Noon it is," Arun said. "We'll do all we can to see that your little one is conceived here in India. Now that that is out of the way, what is your business here at Queen Victoria Hospital? Is it something I can help you with? I am free. Today is my research day."

"Do you have any friends who are forensic pathologists?" Laurie asked.

"I do. A very good friend, in fact: Dr. Vijay Singh. He and I have been friends since childhood. We both wanted to go into forensics. He actually did. He teaches at one of the private medical colleges here in New Delhi."

"Do they have pathology facilities at this medical school?" Jack asked. He was encouraged.

"Absolutely. It's a medical school and a small hospital."

"How about autopsy facilities?" Laurie asked.

"Of course. As I said, it is a medical school. They do quite a few academic autopsies."

Jack and Laurie regarded each other, then both nodded. They knew each other well enough that a significant amount of nonverbal communication occurred between them.

"Arun—do you mind if we call you Arun?" Jack asked.

"I prefer it," Arun said.

"Do you think your friend Vijay might be willing to

allow us to use his facilities? We'd like to do an autopsy."

"You have to have permission to do an autopsy here in India."

"This is a special case," Jack said. "It is not an Indian but rather an American, and the immediate next of kin is here and gives her consent."

"That is a unique request," Arun said. "To be honest, I don't know the legal situation."

"Doing the autopsy, we believe, is very important."

"It could put a halt to a possible serial killer," Laurie said. "What we are concerned about is the existence of an Indian angel-of-death healthcare worker flying under the radar here in Delhi, targeting American medical tourism patients. Now, we were going to go to the involved hospital administrations, but we have learned since getting here that the administrations are, for some ill-advised reason, totally against investigating this problem."

"How have you heard about it?" Arun asked.

"By happenstance a young woman whom I have known for many years is here because her grandmother was the ostensible first victim."

"I think you'd better tell me the whole story," Arun said.

Between the two of them, Laurie and Jack told Arun everything they'd heard the night before from Jennifer and Neil, including the probable attempt on Jennifer's life. Arun was captivated by the story and listened intently, hardly blinking. "And that's it," Jack concluded, and Laurie nodded. "If any cases needed an autopsy, it's

Maria Hernandez's and the two others," Jack added. "Our thinking is, we're dealing with a probable poisoning, which an autopsy can often ascertain, and even suggest the likely agent. Of course, then it has to be confirmed by toxicology. One way or the other, we definitely need to do an autopsy on at least one case, and all three if possible."

"The only toxicology labs here in India are at the public hospitals, like the All India Institute of Medical Sciences, where I am an alumnus, but you wouldn't be able to do an autopsy there. That's for certain. Vijay's facility would be the best bet, and he could arrange for the toxicology to be done. You know, I heard of these two cases here at the Queen Victoria. There is not much chatter about them, but what there is, I did hear. You see, there are very few adverse outcomes in India with medical tourism cases, and when there is, it's almost always a very high-risk case."

"Usually in healthcare serial-killer circumstances," Laurie said, "there's an element of rationality perverted involved, such as a misconstrued desire to prevent suffering, or putting people in jeopardy to get the credit for saving them. Can you think of what could be the rationale here, killing American medical tourists? We certainly can't."

"I can right away," Arun said. "Not everyone in healthcare in India is thrilled with this sudden explosion of the private sector, creating these islands of excellence, like the Queen Victoria Hospital. It's fostering a startlingly divergent two-tiered system. Right now more than eighty percent of healthcare spending is in this relatively small sector, starving the much larger public health system, particularly in arenas like communicable diseases in rural areas. I know a number of academic types who are passionately opposed to the Indian government's subsidy of medical tourism, even if ultimately it is for India's good in relation to foreign exchange. To understand, all you'd have to do is travel from this hospital to a public hospital. It is the equivalent of moving from medical nirvana to a medical underworld."

"That's fascinating," Laurie said. "It never entered my mind to think of it as a zero-sum situation."

"Nor I," said Jack. "That means there are probably radical medical students who are against it as well."

"Without doubt. It's a complicated issue, just like every other issue in a country with a billion people."

"But why would the hospital administration want to block any investigation?" Laurie asked.

"I can't help you there. If I had to guess, it's probably some misguided bureaucrat's decision. That's the usual explanation for irrational behavior in India."

"And why just Americans? You get medical tourists from other countries, right?"

"Absolutely. In fact, it's my belief most come from the rest of Asia, the Middle East, Europe, and South America. Still, it is the USA that has been specifically targeted of late. I believe the government's department of medical tourism is specifically looking to the U.S. as a major source of growth to push it beyond thirty percent per year. We have the capacity. The existing private hospitals are currently underutilized."

"What is your personal feeling about medical tourism?" Laurie asked.

"Personally, I'm against it, unless the profits went for public health. But that's not the case and will never be the case. The profits are being skimmed off by the new megabusinessmen, of which we have more than our share. Plus, in my view the two-tiered system that's being created is ethically untenable."

"Yet you are utilizing the private hospitals," Laurie pointed out.

"I am. I fully admit, but I'm also doing my part for the public hospitals, too. I split my time, working pro bono at the public hospital as an ob-gyn while supporting myself and my family with my private infertility patients. Since there are not too many of us, I've made it a point to join the staff of most private hospitals for my patients' convenience, although I have offices only at two."

"Are you on the staff at the Aesculapian Medical Center?"

"I am. Why do you ask?"

"There was a third death at that hospital related to the two here. We believe whoever is involved must have an association at both institutions. It's what makes us believe we might be dealing with a physician."

"That's a good point," Arun said.

"Since you are not for medical tourism, perhaps you might not be willing to help us solve a mystery that seems to be giving the medical tourism a black eye. It could even be one of your fellow academics or one of your radical students who is at the bottom of it."

"I don't condone this methodology," Arun said categorically. "I'm more than happy to help. In fact, with my interest in forensics, I'll find it intriguing. What's first?"

"The autopsy, without a doubt," Jack said.

"Let me call Vijay," Arun said, picking up his phone.

Chapter 31

Inspector Naresh Prasad was bored and uncomfortable. He'd had his tea, and he'd read the newspaper cover to cover. He had been sitting in the driver's seat of his Ambassador for almost three hours, with no sign of Jennifer Hernandez and no word from the concierge desk. Although he was certain he'd probably bump into her the moment he left the car, he did it anyway, leaving his door ajar.

Standing outside, he stretched, then bent over and almost touched his toes. It was the best he could do. The Sikh doorman waved and smiled. Naresh waved back. Still no Miss Hernandez. He looked back in the car. Although he knew he should show appropriate patience and get back in the car, he couldn't get himself to do it. It was too hot in the car with the sun beating down.

He glanced back at the hotel. What was she doing? Why hadn't she come down? But then he realized he was just assuming she'd not come down, and he was assuming that if she had, then Sumit would have notified him as per his offer to keep him informed. All at once, Naresh decided it was time to find out if she'd been spotted.

Closing his car door, Naresh crossed under the porte cochere, constantly on the lookout for Miss Hernandez. He entered the hotel and, still careful, he went to the concierge desk.

"Good morning, Inspector," Lakshay said. Sumit was busy with a guest.

"She's not appeared?" Naresh demanded, as if it were somehow the fault of the concierges.

"Not as I'm aware. Let me check with my colleague." Lakshay tapped Sumit's arm to get his attention. Lakshay discreetly whispered behind a raised hand.

"No, my colleague concurs. We've not see Miss Hernandez today."

"Can you think of a reason to call her in her room?" Naresh demanded. "I want to know if she is there."

"I cannot," Lakshay said.

"Give me the phone," Naresh demanded. "How do you get the operator?"

Once he had the operator, Naresh asked to speak to Jennifer Hernandez. It took only a few rings. A sleepy voice answered.

"I'm sorry," Naresh said. "I think I have a wrong number."

"That's okay," Jennifer said, and hung up.

Naresh did likewise. She was in her room sleeping, and he wondered what to do.

Sachin Gupta had his driver, Suresh, enter through the employee entrance. There was a gate and a gatehouse. Sachin rolled down the passenger-side window. He could tell the gatekeeper was impressed with the scrupulously clean black Mercedes.

"We're here to see Bhupen Chaturvedi," Sachin said. "He's in maintenance. He forgot his medicine this morning, and we're bringing it to him."

The gatekeeper closed his door. Sachin watched him make a call. A few moments later, he reopened the door. "You can park over against that wall," he said. "Bhupen will meet you on the loading dock."

Sachin thanked the man but then directed Suresh to drive directly to the loading dock. As they pulled up, Bhupen was already there waiting. He directed them to back the car into the neighboring garage that was reserved for maintenance. The identification card he was holding got tossed on the dash. As one of the maintenance supervisors, he was dressed in a crisp dark blue uniform, including a baseball-style cap. He was a medium-complected stocky man with a thick neck. He and Sachin had been friends through high school.

"Are you okay with this?" Sachin asked. "It's going to result in a big blowup and an investigation: American tourist snatched from five-star hotel!"

"What I want to know is whether you brought the money," Bhupen asked.

Sachin produced a sizable roll of rupees and tossed it up to Bhupen, who hastily pocketed it.

"I would think you would be the one worried, driving in here with this fancy car," Bhupen said.

"There are thousands of these black E-Class Mercedes in Delhi, and the plates are fake. By the way, what's the medicine I am supposed to have brought you?"

"My asthma inhaler."

"So what's the situation with the girl? Is she here at the hotel now?"

"Right after you called this morning, I checked. She'd remained in her room. The security chain was still in place. Her jet lag must have caught up with her."

"That's a bit of luck. So I guess we'll do it like we did the last time."

"That's right. I already have the dolly with the big tool chest on the floor. Her room is close to the service elevators. Did you bring your own duct tape?"

Sachin held up a new roll. He also pulled out vinyl gloves, which he handed out to his two minions. Bhupen had his own.

"Are we ready?" Bhupen asked.

"Let's go," Sachin said.

They used the service elevator. No one spoke; there was a certain excitement that had everyone on edge. Emerging onto the ninth floor, they found they were not alone. Down at the passenger elevator was a group of four guests, but by the time Sachin and the others had grouped themselves around the door to room nine twelve, the guests were gone. Bhupen had brought the dolly from where he'd left it in the service-elevator lobby.

Making certain the hall was clear, Bhupen put his ear against the door. "It sounds like she might be in the shower. That would be perfect." Taking out his master key card, and after checking the hallway again, he opened Jennifer's door. Almost immediately the safety chain restricted how far it would open. Everyone could hear the unmistakable sound of the shower. "Perfect," Bhupen whispered. Putting his shoulder against the door and then leaning back, he brought his shoulder against the door in a powerful lunge, hitting the door sharply and without hesitation. All four screws holding the safety chain housing to the doorjamb trim pulled out cleanly. The next second all four men were crowded into the room's tiny foyer and the door was reclosed.

The bathroom was to their immediate left. The door was ajar by three inches, and a certain amount of steam was issuing forth. Sachin pointed to Suresh, the giant, to change places with him. Sachin wanted Suresh to lead going into the bathroom. Sachin would be next, followed by Subrata.

Wrapping his large hand around the edge of the door, Suresh suddenly swung it open and leaped into the room. Within the bathroom was significantly more steam, which he tried to wave out of his face as his momentum carried him into the center of the room.

But the rush was not necessary. The shower stall was at the far back of the room, and thanks to the rushing noise of the water and the dense steam, Jennifer had yet to detect their presence.

Sachin pushed past Suresh and yanked open the shower door. Suresh reached forward into the torrent of water and steam and grabbed whatever he could, which turned out to be an upper arm. Using all his strength, he lifted and pulled, yanking Jennifer out into the bathroom proper. She screamed, but the scream was cut short as the three men fell onto her and a hand was clasped over her mouth.

Jennifer tried to struggle, but it was in vain. She tried to bite but wasn't able to get anything into her mouth, which was swiftly stuffed with a cloth. The roll of duct tape was spun around her head, holding the gag in place. The duct tape went around her torso, wrists, and several places on her legs. A few seconds later the three men stood up, gazing down at their handiwork.

On the floor of the bathroom was a hog-tied, naked wet girl whose terrified eyes were darting from one of her three assailants to the others. It had all happened in the blink of an eye.

"She's a beauty," Sachin said. "What a waste."

Out in the room they could hear Bhupen maneuvering the dolly into the room.

"Okay," Sachin said. "Let's get her in the box and out of here."

The three men grabbed various body parts, lifted, and then with some difficulty got Jennifer out of the bathroom. She tried to struggle, but it was useless. Out in the room, Bhupen had opened the lid of the large toolbox.

"Put her down," Sachin instructed. He looked into the box, then disappeared back into the bathroom, returning with two thick Turkish bathrobes. Bhupen grabbed one and draped it around the inside of the box.

"Perfect," Sachin said. He gestured toward Jennifer and the three picked her up again. Jennifer tried to struggle anew. Terrified, she tried to keep herself from being put in the box by bending at the waist, but the effort was in vain. She also tried to cry out, but the gag reduced her shouts to muffled grunts. Bhupen closed the lid.

"Let me check the hall," Bhupen said. He was back instantly. "All clear."

They maneuvered the dolly out into the hall while Suresh went in and turned off the shower. Suresh then closed the door to the room before catching up to the others. Bhupen pushed the dolly with the toolbox.

"It would be nice if we could guarantee a free elevator all the way down," Sachin said.

"We can," Bhupen said. He took out an elevator key and held it up. "It just has to be empty when it arrives."

The elevator was empty, and after wheeling the dolly into the car, Bhupen used his key to make it go to the basement without stopping. Jennifer thumped a few times but was then still. They exited in the basement and took the tool chest into the maintenance garage. It took only a few minutes to switch Jennifer and the bathrobes from the box to the Mercedes's trunk. She again tried to resist but only briefly.

When they exited the employee lot, the gatekeeper didn't even look up from his newspaper.

"I'd say that was one of our more efficient jobs," Sachin boasted.

"Flawless," Subrata agreed.

Using his mobile phone, Sachin dialed Cal Morgan's number. "We have your guest," he said, when Cal answered. "We're on our way. This is a bit sooner than we expected. I hope you have the money. It was not a cheap assignment."

"Terrific," Cal said. "Don't worry. Your money is waiting for you."

Twenty-seven minutes later, Cal was waiting in the driveway when Sachin's Mercedes pulled in. He held up his hand, and Suresh pulled to a stop right next to him.

"Miss Hernandez will be staying in the garage at the back of the grounds. Can I ride with you to show you where it is?"

"For sure," Sachin said from the front passenger seat. "Hop in the back."

Cal climbed into the car. "Go straight beyond the house," he said to Suresh, pointing out through the windshield. As Suresh accelerated, he added, "I have to give you credit. This is a lot faster than I had anticipated. I thought it might take several days at a minimum."

"We were very lucky. She slept in for us. As a bonus, we brought her very clean."

"What do you mean?"

"You'll see in a minute. Do we take the left up here or the right?"

"The left," Cal said. "The garage is in the middle of that stand of trees."

A few minutes later, Suresh pulled up to a four-bay stone garage with dormers on the second floor. The place was shut up as tight as a drum.

"It doesn't look like it has been used in years," Sachin said. There were foot-high weeds growing in the pebbled area in front of the garage doors.

"I'm sure it hasn't," Cal agreed. He brandished an oversized key. "The basement is like a medieval dungeon. Here's the key."

"How appropriate. How long do you want your guest to remain here?"

"I'm not sure. It's really up to her. I will give you a call."

"It will be easiest at night."

"I assumed as much," Cal said.

They all climbed out of the car. Cal went to a stout side door. He used the key. Beyond the door was a stone stairwell. Just inside was an old-fashioned electrical switch with a rotating knob. He turned it, and the lights went on in the stairway. "Let me get the lights on below as well," Cal said. He hastened down the stairs. At the bottom was a second stout door exactly like the first. It took the same key, and Cal opened it and turned on the inside lights. Behind, Sachin came down the stairs as well.

"What was this used for in Raj times?" Sachin asked.

"No clue." Cal went to the sink to make sure there was water.

The room had a damp, cool feel and smelled like a root cellar. A few cobwebs hung from the ceiling. There was one large room with a sink, and two smaller bedrooms with cots, covered with thin, bare mattresses. There was also a small bathroom containing an old-fashioned toilet with its water-storage tank six feet in the air. The furniture was made of simple, unfinished wood without embellishments.

"Okay," Cal said. "Let's bring her down."

"There's a slight problem. She has no clothes except for a couple of bathrobes."

"How come?" Cal asked.

"She was in the shower when we invited her."

For a moment Cal worried about how to get some clothes for Jennifer but then decided it wasn't necessary.

"She'll have to make do with the bathrobes," Cal said.

Returning to the car, Sachin asked Subrata to open the trunk. As the lid was raised, Jennifer squinted in the sunlight. Her eyes reflected a combination of anger and terror. Sachin had Suresh and Subrata lift her out and carry her down the stairs. Sachin and Cal followed. Cal carried the bathrobes.

"Where to?" Sachin asked.

"On the couch," Cal said, pointing. "And remove the tape."

It took a lot longer to get the duct tape off than it did to get it on, and it was painful in places, but Jennifer did not complain until they removed the gag.

"You fuckers," she snarled the moment she could talk. "Who the hell are you people?"

"That kind of attitude doesn't bode well for your visit," Sachin said to Cal.

"She'll settle down," Cal said confidently.

"Like hell I'll settle down," Jennifer spat. When Suresh removed the last piece of tape from her legs, she leaped to her feet and bolted toward the stairs. Suresh managed to get a hold of her arm, and she reeled around and scratched him with her fingernails. He backhanded her viciously and knocked her down. It was apparent she was dizzy when she sat up; she was swaying slightly and didn't get right to her feet. Her expression was momentarily blank but quickly cleared.

"She might not be the most pleasant guest," Sachin said.

Cal draped one of the bathrobes over her shoulders. "Actually, you don't have to stay here long," he said to Jennifer. "We only want to talk to you, and then you can leave. I'll even tell you what we need. Somehow you have become suspicious of the three medical deaths that occurred Monday night, Tuesday night, and Wednesday night. Something has made you skeptical of the diagnosis on all three. We'd like to know what it is. And that's it." Cal spread his hands and raised his eyebrows. "That's all we want. As soon as you tell us, we'll take you back to the hotel. I wanted to give you a heads-up so you could be thinking about it."

Jennifer glared at Cal. "I'm not going to tell you shit."

"What do you think?" Jack asked. He stepped back. He, Laurie, Neil, and Arun were in the Queen Victoria Hospital basement cooler. With some difficulty, all four of them had gotten Maria Hernandez dressed in the clothes that Neil had brought from the Amal Palace Hotel. Jack had just added the pièce de résistance: his Yankees baseball hat. He had placed it so that the visor was slanted downward and covered most of Maria's face to camouflage her otherworldly color.

"I don't know," Laurie said.

"Hey, she's not going to a beauty pageant," Jack said. "She's only got to get by the guard at the end of the hall."

They had Maria tied in the wheelchair and supported the best they could.

"I'm worried about the smell," Neil said, making a face.

"That we can't do anything about," Jack said. He stepped forward and slanted the hat even more. "Let's do it. If the guard complains, we just have to move a little faster. After all, they are going to know she's gone the moment they look in here."

"Is the van already out back?" Laurie asked.

"It is," Jack said. "Now, here's how we're going to do this. Arun, you leave the hospital via the front door. I don't want you taking any chance of getting into any trouble, which we might for absconding with this corpse."

"Fair enough," Arun said. "I'll go now and come around the back. I want to ride with you so you don't get lost en route to Gangamurthy Medical College."

"Is your friend Dr. Singh going to meet us there?" Laurie asked.

"He is," Arun said.

"Okay, see you outside," Jack said to Arun as Arun opened the heavy insulated door and left. Then Jack turned his attention to Neil. "You push the beauty queen." Glancing at Laurie, he said, "You walk along on the left side between Maria and the guard. Also, be prepared to support her if she starts to sag. I'm going to engage the guard in conversation. He and I are old friends since I've already passed him twice. Is everybody on the same page?"

"Let's do it," Laurie said. She looked at Neil, who had positioned himself behind the wheelchair.

"Let me check out in the hall," Jack said. He pushed open the door and stepped half out. Glancing down at the elevator he saw Arun board. Looking the other direction, he could see the guard sitting in his chair. He saw no one else.

Jack opened the door all the way and motioned for the others to move. "The coast is clear," he said.

No sooner had Neil negotiated the wheelchair over the cooler threshold than several doctors came out of the cafeteria.

"Jesus . . ." Jack voiced. The doctors acknowledged Jack as they passed, deep in conversation. Jack was afraid to look back but forced himself to do so. When he did, he saw that the doctors were already beyond Maria. Neil shrugged. Apparently, there had been no problem. Jack motioned for Neil and Laurie to pick up the pace to get by the cafeteria entrance to avoid any other confrontation.

The guard watched them approach. Jack arrived slightly before the others. "Hello there, young fellow," he said. "You having a busy day down here today? We're going to use this door. My mother is worried about how she looks and doesn't want to run into any old friends."

Jack kept up the chatter as he tried to keep himself between the guard and Maria as they moved past. The guard made a meager gesture of looking at the others, but that was it. "I'll see you later," Jack said, as he backed out of the double doors.

"A piece of cake," Jack mumbled, as he passed the others to get the van's rear doors open. The concealed cord holding Maria had been provided with machinations for a quick release, and with a mere pull on one end, her torso came away from the wheelchair. Among the three of them, they got her into the van and the van doors closed.

Arun appeared from around the building.

"Why don't you drive," Jack said, flipping the keys to Arun. "You know where you are going."

The group piled into the vehicle: Arun behind the wheel, Jack in the front, and Laurie and Neil in the second row.

"How about we get the windows down!" Neil said, impressed that the others could be so stoic.

"Let's not act like we just robbed the bank!" Jack said. "But let's not dillydally, either. What I mean to say is, let's get out of here."

Arun got the van engine going but then stalled the vehicle by not giving it enough gas. Jack rolled his eyes, thinking it was a good thing they hadn't robbed a bank.

"What's Jennifer doing today?" Laurie asked Neil. "Did she mind when Jack called you to bring over Maria's clothes?"

"She was only too happy to have me go," Neil explained. "I think she's only now recovering to a degree from her jet lag. She said she thought she might sleep until noon or even longer and that I wasn't to worry about her. She said if and when she woke up, she thought she'd get some much-needed exercise."

Chapter 32

The oversized key made an oversized sound in the lock when Cal turned it. "We're never going to be able to sneak up on her." He laughed back at Durell, who was behind him. He pulled open the door and supported it until he felt Durell could take it from him. "Lock it behind you with the bolt just in case," he added, as he descended the stairs. At the bottom, he turned and waited for Durell to join him.

"She's a tigress," Cal said. "So we have to be careful. She was also stark naked when they brought her, which blew me away."

"You have my attention," Durell admitted. "Open the door!"

Cal put the key in, turned it, and pushed open the door. Jennifer was nowhere in sight.

Cal and Durell exchanged glances. "Where is she?" Durell whispered.

"How the hell do I know," Cal responded. Cal pushed the door fully open until the doorknob hit the wall. "Miss Hernandez!" Cal called out. "This is not going to help."

The two men listened. There wasn't a sound.

"Shit," Cal said. "We don't need complications." He stepped into the room. Durell followed.

"Let's lock this door, too," Cal said. He got Durell to move so there was room to close the door behind them. He threw the bolt. "She's got to be in one of the bedrooms or the bathroom," Cal said. At least he hoped she'd be in one place or the other. What had him particularly confused was seeing both bathrobes on the couch.

"We can see most of the bathroom," Durell remarked.

"Okay, so one of the bedrooms. Come on!"

Cal walked across the room and approached the doorway. He pushed the door open all the way. The only furniture was the cot, a small night table and an old-fashioned lamp, and a straight-backed chair. There was also a tiny closet, the door of which was ajar. No Jennifer. Turning around, he stepped across the hallway and passed in front of the bathroom in the process. He then checked out the second bedroom. This room was a mirror image of the other except that there was no chair.

Durell, who had come up behind Cal and was looking over his shoulder, noticed the missing chair, and the words had barely come out of his mouth when there was an earsplitting, banshee-like scream that momentarily froze both men. Jennifer had launched herself out of the shadow of the small, shallow closet with one of the legs of the missing chair raised over her head.

Cal was able to react rapidly enough to move his head so that he took the blow on the shoulder. Durell was not quite so lucky. He took a direct hit on the top of the head and staggered backward.

With yet another yell, Jennifer turned back to Cal, but Cal had recovered sufficiently to lunge forward and drive into Jennifer's naked body as if he were an NFL lineman intent on tackling her. And tackle her he did, while she tried desperately to hit him with her chair leg. They ended up on the floor between the wall and the cot, with Jennifer flailing at Cal but without enough arc to hurt him. By then Durell had recovered adequately to step forward and grab the chair leg. He tore it from her grasp. As suddenly as the battle had started, it was over, with both Cal and Durell forcibly restraining Jennifer.

"Holy shit," Cal said. He let go of Jennifer. Durell did the same. All three scrambled to their feet and glared at each other. Durell was holding the chair leg, entertaining the idea of using it on Jennifer the way she'd used it on him. Blood was oozing from his hairline.

"That was not necessary," Cal snarled.

"You are the ones that are keeping me in this Black Hole of Calcutta," Jennifer lashed back.

Durell lowered his weapon, rationality gaining supremacy. But he still glared at Jennifer. Cal returned to the other room, wincing as his fingers found the highly tender spot where Jennifer had hit him on the shoulder, aiming for his head. He grabbed one of the bathrobes he'd seen on the couch and brought it back into the bedroom. He handed it to Jennifer and told her to put it on.

Cal returned to the other room and sat gingerly on the couch, trying to find a comfortable position for his shoulder. Durell broke off from literally challenging Jennifer to give him an excuse to hit her with the chair leg. He followed Cal and sat on the couch as well. Jennifer stalked out after him. She had put on the bathrobe and tied it. She defiantly stood with her arms folded. "Don't expect any Stockholm syndrome from me."

"I left the lights on in here to be nice," Cal said, ignoring her comment. "Next time you resort to violence, the circuit is going to be thrown."

Jennifer didn't respond.

"We came back to hear if you'd given any thought to what I said when I left earlier," Cal said in a tired voice. "We would like to know what made you suspicious about your grandmother's heart attack. That's all. You tell us that and you'll be on your way back to the hotel."

"I'm not telling you bastards shit," Jennifer said. "If you know what's good for you, you'll let me go now."

Cal looked at Durell. "I think she's just going to have to think about her situation before she's going to be cooperative. And I need to get some ice on my shoulder."

"I think you're right," Durell said, regaining his feet. "And I'm getting an egg on my head, so ice would be mighty helpful."

"We'll be back," Cal said to Jennifer. With his right hand trying to immobilize his left shoulder, he, too, got to his feet. He winced.

Jennifer didn't speak as they limped to the door. Nor

did she try anything with Durell still clutching the chair leg.

After Cal locked the upstairs outside door, Durell questioned if being nice to her was the right tactic.

"You're right," Cal said. Going inside the garage's first bay, he opened the circuit-breaker box. It took a bit of a search to find the circuits for the basement, but once he found them, he unscrewed the fuses.

"A little darkness should help," Cal said.

Later, as the two wounded men were crossing the lawn to the bungalow, Cal spoke up: "I told you she was a tigress."

"You did!" Durell agreed. "She took me totally by surprise. I thought she'd be shitting in her pants. By the way, what the hell is the Stockholm syndrome?"

"No idea whatsoever," Cal said. "What do you think the chances are that she's going to talk to us? I'm not as confident as I was initially."

"If I had to guess, I suppose I'd have to say I'm not confident at all."

"We might have to talk Veena into coming to the rescue again," Cal said. "She's already spoken with her."

"That's an idea. She could be the good cop while you and I are the bad cops, you know what I'm saying?"

"I know exactly what you are saying," Cal responded. "And I think it's a terrific idea."

Chapter 33

These are better facilities than we have in New York City," Laurie said, letting her eyes roam around the autopsy room at the private Gangamurthy Medical College. "Our autopsy room is over half a century old. It looks like a movie set for an old horror film by comparison."

Laurie, Jack, Neil, Arun, and Dr. Singh were standing in the postmortem room of the pathology department of the medical school. Everything was new and the very latest. Its hospital, the Gangamurthy Medical Center, was a big player in the medical tourism industry, particularly with cardiac problems and particularly for patients from Dubai and other cities in the Middle East. An extremely grateful Mr. Gangamurthy from Dubai was the major donor, to the tune of one hundred million dollars.

"Unfortunately, I have a lecture in just a few minutes,

and I am going to have to leave you people," Dr. Vijay Singh said. He was a lightly complected man of sizable girth. He was wearing a Western jacket and tie, but a voluminous wattle obscured his necktie's knot. "But I believe we have arranged for everything you might need. My digital camera is on the counter. We even have frozen sections available, as we provide them for the hospital. Jeet, my assistant, will be available if you need anything specific. Arun knows how to contact him, and he'll come right in."

Arun pressed his hands together, bowed, and said, "Namasté."

"I will be off, then," Vijay said. "Enjoy yourselves."

"I'm feeling a little guilty," Jack said, the moment Vijay departed. "Don't you think we should have told him we stole this body and have no official permission to autopsy it?"

"No, because it would have made his decision more difficult," Arun said. "This way he has no responsibility. He can claim he didn't know, which is true. The more important thing is just to get it done without delay."

"Okay, let's do it," Laurie said. She and Jack had donned appropriate suits and gloves. Arun and Neil had just put on gowns. Knowing Maria's history, no one chose to wear isolation hoods.

"You or I?" Jack said, as he gestured toward Maria's naked corpse laid out on the only autopsy table.

"I'll do it," Laurie said. She took the scalpel and began making the traditional Y-shaped autopsy incision.

"Alright. Let's go over this again," Arun said. "I'm

really interested. You said you were considering poisoning."

"We are," Jack admitted. "Because of time constraints we are approaching this case differently than usual. We are starting with a hypothesis and trying to prove if it is right or wrong. Normally, when we do an autopsy we try to keep an open mind so as not to miss anything. Here we are going to see if there is anything specifically confirming poisoning while we confirm or rule out the provisional diagnosis of a heart attack."

"We even have an idea about the specific agent," Laurie said, straightening up from having made the initial incision. She then exchanged the scalpel for the hefty bone clippers.

"Really!" both Arun and Neil voiced simultaneously.

"We do," Jack agreed, as Laurie clipped through the ribs. "First of all, we suspect a healthcare person to be the perpetrator. Having the deaths occur at more than one hospital, we expect it to be a doctor. Since we suspect a doctor, we have to think about drugs since doctors have access to drugs and all three patients had keep-open IVs running. Considering the history of cyanosis, particularly cyanosis that rapidly cleared on the third case during resuscitation, we have to think of curare-like substances used in anesthesia for muscle paralysis."

Laurie finished with the bone clippers and removed the sternum with Jack's help.

"Let's go right for the heart," Laurie said. "If there's evidence of a major heart attack, we might have to completely revise our thoughts."

"I agree," Jack said.

"There's quite a number of drugs that cause respiratory paralysis," Neil said. "Do you favor some over others?"

Laurie and Jack worked rapidly, each anticipating the other's movements. Jack reached for a pan on a side table, and the en bloc dissection of the heart and lungs sloshed into it.

"We do have one drug that we are going to test for specifically," Jack said to Neil, while he watched Laurie free up the heart. "Again, thanks to the resuscitation effort on the third case, where they encountered hyperpyrexia and surprisingly elevated potassium, we're going to concentrate our efforts on succinylcholine, which is known to cause both on occasion. At this moment, unless we find something very unexpected, that is the most promising agent."

"My gosh," Arun said. "This is fascinating."

"There's no heart disease here at all," Laurie remarked. She'd made a series of slices into the cardiac muscle and along the tracks of the major coronary vessels. "Specifically, there's no obstructive disease."

The other three looked over her shoulder. "There is a sprinkling of hemorrhages on the pericardium," Jack said. "That's not pathognomonic of succinylcholine poisoning, but it's consistent."

"There are some on the pleural surfaces of the lungs as well," Laurie said.

"Arun, could you take some photos of this with Vijay's camera?" Jack asked.

"I certainly can."

After the photos were taken, Laurie prepared to take the samples for toxicology. Using separate syringes, she wanted urine, blood, bile, and cerebrospinal fluid.

"There are two other reasons we're thinking succinylcholine," Jack said. "Succinylcholine makes the most sense from a purely diabolical point of view. If the perpetrator is a doctor, as we suspect, he or she would want to use the agent least capable of being detected, and succinylcholine certainly fits the bill. First of all, succinylcholine was probably used during the patients' anesthesia, so even if succinylcholine happened to be found by the likes of us, its presence could be explained. And second, the body deals with succinylcholine very rapidly, which is why in an overdose situation, all you have to do is breathe for the patient for a short time and there's a happy ending."

"But you are still going to run samples?" Arun commented, "even if the body metabolizes succinylcholine rapidly."

"Absolutely," Laurie said, filling a syringe with bile. "If someone uses succinylcholine for nefarious purposes, they invariably inject a major amount, worried they might not be injecting enough. With a large dose, the body's ability to handle it can be overpowered, so not only do you find a host of succinylcholine metabolites in body fluids, you often can find some of the drug itself."

"Succinylcholine has been used in a couple of high-profile forensic cases in the United States," Jack said. "There was a nurse by the name of Higgs who killed his wife in Nevada, and an anesthesiologist by the name of Coppolino who killed his wife in Florida. In the Higgs case the drug was found in the wife's urine, while with Coppolino it was isolated in muscle."

"Well, it will be interesting to see what our toxicologists can do at the All India Institute of Health Sciences. Our head guy has an international reputation."

"Is there some way to get those samples over there?" Laurie said, as she finished obtaining the last sample.

"I'm sure there is," Arun said. "I'll get Jeet to take care of it. I'd imagine the clinical laboratory here at the Gangamurthy Hospital has a delivery service."

With two proficient prosectors at work, the autopsy proceeded apace until Laurie got to the kidneys. After checking them and determining them to be normal in situ, she lopped them out with the knife used for gross dissection. Using the same knife, she opened one with a bifurcating coronal slice, exposing the parenchyma and the calyx.

"Jack, look at this!" she said excitedly.

Jack looked over her shoulder. "That looks odd," he said. "The parenchyma looks sort of waxy."

"Exactly," Laurie said, with even more excitement. "I've seen this before. You know what it turned out to be?"

"Amyloid?" Jack guessed.

"No, silly. That pink stuff is in the tubules. It's in the lumen, not in the cells. Maria suffered acute rhabdomyolysis!"

"Arun!" Jack called excitedly, "call Jeet. We want a frozen section. If this is myosin and we're dealing with an intoxication, as we suspect, this is practically pathognomonic for succinylcholine poisoning."

A half-hour later, Laurie was the first to get to look at the kidney sections. The autopsy had been finished and dictated. Specimens had been fixed, particularly of the kidney and the heart, and the slides would be made. Finally, the body had been placed in a proper mortuary cooler.

"Well," Jack demanded impatiently. Laurie seemed to be taking longer than usual peering into the microscope.

"They are definitely pink casts in the tubules," she said. She leaned back so Jack could look.

"Rhabdomyolysis for sure!" Jack said. He straightened up. "Considering the history, I'd accept that as proof, even without toxicology."

Laurie got up so that Arun and then Neil could look in and see the myosin blocking the kidney tubules.

"So, what are you going to do now?" Arun asked. He was exhilarated to be part of a forensic pathology case, just what he'd dreamed of when he was in high school, before the realities of the field in India had become known to him.

"We should probably be asking you at this point," Jack said. "In the United States, medical examiners operating in an independent capacity would approach either the police or the district attorney or both. This is clearly a criminal situation."

"I don't know what should be done," Arun admitted. "Perhaps I should ask one of my lawyer friends."

"Meanwhile," Laurie said, "we should move quickly to strengthen the case. Hopefully, we'll have scientific proof with the urine we sent to the All India Institute of Health Sciences toxicology department, but that's only with one case. We need to get back to Queen Victoria Hospital and either get a hold of the second body somehow or at a minimum get a urine sample, and we should do the same with the body at the Aesculapian Medical Center. Three cases are much better than one. And we'd better hurry. Jennifer mentioned a noon deadline today."

"Alright, let's do that first," Jack said. "We need proof on more than one body, especially in relation to succinylcholine poisoning. Hell, a body can produce a small amount of succinylcholine just from decomposing."

"I'll take a couple of syringes from here so we'll have them for our samples," Laurie said.

"Good thinking," Jack said.

With unmistakable excitement and a strong sense of common purpose, the foursome piled back into the van for the dash back to the Queen Victoria Hospital. Once again Arun was at the wheel.

Neil pulled out his cell phone. "Now that it's afternoon, I'll give Jen a call," he said. "I can't imagine she could still be sleeping. I know she's going to be excited about all this."

"Good idea," Laurie said. "And let me speak to her as well."

Neil let the phone ring until voicemail picked up. He left a brief message for Jennifer to call him back. "She's probably working out or swimming. I'll try again in a little while."

"She could be having lunch," Laurie suggested.

"You're right," Neil said, pocketing his phone.

When they pulled into the Queen Victoria, Arun drove immediately around to the rear and backed into the same spot.

After eagerly climbing from the van, the group hastily entered the hospital, opening both of the double doors in the process. The elderly man's chair was vacant.

"Maybe he's having lunch," Laurie suggested.

"I hope so," Jack said. "I'll feel guilty if he lost his job over our mischievous activities."

Arun was in the lead. They had to walk single file because the lunchtime cafeteria line snaked all the way out into the hall. They stopped at the cooler where Maria had been stored.

"Should we just ignore everyone and go in?" Arun questioned.

Jack and Laurie exchanged a glance. "You go in, Arun," Laurie said. "Let's not make this a scene."

Laurie, Jack, and Neil moved down the hall a little way. No one paid them any attention.

Arun didn't even get all the way in before he could tell that Benfatti was gone. The cooler was bereft of corpses. He backed out and shut the door. He told the others the bad news.

"There goes our chance for a trifecta," Jack said.

"Let me run upstairs and find out what's going on," Arun said.

"While Arun's doing that, why don't we go up and have a bite to eat in the coffee shop?" Laurie suggested. "Depending on what he finds out, there might not be another chance."

"Good idea," Arun said. "I'll meet you in there."

It took Arun a little longer than he expected, but he also found out more than he had anticipated. By the time he entered the coffee shop, the others already had their sandwiches. The moment he sat down, the waitress appeared at his side. He ordered a sandwich as well.

As soon as the waitress left, he leaned forward over the table. The others leaned in as well. "This is incredible," he said in a low voice, making certain no one else could hear. He looked from one to the other. "First of all, the hospital is furious that Maria Hernandez is gone. They are so furious, that the old man downstairs has been fired."

"Damn," Jack voiced. "I was afraid of that."

"They are also sure that the medical examiners from New York City stole it. Curiously, though, they haven't filed an FIR against you guys."

"What's an FIR?" Laurie asked.

"It's a First Information Report," Arun explained. "It's the first thing that must be done if you want the police to do something. But the police hate to file them because it means work."

"Who are you getting this from?" Jack asked.

"I'm getting it from the hospital CEO," Arun said. "His name is Rajish Bhurgava. We are reasonably good friends. I've known him from our school days."

"If they know we took the body, why aren't they filing the FIR?" Laurie asked.

"I'm not sure I understand, but he said it had something to do with someone very high in the health ministry, a man by the name of Ramesh Srivastava, who'd ordered him not to file. It has to do with fear of the media."

Laurie, Jack, and Neil shared a sustained glance to see if anyone wanted to respond to what Arun had said. Laurie was the only one who spoke up. "Maybe this Ramesh is on the trail of the healthcare serial killer and is afraid of the media alerting him or her too soon in the investigation."

Jack looked askance at Laurie.

"Well, it's just a guess," Laurie offered.

"Let's go on to the next, more important, part," Arun said. "Both Benfatti and the body from the Aesculapian Medical Center hospital, Lucas, have been removed by a magistrate's writ that gives the hospitals the right not only to get them out of the hospital but also to dispose of them as a public nuisance and public danger. But the weirdest part is that they have somehow arranged to have them cremated at the main burning ghat of Varanasi."

"I've heard this word *ghat*," Jack said. "What does it mean?"

"In this sense, it means stone steps on a riverbank," Arun said. "But it also means a hilly range of mountains."

"We're aware of this Varanasi plan," Laurie said. "The hope is that it is special enough to placate the involved families. But I can tell you it didn't have that effect when it was originally offered, at least with two of the families."

"So where is Varanasi from here?" Jacked asked.

"It is southeast of Delhi, about halfway to Kolkata," Arun said.

"How far?"

"Four to five hundred miles," Arun said. "But it's all by major highway."

"Would the bodies be going by truck?" Jack asked.

"For sure," Arun said. "It'll only take eleven and a half hours or so. They will most likely be cremated late tonight or early in the morning. The burning ghats go twenty-four hours a day. But I have to say, it is unusual. Being cremated at Varanasi is generally limited to Hindus. For them, it is exceptionally good karma. If Hindus die in Varanasi and are cremated there, they immediately achieve *moksha*, or enlightenment."

"They must have bribed someone," Laurie suggested.

"Without doubt," Arun said. "They would have to have bribed one of the leading Doms for certain. The Doms are the caste that has exclusive rights over the cremation ghats. Or maybe they bribed one of the Hindu Brahmins. The hospitals would have had to bribe one or the other, or both."

"What's the city like?" Jack asked.

"It's one of the most interesting in India," Arun said. "It is the oldest continuously occupied city in the entire world. Some believe people have been living there for five thousand years. For Hindus, it is the holiest of cities, and especially auspicious for rites of passage, like childhood milestones, marriages, and death."

"What would be the chances of us meeting up with the two corpses if we were to fly to Varanasi?" Jack asked.

"Now, that's a question I can't answer," Arun said. "I

guess reasonably well, especially if you would be willing to spread around a few additional bribes."

"What do you think?" Jack asked Laurie. "It would be good to get at least urine samples, even if we can't do full autopsies."

"Are there flights to Varanasi?" Laurie asked Arun. The idea of a nearly twelve-hour journey was hardly enticing.

"There are, but I have no idea when they leave. Let me check."

While Arun was making his call, Laurie turned to Neil. "Under normal circumstances, we'd ask if you guys wanted to come. But I still think it best Jennifer stays in the hotel."

"I agree," Neil said.

Arun flipped the phone closed. "Several flights have already gone. The last flight is at two-forty-five."

Both Laurie and Jack checked their watches. It was twelve-forty-five. "That's only two hours. Could we make it?" Laurie asked.

"I think so," Arun said, "if we hurry."

"Are you coming?" Laurie asked Arun, as she stood and tossed her napkin on the remains of her sandwich. She also put out more cash than necessary for the lunch.

"I'm having more fun than I've had in years," Arun said. "I wouldn't miss it." As he stood up, he reopened his phone and reconnected with his travel agent. "Thanks for the sandwich," he mentioned to Laurie while his call went through. As they walked to the elevator, he gave instructions to get them three business-class tickets on the flight to Varanasi and two rooms at the Taj Ganges. He gave Jack's and Laurie's names.

When they got to the van, Arun had just finished the arrangement and said he'd meet Jack and Laurie at the Indian Airlines counter at the domestic airport. Then he rushed off to his car.

Jack, Laurie, and Neil piled into the van, Jack behind the wheel. He even left a little rubber in the Queen Victoria driveway, but the rapid driving stopped abruptly at the street. They had forgotten the noontime traffic.

"When we get to the hotel, I've got to take the time to give myself the HCG trigger shot," Laurie said. She was sitting in the front passenger seat.

"Oh, right," Jack responded. "It's good you remembered. I'd totally forgotten."

"You'd also better remember to take along these syringes here on the backseat," Neil said. The bag with the sterile syringes was next to him, wedged between the seat and the seat back.

"Good point," Laurie said. "I might have forgotten them, which would have left us high and dry. Hand them up here!"

Neil passed the bag to Laurie.

"Sorry you and Jennifer can't come with us," Laurie said over her shoulder.

"That's okay. I'll use the afternoon to start looking into booking our return flights. I think the sooner Jennifer is out of here, the better."

"Have her decide on what to do with her grandmother right away," Laurie said. "And then call over to the Gangamurthy Medical College and get it arranged."

"She's pretty well decided on cremation, so we'll do that right away."

With Jack and Laurie keyed up about their upcoming trip, conversation lapsed for the twenty minutes it took to get back to their hotel. Even when they arrived, they didn't speak as they hurried into the lobby.

"You head upstairs," Jack said to Laurie. "I'll arrange transportation to the airport, then be up."

"You got it," Laurie said, and she rushed off.

"And we'll see you guys sometime tomorrow," Jack said to Neil. "You heard where we are staying in Varanasi, and I know Jennifer has Laurie's cell phone number, so keep in touch and keep her here in the hotel!"

"Will do," Neil said.

Since it was a little after one in the afternoon, Neil walked across the lobby and poked his head into the main restaurant, thinking he might see Jennifer.

As he scanned the restaurant's interior, the maître d' caught his eye. "Your companion hasn't been in today," he said to Neil.

Neil thanked him. The Amal Palace Hotel continued to amaze him with its level of service. He'd never been to a hotel where the employees seemed to remember the guests to such an extent.

Wondering if she could be down using the spa facilities, and since the elevator that accessed them was next to the restaurant, Neil boarded and rode down. The elevator door opened at the spa's front desk, and Neil inquired if Jennifer Hernandez was receiving any services, such as a massage, at that moment. Since the answer was no, Neil walked down the hall and checked the stationary bikes: no Jennifer. Continuing on, he exited the spa into the garden and walked to the pool.

With a hazy sun and a temperature hovering in the mid-eighties, the pool was a popular destination, and a number of people were taking advantage of poolside dining. Since he'd not found her elsewhere, Neil was actually surprised not to find her there. It was remarkably pleasant.

Guessing that she must still be in her room and possibly still sleeping, maybe with her phone ringer turned off, Neil debated what to do. If she was still sleeping, she truly needed it, and he wasn't going to wake her. Consequently, he decided to do what he'd wanted to do the night he'd arrived—namely, put an ear to her door. If he heard either her moving around or showering, or the television playing, he'd knock. If all was quiet, he'd let her sleep.

With the decision made, Neil retraced his steps toward the spa entrance. One way or the other, he decided he'd come out to the pool himself.

Chapter **34**

Rather than heading directly to her room after coming through the bungalow's front door, Veena made a beeline for the library. She felt agitated and wanted reassurance, and there was only one person who she felt could provide it, and that was Cal Morgan. He'd already done so several times in regard to the same issue, and she was counting on it again, even though this occasion seemed to her to be the most serious.

As she came through the open door, she was relieved to see him doing paperwork at the library table. She did a double take when she caught sight of Durell stretched out on the couch, a book on his chest, and an ice pack perched on his upper forehead. It was at that moment that Cal became aware of her presence and glanced up. They both spoke at the same time, neither able to understand the other.

"I'm sorry," Veena said nervously, her hand fluttering up to her face.

"No, it's my fault," Cal said, putting down his pencil and grimacing in the process. He had an ice pack balanced on the top of his left shoulder.

There was a moment of awkwardness as they both began to talk concurrently for the second time. Cal chuckled. "You first," he said.

"There was a disturbing development this morning," Veena said. "It has me upset."

Durell swung his legs around and sat up. He was rubbing his eyes; he'd been asleep.

"Tell us what it was!" Cal said.

"Late this morning, Maria Hernandez's body disappeared. The hospital is convinced the two forensic pathologists that Jennifer Hernandez arranged to come to India took it. They must be planning to do an autopsy or they might have already done one. What if they discover she died from succinylcholine?"

"We've been over this before," Cal said, with some frustration. "Especially after this amount of time. I've been assured the human body rapidly gets rid of succinylcholine by breaking it down."

"Also, remember," Durell added, "that if they find some of the breakdown products, it doesn't matter. The woman actually had succinylcholine during her surgery."

"I Googled succinylcholine," Veena said. "There have been cases where people have been convicted of killing their wives with succinylcholine, and its presence was proved by forensic pathologists."

"I read those cases as well," Cal said. "One of them

injected the drug, and it was found in the injection site. We've used an existing IV. The other one, the drug was found in the idiot perpetrator's possession. Come on, Veena! Stop being so paranoid! Durell and I researched this. It's foolproof in our situation. Besides, I've recently read that isolating the drug is not easy. To this day a lot of people question the work of the toxicologist involved in the intramuscular injection case."

"Are both of you completely convinced these New York forensic pathologists are not going to find it?" Veena implored. She wanted to believe, but her guilty mind kept suggesting otherwise.

"I-am-con-vinced," Cal said, pronouncing each syllable in a staccato fashion. He was tired of the issue.

"Yeah, man, it's not going to happen," Durell corroborated.

Veena breathed out noisily, as if deflating, and collapsed into one of the library chairs. She was exhausted from her anxiety.

"Now, we have a favor to ask you," Cal said. "We need your help."

"The way I feel, I can't imagine I could be of any help to anyone."

"We feel differently," Cal said. "Actually, we think you might be the only one that can help us."

"What is it that you need?" Veena asked with a tired voice.

"This morning the same people that we had talk to your father brought us Jennifer Hernandez," Cal said without elaborating. He stayed silent and let his statement sink in.

"Jennifer Hernandez is here at the bungalow?" Veena asked warily, as if she might be frightened that Jennifer was now invading her sanctum.

"She's out in the room under the garage," Durell said.

"Why is she here?" Veena asked, a little frantic. She sat up straight.

"We decided we needed to know what made her suspicious," Cal said. "You're the one it has bothered the most. Right in the beginning, you wanted us to do something about her."

"I didn't want you to bring her here. I wanted you to get her to leave India."

"Well," Cal said, "we need to find out what made her suspicious so that we can change it. We don't want anyone suspicious. I mean, look how it has affected you! You're a wreck. We need you to talk to Hernandez, since you've already spoken with her. We think she'll talk to you, or at least there'll be a better chance, because she won't talk to us."

"No," Veena said definitively. "I don't want to talk with her. She made me feel terrible when I did. Conversing with her reminds me of what I did to her grandmother. Don't make me do it!"

"We don't have much choice," Durell said. "You have to do it. Besides, Cal implied it's for your peace of mind as well as ours."

"It's true, Veena," Cal said. "Plus, I don't think you want us to call off our friends who are leaning on your father, keeping him in line and away from you and your sisters."

"That's not fair!" Veena yelled, color suffusing her cheeks. "You promised that was to be forever."

"What's forever?" Cal questioned. "Come on, Veena. It's not like we're asking you to do something difficult. Hell, she might not even tell you. If that's the case, so be it. But we need to try. We think you'll be able to do it."

"If she tells me, what then?" Veena demanded. "What will happen to her?"

Cal and Durell glanced at each other for a moment. "We call the people that brought her here so that they can take her back."

"Back to her hotel?" Veena asked.

"That's it. Back to her hotel," Durell agreed.

"Alright. I'll talk to her," Veena said, with sudden resolve. "But I cannot promise anything."

"Nor do we expect you to," Cal said. "And we know it is a little hard for you, since she reminds you of her grandmother. That's natural. What's also natural is that we don't want bumps in the road like this in the future, especially when everything is going so well."

"When do you want me to try?"

Cal and Durell looked at each other. It was a question they had not specifically discussed.

Cal shrugged. "No time like the present."

"I want to get out of my uniform and take a shower. How about half an hour."

"Half an hour it is," Cal said.

Veena got up and headed toward the door. Just before she got there, Cal called out, "Thanks, Veena. Once again, you're a lifesaver."

"You're welcome," she said. "We really do have to

find out what made her suspicious. I'm not going through all this again."

"Alright, here's how we're going to do this," Cal said. He, Durell, and Veena had walked to the garage from the house. "First, I'm going to put in the electrical fuses. Then we're all going to walk down the stairs, with me in the lead. I'll unlock the door, and Veena, you step in and call out her name. If she doesn't respond, like last time, say you'll be back when she feels more like talking. Apologize for having to turn out the light again, but say it's the nasty men who insist. And then leave. We might have to do this a few times. We think she has the potential to be violent." Cal shared a glance with Durell, who merely raised his eyebrows and offered a slight nod in agreement.

Everything went as planned. After Cal had opened the door, Veena stepped in and was about to call Jennifer's name when she saw her sitting on the couch. Veena grabbed the door and closed it in Cal's face. She then walked over to Jennifer and sat down next to her.

Neither spoke; they just warily eyed each other. Despite her squinting eyes, Jennifer's face had registered surprised recognition almost from the moment Veena had stepped into the room.

"I believe you understand that there is something specific we have to know," Veena began. She held herself stiffly.

"I understand there is something you would like to know," Jennifer said. "Get me back to my hotel and I'll tell you."

"The deal is you go back to your hotel after you tell us. Otherwise, you have no reason to be cooperative."

"Sorry. You'll just have to trust me."

"I think it is to your advantage to deal with me instead of the two men who run this show."

"You are probably correct, but the fact of the matter is that I don't know any of you people. But I can tell you this, I'm shocked you're involved."

"So that is your position. You refuse to tell me what made you suspicious that your grandmother's death might possibly not have been natural."

"I don't refuse. I offered to tell you but in neutral territory. I don't like being locked up in this bunker."

Veena got to her feet. "I guess you'll just have to wait until morning. I have a strong sense that if you think about it overnight, you will see the benefit of dealing with me and not the others."

"I wouldn't count on it, Nurse Chandra," Jennifer said without moving.

Veena walked back to the door and suddenly wrested it open. Cal almost tumbled into the room from having his ear pressed against it.

"I think she needs some more darkness," Veena said. She pushed by the two men and climbed the stairs.

Cal grabbed the heavy door, and after giving Jennifer a quick glance, pulled it shut, locked it, and followed Durell up the stairs. After locking the upper door, he walked over to where Durell and Veena were chatting.

"That was mighty fast," Cal commented. "Didn't you try to convince her?"

"Not a whole lot. Couldn't you hear through the door?"

"Not very well."

"She's very adamant. At the moment, trying to convince her of anything is a waste of time. My sense is she'll feel differently in the morning, and I told her as much. Another fifteen or sixteen hours in absolute darkness and isolation will do wonders. I don't have to go to the hospital tomorrow, as it is Saturday. I told her what the conditions are, and I told her I'd be back."

The two men looked at each other and nodded. "Sounds good," Cal said, but with a tone that suggested he wasn't convinced.

They walked back to the bungalow. "Are we watching a movie tonight?" Veena asked.

"Yeah, we got a good one," Durell said. "Clint Eastwood, *Unforgiven*."

"I need distraction," Veena said. "I'm still tense from worrying about Maria Hernandez having an autopsy. I can't get it out of my mind."

When they got to the bungalow, Veena headed toward her room. "See you guys at dinner."

Cal and Durell watched her walk away.

"She's really smart," Durell said. "I think she's absolutely correct about the Hernandez woman."

"She's smart alright, but now I'm bothered by her sudden flat affect. That's the way she was when she went off and ODed. We should stop by her room every couple of hours and make sure she's okay. And whoever sees Petra and Santana first, tell them to do the same."

Chapter **35**

A football was just millimeters beyond the grasp of its intended target's fingertips. As a bullet pass from a former college quarterback, it was traveling fast and in a tight spiral when it ricocheted off the surface of the pool. When it touched down to earth the second time, it collided with Neil's butt. Just before the collision Neil was fast asleep, but not after.

Leaping off the poolside lounge chair, Neil was ready to take on the opposing army. The fellow in the pool who'd missed the pass was yelling for Neil to toss him the ball while the ex-quarterback on the other side of the pool was cracking up. In a moment of fury, Neil got the ball and booted it as hard as he could in the direction of the laughing quarterback, but it sailed way over his head and deep into the trees that lined the property.

"Thanks, man," said the none-too-pleased fellow in the pool.

"Don't mention it," Neil replied. He'd recovered enough to feel some degree of guilt. He fumbled for his watch. He'd fallen asleep somewhere around three, after expecting Jennifer to appear at any moment. He'd left several messages on her room's voicemail. The fact that she'd not shown up was beginning to scare him.

"Four-forty," he said out loud. He was shocked. He grabbed his stuff, put on his robe, and headed indoors. As he passed the workout room, he took a look: no Jennifer. When he got on the regular hotel elevator he asked for floor nine. He wanted to check her room before changing out of his bathing suit.

When he arrived at room 912, he rang the bell, pounded on the door, and shook the doorknob without waiting for a response. He put his head to the door. "That's it," he said out loud when he heard nothing.

Descending to his own room, Neil threw on his clothes. When he was fully dressed, he headed for the front desk and asked to see a manager. Typical of the Amal Palace Hotel service, a manager appeared almost by magic. "Good afternoon, sir. I am a guest service officer. My name is Sidharth Mishra. How can I be of assistance?"

"My girlfriend, Jennifer Hernandez, in room nine twelve, was supposed to sleep in today," Neil said urgently, "but this is ridiculous. It's now after five, and she doesn't respond to my calling or pounding on her door."

"I'm very sorry, sir. Let us try to call." Sidharth snapped his fingers at a woman sitting at one of the check-in desks. "Damini, would you mind seeing if you get a response in nine twelve."

"Has she ever done anything like this in the past?" Sidharth questioned Neil, while Damini called.

"Not to me she hasn't," Neil said.

"If there's no answer, we'll head right up there."

"I appreciate it," Neil said.

"There's been no answer," Damini said. "Voicemail has picked up."

"Let's go, then," Sidharth said. He also asked Damini to accompany them.

As they rode up in the elevator, Neil began to wonder nervously if he'd given Jennifer good advice about not getting involved with the police the day before. He knew that in a similar situation back in the United States there would be consequences for leaving the scene of a crime.

"Is there someplace Miss Hernandez might have gone?" Sidharth asked. "Could she have gone shopping, anything like that?"

"I'm sure not," Neil said. He was tempted to mention the possible attempt on her life and that she was afraid to go out of the hotel.

They arrived on the ninth floor and hurried down to 912. Sidharth pointed to the "Do Not Disturb" sign. Neil nodded and said, "It's been there all day."

"Miss Hernandez," Sidharth called out, after ringing the bell. He knocked a few times, after which he took out a master key card. He opened the door and stepped aside for Damini. The woman ducked into the room but immediately reappeared.

"The room is empty," Damini said.

Now Sidharth went in as well. They looked in the main part of the room and in the bathroom. Nothing seemed to be amiss, except the shower door was ajar with a dry towel slung over the top. Sidharth even made a point to feel it.

"It just looks like she merely stepped out," Sidharth said.

Neil had to agree. Except for the shower door and the "Do Not Disturb" sign still displayed, everything appeared normal.

"What would you like us to do, Mr. McCulgan?" Sidharth asked. "Nothing seems overwhelmingly suspicious. Perhaps your friend will be back for dinner."

"Something is wrong," Neil said, shaking his head. He'd advanced into the foyer of the room, and as he turned to leave, his eye caught the damaged trim on the doorjamb where the safety chain had been attached. "Here's something," he said. "The safety chain and its housing are missing."

"You're so right," Sidharth said. He pulled out his mobile and called down to the front desk. "Have security come up to nine twelve on the double."

"I want the police called," Neil said. "I want them called now. I think there has been a kidnapping."

Chapter **36**

"There's no denying that Varanasi is an interesting city," Laurie said. "But that's as far as I'm willing to go." She, Jack, and Arun had just reached the Dasashvamedha ghat on the River Ganges. They had had to walk on a horrendously busy pedestrian shopping street closed to traffic except for official vehicles for what she thought could have been a mile.

The flight from New Delhi had gone reasonably well, although it was delayed by more than a half-hour. It was also very crowded. The ride from the airport to the hotel took almost as long as the plane ride, but both Laurie and Jack had been entranced by the view outside their windows. There had been a constant cavalcade of small, primitive, and crowded commercial shops of a bewildering variety, and the closer they got to the center of the city, the more squalid they became. It was easy for the two pathologists to believe India had a billion people, considering the population density they were witnessing, and also a half-billion stray animals.

Check-in at the hotel went smoothly, particularly because the general manager, Pradeep Bajpai, was an acquaintance of Dr. Ram. And Pradeep had been helpful by providing the contact with a professor at the Banaras Hindu University by the name of Jawahar Krishna, who was willing to be a guide. Jawahar had come directly to the hotel, while the group had an early dinner. The thought was that they might be out a good portion of the night, and they'd better eat while they could.

"It is a city that takes getting used to," Jawahar said, understanding where Laurie was coming from. He was somewhere in his forties or early fifties, with a broad face, bright eyes, and curly gray hair. With his Western-style clothes and flawless English, he could have been a professor at an Ivy League college. It turned out he'd studied at Columbia University for several years.

"I'm alternately impressed with the feeling of religiosity and repulsed by the filth," Laurie continued. "Particularly the excrement, human and otherwise." They had passed numerous cows, stray dogs, and even some goats wandering among the throngs of people, the garbage, and all kinds of trash.

"We make no excuses," Jawahar said. "I'm afraid it has been this way for more than three thousand years and will continue to be like this for the next."

Jawahar had also been particularly helpful for the group's real reason for having come to Varanasi—namely, to try to get access to Benfatti's and Lucas's corpses. As a Shiva scholar, Jawahar was personal friends with one of the leading Brahmin priests of the Manikarnika ghat. The Manikarnika was the major of the two cremation ghats in Varanasi, and where Benfatti and Lucas were undoubtedly being sent. As a go-between, he'd been willing to negotiate with his friend on Jack and Laurie's behalf to be notified by mobile phone when the Americans had arrived and allowed access for enough time to obtain their samples. The price was to be ten thousand rupees, or a little more than two hundred dollars. Jack had tried to have Jawahar find how much the hospitals were paying, but whether the Brahmin knew or not, he wouldn't say.

"So, where are we here?" Jack asked, looking down the tiered steps toward the river. The sun had set behind them. In the faltering light the river was a vast, smooth, oozing body that looked more like crude oil than water. Down at the edge, fifteen to twenty people were bathing. A wide variety of small boats cluttered the shoreline. The current was slow, as evidenced by various slow-moving flotsam. "My God! Is that a human body they are throwing into the water out there, and a cow carcass floating by?"

Jawahar's eyes followed Jack's pointing finger. The objects were about two hundred yards offshore. "I believe you are right," he said. "It's not unusual. There are certain people who are not allowed to be cremated. They are just thrown into the water."

"Like who?" Laurie asked, making a disgusted expression.

"Children under a certain age, pregnant women, lepers, people bitten by snakes, sadhus, and—"

"What are sadhus?" Laurie asked.

Jawahar twisted around and pointed to a line of aged, bearded men with dreadlocks knotted into buns sitting cross-legged alongside the passageway to the ghat. Others were spotted around the ghat. Some wore robes; others were practically naked, wearing only loincloths. "They are self-proclaimed Hindu monks," Jawahar explained. "Some were respectable businessmen earlier in their lives."

"What do they do?" Laurie asked.

"Nothing. They just wander around, indulge in bhang, which is marijuana and yogurt, and meditate. All they own is what they carry around, and they subsist totally on alms."

"To each his own," Jack said. "But back to my question. Where are we?"

"This is the main or most known or the most populated ghat," Jawahar explained. "It's also the focal point of religious activity in Varanasi, as you can see by all the Hindu priests performing their particular religious rites."

About halfway down the stone steps and parallel with the water's edge, there were a series of platforms. Each platform had an orange-robed priest carrying out complicated movements with candlesticks, bells, and lamps. Loud chanting inundated the entire area from a series of speakers strung the length of the ghat. Several thousand people milled about, including other Hindu priests, sadhus, merchants, con artists, children, would-be guides, strolling families, pilgrims from all over India, and tourists.

"I recommend we hire a boat," Jawahar said. "We have plenty of time before we are apt to hear from the Brahmin, but even if we do, we can put in at shore closer to the cremation location."

"Is that the cremation ghat we can just see?" Laurie asked, pointing off toward the north. There was an indistinct glow and apparent smoke snaking up against the darkening mackerel sky.

"That's it," Jawahar agreed. "We'll see it better from the water. I'll find us a boat. When I do, I'll wave." Jawahar headed down the steps toward the river.

"What do you think of Varanasi?" Arun questioned.

"Like I said, it's interesting," Laurie responded. "But it's overwhelming to my Western sensibilities."

"It's like being in a number of centuries all at the same time," Jack commented. He watched a nearby Indian snap open his mobile phone.

The boat ride had been a good idea. For several hours as night fell, they lazed up and down the coastline, mesmerized by the activity on all the ghats, but particularly drawn to the Manikarnika, with its ten to twelve funeral pyres. Silhouetted figures could be seen stoking the fires and sending forth explosions of sparks and smoke into the night sky. Along the waterline were huge stacks of firewood, some of it rare sandalwood.

Slightly elevated above the firewood was the pit where the pyres were built. Above the pit were steps leading up to a sheer masonry wall. Topping the wall was a cantilevered balcony as part of a large conical-towered temple complex. Beside the temple was a squalid palace topped by a nonfunctioning clock tower. Thanks to the fires and the frantic action, the scene projected an image akin to the apocalypse.

It was thirty-five minutes after ten that Laurie's cell phone rang. She'd looked at the time before she handed the phone to Jawahar. She could see it was an Indian number.

Jawahar spoke in Hindi, and only very briefly. He handed the phone back to Laurie.

"Your bodies have arrived," he reported. "The Brahmin has them in a small temple off that large balcony you can see from here. He said we have to come right away."

"Let's do it," Laurie said.

As the boatman oared them in to shore, Jawahar told them they were going to disembark at the Scindia ghat, because females were not allowed at the water's edge of Manikarnika ghat or at the level of the funeral pyres.

"Why on earth is that?" Laurie asked.

"To discourage wives from leaping onto husbands' funeral pyres," Jawahar said. "Traditional India didn't make life easy for widows."

When they landed, Jack and Laurie were fascinated by the huge Shiva temple tilted and half submerged in the Ganges. Along with Arun, they walked over to gaze at it while Jawahar settled up with the boatmen.

In order to get from Scindia ghat to Manikarnika ghat, they had to enter the old section of the city that abutted the ghats for their four-mile extent. As soon as they moved away from the open waterfront, the city became entirely medieval in character, composed of dark, claustrophobic, twisting, yard-wide cobblestone lanes. In contrast to the silky coolness of the Ganges shoreline, they were now engulfed in fetid heat and the smell of old urine and cow dung. It was also crowded with people, cows, and dogs. Laurie wanted to pull into herself like a snail to avoid touching anything. The smell was such that she wanted to mouth-breathe, but fear of infectious disease made her want to breathe through her nose. Seldom had she been so uncomfortable as she tripped after Jawahar, desperately trying to avoid stepping in excrement.

Every so often there would be sudden relief of the claustrophobia as they came upon an illuminated restaurant, an open shop, or a bhang stall lit with a single bare bulb. But mostly it was dark, hot, and smelly.

"Alright, here's the stairway," Jawahar said, coming to such a sudden halt in the darkness that Laurie, who was second, bumped into him. She apologized; he dismissed it.

"These stairs will lead up to that large balcony. I advise you to all stay together. We don't want anyone to get lost."

Laurie couldn't imagine he'd think they might have the inclination to wander.

"There are various hostels up there," Jawahar continued. "Each one supervised by a different Brahmin. They are for the dying. Don't wander into them. There will be a few candles, but otherwise it will be dark. I've brought a flashlight, but we'll only use it when you actually take your sample. Are we all clear?"

Jack and Arun said yes. Laurie stayed quiet. Her mouth and throat had become dry.

"Are you okay, Laurie?" Jack asked. They all could barely see one another.

"I guess," Laurie managed, trying to scare up a bit of saliva to moisten her lips.

"Do you have the money?" Jawahar asked Jack.

"I got it," Jack said, giving his front hip pocket a slap.

"One other thing," Jawahar said. "Don't talk to the Dom."

"Who are the Dom?" Laurie asked.

"The Dom are the Untouchables who from time immemorial have worked the crematoria fires and handled the dead. They live here in the temple with the eternal fire of Shiva. They are dressed in white robes and shave their heads. Don't talk to them. They take their jobs very seriously."

Don't worry, Laurie thought but didn't say. *I'm not talking to anybody.*

Jawahar turned and mounted the stairs, which curved to the left and seemed interminable. When they emerged they were on a balcony with a rudimentary railing. Directly out was the broad expanse of the river, with a nearly full moon rising. Below were the raging fires of the funeral pyres filling the air with sparks, ash, dry heat, and smoke. The Dom could be seen as black figures wielding long sticks as they prodded the fires into miniature infernos. The burning bodies were clearly in evidence in each.

Lying about on the surface of the balcony were thirty or so bodies encased in white muslin shrouds. In the back of the balcony, in a wide concave orientation, were the dark openings of various temples. The center one glowed with the eternal fire of Shiva.

"Let me have the money," Jawahar said, holding out his hand in the moonlight.

Jack complied.

"Everybody stay right here. I'll be right back."

"Good grief," Laurie complained. "This is awful."

"So, people actually come here and live in these caves to die?" Jack asked Arun.

"That was my understanding," Arun said.

Jawahar reappeared. He'd gone into one of the two corner Indian cupolas. "The bodies in question are in that tiny temple next to the stairs we used to get up here," he said. "The Brahmin told us to be quick and not draw attention to ourselves. The problem is that the Dom believe one of their major jobs is to protect the corpses."

"That's all we need," Laurie murmured, as they all moved in the direction they'd come. She could feel herself start to tremble.

When they reached the temple, they ducked in one after the other. They waited until their eyes had adjusted as much as they were going to do. Besides the door opening, there was an unglazed window. Enough moonlight flooded in to see the two bodies side by side. They, too, were shrouded with white muslin.

"You have the syringes?" Jack asked Laurie. Laurie

held them up. She'd taken them from her shoulder bag.
Jack took one. "I'll do one, you do the other. I don't
think we need the flashlight."

They untied the cord holding closed what turned out
to be muslin sacks. Arun helped Laurie while Jawahar
helped Jack pull the sacks down enough to expose the
suprapubic area. Directing the needles straight down just
cephaled of the pubis, both syringes filled with urine.

"A piece of cake," Jack said happily.

After securely capping both syringes, Laurie put them
into her shoulder bag. Then everyone bent to the slightly
more difficult task of getting the bodies back into the
shrouds. Just as they were almost finished, the moonlight suddenly dimmed. Looking up, the group realized
that the door was being blocked by two Dom. "What is
going on in here?" the first demanded.

Jack responded first, getting to his feet and crowding
the Dom out of the doorway. "We're just finishing up.
We're doctors. We wanted to make sure these two were
truly dead. But we're done."

Jawahar, Laurie, and Arun pushed out of the temple
right behind Jack.

Although the Dom were initially confused by Jack's
statement, it didn't last long. "Body thieves!" he yelled
out at the top of his lungs, and tried to grab onto the
front of Jack's shirt.

"Run!" Jack yelled in response. Laurie did not need
further invitation. She threw herself into the stairway, her
legs churning. Jawahar came next, followed by Arun.

Jack gave a karate-style chop to the first Dom's grasping arms, only to have the second latch on to him from the side. At that point Jack used a closed fist, hitting the second Dom square in the face. In the background it looked like Dom were coming out of the stonework. Jack followed with another closed-fist body shot to the first Dom, who buckled. In the next instant Jack was on the stairs.

When he reached the narrow alleyway at the base of the stairs, it took him a moment to see Arun, who'd stayed in sight to wave him on. Jawahar was taking them in the opposite direction that they'd come. Jack ran toward Arun, who'd recommenced running. Behind them they could hear a very vocal horde of Dom coming down the stairs.

In fabulous physical shape, Jack quickly overtook Arun, but then they both ran into Laurie and Jawahar, who'd gotten bogged down in pedestrian traffic. The dark, empty, very narrow lane had butted into a larger but more crowded alley complete with a prone cow chewing its cud. Laurie almost fell over the animal in her haste.

For another five minutes the group pushed and shoved their way to put more distance between themselves and the angered Dom. When they were confident they were no longer being chased, they stopped, each with his or her chest heaving from exertion—everyone, that is, except Jack. They looked at one another, and partially from the anxiety the episode had engendered, they laughed.

After they had recovered their breath, Jawahar led them through the labyrinthine lanes back to Vishwanath

Gali, the shopping street that had initially taken them to the Dasashvamedha ghat. There Jawahar managed to hire two cycle rickshaws, which transported them back to the Taj Ganges hotel.

"What I want to do more than anything else," Laurie was saying as they approached the front desk to get their room keys, "is take a long shower."

"Are you Dr. Laurie Montgomery?" the desk clerk asked before Laurie had a chance to say anything. His tone was exigent, immediately catching Laurie's attention.

"I am," Laurie responded with concern.

"You have several urgent messages. The caller has called three times, and I'm supposed to ask you to respond immediately."

Laurie took the messages with alarm.

"What is it?" Jack asked, with equivalent unease. He looked over her shoulder.

"It's Neil," Laurie said. She looked at Jack. "Do you think it could be about Jennifer?"

As Laurie got her mobile phone out of her bag, the group moved over to a sitting area overlooking the hotel's extensive grounds. Not knowing Neil's cell phone number, she called the Amal Palace Hotel and asked to be put through to Neil's room.

Neil picked up before the first ring had completed, as if he were hovering over the phone.

"Jennifer has been kidnapped," he blurted, even before he was sure it was Laurie.

"Oh, no!" Laurie cried. Hastily, she repeated the news for Jack's benefit.

"It must have been this morning when I was with you guys," Neil said. "When I came back, I thought she was sleeping. I didn't find out she wasn't here until almost six o'clock. I'm so angry with myself I could die."

Neil went on to tell the whole story, including how the missing safety chain was the only clue. That and the fact that nothing is missing from her room.

"Has there been any note? Any demands?" Laurie asked.

"Nothing," Neil admitted. "That's what scares me the most."

"Are the police involved?"

Neil laughed derisively. "They are involved, but a lot of good that's done."

"Why do you say that?"

"They refuse to fill out their First Information Report for twenty-four hours. And an FIR has to be filled out before they do anything. It's like an Indian catch-twenty-two."

"Why won't they fill out an FIR?"

"Get this! They won't fill one out because they've had too much experience, especially with Americans, that whoever is missing, whether supposedly kidnapped or on their own, end up reappearing and all the work required to fill out the FIR is for naught. The lazy bastards are willing to give the kidnappers a twenty-four-hour free getaway time because the paperwork is too demanding. It makes me sick."

"How has the hotel been about it?"

"The hotel has been terrific. They are as upset as I am and have a whole private team on it. They're also busy watching all the security tapes they have for the lobby and the front entrance."

"Well, I hope to God they find something and find it soon," Laurie said. "I'm sorry we're not there."

"Me, too. I'm a wreck with worry."

"At least we got the urine samples we came for," Laurie said.

"I hope you're not too disappointed that at this point, I couldn't give a flying crap about the urine samples."

"I understand completely," Laurie added. "I feel the same. I just mentioned it because we'll be coming back to New Delhi first thing tomorrow morning, and we'll see if we can help you get the local police more involved. Wait, Jack wants to speak with you."

"Listen, Neil," Jack said when he got the phone. "What we have to do tomorrow is get ourselves over to the U.S. embassy and get in touch with one of the consular officers. He or she can then get us together with a regional security officer. They know how to deal with the local police. What you're dealing with is probably no more than a station house officer. What we're going to have to do is get the FBI invited to join in. The FBI's hands are tied until they are invited."

"When will you both get back here?"

"While you were talking to Laurie, I checked. The first flight leaves here at five-forty-five. We should be at the hotel before you're awake."

"Don't count on it. I'm not sure I'm going to sleep at all."

Jack gave the phone back to Laurie.

"I heard that," Laurie said. "You have to sleep. We'll get to the bottom of this. Don't you worry."

After saying good-bye, Laurie disconnected. She looked at Jack. "This is a major disaster."

"I'm afraid so," Jack agreed.

Chapter 37

By three a.m. the bungalow was finally completely quiet. Only an hour earlier, Veena had heard the flat-screen TV in the living room, suggesting that someone couldn't sleep. But whoever it had been had turned it off and had disappeared back to their room.

Avoiding turning on a light, Veena felt for the pillowcase full of clothes she'd put on her night table when she'd turned her lights off at midnight. When her hand touched it, she picked it up, then moved to her bedroom door. Luckily, Samira was spending the night with Durell. Samira had been one of her worries, and for the three hours Veena had lain awake in bed, every time she'd heard a noise she'd worried that it was Samira returning to spend the rest of the night in her own bed, across from Veena's.

Another worry was the key. If it wasn't where she hoped it was, all bets would be off.

Veena cracked her door. The house was silent and remarkably well illuminated from the nearly full fall moon. Moving silently, carrying her shoes in one hand and the pillowcase in the other, Veena moved from the guest wing, where the nurses' bedrooms were, into the main part of the house. She tried to stay in the shadows. When she neared the living room, she slowed and glanced in warily. She knew all too well that when you're living with sixteen people and five servants, you can run into someone in the public spaces at any given time, day or night.

The living room was empty. Encouraged, Veena silently raced down the carpeted hall to the library. Like the living room, the library was dark and empty. Without wasting a moment, Veena dashed to the fireplace. Putting down the pillowcase and her shoes, she took down the Indian-craft papier-mâché box. Since the top fit so snugly, it took a few minutes of effort to get it open enough for her to get her fingernails in the crack. When it did open, it made a popping sound loud enough to cause Veena to freeze. For several minutes she listened to the pulse of the house. It stayed normal.

Lifting the lid and placing it on the mantel, Veena held her breath while slipping her hand into the box. To her relief, her fingers immediately hit up against the oversized key, inspiring her to say a little prayer to Vishnu. Slipping the key into her front pocket, Veena took the time to replace the box's lid and return the box to its exact location.

With her shoes and pillowcase back in her grasp, Veena moved out of the library and darted back down the hall, heading now for the conservatory. It was then that she heard the thunk of the refrigerator door closing. Reflexively, she ducked into the hallway's shadows and froze. And it was a good thing she had. A moment later, Cal emerged into the hall with a fresh Kingfisher beer. He walked past Veena and headed toward the guest wing.

With such a close call, Veena panicked. Although she'd tried to act as normal as she could all evening, she'd known Cal had been suspicious and had even asked her if she were alright on more than one occasion. Later, after she'd excused herself and said she was going to bed, he'd even come to her bedroom with a flimsy excuse. And with him heading in that direction now, she had to assume he was bent on checking her yet again.

As soon as he had disappeared from view, Veena was off again. Now she was up against a time constraint. In the conservatory, she quietly let herself out into the garden, where she put on her shoes, then sprinted across the lawn. She met the driveway just before it entered the trees, and once in the trees, she had to slow to a walk in the darkness. A few minutes later, she reached the garage.

She unlocked the upper door and left it open to take advantage of the flashes of moonlight that filtered down through the trees as the night breezes rustled their leaves. At the base of the stairs it was nearly total darkness, with only a bit of moonlight visible when Veena looked back up to the open door.

She used the key to rap on the door. "Miss Hernandez," she called out. "It is Nurse Chandra." Only then did she struggle to open it. The door swung in to utter blackness. "Miss Hernandez," Veena called again. "I've come to get you out of here. This is no trick, but we must hurry. I have clothes and shoes for you."

Veena felt a hand touch her chest. "Where are the shoes?" Jennifer asked. She was leery, even though Veena said there was no trick.

"I have the shoes and the clothes in a pillowcase. Let's go upstairs and at least take advantage of the moonlight."

"Okay," Jennifer said.

Veena turned and mounted the stairs, moving toward the faint, flickering silver-gray light. She could barely hear Jennifer coming behind with her bare feet. As Veena emerged into the cool night, she glanced back at the house. "Oh, no!" she voiced. Through the trees she could see there were now lights on. A second later, she heard something that made her blood run cold. She heard Cal's voice yell her name out into the night.

Jennifer loomed out of the stairway, peeling off the bathrobe in anticipation of putting on the clothes that Veena had brought.

"There's no time for the shirt and pants," Veena blurted. "But you must have something on your feet." She struggled to get the tennis shoes out of the pillowcase and handed them to Jennifer. Jennifer pulled the bathrobe back on and snatched the shoes from Veena.

"Why the rush?" Jennifer hastily questioned.

"Cal Morgan, the head man, has somehow realized I'm gone. If he hasn't already, he'll soon figure out that I meant all along to come out here and free you."

Jennifer pulled on the tennis shoes. "Where should we go?"

"Back through the trees away from the house. There's a fence, but it's fallen down someplace. We have to find it, and we have to put some distance between us and this bungalow or we're both going to end up back in that basement."

"Let's go," Jennifer said, cinching the bathrobe's belt.

The two women started through the trees. The denser the canopy, the more difficult the going. For about fifty feet, they moved purely by feel, keeping their hands in front of their faces. The main problem was the noise. They sounded like a couple of elephants moving through the brush.

"Veena, come back! We need to talk," wafted over the humid night air. Flashlight beams danced in the darkness, crossing the lawn from the bungalow.

With renewed urgency the women pressed on, eventually colliding with an all-too-robust chain-link fence topped with rusty barbed wire.

"Which way?" Jennifer demanded in a breathless whisper.

"No idea," Veena answered. The flashlight beams were now penetrating the woods.

Making a sudden decision, Jennifer moved to her right, letting her hand trail along the fence. She could hear Veena following her, both women making more noise than they would have preferred. The fence continued on as hale as ever. Just when Jennifer was lamenting that the damaged section of fence must have been in the opposite direction, her hand contact disappeared. Bending down, she could feel that the fence was suddenly horizontal, having fallen outward.

"Here it is," Jennifer whispered forcibly. She stepped on it and it settled more. Advancing timidly, she came to the barbed wire. Although she couldn't see, she took a chance and jumped. Luckily, she cleared it, and she told Veena so. A moment later Veena was next to her, and they pushed on. A few minutes later they broke out of the trees onto one of the wide but deserted avenues in Chanakyapuri.

"We can't stay here," Veena said urgently. "They'll be here any minute in one of the cars. They have four cars."

Just as Veena spoke, a car came around the bend. The women pressed back into the bushes and flattened themselves on the ground. The car slowed, passing at walking speed. The women waited until it had rounded the next corner and disappeared from sight. At that instant they were up and running in the direction from which the car had come. At the next block they crossed the broad avenue and took a smaller street heading away from the bungalow.

"That was one of their vehicles," Veena said between breaths. "They are out cruising for us."

A moment later headlights appeared behind them, forcing them to duck behind a wall at the base of a driveway. Again, they flattened themselves against the ground. It was the same car, moving at the same speed.

The cat-and-mouse game continued until Jennifer

and Veena came across an extensive squatter settlement along a relatively busy road. It was constructed of cardboard, scraps of corrugated metal, tarps, and bolts of fabric. Between the makeshift homes, the earth was beaten bare. It was apparent the commune had been in existence for some time.

"Here!" Veena said, out of breath. They had been running for more than an hour. "We'll be safe here." Without hesitation she entered, walking among the simple shelters and into the depths of the colony. It was quiet except for an occasional baby's cry. But the cry never lasted long. After walking away from the road a hundred or so feet, they met a woman returning from an almost-dry streambed, which was used as the toilet, judging from the smell. Veena spoke to her in Hindi and the woman pointed. After a few more questions, Veena thanked the woman.

"We're in luck," Veena said after the woman moved on. "One of these structures is vacant. The problem is that it is close to the latrine. But we'll be safe."

"Let's move in," Jennifer said. "I don't think I can run anymore."

Five minutes later they found themselves sitting in a lean-to made with a length of cord strung between two trees and hung with a bolt of brightly printed Indian cloth whose ends were held down by heavy stones. Inside, the floor was a jigsaw puzzle of carpet scraps. Veena was leaning up against one tree, Jennifer against the other. Although the smell was rank from the proximity to the polluted streambed, the women felt safe, certainly safer than trying to hail a truck or other vehicle on the open road.

"Sitting down has never felt so good," Jennifer said. They could barely see each other in the half-light of the moon. "I see you are still carrying the clothes."

Veena held up the pillowcase as if she were surprised to see it. She tossed it over to Jennifer. Jennifer reached in and pulled out the shirt and pants. She felt the fabric. "Are these jeans?"

"They are," Veena admitted. "I got them in Santa Monica."

"So you lived in Santa Monica?" Jennifer commented. She eased herself out of the lean-to. Taking off the bathrobe and the sneakers so that she was completely naked, she pulled on the jeans, then the shirt.

Balling up the bathrobe to use to lean against, Jennifer climbed back into the makeshift shelter. She'd glanced briefly at Veena, who was motionless with her eyes closed. After Jennifer had gotten herself as comfortable as she was going to be, she again glanced at Veena. She did a double take. Veena's eyes were wide open and sparkling like diamonds.

"I thought for a minute you were asleep," Jennifer said.

"I need to talk," Veena said.

"Whatever you want," Jennifer responded. "I'm seriously indebted to you. Thank you from the bottom of my heart for rescuing me. But your rescuing me begs the question: What on earth were you doing with those people?"

"It's a long story," Veena said. "I am happy to tell you, but first I need to tell you something about myself and my family so that what I will tell you subsequently might make some sense."

"You have my full attention."

"What I'm going to tell you will bring great shame to my family, but it is no longer a secret. My father abused me throughout my childhood and I did nothing to stop it."

Jennifer recoiled as if Veena had slapped her.

"You may wonder why. The problem is I live in two different worlds, but mostly in the old. In the old India, I am duty-bound to respect my father and obey him no matter what. My life is not for myself. It is for my family, and I'm not to talk about things that would bring shame, like revealing his bad behavior. My father also told me if I did not obey, he would turn to one of my sisters." Veena then went on to tell the whole story about shady Nurses International and the promise to move to America. She told about stealing the patient data and how it turned out to be too good.

"It was at that point that Cal Morgan decided to change what we nurses were doing," Veena explained. "And he told me that he could make sure my father behaved himself with me, my sisters, and my mother forever and bring me to America for a new life if I would do something special for him."

Veena paused and stared at Jennifer. The pause's duration stretched out as Veena tried to find the courage to continue.

"What did Cal Morgan want you to do for him in

return for freeing you from the clutches of your father?" Jennifer asked. She was becoming incensed as the minutes ticked by. She was beginning to fear what she was about to learn.

"He wanted me to kill Maria Hernandez. I killed your grandmother."

Jennifer recoiled for the second time, although this time it was a lightning bolt of pure anger. For a nanosecond she wanted to leap to her feet and strangle the woman in front of her. She'd been correct about her granny's death, and here was the perpetrator within arm's reach. But then somewhat cooler thoughts flooded into her consciousness. Here was a young woman caught in perhaps the worst psychological trap that Jennifer could imagine, especially from having experienced it to a degree herself, but with no chance of freedom.

Jennifer took a series of deep breaths to get herself under even more control. "Why did you save me tonight? Guilt?"

"To some degree," Veena admitted. "I regretted what I did to your grandmother. I even tried to commit suicide, but Cal Morgan saved me."

"A real attempt, or a gesture?" Jennifer asked with little sympathy and some skepticism.

"Very real," Veena said. "But since I was saved, I thought the gods were satisfied. But I felt badly and continued to feel badly and tried to get them to stop. Then, when I was confronted with you and realized they were probably going to get rid of you, it was too much. These people have no morality. They don't kill people themselves but think nothing of having others do it for them. All they think about is achieving their success."

"Since you have told me your secret, I'm going to tell you mine," Jennifer said suddenly. "I, too, was abused by my father. It started at age six. I found it very confusing."

"I was the same," Veena said. "It's always made me feel guilty. Sometimes I used to think I'd brought it on myself."

"Me, too," Jennifer agreed. "But then around the time I was nine I suddenly knew it was all wrong, and I cut my father out of my life. I guess I was lucky. I didn't have any cultural pressures telling me I had to respect him no matter what. Of course, I didn't have any sisters to worry about, either. I can't imagine your situation. It must have been awful. Worse than awful. I cannot even conceive of it."

"It was terrible," Veena agreed. "And as a teenager I tried suicide, but it was definitely more a gesture then. I was trying to get attention, but it didn't work."

"You poor thing," Jennifer said sincerely. "I used to feel sorry for myself because I thought my father had ruined me and no one would want me, but I never even thought about suicide."

A bit more than an hour later it began to get light in the eastern sky, but Jennifer and Veena were unaware until the sun actually rose. All of a sudden they realized they could clearly see each other. They had been talking nonstop for two hours.

Emerging from the lean-to, they looked at each other's faces and, despite the continued threat from Cal et al., they laughed. They were both a mess, with their hair in tangles and actual dirt smeared on their faces, as though they were commandos. "You look like you've been through a battle," Jennifer commented, especially since Veena's garments were as dirty as her face. Jennifer reached back into the lean-to and pulled out the bathrobe. When she shook it out, it looked every bit as bad as Veena's clothing.

As they walked back through the colony, other people were just emerging from the rickety, impermanent shelters. There were mothers with infants, fathers with toddlers, children, and old people.

"When you see this, doesn't it make you sad?" Jennifer questioned.

"No," Veena said. "It's their karma."

Jennifer nodded as if she understood, but she didn't.

As the women approached the road, which was already busy with morning traffic, they became progressively leery. Although at that point in time both thought it unlikely that the Nurses International people would still be out patrolling for them, there was always a chance. To be safe rather than sorry, they kept themselves behind trees while looking up and down the road, which was choked not only with vehicles but also with people. The pedestrians were either walking toward the city or lounging in the morning sun.

"What do you think?" Jennifer asked.

"I think we're free and clear."

"What are you going to do?" Jennifer asked. "Where are you going to go?"

"I don't know," Veena admitted.

"Then I'll tell you where you are going. You're coming back with me and staying in my room until we figure it out. Do we have a deal?"

"We have a deal," Veena said.

It took a while to catch a taxi, but they finally got a driver en route into town to start his day. When they got to the Amal Palace Hotel, Jennifer asked him if he could wait while she got some cash, but Veena paid.

As they walked in, Sumit, the head concierge, caught sight of her and was beside himself. He called out to her with great eagerness: "Welcome, Miss Hernandez! Your friends just came in." He rushed out from behind his desk and with tails flapping ran down to the elevators. A moment later he reappeared with a triumphant look on his face and with Laurie and Jack in tow. He'd nabbed them before they'd managed to catch an elevator.

When Laurie caught sight of Jennifer, she broke into a run. Her smile was from ear to ear. "Jennifer, my goodness!" she shouted, giving Jennifer a sustained hug. Jack did the same.

Jennifer introduced Veena as her savior. "We're going to have showers and then come down for a big breakfast," she added. "You guys want to join us?"

"We'd love to," Laurie said, still shocked but utterly pleased at Jennifer's unexpected arrival. "I'm sure Neil would like to as well."

The foursome proceeded on to the elevators.

"I have a feeling you have quite a story to tell," Laurie said.

"Thanks to Veena, I do," Jennifer said.

They boarded, and the operator pressed seven for

Jack and Laurie and nine for Jennifer. He had an impressive memory.

"I learned a new Indian legal term this morning on the way here in the taxi," Jennifer said. "To turn approver."

"That sounds curious," Laurie said. "What does it mean?"

"It means to turn state's evidence, and Veena is going to do just that."

Epilogue

The atmosphere inside the Toyota Land Cruiser had varied throughout the duration of the drive. When they'd first started out early that morning in New Delhi, there'd been near panic to get under way. Santana in particular had been remarkably agitated, exhorting in a tense voice for the others to hurry. Her big concern was not to wake any of the nurses other than Samira, who'd been sleeping with Durell.

After they'd been in the car for three hours, everyone had significantly mellowed, including Santana. Cal even began to question if they had overreacted, saying there was no way Veena would implicate herself.

"I'd rather be sitting in Kathmandu and be told we overreacted than be sitting in New Delhi and learn we underreacted," Petra had said.

They had had lunch in Lucknow and had tried to hear if there had been any news involving Nurses International that morning. But there had been nothing: no news whatsoever, stimulating a discussion of where Veena had gone, and whether she had gone with the Hernandez woman after freeing her or by herself. There was even talk about what the Hernandez woman knew to tell the authorities. She certainly had limited knowledge of where she'd been held, having escaped in the dead of night, unless Veena specifically told her. Samira doubted she would have, emphasizing that Veena was a team player.

Ultimately, they all had agreed they'd made the best decision to get out of town and out of India until the dust settled, and until they could rationally evaluate the damage they could expect from Veena's flight and Hernandez's escape.

"I'd always had a nagging concern about her," Cal admitted from the third-row seat. "I suppose in retrospect we should have dropped her when we found out about her history. Man, living like that for sixteen years has to knock a few marbles loose."

"If Nurses International is out of business, what do you think SuperiorCare Hospital Corporation and CEO Raymond Housman are going to say?" Petra called from the driver's seat.

"I think they are going to be very disappointed," Cal said. "The program has had a terrific impact on medical tourism this week. It's going to be a tragedy of sorts for them not to get more bang for their buck. Unfortunately, we've burned through a fair amount of cash to get where we are right now."

"It's a good thing you arranged for this contingency

plan, Durell," Santana said. "Otherwise, we'd still be in New Delhi."

"It was Cal's idea," Durell said.

"But you did the work," Cal said.

"We're coming up on Raxaul," Santana said.

Durell cupped his hands around his face and pressed them against the window. "Certainly is flat and tropical, and the opposite of what I had assumed when I started looking into it as the place for us to cross the border."

"What do you think the chances of us having trouble here are?" Petra asked. It was the question they had all avoided asking themselves or the group, but now that they were bearing down on the town, it was becoming progressively more difficult to ignore.

"Minuscule," Cal said finally. "This is such a backwater, people don't even need visas to move in and out of the country. Isn't that what you said, Durell?"

"It's a border crossing, mostly for trucks," Durell said.

"How long do you think we'll have to stay in Kathmandu?" Petra asked.

"Let's see how we feel," Cal said.

"We're now officially in Raxaul," Santana called out. She pointed to a city sign that whipped past.

Silence settled over the hulking SUV. Petra gradually slowed the vehicle. Signs were plentiful. Trucks were parked everywhere. The town itself appeared run-down and dirty. The only people walking the dark streets appeared to be prostitutes.

"Beautiful place," Durell commented, to break the silence.

"We're approaching the customs building," Santana said. Ahead, built in the center of the road, was a nondescript building with areas for vehicles to pull up on either side. A few uniformed border officials sat on empty boxes beneath a bare overhead bulb. A single policeman sat by himself off to one side. He wasn't even holding his rifle. It was leaning against the building. A hundred yards beyond the customs house was a large arched structure spanning the road and defining the border. A half dozen people were walking unimpeded in each direction.

As the Land Cruiser approached, one of the uniformed agents stood up and held up his hand for Petra to stop. Petra lowered her window.

"Car documents," the agent said in a bored voice, "and passports."

They all handed their passports up to Petra. Santana got the car documents from the glove compartment. Petra handed everything out the window.

Without a word, the agent disappeared inside the building. A minute went by, then two. At five minutes Santana spoke up. "Do you think everything is okay?"

No one spoke. Everyone was becoming more and more tense with every passing minute. Their initial optimism of an easy border crossing was rapidly eroding.

Petra was the first to see the police Jeeps in the rearview mirror. There were four of them, and they came rapidly. In the blink of an eye, they boxed in the

Toyota. Out of each jumped four policemen. All except two had their pistols drawn. The last two had assault rifles.

"Out of the vehicle!" the obvious commander barked. His left breast was covered with ribbons. "Hands raised! You are all under arrest."

NOVEMBER 1, 2007
THURSDAY, 6:15 A.M.
NEW YORK CITY, USA

From Laurie's perspective, the worst part of the whole infertility nightmare was the wait. In the first part of the cycle, you were occupied taking the pills or taking the shots and checking the progress with the ultrasound. One way or the other, you were busy and had limited time to obsess. But in the second half of the cycle, it was different. All you could do was wonder: Is this the cycle I'm going to become pregnant, or am I destined to be barren? Even the sound of the word *barren* was disturbing, as though there was something wrong with you, something missing.

As Laurie woke up on that early November morning with the rat-a-tat-tat of rain hitting the window, she wondered if she was pregnant. Like the ten or so preceding cycles, she had high hopes. The hormone shots she'd given herself that month had produced a bumper crop of good-sized follicles.

At the same time, Laurie felt depressed. She'd not

become pregnant in all the other cycles deemed to be equally promising. Why would this one be any different? Wasn't it best to lower hope and expectation? Last month when she'd finally gotten her period, loudly proclaiming she was not pregnant, she'd been ready to give up completely. She feared pregnancy just wasn't going to happen to the over-forty Laurie Montgomery Stapleton.

As she lay there in her warm bed, she could hear Jack singing in the shower. His blitheness in the face of her struggles made them that much more difficult to endure.

"Screw it," Laurie finally called out. She was resigned. She threw back the covers and hurried into the bathroom, where it was warm and steamy. Trying to keep her mind blank and devoid of expectation, Laurie got out one of her hated pregnancy tests. Squatting over the toilet, she wet the wick as the instructions advised. She set the timer and put the stick on the ceramic back of the toilet.

Heading back to the bathroom from the kitchen after turning on the coffeemaker and putting several English muffins in the toaster, Laurie picked up the pregnancy stick but purposefully avoided looking at it so she could devote more attention to turning off the irritating buzzing timer.

Having convinced herself it was negative, Laurie allowed a quick glance at its reading window but then had to look back when her brain said it was positive. For the first time there was a second stripe, and it was loud and clear. Laurie let out a whoop. Instinctively, she knew when the conception had happened. In India, right after

Jennifer had happily appeared at the hotel, Laurie and Jack had made love, and even though later in the day they'd also done intrauterine insemination, Laurie knew it had been the natural way that had produced the happy outcome.

Twisting around, Laurie grabbed the towel bar on the shower door and whipped the door open. She then jumped in, pajamas and all, joining a totally surprised Jack. "We did it!" she yelled. "I'm pregnant!"

MARCH 20, 2008
THURSDAY, 11:45 A.M.
LOS ANGELES, USA

Jennifer got her envelope and resisted the strong urge to tear it open on the spot. After all, its contents would influence the rest of her life. On the front, all it said was *Jennifer M. Hernandez, UCLA David Geffen School of Medicine.* Inside was the result of the match: the process by which the desires of fourth-year medical students and those of the academic medical institutions were correlated to give the most satisfaction to both parties.

The match was so important for the students because where they trained was the biggest single determinant to where they would spend their professional lives.

A number of Jennifer's friends who had already learned about where they were going tried to pressure her into opening her envelope, but she refused. Resisting all manner of persuasion, she broke free of the mostly happy group and dashed out of the auditorium. For mostly superstitious reasons, she was bent on sharing the discovery with her closest friend, Neil McCulgan.

After returning from India, their relationship had blossomed. Although Jennifer rarely had much free time, with her medical student responsibilities amalgamated with her medical-center gainful-employment jobs, what little time she did have she wanted to spend with Neil, provided he wasn't off surfing in some exotic locale.

With her envelope burning a hole in her hand, Jennifer took off for the emergency room. When she arrived, she chased Neil down to a cubicle, where he was working with several residents, practicing intubation on a recently deceased ER patient. Concentrating on his students, he didn't notice her immediately, but when he did, she held up the envelope and coyly waved it. He knew what it was immediately and felt a twinge of depression. He was enjoying their growing friendship even though the physical realm was still very much a work in progress. He knew things had to move on and change, but he wasn't happy with her returning to the East Coast, where he knew she had been set on going since her first year in L.A.

As for Neil's trying the East Coast, the thought had occurred to him, but he fought against it. As much as she liked New York, he liked L.A., especially with his spiritual relationship with surfing. He knew she'd get the match she wanted. She was too good a student and had done particularly well during the fourth-year surgery rotation she'd completed on their return from India.

Cupping his hand over his mouth, he silently and definitely enunciated, "Go to my office."

Jennifer indicated she'd gotten the message. Leaving the cubicle, she walked back to his office. She sat down in his side chair and lifted the envelope up to the overhead light to see if she could make out what the note said. She knew it was like cheating herself, but she couldn't help it.

Neil showed up in just a few minutes. "Well, did you get Columbia?" he asked.

"I haven't opened it yet. I'm superstitious. I wanted to do it in your presence."

"Silly woman! You're going to get what you want."

"I wish I were as confident as you are."

"Well, open it!"

Taking a deep breath, Jennifer ravished the envelope, rudely yanked out the note, opened it, and then cheered. She threw the note into the air and let it waft down to the floor.

"See!" Neil said. "Columbia is lucky to have you." He bent down and picked up the note, glancing at it in the process. He did a double take, shocked. It said "UCLA Medical Center Department of Surgery."

Neil switched from confusedly regarding the note to looking into Jennifer's eyes. "What is this?" he sputtered.

"Oh, yeah, I forgot to tell you. I changed my order of preference. I realized I didn't want to leave now that we're just getting to know each other, but don't worry, there's no pressure."

Neil reached out, grabbed Jennifer in a bear hug, and

by rocking back lifted her off the ground. "I'm thrilled," he said. "And you know what? You're never going to regret it."

Jennifer Hernandez was so excited she had trouble standing in one place. She was pacing outside customs in the arrival area of Los Angeles International Airport. In just a few minutes she'd witness the culmination of months of effort on her part, along with the aid of a number of other people.

"It's hard to imagine that Veena Chandra is about to walk out that door," Neil McCulgan commented. He'd driven Jennifer to the airport.

"There had been a number of times when I was convinced it wasn't going to happen," Jennifer agreed. Almost from the day Jennifer and Neil had returned from India, Jennifer had mounted a crusade to convince UCLA to grant Veena a medical-school scholarship, and the U.S. government to grant a student visa. It was not easy, especially since both institutions initially refused even to consider her application.

At first the biggest hurdle had been Veena's involvement in the Nurses International criminal trial, but that had been ultimately resolved when Veena and the other nurses had been granted immunity by turning state's evidence and testifying against Cal Morgan, Durell Williams, Santana Ramos, and Petra Danderoff.

Next had been the difficulty in arranging for Veena to take the MCAT exam. As it turned out, the effort was well worthwhile, since Veena aced the tests. Her near-perfect score significantly aided her own cause, and once the university began to look favorably on her application, the government was willing to change its tune.

And last but not least had been the effort to raise enough money for airfare and other expenses. Incredibly enough, a significant portion of all this effort had to be accomplished while Jennifer had been immersed in her surgical residency.

"There she is!" Neil called out excitedly, pointing to where Veena had emerged. She was carrying two small cloth bags with all her worldly possessions. She was dressed in ill-fitting jeans and a simple cotton shirt. Regardless, she looked radiant.

Jennifer waved wildly to catch Veena's attention. Veena waved back and started in their direction. As she approached with a broad smile, Jennifer tried to imagine what was going on in her mind. She was finally totally free of her selfish, repulsive, and licentious father, facing the fabulous opportunity to study medicine, which her father had tried to deny her, yet at the same time she was accepting life in a totally different, nonsupportive culture and giving up everything she'd known since she was an infant.

Although there was the slightest similarity to Jennifer's experience leaving New York City and moving to the West Coast, which at the time seemed to her like another culture, if not another country, Veena's experience was going to be a quantum leap more challenging. Veena was moving from a strong group culture to one based mostly on the individual. Jennifer hadn't had to struggle with that and probably wouldn't be able to help. Where she knew she could help was in relation to their similarly horrifying histories of abuse. Jennifer knew all too well the kind of handicaps that such an experience engendered, and she hoped she might be able to teach Veena some of the coping strategies she had learned by trial and error.

Jennifer hoped Veena would be receptive to her help. After all, Veena had taught Jennifer some important life-altering lessons, and she wanted to return the favor. Although at very great cost, Veena had taught Jennifer about redemption and forgiveness in ways she would never have learned otherwise.

Dr. Robin Cook lives and works in Florida.

Penguin Group (USA) Inc.
is proud to present

GREAT READS—GUARANTEED

We are so confident you will love
this book that we are offering a
100% money-back guarantee!

If you are not 100% satisfied with
this publication, Penguin Group (USA) Inc.
will refund your money!
Simply return the book before
October 4, 2009 for a full refund.

M423G0309

ROBIN COOK

"Mixes relevant social issues with murder and mayhem." —*USA Today*

CRISIS

The "master of the medical thriller" (*The New York Times*) shows the profession's dark side: the terrifying story of a doctor who is sucked into the maelstrom of the current medical malpractice crisis...

A partner in an exclusive concierge medical practice, Dr. Craig Bowman has reached an impressive level of success. But this idyllic situation comes to a grinding halt when he's served with a summons for medical negligence—and things get much, much worse.

penguin.com